INQUIRE. LEARN. REFLECT.
(Introductory Engraving of the May 4th Memorial at Kent State)

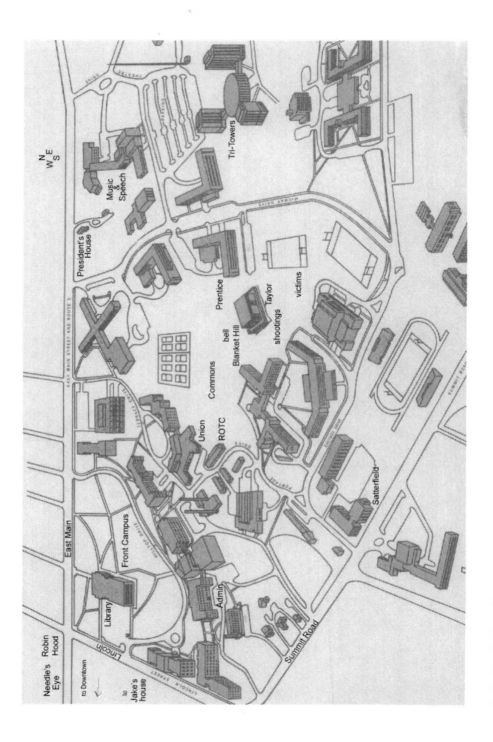

LOVE and WAR at KENT STATE

PART ONE: 1967
A New Life

1

Kent, Ohio
Saturday, September 23, 1967 ...

"No longhairs allowed," said the scowling woman on the front porch. "You look decent now but after you sign the lease, what then?"

Jake had talked to Mrs. Edith Whitcomb on the phone that morning. In a loose matronly dress, her graying brown hair bobby pinned back from her worn face, she'd been waiting at the three-story white frame house on South Willow Street. Jake was ten minutes late for their one o'clock appointment. Mrs. Whitcomb took a long drag on her cigarette and flicked the butt onto the gravel driveway.

Jake wanted to live off campus but close enough to walk. After a two day search he'd finally found the perfect location, a fifteen minute uphill hike to Satterfield Hall, sure to keep him in shape. With classes starting in only a week, the apartment still remained available possibly because the *Record-Courier* ad stated "only professionals need apply." As for his hair, *fashionably shaggy* might have been an appropriate description, collar length in back, his sideburns cut carefully at the curve of his jaw.

"And none of this summer-of-love bullcrap neither," Mrs. Whitcomb added. "I seen it on the news. Can't hardly believe my eyes when I see what's going on up there at that commie college. And most of 'em wanna be teachers? Lord God Almighty!"

No use challenging this angry, salt of the earth woman, Jake thought. *Not only would it be fruitless, she has something I want.* So he smiled, climbed the four steps, held out his hand.

"Jake Ernst. Like I said on the phone, ma'am, I'm starting at the university, grad student in English, teaching freshman comp. Sorry I'm late.

Got held up by the freight train that runs through the center of town. They make them long out here, don't they?"

Not taking his hand, she stepped backward toward the screen door.

"The railroad kept this town alive long as I can remember. Long before that too."

"Thanks so much for waiting."

"Looking at another rental, were ya?"

"Checking out the town, didn't figure on the train. And don't worry, Mrs. Whitcomb, I'm not a hippie."

"Then why ain't you in the Service?"

"I had a deferment for teaching high school and put in my four years. I'm twenty-eight, no longer eligible." Though this wasn't the whole story, it would have to do for this woman.

"Our grandson Tommy is over there fighting for us in Vietnam. A young man should serve his country."

"Handling tenth graders sure felt like service to me."

"Not near the service our Tommy is bein' put through."

"I'm sure that's true. Mrs. Whitcomb, this location is ideal for me. And I'm as professional as it gets. Is the apartment for rent or not?"

She wiped back a strand of hair, studied his face and looked him up and down as if evaluating a used car. He wore pressed slacks, suede desert boots, a tweed sports coat with a button down shirt and a maroon tie.

"Come on, then. You might do. I'm runnin' outta prospects."

Encouraged, Jake followed her into the vestibule, doors on both sides, four mailboxes, a Schwinn ten speed leaning against a wall, and a rack with three umbrellas and a broom. He followed the haggard woman up the banistered stairs to a landing also with two doors. The faint sounds of a flute drifted from behind the one on the left. Mrs. Whitcomb unlocked the other one, and he trailed her in.

"You from here in *Uh-hi-uh*?" she asked.

"Lancaster, Pennsylvania. Near Philly."

"*Ernst*. German name, ain't it? A lot of the Amish moving out here, snatchin' up our land. That your background?"

"Swiss-German, Scotch-Irish and a dash of Hungarian gypsy, pure American."

She looked at him askance. "Can you speak Amish?"

"Not really. But have you heard the expression to 'redd' up a room?"

"Painting ain't allowed here unless with my permission. And certainly not red."

Jake smiled. "No. It means to straighten up a place, to clean it. We say it back home. I like to keep my apartment nice, Mrs. Whitcomb. I *redd* it up all the time. That's about the extent of my Pennsylvania Dutch. Oh, and we say

2

outen the light, you know, use *out* as a verb. And faulty word order: *throw the cow over the fence some hay.*"

"If I'd 'a wanted a grammar lecture, professor, I'd 'a asked for one."

She looked at him as if he might be trying to sell her snake oil. Maybe he was pushing too hard but he wanted this apartment. The place smelled of disinfectant. Sparsely furnished with worn furniture from the forties, an old desk with cubbyholes, its chair on rollers, the apartment had a living room, a bedroom, a large bathroom and a small kitchen that opened to the shared balcony of a fire escape. The steps led down to a cement patio. A fenced in back yard was bordered by maple trees, still green, glowing in the early afternoon sun. A classical flute refrain flowed from the open window of the adjacent unit.

"You keep it really spic 'n span," he said. "Exactly the way I like it. Who will my neighbors be?"

"Next door, a French teacher at the high school been here starting on three years. Engaged to the gym teacher and helps me out watching over the place, tidying up. Downstairs is a biology professor been here eight years now. Other side is a young fella works for the paper over in Ravenna, reports about the college carrying-ons. They all like it quiet."

"Sounds perfect."

"My husband Wayne and me live in Munroe Falls, come over here regular to see everything's proper, reserve the right to look inside without notice, always knock a'course. Things gettin' crazy up there at the college, all these longhairs takin' drugs and protestin' to Kingdom Come, playing jungle music, girls traipsing 'round like hussies. And the boys look like bums, all dirty and hair down over their shoulders. Don't know why the college puts up with it. Ain't no one runnin' things up there. But none a'that in this house, see? That's why we don't hardly never rent to students."

"Think of me as a teacher, Mrs. Whitcomb."

"I could'a rented this apartment long before now, but waitin' for the right tenant. Did you notice how run down the other houses on this block are?

What a shame! Used to be fine family homes like my place here. Know what happened? Students, that's what. Worse for a property than the colored."

"You've found the ideal tenant," Jake said, smiling. Though he didn't like her views, he understood her. She was of the stock he came from, and like so many others of her generation, she saw her way of life slipping away. "So can I move in today, Mrs. Whitcomb? Don't have much, staying at the Cuyahoga Motel on 43-South. Sure is beautiful country around here."

Friday, September 29, six days later ...

"We can all breathe a sigh of relief," said Adele Lockhart, the English Department's coordinator of new teaching assistants, her first words at the introductory meeting in 121 Satterfield Hall. "You'll be glad to hear that the municipal petition to close the Water Street bars didn't get enough signatures, so they'll stay open."

The group cheered.

"Power to the people," someone yelled.

"Yes, how could we survive without J.B.'s? That's the good news. Now," she went on, rubbing her hands, "let's get down to business, shall we?"

A tall, attractive, willowy woman in her early thirties, Adele Lockhart wore her light brown hair frizzed in imitation of an afro. Large hoop earrings dangled beside her pale neck. Her loose yellow top and baggy painter jeans ran counter to her official position. The ragtag group sat in the brand new classroom, paint odor still evident, windows overlooking the University School across Summit Road. Surprised at the casual dress of his new colleagues, Jake sat uncomfortably out of style at the back, the only one of the few males in jacket and tie.

"As I'm sure most of you know," the bright-eyed Miss Lockhart continued, "each state-supported university in Ohio is required by statute to have an open enrollment policy. Democracy in action. So you all better understand from the get-go, this place ain't no Harvard."

The group snickered.

"Meaning that students who enroll here are not at all prepared for the normal rigors of collegiate study. The only entrance requirements: a high school diploma and funds for the ever rising tuition. So, a lot of headaches. Also, this year our freshman enrollment exceeded projections, bloating our class sizes. I'm not saying all this adds up to a pedagogical sweatshop, but..." She slashed a finger across her throat.

"Most of our students commute, so dear old KSU has the atmosphere of a community college. Also creates a terrible parking problem and daily traffic jams. But there's a new bus system, the Loop, which should help us get around. If you drive, make sure you get your parking decal at the staff services office."

She smiled, surveying the room. Her graveyard humor had already captured Jake's admiration.

"The English Department has an official syllabus for English 101, constructed around the turn of the century, so you'll have to do a lot of innovation to keep your students from drifting off in their heads to their last make out session on Blanket Hill. It's a challenge, but can also be quite rewarding."

She coughed comically as if choking on her words. "Now, how many of you have had actual teaching experience?"

Jake and one young woman raised their hands.

"Only two? My God! Both of you please stand. Everyone have a look at these two paragons of classroom instruction. They will be pillars of strength available in matters of crisis, discouragement, confusion and self-doubt." Jake and his compatriot across the room squirmed as others peered at them. "Please be seated, Oh Wise Ones. Afterwards I'd like to have a word with you."

Jake felt himself sweating.

"All right, we'll be meeting an hour and a half every Thursday afternoon to go over the next week's lessons and to deal with any problems. Don't worry, we're not throwing you to the lions, but it wouldn't hurt to have a sword and shield at the ready. Right now, let's have a glance at the official course structure, the original of which is preserved on scrolled parchment somewhere in the catacombs."

Finished covering the course outline, the group took a break for coffee and doughnuts then settled to go over the first week lessons in detail. When they finally disbanded, Jake and the other former teacher stayed behind to confer with Miss Lockhart.

"Please call me Adele," she said. "I'm trying to finish up my dissertation on the folklore of Appalachia along with teaching two sections of business writing and leading this collection of novice instructors. That explains why I look harried. Please tell me who you are, you first, Mr. ..."

"Jake Ernst. Did my undergrad at Penn State, student taught near Philadelphia, then worked four years at Lancaster High, tenth graders. That's about it."

Adele turned to the young woman.

"I'm Lily Lassiter. Graduated from Ohio Wesleyan, then taught two years, all subjects, on the Ponca Sioux Reservation in Nebraska, saving up for grad school."

Lily wore her thick brown hair in a single heavy braid pulled back from her tomboyish face. She epitomized Jake's image of Midwestern wheat field vigor, a vibrant visage from the cover of a Kellogg's box.

"An Indian reservation?" Adele said. "Must have been fascinating."

"That's what I thought before I got there."

"I will depend on both of you for moral support. As first-time teachers the others probably imagine they'll be sitting in cozy circles discussing the moral truths in Hemingway, if, indeed, any can be found there. Let me give you a bit of inside information. Ready?"

Her duo of listeners nodded. Jake liked this woman.

"All right, brace yourselves. You have arrived at an English department rife with tension. Last quarter under the guise of cutting costs, nine tenured profs formed a committee and submitted a plan to fire eight of our fulltime freshman instructors, all of whom had one-year contracts. Wait, the committee didn't say *fire* exactly; they said the contracts wouldn't be renewed. Follow me so far?"

"To save money?" Lily asked.

"It so happens all eight are outspoken critics of the war."

Jake gritted his gut. He'd been here before.

"The committee — we have oodles of committees around here — insisted they'd chosen these particular eight for supposedly not making *adequate progress toward their doctorates*."

"Didn't you say they were fulltime teachers?" Lily asked.

"Exactly," said Adele. "Unlike everyone here today, they weren't pursuing degrees. Hired only to teach."

"Catch 22," Jake said. "That committee couldn't give the real reason."

"Antiwar profs organized in opposition, and the issue raged to a boil until President White himself finally intervened, not in person — he rarely does that — but by vetoing the proposal. Burning scars remain. Labor rights advocates got involved, pushing for faculty unionization. A complete stewing caldron."

"So the teachers didn't get fired," Lily said.

"But egos are still stinging, battle lines drawn. It's hard to remain neutral. Even more fuel on the fire, our freshman class size has risen from twenty-five to thirty-two. Dr. Byron Shenk, my boss, whom we call Lord Byron, sometimes simply The Lord, described our job as 'battling in the trenches.' As you saw on the syllabus, in ten weeks each student has to write five papers and a final. So we'll all be up to our eyeballs in comma splices and run-on sentences. Add to that your research seminars and our Thursday teaching meetings, which require detailed lesson plans. Are you getting the picture?"

"The *trenches*," Lily said dramatically. "But if you want the real trenches, try teaching those angry lost souls on the Ponca reservation."

Jake smiled at the frazzled Adele and took a deep breath, remembering his resolution to his father and himself about keeping his head down. After all, agents of the United States Government might soon show up on his Willow Street doorstep to lug him off for having ripped up his draft card and sent it to the Selective Service office back in Lancaster. What he hadn't told anyone at Kent State was that he'd been fired from his teaching job two months before he'd fully met his deferment. During the draft processing at the army induction center in Indiantown Gap, he'd gone silent, expecting to be hauled off to jail. Instead, he ended up with a group of faking misfits in a psychiatrist's office at Harrisburg General Hospital. After a five minute interview, the shrink told him to go home.

A month later he received a new draft card in the mail designating him 4F, unfit for service, possibly accused of being gay, incorrectly. He protested the classification by ripping up his card under the penalty of a two year federal prison sentence for destruction of government property. Without a response from the draft board, he'd proceeded here to northeast Ohio where officials might appear at any moment to lead him off in handcuffs. The reason he'd been fired from his teaching job was that he openly expressed his objection to the war.

2

Same day …

After his meeting with Adele, Jake headed up two flights of stairs to locate the third floor office he'd been assigned. A young bearded man with a mop of curly black hair already sat at the desk by the window. For a moment Jake thought he would be sharing space with Allen Ginsburg. When he tapped at the entrance of the cramped office, the fellow swiveled on his chair and peered up through horn-rimmed glasses.

"Looks like we'll be sharing this executive suite," Jake said. He introduced himself.

The guy smiled, his sleeves rolled up over wide, hairy forearms. "Tim Updegraft." They shook firmly. "Yeah, I saw you stand up during the meeting, *Oh Wise One*. That woman's a trip."

Jake settled on the chair at the bare desk facing a blank beige wall.

"So you've done some teaching," Tim remarked. "Where's that?"

"Near Philly. You?"

"Graduated from U. of Buffalo in June. Feels weird being at Kent State. We're bitter rivals, if you care about that crap. I was captain of the bowling team, hated these guys. From a Blue Bull to a Golden Flash, Jesus fuck! What brought you all the way to this hole in the wall?"

"Kent is the only place that offered me money. You?"

"Same. With all the new high school grads dodging the draft, the writing program is desperate for warm bodies. Sounds like we're gonna haf'ta earn the big bucks though. You gonna be wearin' a coat and tie every day, make the rest of us look like clodhoppers?"

"Most likely. Got used to it, teaching high school. Anyway, it's good to keep some distance from your students. Gives you a little more authority. I learned that lesson the hard way."

Tim looked at him skeptically. He wore a denim shirt, wrinkled khakis and running shoes, hairy ankles instead of socks.

"What seminars you signed up for?" Tim asked.

"Blake and Modern American Poetry. You?"

"The American Transcendentalists and the Romantics."

"Good combination," Jake said.

"Yeah, I can write one term paper for both classes. Like, 'Shelley and Emerson on Eastern Philosophy,' 'Byron and Thoreau on Nature,' that kinda shit."

"Good strategy. It'll save precious time."

"It's almost lunchtime, wanna head over to the Hood, chow down with a cheese steak and a brew?"

"The Hood?"

"Across from the library. That medieval-looking dive."

As they walked out into the warm autumn air, Jake stood three inches or so taller than his new associate but couldn't match him in girth. Tim looked like an offensive tackle, Jake a wide receiver. As they ambled past Bowman Hall, Jake pulled off his jacket and slung it over his shoulder.

"Have you noticed all the babes in our group?" Tim said. "Some primo tail lies ahead, methinks. How'd you get out of the draft?"

"Teaching deferment. You?"

"Undergrad deferment. Don't know what's gonna happen now that I graduated. My eyesight maybe, but it's only some astigmatism. Crossing my fingers. They gave me an assistantship here, so what the hell, thought I might as well come, see what happens."

"So, you could get an induction notice any day?"

"My doc back home sent in a medical form. If that doesn't work, they'll let me finish out the term at least."

They strolled down a steep incline past the student union.

"They call that place the Hub," Tim said, "but tough getting a seat in there this time of day."

The slope continued on a path between Cartwright and Merrill Halls, then front campus down a seeming endless set of steps in the green park-like setting shaded by old trees. They passed Rockwell Library to East Main.

"Thar she blows," Tim said gruffly, pointing across the street. "The Hood. Pretty gruesome-looking but my roommates claim they serve the best cheese steaks in town."

Jake had noted the odd structure while scoping out the area near his apartment. The Robin Hood Inn occupied the corner of Main and Lincoln, dark brown bricks, a huge, sloping, clapboard roof, turrets, narrow Tudor stain glass windows and heavy wooden doors with prominent hinges and iron hoops.

Inside, dim, dank, the immediate odor of beer, worn slate floors, a long bar, pictures from Robin Hood flicks, crossbows and axes of the Sherwood

Forest era. The noise of conversation, youthful clientele and juke box music announced the place as a premier college hangout. Roughly hewn picnic tables with benches completed the ambiance.

A slender, college age waitress approached, her long brown hair in a ponytail. She wore cutoff jeans and a knotted tee shirt, a cash apron around her waist.

"Hi, guys. I'm Brandi. What can I do 'ya for?"

They ordered cheese steaks with fries, drafts of Rolling Rock. Brandi flounced off, ponytail swishing.

"Light My Fire" came on.

"So what do you think about Morrison's big controversy?" Tim asked, rubbing his tangled whiskers.

"Big controversy?"

"So you didn't hear about the Doors on Ed Sullivan last Sunday night?"

"No TV. What happened?"

"They did the song that's playing on the juke right now. CBS wanted Jim to edit out the word *higher* and he agreed but then on the air he stuck it back in, like he was telling all America to get loaded. What a blast!"

"So, is the network suing him?"

"Who knows? Hey, Jake. You look pretty straight. You ever light up?"

"You mean pot?"

"What else, man? You mean you never...?"

"No."

"Really?"

"Really." He apparently owed his new associate an explanation for this startling anomaly. "My friends and I weren't into it. It wasn't really around that much at Penn State when we were there, at least not that I knew. And they were honors premed students, needed their heads clear. And no arrests. Then I student-taught and joined the professional community. Never got around to getting high." *And don't intend to*, he added in his thoughts.

"Those days are over, my straight arrow officemate 'cause I scored some primo bud. Havin' a humongous bash at our pad tonight. You gotta come."

Brandi set their sandwiches down. "Hey, hot cheeks," Tim said, "party tonight, some wicked-great weed, wanna come?"

"Maybe," she said, smiling. "Write down the address."

"Right on, and bring a couple of your most groovy female compatriots. Plenty of this stuff to go around."

"Like I said, maybe." She sauntered away. The officemates dug in.

"Isn't that dangerous," Jake asked, "giving the address where you'll be smoking marijuana?"

"Giving it to that chick sure isn't."

"Do you know her?"

9

"No," Tim said, melted cheddar smearing his mustache, "but by the look of her eyes, she's stoned as we speak. You know where the Haunted House is?"

"Another bar?"

"No, man. A block up the hill toward town on Depeyster, where the revolutionaries live, SDS types, supposed to be haunted. You've seen *Psycho*, right?"

"The movie?" Jake asked, trying to keep up with Tim's *non sequiturs*. "What's that have to do with Students for a Democratic Society?"

"Nothing, but rumor is, the guy who wrote the screenplay lived right here in Kent, and Hitchcock built a replica of that house for the film."

"No kidding."

"Kent's one claim to fame. A teacher in the English Department lives there now, name of Holly, married to Kent's star political activist, Miles McGill. Me and some other guys from Buffalo, juniors and seniors, have a place right down Brady Street from there. Perfect location, just off the strip."

"The strip?"

"Jesus, man, you need a tour guide. You know, that row of grungy joints along North Water, close to the mill, beside the tracks? Kent State might be the least known college in Ohio, but the strip is the best known party destination. We use to drive all the way over here from Buffalo, man. Chick heaven, guaranteed to get laid. Babes flock here from all over the state for that express purpose. J.B's, Big Daddy's, Orville's, if you like the Harley crowd, any type you want, live music, cheap covers, three-point-two beer so teens can get bombed. You want it, you got it. And our pad not a block up the hill! This town shouldn't be called Kent; it should be called Pussy Paradise."

"Think you'll get any studying done, Tim?"

"Hey, man, *work hard, play hard, die young*, that's my credo. My guys been here a while, on the bowling team, know the ropes, semi radicals but not hardcore. Huge bash this weekend, you gotta come by."

"Sounds good, Tim. But I have two morning classes to teach Monday, gotta get ready. You want to know the most important lesson I learned from four years of teaching?"

Tim paused, mouth half full, stared, seemed to make a categorical judgment of Jake, not a positive one. "Yeah, okay," he said. "What lesson might that be? Wear a tie? Maintain authority?"

"He who is not well-prepared is massacred."

"No problem, man, but this isn't high school. The invite stands. We'll be there nonstop. Hey, how 'bout we arm wrestle for the bill?"

"Arm wrestle? Are you serious?"

"Loser pays."

Jake chuckled.

"You chicken?" Tim asked.

"You're on, but I'll pay my own bill regardless."

"You think you'll beat me, straight arrow man?"

"Tim, you're talking to someone who grew up on a farm, just came from a major tobacco harvest."

"Far out! A farmer boy up against a one-eighty bowler. Let's do it."

Tim called Brandi over to start them, rolled up his sleeve as Jake loosened his tie. They took their positions, locked hands, pressed forearms. Brandi said *Go*, and six seconds later it was over.

"Like I said," Jake reminded his startled opponent, "I'll pay for my own."

Saturday, September 30, next day …

Passing up Tim's party invitation, Jake spent all day and evening holed up in his apartment devising a teaching strategy, preparing his lessons and reading William Blake. During a break, he dashed off a letter to his parents describing his apartment and giving his impression of his new environment.

It's similar to State College, he scribbled, *but rougher, a surprise to me because I thought Ohio would be flat. Rural, woodsy, with busy railroad tracks right through the center of town and a tall ugly white flour mill. And real hilly. And the Cuyahoga River, not much more than a creek. And the campus up above the town. You hardly notice there's a college as you drive on Main Street, looks like a town park, big green lawn, tall trees, then up a steep slope. Only if you look closely can you see yellowish brick buildings that look more like a hospital than a university. Those are the original buildings. At the entrance along the sidewalk is a small boulder where students paint messages, like an outdoor bulletin board; I guess every school has its weird traditions. But on the other side of campus, it's more modern, students going to and fro. And there seems to be a separation between the town and the campus, like two disconnected worlds.*

Oh, and here's an oddity. The squirrels around this place are pitch black, like they've been rolling around in a coal bin, a mutation I guess, but seen as mascots of this area.

Beat my officemate at arm wrestling yesterday thanks to our bouts in the shop, Dad. Anyway, looks okay, start teaching Monday. Love you, J. p.s. If the feds come to pick me up, tell them where I am. Absolutely do not lie. I'm ready to serve my sentence, if or when. Make sure not to do anything to aggravate the situation for the two of you.

3

Sunday, October 1, next day …

Jake sat on his fire escape strumming his worn Martin six string, going through chord structures and picking-sequences. This habit had begun when he was an undergraduate, inspired by the Saturday night, pot free but wine saturated hootenannies in the house he shared with three others. The girl-

11

friend of one of his roomies had led the singalongs and taught him the rudiments of the guitar.

After years of practice he now moved his calloused fingertips and toughened nails deftly over the strings to his favorite songs. He had a nice tenor voice and could easily find the harmony lines that went with the main melodies. All this had developed as a stress-release like a Zen monk might finger a rosary. But in the process Jake had become technically competent as a guitarist and could pick up chords simply by hearing a tune such as, for instance, "Light My Fire." Most rock songs on the radio were ridiculously simple.

Thus, he happened to be lightly strumming the Doors' controversial tune that Sunday evening as the maple trees cast long shadows over the back lawn. He stopped when he heard the screen door of the adjacent unit squeak open. Wearing an apron and drying her hands on a small towel, the French teacher and flutist stepped out onto the balcony.

"Don't stop," she said. "It made doing the dishes enjoyable."

He stood, leaned the instrument aside and smiled. She had golden blond hair straight and silky to her chin, bangs above a tanned forehead, dark blue eyes, her face a longish oval, high cheeks, straight nose and solid chin. No apparent makeup.

"I'm Natasha Van Sollis," she said. "From the mailbox, you must be Jacob Ernst, our new arrival."

"Please call me Jake."

She extended a long, tanned, slender arm and they shook, her palm warm and slightly moist. Besides her apron she wore a tee shirt, jeans and flip-flops, her feet tanned. Jake couldn't miss her stirring natural beauty. Then he noticed the diamond ring on her left hand.

"Are you a professional?" she asked.

"I guess you could say that. I taught high school for a while, have a teaching assistantship in the English Department here at the university."

"I mean with a guitar," she said, smiling.

"With a guitar? Hardly. A habit to pass the time."

"You could have fooled me."

"How about you? With the flute?"

"Heavens no. Played with the marching band and orchestra at Ohio State, though. I hope my practice hasn't disturbed you."

"Not at all. I like it."

An awkward pause ensued.

"I teach over at the high school, a *professional* also."

"The landlady said you're engaged to the phys ed teacher."

Natasha lowered her voice to a mock whisper. "Edith Whitcomb is a bit of a busybody. I'd avoid sharing your secrets with her."

"Thanks for the warning," he whispered in return. "So I won't tell her about the bank I held up this afternoon."

Natasha smiled. "Edith comes around every week to see we haven't destroyed the place. Yes, I'm engaged. Ray Sweeny, coaches cross country and track. e spent the weekend out in the woods with the National Guard. Won't be back till late. He lives with some guys over on Fairchild where I stay most weekends."

Another uncomfortable pause, which again she ended.

"I guess that's your cute little car out there behind my Rambler? What kind is it, anyway?"

"A salvaged 1959 MGA, high school graduation gift from my dad. Did I park you in?"

"Sort of. Would you mind trading places?"

"Not at all. Right now?"

"Yes, and maybe we can make a deal because I use my car every day for work, so maybe you could park yours near the shed, and I can park behind you. I'll leave you enough space to get out."

"No problem."

They met in front to exchange places, Natasha's apron removed, revealing a statuesque figure. Her car sputtered before starting.

"Sounds like you could use a tune-up," Jake said. "I'm good with cars, could do it for you."

"How much?"

"Hey, Natasha, we're neighbors. No charge."

"Ray is a good mechanic, in the armored cav division, but he's swamped with other things. He plans to take it into the shop over Thanksgiving. One of his buddies works there."

Jake said he'd have a look at it the next evening. After they switched parking spaces, they went back upstairs to their separate apartments.

Hmm. Sexy.

It had been a while, the last time two months ago with Ainsley on the night they ended their three year engagement. But this girl, Natasha Van Sollis, would have caught his attention even in the prime days with his fiancée. A weakness of his, he knew. He would have to be careful around here. No doubt about it, attractive young women abounded in Kent, Ohio.

But this was his fresh start. He would give it his all to stay on track, his goal to earn a full doctoral fellowship at a major research university. Thus, he would need top grades and glowing reports from his professors, maybe publish an article. Best to keep his mind on the tasks ahead.

Monday, October 2, next day …

When his alarm rang at six-thirty, he felt ready. He showered, donned the blue shirt and tan slacks he'd ironed before he went to bed, tied his desert boots, knotted his tie, pulled on his sports coat, grabbed his scarred brief case and began the long, steep rise to campus. In the bright sunny morning, he hung a left on Summit Road, traffic with staff headed to work and commuting students arriving. He crossed the intersection at Lincoln, upward past the big, white, bubble-like water tower with the KSU Golden Flash logo and, breathing hard, reached the crest and eased downward. At Portage he turned left and crossed to the main entrance of Satterfield Hall.

With its tall, narrow, steel, rectangular columns, the new three story, L-shaped building, one wing on Summit, the other on Portage, violated the general campus design of institutional yellow brick structures. The landscaping not yet completed, roped off muddy patches lay where lawn and shrubbery would eventually grow.

Inside he climbed the central stairway to a landing, the large window of which looked out over the University School to verdant farmland and timber beyond. On the second floor he went directly to the classroom he'd been assigned for his two classes where he straightened a few chairs, adjusted the blinds so that light could flow in but students wouldn't be distracted by the activity of Bowman Hall across the way. He wrote his name, office number and hours on the chalk board.

Then back at the juncture of the two wings of the building, he entered the grad student lounge, one large table, chairs and padded benches, mail slots, a few TA office doors, and a coffee maker. After pouring a cup and grabbing his mail, he strolled up the stairs to the small office he shared with Tim Updegraft. He tossed a few irrelevant memos into his waste can and browsed over his class rosters, Polish names, Italian, German, Irish, English, zero that seemed non-Caucasian. As he'd walked around campus, he'd seen hardly any blacks.

At two minutes until eight he returned to his classroom. Several students had taken seats, others yet arriving, a buzz of conversation, mixed human smells of perfume, hairspray, deodorant. Several kids were reading the morning *Daily Kent Stater* and some were smoking, having found small tin ashtrays he'd neglected to remove stacked on a window sill.

At precisely eight a few stragglers hurried in and Jake closed the door. Though late arrivals at this early hour would be an annoyance, the plus side was that less motivated students would often fail to arrive at all.

He cleared his throat. The talk faded to silence, all eyes upon him except for one student's head entirely hidden behind the student newspaper. Jake introduced himself and pointed out the blackboard postings, most students writing the info down in their new notebooks. And he'd been correct about his assessment of the roster, not a single African American.

He smiled, paused, noticed the person still buried in the news and winked at the group.

"Young lady," he said to the girl next to the absorbed reader. "Could you tell the young man on your right that the instructor would appreciate his attention?"

A few chuckles arose, and the avid news-worm lowered the pages, tough looking, sandy brown hair slightly over his ears, stubbled cheeks, bristly mustache, and a Yankees tee shirt. The lad grinned.

"Yeah," he said, "looks like it'll be the Cards and Red Sox in the Series."

Jake smiled. "The Sox will have a hard time with Gibson's fast ball."

"Yeah, but they got the Yazz," the kid answered. "Went four for four yesterday."

"Your name?" Jake asked.

"Thurman."

Jake checked the roster. "Thurman? You're not on my list."

"That's my first name. Teachers always get it mixed up. Last name Munson."

Jake found it. "Sorry, Mr. Munson. Tell me, do you like writing?"

"Writing? What'ya mean?"

"You know, recording your thoughts with a pencil or a pen?"

"Don't got thoughts. I'm into baseball. Put off this course for a year, but Coach told me I better get it over with."

Some laughter.

"So tell me, Mr. Munson, why don't you like to write?"

"Never know what to say. Like, I got all these ideas but I just can't think of 'em."

More laughter. Jake smiled, looked around the room, waited, then said, "Can anyone identify with Mr. Munson's point of view?"

Half the hands went up. As if encouraged, the baseball fan looked around, nodding, then added, "I don't see why we have to take this class. Like, why can't we take what we want?"

"Right on," someone added.

"Anyone here actually like to write?" Jake asked.

Three girls and one guy raised their hands.

"And so the rest of you could take it or leave it, is that right?"

"Mostly leave it," someone said.

"Fair enough. But the powers that be have designated this course as a requirement for a degree. I guess they figure educated people should be able to write. Courses in your eventual majors will demand a lot of it. So if you're smart, you'll learn the basics here and get one step ahead of the game."

He explained that drop-add ended the coming Friday, so they could get out if they wanted to, or choose another time or even a different subject. They could even drop it completely.

"Unfortunately, though, as Mr. Munson here is doing, you'll eventually have to *get it out of the way.*"

He looked around, all eyes on him but the smiles gone.

"For those of you who decide to stay, I'll do my part to make the course palatable. I'll go over the syllabus now, then, if you decide to hang around, we'll split up into two person teams and you'll interview your partner and write a paragraph of the five most important facts about that person. Please include their first and last names. This will be ungraded, my way of getting to know you all a little and of taking attendance for today, which, the powers at be require me to do throughout the term. I'm merely a hired hand here, you see? Okay, Mr. Munson?"

The scruffy young man folded the news sheet, put it under his left arm, leaned back and grimaced at Jake.

"Okay, Mr. Munson?" Jake had learned to push such matters to their conclusion.

"Yeah, sure. Whatever."

"Good. I hope you'll stick around. But I still say Yastrzemski's bat is no match for Gibson's arm."

4

Same day ...

After his nine o'clock class, which followed the same procedure as the eight o'clock minus the baseball chat, Jake jogged back to his apartment and drove to an auto parts store in an alley off South Depeyster. He picked up an air filter, a can of carburetor cleaner, and a set of plugs and wires for a 1958 Nash Rambler. He would help his gorgeous next door neighbor whenever he could. Imagining a spark had passed between them on their brief balcony encounter, he even contemplated harmlessly sabotaging her car to make the job last longer. But even for the attention of someone so irresistibly appealing, he couldn't sink to raw deception. Anyway, she was solidly spoken for by someone who drove army tanks, so best to keep a respectful distance.

Back at his office he went through the stack of paragraphs his students had written. They were basically lists, no organization, no transitions, much worse than he expected. Out of his sixty or so students (ten hadn't shown up), only a few papers showed a sense of decent writing. There were, however, several intriguing characters.

In his eight o'clock, one young woman Veronica in her mid-twenties had danced in a Cleveland go-go bar. One fellow had won some trophies racing dirt bikes. Mr. Thurman Munson was on a baseball scholarship, also played on the basketball team and had a girlfriend named Diane back home in Canton. In the next class, a girl had won a 4H blue ribbon for a rhubarb pie, another was a competitive ice dancer, and a young man had a cousin who flew rescue helicopters in Vietnam. Several in both classes were ROTC cadets. In general, the handwriting was atrocious, as was grammar and punctuation. Jake had his work cut out for him.

For lunch he hiked over to the Hood, which was on the way home by front campus and handy from the library. Inside the noisy place, Tim Updegraft stood and waved him over to a table with some of his pals from Buffalo. Brandi, the waitress, took their crude jokes in stride, giving as well as she got. Tim insisted on a rematch of the arm wrestling, even in front of his bowling buddies.

"This farm boy took me by surprise last time," he told them. "Now I'm ready for him."

Except for a few seconds more, the result was the same.

Back home late that afternoon as Jake sat at his desk making notes in the margins of his Blake text, he saw Natasha pull into the driveway. Looking indeed professional in a blue jacket and skirt with a colorful neckerchief, she got out of her car and lugged a large tote and her pocketbook onto the front porch. Jake opened his door as she climbed the inside stairs, envelopes from her mailbox under her arm.

"I can have a look at your car," he said, "while the light's still good."

She smiled and shrugged as if she'd had a long day.

"Kids," she groaned. "I'll give you the keys." She unlocked her door and went inside.

He sat on the top step, sensing something familiar about her, a kind of *déjà vu*. He warned his alter ego to settle down. He was the last thing she needed, he thought. She came out in Bermuda shorts and a sweatshirt.

"Mind if I observe?"

"Be my guest. You're about to witness a genius at work."

"Like Monet at his easel in the Giverny gardens?"

"Exactly. Monet with a socket wrench."

"I look forward to it, *Monsieur Claude*."

Outside, he grabbed a tool kit and flashlight from his trunk and popped the hood of the Rambler.

"Start it up. Let's have a good listen."

She got in and turned on the ignition. The engine sputtered into an uneven rhythm.

"Okay, turn it off." Black moisture lined the seal of the crankcase. He handed her the flashlight, their cheeks nearly touching. He caught a whiff of her nice feminine scent. "Shine it on the engine block. No, that's the radiator.

There in the center." He wiggled his fingers like Groucho as a surgeon warming up, then peered at the motor. "Hmm. You need a valve cover gasket for sure. And when was the last time you changed the air filter?"

She crossed her eyes to demonstrate cluelessness.

"I see," he said. He loosened the wing nut and pulled off the cover, her womanly scent now replaced by that of grease and oil. "Oh, quite a while, huh?"

She shrugged.

"I predicted that, so I got you one. But before I install it, let's do a quick clean of the carburetor." He probed the carb's fuel bowl vent with the cleaner nozzle and gave it a good spray. He adjusted the choke, got behind the wheel and started the engine, which took a few tries. Then, under the hood working the carb, he throttled the engine up and down to get the cleaner all the way through. The motor idled nicely. He added the new air filter and screwed the cover back on.

"You're doing an excellent job holding the light," he said.

"It requires a lot of skill. I must anticipate your moves. Like dancing."

Yeah, he thought, *or other things*. "You should apply for a job as a mechanic's assistant."

"Yes, I think I've missed my calling. This is much more challenging than teaching French poetry to eleventh graders."

"Let's check the ignition system. You need a new battery. See all this gunk built up at the terminals?"

"That snowy stuff?"

"Not good." He cleaned it off. "The coil looks okay; I'll wipe it down. There. Now let's have a look at the distributer cap." He loosened it and popped it off. "Pretty messy, see?" He used a rag to clean the six contacts. "There's arcing damage, so we should replace the cap and rotor. I also got you new plugs and wires, just in case." He pulled off the first cover, ratcheted out the plug, showed her the burnt tip. "I'm gonna change all six of these. Please move the light as I go along."

"You're a real impresario, and I'm sensing your every move."

He glowed inside. After an hour of work, he wiped his hands, stood back.

"Start your engine, *mademoiselle*."

She slid in and turned the key. The car started right up.

"*Voila!*" she said. "You're a genius. *Merci, mon* prince."

If only, he thought but simply said, "Replace that battery, with winter ahead. And have the timing chain cover-gasket checked at a garage. I can do the other stuff here in the driveway. I'll pick up the parts. This fine vintage limousine could use some T.L.C."

"Daddy gave it to me when I was a junior at Ohio State. Haven't done a thing to it except have the oil changed now and then, mostly *then*, I'm sorry to say."

He reached toward her for his flashlight. Their fingers brushed in the exchange.

"A truly transcendent experience, watching you work," she said, smiling.

"*Merci, mon* ... prin-*cess*." He bowed. "I'll be happy to change the belts and hoses too, but the timing gasket will be harder, probably need to take it in. It'll start burning oil if you don't do it soon, all downhill toward Dante's *Inferno* from there."

"You really don't mind doing the work? I'd feel better if I paid you."

"Nah, it's a hobby I picked it up from my old man. He has a shop. But don't worry, I won't hold you indebted."

"Cars and guitars," she said, smiling. "But I insist on at least paying you for the parts."

It was that smile that got to him the most, as if she knew him, as if he knew her, as if they'd met, been together, understood each other. It felt much more now than a spark. They looked at each other, then laughed uncomfortably.

"Have you eaten yet, Jake? I'm going to whip up some pasta and salad. Like to join me?"

Having cleaned up at his place, he knocked on Natasha's door. Her apartment had flowered pillows on the old sofa and chair, dried floral arrangements, and framed prints of landscapes by Manet, Renoir and Gauguin. A desk stood at the front window, folders and texts scattered on the surface, her bags on the chair. At the other side of the desk, a stand held opened print music next to a rack with covered instruments on it.

He sat at her kitchen table, which was covered with a poppy printed cloth, the scent of marinara mixed with leaves burning somewhere in the neighborhood. Her apron on, she assembled a salad of lettuce, carrots, celery and alfalfa sprouts.

"This sauce is Daddy's special recipe," she said. "He does half the cooking at our place, always gives me a jarful when I go home to visit."

"What's his job?"

"Vice-president of a bank in Akron. Ma*ma* has a little sewing shop. She's French. He brought her back from the war, so I grew up speaking both languages."

"Your parents aren't far away. That's nice."

"I like it. I missed them when I was all the way down in Columbus. I'm an only child, so we're a unit. They give me autonomy, though, no dropping in unexpectedly, no prying. Not that there's anything to uncover."

19

She set a small wooden bowl of salad in front of him. "I'll let you put the dressing on it. French or ranch?"

"I think French is appropriate here, thanks."

"Do you speak French at all?"

"I'd like to learn though. I'll have to take it for my doctorate, need to read two foreign languages for research. I already know some German from high school and college."

She set down a plate of linguini covered with a sweet, savory meat sauce. "Okay, then Artiste with a Wrench, let's dig in, shall we? Do you say grace?"

"Not really, heathen that I am."

"Do you mind?"

He bowed his head, closed his eyes and listened to her soothing voice.

"Let us never forget the unity of all mankind. Let us try always to do good, and to remember that kids are just kids. Amen." She looked at him and smiled. "I have to remind myself of these principles every day. They're so easy to forget."

"I was expecting a Baptist prayer, or something like it."

"I'm not religious like that, but my parents go to church, Episcopalian. I guess *I* believe that poor, earthly humanity is all we have. Daddy says he gained his religion in the war, and Ma*ma*, being from France, was Catholic, but Daddy, ruling the roost as he does, felt Episcopalianism is a good compromise. I go when I'm home, though, because Daddy won't have it any other way."

She smiled as if embarrassed by this long speech.

"But you don't buy into it."

"Not really, to Daddy's great dismay. He says he should never have sent me to college, and that if I'd been to war I'd have learned a few things. The church rituals are pretty, though, and the mythology. No, I think there's only *us*, sad to say. And it takes much more faith believing in *us* than believing in God. Are you religious, Jake?"

"Not in the heaven or hell sense," he answered, his mouth full.

"In what sense then?"

"All this," he said, gesturing widely, "had to come from somewhere. Like this delicious meal had a cook, right? And, if you see a painting, you can assume there's a painter. Maybe I worship Tolstoy. Right now I'm devoted to your dad for this spaghetti sauce."

"Tolstoy, really? That's where I got my name. Natasha Kitty."

Jake stopped attacking his dinner. "No kidding?"

"My mother loves Tolstoy. At bedtime when I was a little girl, she read his books to me in French. He wrote them in French, you know. All the Russian aristocracy spoke it."

Jake chuckled. "Your name is great, fantastic. I understand why they might have named you *Natasha*, but why *Kitty* instead of *Anna*?"

"Heaven forbid. Ma*ma* didn't want me to grow up a scarlet woman like Anna. Kitty is the perfect domestic spouse. My parents are like her and Levin. They spat sometimes but their love is unquestioned."

"Literary critics hardly ever notice that pair. In some editions most of their relationship is edited out."

"I know. Maybe because of that first line: 'Happy families are always the same.'"

"But your mom put Natasha first. Natasha is fiery, passionate."

"But she eventually settles down, gives up the dashing Andre for the staid, solid Pierre."

"So which one? I mean..." He realized he might be headed into swirling waters.

"What were you going to ask?"

"Nothing."

She smiled. "I know it was something. Do you want to know which stage I'm in, the fiery or the domestic?"

"It's none of my damn business."

"Please, ask."

"I don't want to pry."

She smiled coquettishly. "Didn't I already tell you there's nothing to uncover? I demand you finish what you started. It's not fair to arouse a girl's curiosity and leave her hanging."

"I was wondering if your gym teacher is Andre or Pierre."

She studied him a moment, then smiled. "I think the trick is to have the proper balance, don't you? Which would you prefer, Anna or Kitty?"

"We're mixing our novels, but I see what you mean about a balance. Sometimes I feel sorry for Karenin."

"That insufferable prig?"

"Anyway, the book could hardly be written today."

"Why do you say that?"

"Because divorce is so easy now," Jake said, "and Anna would certainly retain custody of her son. Problem solved."

"Not really. A man like Vronsky would abandon her sooner or later."

"He wasn't such a bad guy. Nor Karenin. That's the problem, and the magic, in Tolstoy. He writes with empathy for the whole human race, even for insufferable prigs and philandering military officers. Maybe like God. You know, for his creation of *us*, loving something at the heart of each human being no matter how heinously we might defy his expectations."

She smiled at him. That smile. As if it signaled total, instinctive approval. It unsettled but thrilled him.

"This is quite a literary discussion," he said, noticing he'd finished his meal.

"Would you like another helping, Jake?"

Back in his apartment Jake settled at his desk, took a deep breath, held her smile, her whole being, in his mind. He picked up his guitar, strummed a few chord progressions.

Quit it. You don't need this. Already interrupting your schedule, and for what? It's just that, what is it so familiar about her? And could she be feeling it too? No damn way. So stop it. Get a grip. Fix that beat up contraption of hers and count yourself lucky if you get another meal. And put your desperate mind back on Blake.

Tuesday, October 3, next day …

Jake rose again at six-thirty, showered, dressed, grabbed his briefcase and went out into the crisp morning. He wore a suede jacket, the collar up, and strode along Willow then a left onto Summit, two long blocks steeply upward over the crest and down to Satterfield. He picked up his mail in the grad lounge and went upstairs to his office where he noticed Tim's Dr. Pepper can and half eaten doughnut on his already cluttered desk. Alone in the room Jake looked over the syllabus for his modern poetry class coming up in the afternoon, having repeatedly to bring his mind back to William Carlos Williams from thoughts of his next door neighbor.

Natasha Kitty, passion and homemaking. Damn the gym teacher!

But, after all, he would hardly have imagined such a wondrous person to be unattached, would he? He recalled how he'd met Ainsley, at that time the girlfriend of Stephen O'Shea, one of his undergrad roommates. That little obstacle hadn't deterred him. Ainsley hadn't been happy, and Jake thought he could make her so. Thus, he moved slowly, not entirely consciously, trying to win her and finally accomplishing his goal. Maybe his strong reaction to Natasha came simply from his missing Ainsley so much. Over three really fine years, then his own karma coming back, losing her to a Scottish folk singer with curly red hair.

All right, enough of this. Get back to Williams. What's this little poem about a red wheelbarrow all about?

During the entirety of Jake's two office hours neither a student nor Tim appeared, a great advantage of choosing this early time during which he read the entire condensed biographies of both Blake and Williams to obtain an overview of their work and literary reputations. With extra time on his hands, he went through his students' scribblings, making some suggestions in the margins. He realized he soon wouldn't have a free moment on his hands.

Maybe that's why my mind is fixated on Natasha. Soon I'll be too busy to have such absurd feelings. I lost Ainsley because I didn't deserve her. Given another chance, I won't blow it again.

The paint-scented seminar rooms were on the second floor, long polished tables with padded chairs. Professor Thrillwell was ten minutes late, bald, nattily dressed, bowtie, cufflinks, pocket square, not prone to smile nor to apologize for being tardy. Speaking with a New England accent, he went over the syllabus, assigned each student a Blake poem to explicate and left the room saying he'd return in half an hour to collect their renderings.

Jake received a nudge from the person next to him. It was Lily Lassiter, the braided tomboy from the first teaching meeting.

"He's a pompous ass," she whispered. "Don't you think? I doubt he'll be much of a *thrill* at all."

"Quite so," Jake said in a mock voice, leaning his head back and looking down his nose. "Indeed."

Lily chuckled. "That's a good impersonation. If you show me your Bogart, I'll show you my Bacall."

"We better get to work."

"You're right, but it's nice to see a familiar face. Someone told me I shouldn't take this course until I'm in the doctoral program. This guy is a bear. But I love Blake, so thought I'd take the challenge."

Jake was already engrossed in "The Garden of Love," no context, no date, only the words on a mimeographed sheet. He wondered if part of this assignment was to show the professor that they knew what an *explication* was. Jake had learned the word early in his academic career, from Professor Groff in his freshman composition class at Millersville State Teachers College, near his home. He'd taken his first two years there before transferring to Penn State. *Explication* meant neither interpretation nor subjective reaction. Jake read the short poem several times, thought briefly about it, and started writing.

Using first person and viewing in retrospect, the speaker of the poem (Jake avoided saying Blake himself) visited a place called the Garden of Love and saw something he hadn't seen in previous visits. In the middle of the garden stood a chapel where in the past the speaker had played in the grass. But the chapel's gates stood closed with a sign, 'thou shalt not,' over the door, commanding the visitor not to enter. So the speaker decided to enjoy the garden itself with its many flowers, but again saw something new, for instead of flowers, there were graves, tombstones, and black-gowned priests walking ritualistically and tying the speaker's enjoyments and hopes with thorns. The Garden of Love had become a cemetery.

The language is simple and concrete, the narrative easy to understand (except for the final image of the clerics' tying the speaker's joys and desires), the lines short and princi-

pally anapestic trimeter, four to each of the three stanzas, the second and forth lines of Stanzas 1 and 2 perfect rhymes (seen/green and door/bore), but the pattern violated in the final verse with be *in the second line matched with* desires *in the fourth.*

The speaker seems to be writing a parable, the implications of which the reader is left to make for himself.

The explication took Jake fifteen minutes. With the other students still writing furiously, he wondered if he should cover himself by adding an interpretation in case, to Professor Thrillwell, the meaning of the word *explication* also included an analysis of the meaning or meanings created by the narrative itself. Because Jake had time, he added the word *Explication* in front of what he'd already completed, then headed a second section, *Interpretation.*

What meaning can we extract from this seemingly simple parable? First, love changes with experience; the speaker sees something new in the once familiar garden. A chapel *is where worship occurs, but the warning sign over the doorway suggests that love is not to be worshipped. Whereas in the speaker's youth love was lovely ("many flowers bore") now we discover that love is actually the harbinger of death and torment. The speaker himself, growing older, is on the brink of this transition. The dreadful reversal is something that will* happen *not something that has already happened. It is a warning or perhaps a prediction.*

The central metaphor of the poem is that of the paradox of Christ's love, resulting in his crown of briars and his death by torture. Interesting to note is that the speaker presents no hint of resurrection or of the Christian joy in Christ's ascension, leaving, instead, only the stark, ultimate misery produced by youthful love. Could the speaker have lost a wife or lover to death? Does the poem indicate personal betrayal and abandonment? Or is it a blanket statement about the ultimate falsity of the hope that Christianity promises? Finally, does it suggest that Thou Shalt Not Love should be added to the original Ten Commandments?

Jake placed the last period on his essay when the professor strutted back into the room and took his seat at the head of the table.

"Cease writing now. Lay down your writing instruments. Pass me your papers."

He slid the stack of twelve into a folder, put it into his briefcase and rose.

"Have your term paper topics ready for me next class. Always I will be the first to leave, no last second questions, no pursuit down corridors or in elevators. You can drop by my office during the posted hours. Never, and I mean *never*, call me at home. When I am gone, you are dismissed."

He rose and left. Stunned, the students sat silently a moment then gathered their things.

"Don't worry," a woman in her early thirties said benignly, "his bark is much worse than his bite. I took his course on Shelley last quarter and here I am again."

"Coffee in the Union?" Lily asked, trailing Jake out of the room.

"Can't, another seminar coming up." For some reason Annie Oakley came to mind. Lil only needed chaps and spurs.

"Drat," she said. "I wanted to touch base on your teaching approach for our freshmen. What time is your class over?"

"Four."

"May I drop by your office then?"

"Sorry, gotta get back home. I'm tuning up my neighbor's car. I have office hours Thursday eight to ten, would that work?"

She smiled brightly. "It would, professor, sir. Perfectly. I'm an early bird myself."

5

Same day, half an hour later ...

In a green jogging suit Professor Byrne seemed Thrillwell's opposite extreme. He leaned back at the head of the table, darkly bearded, a tennis visor holding back tousled hair and shading his eyes like a poker player's. Most of the students seemed to know him as he greeted them with first names. They called him Drew. Jake had entered the seminar room in the midst of an ongoing rap session.

"Yeah, Chad & Jeremy are insipid but a good choice for Greek Week," the professor said. "Don't want any revolutionary groups in that All-American context."

"They should get Hendrix," said a longhaired guy in a Grateful Dead tee shirt covered with counterculture buttons which included the peace symbol, a marijuana leaf, and Nixon with a Hitler mustache.

"Nah," the teacher answered. "They're a good pick for the frat crowd. They tried for Simon and Garfunkel but came up short. But Ray Charles and Satchmo for homecoming is a real coup, can't complain about that combo." He pulled a pack of Salem from his knapsack, tapped out a cigarette, lit it and inhaled deeply. "Hey, guess we better get this class on the road. You all know, don't you, that the proper way to read Williams is stoned out of your gourd? I'm convinced he wrote his imagist stuff high on something from his little black bag."

"Was weed around in those days?" asked a longhaired, clean-shaven guy in a leather vest over a tee shirt.

"Hell, Jason, the cat was an M.D. Had a whole medicine cabinet full of great shit. As for pot being around, ever listen to those old blues lyrics?"

"Why do you say he was stoned?" asked a young woman, her long brown hair held back by a beaded headband.

"Hey, Wendy, good question. I suppose we should have a look at some of these poems, shouldn't we."

"The one about the wheelbarrow," someone called out.

"Right. That damned wheelbarrow."

"He *must* have been riding high to think that was a poem," Jason said. "*I* could have written that crap."

"Ah," Professor Drew Byrne answered, "but you didn't, did you? First of all, Jason, as you know, there was an influx of Far Eastern ideas into our culture at the beginning of the century, right?"

"Don't know if this poem is Far Eastern but it's certainly Far Out."

The group laughed, Drew among them.

"Far Out," the prof said, smiling, "not to mention Outta Sight and Right On. A good general description of a successful poet. Does anyone in this illustrious gathering of scholarly luminaries care to defend this little poem or whatever we call it?"

Most of the group were still chuckling, so no one volunteered.

"All right. I see someone here I don't recognize." He looked at Jake. "And you are...?"

"Jake Ernst. First term."

"Welcome, Jake. What do you think this poem is about? Why do you think it appears in each and every anthology of modern American poetry?"

Still trying to adjust to the informality of this group, Jake squirmed. "It's kinda like Haiku, but I think Williams was getting at more than merely startling his readers by hitting them with an exotic form."

"What was he getting at, do you think, Jake?"

"It's an image, like you say, but it's not *all* image."

"Go on."

"There's the first line: 'so much depends upon.'"

"Interesting observation. Care to pick up on that, Jason?"

"Like, *so much depends on* our eyesight? That's not profound, is it?"

"You're right on there, man," Drew said. "But Jake is correct that the poem is not a hundred percent visual. So you think he's writing an abbreviated ode to eyesight, is that your idea?"

"Or to common, everyday things," Wendy spoke up.

Drew had apparently dispensed with the formality of his students' raising their hands to be called upon. This was more like sitting around a kitchen table shooting the bull.

"Or to the importance of precise imagery in poetry," someone added.

"Yes," said Drew. "Poets of this era were obsessing about their art. And the image here is the epitome of precision, wouldn't you say?"

"Like a painting," another student said.

"His mother was a painter," Drew added. "Williams himself dabbled at the art. And there was the big exhibition of *avant garde* artists at the New York Armory in 1913. He raves about it in his autobiography."

"So he was painting with words?" Jason asked skeptically.

"Okay," Drew said, "get a piece of paper and draw a picture of this poem. Go ahead, give it a try. Play along with me."

They all did so and passed their results around the table, causing outbreaks of hilarity.

"Now let's get back to my remark about the relationship of this poem to being in an intoxicated state, shall we? I assume by this time in the development of our current culture, all of you have at least *tried* pot, correct?"

Jake did not see the need to reveal his personal deficiency in this countercultural area.

"So you all know that when you have some really good shit, how you notice commonplace things you never really looked at before, know what I mean? Like a painting you always walked by without noticing, or the feel of a fabric, or..."

"My girlfriend's eyelashes," Jason said.

"Or a line in a Dylan song," added Wendy.

"Or a scene in Star Trek."

"Or a rainbow in a drop of dew."

"Or the taste of a cold juicy cherry."

"Okay," Drew said, "so I see we have a bunch of potheads in here." Another outbreak of mirth. "Now does anyone besides yours truly sense a note of celebration in this little poem?"

"The words 'so much,'" Jake heard himself say.

"Ah, our first termer. Explain, Jake, will you?"

"The actual image is precise, but the phrase 'so much' is not. It's like a child's imprecise exuberance."

"Kinda like, 'Oh Wow!'" Wendy said.

"Yeah," added Jason, "like, 'Oh Wow, check out that red wheelbarrow beside the white chickens."

More laughter.

"It happens when you're stoned, right?" Drew asked. "You not only *notice* ordinary things that usually go past you, as Wendy says, but you *celebrate* them. And one more thing: besides the word *depends,* what is the only other verb in the poem?"

"*Glazed,*" someone said.

"Yes, *glazed.* Part verb, part adjective. The red of the wheelbarrow is *glazed* with rain water. Like the water is *part* of the manmade object."

"Like the fusion of the natural world with man's artifact," Wendy said.

"And," someone else added, "*so much depends* on that fusion, nature and man working together rather than at odds with each other."

A silence descended upon the little gathering, each person seeming to contemplate the dimensions of thought created by the tiny poem.

"Oh, Wow!" Jason finally said, breaking the group into laughter again.

Grinning, Drew lit another cigarette. "Now let's have a look at the poem about the plums. But wait, what do you all think of LBJ's raising our taxes ten percent to support the expansion of the war?"

"Boo, hiss," Jason said, and they took off on a discussion of current politics never to get back to the poem about plums.

A few minutes after four Jake strode the several downhill blocks home and immediately drove back to the auto parts store. He picked up a battery, a pack of valve cover gaskets, and a distributor cap and rotor. Back home, the Rambler sat in the driveway. Jake maneuvered his MGA into the spot between it and the storage shed.

At the top of the stairs he knocked on his neighbor's door, eager to give her a repeat performance of his prowess as a mechanic. But he caught her somber expression as soon as she opened up. Rather than inviting him in, she stepped out to the landing.

"I can't," she said, staring at the floorboards. "Sorry."

"Not feeling well?"

"Ray doesn't want me to. Forbids it, actually."

"Hey, it's not a date or anything."

"He's jealous like this," she said, wringing her hands. "I shouldn't have told him, but I didn't see the harm."

"There isn't any harm."

"I know, but he laid down the law."

"Jesus. I'm only trying to help."

"He'll take my car to his friend this weekend."

Jake stepped toward his door. "I got the parts. You can pay me for them, save your guys some trouble."

She shook her head. "I can't, really. I'm sorry, Jake. I guess I was a little too enthusiastic when I told him about my new neighbor. He sensed something he didn't care for."

"I can take the parts back. Sorry if I caused you a problem."

"Not your fault, Jake. It was not only helpful, but ... fun. I'll see you around, okay?"

She backed up to her door, her hand on the knob.

"Yeah, okay, Natasha. See you around."

Blushing, head still down, not having met his eyes once, she went inside. The door clicked. The deadbolt snapped shut.

Fuck this guy. Laying down the law. Gimmie a break.

Minutes later ...

Strumming his guitar, Jake sat on his frayed sofa thinking about the odd conversation on the landing. He felt he'd been caught with his hands in the proverbial cookie jar, which, if the truth be told, wasn't far off the mark. The guy was right to have sensed a threat. Jake would have taken the mystical feeling he had about Natasha as far as she'd allowed. Now he was sure something existed on her part too, which was what her fiancé had picked up.

He felt like going over and knocking on her door. For some ridiculous reason the scene of Benjamin pounding on the church window at the end of *The Graduate* came to mind; crazy, after such little contact with this French teacher with gleaming skin, all affirming smile and affinity to Tolstoy. What a sap he was to fall in love so easily. But she was really something. He would honor her boundaries, though, of course. Their contact had been much too brief not to. He found himself playing the chords to the Beatles' current hit, "Hello, Goodbye."

6

Thursday, October 5, two days later ...

Jake arrived at his office at eight and found Lily Lassiter leaning against the wall of the corridor. In a sweatshirt and jeans, her single braid over her shoulder, she beamed at him with her light brown eyes.

"Top of the morning to ya," she said brightly. "Didn't I warn you I'm an early bird?"

He unlocked the door and ushered her in.

"My officemate is a slob," he said, noticing a half full Pepsi bottle and a crumpled corn chips bag on Tim's desk. "Please, have a seat."

"You should see my roommate over in the grad student dorm. She's an entomologist. I'm afraid I'll wake up one night with ants all over me. She has one of those enclosed ant farms."

"Have you decided on your paper topic for Thrillwell?"

"No, you?"

"Eliot wrote an essay on Blake. I'd like to explore that. My officemate's idea, to write one paper for both classes. I'm taking Modern American Poetry too."

"But Eliot is British, isn't he?"

"That's a gray area. Anyway, what's up?"

She took a deep breath. "I'm terrified of teaching these classes, could use your expertise."

"But you're supposed to be one of the two pillars of strength."

"I taught on a reservation. They just needed a warm body. Ha, in more ways than one."

"Sounds interesting, though."

"More tragic than interesting. I couldn't wait for my contract to end. I did a rain dance for a school, any school, to give me an assistantship. I certainly hope none of the others come to me for teaching advice."

"Okay, Lily..."

"Call me Lil. I'm much more a Lil than a Lily."

As they settled side by side, he caught the scent of peppermint.

"All right, Lil. The key to your class is to keep them busy, damn busy. Keep them looking down at their desktops rather than up at you."

He explained the system he'd developed with his tenth graders, daily quizzes, in-class writings, peer critiques, matching strong students with weak ones, sticking to staggered due-dates for papers so as not to get bogged down with having to correct all the essays at once.

"You can copy my syllabus if you want to." He gave her one and went over it with her.

"But you've got to have some discussion about the stories, don't you?"

"Not really. Give them a good question, avoid ambiguous phrases like 'what do you think, how do you feel, what is your opinion.' You'll be lucky to get most of these kids to see the fine points or to care about them. Focus on what happens in the story, explication rather than interpretation. They'll think a story can mean whatever they want it to."

"Sounds high schoolish."

"I don't think these kids are much beyond high school. You've got to protect yourself, otherwise your teaching will eat up every minute of your time."

An hour had passed and they were still alone.

She smiled. "You chose a good time for your office hours."

"Yeah. I can do my own work."

"You seem cynical about teaching, Jake."

"It's the system. I have sixty-some novice writing students and am expected to do the work for two grad seminars. And for a doctoral fellowship, they'll look much more at my research than my teaching. So what do they expect?"

"You've given me lots to think about. Now may I ask you a question, Jake?"

He swiveled on his chair to face her, nice looking in a straightforward kind of way, a few freckles on her unmade up cheeks. No pretensions, no airs. A nice milk and honey girl.

"A question? Sure. Go ahead."

"Something personal."

"What is it, Lil?"

"First, do you have a girlfriend or wife or something?"

"No. And, not looking for one."

"Got it. But there's a movie in town I'm curious about."

"*Bonnie and Clyde?*"

"No. I read an article in the *Stater* that the film was banned in town last year, but now they're showing it at the Kent Theater on Main Street—*I, a Woman*. It's based on a true story."

He leaned backward, surprised.

"Don't get the wrong idea," she hurriedly added. "I'm not coming on to you or anything. I can't go in there by myself, or with another girl."

"Pretty dreadful reviews of that flick."

"But why would they ban it? Why do they allow the violence like in *Bonnie and Clyde* and ban something about sex? It doesn't make sense. Like Lady Chatterley, like *Peyton Place*. I should be able to see anything that guys can see. Saturday night, how 'bout it? On me."

He studied her. She was solid, looking straight at him, like a challenge.

What's this all about. Something new, a nice looking babe asking me to a porn film.

"In honor of a liberated woman's curiosity," he said. "But I'll pay my own way."

"Super. Let's grab a bite to eat first. They have specials at Hahn's. I'll take the bus downtown and meet you there, like six-thirty?"

"I'll pick you up. But not a date, right?"

"No, of course not. Not a date."

Same day …

Professor Thrillwell's office hours preceded his eleven-to-one seminar. The professor was alone when Jake knocked on the open door. Devouring a sandwich, Thrillwell, in a three piece suit and bow tie, waved him in, motioned to close the door, gestured to take a seat beside the big desk. With a napkin, he wiped mayonnaise from his lips. His office was lined with bookshelves, stuffed and stacked. A Christmas portrait of his wife and two teenage boys sat on his desk. To his right on a pedestal stood a marble bust, of Blake, so Jake assumed.

"Yes, Mr. Ernst?"

"You asked us to drop by with a paper topic."

"You've come up with one this soon?"

"I'd like to get going with my research, if you approve."

"Let me hear your proposal."

"T.S. Eliot wrote his ideas about Blake in a series of essays entitled *The Sacred Wood*, and I'd like to explore some of his claims."

"To what claims do you refer, Mr. Ernst?" He poured coffee from a thermos into a metal cup.

"To the first claim he makes that Blake progressed from a wild man to a traditional poetic voice. I'd like to trace that transition through Blake's development, see if Eliot's contention is true. Eliot simply makes the assertion, doesn't really back it up."

Thrillwell smiled wryly. "An annoying habit of Eliot's, pronouncing from On High."

"And I'd like to dig into the criticism and see if I can find any influence of Blake in Eliot's poems."

"Indeed, indeed. If anything, you may have bitten off more than you can chew, if you'll forgive the cliché. Have you studied Blake?"

"I'm pretty much starting from scratch. I'd appreciate any guidance you could give me."

"Permit me to restrain from giving you my view on Eliot's claim about Blake's journey from the innovative to the conventional. I will be interested in your conclusion, but only if you use Blake's actual work to argue for or against Eliot's contention."

"I'll get on it. But I'm not sure 'conventionality' is the exact word. Eliot seems to be saying that the journey is from roughness to a greatness that rivals Shakespeare."

"Thank you for that distinction. Oh, and Mr. Ernst, may I request that you read the explication you wrote of 'The Chapel of Love' to the class this afternoon?"

Jake sat up. "Okay, but..."

"Yes, Mr. Ernst?"

"Uh, may I ask whether you see it as a good or as a bad example?"

"Let us see what your colleagues have to say, shall we?"

After his disconcerting conference with Thrillwell, Jake strolled by Drew Byrne's office, which was packed with students, several sitting on the floor. The prof, wearing his visor, noticed Jake at the doorway and smiled.

"Join us, man. Plenty of room for one more. We're rapping about the D.C. trip coming up, renting a bus. Interested?"

"When is that?"

"You haven't heard? Big demonstration on the twenty-first. We'll have a helluva time. Get aboard soon; it'll fill up fast."

"I dropped by to talk about my paper for your class. Not a good time."

"Give me your idea, quick. Some of these revolutionaries might get a glimpse of something actually academic."

"Blake's influence on Eliot."

"Bingo. No problem. And you think about that bus trip, all right?"

32

Jake nodded, moved off. He'd been prepared to defend the notion of Eliot's being an American poet even though he'd become a British citizen. No need.

And no need to get involved in a discussion about Vietnam. He'd withdrawn from all that, keeping his head down as his dad had advised. The specter of a visit from the FBI rose in his mind, never being far away. His dad would ask what a mob of motley people walking down a street with cardboard signs could do to end the war. Jake had seen in the university paper that a group met on Wednesdays in front of the Union to protest the war in silence, bringing back memories of the Quakers he once stood with in Lancaster Square, *Protesting in Silence the War in Vietnam*. His school principal having seen him in that muted group was the proximate cause of his teaching job not being renewed and, thus, losing his deferment.

During Thrillwell's class, the professor handed out copies of "The Chapel of Love" and, as predicted, asked Jake to read the part of his little paper labeled *Explication*. Lil beside him, Jake did so, and Thrillwell asked for evaluations. Several students complained that the piece simply paraphrased the poem and offered a description of its form.

"It was well-written though," Lil added in Jake's defense.

Thrillwell then extolled the piece as a perfect example of explication.

"And I might add," he went on, "that Mr. Ernst refers to the *I* in the poem as 'the speaker' not as Blake himself. We must always keep in mind that the first person pronoun of any piece of literature may be a dramatic persona, not necessarily the actual author. Mr. Ernst, however, had the acumen to include an extra section labeled 'Interpretation,' making clear the distinction between the two tasks, which are separate and distinct. Most of you went straight to the latter. Here is a rule: first we explicate, that is, to make sure we agree on what the poem *says*, and only then do we launch into the process of interpretation."

Lil elbowed a congratulatory nudge into Jake's ribs.

"Well done, Mr. Ernst," Thrillwell concluded. "Now let us explore some of the rules of interpretation."

Back at his apartment after the late Thursday afternoon meeting of the new teachers, Jake sat at his desk reading Eliot's long essay when from his window he saw Natasha pull into the driveway. She got out of her car, struggled gathering her bags out of the back, locked the door, and trod up the sidewalk. The autumn breeze lifted her wispy, chin length hair. He didn't like to see her stressed. He heard the door in the foyer below, listened to her footsteps up the stairs and heard her apartment door open and close.

She's right over there, not twenty feet away. And I sit here with an ache in my heart. And where is this guy Ray? They have separate apartments. When are they getting married? Don't they sleep together?

Faintly, he heard the water from her shower.

She's there, streams rushing over her naked body, soap, shampoo. Alone for the night, and here I am, right next door, only a wall between us. Maybe I should ask to borrow some sugar. No, don't be an ass. Honor her decision. But she felt something, "enthusiasm" she'd called it. Jesus. All right, so she felt something, no reason to give her trouble. Just because you want that something and maybe she did too for a moment, doesn't mean it's meant to be.

7

Saturday, October 7, two days later, evening …

Jake showered, pressed his slacks, put them on along with a button-down shirt and a V-neck sweater, and drove to the graduate dorm. When he entered the big lobby, he saw Lil waiting on a leather sofa. Her appearance shocked him. No hint of rodeos here.

The braid had been converted to flowing brown hair over her shoulders. She wore a tight angora sweater and a miniskirt with black tights, and her usual natural complexion had been transformed by makeup into darkly shadowed eyes and glowing red lips

Rising, she smiled. "What's wrong?"

"The new look."

"It's Saturday night. You like?" She twirled.

"Nice." But he wondered what was going on in her mind.

Heads turned as they entered the family restaurant on Main Street close to the theater. She ordered Salisbury steak, he country fried chicken, and they chatted about their classes. She'd altered her syllabus, modeling it after his. Up the incline at the theater they stood in a line almost entirely of males, only a few couples and no unattached females. Smelling of patchouli, Lil gripped his arm.

"Let's make it clear to all these horny guys," she whispered, "that I'm taken."

"I wouldn't put it exactly like that." He allowed her to cling to him.

In the packed cinema she leaned against him. It was a rowdy bunch. The movie, about a turned-on young nurse who seduced any male in her vicinity, excited catcalls and lewd shouts, raucous laughter at the subtitles, guys watching a stag film. In one scene, a man chased the girl in a forest, dressed only in their underwear, and when he caught her he lifted her and smacked her bottom. With each smack, Lil gripped Jake's arm a little tighter.

Jake couldn't deny his own reaction to this crudely crafted movie; seeing all that skin in a public venue was new to him and difficult not to respond to. Clear why it had once been banned in such a small rural town. But censorship boundaries were being lowered. The cute, uninhibited Swedish actress expressed her sexuality without a hint of reserve as if her behavior was perfectly normal.

The noisy crowd flowed out into the breezy night, heading *en masse* down toward the Water Street strip. Jake and Lil moved along with the tide, guys checking her out as they passed.

"Do you know these bars?" she asked. "I've been to Orville's with my roommate. Great bean soup, and pickled eggs in a big jar, but a lot of biker types, and strictly hard rock."

"I've only been to the Robin Hood, up Main, across from the library. Pretty bare bones. Good cheese steaks, though."

"Yuck. But I'd like a drink, somewhere quiet."

"Don't think you'll find much quiet down here tonight."

"Let's drive somewhere? My roommate told me about a Holiday Inn where couples go."

He opened the car door for her, walked around and got in.

"If this isn't a date," he said, smiling, "it sure feels like it."

"Is that such a bad thing?" She leaned against him as pulled into the traffic, south on Water toward the interstate.

Into the countryside, five miles to the interchange, a massive Holiday Inn sign gleamed in the night. The parking lot was full, the place inside dim and subdued. Couples moved on the dance floor to sounds from a five-piece band with a female singer. The booths and tables glowed in candlelight from colored globes. After a rest room break, Lil ordered a daiquiri, Jake, not much of a drinker, a screwdriver. Sitting close at the back of the room, they had no problem talking above the music.

"So what did you think of the movie?" Lil asked.

"Pretty simple concept."

"Sometimes simplicity can be profound, don't you think?"

The candlelight accentuated the red of her lips.

"You think that flick is profound?" he asked.

"How many movies show a woman's sexuality in a positive way? If she sleeps around, she's always punished, like *Splendor in the Grass*, and Natalie Wood was in love, for God's sake. This picture is saying it's all right for a woman to enjoy sex, that it's not at all slutty. We should have the same attitude here in our country. What do you think?"

"Me? I agree there's a double standard."

"Exactly. This movie shows a woman acting exactly like men act. But men get away with it. Women must be the guardians of morality. That stinks. We like sex as much as men do, but we have to act all pure and angelic."

The band started "Light My Fire," unhurriedly, for a slow dance.

"Come on," Lil said, getting up.

She melded against him. He felt her warmth, inhaled her fragrance.

"You're a good dancer," she said. "I like you." She kissed his neck lightly.

He moved her in a leisurely turn, the singer crooning the lyrics.

"Do you like me?" Lil asked.

"Mmm. What's not to like?"

"That movie has me stirred up. I want to be like that girl. We could get a room here."

He realized his little car wouldn't do. She nudged her pelvis against him, then drew him by the hand to the front desk. But the rooms were all taken.

"Your place?" she asked. "Do you have a roommate?"

"No, but..."

"But what?" She looked up at him with her shadowed brown eyes, her full cherry lips.

On the way, she leaned against him as best she could in the bucket seats, her hand working on his groin. In the driveway as he was helping her out, the Rambler came in behind them. Jake looked up, must have appeared like the proverbial deer in headlights. No one got out of the idling Nash. Unable to tell if Natasha was alone or with her fiancé, he nodded at the beams and ushered Lil inside as quickly as he could. Even at the front door, no one had exited the other car, lights now off but motor still running.

The situation broke the lustful mood, but only for a moment. Upstairs, as soon as he'd latched his door, Lil sunk to her knees and unfastened his belt.

Sunday, October 8, next day ...

Jake awoke slowly, glanced at his radio alarm clock, ten past ten. Lil stretched beside him, her lipstick smeared on the pillow, her hair a tangle. He went into the bathroom, too drained to assess the situation. One fact stood out; a wild, naked chick lay in his bed. He was capable of slipping into sexual fervor in a way that clouded his judgment. So now he spent more time than necessary in the john, trying to figure out where this would go from here. With no hint of an answer, he went back to bed.

A sleepy Sunday, he wasn't pressed for a plan. As Lil snored quietly, he searched for feelings toward her that he couldn't find. He didn't want her for a girlfriend. But they'd had a helluva night, no holds barred. She was a super-charged combination of Marigold and Rochelle, two sexy girls from his youth, but he'd never gone to an "art" film with either of them. Lil had asked him to slap her ass, like in the flick. They'd done a lot of stuff he'd never

KENT STATE - 1967

done before, would never have ventured into, simply out of basic respect. Lil was not looking for respect. And he'd been too stirred up to have refused her nearly anything. And she hadn't been quiet about it, either.

Hmm. How thick are these walls?

Not only Lil's squeals but the box spring squeaking and the wood frame rumbling. And they'd laughed a lot, broke out into hilarity, chased each other around the place, did it in the kitchen and the bathroom. Jesus! So much for his reputation with his gorgeous next door neighbor. He hadn't heard a peep from there last night except her door closing as she'd finally gone in, with or without her guy.

Oh, well. There isn't any hope with her anyway.

And what was he supposed to do, live without sex? He recalled his mother's ancient advice: *sex without love is a sin.* With his skill at rationalization, he searched the dimensions still possible within her comment. Was it conceivable to love the game without loving the partner? Even if it were, that certainly hadn't been his mom's meaning. So, new question: is loving sex, in and of itself, a sin? Certainly not in the Swedish film they'd seen.

This question had never arisen with Ainsley because he'd loved her from the first time and every time afterward. Nevertheless, he'd never let loose like last night. And now came that word again, *respect.* He'd never have spanked Ainsley, and some other things, at least not unless she'd asked him. Even then it would have been subject to discussion first. There were boundaries with good girls which disappeared with bad ones. He'd loved Ainsley, and their lovemaking. He didn't love Lil, but had relished the surprises of last night. With Ainsley, though, he'd never had to wrestle with these moral questions when he woke up.

And now, across the way, Natasha, his Ainsley substitute. Given the opportunity, would he perform with her the way he had with Lil last night? Hell, no. She'd never want him to. Or would she? Is that what had led to his losing Ainsley, too much respect, too many assumed boundaries? This thought had never entered his mind before. Last night when Lil had urged him to cross into uncharted territory, he did so without hesitation. It was liberating. Ainsley would never have wanted him to do that kind of stuff, would she?

Weary of self-examination, he lay back. A naked, satiated woman, not bad looking at all, intelligent, aware, lay snoring next to him, her lipstick faded, mascara smeared, looking like a mime after a rough day. He had to get a grip on the situation. It would be a sex thing, nothing more. He'd be clear about that. If he could smack her ass, and etcetera, he could be honest and uncompromising, all about loving the game without loving the partner. He toyed with the analogy. Like an invigorating tennis match with an exhilarating opponent, one to be highly appreciated but not bound up with forever. But wait, he'd never played tennis in his life.

He drifted back into sleep, woke up an hour later to sounds in the bathroom. Lil strolled out, naked, her body well-toned, athletic, her face scrubbed clean, as if being totally unclothed in front of a guy was nothing new to her. He pictured her with Sioux braves in war paint.

She plopped down beside him, breasts bouncing.

"You're good," she said. "Last night was great, top to bottom, inside and out. Was I okay?"

He nodded.

"I decided to throw inhibitions to the wind. Because of that movie. That was new stuff for me, buddy boy. I did exactly what I wanted to do. What do *you* think?"

"Not bad."

"What kind of compliment is that?"

"Sex in overdrive."

"That's more like it. Wow. Overdrive, and then some."

She snuggled against him, kissed his left nipple, twirled a finger in his pubic hair. Soon they were at it again. An hour later, she giggled as he stroked her cheek.

"I'm half starved," she said. "Could eat a mastodon. Anything in your kitchen? Let me guess, an empty pizza box and a flat Coke."

"I'm not that stereotypical, Lil. There's milk, eggs, Jimmy Dean sausage, bread. I take care of myself pretty well."

"Thank God. I feel all scummy, but I have to eat something or I might pass out. I'll throw breakfast together while you lie here and think about me, okay?"

He got up, showered, dried, pulled on boxers and tee shirt. When he came out, sausage, eggs and toast were on the table. Still naked, Lil was already eating.

"I want you to know, Jake," she said, her mouth full, "this is strictly fun and games. Don't get serious on me, okay?"

"Yeah, all right, Lil."

Relieved at her surprising comment, he sat down and dug in.

"I've made some decisions," she said. "Been thinking about it for over a year. Lots of time to introspect on that rotten Indian reservation."

"What decisions?"

"I'm gonna do an experiment. Lifestyle. Like the girl in the film. Do you feel the freedom in the air around this place?"

"Last night, for sure."

"I'm going to exploit it, go where it leads me. I don't want to be tied down."

He took this pleasant news in, along with a succulent forkful of meat. "Disappointed, Jakey boy?"

"I didn't expect any of this. Didn't know I was part of an experiment."

"Not that I won't see you again. You're really something else. Stamina personified, maybe holding back a little, waiting for permission, but I understand. You're a nice guy. You're careful, with those rubbers and all. Sensible, but strong as an elk buck, all that lean muscle."

"Sounds like you're sizing up quarry for the hunt."

"Yep, a real steed. But I have some living to do. So don't try to lay morality on me, or tie me down. Do we understand each other."

"No problem, Lil, but you better be careful. Your idea is a dangerous one. This isn't Sweden after all, and getting pregnant and catching a disease might mess up your future. And not to mention, reputations still count in our profession."

"It should be like Sweden, though. Women should be free to explore, to conquer, to roam, exactly like men. I think that time is coming. I'm going to help it along. Yeah, I'll be careful. Maybe it's merely a phase. Maybe I'll find out I'm wrong. But last night was a fantastic first step."

Tuesday, October 10, two days later …

In Jake's seminar with Drew they spent most the time talking about the protest trip to D.C. Afterwards, Jake strolled along Portage Drive past Bowman and Van Deusen Halls. Below on the Commons some kids played soccer. The trees were turning color. He ambled down the slope between a few ramshackle barracks-like buildings. Dual towering smokestacks of the heating plant gave the campus an industrial aura rather than one of academic tradition. He went into the busy, yellow brick student union where he waited in line and finally ordered a grilled cheese and a Coke, the smoky place certainly no rival for Penn State's spacious counterpart. Then he took the path between Merrill and Lowry Halls and was hit with the lovely view of front campus, its steep, shaded hillside toward the broad, tranquil, leaf strewn lawn. The campus had a double identity, old and new.

He descended a long series of steps to his destination, Rockwell Library, a beige, two-story rectangular building level with East Main Street. Jake knew that the majority of his campus time would be split between there and Satterfield, and though the library and the English Department were a rigorous trek apart, his Willow Street apartment sat midway between them, the walk to the library lacking the uphill climb.

After showing his student card at the front desk, he went through a turnstile and climbed the stairs to the humanities section where he would be doing most of his work. In the crowded reading room, stacks lined the interior wall with long wooden study tables, barely a seat available. Various odors of stressed humanity mixed with the musty, old-book scent amid the low hum of whispers and turned pages. Carved wooden molding lined the ceiling all around with medieval looking chandeliers hanging from chains. Tall windows faced the shaded lawn and a big one at the end of the room showed Main Street about fifty yards away, its frame houses interspersed with stores and student dives, traffic flowing to and from Haymaker Parkway. Dominating that view, cattycornered across the street sprawled the distinctive Tudor style Robin Hood Inn.

The library was no match for Pattee at Penn State, no private study carrels in the stacks. It was much more like the small one at Millersville, but, Jake thought in his literary mood, *as Mercutio said, "Tis enough, twill serve."* He could always use interlibrary loan for materials not housed here, if, that is, he'd ever manage to find a seat.

After browsing in the stacks for books on Blake and Eliot and checking through the Periodical Index for journal articles, he left and took the level, three-block stroll past the Dubois Book Store on Lincoln Street and down College to his place on the corner.

Natasha's car sat in the driveway, and after he checked his mail and headed up the stairs, she came out of her unit, turned her back to lock her door, then whirled and saw him half way up.

"Hi, Natasha."

She wore jeans and a heavy sweater, her straight, golden hair not quite touching her shoulders.

"Oh, it's you."

"Yep. How are you?"

"I noticed you found a girlfriend already. You work fast."

At the landing, he said, "Only a date."

"I should tell you, these walls are pretty thin."

"Hope we didn't disturb you?"

"I turned on the TV."

"Sorry, Natasha. Really. I'm embarrassed."

"Don't be. I wasn't born yesterday. But Ray and I won't give you a problem. I usually stay with him on weekends, but he was at a cross country tournament. He's the coach. Usually I won't even be here, so feel free."

Jake nodded shamefully and unlocked his door as she headed down the stairs.

"Hey, Natasha."

She turned and peered up at him.

"How's the car?"

She smiled. "It starts right up and purrs like a kitten. Thanks. Sorry about that little mix-up. Ray can be possessive. It's difficult for him, you know, being away so much, with the team and the Guard. So sometimes he gets unnecessarily suspicious. Without any reason whatsoever."

8

Thursday, October 12, two days later …

At his morning office hours, after noticing Tim's refuse piling up – the only evidence of his officemate's existence – Jake sat at his comparatively neat desk reading *The Sacred Wood*. He noted elements that demanded further research and realized Thrillwell had been prescient about his having bitten off more than he could chew. In undergrad he'd learned about Dante, Marlowe, and *Hamlet*, but he was clueless about Swinburne's poetry and criticism, Coleridge as critic, Massinger (whom he'd never heard of), Ben Jonson, and Euripides. No worthy prof would let him get away with isolating Eliot's chapter on Blake and ignoring the work as a whole.

Into his second hour, he heard a tap on his open door. He saw a young man who might have been referred to in the current vernacular as a freak, the present costume of frayed bellbottoms, denim shirt, leather vest, long hair and beard, and a leather headband.

The lad stepped inside, bringing with him the smell of pot and Juicy Fruit gum. He stared at Jake through bloodshot eyes.

"How ya doin', professor."

"I'm doing well, thanks. And I'm not a professor. Call me Mr. Ernst. What can I do for you?"

"Ya see, I'm in your nine o'clock class and..."

"Excuse me? I don't recognize you."

"That's because I never made it but..."

Jake motioned for him to take the seat beside his desk.

"In my nine o'clock?"

"Yeah, sir, never got around to coming."

"Your name?"

"Will. Will Markley."

Jake checked the grade sheet. "Yes, I assumed you dropped."

"I should of, but didn't get around to it, so..."

"You missed two weeks of classes. You'd better do the drop action right away, or you'll get a failing grade."

The kid shifted uneasily, coughed. "Ya' see, professor, I found out that if I drop, it puts me under the twelve credits for fulltime. And if I go to part-time, I get drafted, dig? So I wanted to ask you..."

"Ask me what, Will?"

"All I need in this class is a lousy D. I figured you could cut me some slack. Let me do independent study, hand in the papers on my own, see?"

"Sorry, no can do."

"Why's it such a big deal? It's a stupid writing class. I'd probably get a D even if I came every damn time."

Jake chuckled at the kid's gall. "I have rules I must follow, Will. And I don't see the class as stupid. Anyway you must have a 2.0 average to stay in school. D's won't cut it."

"I figure I can pull a B in bio and C's in my other classes. So I figure I can get by with a D in your class."

"Are you in school solely to stay out of the draft?"

"You got it, professor. Like most of the other clowns around this place. I don't need college. I have a good job waitin' in my dad's trucking business, already know dispatch top to bottom. Why not float me a D? Who'll know?"

"Either drop the class or *earn* the D. But to earn it, you'll have to show up. I built in some forgiveness for missed classes, even one paper, but that's as far as I'll go. I had a deferment myself, but I did the work required."

Jake felt a twinge of hypocrisy at this comment, which carried more dimensions than were obvious.

"How 'bout if my dad calls you," Will said, "or better yet, drops by? We can use a writing expert on the payroll, uh, for our advertising and memos and like that."

"Will, I think I've made myself clear."

The kid stared at Jake. "Really? That's it?"

Jake stared back. "Really, that's it."

Will took a deep breath, pulled his head band off, scraped back his mane of thick brown hair, put the band back on.

"This here's a bummer."

"I hope to see you tomorrow in class," Jake said. "If you're trapped here in college, why not try to learn something?"

Will rose. "I'll talk to my old man. He might drop by anyway. We live up the road in Streetboro."

"I'll make a note of our chat in my log, Mr. Markley. And I wish you the best."

Later, Lil's solid braid back in place, her lips and eyelids in their natural state, she sat beside him in Thrillwell's seminar, their knees brushing occasionally as the esteemed scholar lectured about the bios of Blake and his contemporaries, emphasizing the poet's artisan rather than aristocratic roots. Then he passed out more poems for explications, this time having the results presented in the class, most of which, including Lil's but not Jake's, he disparaged without mercy. Lil was in tears afterwards.

"He's a bastard," she said in the hallway, Jake on his way to Professor Drew Byrne's class.

"Wanna do something Saturday?" Jake asked.

She wiped her eyes with a tissue and looked at him, considering. "Sure, Jake. But, I told you, I'm playing the field. Don't expect us to be steadies."

"I'm not expecting you to wear my varsity sweater. Thought you might be up for a chase in the woods."

"The woods? Oh, like in the movie. Hmm. What do you have in mind?"

"I did some exploring the first few days I was here. There's a big lake not too far. We could rent a canoe, find a picnic cove."

She stared at him. "You're a sexy guy, do you know that, Jake?"

"Can take that as a *yes?*"

Saturday, October 14, two days later …

Jake and Lil's trip into the Ohio countryside did, in fact, eventually include a chase. The hillsides red and burnished, the couple beached their canoe on a pebbly inlet and had roast beef sandwiches and red wine.

"See if you can catch me," Lil said. She charged through fallen leaves into a pathless woods.

Grinning like a mythical satyr in pursuit of a wood nymph, Jake raced after her through brambles and thickets, over mossy rocks and fallen trunks. Finally close enough, breathing hard, he grabbed her arm. Laughing, panting, she pulled away and climbed a steep rise on all fours until he grasped an ankle.

"Now force me," she said breathlessly. "If you can."

"Force you?"

"Wrestle me, subdue me." She clutched him in a headlock.

They rolled in the leaves. She was strong but no match for him as she struggled, kicked, flailed, seriously resisting. Only her laughter and happy exaggerated grunts kept him going until finally he turned her face toward him and kissed her even as she kept up the struggle.

The tussle ended with them wrapped passionately together. He took her hard and wild on the leaf covered forest floor. Afterward, still breathing heavily, they lay tangled, leaves in her hair, amazement in her eyes.

"Jesus, Jake," she said, her eyes gleaming, "you're a trip."

"Nothing compared to you."

"Do you feel like you raped me?"

"Hell, no. I'd never do that."

"But I fought you as hard as I could."

"We were playing."

She sat up, raked her hair with her fingers, fastened her bra, buttoned up her flannel shirt and took a deep breath.

"Wow! What fun!"

Jake pulled his jeans up from his ankles, sat, looked through the trees out over the lake.

"Let's think up a scenario in your apartment tonight," she said.

"We can't go there. The walls are pretty thin."

She chuckled. "Did you get some complaints?"

He stood, pulled her up, and they hiked down the slope toward their picnic site.

"So, let's get a room, Lil. I saw a motel outside Ravenna. What kind of scenario?"

Monday, October 16, two days later ...

While Jake was checking his mailbox in the Department office, Drew bopped in wearing his usual visor and jogging suit.

"Hey, there, Jake. What about that bus ride to D.C. this weekend? We have a few seats left, twenty lousy bucks."

"I have too much work."

"You seem detached about the war, never get involved in our debates. What's your stand?"

"I've been through all that back home. Now I need to work on my career."

"Come with me, my office."

Jake followed. The door locked behind them, Drew's office exemplified disorder with its array of books, folders, loose papers, old movie posters on the walls, clothing on a rack, soda cans, and the odor of perspiration from usually being packed with students. Drew pointed to a vinyl settee. Jake sat, and the prof settled on a high-backed chair behind his mess of a desk.

"Here's where I'm coming from about the war," he began, proceeding to hold forth for ten minutes about his studies and conclusions, tracing his argument from the nation's first support of the French, through our replacing them, our subversion of the Geneva Agreement, and the CIA's assassinating General Diem and setting up a puppet government in Saigon. Jake had long ago considered all of it and come to the same conclusions. But, a captive audience, he listened attentively.

"So," Drew concluded, "what do you think?"

"I agree. We're not the good guys over there."

"So let me sign you up for the trip. I'll lend you the bus fare, if you need it."

"It's not that. I really need to work."

"Hey, man, I'll give you all the extensions you need. No sweat in my class."

"But I'm in Professor Thrillwell's class too."

"That reactionary wart. He tried to get a group of instructors fired last term, because they're against the war. The horse's ass. Even in spite of the risk, Jake, some things are worth a sacrifice. We've got to do something about this situation."

"I'm joining the silent protests on Wednesdays, and I'll speak out when asked."

"That ain't shit and you know it, Jake."

"Maybe not, but it's the best I can do right now. Really, Professor Byrne."

"Hey, none of that professor crap around here. *Drew*, get it? With your views about the war, how'd you avoid the draft, Jake? Didn't go, did you?"

"Deferment for high school teaching. But I wrote letters against the war to the newspaper, protested in D.C. with a Unitarian contingent, talked to my students, stood in silence vigils with a group of Quakers. It upset some people, cost me my job. None of my feelings have changed, but I'm on a different tack right now, a new start."

"And while you're on your new tack, innocents are being slaughtered, atrocities committed."

Jake hung his head. "But I'm only one person, and I've made some hard decisions. Please..."

"Those decisions are a copout."

Jake didn't know what to say, felt the guilt that the prof was trying, effectively, to instill.

"I can't go to D.C.," Jake finally said.

"You mean you *won't*. You gave up the fight, for what? Your lousy career, whatever that might be? Hell, when all this is over, the universities won't even exist, as least in their present form. There's a revolution going on, if you haven't noticed, and if you're not part of the solution, you're part of the damn problem."

"Sorry, Drew. Should I drop your class?"

Drew leaned back, pulled the bill of his visor up, wiped his brow, rubbed his tangled dark hair and heaved a deep sigh.

"Drop my class? Don't insult me, Jake. I'm not strong-arming you. Fuck, but who cares about these poets. Something much more important is going on. 'The times they are a'changin', as Dylan says. Tragic that someone with your potential for leadership is too blind to see it." He stared at Jake. "Come on. Reconsider about this trip."

Jake grimaced, shook his head *no*.

"Look, man. I'll give you your A right here and now. And when the time comes, I'll recommend a renewal of your assistantship. But not much use in your coming to the seminar to talk about poetry. Maybe with the extra time, you can get more involved in the Cause."

"Drew, I don't want a free ride."

"Maybe not, but it saves me the trouble of reading that shit you intend to write about Eliot and Blake. Now I have work to do. We're going to make some noise in Washington." He shoved a stapled packet of papers across the desk. "This is a petition for faculty members who espouse the de-escalation of the war. Pretty fucking bland, but can you at least sign it?"

Jake checked it over, hundreds of scrawled signatures, noticed Adele's. He dashed off his signature. "And I'll keep coming to the seminar. And I'll hand in the paper on Eliot. You don't have to read it, but I can't accept a freebie."

Drew pulled his visor back down over his eyes.

"Jesus, man, whatever."

9

Tuesday, October 17, next day …

After his office hours Jake strolled over to the Union where he got a cup of coffee and settled at a window table in the faculty section. He looked out at the Commons. Between classes students walked in various directions across the open space. Though much less formal and marred by crisscrossed, muddy trails, it reminded Jake of the vast lawn in front of Penn State's Old Main. Across the green expanse at the start of a steep rise called Blanket Hill stood a brick structure with a bell, which appeared to be accessible to anyone for any reason whatever. At the top of the slope stood Taylor Hall, modern, polished glass and stone, square columns all around as if in defiance of the overall campus institutional look. At the highest point of the up and down terrain, the building resembled a cross between a gleaming office building and the Parthenon, apparently the new university centerpiece.

He felt a tap on his shoulder, Adele Lockhart, the young Ph.D. candidate in charge of new TA's, a coffee cup in one hand and a briefcase in the other.

"Mind if I join you?"

Jake stood. "Please do."

Her thin hair frizzed, she wore a heavy heather-colored sweater and long feather earrings. Her eyes shone with a bright, merry gray-blue.

"I've been meaning to have a talk with you."

"Uh-oh, what did I do wrong?"

"Nothing like that. I looked over your course schedule. A smart approach. Quite unabashedly minimizing your workload, early morning classes and office hours, in-class writing. You requested those class times, right?"

"Pretty sure they wouldn't be in great demand."

"As I said, smart. And you seem serious about attendance, a quiz every class, no make-ups, dropping the lowest paper score. I like it. I'll try it myself next term, except for the early classes. I'm not a morning person."

Relieved, he smiled. "Okay. Thanks."

"Have any teachers contacted you for advice as I suggested in our opening meeting?"

"Only Lil Lassiter."

"I thought she might have. She submitted a revision of her schedule, quite like yours. She's not very confident, in spite of her teaching position in Nebraska."

"I told her the secret is to keep the local natives busy."

"She was petrified when I observed her class, kept breaking her chalk when she wrote on the board. So let's boost her morale whenever we can."

He didn't mention that he'd been doing quite a bit of morale boosting. Gazing out the window, Adele took a sip of coffee.

"I love it when the trees are like this."

"Me too. What's that bell over there used for?"

"The Victory Bell? The kids ring it when we win a football game. Which is rarely, I might add. But our cross country team is one of the best. Kids ring it to announce a rally, celebrate a birthday, the frat boys use it a lot Friday nights when everyone is smashed. And some people go up and ring it, no reason. It's there, like Edmund Hillary said of Everest. Ask not for whom the bell tolls, Jake, most likely not for thee."

She giggled at her literary humor.

"What do you do for fun, Jake?"

"Play the guitar a little, work on my car, been driving around getting the lay of the land."

"Been to Cleveland yet?"

"A drive-through. I'm not much of a city guy, grew up on a small farm."

"Cleveland is a great town if you know where to go. There's a fantastic jazz club, East Twenty-Fourth Street near Cleveland State, kind of like Birdland in New York. I saw in your file you're from back east, ever been to the Big Apple?"

"Once, but not to Birdland. I walked the Brooklyn Bridge when the sun was coming up."

"Cannonball Adderley is at this club Saturday night, some of us are going. Would you like to come along?"

"Uh..."

"Some of us from English and a few from the Music Department. We could use an extra driver."

"My car only holds one passenger."

47

"That's a little help anyway. I'd dig it if you came. Think it over. Oh, and I'll be observing your nine o'clock tomorrow. Don't sweat it; I have to check on everyone. I like to give my victims a heads up."

"I'll be careful with my chalk."

She smiled sweetly. "You can let me know about Saturday afterwards."

Thirty minutes later ...

Waiting in the seminar room for Thrillwell to arrive, Lil, in her usual seat beside Jake, silently stared out the window.

"I was invited with a group to a jazz club in Cleveland this Saturday," Jake said. "Wanna come?"

"I have a date. Didn't I tell you I'm playing the field? I met a guy in the book store. He's taking me roller skating."

This announcement created no jealous feelings in Jake. It removed any sense of obligation he might have.

"Roller skating, eh? Careful not to bruise that gorgeous posterior."

Wednesday, October 18, next day ...

"You pass with flying colors," Adele said after she'd observed Jake's class. "I liked the way you defined *irony*, got them to see it in the story and then pushed them to give examples from their own lives. That was cool. And getting them to describe perfect revenge, plus the unreliable narrator. Isn't Poe a hoot? They were listening, learning. I'll put a copy of my report in your slot."

"Thanks." Jake slipped papers into his briefcase.

"So, what about Saturday night?"

"That's the day of the big march in Washington. I'm surprised you're not going with Drew's group."

"Drew's troops are too avid for me. I'm strictly nonviolent. People will be there who want to start trouble, some in Drew's crowd too. I do go to the Wednesday vigils, though, put on by the KCEWV?"

"The KC-what?"

"The Kent Committee to End the War in Vietnam, every Wednesday. I know, they should come up with a name that's easier to say."

"I'm going today too. In front of the Union, right?"

"I'll look for you. So what about Saturday night? You going to D.C.?"

"No, I agree about Drew's crew. But I can only take one person."

"That'll be me. Don't want you to get lost. There will be two other cars, but it's hard to stay together in the city. Pick me up at seven, okay?" She smiled, handed him a three-by-five with her address and phone number.

Later, Jake joined her and her friends at the silent vigil where a group numbering thirty or so, faculty members and students, stood side-by-side in in front of the Union. But causing this simple display to be suddenly less than simple, a uniformed officer moved about taking pictures of individual participants. Jake ducked, shifted, held his arm in front of his face, but the cop caught him in an unguarded moment. Jake realized his evasive movements may have excited some extra curiosity.

A student tried to block the camera with his hand and was roughly rebuffed though he continued trailing the cop around, yelling obscenities. Nothing more came of it, but Jake felt uncomfortable having his photograph on record. It wasn't what his father would consider keeping his head down.

Next day in the campus newspaper Jake noticed that the organizers of the vigil had filed an objection to the police photo action. The cops said they wanted to make sure no professional agitators were involved and that the pictures, after being identified, would remain on file. They wanted to prevent events like those at Berkeley from happening here. Only persons with official Kent State status were permitted to demonstrate on campus.

Jake pondered the advisability of his continuing to take part. But in rebellion against being intimidated from expressing his view in such a benign manner, he decided to continue. After all, the damage, if any, had already been done.

Saturday, October 21, two days later ...

When Jake pulled up in front of the small house on South Lincoln, Adele hurried out in loose jeans and a suit jacket, no different than her usual attire except for a cute little Charlie Chaplain hat with a peace button on it. They drove back into town, across the tracks and over the bridge where in an Arby's lot they met two other cars filled with students.

On out Mantua Street, 43-North toward Cleveland, Jake found out that Adele had graduated in the honors division of the University of Wisconsin, where both her parents taught, and that she had received a fellowship at Kent State in a combined master's and doctorate program. Her interest was in Appalachian folklore, particularly bluegrass lyrics and labor unions. Her favorite performer was Pete Seeger.

"He's a guy of courage and integrity," she said. "Did you know he went to Harvard?"

"No." Jake was trying to keep up with the Plymouth Road Runner ahead of him, which often passed dangerously on the rural, two lane road.

"Lost his scholarship, though. Had to drop out, politics. So many of our students think folk music and socialism were invented by Bob Dylan, the dopes. It was really Woody who popularized it. He died last month, did you hear?"

"No."

"He was sick a long time. Pete traveled with him for a while, riding freight cars and camping with hoboes. Pete is the real deal, a genuine hero. Do you think he's hokey, Jake?"

"Isn't that what you mean when you call him *real*?"

"I guess so. He's not trying to be cool, certainly not sexy, not in it for the money, nothing the least commercial about him, totally unhip. He wants to influence the culture, though."

"Yeah, simple words, easy chord structures, straightforward persona. I agree, salt of the earth. Him and Woody Guthrie."

"And so many before them back in the hills, farmers, miners, blacks. You mentioned you play guitar, Jake."

"Only a little. I learned with a lot of Pete's songs because they were easy. But never tried the banjo."

"What about the autoharp, or the fiddle?"

"Only a secondhand six string."

"Do you sing?"

"Not well, but I can pick up harmony. Do you sing, Adele?"

"A bit. Also, autoharp, piano if there's one around. We have a little bluegrass group, Goldenrod, everything Pete Seeger has ever done. Like to get the audience involved, at which Pete's the absolute master. We do picnics, festivals, schools and such. Henry, the guy driving the Plymouth up there, plays fiddle, and his big sidekick, we call him Wash, has an incredible bass voice and can play about anything, total musical genius. Josh plays rhythm guitar and sings, but keeps talking about leaving to play electric stuff, says he can't get girls playing bluegrass. He and Wash argue about it all the time. Wash is purist, like Pete, never forgave Dylan for going electric that night at Newport. We practice in the Music Department. You should come by, maybe jam with us."

"I'm not of that category. But Henry drives like a bat out of hell. Has a death wish, does he?"

"He does everything fast; you should hear him when he plays. By the way, did you see anything on the news today about the demonstration in D.C.?"

"Don't have a TV. Anyway, worked on my car all afternoon. Don't ever buy a British car."

"Over a hundred thousand marchers," Adele said, "and a big confrontation at the Pentagon, six hundred arrested."

"I wonder if Drew Byrne was one of them."

"Wouldn't be surprised. That will create a furor in the Department."

"I didn't like that cop taking pictures the other day," Jake said.

"It's not the first time. They're trying to keep the lid on things around here. Hey, to be expected in this ultra-rightwing state. Don't worry, they can't lock you up for standing on a sidewalk not saying anything."

"No, but..." He caught himself before revealing the nature of his personal plight.

"What?"

"Nothing. So how is it that a bluegrass group is into jazz?"

Jake got left behind at the one traffic light in Streetboro but Adele knew the way into the city to a roughshod neighborhood along a busy street with rundown shops. In the crowded downstairs nightclub, overwhelmingly black, the Kent group, exclusively white, pulled a few tables together and ordered drinks. Jake had never been with so many blacks at once, the place loud with excitement and outrageous super hip costumes. A local trio played rear-ranged blues classics until finally the nationally famous Cannonball Adderley Quintet took the stage. Over the evening, they played three sets, Cannonball wailing on his alto sax, and each member doing solo riffs to the huge delight of the packed, bopping fans.

On the way back to Kent the convoy made no attempt to stay together, and having drunk quite a few bourbon sours, Adele snoozed after they reached 43-South.

"Go straight," she muttered.

At three a.m., Jake stopped in front of Adele's place, shook her shoulder. When she came to, she smiled softly at him.

"Stay with me tonight?"

"I'm bushed. But that was a great evening."

She touched his cheek. "You're so nice and polite, seemed to be taking care of us all."

"Didn't want a race riot."

She smiled. "They're used to us there. Would you walk me to the door?"

On the walkway she leaned against him, her breath somewhat fouled from whiskey and peanuts.

"You could come in, Jake. I'd like that."

"We're both worn out." He gave her a hug. "Sleep tight." He suddenly wondered if Lil had ruined him for mild-mannered sex, which he was certain it would be with Adele.

Half a block from his own apartment, he saw a dark Ford sedan parked in front. Reactively, he hit the brakes and skidded to a stop. He backed up along the curb, turned off his lights and waited. Would they really show up for him at this hour? Apparently they had. Could it be due to the photos at the vigil?

He tried to catch his breath.

Settle down. Think.

He slid the isinglass window back, breathed the chilly air, waited. No sign of movement. No lights in the Ford, no personnel lingering in the street-lights, no burning tips of cigarettes. Ten minutes went by. Nothing but the dark hulk of the big vehicle, its tag blurred by shadows.

Finally it hit Jake that if they wanted him, they'd get him. He'd long ago decided not to flee. What sense would that make? He's the one who'd pro-voked a problem by ripping his 4F card to pieces and sending it to the Selec-tive Service office, explicitly expressing that he did not accept the 4F designa-tion. He'd performed this action fully aware that it was punishable by two years in federal prison.

So here it is. Had they questioned his neighbors? Did they talk to Natasha? It hardly matters, now, does it? Strange that Natasha came to mind as if she were someone to live for, someone who made all the difference. I'm delusional. And why am I sitting here in the dark. Go and face the God damned music.

He pulled back into the quiet street, slowly passed the LTD and turned into the driveway, no sign of anyone. Natasha's Rambler in its usual spot, Jake parked in the small space in front of it as always. He got out, no one around, no one in the Ford.

They must be waiting inside, maybe sitting on the stairs. Fine.

He opened the outside door with his key, a nightlight dimly illuminating the vestibule. No one there. He went up the stairs, which creaked slightly in the silence. Had they gained entrance to his apartment? He unlocked the door, eased it open, turned on the living room light. No sign of intruders, everything in its customary place. From his window he looked down at the sedan, and from this angle in the streetlight, he saw that the plate was from Ohio.

Where were they?

His heart thumping, he peered from the window. A quarter of an hour passed, nothing. The long night caught up with him. He used the bathroom, went into the bedroom, lay down fully clothed, kicked off his shoes and drifted into an uneasy slumber.

10

Sunday, October 22, hours later ...

Jake woke up after noon, felt ragged, suddenly remembered the Ford. He rushed to the front window. Gone. He leaned against the wall.

What the hell?

After some panicked breathing he wandered into the kitchen to boil water for instant coffee. He saw Natasha outside in the back yard, raking leaves. In jeans and a turtleneck sweater, her hair held back by a red head-band, she moved like a dancer with long strokes of the wooden rake. Still in last night's clothes, he grabbed his Instamatic camera and took some snap-shots. For some reason he thought of Tolstoy's Levin having a mystical experience while scything wheat with his peasants.

The job here was a big one, the maples around the property almost bare, the yard covered by a tapestry of red, gold and orange. Jake turned off the burner and changed into khakis and a sweatshirt.

"Good morning," he called from his balcony, the air fresh with a bite of autumn.

She stopped, peered up and shielded her eyes from the sun. "Morning? Have you checked the time?"

"You're right. Good afternoon. Could you use some help?"

"Maybe you'd better recover from your wild date?"

"Not wild, but long. Is there another rake in the shed?"

"Yes. I help Mrs. Whitcomb around here sometimes, window washing, sweeping the porch. She gives me a small cut on the rent."

He bounded down the stairs to the storage shed where he found a metal rake with a number of prongs missing. He pitched in.

"How's the Rambler ramblin'?"

"Great. Thanks again for your expert service."

"Did you add antifreeze yet?"

"I'd better, hadn't I?"

"Yeah, feel chill in the air?" Then with a Scottish accent, he added, "'Winter is a'comin' in, let us sing Goddam, Goddam.'"

"I don't mind winter. Is that from a poem?"

"Robert Burns, I think."

He noticed perspiration on her cheeks, felt her natural, radiant beauty and tried to fall into line with her rhythmic strokes. They pulled the leaves toward a big pile by the back fence.

"Hey," he said. "When I came home last night about three-thirty, I saw a black Ford parked in front."

"Phil's parents, the biology professor downstairs, from Youngstown. They drop by usually on their way to or from a Browns' game, spend the night sometimes."

He breathed a sigh of relief. She focused on her task. For him, yard work was precisely the right thing to untie the knots of stress he'd been feeling.

"Where did you go on your date?" she asked.

"Not exactly a date. Went with a group to a jazz club in Cleveland. Can-nonball Adderley."

"Was it good?"

"Great. Do you like jazz?"

"Don't know much about it. I like Karen Carpenter, and Dionne War-wick. And Tom Jones, he's sexy. Were you with the same girl as two weeks ago?"

"Her? No. Like I said, a group, English majors and folk musicians."

They loaded leaves into a wooden basket which, when full, Jake carried to the pile and dumped.

"I guess it's a good time to be single," she said, both of them raking again.

"How so?"

"Because it seems like morals are loosening up. Everyone free to do their thing."

"But you're one of the lucky ones, Natasha."

"Why do you say that?"

"You've found your mate. It must be really nice."

"I see. Lucky, of course. I was never one to run around. And you, Jake? Are you a freestyler?"

"I wouldn't put it that way."

"How *would* you put it?"

"I guess I'm conflicted."

"Really?"

"I guess I'm looking for that illusive creature they call a soul mate. I thought I'd found her, was engaged, but it didn't work out. What else is new? So, in the meantime, is a guy supposed to live like a monk?"

"When you finally meet this supposed soul mate, do you think she will forgive you?"

"At this point we'll undoubtedly have to forgive each other. My parents have had a pristine relationship, I think, but times have changed. I doubt that marrying a virgin is in the cards for most people of either sex nowadays, especially at our age. I think the real challenge ahead for our generation is staying loyal, faced by all the temptation everywhere. I mean what would you do, Natasha, if you suddenly got a call from Tom Jones?"

She stopped raking. He noticed and stopped too. She glared at him.

"What's wrong?" he asked.

"That was a nasty question."

"Just kidding."

"Your assumption is that I would be disloyal to Ray."

"No, it isn't. But by your comment I assume you'd be tempted, a little at least. You're human, aren't you?"

"And that is a *stupid* question."

"You're right. I know you're human. I've felt it. Hey, Tolstoy's Natasha was human, in spades. She took off with Kuragin, didn't she?"

"I'm getting tired," Natasha said. "I'll finish this job later."

"Don't worry. I'll take care of the leaves. I can see you're upset. I'm sorry for that dumb comment."

"You can finish this or not, I don't care. Here, this rake's much better."

She hurried up the back stairs and into her place through the kitchen door.

During the two hours it took Jake to finish the leaf job, he kept thinking about the apparent error he'd made with Natasha. But each time he went through the steps leading to the offense, he came to the same verdict: not guilty. Which could only indicate he'd accidentally stumbled upon a vulnerability of hers. Her overreaction exposed her self-doubt. Not that this knowledge gave him any comfort, or hope. Then again, maybe it did.

I mean, Tom Jones? A burly, hairy chested, sweating, glitter-costumed Vegas crooner?

That guy as her turn-on placed her as indefensibly human, at least from Jake's perspective. And she was the one who'd started the entire line of conversation by asking him about his date. And then the drama of her fleeing up the stairs.

She must be sitting up there blushing like hell for such an irrational and self-revealing display.

Working from one corner of the yard to another he wondered what would happen if it actually turned out she was having the same feelings for him as he for her. What would he do if one night, late, he heard a tap on his door and there she stood in baby doll pajamas? No, she'd at least break off her engagement before she'd do anything like that. Her attraction to him, if it were there, would uncover a weakness in her feelings toward this guy Ray. She didn't seem the kind to be capable of an ongoing, clandestine affair. Not capable of raw deception. No, not this girl. Or....

And what about himself? Would he accept her like that? Secretly? As the so-called 'backdoor man'? Well, yes. If that's all he could get of this magnificent creature, yes, without doubt. Yes, he was in love with her. Yes, he'd want her entirely, not only in bed but to share mundane moments, like working on her car, chatting over dinner, raking the yard. But if that was not to be, yes, most definitely, he'd take her in secret tidbits and go from there.

After today he firmly believed she felt the same puzzling, wonderful, magical, almost instant attraction as he for her. Maybe he was wrong, and maybe nothing would ever happen, but he simply had the feeling she was, Jesus, the One. Of course, he'd had that feeling before with Ainsley, and long ago in high school with Christine, and he'd been wrong. No, that wasn't correct; his feelings had been true but hadn't worked out. Maybe he'd been deficient in some way, not worthy enough, not expansive enough in his being, undeveloped, naïve, maybe too respectful of boundaries, too something, but

---

not in the truth of his feelings and in his willingness to commit for life. Like his mom and dad.

And here it was again, that marvelous and dangerous sensation far below the level of the intellect, lodged deeply in his heart, and clearly lower down than that. *War and Peace* and baby doll pajamas combined. Christ!

But here it is. And she sees it. And it scares her. And she doesn't know what to do.

So this time she had fled. But if he was patient, another time would come, if by his own non-action all the pressure remained on her. Sure, he could go up there right now, pound on her door, demand a confrontation of their feelings, take her in his arms. But no. If he was too aggressive, she might flee beyond her ability to get back. He must give her no excuses, no easy exit. She needed to stew about this, roll it over, come to the realization without placing the responsibility on him. So all he could do was to wait and to be there when that late-night tap sounded on his door, in one form or another. To have her in any capacity of her choosing, he would be there, and for however long she wished. Done deal. And he knew how it would be. It would be exquisite. *Right. Dream on, you sap.*

11

Tuesday, October 24, two days later ...

Drew's seminar room was packed and buzzing after the big D.C. rally. Monday's *Cleveland Plain Dealer* carried the Associated Press account including photos. A hundred thousand had shown up, a picnic atmosphere at the Lincoln Memorial. Some thirty thousand had marched across the bridge to the Pentagon where there'd been clashes with military police. Looking at the pictures, Jake felt guilty for not having been there. Surely Ainsley and her friends had been, and a contingent of Unitarians and Quakers from Lancaster, while he'd spent the day tuning up his MGA and the evening at a jazz club. Drew was right that he had copped out. Using work as a refuge, he was trying not to think about the war.

Drew and his students had a hilarious time talking about Abbie Hoffman and Jerry Rubin trying to exorcise the evil spirits from the Pentagon and about Allen Ginsberg's attempt to levitate it. Two of Drew's group were among the six hundred arrested and were still being held in an Arlington jail. The seminar members pulled out their wallets and made donations, Jake giving ten dollars. All in the bus had shaken hands with the poet Robert Lowell, a friend of Drew's, who had spoken to the throngs along with Dr. Benjamin Spock and Norman Mailer. Everyone in the professor's seminar room had their own personal accounts, the longhaired woman with the beaded headband passing around a protest flier with the autographs each of Peter, Paul and Mary.

Now and then in the festive classroom Drew met Jake's eyes with a sudden castigating irony that seemed to say, "See what you missed, traitor?" Not a word was spoken that session about the Wallace Stevens poem regarding Key West that had been assigned on the syllabus.

Jake's own students fell into three categories. First were the mainstream, the so-called silent majority, nicely dressed, well-groomed, accepting a traditional approach to college life, pledging fraternities and sororities, going to football games, homecoming, joining clubs. The second group were the hippies, longhaired, pleasure-seeking, apathetic toward their grades and class attendance, pot smoking, into the current music, hip, cool, unshaven, the girls often braless, making-love-not-war. Third were the revolutionaries, politically active, aggressive, complaining, objecting, seeking to upset protocol, and wanting to bring the system down and rebuild it into a socialistic utopia. Rigid boundaries didn't exist among these types, gray areas between them, levels of militancy varying, dress styles blending, worldviews fusing.

Perplexing everything for the young men loomed the draft, and for the young women the loosening of sexual mores. There were no blacks in his classes, no Hispanics, no Asians, only white middle class Ohio kids, most from the immediate vicinity, only a few from out of state.

Ten years older than most of his students, Jake watched from a platform of detachment, not yet quite committed to his own particular viewpoints but focused on establishing a career in what he believed would be the ongoing, more or less traditional establishment. Unlike Professor Drew Byrne, he didn't believe the growing turmoil would destroy the university and other rooted institutions. Sooner or later, Jake felt sure, the war would end, young people would discover they needed jobs to support their families, and violent protesters would realize that the best way to change society lay through evolution, not revolution, by working from within the system. Also, the obvious ill effects of drug use would eventually be seen as a health hazard rather than a route to enlightenment. All the confusion, that is, would fade.

Of course, the big car parked in front of his apartment had reminded him of his own shaky legal status. He understood that at any time he might receive a visit from federal agents. His approach was to follow his dad's advice by moving forward and keeping his head down, thus his refusal to take the bus ride to D.C. He knew his future comfort and his ability to provide for a family depended upon the survival of the Establishment in basically customary terms. And those terms, with some fundamental improvements through societal pressure and legislation, were okay with him. End racial discrimination, equalize the status of women, grant more freedom in personal lifestyles, stay out of needless wars, reduce pollution, pay workers fairly: with all these essential tweaks the nation should be able to continue with enriched lives for all.

He persisted in excelling in his own academic performance. As an undergraduate he'd taken satisfaction from a B average, but not now. Fully prepared, he attended every seminar session even though Drew's meetings resembled current event bull sessions more than incursions into the patterns and meanings in the poems of Williams, Stevens and Frost. Nevertheless, his *A* from Drew already guaranteed, Jake worked diligently on extracting a formalized poetics from Eliot's long essay on the entrenched literary canon, *The Sacred Wood*.

Jake's project for Thrillwell demanded much more, for Jake had to integrate Eliot's views of Blake with the other figures in the piece, most of which Jake had to learn from scratch. A presentation on these subjects in Drew's class would have been stopped short by the others' hooting him out of the room on the basis of irrelevance, but Thrillwell required a half hour presentation with a follow-up inquisition resembling the defense of a doctoral dissertation.

The difference between his two professors could not have been starker, Drew dedicated to converting the universities into institutions for social change and Thrillwell totally invested in maintaining the status quo. Jake realized that he, himself, straddled the fulcrum of these two opposing extremes. He was not unaware, however, of an adage from some ancient wisdom proclaiming that standing in the middle of the road was the most likely place to be squashed.

His position tentatively staked out, Jake spent hours upon hours studying at his usual window table in the library and scribbling information from old texts and scholarly journals onto three-by-five cards. The trick for his term papers, he soon realized, would be selecting and condensing the huge volume of material he was finding. He constructed a schedule in three phases: researching, arranging, and writing, all according to Thrillwell's deadlines. Drew had no cutoff times whatever. At the Willow Street house, no big Fords or registered letters regarding his status with Selective Service had yet arrived.

Thursday, October 26, two days later …
Jake was deeply into reading Blake in his office when he heard a deep voice behind him.

"Mornin'! You Ernst?"

Jake saw a solid, rough looking man in his late forties, polyester suit, tie loose at his collar, a beat-up satchel in hand.

"Yes, sir. I'm Ernst."

"Hi, there. I'm Claude Markley, Wilbur's old man."

"Wilbur? Oh, yes, Will."

Jake stood, shook the visitor's thick, powerful paw, told him to have a seat. He could smell tobacco on the man, mixed with Aqua Velva.

"I feel like I came here hat in hand. Ya see, we need a little help from you, and we don't mean no favor. Don't worry, we'll hold up our end."

"You know, Mr. Markley, I haven't seen your son all quarter, not even the first class. He visited me once here in my office, but since then I haven't seen hide nor hair."

"Yeah, I know. I mean, it's nine in the mornin'. He's a kid."

"I told him to switch the class or even drop it."

"Yeah. But he never got around to all that. What're ya gonna do? Look here, Ernst." He unclasped his briefcase and pulled out a folder. "This here's an ad campaign we wanna run for the local hauling end of the business, and we need some help, English-wise. We figure you're the fella to advise us as a consultant. A thousand bucks, cash."

"Mr. Markley. You know I can't do anything like that."

"Sure ya can. Between you, me and the wall here."

"And I can't pass Will. He's done absolutely nothing."

Markley shoved the folder closer to Jake. "Now see here, young man. We're between a rock and a hard place. He flunks this class, he's a goner, right into the infantry."

"I sympathize with you, but..."

"Now listen up. I served my time, North Africa, drove a God damn truck through thick and..."

"North Africa?"

"That's right, against the Desert Fox hisself, and..."

"My dad was there, wounded. My uncle too, killed, buried there. They were both mechanics."

"Yeah? Look at this here." Markley pulled up his pant leg, lowered his sock. A huge burn scar ran up his calf. "I don't want my boy over there in Indochina, see?" He straightened his clothing, sat up. "And I ain't askin' for no handout. Take a looksee in that folder. You'll find the ad ideas and ten one-hundred-dollar bills."

"Jesus, no, Mr. Markley!" He pushed back the folder, took a breath. "North Africa? My dad might have worked on your truck. Tunisia?"

"Got our butts whipped in them Godforsaken mountains."

Jake leaned back, rubbed his head.

"Look, sir. Forget about this folder. But tell you what. Will missed four papers. If he comes here during my office hours, four times, uses the fifty minutes to write an essay each time, I'll give him a D."

"He ain't no kinda writer, though, ya see?"

"All he has to do is show up and try. We'll forget all the quizzes and missed classes. That's the best I can do. That'll keep him as fulltime, provided he passes his other classes. Think he'll get through those?"

"Says he will. But gettin' him here at nine, I don't know."

"But you do know he'll get up much earlier in the army."

"You got that right, if he gets any sleep at all. Okay then, I'll drag him here myself, Ernst. Your old man and his brother, Tunisia, huh? Ain't that a helluva thing? Look, I'll leave this folder here."

"No, Mr. Markley, no way." Jake backed off, none of his fingerprints about to go there.

12

Tuesday, October 31, five days later …

After a TV dinner Jake was typing up lesson plans when he heard voices and laughter in the downstairs vestibule, soon a knock on his own door. He opened it to find a small witch and a slightly taller skeleton, backed by a pair of grinning adults. Jake had completely forgotten it was Halloween. He stammered, gathered his wits."

The kids giggled. "Trick or treat," the little witch said, holding an opened sack.

Jake met the parents' eyes. "Uh, hold on."

He retreated to his kitchen where he saw two bananas that he grabbed and took to the kids. "I believe in giving witches and skeletons something nutritious." He looked at the parents and shrugged.

"Say thank you to the nice man," said the mom.

"But I want candy," the little witch answered.

"Say thank you," said the dad. "He wants you to be healthy."

Reluctantly, the children accepted the fruit and turned toward the other upstairs door. After closing his, Jake realized that without the bananas he'd be forced to give his subsequent visitors handfuls of corn flakes. The excitement on the landing ended with footsteps down the stairs and another knock on his door.

Christ, now what do I do?

He opened up, Natasha in jeans and a Buckeyes sweatshirt. She held a bag of miniature Hershey bars and smiled benevolently.

"Thought you might be able to use these," she said.

He took an embarrassed breath. "You're a savior."

"We don't get too many goblins, but there will be a few more."

The downstairs door opened and another group entered.

"Why don't we meet them together," Natasha said. "Kill two birds with one stone or something like that. You pull a chair from your place and I'll pull one from mine, and we can wait for them out here on the landing."

"Fantastic! Maybe we can drop their treats down to them."

Three angels of different colors and sizes, and a mom were already climbing the stairs. Like a couple, Jake and Natasha gave them candy. The process happened several more times until there was a lull, during which they sat and waited.

"We're a pretty good team," Jake said.

"They probably think we're a couple. Do you want kids when you find your illusive soul mate?"

"Sure. When's your wedding, anyway?"

"June fifteenth."

"Do you have your dress and all that?"

"Looking at catalogs."

"Big wedding?"

"Yes, in Akron. We both have large extended families, his from Toledo. I'll invite you. You can bring your wild girlfriend."

Jake paused at this comment, which she'd offered with the loveliest of smiles, not quite matching the irony in her tone.

"You're teasing me," he said.

"No, I'm not. I'll invite you, certainly."

"I mean about the wild girlfriend."

She blushed. "Maybe I'm teasing a little. Sorry. Would you prefer one invitation or two? It seems only polite to give you an extra for a guest."

"You don't need to invite me."

"You don't want to come?"

"Honestly? No."

"That's not nice," she said with the same light tone. "Why not?"

Interrupting this line of conversation, an adult-sized Sonny and Cher entered the downstairs foyer, each one knocking on a separate door.

"Quite efficient," Jake whispered.

The downstairs residents opened up and without saying much dropped treats into opened sacks.

"From the university?" Jake said to the visitors.

Peering up, they nodded.

"Care to do a number? How 'bout 'I Got You Babe'?"

Emphatically, they shook their heads *no*. Jake told them to open their bags and he and Natasha dropped candies, not all of them hitting the targets but saving the duo a trip upstairs. They offered thumbs up and left. The upstairs couple resumed their stations.

"Why don't you want to come to my wedding, Jake?"

"Uh, I hardly know you, is all. And, of course, I never met your fiancé, so, um, why not spare your dad the extra expense. I wish you all the best, though."

"I see. So it's my dad's wallet that concerns you?" she asked with the same baiting, disconcerting, mildly irritating tone.

He looked at her, didn't speak. Her smile turned into an amused query of mock innocence.

"What do you want me to say, Natasha?"

"Nothing, nothing at all." Her expression turned matter-of-fact. "I didn't catch your hesitancy to attend, at first. Now I understand. You want to save Daddy some money. That's very considerate."

"Do you think there will be any more trick-or-treaters?" He glanced at his watch, after eight.

"Why? Do you want to escape?"

"No, Natasha, but are you actually waiting for me to say...?"

"To say what, Jake?"

He paused a moment. She seemed quite composed. They stared at each other, both suddenly serious. He rose.

"Thanks for helping me out tonight." He opened his door and started to lift his chair inside.

"Wait." She rose too. "I didn't mean to offend you. I'm sorry if I did."

"I'll come to your wedding if that's what you'd really like."

He went inside and closed the door.

Wednesday, November 8, eight days later …

After his classes Jake joined Adele and the Goldenrod contingent at the silent protest in front of the Union. After the vigil he trailed the group around to the front of Stopher Hall where a more radical crowd was protesting Dow Chemical's job recruitment visit to campus. The fifty or so protestors chanted and held strong signs such as "Dow Murders Children" while senior students in business attire filed in for interviews.

Though loud, the proceedings were orderly, the main feature of this confrontation to be an exchange of manifestos, Ronnie Engle, cochairman of the antiwar committee, presenting the case against Dow's involvement with the war, and the corporation's representative responding with its justification for the continued production of napalm.

With Adele and the massive musical genius known as Wash, Jake stood on the steps of Johnson Hall watching the action.

"It seems this guy Engle and Rachel Gibbs are doing a pretty good job running the Committee," Jake said.

"I don't know," Adele answered. "These signs are pretty harsh."

"Yeah, but they're letting the applicants come and go. Looks peaceful enough. I read in the morning paper that a faculty committee recommended those photos the cops took last week should be destroyed."

"Snowball's chance in hell they'll do that," Wash said.

"It's like battle lines are slowly being drawn," Adele added.

"But they've organized this thing called Vietnam College," Jake said. "A week of classes by profs, pro and con. Rational, educational."

"Sure," Wash said, "to get this apathetic student body off their collective asses."

"But it's not rabblerousing," Jake persisted. "It's based on information, not emotion. At least they're not suggesting we occupy the Administration Building."

"Are you new to the movement?" Adele asked.

"Not really, but I'm trying to stay focused on my mission to create a career."

"Wash thinks our music group should start coming to these things and singing. Try to ease the tension a bit."

"Like Pete Seeger would do," Jake said.

"Yeah," Wash added. "The minute we get violent, we lose. King has the right approach. Pete, too. You know, Pete started the whole 'We Shall Overcome' thing. Get people singing, the pressure is on, and if cops start beating peaceful people singing songs, the blame will fall on the Establishment. Man, that shit at the Pentagon was exactly what we don't need."

"You should bring your guitar and jam with us," Adele said. "We practice Sundays over in the Music and Speech Building, start at one. How 'bout it?"

"I never played with a group. I strum for my own mental health."

Big, bearded Wash burst out in raucous laughter, belly shaking under his bib overalls. "Hey, brother, does that work?"

13

Saturday, November 11, three days later …

At 2:55 a.m., as Jake slept soundly, a racket at his door jolted him awake. In his underwear he stumbled toward the pounding and opened up. Lil stood there, anguish on her face, blood from her nose, left eye swollen to a squint. He helped her inside and settled her on a kitchen chair.

"My God, Lil, what happened?"

"Didn't know where else to..."

He moistened a paper towel and dabbed at the blood on her upper lip. Blood drops stained her jacket.

"Jesus, kiddo, let me get some ice for that eye."

She breathed heavily, her words incoherent. He pressed her brow with cubes wrapped in a hand towel.

"The son of a bitch raped me, Jake."

"Let's get you to the emergency room."

"No!"

"Come on. I'll take you."

"No. I'll be all right. I didn't want to go back to my dorm. I made it over here from the frat house."

"I'll call the police."

"No."

"Why not?"

Her hair was a tangle, lipstick smeared, eye shadow in streaks.

"I'll be okay. Let me rest here. Please?"

"If some bastard raped you, he should be turned in. You can't let him get away with something like that. He hit you damn hard."

"Yes, but..."

"But what?"

"Maybe it was my fault."

"No, Lil. Something like this wasn't your fault. We should report it. And you shouldn't wait around. The longer you wait, the less credible you'll be. They need to do one of those exams."

"No, Jake, I don't want that. Let me rest, please."

Jake's mind reeled. "Jesus. All right, Lil, if that's what you want. But I don't like it. Whatever happened, you didn't ask for this."

"I need to lie down, okay?"

"All right. Come on."

He helped her up, eased her jacket off. She wore the same fuzzy sweater as their first date, now torn at the shoulder, spotted with blood. He led her to his bed, had her lie down and covered her. He pressed the ice pack against her cheek.

"We should call the cops."

"No, Jake, please."

He heard heavy footsteps up the stairs, a loud knock on his door. Before he got there, the pounding came again, then a strong male voice.

"Kent Police!"

Jake opened up. Two officers stood on the landing.

"We were called for a disturbance here," the taller one said, the other standing back on guard.

"Yes, officer. A friend of mine was in a scuffle at a frat party."

"Where is this friend?"

"She's resting."

"Is she all right? Everything okay?"

"She insisted I not call you guys."

"The fella downstairs called it in. We better have a look."

"She'll be pissed at me, but she said some frat guy raped her. I wanted to take her to the emergency room, but she refused."

The cop eased past Jake, the other one following, eyeing Jake up and down. As Jake closed the door, he noticed the two downstairs neighbors peering up. Natasha's door was shut.

Jake started into the bedroom but the shorter cop blocked the way. Jake heard the first officer questioning Lil, who was evasive, insisting she was all right and not wanting to report anything. Finally, she yanked the blanket over her head. The interrogator backed off.

"Not much we can do here," he said to his partner, who was writing in a small notebook. "She don't want to report nothing. Seems a little roughed up but not life-threatening, one helluva shiner though." He looked at Jake. "How do you know this girl?"

"We're in the English Department, grad students."

"Did you cause this damage?"

"Me?" Jake panicked. "No. She showed up, knocked on my door."

"That's what the guy downstairs said," the second cop offered.

"So how'd she end up here?"

"Seeking refuge, I guess. I was asleep."

"She said she was raped at a frat?"

"Yes."

"Which one?"

"Didn't say."

"Did she say who did it, a name?"

"No. She didn't want to report it or go to the hospital, only wanted to rest. I had nothing to do with it."

"Your name?" He was writing on a small pad.

Jake told him.

"Got ID?"

Jake got his wallet from the bedroom, gave it to the officer who wrote info on his pad and handed it back.

"Okay if she stays here?"

"Yeah. But I'm not involved."

"She should come to the station tomorrow, tell us what happened. The longer she waits, the harder it'll be to get the guy."

"That's what I told her, but she isn't too rational at the moment."

"Your girlfriend?"

"No."

"Where's she live?"

"The grad dorm."

"Her name?"

"Lil Lassiter."

"Tell her to come in and fill out a complaint. Don't like to see this rough stuff. Happens too damn often around here."

The officers made some notes and went down the stairs, talking briefly to the tenants below.

Same day …

After noon Jake sat at his desk reading when he heard the toilet flush and the shower start. Ten minutes later Lil came into the living room in Jake's bathrobe, her eye swollen, turned purple.

"I told you not to call the cops."

"The people downstairs did. Guess they're not used to pounding and shouting at three a.m. The officers want you to go to the station and fill out a report. They want to get this guy. You should do it. I'll take you."

"I told you *no*, didn't I?"

"But why?"

She slouched onto the sofa. "Take a guess, Jake."

"I'd rather not play games about this. The guy clobbered you, raped you."

"Speaking of playing games, that's like what we were doing. Last night it got out of hand, is all. When I fought him hard, scratched his damn face, he got pissed, slugged me and … took what he wanted. How do I explain that to the fuzz?"

"Did you tell him to stop?"

"I was half knocked out, Jake."

"Jesus Christ." He swiped a folder onto the floor.

"You like to play rough too," she said.

"Hey, Lil, nothing like that. You know better. Don't compare me with this. It was some mutual nonsense we did."

"I know. Sorry. Like I said, this went too far. This guy didn't quite understand."

"What's his name?"

"You don't need to know."

"Which frat?"

"Are you gonna tattle to the cops?"

"I'm gonna go over there and kick his ass."

"He's a football player."

"So?"

"And he'll have all the brothers around. Forget it, Jake. This isn't the Wild West. I'll have to eat this one. I don't know why I'm so masochistic. Where's something like that come from anyway?"

"How should I know? I'm not a sex counselor. Look, I have a lot of work to do, so get dressed and I'll take you back to your dorm. I guess you can tell your friends you walked into a door. Keep me out of it. I don't want anyone to think I'd do anything like this. By those cops' expressions, I could tell they weren't too sure about me."

As Jake walked Lil to his car, Natasha pulled into the driveway in her Rambler. Lil was holding an ice pack to her eye. Blood stained the shoulder of her white jacket. Natasha got out.

"What's going on?"

"Talk to the people downstairs," Jake said.

Half-hour later...

After Jake returned to his apartment, he heard a light knock on his door. He opened up to see Natasha in a plaid shirt, jeans, pink floppy slippers, her face fresh and natural, her eyes filled with concern.

"Excuse me if I seem nosy, but Phil downstairs said the police were here last night."

"Yeah, you missed all the damn fun."

"What happened with you and your girlfriend? Phil said someone beat her up? It wasn't you, was it?"

"If you think I'm that kind of guy, you shouldn't be visiting me."

"I *don't* think you're that kind of guy. But I am worried about the police coming around. Remember, I told you the walls are thin. I can't forget the first time she was here."

"Jesus, this has nothing to do with me. One of the guys downstairs called the police as soon as she made a fuss at my door. The cops got here five minutes later."

"Jake, can you tell me what happened?"

"Why the hell not?" He stepped aside. "Make yourself at home."

"I shouldn't bother you. You're upset."

"It's okay." He gestured toward the sofa. "Have a seat. Want some instant coffee?"

She shook her head *no*, sat on the edge of the couch. "Tell me why the police were here, and I'll leave you alone."

He dropped onto the decrepit easy chair and told her the story.

"So that's it," he concluded. "She doesn't want to report it. She's a grownup. What 'ya gonna do?"

Natasha smiled gently. "I'm relieved. I told Phil I was sure you didn't beat her up. He saw her outside your door before you let her in. But she looked pretty bad. So, she's not your girlfriend?"

"We dated a couple of times, that's all."

Natasha raised her eyebrows skeptically. "But she's the same one I heard through the walls, isn't she?"

"She's experimenting with liberation, running around, having fun."

"But when she needed help she ran to you."

"I guess she trusts me. We won't be dating again, though, that's for sure. She's apparently extended her tastes beyond my boundaries. I'd never hurt anyone, if that's what you were worried about."

"If I thought that, Jake, I wouldn't be sitting here."

"I guess I care what you think of me."

"Really?"

"You're my next door neighbor. My Halloween partner. I wouldn't want you to think you're living next to a monster. And by the way, I assumed you were with your guy this weekend. He out with the Guard again?"

"Ray and I had a spat. I thought we needed a timeout. So I'm off tonight."

"That's a strange way to put it. Like you don't have to go to work. Wanna talk?"

"It happens sometimes. More, lately. He's irritable. Not happy being only part time in the military. His cross country team lost yesterday. His parents are breaking up. You know, stuff."

"Being with you, he should be happy as hell."

"Do you think so, Jake?"

"I know so."

She smiled weakly. "What a nice thing to say. A girl can use that kind of compliment once in a while."

"Once in a while? I'd..."

"You'd what, Jake?"

"I'd count myself pretty damn lucky."

"You're a sweet guy. That's why I couldn't believe you would ever hurt anyone. A few weeks ago when I heard you through the walls with that girl, you know what I noticed most?"

"Uh, no. Should I?"

"I noticed the laughter. You two were having a lot of fun."

"Anyway, I'd like to show the guy who did that to Lil what's what."

Natasha stretched, filling out her shirt. "Thanks for telling me. I'd better let you get some rest. You look tired."

He rose. "Sorry you had some trouble with Ray."

She rose also. "Are you sorry, Jake? Really?"

"Yes, *really*. Why wouldn't I be?"

"No reason."

"I'd like to feel that you're happy."

She stared at him. "See how sweet you are? Anyway, none of us can be happy all the time, can we?"

She smiled and left.

After strumming his guitar, he stretched out on the sofa and drifted off to sleep, woke up about seven, famished. He remembered that Natasha was over in the next flat, having the night off.

Some time off? Sounds like her relationship is like a factory job.

Tempted to knock on her door and ask her if she'd like to go for something to eat, he looked out his window and saw a black Camaro parked behind her Nash. Ray's car, he assumed. So much for his idea. Probably just as well because several times now he'd been ready to say more to her than he should. Having these kinds of feelings for someone who's to be married in six months wasn't wise.

14

Monday, November 20, nine days later …

Studying during his office hours, still sparsely attended by his students, Jake heard a tap at his opened door, Will Markley.

"The old man told me I had to haul myself out of the sack and get in here, or else."

"Glad you decided to make it, Will. Take off your coat. Have a seat. I hope you're here to do some writing."

"I guess so."

The young man's beard had grown down to his breastbone, making him look like he belonged in the Civil War.

"You understand the deal, correct?"

"Get up at eight-thirty, stagger over here, write four papers."

"Good. Our class is organized around what are referred to as the modes of expository writing, such as description, narration, comparison-contrast, classification, and whatnot."

"Whatever."

"So today I want you to use the first mode. Describe a place, any place. You can use my officemate's desk after we clean up the debris."

Jake got to work on Tim's mess.

"What kinda place you want me to describe?"

"Doesn't matter. What's your favorite place in the world, Will?"

"Wha'd'ya mean?"

"Say you met a girl you really liked, where's a place you'd like to show her?"

"My dorm room, where else?"

"Good. Describe it. Use the five senses."

"Wha'd'ya mean?"

"Seeing, hearing, smelling, touching, tasting."

"How ya taste a dorm room?"

"Do you ever drink three-point-two beer in your room?"

"That shit? No way. Tequila."

"Okay, put that taste in your essay. Describe your room." Tim's desk cleared, Jake handed Will a sheet of lined notebook paper. "Write on every other line, front and back, normal-sized handwriting. You have an hour, maybe make a quick outline of the details before you write, maybe start from the left as you enter your room and go completely around. We call that the spatial approach. Got it?"

"Like, there's my roomie's bunk then his desk, like that?"

"Sure, good idea."

"Who cares about my dorm room?"

"It's an exercise. Go on, do it."

Will sat, rolled up the cuffs of his corduroy shirt. "You got a pencil, man?"

Jake opened his drawer and pulled one out, handed it to him.

"Spelling count?"

"Sure, but you can use a dictionary." He handed the lad the Oxford paperback.

"How can I look it up if I can't spell it?"

"What word don't you know?"

"Barf."

"Use your common sense, and you might find it."

"Two *f*s or one?"

"No more questions. Write the paper."

Jake turned back to his volume on Blake. Ten minutes later Will shoved a scribbled document in front of him.

"I'll be back again on Thursday, like I promised Pop."

"All right, Will. I'm going to ask you to write a narrative. Maybe you can read Chapter Three in your text."

"Never bought a text."

"Maybe borrow one from your roommate."

"He don't have one neither. I don't know why you don't take the lousy grand."

After Will left, Jake looked at the essay, trying to figure out the handwriting.

If ya wanna know bout my room, go in the dore but be carefull not to open to far cuz ya bump the top of my roomies bunk, wake the creep up. Last night he drunk to much teckilla and barffed it all on the floor with his cheese twisties and it smelt like shit. Then his desk with nothin on it cept a model Corrvett hees working on, wastte can filled wit Bud cans, then right angle, window, then closet, then my bed w Cindy Lu naked, legs spread, waitin for me, an im gonna give it too her hard, then my desk, right angle, closet with a lotta crap in it, right angle, Cindy Lu's bike. So thats my room, if ya really wanna know. The End. Will Markley.

Sunday, November 26, six days later ...

To finish the writing phase of his waived term paper for Drew Byrne, Jake had forgone a Thanksgiving trip back to Lancaster, over the protest of his mother. He didn't tell her he was staying in Ohio to write an unnecessary assignment. But he refused to cooperate with the professor's extraordinary gesture of bribing him into antiwar dissent by lessening his academic development. It violated Jake's sense of professionalism. Although he had intended to combine his research with that of his paper for Thrillwell, the two projects turned out to be too different to meet both class requirements, which meant he had to write two quite separate pieces. His goal had been to complete the one for Drew over the break and to have Thrillwell's finished two weeks later, allowing him plenty of time to study for finals and finish grading for his own classes by the end of term in mid-December.

In his apartment he heard no activity from his neighbors and assumed they'd gone to their families for turkey and pumpkin pie. As he retyped his bibliography, his phone rang, a rare occurrence. It was Adele, who invited him to jam with Goldenrod. Josh, their rhythm guitarist, had gone home too.

"I'm not anywhere near your caliber," Jake said.

"How do you know that, Jake, without giving it a try?"

"Because I've never played with a group."

"Do you know the chords for 'This Land Is Your Land'? Didn't you tell me you learned with Pete's songs?"

"Yes, but..."

"No buts. The orchestra practice room in Music and Speech. The building is locked up, but I have a key, so meet us in front at one. Don't give me any crap about it," she ended playfully.

Why not do it? Maybe it's time to test my skill. I'll go over there, screw up enough, and Adele will leave me out of it.

He drove to the sprawling building, a combination performance center and classroom conglomeration at the northeast corner of campus. Adele was waiting outside for him. She led him through unlit corridors to the three-tiered practice room. It smelled of chalk dust and old paper. Music stands and folding chairs cluttered the place, a kettle drum and pair of covered tubas in the back.

They warmed up with standard pieces, "Blue Moon of Kentucky," A, D and E chords, simple enough, except these players had little quirks in the rhythm, sudden pauses, Jake's job to keep the beat as a bass player might do.

71

They didn't have a drummer, although Adele tapped a tambourine against her thigh as she sang, switching sometimes to strumming an autoharp.

Jake enjoyed the session, especially as these nice people tolerated his slipups, realizing most of his miscues were caused by the idiosyncrasies of their own arrangements. But he hung in there. His not having done this before, what did they expect?

They were good, too, authentic in their hillbilly twang. Wash, a lumbering, more than heavyset bearded guy in bib overalls, played amazing licks on the banjo then picked up a mandolin and did the same. Henry, a tall skinny guy with muttonchops, played a lively fiddle. Afterwards, they all went over to Adele's apartment and had turkey leftovers with a Woody Guthrie album on the stereo. They talked about Seeger's current attempt to clean up the Hudson River by building a sloop and sailing from Albany to Manhattan as a sailing troubadour. It became clear that Adele and Wash had started something up together. Jake left comforted that she'd found someone, Wash staying behind, both of them waving goodbye like a happily married couple.

That evening as Jake slouched in his easy chair reading, a light knock sounded on his door. In a flash he had the irrational thought that it was Natasha about to tell him the engagement was off, but he found Lil standing there in a wool cap, a winter scarf around her neck. His heart sank, but he let her in.

She'd missed two seminar meetings with Thrillwell as her eye healed, after which she seemed her normal perky self. She'd apparently intuitively inferred that Jake wasn't interested in renewing their sexual games. But now, her winter garments draped over his desk chair, she stretched out on his sofa in a gold paisley jumpsuit.

"I went for a walk," she said, "and saw your light. Thought I might come up and amuse you."

While water for tea heated up, Jake sat on the easy chair.

"I can't get that rough night a few weeks ago out of my head, Lil."

"Yeah, that wasn't amusing, was it?"

"Not at all. Everything okay?"

"No more frat parties for me. Those guys have no imagination, no innuendos whatsoever, like bears devouring fawns. So what about you, Jake. How's your sex life?"

"Not a lot of free time."

"So how 'bout tonight?"

"No, Lil. I think the police and everything else that night ruined it for me. Your style can get a guy in trouble. I guess I have a few boundaries."

"And I pushed you over them, is that it?"

The whistle of the teapot went off. He suggested they sit at the kitchen table, so she followed him there, sat as he gave her a teabag and poured water into one of Edith Whitcomb's chipped cups.

"Lil, I came here to establish a career. I don't want anything to threaten that. I've already had my picture taken at a protest vigil, and the police come here to my pad. Not a good start. I don't need any more sex adventures. And if I were you, I'd be damned careful."

"Yeah, this place is like a jungle with a bunch of horny gorillas."

"Maybe find a steady partner, someone who isn't going to give you a black eye."

"Steady, ugh. Takes all the fun out of it, Jake. Too predictable. I know I'm playing with fire, but dammit I like the risk. There's a poetry reading Tuesday afternoon, a coffee hour afterward. I'm definitely planning to hang around academic types rather than the brutes at the bars. Are you going to the reading? Some guy from the University of Tennessee."

"There's an antiwar panel at the same time. So I'm conflicted."

"I thought if the guy's cool, even if he's older, he might be lonely far away from home, up for a daring sexy lover of verse."

Jake felt relieved she wasn't going to go nuts because of his rejecting another wrestling match.

"You're an interesting woman, Lil."

"I sure don't want to be Melba toast. I guess I'm still searching for my 'erotic boundaries,' as you put it. One thing I learned for sure is that drunken beer bashes with football types are certainly not within them. I'll let you know how it goes with this visiting poet. Hey, there's a Bob Dylan flick playing at the Kent, supposed to be pretty good. We could catch the late show."

"Yeah, Lil, that sounds fine."

"I love Dylan, don't you?"

"I think he's kind of counterfeit, like he stole his image from the real McCoys."

"The Real McCoys? Is that a group?"

He laughed. "No Lil. Pete Seeger, Woody Guthrie. And there's a verse in 'The Times They are A-Changing' that's hard to forgive."

"Which verse is that, as if Dylan needs your forgiveness?"

"The one about 'mothers and fathers throughout the land.' He totally misunderstands the parents he's talking about. They've been through shit he couldn't imagine, and they have wisdom, and more, they love their kids, and to trample on that love is disgraceful. In general, of course, there are bad parents in every generation, but I happen to believe that ours are especially great people. And I don't like the way a punk like Bobby Zimmerman from a middle class family in Minnesota crassly dismisses them. He's plain wrong."

"Wow, Jake, that came out of nowhere. You feel passionate about this subject. So I guess you don't want to go to his film."

He took a breath to settle down, having let loose a fury that had been stored in some obscure compartment of his brain.

"No, let's go."

"But why? We could always stay here and ... oh, I get it. You want to get me the hell out of here."

"Let's have an understanding. You conduct your liberation experiment with me having been your first lab rat. I'd like to see the film because the guy is becoming a cultural force I'm trying to understand. People rebelling, grabbing on to clever phrases that they substitute for reasoned arguments. Like, 'ignore your parents' – Jesus!"

Lil smiled indulgently. "You're right about one thing, Jake. The boy sure can't sing. But you're much more to me than a lab rat."

15

Tuesday, November 28, two days later ...

During Jake's office hours, Will returned. Not taking off his coat, he pulled a folded paper out of the back pocket of his jeans and handed it to Jake.

"My second assignment, a story like you said, okay?"

"Not okay, Will. You have to write your paper here, in my presence."

"Why?"

"Obvious reasons."

"Like what?"

"Like, how do I know you wrote this?"

"It's in my handwriting. Take a look."

"Sorry. Let's clear the pizza box off my officemate's desk, and you can get to work."

"But I already spent half an hour on this thing last night."

"If you want credit for it, Will, you'll have to write it again, here, and I'll hold on to this version until you finish."

"Fuck, man! What are you, some kind of dictator?"

"If you want your D, you'll write your papers here."

"I was smashed when I wrote that. I forget the whole thing."

"So write a different story. Did you read the chapter on narration?"

"No. I forgot."

"A narrative is something that happened or might have happened, true or not, doesn't matter. Write it chronologically."

"What's that?"

"In the order it happened. Here's some paper."

Will sulked, muttered something unintelligible. "Fuck, do you have a pencil I can use?"

While the young man worked, Jake compared the handwriting of the paper he'd just handed him with the one he'd written a few days before. Except that they were both nearly illegible, they didn't match at all. If it weren't for the kid's dad, Jake would have thrown him out of the place.

After his two seminars Jake returned to his office to find Tim at his desk, the first time he'd actually seen him since their second arm wrestling match at the Hood. His hair had grown longer in dark curls, his shirt and khaki slacks wrinkled as if he'd slept in them.

Not looking up, Tim said, "You always move my things around."

"Just your trash. One of my students is doing makeup work. Used your desk. Is that all right?"

"Whatever. You'll be getting a new office bud next term anyway."

"What do you mean?"

"I got God damned fucking drafted."

Jake sat down and swiveled his chair toward his burly partner. "But why? Grad school deferment has been approved. I read about the policy a couple weeks ago."

"But TA's aren't fulltime."

"Right. Can't you switch?"

"Too damn late. Anyway, don't have the bread. I'm up shit creek without a paddle."

"Didn't you tell me you have a doctor's letter about your eyes?"

"No dice."

"So, you're going?"

"What else? I don't want to, but I'm not a coward, not running off to Canada or anything. They're letting me finish my term, at least. The Grad Office confirmed my job here. So it's the induction center in Cleveland, January third. That's it, tough shit."

"Sorry to hear it, Tim. I'm sure you don't support the war."

"That's not exactly true. I just didn't care about it, until now. I guess the government knows more about it than these protesters. I'll go and do my duty. If I don't, somebody else will have to."

The last statement hit Jake where it hurt, but he held back from trying to talk Tim out of going. He seemed to have weighed his alternatives.

"Did you hear about the big demonstration next weekend," Jake asked, "at the Cleveland Induction Center?"

"Yeah, they're taking buses from here, right? I'm not going with those clowns. I didn't figure you're into protesting, Jake. I thought you're out of the whole thing."

"But I don't believe in the war."

"So are you going to Cleveland? Sounds like a big party to me."

"No, I'm not going. There's liable to be trouble. I favor reasoned argument, like the faculty antiwar committee is trying, learning sessions, work for political candidates, open letters like the one to LBJ they published the other day, the silent vigil. The war was a mistake from the beginning."

"But we can't let the communists take over the whole world, can we?"

The two discussed the issues for another hour, Tim resigned to his fate beyond reasoning him out of it. It seemed a decision based upon rational judgment in spite of his irritation with having to go. With his own murky escape, Jake felt like a hypocrite, his persuasions halfhearted.

By the time the discussion ended, the moment came for Jake to decide about attending the poetry reading there in Satterfield or the antiwar panel across campus. The frigid weather made the decision a simple one.

"If I don't see you again, Tim, I hope everything works out for you."

"I'd just like one more try at arm wrestling."

They lined up for battle at Tim's desk. No change in the outcome.

At the reading, Lil, all dolled up, sat attentively in the front row. Professor T. Milford Bent, a Christian ethics proponent, presented the war only in terms of the unchristian methods being used by both sides. Jake thought the man's message was muddled, but some of the images in his poems were brilliant. Lil applauded ardently after each rendering. The poet wore a three-piece tweed suit and had the kind of head that inspired sculptors to create bronze busts. He read with a lilting baritone voice that didn't need a microphone and stayed true to the regular meter and rhyme with which his verses had been constructed.

Jake's main purpose for attending was that the bigwigs in the Department were there, Thrillwell included, and that he received some brownie points by being seen by them. Readings, lectures, discussions, coffee hours were the kind of obligatory assemblies that lay ahead in his career. The Department's growing antiwar contingent would be at the Vietnam panel.

Now and then Lil's eyes met Jake's with an ironic gleam. She'd purchased Professor Bent's volume of poems, had him sign it, and ended up the only female in a sparse circle seated around the dignitary as the others, Jake among them, filtered out.

Wednesday, December 6, eight days later ...

As Jake's nine o'clock let out, Adele came into the room, a serious expression in her eyes.

"We need your guitar, Jake."

"No problem. I'll go home and get it."

She smiled. "Not the instrument, silly. You, playing it."

"You're kidding."

"Josh finally flaked out to play rock 'n roll."

"But I only practiced with you guys once, with unimpressive results."

"With *impressive* results. You're good. Sure, you'll get better, but we need you today."

"Today?"

"You know about the big rally, right? For the trip to the induction center on Friday?"

"Yeah, I read about it."

"Here's Wash's idea. He believes things are going to get out of hand around here. The two antiwar groups are growing, both recruiting followers, and there's this whole antidraft program all over the country this week. Wash says it's like a lit fuse. He believes our playing will calm emotions, a counter-balance to the vitriol. See?"

"So he wants to perform at the demonstration today?"

"Play in the background. Like Pete would do if he were here. But we'll be really thin without a rhythm guitar, and we need your voice as well."

"My voice?"

"For back up. You're good at harmony."

"Jesus, Adele, this is coming at me from out of the blue."

"It doesn't have to be a permanent commitment, Jake. For today, all right?"

"All right. It might calm things down. But the activists might get ticked off when they're making speeches."

"We won't play while they're talking, and we'll stay in the background, on the other side of the crowd. Go get your guitar and meet us at the Union."

About two hundred people gathered in front of the HUB, Goldenrod across the street performing the Pete Seeger songbook, Jake humming harmony when he didn't know the words and struggling to follow the group's syncopation. Some people actually sang along. Pete would have been proud. When the leaders of the demonstration spoke, the group let their voices go silent.

A grad student in political science made a major point. He'd conducted a statistically valid poll of KSU students, finding that only twenty-two percent of the student body believed in the present war policy, while fifty-one percent disagreed, twenty-seven percent abstaining.

"Now," the speaker bellowed, a tall, slim fellow with long dark sideburns and mustache, his eyes covered with sun glasses, "with a majority of this campus behind our cause, it's time to step up or game. We need less speeches and more action."

"That's Holly McGill's other half," Adele said.

"Holly McGill?"

"She's one of the most popular lecturers in the English Department, working on her Ph.D. One of the sweetest people you'll ever meet. They live in the famous Haunted House, with some other activist types. She does all the cooking and housework for those madmen."

During the frequent disorganized time lapses when participants milled and chatted, Goldenrod played, not loudly, not with mikes, but with passion, with energy. No one objected. People thought the group was part of the program even though they were far away from the speaker's stand. Two buses would leave that Friday to join Saturday's masses demonstrating at the Cleveland Induction Center. Overnight housing would be provided free of charge.

The members of Goldenrod would not be among them, but Wash, thrilled at the reception their impromptu performance received, wanted to make sure the group did the same at all the local rabblerousing, Jake included if he consented. Impressed with Wash's thinking, Jake was pleased to agree, though he would need a lot of practice and memorizing.

16

Saturday, December 15, ten days later ...

Jake awoke to what he recognized as the rattling of a snow plow. He looked out his window and saw the neighborhood buried in white. The forecast had been for snow but nothing like this. And it wasn't one of those romantic first snows with big flakes drifting down tickling one's nose. These were small, cold flakes being blown by gusts of wind, piling in drifts against hedges and homes. His MGA was practically covered, his neighbor's Rambler submerged up to the hood. The plows had blocked the driveways with heaps of the white stuff.

The radio said that predictions had been inaccurate as they often were along the Great Lakes, seven inches so far and perhaps three more to come. There was no way Jake would be able to make the Christmas break drive back to eastern Pennsylvania.

The term had closed the day before with a flurry of paper pushing, Jake's freshman grades finally submitted. Of his original seventy students, he'd given eight A's, seventeen B's, twenty-seven C's, nine D's, and four F's, the latter only for those who either failed to complete the course or never showed up at all. Five students had officially dropped. So the Bell Curve was skewed slightly to the high end but not so that anyone in Admin would accuse him of being too soft a grader. He still cringed at having passed Will, but that had been a moral compromise in favor of Mr. Claude Markley's having served in the same desert arena as Jake's dad. He had the scars to prove it. As for Jake's own classwork, he had nailed down aces in both his seminars. So he'd been planning to make the drive home to report success to his parents.

A plow rumbled by, adding to the blockage of snow in front of driveways, wind blustering, flakes flying sideways more than downward. But rather than annoyance Jake felt the odd pleasure that comes when one's will is utterly blocked, submission the only option. So without need to set the alarm, Jake settled back under the covers and drifted into a well-needed sleep.

When he woke up about eleven, the blizzard had become flurries in a gray, cold sky, difficult to know if the flakes were still falling or only being hurtled about by the wind. One thing sure, he needed to dig his car out before the snow melted through the faulty seals in the vinyl top. After bacon and eggs, he pulled on long johns, jeans, sweatshirt, pullover cap and hiking boots, went down the back stairs kicking the snow away as he descended, feeling the bite of the wind. He trod through the deep cover of white to the utility shed where he was certain he'd find a shovel. But the shed was padlocked.

Then he heard Natasha's voice. "I'll bring the key." She stood in her back doorway gripping a bathrobe tightly around her neck, her blond hair lifted by the breeze. "Let me pull something on."

He plodded around to the driveway to assess the damage, his car a mere impressionistic snow sculpture. As sentimental as he felt at his dad's heartfelt gift over ten years before, this vehicle, with all its engineering deficiencies, had become a constant exasperation.

Time for a change. I'll have to talk to Dad when I get home. Hope he'll understand.

His father, who held onto things until they literally fell apart, would probably insist that with a few tweaks and rebuilding, the worn-out crate would be as good as new. With his gloved hands, Jake cleared a path through the drift to see the windshield. Another plow roared by adding to the obstruction of the way out.

When Natasha called from the back yard, Jake followed his own snow prints back where in the dimness of the shed they found a snow shovel and a garden spade. Bundled up, she smiled, her cheeks glowing rosy from the cold.

"Too bad this came on the weekend," she said. "I was hoping to get Monday off from school. Don't you just love snow days?"

"I bet you get a lot of them in these parts."

"And we cherish each and every one like little gifts from God."

"Do you think the worst of this is over?" Jake asked.

"That's what the radio says."

"Yeah, but they said this might be only three inches."

After she followed Jake's path back to the front, they got to work clearing their cars. A few other neighbors, mostly students, toiled with shovels and snow blowers.

After about an hour's hard labor, the pair had cleared both vehicles, snow piled high at the edge of the yard. The driveway itself and the white wall left by the plows yet to be dealt with, Natasha suggested a break for coffee. They trekked back and climbed the rear stairs to her place where they used a broom to sweep each other's clothes. Their exertion had more than neutralized the freezing wind, and Jake sat at her kitchen table feeling his long underwear soaked in sweat. The coffeepot gurgling, Natasha pulled off her turtleneck to her tee shirt which Jake couldn't help but notice clinging to her bra beneath.

"Excuse me," he said, "none of my business, but I've been wondering why your fiancé hasn't shown up to lend a hand."

"It's his weekend with the Guard. I'm sure they're having a grand old time clearing the interstate."

"I'm sure that's good practice for Vietnam."

She smiled, her complexion radiant with health. "He hates being stuck in the Guard, says he should have enlisted, tried for officer training."

"Don't most guys go into the Guard to get out of the draft?"

"Ray is quite patriotic. Wanted to go. His mother and I talked him out of it. He joined the Guard to placate me, blames me for it sometimes."

"Stuck here with you, huh? He should count himself fortunate. So he believes in the war?"

"His dad got a Bronze Star from D-Day. The military is a tradition in their family. They have an ancient photo of an ancestor at Antietam, holding a musket. His granddad was at Ypres in the First World War. You know, courage and honor, all that? And poor Ray had to duck out because of his girl." She paused. "Now don't you dare say something dumb like you always do."

"Something dumb? Like what?"

"You know what I mean."

"Give me an example."

"Like, for me you'd give up going to war in a heartbeat."

Jake leaned back in his seat to evaluate this new turn in their repartee. Then he hung his head.

"Have I been that obvious?"

She smiled. "I'm afraid so, Jake." She poured coffee into mugs. "Milk and sugar?"

"Black is fine."

She placed his steaming mug in front of him and sat down with hers across the table.

"Okay then," he said, ignoring his brew. "Those idle comments weren't intended to be dumb. There was truth in them. Sorry, if I offended you, but actually..."

She smiled tolerantly.

"If you really want to know," he picked up, "I felt something from you too. And didn't think it was dumb in the slightest. A little dangerous for you, is all."

"When did you feel *something* from me?"

"Fixing your spark plugs, raking leaves, on the front stairs coming and going, Halloween, your curiosity about my dating life. Ray felt it from you too, apparently. Got on your case about it."

She stared at him, no smile, some sadness. She took a sip of her coffee.

"So there *is* something," she said. "Yes, both ways, isn't there?"

"No doubt."

"Yes, no doubt." She grimaced in distaste, not from the coffee.

Jake peered at the steam rising from his mug.

"But you know it's impossible, don't you, Jake?"

"A man can dream, can't he?"

"See? That's what I mean about saying dumb things."

"What's dumb about it?"

"Like you think it's not something serious."

"If it's impossible, what's left but graveyard humor?"

"Not rubbing it in would be more gracious."

"Maybe you're right about that. But until this little chat, we've been skirting the issue. And anyway..."

"Jake, you're always starting a statement and then not finishing it."

"That's because I'm afraid you don't want to hear it."

"It's what we're talking about in this *little chat* as you sarcastically put it. So tell me."

"Okay then. Maybe it's not as impossible as you think."

She paused, apparently to let this sink in. "My God, Jake!"

"Is it such a shocking thought?"

"You can say it because you're free. If you were in my position, you'd see it in a different light."

"As being impossible?"

"Absolutely impossible. There's too much at stake."

"All right, it's God-damned impossible. That's why I haven't been in hot pursuit."

"And you haven't been?"

"Natasha, now that this is out in the open, do you have any idea how many times I wanted to knock on your door, how often I've thought of you over here, only a thin wall between us? How when we're side by side I wanted to take you in my arms? You're right, our perspectives are different, and believe it or not, dumb comments aside, I've honored yours. And will, of course. I'm not going to attack you. Christ!"

"I wasn't sure of that after I heard, and then actually saw, what happened to your girlfriend."

"She's not my girlfriend, dammit. And I didn't hurt her and never would."

"I'm sorry, Jake. I didn't mean that. I know you wouldn't."

"Do you think I didn't feel your jealousy? Did you want me to be loyal to an impossible situation? Celibacy isn't my thing. I'm sorry, but I'm a normal, twenty-eight-year-old, single guy."

"Of course you are, Jake."

"And I never attacked Lil. We were fooling around and, whatever it was, I'm glad it's damned over."

"All right, all right, Jake. Calm down. I remember listening to the two of you laughing. Let's look at this whole situation like rational adults, shall we?"

"Sure, I'll try, but there's more going on here than rationality."

"Yes, like you're seeing this as something possible."

"I not only see it as possible, Natasha, but..."

She huffed. "There you go again, Jake, leaving off your sentence. But ... what?"

"But as ... inevitable."

"What?" She rose, backed up against the sink. "What did you say?"

"You heard me," Jake said, rising too. "And don't count that as one of my so-called dumb comments. When a man and a woman feel what we've been feeling, the crack in the dam will open. It's inevitable."

"Are you out of your mind?"

"Are you out of yours to deny it?"

"What are you referring to as a crack in the dam?"

"Your feelings for me. If you were happy with Ray, you wouldn't have these feelings. The dam is your obligation, and the crack in it is your desire."

"Stop it, Jake. You sound conceited."

They stared at each other, Jake feeling he'd never seen a woman as superb as the one before him at this moment.

"I'll go back to my apartment if you want me to," he said.

She sighed as if in resignation of something. "No, please sit down and drink your coffee. We have work to do outside. I think you have a highly overinflated impression of your magical charm. The dam is strong, and will remain intact."

Jake and Natasha worked on clearing the driveway, eventually attacking the plow-made barrier, the wind calming and even momentary patches of blue sky. A spirit of comradeship prevailed with neighbors out, mostly undergrads, joking, drinking beer, laughing, laboring together. Jake had a new kind of breakthrough energy rivaled only in his memory by the moment of his and Ainsley's coming together. He felt united with Natasha now, regardless of the consequences, their future entirely in her hands.

He knew not to press the issue. It was there, implicitly, that immensity of pressure against the metaphorical dam. She held the switch that would release the floodgates, she and only she. He would wait. So he shoveled with manly vigor, joked with the neighbors, enjoyed every fabulous moment of Natasha working by his side and of the both of them getting involved in a snowball fight, one side of the street versus the other. He knew without doubt that she was what he yearned his future to be. And he thought but didn't say, *You see, don't you, Natasha, that right here this moment is what our being together would be like?*

Finally, nearing dusk, they completed their toil and started the cars to let the engines warm. As they leaned against their respective vehicles, they smiled at each other.

"So, what now?" she said. "And don't say, 'the inevitable.'"

"Would you like to go someplace for dinner?"

"I can't be seen out and about with you, Jake."

"Right. *Ulysses* is playing at the Kent. It's dark in there."

"The Civil War?"

"No, James Joyce's novel, the screenplay highly edited according to reviews."

"We'll still have to go in and out of the theater," she reminded him. "I know. Let me cook something."

"Great idea. You're a wonderful cook."

"And lay off the compliments, okay?"

He bowed, flourished. "Your wish is my command, *mademoiselle*."

She shook her head at his foolishness. "Then after we eat, why don't we play Scrabble?"

"Sounds delightful."

She flashed an in-spite-of-herself grin. "Jesus, please hide your glee, okay? It's like you think you've won a duel against me."

17

An hour later ...

After a shower, Jake checked his watch eager for the allotted time to pass. In the meantime he tidied up his place. Then, in a pressed dress shirt and gabardine slacks, his hair still damp, combed back covering the top halves of his ears, his longish sideburns neatly clipped, he slapped some English Leather on his neck and knocked on Natasha's door.

"It's open," she yelled from the kitchen.

As soon as he entered, the delicious aroma of marinara hit him. Gershwin's *American in Paris* played on a stereo. She stood at the stove, slacks and blouse partially covered with an apron, her hair pulled back in a short ponytail.

"Food smells terrific," he said.

"Almost ready. Have a seat. Didn't have much, planned on grocery shopping today. But I did find a lonely can of peas in the cupboard."

"I'm so hungry, raw turnips would do."

"I have a bottle of Chianti I've been saving. Would you like some?"

"Only if you would."

"But of course, *monsieur.*" She turned and smiled.

"What were you saving the wine for?"

"The holidays coming up. Now's the perfect time."

Jake ate with gusto, to his hostess's apparent delight.

"You look nice, Jake."

"So do you, Natasha. But you'd look nice covered with coal dust."

"Enough of that," she said smiling.

"I'm sure you get that kind of remark everywhere you go."

"Don't be silly."

"Don't guys hit on you all the time?"

"Not when they see my engagement ring."

"Your male students must have giant crushes."

"Jake, stop it." She blushed in the candlelight. "I don't care for juvenile flattery. Let's have a pleasant evening, shall we?"

Sensing a mild setback, Jake focused on his chicken breast. He had, indeed, been being juvenile and felt gladdened she was above such comments. He was embarrassed that he hadn't realized it. After the meal she cleared away the dishes and set cups of chilled chocolate pudding on the table. Jake refilled their wine glasses.

"So," she said, "how did your classes go this term?"

"The ones I taught or the ones I took?"

"Start with the ones you taught."

As they ate their dessert, he told her about Will Markley. She laughed at the tale.

"His writing is really that dreadful?"

"Yeah, no way he deserved to pass."

"I think you did the right thing. At least you didn't take the bribe."

"I did it for his dad. The war is forcing all of us into moral dilemmas."

She suggested they move into the living room where she ushered him to an easy chair and flipped the album to *Rhapsody in Blue*. Apron discarded, she set the half full wine bottle on a coffee table alongside a Scrabble board. She settled on the sofa.

"You didn't tell me about the classes you *took*, Jake."

"That's a pretty boring subject." But he filled her in on the polar opposite profs he'd had. "Ever read any T.S. Eliot?"

"Of course. What's that line? – 'In the room the women come and go, talking about Michelangelo'?"

"Yeah, 'Prufrock' is jam-packed with quotable lines."

"'Do I dare to eat a peach?'"

"'Shall I walk along the beach,'" he echoed. "'Shall I wear the bottoms of my trousers rolled?'"

"Poor J. Alfred," Natasha said. "Such lonely soul."

"So, being a French teacher, I'm sure you're into the French poets."

"We had to study the major ones – Rimbaud, Valery, Hugo, of course, Mallarme, but my favorite is Anais Nin."

"Anais Nin?"

"Does that surprise you?"

"Wasn't she into a *manage-et-trois* with Henry Miller and his wife?"

"You know so little of me, Jake."

"Maybe, but I highly doubt you're into threesomes. I do know the most important thing about you, though."

She smiled, sipped her wine, looked at him. "That comment is too intriguing to resist, although I think I should."

"All right, let's play Scrabble. But no using French words."

"I happen to have the official dictionary. We'll use only words from there, but..."

"You ended a sentence without finishing it," Jake pointed out.

"Yes, I guess I did, didn't I?"

"So who makes the first word? You are about to be overwhelmed by my verbal acuity."

"Wait just a minute, Jake. What is this *most important thing* you claim to know about me?"

Not much of a drinker, Jake was feeling the wine.

"Maybe I should keep it to myself. Like a secret weapon."

"I don't think so. And whatever you think this *weapon* is, I'm sure you're not correct."

"I'm correct, all right."

"I've never been involved in a *manage-et-trois*, if that's where you're going."

"No, I'm sure of that. I have no idea of your dark secrets."

"Out with it. No secret weapons allowed."

"I think we should play Scrabble."

"Stop teasing me, you jerk," she said smiling. "Tell me."

"Okay, only if you insist."

"Yes, I insist."

He mock cleared his throat. "All right, Natasha, you're correct that I don't know much about you, like your favorite poet being Anais Nin, but I do know the key thing."

"Yes, damn you, Jake. So you said. And what do you think this key thing is?"

"The key thing is that ... I know how ... to give you ... a happy life."

She stared at him. She let out a puff of air, leaned back, studied him as if taking stock.

"Very amusing, Jake. Another of your dumb remarks. Do you really think that because I told you I like Nin's poetry, your supposed prowess in bed will give me a happy life?"

"No. Nothing to do with Nin and prowess in bed. I'd never reduce someone of your quality to that level."

"Oh, really?"

"Now on to our word game."

"No, Jake. Okay, you caught my vain curiosity. What, exactly, do you think will give me a happy life?"

"It's not one thing. It's a medley of things. A cocktail, as it were."

She smirked. "And of what, pray tell, does this medley consist?"

"Pay attention, there will be a quiz." The wine was loosening his usual inhibitions, but it felt good to speak his mind to her at last. He spoke into her listening eyes. "The medley consists of a man who will give you adoration, devotion, protection, respect, loyalty, equality, children, a great home, companionship through old age, and complete freedom in the bedroom. There may be more ingredients that elude me at the moment. But, to sum it up, an ideal love."

Gershwin's symphony ended. Natasha stared at Jake as if evaluating his sanity.

"Jesus, Jake," she said. "What ... I mean, what are you talking about? This transcends dumb. It's ... it's ridiculous."

"No it's not."

"Ridiculous. Just ... ridiculous."

He leaned forward across his pudding cup. "Why is it ridiculous?"

"Because ... first of all no man, not even you with all your delusions of grandeur could possibly provide all that, and second, because ... there's no such thing as an *ideal* anything. Life is a compromise, we have to take the good with the bad, if we're actually being serious here."

"You don't really believe that."

"Jake, where on earth do you get off telling me what I really believe and what I don't?"

He now realized he'd trapped himself in a full scale debate. "I know, that's all."

"That's hard to reject," she scoffed, "some intuitive, spiritually revealed insight from a silly mind."

"It all comes down to your name," Jake said. "Natasha-Kitty. You know all about it from old Leo."

She let out a breathy laugh, as if from relief. "I get it. Characters from a book."

"Don't you believe we can know of things from books? But I have another source, a very reliable one."

"And what in the world is that?"

"The way my dad loves my mom. I grew up with it. It got into my bloodstream, my soul, by osmosis."

This statement seemed to engulf the conversation in a sudden aura of sanctity.

"Oh, Jake, you absurd romantic. How your heart must have been broken, and how it will be again! There is nothing ideal in this world, and forgive me for saying it, but I'm sure your parents don't live up to that description. Levin and Kitty are romantic illusions. Have you any idea of how Tolstoy and his wife actually got along, how every married couple gets along, except maybe your idea of your parents?"

Jake took a deep, confident breath, leaned back on in his chair, and absorbed the sincerity and sadness in Natasha's eyes.

"My heart's already been broken, Natasha. But that was before I met you. And *you* cannot possibly break my heart."

"Golly, Jake, of course not, how could I? We're not even together, despite your sense of inevitability."

Tipsy or not, he felt free to speak his mind.

"Our being together doesn't matter, Natasha. You exist. I know of you. That's permanent, it's knowledge. It's not how you feel about me that matters but how I feel about you. It's how I think about you every day, every time I open my door and see yours, every time I see your old wreck of a vehicle, every time I think of you in your apartment, doing things, whatever they are – washing dishes, reading in bed, taking a bath – not to mention the little bit of time we actually shared together, like this exact moment and that sad, terrified look in your eyes."

She seemed about to say something, but he beat her to it.

"And now that I'm considering it, you must remember that Kitty didn't go for Levin at first, she thought she was in love with Vronsky. But that didn't change his love for her, not even for an instant. You are what you are, Natasha, and I'm not saying you're perfect, only that you're perfect for me. And if you don't believe it's possible for someone to feel this way about you, then you're the sad one, stuck in your world of compromise, and not seeing the escape from that misery even when it's staring you right in the face."

"Jake, stop it. Stop it. You've had too much wine. I guess you're not used to drinking, or something. I think maybe you should go home and sleep it off."

Jake nodded. "All right, Natasha, maybe I had just enough wine to be able to tell you how I feel. And I guess it's time you knew. Sure, I'll go. And I won't bother you. I won't pursue you. And tomorrow I'll leave for home for a couple of weeks. And maybe when I come back, I'll see you around, and maybe you'll get married in June and plod on with your life of compromise, but that won't change one iota of how I feel and what I know."

He stood up.

"Sorry I ruined the Scrabble game," he added glumly. "Have a wonderful Christmas."

18

Minutes later ...

After Jake left Natasha's apartment, rather than pulling his hair out, he grabbed his guitar and pounded out a long version of "If I Had a Hammer." Why on earth, he wondered as he strummed, had he revealed his deepest thoughts to her? How stupid could he be? What could he have expected but her panic and fright? Jesus Christ! Or but what he got, a realistic evaluation of his absurd hopes and dreams. She had her feet on the ground, and he lived somewhere in the ethereal clouds. And now he'd lost it all. He'd pushed her beyond her power to get back to where they'd been, nice neighbors with some unspoken fantasies. Worse, he wondered if she was right about his having over idealized his parents' relationship. Maybe what he wanted, or thought he wanted, was sheer lunacy. Maybe that was why he'd lost the two women he'd loved, and now the third. They knew they couldn't live up to his imaginary love story.

So what's left? Life as a tennis match? Enjoying the game for the game, not for the player across the net?

He knew he wouldn't be able to sleep after the atrocity he'd just committed, so he changed into warm clothes for a late night walk. As he tied his bootlaces, he heard a light knock on his door – Natasha, her face gleaming with cold cream. She stood there meekly, wrapped in a terrycloth bathrobe, with long pajamas and her fluffy pink slippers.

"I don't want to end our conversation the way we did. May I come in?"

He stepped aside. She entered.

"Looks like you're going out, Jake."

"I couldn't sleep."

"I heard you playing the guitar. It sounded angry."

"At myself, not you."

"Are you going to see that girl?"

"Lil? How many times must I tell you? She's only a friend, not even that."

"I can see you're upset. May I come along on your walk? I'll be ready in a jiff."

"What, God forbid, if someone sees you with me?"

"Everyone is snowed in."

"I'll be on the porch."

Though the cold bit his cheeks, the wind had calmed. The whiteness shone in the streetlights as the pair strolled on mostly cleared sidewalks, up College, north on Lincoln to Main, past the library, the university's paths still snow covered, closed for the break. Local kids were sledding down the steep slope from Kent Hall, their shrieks and laughter piercing the silence, parents huddled below on the library porch. Across the street, the garish neon of the all-night Hot Dog King reflected off the white.

"Let's get some hot chocolate," Natasha said. "I'm freezing."

"Are you sure you won't be observed?"

"Let's not sit by the window, anyway. Hardly a soul out driving around tonight. And guess I could simply say I went for a walk with my neighbor."

"A neighbor you're not supposed to be too enthusiastic about."

"It's not like going to the movies together."

Coats opened, scarves unwrapped, caps off, they sat in a booth, the only patrons there, the attendant behind the counter reading a *Mad* magazine.

Their steaming drinks before them, Natasha said, "I wasn't nice to you this evening. I'm sorry, Jake."

"I was too open, putting pressure on you. What else could you have done but defend yourself?"

"You did seem a bit smug," she said, "but I'm sure you were expressing your real feelings."

"You're correct on both accounts."

He took a sip – searing hot, delicious.

"Even so," she said, "I should have butted out of your parents' relationship. I guess it sounded too good to be true."

"I'm not saying they don't argue, or that they're happy each and every minute. It's just that..."

Natasha waited. "Please finish your sentences, Jake."

"Finishing my sentences is what gets me in trouble."

"You're not in any trouble."

"Sure feels like it, or did before you knocked on my door in your slippers."

"I couldn't let it end like that. So you started to say something about your mom and dad."

"They're rooted in one another. It's what they live for, their purpose, extended to me, of course. Our family."

"Not too different from my parents, really. I don't know why I responded the way I did."

"Because I was using that picture to pressure you."

"Pressure me for what?"

Instead of speaking, he gave her a look.

"Bed, Jake? Were all those beautiful words only a seduction speech?"

He felt heat at his neck, much more than from the hot chocolate and the warmth of the tacky restaurant.

"No, dammit, much more than bed. I'd ... like to make you happy. Exactly what I said, the whole bourgeois cliché."

"I'm sure that's not how you view it."

He looked at her face, her rosy skin, vibrant blue eyes. "You're right, that's a lousy way to say it. But my ridiculous romantic viewpoint is coming under heavy attack these days, like there are more cosmic things to be concerned about."

"Those cosmic things *are* important, Jake, civil rights, the war, drugs, moral decay, all of it. Something serious is happening in our country."

"Yeah, don't I know it!"

"You're right in there with John Lennon, Jake—'Love is all you need.'"

He smiled. "And that reduces it to a platitude."

They retraced their tracks beside the silent campus. Natasha grasped Jake's arm and held it as they trod onward. The intimacy surprised him, warmed him.

"So you really want to go to bed with me, Jake?"

He said nothing, kept moving to cover up his astonishment.

"Answer me. Do you, really?"

"It wasn't a seduction speech, Natasha."

"That doesn't answer my question."

"Do I want to go to bed with you? Jesus, what do you think?"

"I think, you're not thinking clearly."

"Sure, I'll give you that."

"For you, it's simple, but not at all for me."

"I know."

"What would you think of me?"

"I believe I already explained that."

"If I gave in to these strong feelings and then continued with Ray, what would that make me, Jake? The dam would crack wide open and the flood would destroy everything in its path, all three of us, my parents, Ray's parents. See what I mean?"

"Yeah, I see, but..."

"There you go again, not finishing your thought."

"That thought's not worth finishing."

"You're imagining my breaking my engagement with Ray and moving in with you. Right?"

"I'm not that crazy, I guess."

"You once asked me what I'd do if Tom Jones called me up, remember?"

"And you were offended, rightfully so, and fled up the stairs."

"I thought about it afterwards and came to the conclusion that under such overwhelming circumstances, the conditions exactly right, I might, hypothetically, be capable of a one night stand with Tom Jones. But I highly doubt that's what you have in mind. If I did such a thing with someone, Tom or maybe you, say only one night, no one to know, I'd only have to live with *myself*. Other than to my conscience, there'd be no destruction. But a one night stand isn't at all what you have in mind, is it, Jake?"

"I guess I wasn't thinking that far ahead."

"Yes, and I highly doubt someone in Tom Jones's category is going to call me. Not that you're not handsome, Jake, and not that I don't find you extremely sexy."

She squeezed his arm and lay her head on his shoulder as they plodded down Willow Street.

"Maybe if we had met in undergrad," he said.

"I've been with Ray, on and off, since the first week of my freshman year at OSU. He and I have a history, Jake, and a lot of wonderful times."

"I wish I'd met you in first grade. Then, I absolutely know there'd have been no ons-and-offs. At least from my side."

"First grade? What a cute idea! Haven't you ever been in love, Jake?"

"Twice. But there were no ons-and-offs, only offs and a major screw up on my part."

Natasha did not pursue this point as they walked on down to Willow. Two plows rumbled past.

"I want to get to know you, Jake. What you've been saying tonight intrigues me. I know it's not only seduction. But we need some time, as neighbors. After all, this thing we feel is coming from somewhere exciting but dangerous, and if we act on it at this point, we'll regret it. It will end up tragic. We could leap into something that could satisfy itself in a mere twenty minutes, and then find out things about each other that could change everything, and there'd be nothing left but T.S. Eliot's wasteland. I know instinctively you're a good person, Jake, but..."

"I know the same thing instinctively about you too, Natasha."

"But instincts are not what we should bet our lives on, are they?"

"I know you're trying to let me down gently. It figures. That's the kind of lovely person you are."

"Don't think of it like that. But we need some friendship time to get to know each other. I can handle that. And it would be much better to end up good friends for life than lovers for twenty minutes, don't you think so?"

He knew she was skillfully guiding him out of his adolescent urge to simply possess her. Her charming manner made him cherish her even more.

"Don't you think so, Jake?"

"Maybe, but one thing I *do* know—it wouldn't last only twenty minutes."

LOVE and WAR at KENT STATE

PART TWO: 1968
Tasha

19

Tuesday, January 9, 1968, after Christmas break …

Jake read the *Stater* at his office desk, the one once belonging to Tim, who'd been inducted into the Armed Services of the United States, the desk having been commandeered by Jake because of the window. He had yet to meet his new officemate but could tell by the arrangement of his own former desk that the new TA happened to be an attractive young black woman, apparently a graduate of Oberlin. He knew this because of the framed photographs on either side of the reading lamp. One pictured a beautiful black girl between two whites, sorority sisters by the Greek letters on their shirts. The other picture showed the same young woman between two adults, presumably her parents.

By the meticulous arrangement of desk accoutrements Jake knew he wouldn't have to be cleaning up debris. Tim would no doubt learn neatness in the army. Jake's new officemate had centered a nameplate perfectly beneath the amber covered lightshade – Carmen Ella Curlew. She would be the only African American among the grad student teachers of freshman composition.

Should be interesting.

Jake felt guilty about having captured the window desk even though he'd done so before he knew who the new arrival would be. Of course, she'd have no idea about his selfish act, but that fact didn't make him feel any better. He'd taken for granted Tim's replacement would be male.

Engrossed in an Associated Press article about broad scale attacks by the Viet Cong all over South Vietnam, referred to as the Tet Offensive, he heard a tap on his opened door, Adele.

"You're up bright and early, Jake."

93

"That makes a pair of us. Come in, have a seat."

Her light brown hair frizzed out as usual, feather earrings dangling, she said, "Can't chat. I thought you'd like to know that I put your name in for my job next fall. I'll need every minute to prepare for my comps. Then my dissertation and I'll be out of this hellhole. You're clearly the best one to take over the torture."

"I'm flattered, Adele, especially since you make the position sound so lovely. But no thanks."

"I figured you'd say that, which is why I didn't discuss it with you. You'll take the job, though. I'm sure." Her eyes brightened with confidence.

"You're sure, are you? And why's that?"

"Because you're ambitious. Because you're damned good. Because you're needed. And because you're sensible. All of which will force you to accept. We'll have plenty of time to go over the ropes. Oh, and one more thing. Wash wants some time with you about our group. There's a folk festival two weekends from now. Of course we're performing, and we need you. He wants you to practice a few things."

"I'm not ready for that and you know it."

"Beggars can't be choosers. We need you for backup and harmony. Josh isn't coming back; he's getting into electric stuff. He and Wash had it out the other day. Wash needs a couple of hours with you as soon as you can. He was hoping tonight before the term really takes off. Okay? Okay!" She smiled warmly. "Come over to the house at six. I'll make you some Pennsylvania Dutch chicken and waffles. See ya bye."

Before he could object, she was off.

Doubtful about the bureaucratic promotion, if an *advancement* it was, Jake reminded himself that he was there to pull the grades and win a fellowship at a classier school. He didn't need distractions like time consuming administrative duties and learning how to play bluegrass rhythm guitar. He had prepared the new term in the same rigid configuration as the previous one: his classes and office hours in the early mornings, his two seminars back to back, one on the Romantics, the other on Thoreau and Emerson, again with combined research projects in mind. For the silent vigils and related matters, he'd kept Wednesday afternoons free, which seemed to be the usual time for anti-war events.

At home with his parents over break, he'd sent a letter to Lancaster's Selective Service Office, providing his current address and phone number in Kent. He didn't want concerned officials bothering his folks, whom he feared would try to protect him. He wanted to remove that option from their thinking. Ready and willing to serve any sentence meted out, he wanted to forestall the possible accusation of his evading capture.

He'd had a quiet time, enjoying his mother's cooking, working in the shop with his dad, playing poker with some of his high school pals, practicing Goldenrod's songbook, reading Ralph Waldo's essays, and trying unsuccessfully to keep Natasha out of his thoughts. In fact, she'd become part of his permanent but subtle awareness. Though tempted to phone Ainsley, his ex-fiancé, at her estate near D.C., which was soon to become a progressive school in the model of Summerhill, he decided to leave well enough alone. She'd found a new man with whom she was planning the project, so contact would only be awkward for all involved.

The two days since he'd been back in Ohio, he and Natasha's paths hadn't crossed. He didn't want to pressure her about what she'd referred to as *neighborly time* together. As far as he was concerned, he'd known everything he needed to know the first time he laid eyes on her. He'd simply had to restrain himself from pounding on her door and taking her into his arms. He recalled their walk in the snow, her leaning against him holding his arm, her scent, her stirring feminine pliability as they'd hugged good night, her marvelous common sense. How could he even put these feelings into words? But it all came down to the depressing fact, so plainly and correctly expressed by her, that he was free and she was not.

God damn that simple fact to hell!

He'd fantasized her breaking up with Ray over vacation and waiting on his doorstep when he returned. A fantasy was all it turned out to be. Anyway, he would not exert his presence on her. He'd wait for their paths to cross naturally or to hear her knock on his door. She was entirely in charge of what would become of them. Any push from his part would risk driving her away entirely, a risk he wasn't willing to take. Thank heavens, she'd allowed him to survive that maudlin speech at her kitchen table.

Cool it, he had to constantly remind himself. But had she thought of him at all? The feelings existed, of that he had no doubts. How long could she go on denying what he knew to be a certain truth?

Enough, already, he thought, leafing through the daily college paper where he caught glimpse of the small headline: *Tolstoy's Daughter to Appear.* Alexandra Tolstoya's presentation would take place a week away, seven-thirty in Bowman Hall.

Hmm. Would he not be derelict of his duty not to inform Natasha of this fortuitous event? Her name had come from the Russian writer. Jake and she had interwoven Leo's work in their flirtations. Yes, flirtations. What else could he call their conversations? It wouldn't be a date, would it? Not at all, simply two interested parties attending a presentation of strong mutual interest. Like two birdwatchers having the opportunity to spot the dance of the rare whooping crane. Something not to be missed. How could she refuse?

He clipped the announcement and put it in his wallet. He'd give it to her this evening. No, he wouldn't have time in case she invited him in. He'd promised to meet with Wash. So, tomorrow. He'd give it to her tomorrow when she came home from her job. Perfect!

But wait. Hold on. Inviting her to Countess Alexandra's talk would seem like asking her out. And there would be expectations of spending some moments together to catch up on their holiday breaks. It would look much too obvious. No, maybe it would be better to simply slip the announcement under her door. That way, if they happened to meet up at the occasion it would appear a coincidence of sorts, at least not a planned outing together. She would find the clipping, and if she wanted to discuss it further, she could come to him. Yes, sliding the article under her door would only be supplying her with information, not asking her to join him. His restraint would seem admirable. She'd see him as upright. No pressure whatsoever.

That evening after a tasty home cooked meal, Jake and Wash sat in Adele's kitchen, Wash demonstrating how to get more life out of chords, giving them vibrations resembling voice vibrato.

"Make them sing," he said. "Don't press them against the fret too tight. And at the end, or in pauses, let them linger. Give them voice."

Jake struggled to get the idea, paying too much attention to this subtle technique rather than to the chords themselves but at least picking up the concept.

"It's all muscle memory," Wash explained in his gentle giant manner. "Work on it. I know there's not much time. And pay attention to our sheet music, my and Henry's arrangements, because we add some syncopation, especially at the ends, and chords coming in there will sound like mistakes. Here's the song list for Friday night, okay? Only four numbers. There are a lot of acts. We're the only pure bluegrass, all the others are trying to sound like the Kingston Trio or P,P&M. We're the real deal. And we're gonna try to do a Seeger singalong kinda trip, though kids these days don't think it's cool. But the older ones in the audience will get into it, along with the true-blue country music types."

"All four-four time?" Jake asked.

Wash smiled. "Yeah, very basic. We won't rush you. And somewhere along the way, you should learn the G-run. You know, Lester Flatt's little invention? Easy to slide down to D and back up. It'll cover you in almost every situation. You know it, right?"

"No, sorry," Jake answered nervously.

"Here, let me show you."

"You need to find someone good," Jake protested. "I don't do slides and runs. My guitar is only a time killer for me, like space to think in."

96

"Bluegrass musicians are hard to find, *kemo sabe*, and you brush and pull chords like nobody's brother. When you learn to add a touch of musicianship and a few simple riffs, you'll be terrific. Plus you got a great voice. Why didn't you ever learn this stuff, anyway?"

"Besides apartment singalongs, never even thought about it."

"Start thinking about it, okay?"

"Isn't it a blast, playing with us?" Adele piped in.

Wednesday, January 10, next day ...

At his kitchen table Jake was finishing up a Salisbury steak TV dinner when he heard a shave-and-a-haircut-two-bits knock on his door. Thinking his clipping tactic had born fruit, he jumped up from his chair, forced himself to take a breath and strolled into the living room.

And there she was, golden haired, blush cheeked, blue eyed in the dim light of the landing, holding up a ragged piece of newsprint.

She smiled. "This slip of paper mysteriously showed up under my door. Would you happen to know anything about it?"

"Who me? Not a bit. What is it?"

He stood back and gallantly gestured for her to enter, which she did.

"Something smells good," she said.

"Swanson."

"Poor man! How sad that you must eat that poison!"

"Bachelor's best friend. Care to stay a minute, or are you on the run?"

"I can spare a minute. Sorry I haven't dropped by before. I've been swamped with a student teacher, my first one. She's from U. of Akron."

She sat at his kitchen table. He put water on for tea.

"I was nervous when I first started student teaching," he said. "I remember all the girls had notebooks with pictures of the Beatles on the covers."

"Pictures of the Beatles made you nervous?"

"No, but it's an image I recall of that first day."

"Something tells me you were terrific."

"It took a while. I thought I'd floor them with my nice guy-ness, but soon learned that being their best friend doesn't work."

"No, you have to put the fear of God into them, then you can loosen up, slowly."

"If you'd taught when I was a student, I'd have majored in French."

With a stern look, she said, "Now enough of that tone, young man." She waggled an index finger.

"Somehow," he said, "I can't see you as a stern taskmaster."

"You'd be surprised." She laid the article on the table. "So, about this. She must be in her eighties."

"I didn't know she was out lecturing. Actually, didn't know a thing about her."

"Nor I. But this meeting is not to be missed. Whoever slipped it under my door must have known that."

"I would guess so."

"Wednesday nights are good for me. Ray has his Guard meeting over at the Ravenna armory. Might you be interested in going together?"

He shrugged. "I guess that could be arranged."

"I was thinking I could make dinner beforehand, maybe with a glass of wine?"

"I suppose I could deal with that."

"We should dress nicely," she added. "In the presence of royalty. And if she's promoting a book, I'd like to have a copy for her to sign. Do you think DuBois will have it?"

"I shall check, milady."

"I shall reimburse you, kind sir."

They prepared their Earl Grey tea.

"So," she said, "how was your break?"

"It was nice to be home. Yours?"

"A mix. Nice at my house, pretty rough at his."

"You said he's having some troubles."

"He's struggling. I wish I could help him, but I'm part of the problem."

Jake's attention perked up, but he took a calm sip of tea and waited.

"I think I told you he compromised his patriotic spirit for me."

"You mean he'd rather be ducking bullets halfway around the world than spending his time with you?"

"He feels emasculated. He's a sensitive guy, but an athlete too, so a bit macho. And his family tradition has been deeply ingrained. I told you about all those military pictures on their mantle."

Trying to learn the art of restraint, Jake held back from asking why she didn't just let Ray go to Vietnam.

"Is it wrong of me to be holding him back, Jake?"

He knew what he wanted to say, but said instead, "Didn't you once explain to me that compromise is part of any successful relationship?"

"How diplomatic of you, Jake!"

"What would you like me to say? That there are moments in a man's life when he must do what he must do? Like, where would we be if Coretta King had held Martin back from marching in Selma?"

"I don't think this is quite as dramatic. You believe I should let him go and pray day and night that he comes home alive."

"You're putting me in an awkward position, Natasha. If you're thinking I'd like Ray out of the picture in that particular way, you're wrong."

She sighed. "Here we go again, Jake, back to us. And I'm not blaming you. It's the elephant in the room whenever we're together. I'll confess it; I missed you over the holidays. But don't you think it's honorable of him to want to go? Heroic? Brave?"

"But also deceived. It's what governments do to their young men so they'll be willing to go and die. And I'm not saying it's not necessary sometimes. World War Two was necessary. Only we shouldn't be so persuaded by propaganda that we can't make informed distinctions."

"He says the protestors are cowards who want to stay home and smoke pot."

"In some cases, but not in all. I think resistance in the face of stupidity backed up by power is equally brave. This war is wrong. I feel sorry for the poor jerks who are tricked into it, and I hate the politicians responsible for the lies."

She shook her head. "Boy, I hope you and Ray never meet up. Or you and Daddy."

"I'm against the perpetrators, not the soldiers."

"So you resisted the draft, Jake?"

"The government gave me the option of fulfilling my duty by teaching. So that's what I did."

"No regrets?"

"Some, but that's a long story, not relevant. So," he took another sip, "are you the only roadblock to Ray's changing to fulltime? Can Guard members make such a switch?"

"Probably."

"And you'd wait, like you say, worried to death but loyal?"

"I guess I'd have to. But, Jake..."

"Finish your sentences, please."

"The pull for me to come over here late at night and knock on your door, well, I can't tell you."

Breathless at this confession, he studied her. When he gathered the wherewithal to respond, he said, "You know, don't you, that I'd open the door without hesitation. From now on I'll leave it unlocked."

She took a deep, frustrated breath. "But, my God, Jake! What then?"

He felt his body responding to this line of conversation.

What a joy it would be, but wait, hold on. This is only a damn discussion.

And she was right, wasn't she, about the repercussions? It could ruin everything he actually wanted. But his body didn't seem to care. And the decision had to be, he fought to reason, her choice. Otherwise it would all crash down on him, and he'd lose everything.

Christ! Look at her eyes, moist, sad, in turmoil.

Had he ever seen anything more beautiful? He leaned back, a foot farther away from her, fighting his arousal, trying to think of what to do, afraid simply to follow his impulse to get off his chair and grab her. But she was right to worry. He had to think of her situation.

"You really love Ray, don't you?" he heard himself ask.

She gushed her response as if his question was a huge kindness granted her in a time of dire stress. "Yes. Yes, Jake, I really do. I know him, we've shared so much, he's such a good man, nothing I can fairly fault him with. I respect him, cherish him. So I don't understand..."

"Don't understand what?"

With her hand she motioned back and forth between them. "This. Us." Pleading shone in her moist eyes as if she wanted him to explain it.

But what could he do but both pity her and want to ravish her in the same instant?

"Man," he said softly, "this is tough."

They stared at each other in a kind of exquisite mutual anguish.

"One thing is sure," he said. "Whatever you do, it has to be the *right* thing. Because if you do the *wrong* thing, you'll punish yourself without mercy. That's the kind of beautiful human being you are. The reason you don't follow your urge to knock on my door is that you think it would be wrong. I understand it. Not all of me wants to understand it, believe me, but my brain and my caring for you do."

"Jake, I'm not as good as you think I am."

"That's because you want to do something that you think is immoral. So it's important here to do what is right."

She huffed. "And what is that?"

"I'll tell you the way I would tell my sister, if I had one. With my own feelings, my self-interest out of the picture. Jesus! But here is what is right. Are you sure you want to listen to it?"

"Yes. What is right, Jake?"

"You must let Ray go to war. You're preventing something that is key to his self-image, you are breaking him, and you'll end up with a broken man. I know you're afraid for him, but this is classic, Natasha. It's Odysseus, it's Natasha and Prince Andre, the tale of hearth versus duty. You must let him do what he thinks is his obligation, and you must endure the consequences, a possible breakup, his disillusionment, even, God forbid, his death. I respect his sense of honor, and you must too. By trying to protect him, you're killing him slowly. Out of trying to placate you, he's slowly, miserably, dying. At least if he dies in the jungle, he'll be a hero."

She rose, went to the kitchen door, parted the window curtains and gazed out. "Do you think it'll snow tonight?"

Jake didn't answer. He wriggled in his jeans to make himself more comfortable.

"What do you think about the war, Natasha?"

"The government says we must fight it, so I guess they know what's best. I certainly don't."

"So you'd try to keep him out of it no matter what it's all about. Even World War Two?"

She shrugged, her back still toward him.

"You're not protecting him, Natasha. You're protecting yourself and destroying his manhood in the process."

"His manhood," she scoffed. "Anyway, he's in the National Guard. They could call him up any time. Isn't that enough?"

"Apparently not for him. He needs to go, and with your blessing. You must try to understand. Men and women are not the same. But, hey, plenty of women have had a sense of duty beyond their home, and their men had to understand. Let him go; he'll be happy and love you all the more for it. Hell, my mom even tried to keep me from coming here to safe, unthreatening Kent. Protecting those you love is in your nature as a woman."

Natasha shrugged again, looking out. "The weatherman says we'll get two inches." She closed the curtains, turned. "And you're saying all of this without any self-interest?"

"I'm trying. Like I said, I'd say this to my own sister. Ray needs to go to war and get his picture up on that mantle."

"It's so stupid."

Jake's agitation was settling down. He could stand up now without embarrassment.

She smiled. "It's not like I think you're Tom Jones, Jake. I don't think coming over here late at night is wrong in the one night stand sense. But...."

"Right, I'm no Tom Jones. Jeez, no. I do bluegrass. No bluegrass in Vegas."

"I didn't mean it that way. As I said before, an illicit fling is not outside my boundaries if *I'm* the only one who has to bear the consequences."

"Uh, so changing the subject," he said. "Are we on for the countess next Wednesday? That candlelight dinner you suggested?"

"Of course, but did I say anything about candlelight?"

20

Tuesday, January 16, one week later ...

At his office desk Jake noticed the *Daily Stater*'s announcement of the folk festival coming up, billed as the first annual, Goldenrod to perform at seven Friday night. Wash would teach lessons on the banjo at a Saturday afternoon symposium, Adele the autoharp. Rather than playing with the group, Jake knew he should be taking such instruction himself. Lester Flatt's G-run, was Wash kidding? Jake's fingers weren't cooperating with runs, slides, riffs. He could strum, both down and up, pick a single string and brush the rest, but he lingered far away from what a bluegrass rhythm guitarist had to do. By practicing in his apartment all weekend, he'd learned the chords and words to the four numbers they'd be performing.

Since his conversation with Natasha, she seemed to have fallen off the map. Her car wasn't in the driveway at night. She hadn't been around all weekend. He couldn't wait to see her for the Tolstoy lecture, had bought two copies of the Countess's book, *Tolstoy: A Life of My Father*. But he fretted about Natasha's sudden, prolonged disappearance. Had she taken his advice about preserving her fiancé's manhood? Would Jake be held responsible for the fallout?

He laid the newspaper aside and started correcting the term's first stack of student essays. After a while he heard the entrance flurry of his new officemate, the thump of a briefcase, the squeak of her swivel chair, her breathing as if from exertion. But no greeting.

He turned and saw her sliding folders into her file drawer. Her hair was in a short Afro, unlike the coiffured look in the desk photos. She wore African looking earrings with a navy blue suit and polished pumps.

"Good morning," he said.

"Hi." She kept working, didn't turn.

"I'm Jake Ernst."

"I know. It's on the plastic plate by the door."

"Oh, right. Yours will be there soon. So, you're settling in okay?"

"Sure, why not?"

"Can I be of any help?"

"No. I'm good."

She was slipping what seemed like student essays into the folders, not yet having looked around at him.

"I thought you might rather have this desk," he went on, "here by the window. I kind of appropriated it because the guy from last term was drafted. I didn't expect a young lady."

"What difference does my gender make?"

"Uh, none, I guess. I'm offering it, is all."

"I'm fine."

"All right, Carmen. Let me know if you..."

"Ella. I'm Ella, okay?"

"Oh. After the singer? She's the greatest."

She whirled and glared at him. "What makes you think I'm named after her, because I'm black and she's black? Don't start, okay? I'm Ella because I'm Ella. Why are you Jacob? After Jacob's Ladder? I doubt it."

Finished with her project, she grabbed her case and left, her shoes clicking crisply in the hallway. He might as well have directly disparaged her race. Stunned, he stared at the opened door.

Wednesday, January 17, next day …

Jake taught his two morning classes and in a lightly falling snow joined the vigil in front of the Union. Then he walked back to his place, expecting Natasha to finally show up for their get-together that evening. Due to her seeming disappearance, he'd been tempted to call Theodore Roosevelt High to inquire about her but thought it might be an unwarranted intrusion. He assured himself she would show up in time for the Countess's presentation. Clearly, though, something had been going on since their conversation about Ray's situation.

Working on the music and watching out the window for her to pull into the driveway, Jake waited. Though he enjoyed performing with Goldenrod, he hoped they would soon find a better guitarist. His nerves were fraying at the prospect of being on stage in a big auditorium. Groups would be performing from all over Ohio. So leaving slides and riffs for a later time, he practiced the four tunes and watched out the window.

By six-thirty Natasha still hadn't arrived, the presentation only an hour away. So much for the dinner, but she'd certainly show up for the lecture. At seven-fifteen, still no Natasha. All right, she'd meet him at the event. In slacks, tie and sports coat, he pulled on his parka and drove to Bowman Hall where a small group waited for the arrival of the Countess, Natasha not among them.

Now Jake knew something crucial must be occurring in her love life. Or there'd been an accident, an illness. A flu epidemic was ravaging the area, a dorm virtually quarantined. Maybe that was it.

Professor Tillich of the Russian Department ushered Alexandra Tolstoya into the room. Stout, elderly, in a black suit with a white blouse high on her neck, a cameo broach, her thick, gleaming silver hair swept back over her ears into a thick bun, rimless glasses, a wide smile on her large, rosy face, she took her seat. She grinned during her introduction and in a heavy Russian accent proceeded to give a general bio of her dad. She'd been at the famous railway station where Tolstoy passed away, alienated beyond repair from his wife, who had followed him there on the next train. He'd left a chaotic situation in his wake. The Countess's eyes filled with tears as she recounted the experience. His personal secretary, she'd been twenty-four at the time, caught in the middle of the war between her parents.

After a short break she went on to discuss the foundation she'd created after becoming an American citizen, mostly to refine and liberalize the United States immigration laws dealing with political dissidents. Located on a farm north of New York City, the foundation provided assimilation services for all those coming to America, fleeing persecution as she had done. She encouraged donations. Brochures were passed out.

After Q & A, she sat at a table and signed books. Jake stood in line, still holding the hope that Natasha would rush in all flustered about being late. He laid the two books he'd bought in front of the Countess's large, solid hands.

"And your name, young fellow?" she asked, grinning up at him through thick spectacles, her gray eyes gleaming with cordiality.

"Jake," he said. "I appreciated your words tonight. I had no idea you helped Nabokov and Rachmaninoff escape the Soviet."

"Yes, and our foundation has been of help to many more and continues to do so."

"This book is for a friend of mine who teaches French at the high school. Her mother is from France, loved your father's books and named her Natasha Kitty."

"Of all things. I am sure you know that my father renounced those novels, part of the tragedy of his life. He gave his royalties away as well. How it infuriated Ma*ma*! I will address this to *Tasha*."

In her shadow on the page she scribbled something in French not readable to Jake.

"I'll find out more about your foundation," he said into her wise smile.

"You must come and visit."

"Yes, I know that Pete Seeger lives nearby."

"Of course, he has come to sing at our farm many times. My father would have adored him. Mr. Seeger holds the same view of what society should be without all the religious dogma."

Jake wrapped his two books again, put on his coat and wandered forlornly out into the snow.

What was happening with Natasha? *Tasha.* He liked it, but where was she? When he climbed the stairs to his place he saw a note taped to his door: *I got a phone call from Miss Van Sollis. She said she's wrapped up with her work and hoped you enjoyed the lecture. Incidentally, I'd like to request that you refrain from playing your guitar after 10 pm.* The note was signed, *Dr. Phil Kilbride, downstairs.*

Relieved that she was okay, at least, and wouldn't have blatantly stood him up, he went inside. Before the note, he'd been about to make those calls to the hospital and the police department. But something was going on, for sure, and he'd have to be patient until he found out what. He felt certain it had something to do with their last conversation about Ray's sense of manhood.

After eleven, in sweatpants and tee shirt, Jake, grading papers, heard footsteps up the stairs and a knock on his door. Finally, she was there. He jumped out of his chair and opened the door. It was Lil Lassiter, bundled up, her cap frosted with snow, a bright smile on her tomboy face.

Adjusting to the disappointment, he tried to appear pleased and ushered her in.

"Lil, long time no see."

"Yes, time for a visit, I thought. Since we're not sharing classes this term, figured I should check in."

He put milk on the stove to mix with chocolate syrup. They sat at his kitchen table.

"So how was your break?" he asked, trying to find a good excuse to make this encounter brief.

"Chat-ta-noo-ga, baby!" she said.

"You mean with that Christian poet?"

"You bet your fabulous ass. Christians really get into sin, know the difference between what's natural and what's plain down 'n dirty."

He mixed their hot chocolate, set their cups on the table and sat.

"So he's your guy now? You don't seem the type for a long distance relationship."

She slurped. "That's the beauty of it, Jake. I can jaunt off to Tennessee any time I want to, and also do what I like around here. Cake and eat it too, dig?"

"Yeah, dig."

"So, are you up for a little extracurricular activity?" she asked with an alluring smile.

"No, Lil, not really. After that last little incident, I'd rather keep you at arm's length."

"Found someone else, have you?"

"Only in my dreams."

"You have a crush on someone?"

"Something like that."

"Someone in the Department? I see you with Adele sometimes."

"No."

"Don't you love twenty questions? Should we keep playing, or are you going the spill the beans?"

"As long as we're using clichés, I'll keep the cat in the bag for now."

"So you're holding that powerful sexual energy all bottled up? Maybe I could help you out. A little meaningless fooling around."

"Sorry."

"A nice hot bath, a geisha massage?"

"No, thanks."

"Damn you." She smiled. "Okay, tell me about this crush you have."

"Nothing worth discussing. Anyway, how's your lifestyle experiment going? Nothing changed after that attack?"

"Nothing changed except no more frat parties. But I'm doing what I want, not submitting to the sexual oppression of the white male, double standard regime."

"Like the girl in *I, a Woman*."

"Pretty much, yes. You can hardly condemn me, since you avidly partook if I remember correctly."

"That was before..."

"Your crush."

"Before the police coming here. I wish you the best, though. The thing with the poet isn't romantic?"

"Romantic? Hell, no, we defile each other, roll in filth, pigs in shit. Quite joyous, actually. Poetic degradation. Ever read James Joyce's letters to his wife?"

"Haven't had the pleasure."

"Read them. You'll get the picture. My Chattanooga poet reads them to me sometimes as foreplay."

She finished her drink.

"So I have some work to do," Jake said.

"Your exit signal."

"Want a ride back to your dorm?"

"Are you kidding? With the bars still open? I'll head down to the Ron-De-Vou, find a nice, shy grad student and blow his everlovin' mind."

As he opened the door to usher Lil out, Natasha, looking haggard, was trudging up the stairs. The two women glanced at each other as they passed. On the landing Natasha glared at Jake.

"Natasha..."

"Never mind. I'm too worn out for any of it." She put the key in her lock.

"But..."

She opened the door then closed it behind her.

Jake stood forlornly on the landing staring at a door that might as well have suddenly become the Great Wall of China. He wanted nothing more than to break it down and comfort the woman he loved. But comfort her from what? Heartbreak? Frustration? Anger? At him? Had *he* caused whatever it was? Would knocking on that two inch barrier be a violation of their friendship? Would it piss her off beyond his redemption?

He took a deep breath, tried to reason it out, didn't want to make a crucial mistake. If his urge was to satisfy his curiosity about what had been going on the last week, his pushing the issue would only be selfish. If it was to assuage her suffering, that would be okay if she were ill or injured, but if she wanted his comfort she knew where he was and she knew he would open his arms to her, or simply listen. Neither case justified his pursuing her at this moment. She said she was worn out. That required rest, not further exertion. He'd have to get a grip, and wait. But what if, heaven forbid, she thought he and Lil...?

He'd been grinding his knuckles, stopped it, heaved another deep breath. Inside his apartment he wrote a note: *Tasha, I'm here for you. I have your book signed by the Countess. Hope to talk to you soon. Yours, Prince Andre.* He slipped it under her door.

He lay in bed trying to read an Emerson essay; nothing put him to sleep faster, except perhaps a novel by Joseph Conrad.

21

Thursday, January 18, next day ...

On his way out to hike to Satterfield Jake found a note slipped under his door: *Dear Prince Andre, Sorry for my mood last night. Hope you had fun with your girlfriend. I can hardly blame you, can I? Let's have that dinner I promised, this evening, unless you have plans!! Tasha.*

At first he smiled. Was there still hope? But then her referring to Lil as his girlfriend irked him. Did she believe it? He'd have to straighten out that little jibe the first moment he could. And did the point about blame indicate she'd been romping in bed with Ray? Nevertheless, they would have dinner. Great. He had a bad habit of over thinking things.

In the snow that had whitened the neighborhood, he noticed the Rambler's tracks out of the driveway.

He spent an agitated day. Toward the end of his office hours, unattended by students as usual, Ella popped in, her hours directly following his. Saying nothing, she settled at her desk. Not wanting to have an entire term of silence with his officemate, he offered a simple good morning.

"Yeah, okay," she answered, not looking around.

"What classes are you taking, Ella?"

"You don't have to be concerned about that."

All right, then, he wouldn't be, but her tone constituted another irritant to this day. Did she dislike him simply because he was white?

He soon left to attend Dr. Worthington's seminar on the Romantics, starting with none other than Blake, in which Jake was well-grounded. But Worthington read time worn lectures, stumbling repeatedly in a monotone while all his students constantly checked their watches. Next came Professor Bibble's class on Emerson and Thoreau, during which Jake couldn't keep his mind from drifting to Natasha's apparent ordeal and her enigmatic invitation. So they would have dinner together; the situation would clarify itself there.

A small, wiry man, clean shaven with a crew cut and a ferret like face, Bibble spent most of the two hours recounting his having, in his youth, hiked the entire length of the Appalachian Trail as if the experience had parallels to Henry David's meditations at Walden Pond.

Finally Jake grabbed a sandwich and carted his guitar over to the music building where Goldenrod rehearsed "Shady Grove," "Blue Moon of Kentucky," "Roll in My Sweet Baby's Arms," and the final song, "Good Night Irene," which was to be an audience participation piece *a la* Pete Seeger. Jake had the chords down pat, but no runs, and he backed up the vocals with harmony. Still, he felt nervous and wanted them to find a competent player as soon as possible. Adele had a way of exploiting his helpful nature, but one of these days he'd have to confront that tactic. At least the rehearsal took his mind off his next door neighbor, but all that flooded back as soon as he began the bitter cold trek across the up and down campus toward home.

Pleased to see Natasha's car in the driveway, he climbed the stairs to find a Post-It on his door: *Seven, please, monsieur.* Two hours away.

Unable to concentrate on his studies and not wanting to grade essays, he paced a bit then sat down with his guitar. What would Natasha have to say? He idly twiddled the strings in half an effort to get the famous G-run down, only eight damn notes, but his fingers weren't accustomed to picking individual strings. Precise timing was needed too. So while he toyed, he idly pondered his fate. Then something suddenly caught his attention.

He'd done it!

He tried again, and there the sequence was, almost. But not like the last run through. He tried again, no, not quite. Again. Once more. Then there it was, smooth, perfect. It was coming. He'd get there. Not in time for the concert, of course, but he saw it was possible. He tried again, yes, there it surely was. Maybe he could even slide it down to a D-run. No, that was a long way off.

A soft knock sounded on his door. He checked his watch, 7:15. Damn it! He hadn't showered, shaved, changed his clothes. He opened up, apologized.

Natasha smiled sweetly. "I thought you might be getting revenge for my standing you up last night."

"Never," he said. "I lost track of time. Sorry."

"Yes, I heard you, same thing again and again. Anyway, chow's on."

"I'm there. Five minutes, okay?"

He brushed his teeth, ran a comb through his hair, rubbed some deodorant under his arms, changed his slacks and shirt, grabbed her autographed book and rapped on her door.

With Segovia playing Bach on the stereo, she led him to the kitchen where the table was set with a red cloth, a candle burning, small salads, goblets, an uncorked bottle of red wine. In slacks and ski sweater, she set cups of soup at their places and sat down. She'd parted her hair in the middle and curled out the ends at her shoulders, making a perfect frame for her face, subtly made up, no signs of stress and strain.

"Pour us some wine, your highness, *s'il vous plaît.*"

He mock sniffed, swirled, tasted and poured.

Grinning, lifting her glass, she said, "To the Countess, with my apologies to you, *mon voisin.*"

"What's French for likewise?" he asked.

"*Aussi,*" she answered. "But not appropriate here because you owe me no apologies."

"Ah. So what would be appropriate, *mon* teach-*eur?*"

She smiled. "How about *cheers? Santé.*"

"*Mon* French needs some work. *Santé*, it is."

They clinked. The aroma of the soup tantalized him, spicy with lentils and tomatoes. Then came plates with chicken cordon bleu and a vegetable medley of carrots, celery, broccoli and snap peas. He was hungry, and it was delicious. But nothing could have overcome his delight and his anticipation of what this magical setting seemed to hold in store.

"You're really a good cook," he said. "*Tres bien.*" He pressed his thumb and finger together and kissed.

"*Merci, mon prince,*" she said, smiling. "May I see my book?"

He handed it to her, and she opened to the cover page, read, and looked up at him.

"That is so very nice."

"What's it say?"

"You didn't read it?"

"My French isn't strong. For me she only wrote, 'Best wishes.'"

"'To Tasha, Welcome to our family. May you find your Pierre.' Then her signature."

"Wow! You're a Tolstoy."

"What was she like?"

He described the meeting and the Countess, told her about the Tolstoy farm in upstate New York.

"I kept thinking you might rush in out of breath," he added.

"Extremely sorry about that. I did manage to get away to call Phil downstairs. That was the best I could do. I sensed your feelings, though, as if they were my own."

She suggested dessert in the living room and asked him to take their wine and turn the record over. "I picked up some éclairs at the bakery downtown," she said, motioning for him to sit in the easy chair. After bringing in the dessert and the candle, she settled on the sofa.

"Now, we can talk."

To him, the evening so far had already said it all, but he well-understood the difference between their situations and he recalled the ambiguities in her note.

"First," he blurted, "that was only a brief, unexpected visit from Lil. Nothing happened, no way in hell."

"Don't worry about that."

Not at all relieved, he went on. "What's been happening? I've been really worried."

"I know. But this was the most difficult time I've ever experienced – tugging and pulling, resolved, confused, heart torn, mind-run-ragged, traveling to his home in Toledo, two homes there, his parents splitting. Now I know what people mean when they say, *Holy Toledo*. And it all started with trying to do the right thing, which you told me to do. Don't worry, I don't hold you responsible. It was my choice, entirely. But I'm not sure it was the best one."

"You released him to his patriotic mission?"

"That's how it started. I said I'd stand by him, wait for him. We were sitting in his car after school. I told him I was willing to be a warrior's wife, waiting faithfully by the hearth." By the end of this explanation her tone had turned sour.

"How'd he react?"

"Mixed. You know, how you think you really want something until you actually get it? That's how he responded. I had to convince him that I really meant what I said."

"Did you really mean it?"

"Yes and no, but I think I convinced him. It took a while. I mentioned Odysseus. We sat in the school lot until after midnight. The security guard told us to leave."

"I respect you, Natasha. It took courage to tell him that."

"Yes, once you say such a thing, you can hardly take it back, can you?"

"No, I guess not."

"Then I stayed with him. It was emotional. We took two days off school to see his parents, especially his mother who condemned me as a once ally who'd deserted her. Back and forth, yelling, crying, debating. But one thing emerged from it clearly."

"What was that?"

"He really, truly wants to go. I hesitate to put it into his actual words."

"It's all right, go ahead."

"He said that for the last three years he's been feeling ... pussy-whipped."

"Jesus, he put it that way?"

"A direct quote. And he was clear he'd made up his mind weeks before to transfer to active service, had already filled out the forms, but hadn't submitted them. I think we all felt a little abandoned. He said he was doing it with or without our support. He was like a mustang let out of a corral. There was only one thing on his mind, and it wasn't us. And, this is a horrible thing to say but..."

"Go ahead, say it."

"I didn't like him much after that. He resented my and his mom's having pressured him into joining the Guard. He didn't see the love behind that. He thought we'd been trying to possess him, didn't recognize his needs. I can see his point, I guess. Like you explained to me, Jake. How'd you come to be such a wise person anyway?"

"Anything but wise. I've read a lot of books about moral quandary, and had a few incidents myself."

"Don't make light of your insight. Maybe Ray's mother and I aren't happy, but he certainly is. The forms have been submitted, this thing called the Tet Offensive has activated a lot of Guard companies, and lots of other guys are transferring to A.D. too. I guess the time is ripe."

"A.D.?"

"Active duty."

She offered a melancholy smile. "Anyway, after this epic struggle, all decisions have been made. But you know something, Jake?"

"No, what?"

"A girl doesn't like to hear, 'I don't care if you support me or not, I'm going to do what I'm going to do.' It doesn't sit well. And I..."

She gulped her wine, stared at the candle flame, the rim of the goblet still pressed to her lips.

"Go on," Jake said.

"I couldn't sleep with him after that, not even in the same bed."

As sad as this fact seemed to her, Jake couldn't hold back the wave of pleasure sweeping through him.

"If he'd been willing or able to see the sacrifice I was giving him, to appreciate the fact that I was ready to wait for him, it would have been different. But it was like I'd wasted three years of his life. It was resentment and blame he felt, not love. And suddenly, would you believe this? Suddenly I didn't love him anymore, just like that." She snapped her fingers. "I can't believe that all he and I had shared was gone, in an instant."

"Yeah, that's sad," Jake said, not believing his words.

"I see him at school but don't even want to talk to him. He seems completely at ease knowing his taking this attitude means losing me. He could have had both, maybe, but he slammed the door in my face. So how can I love him, Jake, how can I?"

His slacks suddenly becoming highly restrictive, Jake emptied the wine bottle into their glasses. She noticed the gesture, looked at him, took a long swallow.

"But, I'm not going to go to bed with you tonight, Jake."

He straightened at the sudden change of topic, wriggled a little.

"Sure. All right."

"You *do* want to go to bed with me, don't you?"

"Yes."

"You have from the first time we met that day on our balconies."

"Yes, you're right about that."

"Not knowing a thing about me except I looked good to you."

He let out a breath, attempted a smile. "Yes, maybe it was the apron."

She sighed, shook her head. "You guys."

"It wasn't completely like that, Natasha, and it certainly isn't like that now."

"Yes, well. I've told you my situation, probably still up in the air, but doesn't feel like it. Feels like everything's been settled. So. Now let's talk about you."

"Like I told you," he gushed, "she's not my girlfriend. I slept with her twice, but not after the police showed up that night. She was a diversion, like a tennis game."

Natasha sat back. "A tennis game?"

"Yeah, when you enjoy the activity but aren't in love with the other player. Is that a weird idea?"

"You can do that?"

"If I have no reason not to."

"So that girl is like a tennis partner? Only the game you play is sex?"

"*Was.* Her name's Lil. Yes, a tennis partner, in a manner of speaking. And the other night she dropped by, for a match, but there's no way. I'm not interested in playing games these days, Natasha."

"Why not?"

"What do you mean, 'why not'?"

"Why not?"

"Jesus! Because of you – us! Don't you know that? Are you kidding me?"

"Don't get mad, Jake. A girl has to hear the words."

"But you gave me some reason to hope, didn't you?"

"Yes, I certainly did. But not tonight."

"Okay, I heard you. On your own time, if ever."

"First, if these three years with Ray are really over, I'm on the rebound, need some time for things to settle. Second, I need to know you better."

"Sure, I respect that."

"Our situations are different. Apparently our values, too."

"Yes, of course."

A pause followed, each looking at the other but saying nothing until she broke the silence.

"I *would* like you to hold me, though. I haven't been nicely held through this whole ordeal. Everyone's mad at me."

"I'm not."

She laughed. "What a surprise! That's why I'd like you to please come here and sit beside me."

He couldn't move fast enough. Then she was in his arms, molding to him, clinging to him, he to her, feeling her pliability, her resonance, softness, warmth, feeling the pressure of her cheek against his, inhaling her fragrance.

"Oh, God!" she said. "Oh, Jake!"

They held, released momentarily, held again, pulled back. Their eyes met, their faces close, their bodies as one. He found her lips with his, heard a moan from deep in her throat and kissed her as if taking possession of a magical being deeply yearned for over eons of time. They became avid. Finally, she wrangled away.

"Oh, my God! Have I ever felt like this? No, never."

Breathing heavily, she adjusted her sweater, backed farther away, gazed at him, startled.

"That's all for tonight, Jake, or I'll burst, I'll just burst."

22

Friday, January 19, next day …

Goldenrod's set went off without a hitch, Wash and Adele carrying the weight and Jake in the background singing harmony and strumming the beat, changing chords effortlessly. Wash did long riffs on the banjo, the mandolin and guitar. Henry did runs on the fiddle and Adele on the autoharp, and to Jake's surprise the group got the audience into singing and swaying along to their last number. The crowd cheered and clapped, but the best part was that Natasha sat among them in the second row of the vast auditorium. In the casual atmosphere, groups came on and left, rearranging chairs and mikes during transitions, musicians in the wings with their instruments, some sitting in the audience before and after their performances.

With his six string Jake edged to the seat beside his gorgeous, excited neighbor.

"You're really good," she said with a wide smile.

"No, but I made it through. I'm glad you came."

"I couldn't miss your debut, could I?"

"Sure, you could. But I'm glad you didn't."

The lights lowered for a Joan Baez lookalike solo with her guitar and operatic soprano voice in contrast to Adele's raspy mountain sound. Natasha leaned against him in the darkness.

"How have you felt since last night?" she asked as they left.

"Happy. Wondering if things between you and Ray are really settled."

"Seems so. We're both swamped, haven't talked."

"He owes you an apology."

"He thinks I owe him one. I'm afraid our views are irreconcilable on the matter."

In his car, Jake said, "Should we stop at the Robin Hood for a drink?"

"To celebrate your success? We should, but I'm still not ready for anything public. Anyway that place will be packed on a Friday. It will get back to him. And he can be volatile. How 'bout your place? I have a bottle of Zinfandel we can share."

Music to Jake's ears.

At the house she went into her place to freshen up. He grabbed a quick shower to rinse off the sweat he'd shed on stage. In jeans and long tee shirt, striped socks and fluffy slippers, she came back holding strawberry cheesecake and wine. While he got dishes from the kitchen, he heard her ask, "Do you mind if I look at the pictures in your wallet lying here?"

"No problem. But keep your mitts off the two dollars."

He set the plates and tumblers on the coffee table.

"Who are these people?" she asked. "I guess the two older ones together are your parents, right?"

"Yes. Virginia and Martin."

"Still in love?"

"I'm sure."

"No upheavals?"

"Now and then, when my dad was drafted, and then when he came home with his arm in a sling. But upheavals of fear and sorrow, not conflict. I've seen them argue but never fight. I guess because my dad sees her as always in the right."

"The man of my dreams. Thank God he came home from the war. Who's this, at the ping pong table?"

"Amber. My first girlfriend. High school."

"She's cute. And this? Looks like the prom."

"Christine. My first major crush."

"Strange you still carry your old girlfriends with you."

"Those photos represent lessons learned," he said. "I like to keep those lessons close."

"Who's the gentleman? He looks a little scary."

"Professor Groff, a mentor of sorts."

"How so?" she asked, grinning at her professor-like phrasing.

"Indeed!" he echoed her tone. "He introduced me to literary studies, what to look for, methods of analysis, how to judge. Without him and my senior English teacher in high school, I'd probably be teaching math. But, he's a homosexual, and he taught me..."

"Don't say it."

"No, not that. I'd never been exposed to gays before college, and I learned acceptance, tolerance. They pay a hell of a price for their existence. Hey, come on, let's give that cheesecake a try."

He pulled some cushions from the sofa to the floor and they sat on them, picnic style. He told her about his trip to the Big Apple where he'd ended up in a bar for gays and transsexuals, Groff joyously among them, how he'd learned to accept them as he would foreigners simply enjoying their cultures.

"In high school," he explained, "I'd done a paper on Armenia, so I called them Queer-menians and let it go at that, like they're from a foreign country with odd traditions."

She giggled, then turned serious. "There was a gay kid in my high school. He got beat up all the time, but it didn't stop him from walking like a girl."

"They have to be brave," Jake said. "They're treated like vermin."

It was an evening of biography, her getting to know his past, becoming used to being with him. Though eager for another of those hugs and more, he held back, told her what she wanted to know about his past, especially his engagement to Ainsley. But he spoke only in answer to her prompts. Daphne's abortion and his present tenuous situation with the Selective Service never came up.

"I thought you might carry a rubber. Isn't it a staple of most guys' wallets?"

"I defy the stereotypes."

"Some girls in my classes carry them in their purse. But a lot of them simply get pregnant. It's becoming a problem."

He verged on telling her the Daphne tale, but held back. Toward two in the morning, she yawned, smiled, apologized. He realized the magic moment would not arrive, but they embraced tightly at his door before she went back to her place. He was sure she had some secrets too. Who at their age didn't? But not necessary to know them. He wanted to keep her in his mind exactly as he envisioned her. And he realized the danger of her jumping from one complex relationship directly into another. As far as any secrets she might hold, none of them would deter him for a moment, not even something as hypothetically outrageous as her having once belonged to a witchcraft coven that sacrificed kittens to the devil.

Sunday, January 28, a week and a half later ...

Jake rose at eight. Yawning, he gazed out his bedroom window. Overnight a blizzard had swept in from Lake Erie. The world lay knee deep in snow, a howling wind sweeping it into giant drifts. From his frost-lined window he saw both cars merely as shapes under a cover of white, the identical scene played out some weeks before, having served as part of his slow, romantic unification with his neighbor. He'd been longing for a different form of that unification, however, and saw this instance of shoveling as an impending chore. With another week of Natasha's separation from Ray, and a school drama project now out of the way, Jake had envisioned today as smooth sailing ahead.

Instead, he readied his spirit for a few hours of shared labor that could only bring them closer. Other than several notes slipped under doors about their schedules, they'd had no contact due to her time consuming junior class performance of *Romeo and Juliet* finally held the last two evenings. Though Jake offered to attend for moral support, she wanted him to keep his distance since Ray would be there with a group of teachers as ushers.

Natasha had written on a slip of paper that the show was sure to be embarrassing. She was certain Romeo was going to have some trouble with his lines, not to mention all his buddies heckling him from the audience.

Jake had spent the week in his regular routine. Nationally, Air Force Reservists were being called up because of the North Koreans having captured an American Navy ship, the Pueblo. Closer to home, his officemate Ella had been involved in a black activist's visit to campus to talk about the right of blacks to react violently to their oppression. She'd left a leaflet on his desk. It was the first activity by the campus African American organization since Jake had arrived at KSU, but he was content to read about the presentation in the daily paper.

Pictures of the folk festival appeared there too, one of Goldenrod, Jake barely visible in the background, which he'd clipped and sent to his parents. He attended the weekly vigil at the Union, which blacks seemed long ago to have decided to avoid. And the Political Science Club published a campus poll indicating that a great majority of students viewed premarital sex as perfectly moral, only sixteen percent having said otherwise.

At eleven that morning when he finally heard Natasha's knock on his door, he found her on the landing in bathrobe and pajamas, sleepily rubbing her eyes.

"I'm sure you already ate, but why don't you join me while I do. I'm famished, making pancakes."

She didn't have to ask twice. At her table, she confirmed that most of her fears about the performance had borne out.

"The balcony scene was utter disaster," she said. "The ladder broke. But with everything, I'm sure stardom lies ahead for the girl who played Juliet. It's certainly the last time I'll ever allow a boy from the football team to play a lead, maybe even to walk on stage. His teammates were merciless. The chaperones had to escort them out."

Enjoying her flapjacks and maple syrup, Jake listened as she described all the *faux pas* of the two shows. During the day, the wind settled down making the dig out easier. They took a break to construct a snowman in the front yard, using buttons from her sewing kit and a carrot from her fridge for eyes and nose. Jake felt the joy of a family man, stealing a mutually avid kiss in the dimness of the tool shed, their winter clothes as barriers from finding each other's bodies.

As he started to unzip her jacket, she whispered a soft, "Not here, Jake. But we will. Tonight."

He spent the remainder of their chore imagining what lay ahead. In the late afternoon they took a pause from each other and joined up again for dinner in her place, salads and spaghetti with her dad's delicious marinara sauce.

"I have a few more questions," she said as they ate, "about those snapshots in your wallet."

He took a deep breath. He thought questions would be better after, not before, their evening ahead.

"Questions? Such as," he said in their mock professorial tone.

"You know, Jake, don't you, that I'm not in a position to make a commitment at this time?"

"I don't need a commitment."

"Yes, I know you like to play tennis, but..."

"I didn't mean it like that. This isn't tennis."

"I guess I'm scared."

"What about?"

"You've had a lot of experience and, yes, I've slept with three guys, and made out with others, but it's all been rather straightforward, and you've been with that girl, Lil, and with those in the pictures, and who knows how many others, and I'm not sure I can measure up."

"Hey, Natasha, I..."

"Jake, I'd like you to call me *Tasha*. Would you? Ever since I saw it from the Countess, I've liked it. This is a new start for me. I'd like to be Tasha with you."

He smiled. "All right ... Tasha. I like it too. Anyway, I want you to know that being with you, whatever way, straightforward, all crooked, even not at all if you're not ready, is okay with me. I'd be happy making snowmen with you."

She laughed softly. "I don't believe that, Jake."

"I don't want any pressure on you."

"But I feel pressure, like stage fright. I want..." She looked at him, a fork-ful of pasta half way to her mouth.

"Stage fright, Tasha?"

"I want to be the best you ever had. Something that will erase all the others from your mind."

"You already are that. I've felt things before. You have too, of course. But honestly, I've never felt anything as strong as this. And I don't care if it's even a worse disaster than the balcony scene, it doesn't matter. Don't worry about me, please. Maybe we should wait, until you're really certain."

"No," she answered quickly. "I don't want to wait. I want to sleep with you every night. I want to share meals with you, be with you, at least for now. You're a world I want to explore, Jake, a person I want to know, in every way. But I can't predict the future. Right now I'm overwhelmed with feel-ings, and feelings can change."

Jake wanted to stop eating, charge to the other side of the table and seize her. But he toyed with the iceberg lettuce in his salad.

"I understand you're not ready for a commitment. And you're right that it's *your* situation that's complicated, not mine. So we'll take it exactly as you want it. There's no hurry and no expectations. You're not going on stage."

She stared at him, tears welling, took a deep breath. "Then I'll come to you, Jake. At ten o'clock I'll knock on your door."

"Ten o'clock? That's over three hours."

"I know how long it is, Jake. But it's how long I need, okay?"

"Yes, Tasha. I'll wait for you, until 1970 if need be."

She smiled. "And I want candlelight, and music (something Brazilian, maybe) and red wine, deep, robust. And you, Jake, I want you."

Her tears flowed freely now, but Jake sensed she didn't want him to embrace her, so he gave her space. She smiled apologetically, wiped her cheeks with a napkin. Whatever he'd seen and done with the women in his past, he'd never come anywhere close to something like this.

Back at his place he had the problem of not having a Brazilian record, candles or wine. So he had some shopping to do at seven o'clock on a snow-covered Sunday night. There was an all-night music mart on Main Street geared for students, and a corner grocery store across the tracks on West Main. As for the wine, what was he to do? He called Adele, said it was a romantic emergency, which set her howling.

"We have half a bottle of T-bird in the fridge," she said.

"Anything will do."

In his MGA he swerved on the slippery streets, gathering up Natasha's required materials, enduring Adele and Wash's wry smiles, and returning to his place about nine. There, he showered, changed his sheets, moved his record player to the bedroom, poured heated wax into saucers, stuck the candles in them, brushed his teeth the third time, checked his armpits. For him, the whole event atmosphere was totally unnecessary; he'd have been happy to do it with her on the dirt floor of the tool shed. But he'd play along. Hoping the Thunderbird would meet her standards, he set the stage.

No Hugh Hefner, he felt ridiculous in pajamas, so without underwear, he slapped some cologne on his chest and pulled on jeans and a sweatshirt. He wondered if she wasn't expecting much too much from him; he was no Tom Jones, either. The next half hour seemed the longest of his life. Then at 9:55, he poured the wine into tumblers, put on a Stan Getz album entitled "The Girl from Ipanema," lit the three candles and turned out the bedroom light.

He waited in the dimly lit living room wondering if her knock would actually come. With time to weigh her options, she'd probably changed her mind. But at exactly ten, the light knock sounded. And he'd never seen anything quite like what he saw when he opened the door. After slipping in, she pressed a finger to his lips to tell him to keep quiet. She'd parted her silky blond hair on the side and swept it over her forehead. It twinkled with glitter. Mascara lined her eyes and curved outward and upward from the corners like a mask at a costume ball. A deep crimson glowed on her plump lips. And she wore a low cut, fishnet body stocking down to a pair of stiletto heels. Smelling richly of an earthy musk perfume, she gazed at him with quiet, serious, deep blue eyes. It was all as if she'd used her several hours alone to become Bridgett Bardot!

Catlike, she eased against him, her whole length, lay back her head and parted her lips. Not taking a moment longer to assess her transformation, he lowered his mouth to hers, devoured it. She pulled back, took his hand and led him to the bedroom. In silence she pulled him to the bedside and shoved him to sit on the edge. She pulled off his shirt, opened his jeans and tugged them off to the floor.

"Lie back," she whispered. "Let me see your body."

He swallowed, did as she said.

"Mmm." She licked her lips.

Who is this person. What a fantastic surprise!

She took hold of him, gripped him. "I knew you were beautiful," she purred, stroking him. "I want to put wine on you and lick it off."

She did so, Jake struggling to take this all in. But he managed.

She backed off, leered at him to the sounds of guitar and saxophone, flowing Portuguese words. She moved to the music, a slow, writhing samba. She pulled down the straps of her outfit, showed her breasts, rubbed wine on her nipples, turned and tugged the piece down over her hips showing the curved line of her back to the cleft of her buttocks. She shook her ass, shimmied, smacked lightly, kicked off her shoes, and dived next to Jake, her knees beside his head.

"Pull off my clothes," she said. "Kiss my toes."

He complied, as she did the same to him.

"Now stand up," she said, "and watch me."

He did so. She squirmed on the bed, toyed with her breasts, opened her legs.

"I want you to see ... everything."

She parted her labia, stroked herself wantonly.

"You too," she said, "the way you do when you think of me."

Having had not a little experience with this, he did as directed.

"Come closer. Let me taste you."

She kissed and licked him, stroking all the while.

"Stop," he said. "You'll make me come."

He lay beside her, kissed her breasts, tasted the wine on her nipples, slid down to her navel, opened her legs and moved his tongue into her. She whimpered and moaned.

"I imagined this so many times," he whispered.

"Oh, Jake, me too. I want you inside me. Now."

She helped him slip it in. They kissed as he nudged fully inside, and they pressed against each other, wriggling. First that position, then another, then another, yet another, her on bottom, then on top, then from behind, every way he knew about. Then with her over him, her breasts brushing his lips as she moved to her own rhythm. She moaned deeply, clenched him hard, shuddered and climaxed, her pulsations going on for a minute, two, her lips on his neck, her teeth biting until she began to settle and finally collapsed on top of him as if she'd passed out.

Exhausted, exuberant, he felt her weight on him, didn't want to move her, overjoyed to be nearly smothered by her hair, her skin, her sexy smell, her labored breath. The music had long stopped, the hurricane candles now flickering near their ends.

He heard her whisper, "Did you...?"

"No. I don't want to stop yet. Do you know how long I waited for this? Maybe my whole life."

"Oh, my God, Jake! More?"

"I can't get enough of you."

If nothing else were to unite them, he was determined to make this night create an inseparable bond.

He rolled her off him onto her back and pushed into her again, pulled her knees up, her ankles by her ears, and thrust into her again and again as if now it was his turn to possess her, again and again, turning her around and doing it from behind, deeply, as hard as he could. Almost forgetting her in his own need, he rolled her over on her back again and went on and on until he felt his explosion building like a seething fuse..."

"Open your mouth," he said, looking into her eyes.

"Oh, my God."

Her turn to obey him, he stared down at her. With a wild look in her eyes, she parted her lips.

Still feeling about to burst, still pushing into her, he said, "Show me your tongue."

She showed him, pink, ruby red, the flash of her teeth, the darkness of her throat.

"Move it around."

As she waggled her tongue obscenely, he felt it about to happen, blurring his mind, losing control.

Glint in her eyes, she moved her tongue like a challenge, like a serpent's, and as his release neared he pulled out, found her mouth, nudged in and let it all go. She kept it inside, stroked him, getting every drop, groaning, swallowing, not stopping even afterward, but licking and slurping as if in voracious jubilance.

Utterly drained, he rolled off onto his back, and she bent down again and kept kissing him until finally under the pressure of her lips and tongue, he was hard once more.

She pulled away from him with a humorous pop.

"Can we wait a little while?" she asked, looking up at him. "I ... I don't think I can right now."

He realized he was dripping with sweat. The room had almost darkened, a few flickers left in the candles. He pulled her up to him, and they lay breathing in the near darkness.

"My God, Jake!" she whispered, as if sharing a deep, dark secret. "No one ever made me do anything remotely like that before. And you were right — it certainly wasn't any twenty minutes."

"Tasha," he muttered, holding her. "Tasha, my Tasha."

23

Monday, January 29, next day ...

Jake's radio alarm went off at 6:30, and as he rolled over to turn it off, he heard the announcement that schools and campus were closed because of more snow. He snapped the radio off and turned back to Natasha, who had stirred slightly. She smiled.

"What lovely news!" she said, snuggling back under the covers and closing her eyes.

When Jake felt her naked warmth against him, he looked at her, thrilled to see her golden hair fanned on the pillow. He was awakening from what felt like a glorious dream to find that it wasn't a dream but a reality. And what a reality it was! Glitter in her hair, mascara now run amok on her cheeks, a metallic, fishnet body stocking wadded on the floor. She'd transitioned from the serene, stately, aproned, innocent house frau he'd first seen that September day on her balcony, dishcloth in her hands, to a wanton harlot from the pages of *Penthouse*. Despite the underlying comedy in that transformation, her motive endeared her to him eons beyond his feelings before this night had occurred. Why? Because more than any words could express, it showed her love for him.

She loved him. For something intuitive told him this was not her usual bedroom *modus operandi*, but that she'd extended herself far beyond her customary element. Of course, he could be wrong. What she'd shown last night might well be her boudoir identity, but no matter. Correct or not, Jake felt breathlessly happy, one of those incredibly rare moments in a person's existence that defies prediction and that sanctifies every single instant in the past that has led one's journey, no matter how rocky, to this exact point in time.

He was now on a rushing river, beyond his control, nothing left but to ride the transcendent rapids to whatever conclusion lay ahead. He might find himself whirling over the brim of Niagara Falls into a drowning doom, or floating eventually on calmer waters in easeful bliss. No matter, what will be, will be.

In the bathroom he noticed dark smears of mascara on his stomach and thighs, lipstick marks too. He breathed her scent on him, didn't want to wash it off. He'd stay precisely as he was. After relieving himself, he returned to bed and lay there gazing at her disheveled face, her chest rising and falling under the covers. He drifted into a deep slumber, awakening sometime later to strong sexual feelings and finding her stroking him beneath the blankets.

She smiled into his eyes.

"You are a very, very sexy man, Mr. Ernst. Or maybe sex crazed. Or the perfect combination. And I think I'm ready for more right now, and it seems you are too."

He was. But this time no production element was involved. This time they made love the old fashioned way, no need for sidelights, no need at all. Nothing more to prove on either side. Afterward, they lay, heads on the pillow, staring into one another's eyes.

She giggled, then laughed, then howled. He laughed too.

"Holy Moly Alabama!" she said.

"Alabama? Why Alabama?"

"It's what Daddy always says."

He smiled. "You really blew my mind with that French sex kitten look."

"Not what you expected, was it?"

"Not at all."

"Thought I'd be a meek babushka?"

"Where'd you find that outfit? I doubt anywhere around Kent."

"If I tell you, do you promise not to gloat?"

"Why would I gloat?"

"Do you promise or not?"

"I promise."

"I don't think most girls would tell you something like this, but I trust you, and maybe it's something you should know."

"Then tell me."

She rustled under the blankets, propped her chin on her elbow, her absurdly smeared face a few inches away.

"After I heard you singing 'Light My Fire' that first day on the balcony and then when I helped you fix my car, I felt very, *very* attracted to you. But I felt guilty about it, you know, because of Ray, and then when I heard you with that other girl through the wall, I had an idea what you liked and felt even more attracted, especially by all the laughter, and so I ordered that leotard thing from a Fredrick's of Hollywood catalog, uh, in case we might, you know, eventually..."

"Is that true?"

"I'm telling you so you don't think I ever did anything like that, you know, so slutty, with anyone before, not even Ray."

"I don't care if you did. you've had a life before this."

"Yes, and you have too. But Ray would kick me out of his house if I ever tried anything like that."

"I doubt it."

"He would. But I knew you wouldn't because of something you once told me."

"What was that?"

"Remember that speech you gave about knowing what would make me happy?"

"Vaguely. You were driving me out of my gourd."

"You said all these things you were going to give me and one of the things on your list was 'absolute freedom in the bedroom.' I knew then you were into kinky stuff."

"I don't care about that. It's not about what I like in the bedroom, it's about..."

"If not you, who *is* it about, Jake?"

"My partner, you."

"So you thought I was into kinky stuff, did you?"

He chuckled. "I guess I was covering all my bases. Tasha, you and I here like this isn't about kinky. It's about us. I'll take it any way you want it. I don't expect sequins in your hair and striptease dances to Brazilian jazz."

"Don't tell me you didn't enjoy it. I saw the results."

"Only that I don't expect it. You're a turn-on enough for me even in your galoshes. And right now, I'm hungry. Could eat a horse. Would you be kind enough to whip up some more of your incredible pancakes?"

"Of course, and we can celebrate that most wonderful of God's gifts, a snow day."

She rose and sauntered sassily to the bathroom. A second after the door closed, she screamed.

"Oh, my God! My face!"

Tuesday, February 13, two weeks later ...

Out of breath, Ella stormed into the office. Rather than taking the elevator, she usually climbed the stairs, but her frenzied state indicated more than rigorous exercise.

"I'm sure you heard," she said.

"About?" He continued grading a paper.

"Maybe you didn't then. I noticed you didn't come to Brother Austin's presentation on the right of violent resistance, and this racist rag they call a college paper around here didn't cover it, not a single word. This place might as well be back to the plantation."

Jake swiveled his chair to face her.

"Is that what I should have heard about? The *Stater* not covering Austin's speech?"

She huffed. "Don't bother yourself about it."

"About what? Come on, Ella, tell me."

"It went down last Thursday, for Lord's sake. Of course, it wouldn't make the papers around here."

"What went down?"

She turned to meet his eyes. "Three beautiful brothers shot and killed, twenty more wounded."

"Where did this happen?"

She almost spit in her disgust at his ignorance. "South Carolina State. About a bowling alley don't allow us. Police shot into a campus protest. Yeah, the kids threw some bottles, so what, flipped the bird, made a bonfire like a football party, and the pigs fired straight in, lied about a sniper shooting at them, the same old shit about outside agitators. The kids wanted to go bowling. Fuck!"

She'd started in frustration to explain this all to Jake but ended looking at the floor as if talking to herself.

"Three beautiful black brothers," she added in despair, "one only in high school."

Listening, Jake made the assumption that, for her, *brothers* meant neither blood relatives nor members of a frat.

"I'm sorry, Ella. Really, I haven't heard a word about it. I've been really busy." And by *busy* he didn't mean only with his schoolwork. The joy of being with Natasha had been his all-consuming interest for the past few weeks.

"Uh-*huh*! Busy. I'm sure. But with anything that matters? With the struggle for justice, with the fight for human rights? No, you more worried about dangling participles and split infinitives. I'm sure you were into Johnny Carson's visit to campus last Saturday."

He checked his watch. She noticed the move and winced with annoyance.

"Look, Ella, I didn't go to see Carson, or Marvin Gaye before that. My ... ah, work comes first. I'd like to talk to you about all this, but my seminar is about to start."

"And I'm sure you never miss out on a class, with all the urgent areas of literature being discussed."

"My classes aren't all that urgent compared to what happened at South Carolina, but..."

"South Carolina *State*. It's a black university, in case you didn't know."

"Okay, I didn't know, sorry." He was about to say, *lynch me*, but wisely caught himself.

"Orangeburg," she added.

"Right. I'd like to know more about it, but you're correct that I don't skip my seminars. Please don't close me out, though, Ella. And even if you're probably right to put me into the stereotype of all white people, I'm concerned, I really am, and if you're willing to be a little patient with me you'll probably have an ally, if that even matters at this point."

"An ally? No, it doesn't matter. Whatever happens, we're going to have to do it by our own selves."

She turned back toward her desk, leaned forward, crossed her arms on the large blotter and lay her cheek on her wrists.

Ella's disturbing news about Orangeburg, however, and the difficulties in their relationship did little to dent Jake's eagerness to get back home for dinner with Natasha. The last two weeks had been a whirlwind of romance, vigorous sex and shared intimacy, talking and working. Natasha still hesitant to be seen with her new lover in public, they'd lain in each other's beds, she working on lesson plans and he reading the voluminous writings of the American Transcendentalists, all their time enclosed in their mutual, next-door love nests.

This little room, our universe, John Donne had written.

Her unwillingness to discuss Ray left Jake with the general impression that her once fiancé was waiting for his transfer papers to go through so he could get into the action of serving his country halfway around the world. In the meantime, Natasha mentioned that the two of them occasionally passed each other silently in the workplace they shared.

But not going out was all fine with Jake. He'd be happy being with his Tasha in a cave.

Over a meal of ham steak and green beans, he told her of his office run-in with Ella, explained what she'd told him of the Orangeburg events, of which Tasha had been totally ignorant as well.

"It should be big news," he said.

"Maybe it was. I haven't read the paper since our night at Carnival in your bedroom."

He smiled. "You're all the news I've been able to handle."

"What do you think your officemate wants from you?"

"Don't know. Maybe for me to know I'm an example of apathetic whites. But I don't think blacks will solve anything by violence. Except maybe get attention. King is smart, make the whites do the violence. But I doubt blacks will get anywhere by burning buildings and shooting cops. The establishment is much too strong. Like when those white protestors attacked the Pentagon last October. Yes, they got attention, but it's negative attention. How does that help?"

"Okay," Natasha said, cutting a piece of ham, "but the civil rights protests and the antiwar demonstrations aren't the same. The blacks have a real cause. The other is simple politics."

"Yes, but the politics of life and death. Our government is wrong about the war."

"Why do you say that, Jake?"

This question gave him the platform to deliver a lecture about all the research he'd done on Vietnam and how he'd come to his stance against American involvement. Tasha responded with a smile at his ardor, if not his argument. He noticed the difference.

"So, you don't agree?" he asked.

"I think the government understands more about the situation than we do. I think there are secrets that if you knew them, Jake, you might change your mind."

"What kind of secrets?"

"Like what the Russians are up to, and the Chinese, about communism wanting to take over the world. Of course, if they're secrets, how would I know them, but I'm just saying."

"Sounds like Ray talk."

"Maybe, yes. He believes in the war. So does Daddy. I haven't conducted any conclusive studies of my own. But it's pretty clear that people in a position to know feel convinced we need to be there and win. I don't know, I'm only a lowly guardian of the hearth." She rose to clear the dishes. "But I'm glad you made the sensible decision to serve your time teaching. That was smart. You did your duty as the government saw it and you're free and clear, as long as you don't storm the White House or anything."

Her statement gave Jake pause. Was this the time to come clean about the possibility of his getting a visit from the FBI and being hauled away to incarceration? Although time passing seemed to be making this prospect less and less a concern, maybe Tasha had a right to know, and maybe now was the moment to confess.

He rose and dried the plates and pans as she washed them, their hips touching. Any nudge, any brushing of her clothes or skin, her scent, aroused him. Soon he wrapped her in his arms and, her sudsy hands left wet, all but dragged her to her lacy, flowery bedroom.

24

Thursday, February 22, nine days later …

At yet another protest against Dow Chemical's job recruiters, Jake leaned against the bricks of Bowman Hall, zippered in a down parka and, with fingers cut-off gloves, strummed rhythm for Goldenrod, part of Wash's ongoing effort to keep the lid on things. About forty vocal protesters carried signs and chanted while another two hundred or so students gawked, many jeering the activists. Ella's attitude had made Jake more race conscious, so he marveled that all antiwar rallies were virtually void of African American participation. Today was an exception, however, in that a black army veteran gave one of the speeches, emphasizing his personal observations of how napalm obliterates forests and rice fields and fries villagers, young and old, gender be damned, to a crisp.

"Is this guy a student here?" Jake asked Adele. "A faculty member?"

"Don't think so. Never saw him before."

"Why don't the campus blacks show up at these things?"

"Who knows? Their group is tightknit. I'm surprised to see a black kid is running for student vice-president. Most of them probably regard him as an Oreo."

"An Oreo?"

"Take a guess."

"No idea."

"Black on the outside, white on the inside."

"Ah, I get it. What about the guy who's playing Othello in the university production?"

"That's Joe Lynn. Yes, I think he's involved with BUS."

"Huh? Bus?"

"Black United Students – BUS. Where have you been? Are you going to the play?"

"I think I'd better. My officemate will be pissed if I don't, more evidence of my white apathy. I wonder if they regard Shakespeare as a racist."

"The whole world was racist then. Around here, the black organization is all about non-assimilation. They act in unison, independent of the white groups. There are so few of them, like three percent, and their ruling clique snatches up the new ones as soon as they set foot in this place."

The Vietnam War vet's speech concluded to respectful applause, no jeers, and Goldenrod broke into "This Land Is Your Land." As Jake strummed, he mused about Native Americans having been left out of this Woody Guthrie song. It's actually *their* land, Jake thought. The Europeans stole it from them, killed off millions with rifles, smallpox, broken treaties and dead end reservations.

After the protest dispersed, the music group convened in the Union to get warm over coffee. The conversation returned to campus activism.

"These antiwar leaders are slick," Wash said. "They're lying back, gathering their forces. The Wednesday vigils are kept cool to draw moderates in. Rachel's ultimate goal is to radicalize the campus, but she knows this is a conservative stronghold. Though most kids think the war is wrong, they're not ready to stop partying and do much about it."

"Yeah," Henry, the fiddler, added, "they keep the faculty group separate from the student group with petitions, letters, teaching days so the profs don't get in serious trouble But those guys out there today are serious, SDS, Young Socialist Alliance. Wash is right. They have a national game plan, taking their time, looking all kosher-like, following administrative policy but bringing in outside speakers, putting them up at the Haunted House, building their strength."

Jake remembered Tim telling him about that place, the Alfred Hitchcock house, apparently the home of deeply committed agitators, some from campus, some not. Adele had mentioned that an English instructor was married to a leading revolutionary and did all the housework.

"Who's that Rachel person you mentioned, Wash?" Jake asked.

"Rachel Gibbs. Political science, grad student. She and Ronnie Engle keep the protests coming. They're no dummies, one step at a time slowly upping the ante. Hey anyway, Troop, I got a call from the Needle's Eye. They saw us at the festival, want us to lead their Saturday night hootenanny in two weeks, put it on your schedule."

Thursday, March 7, two weeks later ...

In 121 Satterfield, Jake waited with a sparse group for a visiting Browning expert, famous in lit circles for his dramatic readings of the Victorian poet's works. Jake made a strategic habit of being seen at all Department functions. As he waited, his mind dwelled on the erotic roleplay Tasha had come up with last night. Lil suddenly sat down next to him, her earthy perfume having signaled her arrival before her actual presence.

"Hi, Lover," she said softly, "how's it hanging?"

As she pulled off her coat and scarf, he noticed she wore a tight angora sweater, clinging ski pants, heavy makeup, her usual single braid loosened so that her brown hair framed her peaches-and-cream face.

"You look like you're on the hunt," Jake said.

"Don't worry, not for you. I have much bigger game in mind."

"What happened to the professor in Tennessee?"

"No harm in adding to the smorgasbord, is there?"

"So you've been reading up on your Browning?"

"Need you ask? He and Liz had quite a torrid thing going. And this guy is not only a prof but an actor. Could make for some interesting times."

"You're quite the operator, Lil."

"Yep. Except for the occasional dud, life is a ball. And you? Getting any?"

"I wouldn't put it that way."

"Really, how would you...," but the special guest's entrance allowed Jake to escape this line of banter.

Introduced by Chairman Armand Rudolf Madison, the speaker was a bearded, burly, robust fellow with flowing dark hair that touched the shoulder of his black turtleneck. He resembled the Victorian poet himself.

Shouldn't be much of a problem for Lil's prowling, Jake thought. And during the presentation, Jake heard some lines he noted for Tasha:

It is twelve o'clock/I shall hear her knock/in the worst of a storm's uproar./I shall pull her through the door/I shall have her for evermore!

After the reading the small group adjourned for coffee and *hors d'oeuvres*, several in a signing line with the professor's book on Browning's poems. Lil stood last, and as Jake left she gave him a wicked wink.

That evening before dropping over to Tasha's place for dinner, Jake sat at his desk copying the Browning lines to give her, but the last word, *evermore*, gave him pause. Certain that she hadn't yet reached the eternity point in their relationship, he figured he'd better hold these lines in abeyance. Though within the contained boundaries of their no longer separate second floor digs they seemed a solid couple, he needn't press the issue. Whatever they had together, she was in charge. Where they went from here would be up to her. He'd have to wait for her signals, and at the current moment he had plenty to be satisfied with. Tonight, after dinner and their work and studies, they planned a Scrabble game, dirty words permitted. If he'd thought in the beginning she was strictly a traditional girl, he'd been, to his present delight, utterly mistaken.

The phone rang, Adele in a panic.

"Wash caught this flu that's going around. He won't be in shape for the Saturday gig at the Eye. You're gonna have to sing lead."

Jake caught his breath. "But Wash is our star. It'll be like Dion and the Belmonts without Dion."

"It's only a singalong, not like a performance. The instrumentals aren't important, but they motivate the crowd. I'm gonna print up a sheaf of lyrics to pass out. But we'll need you in front. I called to give you due warning."

He considered this development. He didn't see where he could make room for the ever-growing involvement in Goldenrod. As for Saturday night, he'd been in many informal hootenannies back at his Penn State apartment, though hadn't led any of them. But easy enough to announce the song, play the key and get going.

Would Tasha venture out with him? The Needle's Eye, in a church basement on East Main next to the Robin Hood, would hardly pose the problem of Ray or his friends spotting them together, would it?

Tuesday, March 26, three weeks later ...

Winter quarter completed, spring term now underway, Jake had with two more freshman classes to teach, two more seminars to deal with, and his usual scheduling parameters, sat in his office checking over the first day offerings of his students when he heard a tap on his opened door. A wisp of a young woman in sweater and jeans, close cropped brown hair, rosy cheeks and round granny glasses stepped in, right hand extended.

"Rachel Gibbs," she said as they shook.

Jake remembered the name from his conversation about campus activists and from having seen it numerous times in the *Stater*. He gestured for her to have a seat.

"I noticed your signature on Drew's faculty petition to end the war," she said. "Thought it was time for us to meet."

"I've seen your name as well. Listened to you at the protest podium."

"Adele tells me you've joined their music group. We really appreciate Goldenrod's presence at our little gatherings. Here's the thing, Jake. You know, there's no doubt that this campus is pretty Godforsaken as far as social awareness is concerned. The kids here are more interested in beauty pageants and beer bashes than what's happening in the country, and we're trying to ratchet up awareness."

"I've sensed that."

"And you're one of us, correct?"

"To a degree. I also signed the faculty petition to support Eugene McCarthy in the presidential race."

"Like he has any fucking chance at all," Rachel said.

"He might. Johnson is unpopular."

"But he already beat McCarthy in the New Hampshire primary."

"Not by much," Jake said."

"We have to circumvent normal politics unless we're willing to see the war drag out with hundreds of thousands more casualties. So, let me get to the point of my visit."

"Please."

She rubbed her palms together, her small hands plain, no rings, no nail polish.

"I'd like to drop by your two freshman classes, introduce the KCEWV, let them know what we're doing, how they can get involved. Figure if we can get them interested before they fall into the abyss of Kent apathy, we'll be one step closer in making a difference."

"I see."

"Nothing rabblerousing. I'll hand out a flier, let them know we're not communists, present our schedule of events for the term."

Instinctively Jake hesitated. Rachel apparently picked up his misgivings.

"We cleared it with Adele, of course, as coordinator of the freshman program."

"How long do you need in my class?"

"Why are you resistant, Jake?"

"I have my classes down to a tight schedule, don't want to get behind."

"Is that all?"

"Not completely. I guess I believe all this should be done outside the classroom. If I allow you to do your thing, I'll have to allow the opposite view, and my class will become an ongoing debate about the war. I'm supposed to be introducing them to literature and teaching them academic writing. That's what I'm being paid for, and what I signed up to do."

"Come on, Jake," Rachel said, "don't give me that line. We're here to teach kids how to think, and what better way to do that than to get them involved with the crucial life and death issue in our society? Where's your conscience? Frankly, I'm shocked at your attitude."

Her own attitude at this moment locked him into his.

"Look, Miss Gibbs, if you..."

"Rachel. I'm Rachel, for God's sake."

"Okay, Rachel, if the Department will let you set up a table in the hall outside my classroom, talk to students before and after my class, no problem. I'll tell them you're out there. If they ask me my view, I'll be open with them about my opposition to the war. If they want to use class time to discuss the issues, I'll allow it, even let them write about it, one viewpoint or the other. But while the war goes on, students still need to get an education, and I'm not in charge of the curriculum. I'm a hired hand, and I accept that status."

"Are you bullshitting me?" she said, disbelief in her alert brown eyes.

"Sorry to disappoint you."

"I can't fucking believe this. Seven freshman teachers have already committed to having us make presentations. What, are you trying to protect your own ass?"

"I'm trying to do my job. We obviously see our responsibilities differently."

"I think we're responsible for saving lives."

"But there are different ways of doing that. Our country is still going to be here after the war ends, and people will have to be prepared to carry our society onward."

"But not the way it has been, for fuck sake. Don't you see there's a revolution going on? It's not going to be the same world, and our job is to shape the new one along humanitarian lines. We're going to change the world with or without you, Jake."

"We're not talking about who I'm with. I'm against the war, have spoken out against it, have taken hits for it, and want to end the killing and suffering as much as you do. Right now we're talking about a tactic you wish to employ in my classroom. It's as simple as that."

She stared at him, huffed, rose and stormed out.

Breathing hard, Ella came in. "What was *that* all about?"

"Nothing important. Did anyone come to you about making an antiwar presentation in your classes?"

"No. Is that what that chick wanted?"

"That was Rachel Gibbs, head of the student antiwar group. She wants her troops to speak to our classes about protesting on campus."

"Why's she so pissed off?"

"Because I told her *no*. We shouldn't be using freshman English to promote our personal political views."

"Wow, you really are part of the lily white establishment, aren't you?"

"Not completely."

"Could'a fooled me. Are you saying I shouldn't let them speak in my classes?"

"No. That's entirely up to you. It's how I run my own, that's all."

"But..." She stopped suddenly.

"But?"

"There's a rumor going around."

"A rumor?"

"That you'll have Adele's job next year."

"I've already turned that down."

"It's the rumor, anyway."

"Look, Ella, Adele, has left the protest matter in each teacher's hands. Academic freedom, right? I agree. I'm sure she has consulted the higher ups, and they've endorsed her policy. You use your judgement, I'll use mine, even if it mistakenly places me in the lily white establishment."

"Okay, different strokes. That chick sure was pissed off, though."

"Incidentally, Ella, ever since our discussion about Orangeburg I've been checking the *Washington Post*, and I'm sure you're aware of the Howard University situation."

"I'm aware of it all right. Man, I wish I'd been accepted there."

"Incidentally, I caught the *Othello* performance the other night. Did you happen to see it?"

"And you're bringing that up because...?"

"Never mind then."

"Because the star happens to be black?"

"And because we're both English majors. Joe Lynn did a great job."

"You apparently didn't see the *Stater's* review. Said he was terrible, mispronounced words, overused gestures, not close to Iago's performance, the white guy's, of course."

"They must have seen a different show than I did."

"And of course the reviewer sang praises about Joe's physique, called him 'beautiful.' So damn typical of Whitey's views it makes me want to scream."

133

"Why don't you write a letter to the editor?"

"That'll sure change things."

"Better than stewing about it."

"We're doing a lot more than *stewing* about our situation in this white enclave. We have big plans that will set this place on its honky white ass."

25

Sunday, March 31, five days later ...

Jake and Tasha settled on her sofa in anticipation of the "Smothers Brothers Comedy Hour" when the screen changed to a desk in the White House. President Johnson appeared as part of a special report. He spoke at length about the war, almost pleading Ho Chi Min to come to the negotiating table. He talked about various peace offers he'd made and, to Jake's disgust, about the nobility of the U.S.'s effort to secure South Vietnam's independence.

"They were never two countries," Jake shouted at the black and white TV screen.

"Shhh!" Tasha said, nudging his ribs. "I want to hear this."

The President said he would stop bombing the North if they stopped sending troops into the South. He praised the bravery of American soldiers and said they were fighting for the security of all Southeast Asia. He also stated the need for increased tax revenues to pay for the war and to reduce the nation's twenty billion dollar deficit.

Jake was beside himself at the raw deception he believed Johnson was presenting to the American people. But then the tone of the speech changed. The President addressed the divisions in the country, the misgivings of citizens, and then, surprise of surprises, he announced his refusal to run or to accept the nomination for the 1968 election.

In his south Texas twang, LBJ said he was bowing out!

It took Jake hardly a second to reach the conclusion that the dissent in the nation had driven him to resign. Of course, the President couched the move as a way to devote his fulltime to reaching a peace rather than to the distractions of running in a political campaign, but to Jake the message was crystal clear: the protestors had driven him from office.

Following the speech, commentators recapped and interpreted, but Jake could feel the wave of celebration that must have been rippling through certain segments of the country. And in particular the backers of Senator Eugene McCarthy.

"The first step to a peace settlement," Jake pontificated to a worried looking Tasha, "is to have a real peace president, someone who wants to reunite an artificially divided country rather than establishing two nations where there were never two at all."

Toward the middle of Johnson's lengthy speech, Tasha had edged away from him to the far end of the couch, having wriggled out of their embrace.

"But he said," she commented, "we won't leave until the South is their own country."

Jake took a breath from his excitement. He stood, paced, looked out the window at the street half expecting to see people coming out of their houses to dance, cars flashing lights and honking horns. Of course, the street was as dark and quiet as usual.

"Never two countries," he said. "After the French gave up, a treaty was made in Geneva to separate Vietnam *temporarily* to allow time for a national election to select a president. When the U.S. saw that the president would definitely be Ho Chi Min, we disrupted the election, installed a puppet government in the South, and proclaimed that the North was invading the South. We subverted the Geneva Accords."

"But why would we do something like that?" Tasha nearly shouted in frustration.

"Because Ho is a communist, and Russia is communist and we think they're trying to take over the world and that if they get Vietnam, soon they'll be invading San Francisco. It's so God damned stupid! Ho is a nationalist. He'd fight as hard against Russia and China as he's fighting against us and as he did against the French. He wants Vietnam for the Vietnamese. You see?"

Tasha stared, a hint of horror in her eyes.

"But isn't that only *your* theory?" she asked. "The President explained a different theory. What makes you think you know more than the President, Jake?"

Jake went back and sat beside her. When he moved to hold her, she moved away.

"Answer me, Jake."

"Because I studied it, read whatever I could, listened to professors who explored the topic rationally, historically, factually. Some people believe the reason JFK was killed is because he wanted to get out of Vietnam, that he knew it was a mistake."

"That our own government killed him? Are you crazy?"

"Some people believe it."

"What do *you* believe?"

"I doubt one jerk with a gun bought from the Sears catalog could have managed it. I believe the Warren Report might be a cover-up. But who knows? Some witnesses say there was a second shooter..."

"So you don't trust anything the government says, Jake? They're lying to us? Why would they do that?"

Jake looked at her, her hair still disheveled from their earlier lovemaking, her naked legs from under her robe, her eyes full of concern.

"I don't know why they would do it, but you're right, I don't trust them. Eisenhower warned us not to trust the military industrial complex, that its financial interests are wrapped up in the government so tightly that their money rules politicians, and that the Pentagon and FBI are the ones really running things, not the elected officials. But I don't know that. I only know what I've read and heard from people I trust more than politicians. I don't know about who killed Kennedy, but about Vietnam I think it could have been merely one judgment error piled on another until it became impossible to admit we were wrong, too invested to back out. So to save face, we push on. And maybe there *are* some people high up who actually believe that a communist Vietnam is a threat to us. But those people are plain wrong."

"And you know they're wrong? You're the authority?"

"Tasha, I'm a citizen who's done his homework. Our country wasn't designed for people to blindly accept what the government says. We're supposed to think, and to operate from the truth. We make our choices on the best information we can get, which is why we have freedom of speech and press. The idea that South and North Vietnam are separate countries is a lie, Tasha. It's a lie that our government has been telling us. And if they're lying about that, which is supposedly the basis of our involvement over there, what else are they lying about? Maybe that's why Johnson wants out, to make way for a peacemaker, like McCarthy or Bobby Kennedy."

Tasha shook her head forlornly, seemed about to cry. "I don't know what to think. My family is Republican. All our neighbors are Republican. They'd be upset if they knew I was involved with someone who has such ideas."

Jake waited. He held her hand, her long fingers, clean clear nails, her engagement ring having been removed weeks ago.

"You're thinking of Ray, aren't you?"

"A little."

"Johnson said he's sending more troops. Maybe that means him."

"There's some delay with Ray's transfer. He doesn't know why. He's upset about it."

"You've talked with him?"

"The other day, after school. In the cafeteria."

"You didn't mention it to me."

"Didn't see a reason to. It doesn't change anything between us."

"Are you sure? I mean because I'm a political radical, and he's a prospective war hero?"

"You two are certainly on opposite sides."

"Does he know you're seeing me?"

She smiled, moved closer to him. "No. Right now, you're my delicious secret. And honestly, I used to think I knew about the war, even though I didn't want Ray to go. I thought his being in the Guard was honorable enough. And now I listen to you, and I wonder. I guess I'm not one of those citizens who distrusts the government enough to doubt them. Now I don't know what to think."

By this time the Smothers Brothers were back on, introducing a country singer named Glen Campbell. Jake listened to a song called "Wichita Lineman." It was a song that at that moment, Tasha leaning into him, the warmth of her body, her scent, her confusion, defined something for him, something deep and eternal – *I need you more than want you, and I want you for all time* – words he nearly repeated to her, but held back.

Thursday, April 4, four days later …
Jake and Tasha were washing the dishes of their late supper when they heard a pause in Walter Cronkite's news presentation from the TV in the living room: Special Report. Dan Rather introduced himself and said: *The Reverend Martin Luther King was shot to death as he stood on a balcony in Memphis, Tennessee.*

Jake immediately moved to the living room and saw a King colleague describe what happened: a motel, the entourage waiting for their leader to come out of his second floor room, a sound like a firecracker, King wounded badly in the neck. More details: a young white man fleeing the scene, a rifle found, a car driven off with two other Caucasians.

Tasha joined Jake, leaning against him.

"Oh, my God!" she said. "Jake, I'm scared. There's going to be trouble everywhere, like the Hough Riots a couple years ago."

"Hough Riots?"

"In Cleveland, you know?"

Actually, he didn't know.

"There was trouble in the black section of Akron too, and Columbus. This will start it all over again."

"Is there a black section here in Kent?"

"A small one, not enough to cause trouble. I feel sorry for them, but scared too."

Jake thought of Ella, wondered the horror she must be feeling.

"Things are getting so crazy," Tasha said.

Sitting close on the sofa, they learned that King had gone back to Memphis in support of striking sanitary workers after having marched with them several days before. His goal was to unite the blacks and whites in the ongoing, often violent dispute. Now he was dead. And despite President Johnson's televised appeal for restraint, would the killing ignite hostility across the country? Robert Kennedy, campaigning for the Democratic nomination for president, was due to speak in Cleveland the next day and to make a quick stop at Kent State on Monday.

Later, lying with Tasha in her bed, Jake held her as if protecting her from a perilous world. President Kennedy, Malcolm X, now this. Kill your opponent, simple as that.

"Do you know many Negroes?" Tasha asked, her back to him, wrapped in his arms.

"No. There were no blacks in my small town, none in the schools I went to. Zero. I had them as students at Lancaster High, though, met with worried parents, some angry ones. But never a black friend, sorry to say."

"But you said your officemate is black."

"Hardly a close friend. What about you?"

"Daddy insisted I go to a private school. No blacks. And none in my sorority at State either. We didn't think much about civil rights. Things were simpler then. Not right, just simpler."

"But you believe in equality, don't you?"

"Of course, Jake, but it's going to take a lot of changes in the educational system to have equality. I mean, on the whole, blacks are far behind."

"Yeah, because of oppression, segregated schools with no funds."

"Sure, there are reasons, but they're still behind, I mean in general. My best student is a Negro girl, learned French as a child in New Orleans. Going to Paris as an exchange student next fall. But she's the exception that proves the rule."

"You folks still use the word *Negro* out here?"

"The president called them Negroes in his speech, Walter Cronkite used that term. It feels awkward calling them African Americans, or Afros, or whatever. *Blacks* is weird because most of them aren't black. What do you call them, Jake?"

"Blacks. African Americans. Seems those are the terms they prefer. I guess they should have the right to determine what they like to be called."

"I'm not prejudiced, if that's what you think, Jake."

He held her tighter. "I don't think that."

"I'm for equal rights all around. They've gotten a raw deal, but catching up won't be easy. There are tons of racists around here. Negroes ... sorry, blacks ... are going to need special help, and whites will claim reverse racism. I don't see a way out."

"Johnson's Civil Rights Acts will help," Jake said. "Got to give him credit for that."

"But passing laws doesn't change hearts. People find ways to get around regulations. Anyway, I'm scared." She pulled away from Jake, got out of bed. "I want to phone my parents, see what's happening in Akron."

After her call, she came back to bed. Everything was quiet in her home town, so far at least.

Monday, April 8 four days later …

As Jake's eight o'clock class left, clearing the room for his nine o'clock, Adele pushed her way in against the flow.

"There's a march later," she said. "Wash and I and Henry are joining, over to the black section in town. Wanna come?"

"Organized by the Black Union?"

"I don't think so."

"The antiwar committee?"

"No, spontaneous. Starts in front of McDowell at eleven."

"I'll be there."

"Such a terrible thing."

"Yes, horrible."

"We gotta get behind Bobby," she said.

"What about McCarthy?"

"He has courage, but Bobby has spark. You need spark to win elections. He gave a beautiful speech at the City Club in Cleveland Friday. And they're saying he kept things calm in Indianapolis Thursday night, announced the assassination to the crowd. Cancelled his trip here today, though. Things are getting serious. Violence all over the country. They keep posting info in the window of the *Stater's* office over in Taylor Hall."

His nine o'clock students, all white, were seated. Adele left. Jake looked at the thirty somber faces before him.

"Whether you agree with King's ideas or not," he said, "I think we can all agree that murdering our opponents is no way to settle arguments. We must use language, persuasion, elections. Like King said in Memphis, freedom of speech, of assembly, of the press. And nonviolence. He knew that the numbers were overwhelmingly against him, so he had to change the odds by reaching the white population, the ones who had good hearts, fair minds, but who were simply ignorant of the real injustice of segregation. Now who knows what will happen – cities on fire and people running for their guns? The last thing King wanted was a race war, which he knew his side would lose."

Each student in the room was staring at him.

"A lot of profs have cancelled their classes today," someone piped up.

"I'm not one of them."

A general moan sounded.

"We're on a tight schedule here, so we'll plod on. You can leave, but it will count as an absence. It may not seem like it, but your education is part of the solution to our country's problems. That's what I believe. I hear there's a

139

march scheduled for eleven. I'm going. Everyone is welcome. And feel free to use these horrible events in your essays, but stick to the rules of effective argumentation, presenting facts, not just emotion."

"Maybe it was good that he got killed," a male voice was heard.

The room grew dead silent, people looking around for the speaker, a student near the back with a crew cut and button down shirt.

Jake burst out. "Anyone who thinks that is a damn fool." He caught himself. "Look, everyone is entitled to his own opinion, but..."

"I mean, for the Negro cause," the lad said calmly. "He'll be a martyr now. He mentioned it in that big speech he gave in Washington, that he wouldn't reach the mountaintop with his people. He was always putting himself in dangerous spots, like he was asking for it."

"In here," Jake said, settling down, "let's not take class time to argue political issues. Do it in your essays. Remember the standard rules of effective argument, evidence and more evidence. Now open your text to Chapter Three."

As they turned pages Jake wondered if he'd chosen the correct track in this instance. Maybe he should use the situation as a learning moment.

No, the moment is too sacred. We'll move on with the job of education.

He remembered reading in last term's American Transcendentalism course, Thoreau, perhaps, that three equal forces exist in nature: creation, destruction and maintenance. Each and every action requires all three. What society seems to be lacking today is the third.

Maintaining continuity is my role, but is it the right role or simply the one I know best and cling to for my own comfort?

That day's march started with a small muted group almost exclusively white wending its way through campus, gathering others along the walkways to Summit Road, on to Franklin, left to Dodge, then right two blocks to the Union Baptist Church. The black pastor in the small Kent ghetto apologized for not having enough space to invite everyone in. Through a bullhorn, he delivered an outdoor sermon-like speech to the orderly crowd. They ended by locking arms and singing "We Shall Overcome." Standing between Jake and Wash, Adele wept. Tears welled in Jake's eyes too.

As the mourners retraced their steps on the way back to campus in the crisp spring air, Jake wondered what he could do to help the black cause. He had no idea, as he had no idea what power he had to stop the war. Except to stay loyal to his position and to behave accordingly. Blacks would have to lead in their own liberation. It seemed clear that Ella wanted him to butt out, that she constantly reminded him of his ignorance of black culture. Jake realized he was the epitome of the result of a segregated society – total witlessness.

26

Easter Sunday, April 14, one week later …

In heavy hooded yellow raincoats, Jake and Tasha stood at the railing of a tourist boat called Maid of the Mist, the roar of Niagara Falls too loud for them to speak but not loud enough to keep the wide grins from their faces. Soon they were doused in spray, suddenly chilled to the bone on the otherwise lovely spring day. Finally out of the tumult but still in the roar, they smiled at each other, a mutual joy that said several things: that this was indeed one of the wonders of nature, that feeling its power was awesome, and that a great part of their exhilaration was being there together. In fact, for Jake the moment constituted the single happiest of his life.

No, they weren't on their honeymoon, but you couldn't have proven that from their behavior and from the several new outfits Tasha had brought along from Frederick's of Hollywood. No engagement prospects, however, had arisen from either of their sides although Jake would have married her without hesitation. No words with even the vaguest of such references had been spoken. The magnificent falls was simply an outing over Easter break from both their schools, a slow sightseeing drive along the lake – Lake Shore Boulevard out of Cleveland, Route 531 to Erie where they spent Friday night, along Route 5 to Buffalo and onward to their motel in Grand Island. Finally, Sunday, to the wondrous roar and mist.

"I can't believe you've never been here," Tasha said, their rain gear returned and their shivering calming as they got into Jake's car in the packed lot.

"I'm not much of a world traveler."

"My parents spent their honeymoon here," she said. "They were married in France but didn't have time to celebrate properly there. Then they took me here when I was seven. Where's the farthest you've ever been from home?"

"Hmm. Kent, I guess, maybe here, don't know which is farther. I know D.C., though, and been to New York City. A week in the Poconos, too. And the Jersey shore."

"Never flew on a plane?"

"No, never. You?"

"For my high school graduation present my mother took me to France. I met all her relatives in Lyon. In my senior year at OSU, I went back again with the French honors students, a two week tour, London, Madrid, Rome and Paris again. I'd love to show you the City of Lights, Jake."

"I'll take you up on that."

"Being out of Kent this weekend has been magical. Like freedom. We've been cooped up, afraid to go anywhere."

"Speak for yourself. I'm not afraid."

"True, you've no reason to be, but I'm not ready for the announcement I'd be making by being seen around town holding hands with you."

"Hey, I'm not complaining. But do you have any prediction about when that might change?"

She held his hand, which was resting on the stick shift he was using in the heavy traffic toward the interstate in Buffalo.

"No prediction. And let's not spoil this fantastic time by talking about it, shall we?"

In spite of the slight tone of foreboding in her voice, he was quick to agree in his mock-haughty professorial attitude. "Quite right. Indeed, we shan't explore that topic further. I forbid it."

Smiling, she moved her hand to his thigh as they settled in for the eighty mile drive home on I-90.

Tuesday, April 23, nine days later ...

The air changed suddenly in Jake's office. Sensing a presence, he turned and saw a short, stocky guy with bushy hair and long pointed sideburns. His intense eyes were slightly squinted, and he wore fatigues, a striped tee shirt and a red neckerchief. Jake had seen him as a frenetic key speaker at rallies.

"Hey, there," the fellow said, standing in the doorway. "Ronnie Engle, how's it going?"

"Going well. What's up?"

"You heard about Friday's strike, right?"

"Saw the signs."

"Cancelling your classes, right?"

"No, not that."

"Wha'd'ya mean?"

Jake swiveled his chair to face Engle directly. "I mean, not cancelling my classes."

"Why the hell not? It's a strike. That means refusing to work. So cancel them."

"Sorry."

"You mean you're acting against us?"

"I'm against the war, but I'm not being paid to cancel classes. I'll be in my classroom. If students don't want to come, that's up to them. If I cancel my classes, it would hardly be a strike for them, would it? They're the ones who should refuse to work, not the instructors."

"Shit, man!" Engle stepped in from the doorway, twirled Ella's chair and sat in the middle of the small room. "Adele's joining us, and she directs your gig here. What more do you want?"

"That's her choice. But I'm hired to teach. I protest on my free time."

"What kind of half-assed commitment is that?"

"Look, I've already had this conversation with your partner."

"My partner? Who would that be?"

"Miss Gibbs."

"Rachel, yeah, she told me about you. Sign all the petitions but don't do squat."

Ella burst in, out of breath. She quickly took in the scene.

"You're in my chair," she said to Ronnie.

"There's another one beside your desk," he said, turning back toward Jake.

"I want that one. It's mine."

"Incorrect. Technically, it belongs to the university."

"Give it to me."

Engle shrugged, rose. "Jesus, here, take it." He shoved it toward her on its rollers. "You're striking Friday, right?"

"Not sure yet," she said.

"So BUS hasn't sent out the word, given you permission?"

"It's my decision."

"Don't give me that. Why are you people always holding back? We need a unified front."

"Led by you and SDS?"

Jake felt compelled to interrupt. "We have work to do here, Ronnie. I'll give the strike some thought, okay? Why don't you head out?"

"Jesus Christ, don't you know what's going on in the world, innocent people dying, our government trying to colonize the whole damn planet? Teaching your little writing classes ain't shit. They don't matter. What matters is committing totally to the Movement. Get with it, for fuck sake."

He loped out of the office, muttering down the corridor.

"The famous Ronnie Engle?" Ella said. "What a jerk!" She wheeled her chair to her desk and plopped down on it.

Jake turned back to the stack of essays he was grading.

"So I take it you're not into the strike," Ella said. "It's a national event, you know?"

"I'll teach my classes. Then I'll go to the rally. I play guitar for a bluegrass group. We do Pete Seeger stuff to keep the emotion on an even keel."

"Bluegrass. That figures."

"Did you get my note about King?"

"Nice words. Nice, nice and more nice. Makes me wanna puke."

143

"Ella, what am I supposed to do? I can't help it I'm white. How can someone like me be of use to your struggle?"

"You can't be of use. In spite of your nice tries, you're useless. If you'd gone to hear Brother Boutelle the other night, you'd understand."

"I read his comments in the paper. A black nation isn't realistic, is it? Isn't that what Liberia was all about?"

"We don't need a nation. What we do need is a unified black nationwide community. Maybe you can use your vast influence to make that happen."

"I'm trying to be your friend, Ella. No need for constant sarcasm."

"Excuse me? I'll use sarcasm if I want to. Our people, as Sir Ronnie refers to us, have to stand up for ourselves. And if we decide to strike, which we probably won't, you better not hold it against me when you're the director of this program. But, wait, maybe some hillbilly music will be an incentive for *my people* to get out there. I'll have to tell *my people*; they'll be so excited."

Her dismissive tone always stabbed his heart. Didn't she know they needed white support to reach their goals? King knew it. But where will all this talk of Black Nationalism, violent black response, get them? Except shot. What was becoming of the idea of peace and love? Where was the strength and courage to use King's approach? But maybe the only thing that approach had accomplished was getting him shot also.

As Jake was packing his briefcase to leave, Ella cleared her throat, seeming to have something to say. She turned toward him and gestured for him to close the door. Three of her students were waiting in the hall.

"She'll be right with you," he said, pulling it shut.

"But I have a question," Ella said with a sincerity she'd never shown before.

"Go ahead."

"I don't think I've ever seen you have a student conference. Yet, my kids are lined up outside. You just use your time to grade papers. So, what's the secret?"

"The hours."

"You mean you schedule early morning so students won't come?"

"They seem to be able to work things out on their own, considering the alternative of using their alarm clocks."

"That's crass."

"It's survival, well within the rules."

"So that's it? Schedule early hours?"

"Early classes, too. I lose a dozen or so students to drop/add every term. And the ones who show up are too sleepy to cause problems."

"Damn! That's corrupt."

"If you make your syllabus and assignments clear and if you keep your class discussion time around explication rather than interpretation, and if you follow the writing textbook to the letter, they don't have many questions. Look, Ella, there's a trap you can easily fall into that will hurt your career. If you put all your chips into teaching these classes, you won't have time for your seminars."

"Yes, I noticed that."

"And if your goal is to teach in college, it's your research that matters. Have you noticed the teaching techniques of your profs? Pitiful, right? They got here because of their articles, not their pedagogical expertise. And anyway, my student evaluations have been coming in strong. Kids appreciate clarity. They can discuss philosophy when they get into their majors."

She looked at him with a skeptical smile. "All right, thanks, I guess. I don't agree, but I see your point. I hardly have time to breathe. They keep coming in here asking what to write about."

"Make your topics absolutely clear, related to the readings, open book, no more than two choices, and have them write in class. hat way they don't have time to think too much and it's five easy lesson plans each term."

"Shit, Jack! You're subversive."

"Jack? Oh, like Ray Charles? Hit the road, Jack?"

She flashed him a look. "Don't start. It's an expression."

"I learned all these survival skills teaching high school sophomores, and most of the kids here aren't much above that level. And before you can help other people, you must make sure you're okay yourself."

"Yeah, right, I have to agree with you there," she said. "Uh, do you happen to have an extra copy of your syllabus? I'll look it over. Adele told me it's not bad."

When Jake left the office, six of Ella's students were waiting.

Wednesday, April 24, next day …

Jake and Tasha waited in the lecture hall for the arrival of the acclaimed poet, Denise Levertov. He'd convinced Tasha that Ray or his friends would probably not be present for the occasion just as they hadn't been to the folk festival or the hootenanny at the Needle's Eye.

"This would be like a foreign country to him," she agreed.

They'd purchased Levertov's two most recent collections of poems, *O Taste and See* and *The Sorrow Dance*.

Jake noticed Lil seated in the front row, having assumed, it seemed, a new identity as a Hindu princess. Her now waist long hair had been crinkled into short waves, with several thin braids, her skin tan, dangling brass earrings, bangles on her wrists, sandals, a leather anklet, a gauzy top and a long Indian skirt. Beautiful, Jake thought, then quickly realized who she actually was. But could she possibly be on the hunt for the famous poetess?

Lil turned, caught Jake's eye and gave him a wicked little finger wave.

145

"Who's that?" Tasha asked.

"Lil."

"Oh, her. Looks like queen of Sheba."

"Yeah, doesn't she?"

"Do you ever think of her?"

"No. But I see her around sometimes."

Ms. Levertov arrived with an entourage and was introduced by the Department Chairman, who gave an extensive bio of the guest's having grown up in England after her father fled Russia as a persecuted Jewish intellectual. Later, after marrying an American, she emigrated to the States.

Wrapped in a thin shawl, she was a small, plain woman, gap-toothed, humble, no appearance whatever of celebrity, her curly hair cut short. She read with a clear Americanized voice, her precise imagery unabashedly influenced by William Carlos Williams but fiercely expressing her antiwar sentiments. After her poems she announced that she'd be joining an antidraft panel the following evening, which she invited everyone to attend. She mentioned a string of leftwing affiliations.

Books signed, Lil last in line with hers, Jake wondered if his former playmate now included women on her private agenda. Then he and Tasha stepped across the portal of Satterfield Hall into a luscious April night.

"*I saw paradise in the dust of the street.* That line is straight from Williams," Jake said. "That's his whole message, the divinity of the commonplace."

"*Your lovely body grows in tendrils,*" Tasha quoted, "*half in darkness.* That line reminds me of how I feel about you, Jake. I'm glad she read at least one love poem." She leaned against him as they strolled down the hill in the moonlit night.

He pulled her closer. Rare, such a comment, for they seldom voiced their feelings for each other, somehow silently fearing such expressions, as if, perhaps, words couldn't contain them. But what she'd just said stirred him deeply. He let the silence of the moonlight be his answer.

When they turned from Summit onto Willow, she stopped suddenly.

"Oh, no!"

"What's wrong?"

"That's Ray's car in front of our place."

She pulled Jake into a shadow. "Oh, Jake. I don't want him to see us together. Please."

"Maybe it's time."

"I'm not ready. Please, I beg you, Jake. Let me go on alone. I'll tell him it was such a beautiful night I decided to go for a walk, picked up this book in the bookstore. Please, Jake, walk around the block, come in when we're inside, okay?"

"But..."

"Don't argue, Jake. Let's make this as simple as we can. Please." She hugged him hard and trotted off.

27

Thursday, April 25, a few hours later ...

Jake tried to sleep but failed. At two-thirty, muffled voices still came through the walls. He'd taken a walk around the block after she left him, got in about eleven. Ray was still there. She'd insisted several times that he wasn't violent toward her though he was jealous and possessive. Jake wondered what they were talking about, why so long, and felt an irrepressible dread. But what could he do but wait and hope that she'd come to him after the intruder left? Outside under the streetlight, the guy's black Camaro remained like an omen of evil.

Jake paced, picked up his guitar, quietly practiced a few unoriginal riffs. He wasn't far from being able to add them to his sparse repertoire. Then he paced some more, the muffled voices going on and on, sometimes rising in volume then dropping off again, but the words never discernible. He subdued the impulse to go knock on her door but remained on guard in case she needed help. Three o'clock passed, four o'clock; soon they'd have to leave for work. Whatever happened, the coming day would be a drag. He hoped they'd end soon and she would eventually fill him in about what this extremely lengthy powwow was all about.

But even at seven-thirty, time to depart for his office hours, they were still at it, apparently not intending to go to their own jobs. Whatever it was, it was clearly serious. Jake had to leave, the dark muscle car still ominously in its spot.

Having pulled all-nighters many times before, Jake was surprised at the depth of his exhaustion, realizing that part of it must be from the state of his emotions. Could she actually be getting back together with the guy? Had she told Ray about him? Could Ray live with that? Could she go back to him after having been so intensely involved with someone else? Could Ray forgive her? Could she forgive herself? She and Ray had been together for five years, engaged for two, the invitations sent out for their June wedding, dress fitted, band booked, church and reception hall set up. Jake hadn't questioned her about all that, assuming cancellations had been taken care of. But maybe he was wrong. Maybe everything was madly still in place. Maybe the inertia of history was impossible to resist. Jesus! Would he have to live without her? Could he, possibly?

All this sped through his weary mind as he sipped his second cup of coffee and peered at an atrociously written student essay about a Little League game in which the writer's dad had run onto the field and kicked dirt on the umpire. Being barraged with such essays was a high initiation price for entrance into the advanced levels of academia. And his fatigue and prospect of doom didn't help his concentration. What was happening with Tasha?

A tap on his door caught his attention, a couple peering into the office. Jake recognized them from their reputations as leaders of the antiwar committee, Miles and Holly McGill, he from Political Science and she a popular lit instructor. For some reason these SDS types were leaning hard on him. Jake told them to take seats on the two chairs in the office used for student conferences.

"We're here to apologize for Ronnie's behavior the other morning," Holly said. "He needs to work on his social skills."

"Yeah," Miles added. "We'd like to make it up to you by inviting you over to our place for grub tonight. We're having a few faculty people to discuss the strike tomorrow, thought you might want to meet them, get an accurate picture of where we're coming from."

"I made my position clear to Ronnie."

"But a little more exposure wouldn't hurt," Holly said. She was attractive, long straight dark hair, nicely dressed, her lovely face marred slightly by a faint scar on her right cheek, her mouth not quite even as if her jaw was a tad misaligned. "We'd like to get to know you, and for you to get to know us. We understand you share our views but have some problems with our methods."

Jake stifled a yawn. "Sorry, long night last night. Thanks for your interest, but I'm going to toe the line, at least for now. I have some, uh, personal matters, so tonight's not good for me. And right now I have a pile of papers to grade."

"I know how that goes," Holly said. "The invitation is open." She handed him a business card. "You've probably heard of the Haunted House. That's us, the most dynamic place in town. We'd like to hear your ideas, get to know you, and vice versa. Are you sure you can't make it? We'll have pizza from Pisanello's, informal, and clear the air for each other."

"Maybe some other time."

"You really fear us, don't you?" Miles said less cordially. He was tall, lean, sloppily dressed as if his appearance was the last thing on his mind. His dark hair hung loose and stringy, and his moustache drooped around the corners of his mouth. Sunglasses hid his eyes.

"Fear you?" Jake said. "Not at all."

"You should be seeking the real skinny about what's going on around here," Miles said. "Tomorrow will be a breakout day, and we'd like you to be part of our plans. Adele says you're in line for leadership over here. We have other committed faculty people. Drew Byrne has mentioned you to us. So we'd like to have you aboard."

"I'm not joining SDS," Jake said. "Thanks for coming by, but I have work to do."

Holly smiled. "All right. Adele says your band is playing tomorrow. We really appreciate it. Please keep an eye on us. I think you'll see the power we're slowly generating around here and the difference it will make. I'm sure you'll join us, and you're welcome to pop over for our evening feast any time. I usually do a lot better than pizza, believe me. Maybe you'd be more comfortable if Wash and Adele were there. Would you?"

"Look, I've had a bad night, I'm busy, and..."

"Right," Holly said, still smiling. "Keep us in mind, okay?"

Miles was about to say something, but Holly put a hand over his mouth and gestured with her head that it was time for them to leave. She extended a pale, slender hand to shake. Jake complied, shook Miles's also, and the two, careful to replace the chairs, were gone.

Why do they see me as such a valuable commodity? What's all this about leadership in the Department? And what the hell do they think I'll bring to SDS?

The day dragged on, Jake unable to keep his mind off Tasha, kept going over possible scenarios, concluding that she was wrangling with her ex-fiancé about their breakup, finalizing things. He puzzled over whether she would tell Ray about him. She'd been careful about their public exposure, venturing out into the world at large only a few times, but had basked in the freedom she felt on their trip to Niagara. How would Ray react if she told him she was sending away for sexy nighties to wear for her new lover? And was she safe? Would they be able to talk about it tonight?

She didn't come home that night, however. He waited, paced, played his guitar, tried to read Chaucer but couldn't. He wanted to drive to Ray's place to see if her car was there but had never found out exactly where he lived. Finally due to sheer exhaustion, he drifted into a restless sleep.

Friday, April 26, next day ...

Jake's radio alarm woke him at 6:30 with Bobby Goldsboro's hit "Honey," sentimental pap, Jake thought, but he took note of the line, *I'd be with her if I could.* He rolled and hit the off-button then popped to his feet and looked out the window only to discover Tasha's Rambler still wasn't there. Tired enough to wish he'd honored the McGill's wish for him to cancel his classes for the big student strike, he rubbed the sleep from his eyes and decided to call the high school later to make sure Tasha was all right. He believed she'd have called him if she could, but that doing so would have announced the relationship to Ray. That, and the possibility of her having been incapacitated were the only reasons he could fathom that he hadn't heard from her. She probably thought he'd understand and be patient.

Lugging his satchel and his guitar in its case, he climbed through a gray morning mist to Satterfield where he got coffee from the grad student lounge and took the elevator to the third floor. He went over his lesson plans for the day, a discussion of Twain's "The Celebrated Jumping Frog of Calaveras County." He glanced at his usual presentation about the relative pronouns *who*, *whom*, *that* and *which*, planning to demonstrate the use of adjective clauses to combine simple sentences.

How thrilling! And how relevant!

He opened the *Stater* to a double page photo spread depicting what appeared to be the KSU spring rite of mud fights on campus. The article included a warning from the dean of students that such celebrations of rebirth could result in dismissal from the university as well as in charges for assault and destruction of property. There was nothing in the paper about the student strike and its accompanying rally to occur that afternoon in front of Stopher Hall.

Jake hoped the event would be called off due to the rain. No such luck, however. After his sparsely-attended classes, as always Goldenrod assembled with their instruments under a roof some distance across the lawn. Roughly a hundred strikers and quite a few opponents gathered for the scheduled speeches. A folk music duo, Nash Ramblers, tried to perform under a raised tarp, but there was trouble with the speaker system. Committee members rushed about. A heavyset guy with wire-rimmed glasses shouted that the administration had failed to provide the promised PA system. He ranted about how university officials continually sabotage the Committee's events.

Suddenly James Brown's "I Got the Feelin'" blasted from a second floor window of Stopher. Half an hour later substitute sound equipment was set up, but the loud sounds of funk continued to interrupt, changing the somber mood into time to boogie down. Engle and McGill rushed to the building, and soon the music stopped. Engle appeared at the dorm window and hurled out a black thirty-three like a Frisbee. Funk quieted, presenters began, the first a priest from the local Catholic Church, who abruptly stopped his talk, ducking and grasping his neck.

People pointed toward a third floor dorm window. Someone shouted, "BBs!"

No police presence, tiny Rachel Gibbs raced toward the entrance followed by a few others, and Wash signaled their group to play "Blowin' in the Wind." Things came to a standstill until Rachel returned, holding up several boxes of BB pellets.

She shouted, "That fucking creep says that the next time it'll be a machine gun."

Campus security showed up and went into the dorm. Rain poured down. Soon drenched, the most avid of the strikers withdrew to the relative safety of the Union's commuter lounge while frat brothers and sorority sisters battled in the mud of the Commons. In the Union Jake found a pay phone, looked up the number for the high school and dialed.

He asked the secretary if Natasha Van Sollis had come to work that day.

"Of course," she answered. "What seems to be the problem?"

"Is she all right?"

"Who's calling, please?"

Jake hung up.

Back home, rather than taking the time to dry off, he drove directly across town to the school on Mantua Street, which was leaving out as he arrived, a line of school buses and vehicles with parents picking up their kids. Aware that his sports car would be easy to spot, Jake cruised by and turned around in the cemetery lane across the street, hoping to catch a glimpse of Tasha on his way back. The parking lot was crowded with student drivers but he spotted Tasha's car parked beside Ray's. He left his MGA half a block away and jogged to the lot where he stood behind a sycamore tree off the entrance, getting soaked in the steady drizzle.

Half an hour later he saw them come out the back door, Tasha as if fleeing and Ray pursuing. They stopped in front of their cars, seemed to argue, Ray despondent, Tasha adamant, until she got into her car and drove away. Ray stood in the rain watching, then slammed his fist into the rear fender of the Camaro and fell to his knees gripping his hand in pain. Jake sprinted back to his car and headed for home as fast as he could. But he missed crossing the tracks as one of the longest and slowest freight trains in history inched its way through the center of town.

Finally, thirty minutes later, back at the house on Willow Street, he felt his heart sink as he saw Tasha's empty parking space. Where was she? His first impulses was to drive around town looking for her, all over the state if necessary. Instead, deflated, he climbed the stairs to his pad, unlocked the door and discovered a lavender envelope on the floor, his name written in a hurried scrawl.

He ripped it open.

Dearest Jake, I was so hoping you'd be here. Where are you? I haven't been free to call you, and feel a desperate need to be with my family. So I'm going to Akron. Please don't worry. I'm okay. Just a big mess to take care of and need my daddy's wisdom. I beg you not to give up on me, if you haven't already. our Tasha.

28

Saturday, April 27, next day ...

Yesterday's showers had burst the world into rich springtime green, fruit trees in bloom, the street out front glistening in the morning sun. Jake had spent an agitated night in hope of a phone call from Tasha.

Okay, she'd been stuck with Ray unable to get a few minutes to call, but what is the problem now? Maybe she's embroiled in complicated discussions with her parents. But what about?

Then it struck him.

Could she be pregnant?

He counted the days they'd been together. He certainly believed that he'd been the only one since her crazy, wonderful Bridgette Bardot performance. So if she was pregnant, the child would surely be his. Or would it? Was it conceivable that she'd slept with Ray during that time? Hell no! If she was pregnant, it would with him. After their first night in bed together, she'd insisted she was on the pill, had been since college. But Jake had been deceived in such matters before, leading to the sordid situation with Daphne and Reverend Martino back in Lancaster. But, Jesus, Tasha was no Daphne.

Tasha, pregnant? What would he do? This time he would fight. In contrast with Daphne, his feeling for Tasha was no one night stand, no sudden loss of moral command. Not hardly. But still, such things were purely in the woman's control, her body, after all. But he'd fight. First, he'd fight for marriage, but if not that, at least for the baby's life. If necessary he'd take the child home to his parents' farm, and he'd stay there and raise it in health and happiness. There were worse fates than living out his life on that fertile land.

Such dour thoughts plagued him all morning. Goldenrod was scheduled to lead another Saturday night singalong at the Eye, and during his tragic musings he kept going over guitar runs he was perfecting for two pieces in their standard collection of songs. He might ask Wash if he could try one of them tonight. As he thought about Tasha, his fingers flowed almost automatically through the riffs, both played off the G-run and, after a dozen bars, fusing back into it.

About eleven that morning his phone rang. He almost knocked over the coffee table in his rush to answer it.

No, she wasn't pregnant. That scenario didn't come up. The big mess she'd been dealing with was that Ray's transfer to active duty had been denied, something about his unit's specialty in armored transport not being a priority in the current fighting. Instead, they needed helicopter pilots and air support. Air National Guardsmen were being activated, not tank men.

Ray was crushed, bitter. He wanted his fiancée back. He would never have given her up except for active duty, would never have said the things he had if he thought his desire to go to the action would be denied. He'd been begging and weeping, and Tasha had felt a need to comfort him, to endure the new circumstances between them until matters were settled.

"So you told him about us?" Jake asked on the phone.

"Heavens no. He was close enough to the brink without that."

"What brink?"

"Losing it completely. He's feeling stripped of everything he cared about. It got so my only escape was to come home. Daddy wants me to go back to him, but how can I do that? I'm scared for Ray, though. I'm afraid of what he might do."

"Like what? Suicide?"

"Or something violent."

"To you?"

"I doubt it, but ... maybe. He's in a bad state. And if I told him about you, he'd have a definite target. He's barely able to hold it together to teach his classes. I've never seen him like this. So I've stayed with him, trying to talk it through, but it got us nowhere because I simply can't go back."

This begged the question of whether she'd slept with Ray, a question Jake didn't have the courage to ask.

How would that change things? Would she have been caring enough toward Ray to do that to comfort him?

He suddenly realized how little, really, he knew her. And, dammit, how little he knew about women.

"When will I see you?" he asked.

"I don't know. As soon as possible."

"Can I come to Akron? Like immediately?"

"No. Don't do that."

"Didn't you tell your parents about us?"

"No, Jake."

"Isn't it important?"

"It's the central issue. But it would be like lighting a fire. Here at home and in Kent. My parents are trying to talk me back to Ray. They love him dearly, think we shouldn't change our original wedding plans. After all, everything's still set."

"You're not going to do anything so crazy, are you?"

"No. Not after ... I couldn't even let him touch me, Jake. I mean, not even after all the times I'd been with him. No, I see him in a whole different light, since ... you and me. Yes, I held him, slept in the same bed, clothing on, fighting him off, but I managed it."

"So if you didn't tell your parents about us," Jake said, "what did you tell them?"

"That I don't love him anymore. And when they tell me he was trying to make a noble sacrifice for his country, I can only explain that when he turned on me, blaming me for holding him back, for being selfish, and that he'd decided to go to active duty even before discussing it with me, they tell me that such things come up in relationships sometimes and I should forgive him. But the real problem is..."

"Is what, Tasha?"

There was a pause. Then as if having suddenly been thrown off course, she said, "I love it when you call me that."

"What is the real problem, Tasha?"

"You. You're the real problem. The problem is I'm in love with you. Totally."

How Jake wished at that moment he had her physical presence instead of a black, corded wall phone! He'd have crushed her to him, somehow integrating them into a single body.

"Jake, are you there?"

"Yes. I'm in love with you too, Tasha. Totally."

"But..."

"But, what, Tasha?"

"But now is not the time to tell them, Jake. I can't. They'll just have to see me as stubborn and unforgiving. Even if you'd never have come into the picture, I don't know if I'd be able to go back with him, but I highly doubt it. It certainly wouldn't be the same. He insists he was wrong about accusing me of selfishness, but I remember his voice, his face, as if he despised me. And now, seeing him like this, so weak, so out of control, panicked. I feel sorry for him, concerned, but he's not the man for me, Jake. You are."

"Then you should tell them. After all, it's..." He paused.

"Were you about to say *inevitable*, Jake?"

"Yes, inevitable."

"It's the right word, but now isn't the right time. Bear with me. Eventually, they're going to have to accept the inevitability of my staunch refusal to start over with him. For now, let them misunderstand my motives. Maybe later I can let the truth out, but for now you're my dark secret, Jake. Dark and wonderful. And I beg you not to give up on me, not to find another tennis partner."

Jake's heart stung. "You're not a tennis partner. Don't even think that."

"I know. I was going for a touch of levity."

"I want to see you, hold you."

"I want nothing else," she answered. "When I see this situation through, we'll have such a reunion that Edith Whitcomb will evict us for making too much racket."

"Let's make it soon. I'll be happy to live in a tent with you."

"You're strong, Jake. Not like Ray. I don't love him now. I love you. I don't know if I like what that says about me. But it's you, my Prince Andre."

After they hung up Jake collapsed on his sofa, suddenly realizing that in the book Prince Andre was killed in battle. Natasha ended up with Pierre.

He recalled that in his past loves with both Christine and Ainsley, he hadn't fought to keep the relationship together. After Christine had sent him a Dear John letter his first semester in college, he'd given up. His roommate Chuck accused him of cowardice. "Send her flowers," he'd said, "stand under her window in the rain. Girls go nuts over that kind of stuff."

But Jake had merely accepted his fate. Not this time, though. This time he'd fight to the bitter end and if his heart were to be crushed for all time, then that would be his own personal inevitability. And lying there, eyes closed, ingesting Tasha's being almost as if she were present, he accepted that risk, fully.

The Needle's Eye was a coffee house in a church basement across from campus. The light was low, candles on the tables, a small stage, no alcohol but exotic teas, java blends and cider ordered at the counter of the kitchen and carried by patrons back to their tables. The church's idea was to use the current trend to draw spiritual seekers to Christ. They downplayed the religious aspects, however, obviously feeling that being set in a church facility was message enough. Too bland for serious radicals and revolutionaries like Gibbs, Engle and the McGills, the place attracted a mixture of flower children who smoked reefer outside behind bushes. Also, too-young-to-drink conservative Kingston Trio types who hadn't yet caught on to Dylan. And church members, some even middle-aged or older, hanging out to reach the young, hip and alienated.

With such an eclectic group, the place was always crowded, whether for a left leaning documentary, a panel discussion of liberal profs, or folk music. During program breaks, it was abuzz with conversation.

In the closet-sized warmup room, Wash listened to Jake's riff for "Sloop John B," grinned, patted his protégé's back and nodded approval.

"Yeah, man. We'll back off after the third chorus and you do it. It's good, real good, and original too. Right on! Now we'll have to work on your stage presence."

As far as stage presence, it was all Wash, who was simply too big to ignore and who wore bib overalls and work boots, a red bandana over his head, his hair pulled back in a ponytail, and his thick, unkempt beard splayed out over his chest. Adele was up front beside him, a mere matronly, feminine shadow in his large presence. Henry stood to Wash's left, a few steps back except when he came front for his fiddle solos, and Jake, dressed as he always did, button down shirt, pressed slacks and desert boots, his hair parted on the side and combed neatly. He flanked Adele, slightly behind her. He wondered what Wash had in mind regarding his *presence*. Was he going to have him dress up like a mountaineer?

Jake's run during the song went off perfectly, even drawing some applause, nothing compared to Wash or Henry, but, hey, a start. Something to build on. Something to take his mind off other matters, like when the hell he'd see his woman again, wondering if she was sleeping in the same bed as his rival, clothed or not, whether her parents and said-rival would accept *no* as her answer and retract the wedding invitations.

After the hootenanny, the group sat at a table sipping cider and nibbling banana nut muffins in celebration of Jake's small but breakout performance. A Leadbelly album played, and two apparently married couples at the next table discussed the current film in town, *Guess Who's Coming to Dinner*.

Jake felt a tap on his shoulder and turned to see a pretty, very pretty, hippie girl, longhaired, fresh-faced, hazel eyed, smiling. She handed him a program of the night's performance.

"Hi, would you sign this, please?"

"Sign it?"

Adele nudged him. "She wants your autograph, Dumbo."

He looked at the lovely girl, probably still in high school. "Really?"

"Would you, please?" Blushing, she handed him a pen.

Next to the song he'd riffed on, he scribbled his name, his neck warming with embarrassment. He handed it back along with the ballpoint. Their fingers touched. She giggled and hurried off as if she'd won a dare.

Wash smiled tolerantly. "With Josh gone, you'll be the new babe magnet. Every group needs one. I've been working on Adele to spruce herself up a little, add some sex appeal, but purist that she is, she insists it's not appropriate for a true bluegrass group. She wants to look like a dowdy housewife, mother of eight, hanging out the laundry. What do you think we should do with Jake, Adele?"

"Apparently he's doing fine."

"You know, a little more stage charisma, within your purist boundaries, of course."

"Jeans," she said.

"Jeans, absolutely," Wash answered. "And not loose ones either."

"And a plaid shirt, sleeves rolled up. Suspenders, maybe."

"Yeah," Henry added. "Like he came back from splitting logs, tall and gangly. The Abe Lincoln look."

"Western boots?" Wash asked.

"No," Adele said. "Work shoes."

"How 'bout barefoot," Henry said with a smirk. "Hog shit between his toes."

"No," Adele said as if Eric's idea were serious. "Barefoot isn't practical, not comfortable. Any ideas for footwear, Jake?"

"Snowshoes. An Alaskan husky by my side."

29

Tuesday, April 30, three days later …

Tasha had phoned Sunday night to say she was staying in Akron for a few days, still trying to work things out, had called her principal to get a sub for her classes. She'd never missed a day before.

"My life is upside down," she'd lamented.

She adamantly rejected Jake's idea for him to go to Akron and hole up in a motel, so what else could he do but wait and stick to his schedule?

Schedules are useful in a crisis.

Ella bounced into the office, breathless as usual from her vigorous climb up the stairs.

"So what did you think about last Friday's fiasco?" she asked.

"The strike?"

"BBs, can you believe that?"

"I didn't see you out there."

"No. The Committee keep trying to suck us in. It irks them no end that we don't want any part of them."

"Suck you in, how?"

"Like in their demands, they always tack on civil rights at the end of the list, as if they give a damn about us."

"But you guys are against the war, aren't you?"

She gave him a look.

"What?" he asked.

"Yes, we're against the war. God! Ali said it best — no Vietnamese ever called us *nigger* — but that doesn't mean we'd ever team up with this group of honkies. Did you see that their leader Miss Gibbs was arrested for spraying graffiti on a dorm wall? Damn, that's Mickey Mouse!"

"Yes, true. But, excuse me, I hardly ever see anything from Black United Students. Are you trying to make your statement by boycotting the antiwar committee? That's a pretty quiet statement."

"We'll make a statement, don't bother about that. We've got something planned that'll extend far beyond this little insignificant white commune."

"Something planned? Such as?"

"Wait and see. You won't miss it, believe me. And as far as the antiwar committee, with their esteemed chairwoman in jail for illegal use of paint, and that sad excuse for a strike, they're history around here, and we're about to step onto center stage."

A solid knock on the open door turned both their heads. They saw a fully bearded young man in a leather vest. Jake suddenly remembered him, Will Markley, whose father had tried to bribe Jake his first term.

Ella turned to her desk, and Jake hesitantly welcomed Will in. The young man eyed Ella.

"Can I talk to you in private, professor?"

"Here will be fine," Jake said.

"No. Private. Can you come out in the hall?"

Ella turned. "It's okay, *professor*. Like I could give a damn."

Reluctantly, Jake left with Will and followed him down the empty corridor.

"I'm gonna sign up for your summer class," Will said. "I saw you're teaching 102. Same deal as last time, okay? Even though I don't see why I have to come to your office and write those stupid papers."

"Absolutely not the same deal. That was a onetime thing. And it wasn't for you, it was for your dad."

"He's *still* my dad."

"No deal."

Will studied him with a threatening stare.

"No deal," Jake said again. "No way in hell."

"I could report you."

"For what?"

"For accepting money."

"I didn't accept money. What are you talking about?"

"You know fucking well what I'm talking about?"

"Did your dad tell you I accepted money?"

"Damn straight."

"No he didn't. I did your dad a favor, for his service in North Africa. Report me all you want, but your dad will verify the situation. He's a man of honor, which doesn't seem to have rubbed off on his son."

"I wouldn't bet on his honor. But he *is* a respected businessman, in the Lion's Club and VFW."

Jake took a step back toward his office, paused, noted Will's confident smirk. "Tell you what, you creep. I'm going to report this feeble attempt at extortion to my director. We'll call your dad and clarify the whole thing."

"I wouldn't do that if I were you. If I were you, I'd play ball."

By the end of this sentence Jake was almost back to his office where he went in and sat down hard on his chair. With Ella deep in a conference with a student, Jake gathered his things for his Chaucer seminar and left.

That night he got a call from Tasha. After she'd convinced her parents she wasn't going through with the marriage, she said she would spend the next several days with her mom sending out retractions and canceling arrangements with various wedding vendors. On the phone Ray had objected furiously, even gone to Akron and after a long conference with her father was gently sent away. Tasha's parents asked him not to call for the time being and sadly insisted that their daughter refused to go through with the wedding. Tasha said she'd return to Kent the following Sunday.

"Can't wait to be with you again," she said in tears.

And how!

Friday, May 3, three days later ...

Afternoon classes had been officially let out for a presentation by Vice-president Hubert Humphrey in his kickoff speech for his presidential campaign. How Kent State had been selected for this prestigious event was beyond Jake's ken, but apparently northeastern Ohio with its many labor unions and Democratic voters was a good place for the Minnesotan to begin. The university was one of a plethora of regional stops that weekend, including motorcades to and from the campus out of the Akron airport.

Humphrey would give a fifteen minute speech then submit to questions by a four person panel that included two political science faculty members and the president and vice-president of the student body.

At one-thirty Jake sat with Adele and Wash in the filled-to-capacity field house with various dignitaries seated on a dais awaiting the esteemed guest. The event was giddily regarded by the university administration as a national spotlight for the school, which a widely grinning Hubert Humphrey eventually pointed out to the abundant media representatives was the twenty-sixth largest university in the nation. President White introduced the honored guest in the most ebullient terms imaginable. The rapt audience listened as Humphrey thanked the campus hosts and the area's Democratic politicians for their hospitality. One could not doubt the engaging enthusiasm of the Vice-president, who was interrupted often by enthusiastic applause.

Among those less enthusiastic, however, Jake saw Humphrey as a mouthpiece of Johnson's policy, strong for civil rights, yes, but equally strong for the war even though at this event he announced the beginning of peace talks in Paris. Jake viewed these oft-mentioned talks simply as an invitation for Ho Chi Min to surrender half of Vietnam as a U.S. colony.

Then something astounding happened.

During the applause at the end of Humphrey's official comments, a group of fifty or so black students who had been sitting together, Ella among them, rose and silently strode out of the gymnasium by a back door, stunning the huge audience to quiet and confusion. Boos erupted. Another more ragtag group of students, this time white ones led by McGill and Engle, hustled behind the blacks among even stronger boos. The country's vice-president wittily quipped that he was glad the gym had so many convenient exits. Media flashes went off during the disturbance, and several mobile TV cameramen rushed after the dissenters.

Ella's former comment about taking center stage hit Jake like a brick.

It took a few minutes for things to settle down and for the panel to resume, one member of which happened to be the black vice-president of the student body, the person Adele had once referred to as an Oreo. Young Mr. Pickett was last to ask his question: how his former excitement about the Administration's civil rights legislation could be renewed in the light of King's assassination and its ongoing violent aftermath. Humphrey heaped lavish praise upon the young inquisitor and asked him to apply for a job in his campaign.

Wild enthusiasm greeted this response, though as Jake looked around the field house he now saw barely a single African American face. Even more to the point in Jake's mind was that after Humphrey's waving, smiling exit, the audience's buzz included little about his speech but much about the walkout.

Later, as Jake ate a TV dinner in his kitchen, the evening radio news verified his feelings. The lead on NBC: "A walkout by Kent students mars Humphrey's kickoff speech."

Sunday, May 5, two days later …

Jake kept glancing out the window while at his desk trying to dissect the Middle English of Chaucer's "Miller's Tale," thought to be the quintessential example to the ancient poet's ribaldry. At about three-thirty Tasha pulled into the driveway. Knowing better than to rush down the stairs to pull her into his arms, he watched as she lugged a bulging tote onto the porch. With his door opened a crack, he watched her climb the steps until she noticed him peeking out. She smiled brightly. He stepped onto the landing and helped her with her bag.

"Give me a minute," she said softly, looking tired underneath her grin. "I'll come over soon. Oh, how I missed you!" As they parted, she grasped his hand for a fleeting moment.

Minutes passed like hours, but finally she tapped on his door and was where she belonged, firmly pressed against him wrapped in his arms. It was a hug like no other he'd ever received, desperate, passionate, like salvation for both of them. Her familiar scent, her ardor and his, almost overwhelmed him. They held firmly, unrelentingly for long, miraculous moments.

Slowly coming to his senses, he needed to look at her and so lay his head back enough to see her eyes, tearful, yearning, relieved. Then he grasped her even stronger than before. More than an erotic moment, it was a true home-coming, their agonizing separation arriving at last to a longed-for end.

"Oh, my God!" she murmured. "You feel so wonderful, Jake."

"You feel even more wonderful."

"No I couldn't possibly. It's you."

"No, it's you."

They backed away a few inches, peered at each other and burst out laughing.

"Yes," he said. "Let's not start this reunion with an argument."

They moved backward to arm's length. "You wouldn't happen to have anything alcoholic to drink, would you?" she asked, her cheeks streaked with tears.

"Some of that Thunderbird we never finished."

"That will be heavenly," she said, smiling.

After rooting the bottle from the fridge, he gave it a whiff and guessed it wasn't rank enough to throw out. He emptied it into two quarter full tumblers and took the glasses into the living room where she had settled cross-legged on the sofa.

"This might put an end to us," he said, handing her a glass.

"No. It will be a beginning."

"To our beginning, then."

They clinked, and as he sipped, she downed all of hers. "Ah, I needed that." She looked at him. "And now I need you, Jake. Come, my darling prince, and take me to your lair of love."

"Your wish is my command, milady. I need you just as much."

"No, not possible."

"Yes, more possible."

"No, I think not."

The dispute ended as they landed on the bed.

30

Wednesday, May 15, ten days later ...

At the weekly silent vigil against the war, Jake whispered to Adele that he needed to talk to her.

"Good," she replied. "I need to talk to you too."

After the protesters dispersed, the pair went into the Union snack shop and, iced tea in hands, settled at a table with a view of the Commons, now crowded with students studying on blankets, throwing Frisbees and relaxing in the sun.

"You first," Adele said.

Jake told her about his conversation with Will Markley and briefed her fully on the situation.

"Are you sure you didn't take the thousand bucks?" she asked with a wink.

Jake smiled. "I didn't touch that envelope, but I can't prove it. There might be a problem if the dad backs up the son."

"The kid's bluffing. He still has to pass 102. How would stringing you up help him accomplish that? And I fully understand why you partially gave in to his father. You got the kid to do *something*, at least."

"Yeah, to rise and shine those mornings. He even had the gall to bring in one essay that someone else had written. I have it in his file."

"He's lucky he ran into you instead of me. I don't think it'll come to beans. Now, my turn. Lord Byron needs to talk to you about taking over for me as coordinator of the first year TA's. Actually he's expanding the job to all of them."

"Adele, I don't want that job."

"But think about how it will help your career. See it as an honor, really, considering you're only in the M.A. program. But your maturity and your teaching experience makes you the best choice. All the teachers who came to you for help praised your advice. And I gave Dr. Shenk your syllabus, much of which I suggested be incorporated into that ancient tome we use now. He charged me to ask you to meet him in his office after your second seminar tomorrow, around three, right?"

"How many hours a week do you spend on that job?"

"Let's see, there's the weekly meeting Thursday afternoons and then one class visitation with follow-up for each TA, then office hours, which I minimize by farming advice conferences out to volunteers like you and occasionally Lil. Also a few reports to the Lord, who's a real straight arrow but a good enough guy. I'd say six hours or so weekly. Incidentally, I probably shouldn't tell you this, but..."

"Shouldn't tell me what?"

"I promised her I wouldn't."

"Out with it, Adele."

"But keep this under your hat."

"My hat? Sure, sure."

"Ella Curlew told me in strictest confidence that you helped her. She was having time issues and you gave her some useful tips. I guess she didn't want you to have the satisfaction of..."

"Black Pride, no doubt."

"And mentioning hats, Wash and I were discussing your stage persona. We thought one of those patchwork Ivy caps, with the short bill, you know? Levis, plaid shirt, vest, cap and the desert boots you usually wear. What do you think? I mean now that you'll be stepping forward for riffs. Think of all the autographs you'll be handing out to young chickadees."

"Jesus, Adele, what are we, the Mamas and the Papas?"

"And he mentioned giving you a vocal solo too. You have a fine tenor voice, Jake, in case you didn't know. We have a couple summer gigs booked, fairs, picnics and such, maybe even the Blind Owl. Some pretty big names play there. We're glad you'll be around."

"Thanks, but I'm running out of extra hours here."

"And as for this kid Will, don't give it a second thought. Certainly no need to mention it to Shenk. But I'll make an official note in my log that you reported it to me, even postdate it if you'd like."

"Hell no. I want everything strictly legit."

Thursday, May 16, next day ...

The picture of orderliness, Professor Byron Shenk's first floor office consisted of a lobby with a dignified, mid-fifties secretary-receptionist named Nan and an inner sanctum lined with bookshelves of extensive material on the English Victorian Age, Classical rhetoric, linguistics and contemporary pedagogical methodology on college writing. The Director of Freshman Composition wore a three piece tweed suit and sat in a high backed leather chair. The room had a strong odor of pipe tobacco, and indeed the one side of the vast, glass-topped desk had an extensive array of pipe smoking paraphernalia.

The man himself had slicked-back salt and pepper hair, a chiseled face, dimpled chin, and calm dark eyes. Behind him on the wall hung a portrait of George Lyman Kittredge, whom Jake recognized as a heroic figure to all serious scholars of literature.

After shaking hands Jake and the professor settled face-to-face across the desk, Jake having declined Nan's polite invitation for coffee.

"You know, Mr. Ernst, we're sorry to be losing Adele. She's done a peach of a job for us."

"Yes, she's great."

"So her recommendation goes a long way. She tells me you might need some persuasion to take over her duties."

"I'm primarily interested in my scholarship. I like teaching, but I know what counts most in terms of my career path."

"Most assuredly. And you might be surprised that I agree with your concern. For now, I think you have the sensible outlook. But you know, there's an increasing interest in rhetoric. Graduate students are expected to publish but seldom have the writing tools. Also, research about business is showing how woefully unprepared recruits are for the rigors of writing in middle management positions. All in all, the teaching of composition is an up and coming industry. You might keep that in mind."

"Yes, but aren't such people coming out of colleges of education rather than liberal arts?"

"Indeed. And they scorn us, as we do them. Wisdom tells me we must bridge that crevasse. The old humanities' attitude is that it is the student's job to learn, not the professor's to teach. But as young Bob Dylan says, 'The times they are a'changin.'"

He chuckled at his use of a current counterculture voice. At Jake's indulgent smile, he went on. "Do let's bypass the chitchat, shall we? Do you accept the position, or not?"

"I thank you for the offer, but Adele tells me that due to enrollment figures she was forced to teach an extra class with no extra compensation. How are the figures shaping up for next fall?"

"Quite right. Several issues were involved. There for a while, we thought the senior department members were going to sack eight of our experienced teachers due to their ... frankly, due to what these traditional faculty members viewed as their anti-American sentiments. Also, Admissions sadly underestimated how many young men were flocking to college to avoid the draft. So we were forced to deal with enrollment far above expectations. Thank heavens, President White nixed the firings, so we got by. I think it's safe to say we can even reduce your classes to only one per term since we've now included all TA's and, to the best of my hopes, done a much better job of predicting enrollment."

"Only one class to teach per term?"

"I must say, however, that with the nation in crisis, things are not entirely predictable. As you know, the deferment for graduate students has been entirely eliminated and although there are rumors of peace talks, the war could escalate tomorrow. It's possible that sacrifices will be in order. We'll expect your cooperation. We are quite grateful for Adele's, which will be reflected in our recommendations for a future tenure track position." He paused, smiled at Jake. "So you will come on board?"

"I will."

"Excellent! And I take it we can count on your moderate approach to the war debate? I've done a bit of checking, nothing worthy of CIA status, but..."

Jake squirmed. "A bit of checking?"

"I saw your signature on the faculty petition against the war, noticed that campus security has your photograph in their file from the Wednesday protests, and that you even play in Adele's group at the student committee's rallies. But Drew Byrne was sorely disappointed in what he calls your lack of commitment, and we were happy to see that you didn't cancel your classes for the now infamous strike. Of course, you are welcome to your views; we only trust that you will stand firm on your temperate approach, as Adele has stood on hers."

"Yes, sir, you can, because it expresses my true beliefs." Jake quickly rejected the idea of mentioning his nebulous status with Selective Service, for which he might be picked up to serve a prison sentence at any time. He decided not to mention it because as time had gone by with no reaction from the draft board, he'd almost forgotten about this chink in his armor.

"Good. Good," the professor said. "We can only hope that now, with the apparent demise of the KCEWV – couldn't they have chosen an acronym? But due to the strike debacle, we won't have trouble with Black United Students. Their little walkout stunt with Humphrey has put us on the national stage, quite an embarrassment. President White is still blushing. But I greatly respect the man. He immediately set up a meeting with black leaders, and the scuttlebutt is that he's going to approve a Negro faculty member in the Spanish Department to act as a liaison between them and the administration, which was one of their demands."

"Yes, it's a good step, but that demand was the very last on their list."

"A token concession, but one feasibly implemented. The others are outlandish, but being taken under consideration."

"I hadn't realized," Jake said, "that several fraternities and sororities have actual clauses in their constitutions preventing blacks from joining."

"Ah, nor did I. Definitely something to investigate. Now one more thing, Mr. Ernst. Adele has been raising havoc about the state of the 101-102 syllabi. I agree. They're sadly outdated. She has shown me yours. Of course, many of your methods, daily quizzes and such, are idiosyncratic, perhaps not useful as a general rule. But some are quite applicable, especially considering we're an open admissions university, and, thus, the writing levels of our entering minions sadly inadequate. We especially like the idea of in-class writing assignments, which will minimize the stressful and time consuming issue of plagiarism. Would you be able to spare the time this summer to join a committee to revise the syllabi? We'd like to use the updated version for our fall classes."

"But I'll still be assigned two classes to teach this summer?"

"Yes, Mr. Ernst. May I call you Jake?"

Jake nodded.

"It's too late to change the summer teaching assignments. So, agreed? And of course you and I as well as the Freshman Writing Committee will have some work to do in order to prepare you for your new position."

Though hardly able to back out now, Jake wriggled at the thought of giving up a single free moment he might spend with Tasha over her summer break.

Sunday, May 25, nine days later ...

At three in the morning, Jake pulled his MGA into his parking spot, Tasha waking up beside him from dozing on their way back from Cleveland. They'd been to the Agora Ball Room for a Ramsey Lewis concert then stopped off at the jazz café Jake had visited with Adele and the Goldenrod crew soon after he'd arrived in Kent. Tasha rubbed her eyes. As Jake was on his way around the car to open her door, he heard the screech of tires. He turned to see a black Camaro skidding to a stop along the curb.

The lean, wiry guy he'd seen at the high school, now wearing a jogging suit and headband, leapt out of the vehicle and charged across the lawn. Jake's hackles immediately rose. Adrenaline rushed. He readied himself for combat.

"What the hell's going on here?" Ray yelled in the near darkness.

Jake stationed himself between Ray and Tasha. The intruder stopped in his tracks. He glared at Jake. Tasha's voice sounded from the driveway.

"Cool it, Ray. Just cool it."

"Where were you?" Ray asked, craning to see around Jake.

"It's none of your concern."

"None of my concern? Everything about you is my concern."

Jake played a blocking game, keeping the ex-couple separated.

"Calm down and go home," Tasha ordered.

"Christ, you're dressed like a whore."

"You'll wake up the neighborhood. Someone will call the police."

"Fuck the police." He caught Jake's eye, at this moment a standoff, Jake the taller, a tad broader. "What're you doing with my girl?"

Lights came on in the biology prof's window, also in the house across the street.

"You've been drinking," Tasha said. "Go on home before you get into trouble."

"I want answers, Natasha. I thought we were taking time to work things out. Now you're running around on me."

"We'll talk about it tomorrow. Please, Ray, get out of here. Now!"

In bathrobe and slippers Phil came out onto the porch. "Should I dial emergency?"

"No," Tasha said, "please don't. He's leaving. Aren't you, Ray?"

He took a step back, the glass packs of his Chevy rumbling as it idled.

"You could lose your job, Ray. I'll call you in the afternoon."

"What time?"

"Dammit, Ray. Two o'clock. Now go."

He eyed Jake again. "Can't believe you're going out with a damn mechanic," he said through Jake's blockade.

With the guy's military training, Jake wasn't sure he could take him, but he'd try.

"Fuck!" Ray said. "I don't believe this. I wanted to talk to you about something tonight, something important."

Jake heard a siren from the direction of downtown. At the sound, Ray, retreated to his car, slammed the door and peeled out. Tasha and Jake hurried into the house, assuring Phil everything was all right. Shaking his head with annoyance, Phil went back into his place.

From Tasha's apartment window Jake peered out through the crack in the curtains as the cruiser, lights flashing, pulled to a stop out front, the house now dark. The neighbor from across the street came over and conferred with the two officers who then got into their vehicle. Though the flashing lights went out, they sat in the car for ten more minutes before pulling away.

"It was only a matter of time until you two met," Tasha said, bath water running as she pulled off her clothes. "Did I really look like a whore?"

"Sexy. But not in bad taste."

"It was jazz, after all. But I would never have gone to jazz with him, and never dressed like tonight. He's strictly a country music type, and doesn't like me looking sexy when we go out. Was my top too low-cut?"

"Let's just say, I had a hard time concentrating on the music."

"Come on, get in the bath with me."

"Does he think you two are still together, taking a timeout?"

"Who knows what he thinks?"

"I mean, haven't you definitively broken up with him?"

"Maybe not definitively enough for his mind. Come on, will you? Let's erase this little incident with some bubble bath."

"So you'll straighten things out later?"

"But I don't want to tell him about us. God knows how he'll react. I'll make him believe we're just neighbors and pals."

"I thought I was going to have to put him in his place out there."

"I better warn you, he fights dirty. And, Jake, we want to avoid such things, at all costs."

"Maybe that's what he needs."

"It's not. Anyway, he has friends. And access to firearms. And without the Guard, he'll feel like nothing, and an arrest for brawling would end it. We need to avoid raging testosterone, okay? You'll both end up in jail, or worse."

"Access to firearms?"

"He's in the Guard, remember? Besides, everyone hunts around here. Come on, Jake, the water's getting cold. We'll take care of the hormones, just you and I. Let's wash each other all over."

31

Later that day …

Naked, Jake and Tasha lolled in bed, the radio on as they read through sections of the *New York Times.* At two-thirty her phone rang.

"Oh, God!" she said. "I completely forgot I told Ray I'd call." On her way to the other room, she added, "Grab your clothes and get out of here."

Hoping to assess the phone conversation, Jake took his time. She demanded to meet Ray at the Brown Derby in an effort, Jake supposed, to keep emotions publicly contained. No, she didn't want Ray to pick her up. She'd meet him at the restaurant. With Ray on the line, Jake saw no reason to vacate her place. A phone argument ensued about meeting in public rather than privately. When she hung up, she was surprised to see Jake still there.

She waved at him to leave.

"Thought you might need backup," he said. "I could wait for you outside the restaurant."

"He'll spot your car. I'll be fine."

"Are you sure?"

"I'm sure. Now go, please."

Back in his place Jake made instant coffee. He hated waiting like this, not settling things together as a couple. He'd thought they would be undiscovered in Cleveland, hadn't predicted Ray would stalk her. He'd evidently waited on the next block for their return.

Friends with firearms, eh? Could it possibly go that far?

He heard Tasha's door close, her footsteps down the stairs, watched from his window as she got into her Rambler and left. She was smart, though, because what could go wrong in a busy family restaurant? He'd try to get some work done, check his Chaucer paper for typos, whiteout lavishly employed. Such precision work, like proofreading and strumming his guitar, often took his mind off his worries.

When his phone rang he leapt to answer. But it was Lil.

"Such springtime magnificence," she said cheerily, "thought you might be up for another canoe ride on that lake, remember?"

"No," he barked. "That's off between us, completely off."

"Okay, okay, don't bite my head off, cowboy, thought you might say that, but listen to this. I'm here with a gorgeous sex angel named Shari, right out of that novel *Candy*. We're up for some fun and games, like the Doublemint twins, dig?"

"Forget it, Lil."

"All right, Jake. I wanted to give you the right of first refusal."

"I gotta go."

"So what's going on, you found someone? I've seen you at a couple of readings with a hot looking blond."

"None of your concern, Lil." He hung up.

Jesus – Lil. Wonder if she ended up in the sack with Denise Levertov.

But his main thoughts were of Tasha working things out with Ray at the restaurant.

When he heard the downstairs door open and close, he jumped up, saw the Nash back in its spot and rushed to open up as Tasha reached the landing. She glanced sadly at him with reddened eyes.

"Let me freshen up. I'll be over in a minute."

That minute became half an hour, but finally a tap sounded on his unlocked door. She came in wearing a bathrobe and slippers, her wet hair slicked back. Having to shower the cigarette smoke off her from the restaurant was her excuse for the delay. They settled on his sofa.

"You've been crying," he said.

"Ray is coming apart at the seams, lost his hopes for active duty. And the mess with me. And he was called into the principal's office for smacking a hoodlum in his P.E. class. I've never seen him like this."

"All his own doing, isn't it?"

"I wouldn't say that, no."

"Why not?"

"Because I had inappropriate feelings for you long before all this came down."

"Inappropriate?"

"You know what I mean."

"I'd call them *natural* feelings, utterly appropriate."

"All right, whatever. But I was engaged, and I betrayed him."

"Not until he turned against you. And don't call it *betrayal.*"

"I followed your advice, Jake. That's what caused the whole muddle."

"But didn't you tell me he'd already decided to apply for active duty even before you released him? And didn't you tell him you'd stand by him if he went?"

"Stop defending you-and-me, Jake. The poor guy is really suffering. And I'm the cause of it."

"No you're not, Tasha."

"Don't call me that right now."

Jake paused, took a deep breath. He knew this was a crisis point. His reaction would be critical.

Cautiously, he said, "So, you're feeling sorry for him. That's understandable."

"Back then he said some rough things to me, but it was from frustration. He didn't really mean them. His tone is totally different now."

"But it's true that he was going to apply for fulltime regardless of your feelings, isn't it?"

"But even so..."

"Even so, what?"

"His desire to serve is noble."

When Jake moved to hold her, she backed away. Her feelings at the moment were genuine. To fight against them would be a mistake. No way could he pull her out of this mood right now.

"I understand your frame of mind," he said with difficulty. "I don't blame you."

"Don't you, Jake?"

"This has always been easier for me than for you. How can I help?"

There was a glimmer of a smile, a melancholy one. "Oh, Jake, you're such a perfect darling."

"I don't like the sound of that."

"I don't think we should see each other for a while."

Not to panic, he nodded reflectively. "Are you going back to him?"

"I need some time to think."

"So, you're considering it?"

She sighed, gazed at him. "I ... really don't think I have a right to be happy right now. Not while he's breaking apart because of me. At first when you and I got together, I thought he was overjoyed to be rid of me, that he would be proudly marching off for active duty, and I could be free to express what I'd been feeling for you, but..."

"*But*," Jake began, hoping logic might work, "shouldn't that tell you something crucial, Tasha – sorry – *Natasha*?"

"Something crucial, Jake? And what's that?"

"He'd have been happy to leave you. It's his disappointment with losing out on his chance to get into the action that's causing his breakdown, not his love for you. He didn't reach his main goal, and now he's trying to minimize his losses."

"I guess his reasons don't matter. He's miserable, and I feel guilty for enjoying myself so much."

"Perfectly reasonable. But let me ask you one question."

"What question is that?"

He took her hand, and she let him, a small step that gave him confidence.

"Say he suddenly gets notice they reversed their decision and accepted him. Would that change things?"

She stared at him. "That *is* a good question, Jake."

"You'd be right back where all this started, wouldn't you?"

"Maybe."

"You have no doubt that he'd go, do you?"

"No doubt at all."

"You see? You're not his *first* love. You're a consolation prize."

Another sigh, but her hand was still in his, a part of her like absolutely every other part of her he cherished.

"Hmm," she muttered. "A consolation prize. That's what I am."

"Right? Correct?"

She eased her hand out of his. "I guess so, but..."

"Yes, go on?"

"What would *you* do, Jake, if someone important to you, whether you loved them or whether they were simply drowning and reaching for you to save them? What would you do?"

"I see where you're going. And it shows what a beautiful person you are. But there are two points to think about."

She smiled, less melancholically than before. "You're so rational, Jake. What two points?"

"First, yes, I'd try to save them, but not if it would drown me also, not if I couldn't swim or weren't strong enough to pull them out but would be pulled in myself. I'd do what I could, yell for help, call emergency, try to find a rope or a tree branch or..."

"Okay, okay, I see your first point. What's the second one?"

"The second point is that, well, he may be frustrated, true, but he's not *drowning*. Your analogy isn't apt in his case. He has the same options all of us have when we're deeply disappointed. He has family, friends, counselors if need be, work responsibilities, his own inner strength, and he even has you if he can accept your friendship instead of your whole being. It may be difficult for him right now, but it's not a life-or-death situation, or damned well shouldn't be. If it is, he's weak and unreliable, neither of which should be acceptable to you, or God forbid, to the military."

"Hmm, that *may* be a good point."

"Your going back to him might satisfy some part of him, for the moment, but it won't take care of the main part."

"The main part?"

"He's using you, Tasha, to satisfy some speck of his pride, but he's not thinking of the most important thing."

"Going to the war, you mean?"

"No. Beautiful person that you are, Tasha, *you're* thinking about *his* needs, but don't you see? – He's not thinking one iota about *yours*."

Their gazes seemed locked. Instinctively, Jake understood it was time for silence. Her eyes grew wider. Then her feelings for him seemed to flood back and she fell into his arms, pressed against him and wept. He held her as she shook with sobs.

"Oh, Jake," she murmured into his chest. "Oh, my wonderful Jake!"

After they passionately consummated this reunion of sorts, Tasha dozed off and Jake lay beside her, relieved, exhilarated, more in love than he'd ever imagined love could be. Not only thrilled for having won her back as she'd been drifting away, he also realized he might have saved her from being pulled into the quicksand of Ray's inadequacies. But spoiling his sense of victory, he almost immediately recognized, direly so, that he'd been withholding several vital pieces of information from this extraordinary creature lying next to him. His impulse was to wake her immediately and reveal them, but he held back. She'd been through enough for one day, so why add to the stress? Yet, with further thought, he felt he couldn't hold these confessions back much longer.

In the dimming light of the afternoon, he wondered why he'd let his secrets go so long. Maybe because he was scared to tell her, or the right moment hadn't come up, or he hadn't seen the two of them committed enough as a couple to bring up such personal truths. After all, she hadn't probed for deep confessions. But something huge seemed to have happened today, which changed things, and now he felt she had an essential right to know, that his telling her later might give her reason to reject him.

Her breathing came heavily, her bare chest rising and falling, a strand of golden hair across her brow, her lipstick faded from their ardent kisses. He felt the feeling from Frost's poem – a cup filled just above the brim. When she woke, he would tell her, let her judge, test her forgiveness, for now was the time for her to be fully informed.

Though restless with his decision, he continued beside her in darkness, feeling her length against him. He dozed off. When he woke, she was gone. Two hours had passed. He noticed a light in his kitchen, jumped up, pulled on his boxers and found her naked at the table devouring Cheerios in a bowl of milk. She looked up, smiled.

"I was famished. This was all I could find. Join me?"

"I need to talk to you, Tasha."

"About our earlier conversation? My head's still spinning about that."

He sat down across the table, took a breath. "Not about that. Something else, important. I know you've been through a lot today but that's part of the reason this won't wait."

She pushed her dish away. "Let me put my robe on. I feel vulnerable all bare like this. And how 'bout you put on a tee shirt."

Both clothed, they sat back down in the kitchen.

"Now what's this about?" she said.

"Two things I haven't told you about."

She reached across the table for his hand. "Are you an ax-murderer or something?"

"First, I wasn't completely honest about my situation with the draft."

"Not honest? I don' like the sound of that. You had a teaching deferment, right?"

"But actually it was canceled three months before my four year commitment was up. My teaching contract wasn't renewed because I expressed my views against the war. The three month gap between the end of my contract and my twenty-eighth birthday allowed the draft board to come after me."

He told her the entire story, having eventually been declared 4F for nebulous reasons by a civilian psychiatrist the day of his induction into the army.

"That shrink might have thought I was gay," Jake said.

After listening to this fifteen minute presentation, not releasing his hand, she smiled.

"I have good reason to believe you're not gay. Why did he think so?"

"He couldn't find any other reason the induction people sent me to his office with a bunch of goons. He didn't buy the simple truth that I opposed the war, said that all I would have to do is admit I'm gay and he'd automatically designate a 4F. He asked me again if I had homosexual tendencies, and I said absolutely not."

"So," Natasha said, "you're not gay, were never gay?"

"Correct."

"But he told the government you were."

"I'm assuming that was his reasoning."

"Were you acting effeminate?"

"No. Some dopes there were acting crazy. I did go into silence, though, at the induction center. Refused to speak or move. Expected to be arrested and go to jail. But they sent me to the shrink with a group of nut cases."

"I see. And you got a 4F." She looked at him, smiled. "I'm glad. We won't tell Daddy, though, when the time comes."

"But it's not quite the end of the story. I didn't think it was proper to get out of military service because of a 4F. My only so-called deficiency was my strong objection to the war, so when I got my card and saw the new designation, I ripped it up and sent it back. That's a crime, destroying government property, punishable by two years in federal prison."

"You mean you've been to prison?"

"I never heard from them. But, see, Tasha, they could possibly pick me up at any time and prosecute me. That was the chance I took. I think you should be aware of that possibility, is all. Whenever I talk about my draft status, I merely mention my deferment, not that I could still go to jail."

She squeezed his now sweaty hand and grinned. "Then I'll have to bake you a cake with a file inside, won't I? What's the other thing in your deep, dark past?"

He pulled his hand away. He doubted she'd respond with the same frivolity to Point Two.

"All right. You know I was engaged once, right?"

"Yes, to the Ava Gardner look alike in your wallet?"

"I removed those pictures, by the way."

"Go on about your engagement."

"We were together three years, but not day in, day out. I was in Lancaster and she lived near D.C."

He went on to describe the results of his one night stand with Daphne Todd, that Daphne had lied to him about being on the pill, become pregnant and, against his objections, had an abortion. He explained that he eventually helped set it up, cooperated with it, and partially paid for it.

"I was sick about it the whole time," he concluded, "and still am. But she wouldn't have it any other way. At the final moment I tried to stop it but wasn't able to."

She came around the table and pressed his head to her chest.

"But why would she tell you she was on the pill when she wasn't?"

"She and her pastor boyfriend used the rhythm method and she thought she was okay. That's what she said. And she didn't like the feel of condoms, thought I might insist on using one, which I would have."

Tasha backed away. He looked up at her.

"I don't like to imagine you in bed with other women," she said. "I was so jealous of that nasty girl Lil the night I heard you two romping around in your apartment."

He nodded. "I don't like the picture of you in bed with Ray either. But at our ages we can hardly expect each other to be virgins, can we?"

"I guess not."

He added that when she'd gone off to Akron without explaining why, he thought she might be pregnant and decided in his imagination to fight any ideas of an abortion, or if it was his, he would demand to take part in its upbringing.

"What do you mean if it was *yours*?" she asked.

He wriggled. "I counted the days, and realized it had to be, unless..."

"Unless what?"

"I thought you might have slept with Ray again, or, hell, I don't know, Tom Jones or someone."

With humor, she whapped him on his skull.

"How dare you think such a thing of me? I was having difficulty enough going to bed with *you*, and before I actually did, I felt guilty even thinking about it, which I confess I did a lot."

"How was I supposed to know? Anyway, you weren't pregnant, so the point is moot. But I wasn't about to cause our possible child's hypothetical death."

She chuckled. "And you thought these two confessions would make me stop loving you, Jake?"

"Tasha, you almost did today."

She whapped him again. "Stop loving you, Jake? Stop *seeing* you maybe, brokenhearted for sure, but you did quite a clever job talking me out of that possibility a few hours ago, didn't you? Stop loving you, though? I don't see how that's possible. I thought you were going to tell me you went to bed with that Lil person again. You didn't do that, did you?"

"Jesus, no, Tasha."

"Not even tempted?"

"Not at all."

"Guaranteed?"

"Guaranteed."

"So stop being an ass, okay? Now, may I get a fresh bowl of cereal since it's the only thing you have to eat around this place?"

32

Wednesday, June 5, eleven days later …

After midnight Jake and Tasha lay in each other's arms in the dim light of the TV, which they'd moved into her bedroom. They were breathless and sweating from a marathon lovemaking session. A "Tonight Show" rerun was on when a news flash interrupted Johnny's Carnac the Magnificent bit: the California Democratic primary returns were in with Robert Kennedy having defeated Eugene McCarthy. Bobby came on and thanked his staff and volunteers, particularly the black community, for their help and support. The L.A. crowd was ecstatic as the senator continued his victory speech.

"That about does it for McCarthy," Jake said.

"My parents are for Nixon," Tasha said, snuggling against Jake. "Hardcore Republicans."

"Who are you for?"

"I'm not much interested in politics."

"Did you vote for Goldwater?"

"I didn't vote. That was my term in France."

On TV, Kennedy was saying that the American people want change, are looking for a new direction, hoping for peace in Vietnam. Then, to a jubilant ballroom audience, he said, "On to Chicago!" After he left the stage, a few news commentators began an analysis of the election results. Jake rose, went into the kitchen and got a Coke from the fridge. Back in the bedroom, the bed was empty. He heard the shower start. He took a long swallow and turned his attention to the television screen.

Mayhem erupted in the ballroom. An announcer said there'd been a shooting, no reason to worry, but that the senator had been hit in the shoulder and four others wounded. Shrieking and yelling ensued. The announcer said Bobby had been shot in the hip, blood on his face, his eyes open. Another announcer, Charles Quinn, took over. Kennedy had been shot in the head. Someone shouted, "No, no, no!" Someone else yelled for a doctor.

Wrapped in a towel, Tasha came into the bedroom, drying her hair.

"What's going on?"

"Kennedy's been shot."

She gasped.

"Yeah, in the head."

"Holy Mother of God!" She sat on the edge of the bed.

"They said it's nothing to worry about."

The voice of yet another announcer came on, describing a piece of unedited footage about to run, then the visual of Bobby on the floor, blood all around his face, in a kitchen, people screaming, general bedlam, someone waving a fan at the candidate's scalp, trying to pull hair from the wound, a harried Ethyl Kennedy pushing her way through, a doctor attending, then a camera cut to a second bleeding man on the floor. Holding a bull horn, a man saying his name was Dick Tuck yelled for everyone to get out, no one listening, people cussing loudly, the senator lying there all bloody. Soon he was on a gurney, Ethyl by his side, being shoved into an ambulance. No one knew who the shooter was, Tuck announced.

Tasha leaned against Jake, her wet hair on his shoulder, both riveted to the screen.

"My, God!" she said. "They kill everyone."

Jake pulled her closer as if something might come hurtling toward them from the TV set.

"So it'll be Humphrey who wins," he said.

"What about your guy, McCarthy?"

"Too plainspoken. No, it'll be old Hubert, a surrogate of Johnson, the whole machine behind him. But the peace talks he's touting are merely a demand for Ho to surrender. The war will go on no matter who our president is."

Partially recovered, Tasha resumed drying her hair. Jake caught the aroma of oranges from her shampoo.

"Those poor Kennedys," she said. "How much can one family take? Let's hope he lives. Where were you when Jack Kennedy was killed?"

"A junior at Penn State. I was walking down the street with a friend, after lunch, cold, drizzly, and a bunch of people were watching a TV at the window of an appliance store. Someone there told us." He paused. "Where were you, Tasha?"

"That was my freshman year. I was pledging Tri Delt, and we pledges were cleaning up after a luncheon and one of the sisters ran into the room and told us. Then we went downstairs to the party room and saw it on TV. Anyway, jeez. Was the friend you were with a girlfriend?"

"Not exactly."

"Come on, tell me."

"Someone casual."

"Were you having sex with her?"

He smiled. "No, we were outside in the rain."

She elbowed him. "You know what I mean. So you were, weren't you?"

"Why do you want to know, Tasha?"

"Tell me. Are you scared to?"

"I'm trying to listen to this news."

"Yes, and I'm trying not to. Was she one of the girls in your wallet?"

"Not at all," Jake said. "She didn't teach me any big lessons about my life. Didn't I tell you I took those pictures out?"

A live interview with the head cop came on. They had a suspect, showed a clip of a small, swarthy, dark haired man. The clip switched to the chaotic ballroom, people running around, yelling, swearing. Kennedy was undergoing surgery, Ethyl at the hospital waiting.

"What was her name?" Tasha asked.

"Whose name?"

She sighed in frustration. "This casual chick."

"Rochelle."

"How'd you meet her?"

"Jesus, Tasha, this is not the time for such talk."

"All right, tell me this. How many girls have you slept with besides *casual* Rochelle?"

"Are you serious? Come on, let's turn the TV off and get some sleep. We both have busy days tomorrow."

"You're such a coward, Jake. Do you think I'll break up with you if you tell me?"

"Why do you want to know?"

"All right, since you're evading. I'm a pretty good judge of these matters, so let me guess." Before he could object, she said, "Twenty. Yes, I'd say twenty."

"No, Tasha, not twenty. Do you really want to know?"

She squeezed one of his nipples. "Yes, urgently."

"Ninety-three."

"Shut up. Be serious."

It was about 2:30 a.m. A man named Frank Mankowitz came on, said he was director of Bobby's campaign. The senator had a serious wound in his brain. The operation was ongoing. He wasn't conscious, in critical condition, his wife with him. The coverage went to a live shot outside the hospital, a crowd lingering, nothing to do but wait.

"Tell me how many, truly," Tasha demanded.

Jake could not relate to her foolishness.

"In my final count," he asked, "do you mean all the way, or including heavy petting?"

She seemed to notice his somber mood, but went on regardless. "Both."

"Six then, including you. How many are on your list?"

"Oh, Jake, this night is too solemn for such things. Hold me, please."

He was happy to do so. He really didn't want to know her final count. He got up, turned off the television and went back to bed. They pulled the covers up and lay together.

"I'm so glad we're lovers," she said softly. "Really, Jake, meeting you has been a miracle."

"For me too."

"Those girls were lucky to be with you, but I'm the luckiest one."

"No, I'm the luckiest guy. It seems as if all the forces of my life brought me here to Kent, to an apartment next to yours."

"You're right about a busy day tomorrow. At the high school we have to get ready for commencement. Don't you want to know how many guys I've been with?"

"I think you already told me, three. But I'm not really concerned about that."

"Why not?"

"All this news tonight is too somber."

"You're right, the number in the all-the-way column is now three. But I was a heavy petter in high school. You know, back seats, hayrides."

"Stop, Tasha. It's not important."

"But do I satisfy you, Jake?"

"Jesus, yes, Tasha. I've never been so happy."

"Is there something you'd like to do that we haven't done yet?"

"No."

"If there is, will you tell me?"

"There isn't."

"What about with Rochelle, or Ava Gardner?"

"No."

"If there is, will you tell me?"

"Tasha, let's go to sleep."

"I don't want you to have done anything with someone else that we haven't done, okay?"

"Sure, okay."

"I want us to do everything imaginable so you won't ever want anyone else."

"I don't want anyone else. It's not about the things we do in bed. It's much more than that. You're the one, Tasha. You're the one for me."

She wriggled a little against him and drifted off. He lay awake in the darkness. The world was quiet. Turn off a machine and all the chaos gone. And what was to happen with this world? What madness was yet to come? Would there be a revolution? A real one, with a new government? And who would rule this new world? The conservatives, the Nazis? An ultra-left junta run by Dr. Spock and Noam Chomsky? Would China and the Soviets unite and let the nukes fly toward us, we the same toward them? What will happen? A race war? Another depression, whole scale destruction, the obliteration of humanity? Such were the horrors that drifted through his mind.

He closed his eyes, thought of his father. *History is something that happens to us*, he'd once told Jake. *We're the little people. History takes us where it wants to go and we try to survive in the current.*

But this present current seemed to be rushing toward a falls as deadly as Niagara.

Tasha plopped her thigh over his as if he were part of the bed, natural, so intimate as to be utterly unconscious, but not to him. He inhaled the orange blossoms in her hair, heard her soft breathing, shivered with an uncontainable joy. Tasha. Yes, this unity is what he will live for, fight for, lying here together exactly like this.

33

Friday, July 12, six weeks later …

The four members of Goldenrod with Tasha at Jake's side clustered at one of the small tables in the cramped church basement turned coffeehouse known as the Needle's Eye: *easier for a camel to go through the eye of a needle than for a rich man to enter the Kingdom of Heaven*, or something like that. I'll never be rich, Jake thought, so I might have a chance. After a film about SDS, they'd performed a few protest songs and transitioned into authentic Appalachian bluegrass. Jake wore his new stage outfit, Ivy cap, a James Taylor "hangdog" look as Adele had described it. He'd played two new runs and now at their table had just downed a glass of cold cider.

179

Though during the last few days in the Glenville section of Cleveland a shootout between blacks and police had erupted, the summer was passing quietly forty miles southeast in the City of Trees. Jake was teaching two classes of composition and taking a seminar on Dryden and Pope, their political satire relevant to present times. Tasha was teaching summer school French to three students who'd failed her eleventh grade class, and she was also meeting with a group of visiting French college students living in Prentice Hall. Tomorrow she and Jake would be the escorts taking them shopping at Akron's Summit Mall. Ray was presently embroiled in a two week training course in West Virginia, thus allowing Tasha more freedom to be out with Jake. Nevertheless, she fretted about one of his friends seeing her and reporting to Ray when he returned.

"So," Wash said, sweating from the performance, "the fall music festival will have a folk contest, not only jazz this year. We'll enter that, right everyone?"

"Pure bluegrass won't stand a chance," Henry said. "We should spice things up."

"We ain't gonna plug in, if that's what you have on your mind," Wash answered.

"Not plugging. But something more in line with the times."

"No," Adele insisted. "Authentic, that's us. That's what we have over everyone else. You saw how this place was rockin'."

"Sure," Henry said. "We're the only show here at the moment. But at the festival there'll be a lot of competition. We should start doing some of our own stuff, something present day."

"I don't know about that," Adele said, "but we could improve our stage presence."

"Yeah," Henry added. "Now we look like three scarecrows standing around a mountain."

They all laughed.

"I'm trying my best to trim down," Wash said.

"You'll have to give up more than Twinkies," Adele answered.

Wash turned to Tasha. "And what about you, young lady? Do you sing, play, tap a tambourine? We could use another female." He turned to Adele. "No offense, hon."

"But you're right," she answered. "Tasha would brighten things up, no doubt."

"I played the flute and piccolo in the orchestra at Ohio State. But nothing like this. Anyway, I'd be terrified."

"Ever play the recorder?" Adele asked.

"In junior high, then I learned the flute."

"These songs ain't Bach," Wash said. "If you can play Sousa, you can play our stuff."

"Why didn't you tell us this, Jake?" Adele asked.

"Because I didn't know she'd be interested. She can sing, too, a fierce imitation of Janis Joplin after a couple glasses of wine. You should hear her rendition of 'Me and Bobby McGee.'"

"I play mainly classical," Tasha said, "and for fun, privately, a little swing, some jazz, nothing improvisational. Last fall I learned 'Light My Fire,' though." She nudged Jake in the ribs.

"That's a start," Wash said, grinning. "Join us Sunday, bring your instrument. Jake can show you some of our music. For the fun of it."

Tasha was blushing. "No, I can't. I'm much too busy with our French guests. And I've never even thought of being in a group. I have stage fright like crazy, even teaching my first classes each fall."

Jake felt a tug on his shirt and turned to see the same high school hippie who'd introduced herself to him last time at the Eye.

"Hi," she said, smiling. "You were sooo good tonight. Far out, really, for sure. I love the cap. You look outta sight."

"Well, thanks," he answered, noticing Tasha's surprised expression.

"I'm Audrey. My dad is the head minister here. Could you sign this program for my friend Crystal? She's too shy to ask."

She handed him the sheet and a ballpoint. Though he felt uncomfortable signing a schedule featuring a partisan SDS movie, he scribbled his name. And Miles McGill of SDS fame was scheduled to speak here next weekend. The girl lingered a second, giggled and hurried off. Meanwhile, quizzically, Tasha stared at Jake.

Later in the car she said, "Maybe I'd better try out for your group, to keep an eye on you when you're at the Eye. I think I'll dig that ancient recorder out of my closet when we're in Akron tomorrow. We have to pass right by our house on the way to the mall. I'll call Ma*ma* and tell her to make some lemonade. The girls can meet a real American family with a *femme au foyer* who grew up in their country."

"Why didn't you tell me you might like to join our group?" Jake said.

"You never asked, and actually until Wash said something, it hadn't entered my mind. But here's the real question, Jake — why didn't you tell me cutesy flower girls have been hovering around you?"

Saturday, July 13, next day …

Jake rode shotgun in the university van, Tasha in the middle, the official school driver at the wheel. She'd warned Jake that she hadn't told her parents about them, that it was too soon, that they were still recovering from the cancellation of the wedding. As farms, woods and small towns passed by, in

181

the back seats ten college girls from Strasbourg chattered in French. In less than half an hour, the vehicle pulled into the driveway of a split level suburban home with a large, well-manicured lawn. On edge because it was the first time he would meet his sweetheart's family, Jake got out as Tasha's parents emerged from the front door. An Irish setter ran to Tasha, its tail wagging furiously.

Tasha introduced Jake as her next door neighbor who kindly agreed to come along as a chaperone, no indication that he was any more to her than that. Jake played the role, noting that the family seemed ideally comfortable. Mrs. Van Sollis had set up a lovely refreshment table in their downstairs recreation room. She beamed as she chatted with the visitors in her native language. Mr. Van Sollis, solidly built under his well-trimmed flat top, engaged Jake in conversation about the goings on at Kent.

"Is it as infested with longhaired troublemakers as our college here in Akron?" he asked.

"Kent doesn't seem at all radical," Jake answered. "Some rallies occasionally, more hecklers than participants, a weekly silent protest, some resistance against recruiters from Dow Chemical, antiwar lectures and whatnot..."

"Sounds like quite a bit to me," Van Sollis said.

"But most of the kids are more interested in parties and the downtown bars."

"Yeah, that strip on Water Street is famous statewide. I suppose you were in the Service, right?"

"No, I served out a deferment for high school teaching."

The tall, handsome man gave Jake a skeptical glance. "But, of course, you support the effort. Gotta stop the commie bastards dead in their tracks, right?"

Neck deep in Nixon country, Jake figured it was no place to engage in political debate.

"Dealing with those matters aren't included in my job description."

"Which *is*?"

"Working on my master's and teaching freshman writing. That's about all I can handle."

"I see. Anything going on between you and my daughter?"

Stunned, Jake quickly answered, "We live next door to each other."

"I guess you know about her big breakup, right?"

"Not much."

"We hadda cancel the whole shebang. Pretty damn embarrassing. Ever meet Ray Sweeny?"

"No. I helped Natasha with her car once, needed a tune-up."

"She's like her mom, neglectful of things mechanical. Ray's a man of honor, not a fella to be satisfied with a teaching deferment. He's busting his gut to get over there in the real deal. Don't know why my daughter doesn't respect that."

Jake only nodded.

"Kinda surprised she brought you along today."

"She said she needed some support with these kids," Jake answered, shifting his stance and noticing that the big room was getting warmer.

Sipping lemonade, the two men stood in silence, seeming to have run out of things to say. Thankfully to Jake, the stop at the Van Sollis residence didn't last long.

Soon walking together in the gleaming indoor shopping center, Tasha wanted to know what Jake and her father had been talking about.

"He asked me if anything was going on between you and me, and I said you dance the samba and lick wine off me every night."

She stopped in her tracks. "You said what?"

He smiled. "No, I blabbered that I'd tuned up your Rambler."

"Don't scare me like that." She punched him on the shoulder. "That's not all you've tuned up."

Jake remained stoic. "I'm afraid your dad and I aren't on the same page, politically."

"No, not even in the same library." She added, "My old recorder won't do. I'll pick up a new one here at the music store. I can break in this credit card Daddy got for me at his bank. Never had one before, how 'bout you?"

"No."

"Pretty groovy. You can buy things without cash."

Friday, August 23, six weeks later ...

Home from an all-afternoon conference with Dr. Shenk of Rhetoric and Composition in an orientation for his new position as the coordinator of arriving TA's, Jake climbed the stairs holding what he knew was a birthday card from his parents. On the landing in front of his apartment he caught the whiff of something baking from Tasha' place. Inside his own, he opened the standard Hallmark card to find a check for a hundred dollars in spite of his insistence that he was doing fine financially. He hadn't written to them about Tasha. He and his upstairs neighbor had become a couple, yes, but the outcome was not yet certain. No use giving his mom another reason for later disappointment. She'd been crushed at the breakup with Ainsley.

As Jake had watched the riots on TV at the Democratic Convention in Chicago, he'd thought about his dad. On the quiet summer campus, there'd been talk of a group visiting the Windy City to protest, but Jake hadn't imagined anything like the clouds of tear gas, the beatings, and protestors being dragged off and hauled away in paddy wagons.

At his apartment, he showered, pulled on shorts and tee shirt, tapped on Tasha's unlocked door and went in to the savory aroma of lemon cake. A classical flute piece played on the stereo. Wearing an apron, she was in the kitchen putting on the final touches of white frosting.

"Smells great," he said.

"Twenty-nine candles, right?" she asked, smiling, a strand of golden hair drooping over her brow. She blew it aside. "Besides your favorite pasta and this cake, what would you like to do tonight? Please let's not watch more of that Chicago mayhem."

"Do you really want to know what I'd like?" he asked with a croon.

"Yes, you dear man, I would. But I have an idea by that sexy tone of voice. We do that every night. I mean what else?"

"It's my birthday, right?"

"What is on that demented mind of yours?"

"Remember our first night together?"

"How could I ever forget that?" She speared candles into the cake.

"I'd like a repeat performance of your 'Girl from Ipanema' act."

She gave him a sultry stare. "You would, would you?"

"Yes. An exact rendition, Bridgette Bardot and all."

"I think that can be arranged. Do we have to drink Thunderbird, though"

"Absolutely. I want it exact, one of the finest moments of my life. I'll go over to the State Store and get the wine."

"And you want the makeup and all?"

"Yes. Do you still have that outfit?"

"And do you still have that samba record?"

34

Monday, October 28, five weeks later ...

In his mailbox at the grad student lounge Jake found a sealed letter with his handwritten name on it. Puzzled, he sat down at the big table and opened the envelope. It was from Dr. Byron Shenk, his new boss. The text was handwritten also.

Jake: For some reason your name appeared on a list that ended up in the U.S. House Committee on Internal Security, formerly the House Un-American Activities Comm.

Jake felt a surging cold chill, put the paper down, looked around the lounge, three grad students huddled on a corner bench, laughing and drinking coffee.

He flattened the sheet on the tabletop and continued reading: *They've sent an investigator here (you're not alone on the list) who is quietly interviewing this hand-picked university-wide group. Admin is keeping it hush-hush for the moment, and this man, Boris Wettman, wants to speak with you today in your office, 4 pm. I think it would be a good idea for you to be there, cooperate fully, and keep the meeting to yourself.*

Throughout the day in his freshman class, in his evaluation observations of two new TA's, and in his seminar on Hawthorne and Melville, Jake felt a knot in his gut. What the hell was this? The House Un-American Activities Committee of Joe McCarthy fame? Jesus! Maybe this guy Wettman had arrived in lieu of the FBI with handcuffs in a black sedan. If so, Jake's life was about to change precisely when he'd thought it couldn't be flowing along any better.

At three forty-five Jake sat behind his desk, unsuccessfully trying to correct the plethora of errors on a freshman essay, a process analysis assignment, this one from a young lady on how to make pumpkin pie. Jake feared it was the last such paper he'd be reading for quite some time and realized how blessed he was to be delving into even horribly flawed prose. He now had a small private office on Satterfield's ground floor, his window looking out on some still green barberry shrubs.

At precisely four, a small, roundish man in trench coat and fedora, horn rimmed glasses, appeared at Jake's opened door.

"Wettman," he announced, "for our appointment."

Jake rose. "Come in. Have a seat."

"Mind if I close this door?"

Without permission, he did so, took off his hat revealing thick dark hair parted in the middle. "I'll take off my coat too, if you don't mind. I was over at the Art Department. Nice campus, but the students here must be in good shape with all these hills. Walking over here, I noticed those two tall smoke stacks. What're they all about?"

"The power plant," Jake answered as Wettman hung his outer garments on the coat rack. He sat down on the chair in front of Jake's battered desk.

"They make this place look like a Chevy plant. Burn coal, do they?"

"I see the trucks coming and going. What is this about?"

"Right to the point, eh? Okay, I'm Bo Wettman, you can call me Bo. Like to keep these things friendly. I guess you've been alerted by Dr. Shenk? I hear they refer to him as 'the Lord.'"

"He mentioned you wanted to meet, but not what about."

"Okay, I'll fill you in. Ya see, Congress is a little concerned about what's been going on in the academic communities, you know, uprisings, taking over buildings, burnings — you name it. There was that degenerate commie kid at Berkeley, then the Columbia thing. Getting ridiculous, these SDSers threatening to overthrow the U.S. Government. You know what I'm talking about, right?"

He gave Jake a shrewd look as if his last comment wasn't really a question.

"Somewhat."

Wettman scoffed. "*Somewhat.* Right. Anyway, the Government is concerned. We've been keeping our eyes open, but now we're into a full-scale investigation, need a little help. I'm gonna be here for a few weeks, observing, doing interviews with some people, then report back to the Subcommittee."

"Uh, why me?" Jake said, fearing the answer yet wanting to be sure.

"Mind if I smoke?" Wettman said, his hand already inside his navy blue blazer. He held a pack of Marlboro across the desk.

"No, don't smoke."

"I need an ashtray."

Jake had nothing but a Styrofoam coffee cup from the morning. He placed it near his thoroughly unwanted guest. Wettman smiled.

"No idea, *why you?* Really?"

"Is it because I've voiced my opinion about the war?"

Wettman guffawed. "You know it goes a little deeper than that."

"What then?"

"Let's say that whatever there is to know about you, we know. Let's assume that, shall we, as a matter of course. But I couldn't care a rat's ass about your views on the war."

"What's going on, then?"

"Let me ask you this, Ernst. Are you onboard with this absurd notion of violent overthrow of the U.S. Government?"

Jake hated having to answer any of this man's questions, even directions to the john, should he ask. But it was bound to have come to something like this, the man's inquires like metaphoric shackles.

"No, I'm not onboard with anything like that."

"Of course, you'd say that. Remember those three letters you wrote to the editor of your hometown paper?"

Jake was stunned to silence.

"They show you read up on the war, think you know something about what you read, the public information available, assumed you know it all, which you certainly do not."

Jake's mind became dizzy at Wettman's reference to those ancient letters. If he knew about them, he knew everything. So, all right, he was going to prison. This guy was toying with him like a sadistic child de-winging a housefly.

"Anyway, I only wish you clowns could sit in on some of our closed sessions on national security. Your minds would be turned upside down in a matter of minutes. But you don't know what's going on and are too dumb to trust those who do. We sure don't want our government overturned, either by you bums or by foreign powers intent on taking away the freedoms you're enjoying by spouting about things you don't have a clue."

"I suppose you're here to take me somewhere today. Will I have some time to straighten up my affairs?"

"Take you somewhere? Hell, no. We like you right here in this crap office with no God-damned ashtray." He tapped his ash into the coffee cup.

Jake's temper was rising above his fear. "So, what's going on then?"

"Ernst, I'm glad you realize I could take you *somewhere* if I wanted to. It's good that you know that. But no, all we're trying to do is open lines of communication. We have your name on the charter of a faculty group against the war, also photos of you in a demonstration, not to mention playing the guitar in a group supporting SDS rallies. You don't seem to be a troublemaker. Not a true blue pro-voc-a-teur. You seem to be getting on with your life, good grades, good teaching evaluations, gaining stature, even shacking up with one incredible looking piece of..."

Jake rose. "Get out of here."

Wettman took a calm drag of his cigarette, sighed.

"Sit down, Ernst. That *was* a crude comment. Sorry to get your dander up."

Jake remained standing. "We're finished here. If you want to take me to jail, let's go."

Wettman chuckled. "Come on, man. I don't want to mess up your lovely little life. You're no threat, only misguided, basically exercising your constitutional rights. Other than that temperamental little package you sent to your draft board, we don't have anything on you. Sit down. Relax."

Jake stood there, immobilized. He guessed that's exactly how Wettman wanted him to feel, already imprisoned. He sat.

"Here's the plan," Wettman said, dropping his cigarette butt into the cup with a sizzle. "Like I said, lines of communication. Somehow I got the damned job of following Mark Rudd around the country. You know who Mark Rudd is?"

Jake took a deep breath. He had the option of being silent, taking his punishment. He thought of Tasha, who at this moment was probably on her way home from the high school, expecting him there soon. They were planning to see a rerun of *The Graduate* tonight at the Kent Theater, a rare evening out.

"Mark Rudd," Jake repeated grimly, "the guy at Columbia?"

Wettman smiled as if in victory. Jake hated him, quelled his rage.

"Right on, brother. Columbia, precisely. Also national president of SDS. And he happens to be speaking at this Podunk campus tomorrow. We want to know what he says. Of course, I'll be there, unrecognizable, but we also want to know the aftermath. We need to learn what these serious, but deranged, revolutionaries are up to here in the country's back woods. Like I say, lines of communication. The truth, that's all. I can't be everywhere at the same time and, believe me, these knuckleheads get around. We need a few select contacts who can keep us informed. And in your case, particularly regarding the faculty."

His options blurred, Jake sat quietly, staring at the essay about pumpkin pie.

"Don't think of yourself as a snitch, Ernst. We don't intend for you to subvert SDS operations, nothing like that. Simply channel information about what they're up to, information generally available, a kind of stringer reporter. You won't be alone, but you won't know our other contacts. We want several independent lines coming in. We know you live above a journalist for the local rag they put out over in Ravenna. Might pick up some useful bits from him, in passing conversation, of course. He damn well needn't know about me."

"These other people are being blackmailed too?" Jake asked hoarsely.

"Blackmailed? There's a nasty word. No, Ernst, you're completely free to make your own choices. None of us forced you to send that little package to Selective Service, a felony, if you didn't know. You were free and clear with a snazzy little swishy 4F before you did that..."

"Being against the war," Jake cut in, "doesn't mean you're swishy."

"A yella-belly, at least."

"Not that either."

"What-the-hell-ever. So the irony is that you find yourself in the grips of your own provocation, pretty flimsy though it was. We expect you to attend the happenings around here as an objective observer, no infiltration, no cloak and dagger, just what's being said and who's saying it, stuff any marginal but observant witness would know. We won't be wiring you up, nothing like that. Tell us what you see and hear, read in the paper, so we can make an absolutely objective evaluation of the internal threat to our nation beaming out from this one horse hamlet. Hey, like you're writing home to Dad, who incidentally was a model soldier."

"Leave my dad out of it."

"I'm just saying, unlike you, he served his country."

"That war was nothing like Vietnam."

"Shut the hell up and listen, *compadre*. We don't care crap about your feelings about it. You're as harmless as a wounded hare, and if you turn out not to be, we can neutralize your ass any time it's necessary. We're telling you to continue exactly as you have been, no change, out there like always, watching, listening, even singing a few Seeger tunes, why not? Is what we want so unreasonable? Isn't it all part of our democratic way of life?"

Wettman rose.

"That about does it, buddy-boy. Hey, I know you don't like being put over a barrel. Who does? But it's a barrel of your own stupid making. And now you have a simple choice: serve your country in a completely patriotic and reasonable manner, or sit in the hoosegow jerking off about that primo looking girlfriend of yours. Seems like a no-brainer to me."

Jake sat seething as Wettman took his time putting on his coat and hat. He turned.

"Cheer up, Ernst. I'll know you're onboard if I see you at the Rudd nonsense tomorrow. Then we'll be in touch." He grinned, tipped his hat. "One way or another."

Almost unable to contain his rage, Jake stood, breathing hard. He felt like smashing his guitar leaning in the corner.

No, calm down. Now is not the time for temper. Now is the time for thought. Yes, the man is hateful, but his personality, his intonation, his insinuations are not the same as the situation. There's a lot at stake. Get a grip on yourself and use your brain.

Using his brain wasn't easy for Jake even as he walked homeward in the late afternoon chill, the aroma of burning leaves in the air. Down the hill, four kids whizzed past him on skateboards, a new fad, scooters without handlebars. The brilliant autumn colors had faded to crisp shades of brown.

Should he tell Tasha about Wettman? No, not yet. Not until he figured it all out. He had to measure his options. One choice was simply to defy the louse and go to jail now; after all, he'd known this day might come.

The compliance option was out of the question. But wait, was it? The guy kept using the word *objective*. He wanted objective reports, not spying, he said. Jake wouldn't have to *infiltrate*, only report. Other than Wettman's tone, what was wrong with that? He'd been hanging around these rallies anyway, with Goldenrod. He read the *Daily Stater*, heard conversations. Shouldn't the government know this stuff anyway? Did he believe in the violent overthrow of the federal government? Certainly not. Was he in tune with these SDSers? No way. Would he want them running things? God forbid!

If he could get beyond his personal distaste for this slimeball and look only at the assignment, maybe he could carry on without having to give up what he'd managed to create for himself this last year. Tasha had joked away his problem with the draft board; she'd bring him a file hidden in a cake, she said. But two years away from her wouldn't be a joke for either of them. He'd lose her. That might happen anyway. The Ray issue was anything but resolved. Jake and Tasha were still hiding from him as he cruised by their house in his Camaro. Tonight's movie date constituted a rare local outing. They'd spent the summer camping in the Cuyahoga Valley National Park, enjoying concerts at the Blossom Music Center, and descending the stairs into the cramped confines of the Needle's Eye, all of which were hardly any of Ray's haunts. Also, Jake had met Tasha's parents with the French girls, briefly but an inroad nonetheless. Progress was being made. They'd become a couple, no doubt. All they needed was for Ray to get his appeals for fulltime army status approved, or to find another girl.

Jake strolled off Summit onto South Willow, a block from home. He saw the Rambler in the driveway. The fact was that until this afternoon's confrontation with Wettman, Jake had been happier than ever before. In his eyes, his future had been clear sailing ahead. So what harm in playing along with Wettman's extortion? Report what everyone already knew, maybe even highlight the logic against the war. Show these people that the antiwar fervor had a logical base.

Wettman had intimated that national leaders were following a secret logic, knew something vital but undisclosed about our reasons for fighting the Vietnamese. Okay, then, why don't they disclose it? If they could change our thinking, really convince us of the vital danger of a communist Vietnam, then why the hell don't they? What overwhelming security secrets are they hiding?

If all they wanted from him was an objective report, what would be the harm? He might even do some good. That is, of course, if Wettman was being truthful about not spying, about being simply factual. With all the rumors, even propaganda, about outside agitators, professional anarchists infiltrating the nation's academic institutions, maybe Jake could set the record straight. For he'd not seen or heard any evidence of the sort. If it was truth they wanted, he could give it to them without violating his conscience, couldn't he?

Such were the considerations that swirled through his mind as he sat in the dark theater next to his true love watching poor Benjamin dealing with his. And as they left the theater, Jake saw no reason to bring any of this up with Tasha.

"You seem in an unusually somber mood tonight," she said on their way home in Jake's car. "Didn't laugh at a single joke. Is anything wrong?"

"I saw that film before," he answered. "I wonder what their life will be like after that bus ride. And I should tell you, Tasha, tomorrow night I'm going over to the auditorium and listen to this Mark Rudd character."

"Mark Rudd? Who's that?"

"He's the guy that led the Columbia shutdown last spring. I'm curious about what he has to say."

"Okay, sweetheart. No problem. I'll practice my new recorder."

35

Tuesday, October 29, next day ...

Over a thousand students and faculty crowded into the University Theater to hear Mark Rudd, many of them SDSers by their oddly military outfits but most of them curious spectators. Young, fresh faced, clean-shaven, shorthaired, Mr. Rudd gave an impassioned but disjointed speech filled with profanity about what happened at Columbia. He framed the presentation from the perspective of SDS's national goals. The spring protest at Columbia had closed down the university for a number of days, which Rudd felt had been a profound success. The dispute was ostensibly about defense research and an attempt to create a white enclave by replacing a local Harlem park with a university gym. Rudd theorized that America's academic institutions were not neutral but intensely political in favor of the military industrial complex. As national president of SDS, he went on to define the group's goal as not to seize power but to radicalize, to make people think. He announced an SDS program to initiate student strikes against the upcoming election between Nixon and Humphrey. Then he made a pitch for contributions for his legal defense fund regarding the charges pending against him for his role in the Columbia shutdown.

He showed a film about that disruption, and in true Kent style, most of the audience cheered when the NYPD attacked the demonstrators. Jake knew that apathetic Kent State was no Columbia or Berkeley, that the radical voices though loud were few and mostly scorned, the rallies consisting mainly of unsympathetic bystanders looking for amusement as they changed classes and heckled the speakers – certainly nothing for the U.S. Congress to be worried about.

During Rudd's presentation Jake, who leaned against the back wall of the auditorium, looked around for Wettman, who'd been correct that he wouldn't be visible, apparently the master of disguise if, in fact, he was there at all. Jake detested Rudd's approach, especially the lack of organization and the bad language, almost as if disrupting spoken English was a more important goal than the radicalization of his listeners' political thought. Jake finally concluded that the event could not have had much effect on the viewpoints of the audience.

Walking home under the streetlights, the traffic sparse, a cold breeze in his face, Jake wondered if he should mention Wettman to Tasha. He also wondered if he should contact a lawyer. Of course, his case with the torn up draft card was open and shut. He'd as much as invited the FBI to pick him up. Was this deal with Wettman supposed to absolve him of his crime? Or would it be held over his head like the sword of Damocles until the federal statute of limitations ran out in August, 1972. Would his task be simply to report events like tonight, or would it escalate? After all, the *Stater* would report what happened, along with the *Courier-Gazette* and the Akron daily, so why not simply cut out their articles and editorials and give them to Wettman? The reporters would do a much more thorough job. Jake also wondered when he would meet the horse's ass again?

No, better not get Tasha involved until he knew more about this deal with the devil. He realized, however, that delay about telling her was flirting with disaster for by now they knew virtually everything about each other, and one of the things he loved about her was her penchant for the truth. She'd probed deeply, often in the lazy aftermath of their lovemaking, about every detail of his life, even exact minutiae of his sexual experiences. She seemed much more intrigued than jealous about them. He, on the other hand, had been less inquisitive, more jealous than captivated. So holding back on Wettman carried a heavy risk. And after all, she deserved to know about the possible consequences of her involvement with this fugitive from justice.

Wednesday, October 30, next day ...

Wettman strolled into Jake's office a few minutes after eight. Without a word, he hung his coat and hat on the rack and settled onto the ragged chair in front of Jake's desk.

"Pretty smart," he said, "holding court early in the a.m. No one shows, right?"

"I have some questions," Jake said.

"Did you hold on to that coffee cup from yesterday?" Wettman pulled his smokes out of his jacket pocket.

"The staff cleans up every night."

"Your cup seems half full. Don't wanna deprive you of your caffeine fix. Mind grabbing me a cup from the lounge?"

"I do mind."

"Why? Think I'll snoop around your office."

"Exactly."

"What'll I find?"

"I don't like the violation of my privacy."

Wettman chuckled. "You're a piece of work, Ernst. Okay, I'm not gonna drop ashes on your floor, so would you like another cup of coffee? I can pick one up for you."

"No."

"You know, Ernst, this doesn't have to be an adversarial relationship. We both understand you're going to accept our little deal, so why not make it friendly? Hang on, I'll be right back. I'll bring some empty cups for our future talks."

When Wettman left, Jake was sorely tempted to check the guy's coat pockets but suppressed the impulse. He hated the arrogant slug. He realized that if the campus leftists found out he was associated with a congressional agent he'd be deemed a traitor even if his reports would be purely objective. Guilt by association.

Wettman came back with a small stack of Styrofoam containers, one filled with coffee for himself.

"Ran into Holly McGill in the lounge," he said. "Of course, she doesn't know me from Adam. Quite a dish. Wouldn't think her capable of leading a revolution, would you?"

"Don't know her well."

"Yeah, you got your hands full already."

"Don't make such references to my love life. That is if you're being honest about wanting this to be an amicable process."

Wettman slurped his coffee and winced. "Christ, how do you people drink this stuff? Amicable, eh? All right, sounds like you're warming up to the idea. You said you have some questions." With a chrome lighter he deftly lit a cigarette and pointed out the Congressional insignia. "Dick Nixon gave me this lighter. Christmas gift. I'm sure you know he's an anticommunist force. Gained his *bona fides* from his work on the Alger Hiss case."

"How long are you going to hold my crime over me? Will my cooperation with you absolve it?"

"Concerned about your hide, eh? Should'a thought about that sooner. There's no absolution. I guess you can say it depends on your performance. *Thank-yous* are always in order. Speaking of performances, wha'd'ya think of Rudd's last night. I saw you yawning there in the back. I thought the place was quite lively."

"Then you probably noticed that more people were there for the fun of it than were likely to become radicalized. Why are you worried about this place. Yes, there are a handful of hardcore leftists, but they're the same old crew. Everybody knows their spiel."

"Here's what I do know," Wettman said, exhaling smoke from his nostrils. "The overall SDS plan follows the steps of professional revolutionary planners, guided by internationals connected to the Soviets. It's not the Vietnamese we're fighting over there but the God-damned Ruskies. It's the strategy learned and executed flawlessly by Fidel. He started with twelve Soviet trained Marxists. So, their strategy works, get it? At first they seem harmless, print pamphlets, talk about constitutional freedoms, 'educate' the masses. Then they raise the rhetoric, excite emotions around cleverly selected causes, convert a few pig farmers, like Columbia University's tearing down a neighborhood park. All this to engage the sympathies of otherwise good citizens. Yeah, their causes might even be good ones. That's what pulls the moderates into their clutches. Then they arrange events to expose the hypocrisy or inadequacy of administrators, law enforcement, government. Man-oh-man, are the universities ever ripe for that step."

"I don't need this lecture," Jake said, finishing off his coffee.

"And remember, Fidel and Che started not in Havana but out in the boondocks, and what word better describes Kent, Ohio?"

"Are you suggesting that Soviet leaders have designated Kent for the beginning of America's overthrow? I don't need this crap."

Wettman scoffed. "You can say that again. You've been well-indoctrinated. We know of your association with one Stephen McShea, have a picture of you marching in a parade with him back at good old Joe-Pa U. He fled to Canada with the rest of the yellowbellies, sitting there in Vancouver organizing protests in the U.S., and we're waiting for him to cross back over the border. Then we'll nab his ass."

Jake tried to hold back his shocked reaction to this background information. The work they'd done on him was scary. He felt scared.

"Yeah," Wettman continued, "and we're aware of the little cadre on that farm outside of D.C. They say they're building a school, but we know what they're up to. We've got the full dope on you and your crowd, Ernst."

Christ, they know about Ainsley!

"Then spare me the treatise on revolutionary methodology," Jake said, trying to keep his voice even.

"Yeah, we even know your sordid connection with Martino, the Unitarian commie in your hometown, and lovely Miss Dobbs and her so-called draft counseling. Not to mention the faggot professor you used to hang out with. And your arrest record for wrecking a nativity display."

"Okay, you've made your point."

"All right, then you needn't be concerned with absolution. There's no deal for you here."

"So if I'll have to go to jail eventually, I might as well go tomorrow. You say you don't want me to spy, but of course that's what you want. You say it's objective reporting, but then why don't you subscribe to the student newspaper? No, I won't do it. Put me in jail."

"Hey, Ernst, calm down, relax."

"And I'll tell the campus about this, talk to a reporter, that you're recruiting informants. They should know what you're up to. You say there are others, right, and..."

A knock sounded at the door, causing Wettman to whirl.

"A student," Jake said, his ire having warmed him. "Come back later with your troops. There's no revolution here, only a couple of scruffy poly-sci majors, certainly no rivals of Fidel and Che. You don't need spies at Kent. Now get out of my office."

"Cool your jets, Ernst. I gotta go anyway. We'll talk again."

"I'm ready for prison, anytime. I'll have an attorney and be willing to talk to the press. Now, I have a student who needs some writing help."

"Okay, I'll have a little chat with your family back on the farm. And we'll take it from there."

"And fuck you, Wettman," Jake said furiously between his teeth. "You've just radicalized a moderate."

The student, one Steve Stone, was a baseball player whom Thurman Munson had brought to Jake's office and introduced as a prospective freshman for Jake's 101 class. Thurman had been in Jake's first class, a year before and was now playing pro ball on a Yankees' minor league team. Steve, a neat, clean-shaven kid wearing a jacket with Greek letters, was concerned about passing Jake's current 102 class in order to maintain his baseball scholarship. He'd written a process essay on how to get away with throwing a spitball.

A much more motivated student than Munson, he'd turned down a chance to pitch for the White Sox in order to get his degree. His writing still needed improvement. Besides being much too general, the paper was rife with fragments and run-on sentences, showing how little he'd picked up from the earlier course. But unlike Thurman, the young man was sincere about more than mere athletics, sincere enough, at least, to get out of bed at eight-thirty in the morning to seek help. Jake, however, now had serious reason to worry that he, himself, wouldn't be around tomorrow to help any of his students.

36

Wednesday, November 13, five weeks later ...

At two-thirty, Jake had left his Spenser seminar and was trekking across campus toward the library when he saw a teeming crowd of students gathered at the entrance of the Administration Building. Down the steep slope in front of the columned entrance, about fifty black students clustered on the steps. Jake saw a banner: STOP OAKLAND P.D. RECRUITING.

What's this all about? Kent is pretty far away from California for them to be recruiting here. And BUS is stretching pretty far for another cause.

Not much was happening, a ragtag group but odd for blacks to be out in force, bundled up against the cold and milling about with their sign. Spectators had begun to congregate for the show. Occasionally a visitor to the building was forced to detour around the protestors to a side door. But soon the group rose, formed a line and began moving up the lane toward Terrace Drive, where Jake and others were watching.

Someone tugged his coat sleeve, Adele, who said, "Come on, let's see what's going on."

"Can't," Jake said. "Work to do at the library."

"They're headed for the Union, where the recruiters work. You have to go by there anyway."

Edged along by the flow, he and Adele trailed behind the procession.

"What's it matter who's recruiting?" Jake said. "It's not Dow, after all, not napalm or anything."

"Yeah, but there was all that Black Panther drama that went down in Oakland, Huey Newton and all. The university's law enforcement program is a perfect place to hire cops."

"I didn't even know we had a law enforcement program."

The pair moved along with the crowd, Adele intent on what was happening. "You know how SDS has been trying to join forces with BUS. Maybe that's what this is all about. Let's check it out."

On his way in any case, Jake tagged along. A crowd had already gathered at the Union, mostly spectators, who were always more subdued when blacks were involved, whether out of respect or downright fear. Many of the activists went into the building while others lingered outside.

Since his stand against Wettman several weeks before, Jake's life had changed. He was waiting for the sword to fall but had heard nothing. He guessed they were making him stew. Or, that the long arms of the law moved slowly. Nevertheless, he didn't need to be mixed up in another demonstration. He'd been radicalized but not in the typical way. He felt no need to get out here and raise hell, carrying signs and blocking doorways. If anything, he'd become more of a determined moderate.

He'd been honest with Wettman when he said he didn't believe in revolution or in the country being taken over by Mark Rudd types. But that hardly placed him in the Wettman/Nixon camp. He felt the war should be stopped, but not by violently overthrowing the government. That route had no chance of success. Nor did he want to go to prison for longer than absolutely necessary. So he'd been moving through his life as if under mild sedation, waiting for the next step and trying to keep Tasha from noticing his mood. If nothing were to happen, she needn't be bothered about the situation. And he hardly believed he could keep up their relationship from behind bars. With her family being entrenched Republicans, he had enough to overcome. Her sticking with a convicted felon would be too much to hope for.

A sedan pulled to the area from the direction of Admin, and several suited white males got out. Jake recognized one of them as Matson, Dean of Students, a slim, dark haired, button down type who looked as if he might be working for the FBI. Pulling his collar up against the cold, Jake soon saw four patrol cars, lights flashing, pulling up the hill from the direction of Lincoln Street. What now? Uniformed patrolmen with billy clubs made their way through the crowd into the building. Wash joined Jake and Adele.

"What's going on?" the big man asked, the sky darkening with the first hint of nightfall.

"Matson is in there talking with BUS," Adele answered. "BUS members don't seem to be leaving. SDS is in there too, announcing demands. They yelled to everyone about requiring the Oakland recruiters to get off campus for good."

Soon a grim Dean Matson came out, escorted by cops.

"Ten minutes," someone yelled from the doorway. "He's gonna talk to President White. Back in ten. Hang tough, everyone."

Someone in the crowd yelled back, "You guys are blocking *our* rights. We have every right to talk to recruiters."

"Yeah," someone else heckled, "if you don't like our country, why don't you move to Russia?"

"Looks like BUS and SDS have finally coalesced," Adele said. "They're all in there together."

"Not getting much support from the whites out here," Wash added.

A bearded white guy came out in a pea coat and wool cap. Adele knew him.

"Hey, Barry," she said as he approached. "What happened in there?"

"Same old shit. Matson told us we're violating the Student Conduct Code, we'll all be disciplined. What else is new? Said the recruiter pigs have a right to be here. Those blacks in there are serious, though. Good to see them finally get into the action. Made a ring three deep, locked arms, their chicks in the middle, protected. They had an outta-sight game plan. We followed their lead."

Jake wondered if Ella, his former officemate, was there.

"Any violence?" Wash asked.

"Not besides some elbowing. Hey, gotta go. Organizing a campus march for later. Matson says he'll be back in a couple of minutes. Gimmie a break, these guys take hours, days, not minutes. They're gonna let our guys wait around in there, get bored, in the meantime the pigs snapping cameras and taking names. Damn! This is exactly what we been waiting for!"

He pushed his way through the onlookers.

"Could get serious," Adele said.

"I'm going to the library," Jake answered, buttoning his collar against the cold. "This group will soon be frozen back to their dorms. You guys keep your heads down, okay?"

197

Thursday, November 14, next day ...

As soon as Jake arrived at Satterfield shortly before eight, he grabbed a cup of coffee and the student paper from the lounge and settled at his desk to find out what had happened the night before. Barry, the SDSer, had been right about Matson's conference with White taking more than ten minutes. According to the front page article, it had taken three hours, with the president deploring the sit-in, reinforcing Matson's reference to the official student conduct code and insisting the recruiters had every right to be on campus.

After that, the students had marched around campus, greeted by hecklers, scuffling at several dorms, pelted by water balloons from windows of the tall Tri-Towers residence halls and conducting a final rally at the plaza there called the Pit. The *Stater*'s editorial took the side of the recruiters, saying the protestors were violating the democratic rights of the student body in general. Also, the student government's vice-president, Mr. Pickett, the so-called Oreo, along with other blacks in the organization, resigned. They said that student government was "pseudo."

Tensions were bubbling up. The BUS organization planned a general meeting that night to answer questions about the Oakland recruiters and to discuss the issues with anyone who wanted to participate.

In his eight o'clock writing class, Jake's students were buried in the *Stater*'s account. Few looked up when Jake cleared his voice for the class to begin. He waited, tried again. Finally, Audrey Kraft spoke, by far his best student, long straight dark hair, hazel eyes, statuesque, confident and vaguely familiar from the first day. Jake tried to remember where he'd seen her before. And oddly, since that first day, she often smiled as if she recognized him, too.

"What do you think of the protests yesterday, Mr. Ernst?" she asked.

The other students looked up from their reading. Jake took a moment. This was the first time he'd been directly asked a question on the matter of campus goings-on. He'd carefully organized his class time to avoid matters not directly concerned with the course syllabus, and until this moment the strategy had worked perfectly.

"Uh, what do I think?"

"Yeah, I saw you out there in front of the Union. Do you support BUS?"

With all his structured planning, he was oddly ill-prepared to answer Audrey's forthright query.

"I, uh, appreciate the question," he said, "but about the recruiters, I don't understand why they came all the way here from Oakland, California. Probably because of our law enforcement program."

"Do you think KSU should even have that kind of program?" Audrey persisted.

"Why not? I'm sure it's a valid field of enquiry. But..."

"Do you think we should have Rotcy?" This was the voice of a slight, tousle haired, bright-eyed lad, Aaron Burkhart, who seemed in their comings and goings to be attached to Audrey's hip. The pair always sat together at the back of the room.

Jake took a breath. "Look, I can understand your curiosity about your teachers' views, but I'm being paid to help you people improve your writing for your academic future here. And there's not much time, only ten weeks, so there's really not a moment to spare, and..."

"Come on, Mr. Ernst," said Audrey. "Where do you stand? Were you in the war? Do you believe we should be in Vietnam? Do you support President White's stand against the blacks?"

Jake's mind was racing. He really needed to get on with the day's lessons.

"Tell you what, Audrey, everyone. I understand how you might think that these issues supersede how to construct topic sentences, but I'm hired here to do a particular job, not to share my personal opinions."

"Who's going to guide us, if not our teachers?" Aaron asked.

"I'm not wise enough to guide anyone. I have enough trouble guiding myself. I'm much more interested in what you're thinking than you should be about my thoughts. But I'll tell you what. If you're really interested in discussing these issues, you can bring them up as topics in your essays and I'll evaluate the effectiveness of your arguments. That's in line with my job. But as far as guidance in your confrontation with campus issues, I'll have to draw the line about using our class time for that."

"Boo, hiss," Audrey said, half-lightheartedly, her tone a great relief to Jake. She flashed him that knowing smile.

He smiled back, relaxed. "Look, there are plenty of activist professors, and plenty of conservative ones, and a lot who are only concerned about doing their research. But if you would like to have a forum with me in which to discuss all these important matters going on around campus, I'll set up a special time when you can come by my office and talk. You might be as helpful to me as I to you, and maybe we can work out our ideas rationally, without emotion. How about, uh, Wednesdays, say, three pm? My door will be open to anyone who wants to talk. Now let's get on to what we're all here for. Please open your textbooks to Chapter Six."

Most of the students seemed comfortable to get on with the class but the expressions of wry skepticism on the faces of Audrey and Aaron, two excellent students, struck him to his core. Anyway, it was likely he wouldn't be around for his office forum at all.

Monday, November 18, four days later ...

Late afternoon during his Spenser seminar, when one of the grad students was presenting an interpretation of Redcrosse Knight's famous premature ejaculation scene, two students leapt up and peered out the window. Others followed. Startled, Jake rose too and saw a line of hundreds of students bundled up to fight the cold and gloom. They were filing past Bowman Hall toward front campus. The procession went on and on, no ruckus to be seen, quite solemn, but with reporters and TV cameras.

Several students hurried out of the seminar room, others gathering their things and leaving also. Only three of the fifteen, including Jake, remained. Professor Grimsley furiously wrote notes as if recording attendance.

"Are they more interested in agitating against the so-called establishment than in building their careers?" He looked up from his paper with tired, watery gray eyes. "Now that I took role, shall we get on with it? Continue, Miss Southerly, with your impressions of our noble knight's quite ineffective response to the charms of Una. Unless I'm mistaken, it's the real reason we're here."

Restlessly, shocked at Grimsley's persistence at what Jake for the moment felt was Spenser's utter irrelevance, Jake tried to listen. But where were all those students going? And why?

The seminar finally over, Jake ran down the stairs to his office, grabbed his coat and rushed out into the wintry daylight. Many department members were gathered at the entrance, looking toward Bowman, Lil Lassiter among them.

"What's going on, Lil?"

"Oh, hi, Jake. They're leaving the campus. The blacks. They're supposedly getting onto buses to Akron U. Something about setting up a Kent campus in exile."

"In exile?"

"A church over there. They demanded amnesty from that recruiting sit-in last Thursday. White said those who'd been identified would be punished according to the Code of Conduct, hearings and whatnot, twenty so far. Says he won't give amnesty by coercion. Rules are rules."

"Yeah, I heard about that on Friday. White really toes the line, doesn't he? So, no kidding, they're all just walking out?"

"Incredible, isn't it? Some black faculty are going with them. Professor Levitt over in Soc called them beautiful, supports the boycott all the way, some other profs too. Says he won't teach class until they come back." Lil smiled up at Jake, her cheeks rosy from the cold, her standard single braid over her shoulder from beneath her hood. "Anyway, Jake Ernst, I haven't talked with you in a month of Sundays. How the hell are you?"

"I'm okay. Afraid to ask you the same."

"Having the time of my life. Don't all these agitators know Kent is a party school? I'd love to get together with you again. You up for that?"

"No."

"Chicken," she teased. "I live with some ultra-cool freaks in a house on South Depeyster. Party every weekend, and I do mean *par-tee*. You have an open invitation. Bring along that blond knockout of yours."

37

Wednesday, November 20, two days later …

At three o'clock, lo and behold, four of Jake's writing students showed up for the discussion session he'd suggested. He had to forage a few chairs from neighboring offices even though the kids said the floor would do fine. But Jake feared that a faculty member strolling by might be shocked to see a group of freshman gathered at his feet. He was wise enough to know that over-popularity with one' students constituted a danger from some. He didn't want to be charged with pandering, an accusation Drew Byrne, his former prof, now more of an activist than ever, was constantly enduring. But Drew had tenure.

When Jake asked who wanted to start the discussion, Audrey Kraft spoke up, her blue-green eyes fresh and radiant in her lovely but serious face.

"Mr. Ernst, don't you remember me?"

"Uh, you seem familiar, Audrey, but I don't remember from where."

She handed him a folded a program from the Needle's Eye. He saw the autograph he'd written.

"Oh, you're that cute kid?"

"That's me."

"Wow, Audrey. I'll be."

"My parents moved to Maryland, but I decided to stay right here for college."

"Now I know why you looked familiar. Glad to see you again."

"So, Mr. Ernst, do you agree with White's handling of the black exile?"

"I don't think we can call it an *exile* exactly. They left voluntarily, didn't they? Maybe *exodus* would be better. Anyway, what do *you* think about it, Audrey?"

"I think White bungled the whole thing. First he says they'll get punished, now he gives them amnesty so they'll come back."

"What else was he supposed to do if they couldn't find any evidence against anyone?" Steve Stone asked, a surprise attendee at the little meeting.

"Then he shouldn't have threatened them in the first place," Aaron said, sitting close to Audrey. "He had twenty names. That's why they felt the need to split."

The fourth student was a meek young lady with a pale, unmade-up face and mousey brown hair.

"What do you think, Naomi?" Jake asked her.

"I don't know what to think," she answered shyly. "I feel scared all the time. I'm thinking of dropping out and going home."

"Come on, Mr. Ernst," Audrey said. "Give us your opinion. We're rapping. You're not in the classroom now."

"I'm kind of in Naomi's position, don't know what to think. I was shocked by their walking out. I've thought that BUS has been pretty quiet since I got here last fall, holding back on rallies and such, keeping their distance from SDS."

"What about when they stormed out on Humphrey?" Audrey asked.

"Yeah," said Aaron, "and SDS jumped right in."

"I'm more inclined," Jake said, "to go along with BUS than SDS."

"Why's that?" Steve asked.

"Because the blacks have a real gripe about civil rights. This is only an impression, but the SDSers seem like spoiled brats who can't get their way."

"But what about the war?" Audrey spoke up. "Isn't that a real gripe?"

"It is. But I have a feeling SDS would be raising hell even if peace were declared tomorrow. Just an impression from how they present themselves. And the way Mark Rudd talked. They're using the war for something much larger."

"What do you mean?" asked Naomi.

"How he mutilated the English language, and..."

"That's because you're an English teacher," Steve said. "You're prejudiced."

The little group laughed.

"Quite right, Steve, but Rudd confessed that SDS wasn't aiming at taking over the country, but at radicalization, at making people think. They jumped on the Columbia gym project the way our activists jumped on the Oakland recruiters last Monday."

"Have you been to SDS headquarters, over at the Haunted House?" Audrey asked.

"No. Have you?"

"Aaron and I go over there sometimes. It's a blast actually, all kinds of weirdoes running around, sliding down banisters, a keg always open, a lot of hot arguments, even fights, visitors coming and going. Holly makes good food, though. Mark Rudd stayed there."

"What do you think about all this, Steve?" Aaron asked.

"I understand being against the war. But why not trust the government? I mean how do these radicals know more than the president and the military?"

"But I notice you haven't joined the army," Aaron said wryly.

"Because I wanna play baseball. But I'd like to understand what's going on. Most of the guys in my frat don't have a clue and don't want to. Just party and duck the draft."

Onward the conversation went, Audrey and Aaron taking the opportunity to inform Steve of the politics of world domination and Naomi meekly listening as if having sought in this little huddle merely a place of relative intellectual calm.

Jake listened too. Audrey and Aaron knew their stuff and presented it logically and accurately. Steve, clearly hearing the case in detail for the first time, asked questions, didn't argue.

"I didn't know much about any of this," the baseball star said.

"Me either," echoed Naomi.

"Anyway," Audrey said. "I completely agree with the *Stater* editorial today that White blew this whole BUS thing. First he came out all big about law and order. Then he backed down. In their backrooms he and Matson found a way out – 'not enough evidence to prosecute.' And he's calling in the Civil Rights Commission to study racism here. They'll find a lot of it too. White backed down, gave BUS what they wanted, amnesty. And now the campus is buzzing about the issues. Chalk one up for the good guys. The blacks are coming back tomorrow, and Aaron and I will be at the front gate to greet them."

"Yeah," Aaron chimed in, "there's a prof in the Soc department, Jonah Levitt, that canceled all his classes until the blacks come back. Why didn't you do that, Mr. Ernst?"

"Because I'm only a TA not a professor with tenure, and I'm being paid to teach your class. You know the attendance policy. It gives you some days off if you want to take them. But don't you think civil disobedience requires a penalty? If you break the law or the Code of Conduct, you should expect to pay for it, shouldn't you?"

"I guess so," Aaron said glumly.

"So," Audrey said, "you think they shouldn't get amnesty?"

"Like the president said in his comments, there's no need for amnesty if there's no evidence of a violation. It's a neat little package the administration has come up with to solve their problem."

"Even though anyone with any brains can see right through it?" Audrey asked. "They can't have all the Negroes leave the university, can they?"

"No," Jake said, "they can't. They'd probably be happy to let the SDSers go, but not the blacks."

At quarter after four he finally had to end the session, at which time Steve and Aaron returned the pilfered chairs to the offices next door. The group agreed to meet again next week.

But will I still be working here? Wettman must be filling his notebooks on the black exodus.

Thursday, November 21, next day …

After his weekly meeting with the new TA's, Jake took a detour from his schedule to walk over to the Administration Building along with Adele. The returning blacks were greeted not only with cheers and tears but with a sudden burst of sunshine from behind the clouds that had been covering the area for over a week. The victors had returned. Jake spotted Ella on the steps of the building, ebullient, now with an evident afro. She was dancing, both fists in the air, and exchanging hugs among the victorious group.

Jake and Adele listened to a black dean explain that these self-exiled students would be part of an "experiment in democracy." They would create a new atmosphere of communication and understanding on campus. Neither Matson nor White were in attendance, however. Adele was in tears. Jake held her close. Not a shred of doubt existed in his mind that blacks on campus had been an unheard-from and ignored minority. Clearly, their status had changed. Lesson? Well-managed protest works.

"Last spring I had a black officemate," Jake said to Adele, who leaned against him, teary-eyed.

"Ella."

"She told me BUS was merely biding their time, waiting for the right moment to strike. She said it would be something big."

"Damn big," Adele answered. "This is beautiful, one of the most beautiful things I've ever seen. Now we all have hope that the university will develop a conscience. They finally did the right thing. But White should be out here. Why does he hide from real student contact? Matson should be here too, eating a little crow."

"They probably want a black administrator to manage things."

"But they need to show their hearts as well as their negotiating expertise, show their desire to genuinely connect with their students rather than appeasing them. And wait and see, the Oakland recruiters, if they're brave enough, will be back again next quarter. That's where White's real test will happen. He's granted amnesty but said nothing about the recruiting policy."

Jake saw Audrey and Aaron in the crowd, waved to them. Beaming in the sunlight, they waved back.

"Why aren't we with Goldenrod out here," Adele asked, "playing 'When Johnny Comes Marching Home'?"

Saturday, November 23, two days later ...

Jake and Tasha lay in her bed. They'd been to see *West Side Story* at the Kent Theater, come back to her place, showered together and made love, which they did at least once every day, sometimes twice. Their sex was prolonged, varied, imaginative, never routine. And moments like this, lying in each other's arms afterwards, silent, fulfilled, unified, were the best moments Jake had ever known.

"Somewhere there's a place for us," he whispered, echoing Tony and Maria's song.

She answered by edging closer against him.

"Thanksgiving break," he said. "We both have a few days. Why don't you come home with me, meet my parents?"

"I can't. Have to go to Akron to see mine."

The candle flickered out, leaving them in darkness.

"Anyway, I'm not ready for that. And I'd invite you home, but my parents aren't ready for that either. I like us right exactly where we are, here in our hideaway."

"We can't stay here forever," Jake said.

"Oh, how I wish we could! I've never known anything more perfect."

A flash of worry surged through him. In spite of the hopeful breakthrough for campus blacks, the world outside this room was anything but perfect. After a while her breathing told him she was asleep. Their relationship was boxed in. There was his impending arrest. And her parents' pro-Ray attitude, still mourning the breakup, bearing the humiliation of the terminated wedding, not about to warm up to someone like Jake. And there was Tasha's reluctance to burst into another life. Jake fretted that he may be merely a kind of tranquilizer for her, rather than a future.

In contrast, he saw her as his route to a solid family life. He longed to be out in the open, not slinking around trying to avoid a stalking Ray, not to mention his own hesitancy to speak of Tasha with his mom and dad.

He pondered, longed for the day Tasha and he could be a couple in the most mundane, bourgeois sense. What will occur to set them free?

Then came the dark note of his being about to lose his physical freedom. He decided that since he and Tasha were about to separate for the holiday, he should head home by himself. It had been over a year since he'd been there, and his parents should know his present status with the government. About Tasha, he would be tightlipped, though. He wasn't sure enough about her to worry his mother, who had endured enough pain from his broken romances. And he needed to talk to his dad about getting another car. He'd been holding on to the MGA only out of sentimentality for its having been a gift from his father.

Sunday, December 1, a week later ...

In the gloom of evening after six, after a long drive back from Pennsylvania, Jake pulled into the driveway in a '65 brown and beige Volkswagen camper, freshly tuned up by him and his dad in his dad's shop. Though it lacked the stylish appeal of his sports car, it was the epitome of practicality and utility. He imagined all kinds of private getaways with the woman he loved. Among the wondrous features also was the rear mounted engine which made it grip in the snow and rain. Jake's dad would sell the MGA and send Jake the proceeds. Tasha's decrepit Rambler was not in the driveway, however.

He grabbed his duffle bag, took the junk mail from his mailbox and climbed the stairs. When he opened his door, he found an envelope on the floor, his name written in Tasha's graceful penmanship. He knew immediately that this was not good. He picked it up and backed out, sitting down on the top step and staring at the envelope. Finally he tore off an edge and pulled the letter out. It was handwritten, four pages front and back in lavender ink certainly from the fountain pen she cherished, a college graduation gift from her dad.

As he read through the pages his heart shriveled and his head drooped more and more. In sum: she'd moved in with Ray. In sum: Ray needed her, Jake did not. Not that Jake wouldn't be devastated, she'd written, but he would survive. Ray, in sum, would not. He'd actually been at her home in Akron to greet her return, waiting with her parents. In sum: she would miss Jake more than she could express but under the relentless pressure of the long weekend her "duty" had been made clear to her. She'd finally surrendered to her "fate." She couldn't bear seeing Jake, telling him face to face, would falter, collapse into his "strong, tender" arms.

That very day, as he'd driven the Pennsylvania Turnpike filled with the anticipation of seeing her again, she, Ray, and her parents had helped her move to a little house at Twin Lakes, her folks relenting to accept their daughter cohabitating with her fiancé before their marriage on New Year's Day. That's right, their marriage.

Jake sat on the landing, her letter in his hand. He wanted to cry out in anguish. He wanted to bellow his hurt. Instead, he stumbled to his van and headed across the river and out Mantua toward Twin Lakes. He drove over several off-roads until he saw her Nash and Ray's Camaro side by side in front of a small clapboard house. Sitting in the VW, he stared at the lighted windows veined by the shadows of bare branches. Tasha, there, inside. But gone from him. Could the adjacent cars be more definite?

He remembered the words she'd written: *Please don't seek me out, dear Jake. Please don't. No scenes, I beg you. It will be no use, no use at all. What I am doing is the right thing, maybe not the happy thing, but the right one. I am where I belong. But never, ever, for all of your life, which I know will be a great one, no, never, ever doubt I love you and that I will never love anyone the way I love you.*

Then had come the I'll never forget the wonderful, transcendent times, etc., more God-damned *etcetera*, growing more and more impossible to read through his blurred vision.

Now he sat there in snow flurries, engine running, soon bound to draw attention from the picturesque bungalow. He'd vowed to fight if this happened to him again. But how could he fight something that appeared so final? She and Ray must have slept together, maybe were in bed at that exact moment.

With that image in his swirling mind, he knew there'd be no winning her back. The image flashed, a bullet through the brain. Tasha was gone. On his way back toward Kent, he pulled into the lakeside lot of a darkened tavern, got out, stared across the black water, snowflakes falling all around. Then he let out his bawl of torment like a mortally wounded mammoth howling across the universe.

LOVE and WAR at KENT STATE

PART THREE: 1969
A Seething Cauldron

38

Tuesday, January 21, seven weeks later ...

Headed home from the library in a frigid, depressing dusk, Jake walked quickly but carefully on the icy sidewalks along Willow Street. Three things had sustained him through his rancorous, heart-torn grief at Tasha's abandonment: his teaching, his studies and his music. Though Tasha had practiced her recorder, even rehearsed with the group, she'd never played in public with Goldenrod. But the foursome was gaining notoriety, and the obligation to perform on stage and to teach his freshmen, provided the sustenance he needed to survive the emotional depths of losing the one he'd felt sure would be the "inevitable" purpose of his life. *Inevitable*—what a joke! So far, at least, he'd plodded along as he was now doing in the bitter cold that had frozen northeastern Ohio almost to a standstill.

Yesterday in the Student Union he'd watched Nixon's inauguration speech on NBC. Though he felt the monumental hypocrisy of the new president's words, of his quoting Archibald MacLeish, one of Jake's favorite poets, Jake had held himself back from joining the futile chorus of boos erupting from the Kent student audience in the packed cafeteria. Virtually everyone in the room understood that Tricky Dick's appeal to Ho Chi Min for peace was merely a demand for surrender—submit to us and the war will end. And the students knew also that the nation's new president's solicitation for a quieting of voices so that "words" could be heard simply constituted his wish for dissidents to shut the hell up.

Now, only what Jake saw as his duties kept him on track. How he could ever be happy again, he could not fathom. Strong in his mind was the possibility of retreat to his father's land, tilling the soil and repairing machinery,

208

work of the hands, labor of his forbearers, honorable and eternal. But for the next year or so, there was toil of a different sort to be done here in this frozen little town on this troubled little campus. Not one to desert his responsibilities, he" decided to plod onward to the completion of his program.

And besides, he might be arrested at any time. What was taking so long? Odd, but he almost wished for the relief prison might bring.

As it happened this frozen evening, he reached the steps of his house at the same moment as Billy Kaplan, his rarely encountered downstairs neighbor, bicycle rider and reporter for the local daily paper published over in Ravenna. A wiry, dark haired, constantly in motion man about Jake's age, Billy seemed always on the go, early mornings and late nights. From articles in the *Courier*, Jake deduced that Billy's job was to cover KSU sports. He'd done extensive articles on Thurman Munson, both while the baseball star was at Kent and when he'd put on the pinstripes. He'd even interviewed Jake about Thurman as a freshman writing student, requesting some of his essays. Jake had explained that student essays were always returned to their authors and that Billy would have to get them from Thurman himself. Billy had talked to Jake about Steve Stone as well.

"Hey, Jake," Billy said this present evening inside the chilly vestibule of the house they shared. "I gotta talk to you. Join me for a minute, okay?"

Hardly in the mood for his neighbor's frenetic personality, Jake searched for an excuse. Noticing the hesitation, Billy added, "Come on, man, only a minute." He held the door of his apartment wide open and gestured grandly for Jake to enter.

The place was a maelstrom of papers and folders, stacks of newspapers, black and white sports photos tacked all over the walls, and the stink of cigarettes, overflowing ashtrays at various strategic spots.

"Ditch the coat for a minute," Billy said, wiping some papers from an easy chair and turning his desk chair around. "Have a seat."

"What's up?" Jake said, remaining by the door in his coat.

"Okay, okay. You're in a hurry, I get it. No problem, Jake. But things are heating up on campus ever since the BUS Walkout, y'know, sure you noticed. I'd like to get your view of things. My boss wants me to start gettin' in on stuff like that. Saw one of the English profs got arrested at the inauguration parade in D.C. yesterday, Drew Byrne. You know the guy?"

"Not really. Took a course from him my first term here."

"A real radical, huh?"

"Pretty much."

"A lotta that type in the English Department, huh?"

"Like every department."

"Yeah, especially Soc, don't even need to mention PolySci, Christ Almighty! Come on, take your coat off, have a seat. I'll heat up some coffee. Hope you like it two days old. Gotta age it, you know, like fine vino."

"I have work."

Billy's coat was draped on the sofa, its owner lighting a Camel.

"Okay, okay, sure you have work, but, hey man, what's your stand on things?"

"Against the war, that's about it. Keeping my nose to the grindstone."

"Yeah, yeah, probably smart. Okay, okay, look, I know you're busy, but sometime when you have a minute, can we rap? Hey, you know, off the record, deep background, right? You hear the whispering, hell, man, even the shouts, around Satterfield, right? Maybe you hear things the public might oughtta know, help your cause. Think about it, okay? Slide a note under my door if you'd like to share, strictly anonymous."

"I don't know about that," Jake said backing into the vestibule.

"Okay, okay. Hey, what happened to the French chick lived up upstairs with you?"

"Moved out. Got married."

"Man, I thought you two were like that." He crossed his fingers.

"No. Only friends."

"Yeah, right. I'd like a friend like her. Okay, okay, see you're trying to escape. I won't bug you, but I'm outta my league covering this political shit, prefer the hardwood, the wrestling mats, volleyball court. You could help me out with the intellectual stuff. Yeah, yeah, you're antsy, I get it. Have a nice evening."

"You too, Bill."

"Hey, call me Billy. Everybody does." He started lighting another cigarette with the former one.

The guy reminded Jake of Ratso from *Midnight Cowboy*.

Jake pulled the door closed and headed up the stairs, now sweating beneath his eiderdown parka. In his place he wearily took it off along with his wool cap, sat down, untied his boots, kicked them off, and leaned back in the dim light of his living room.

Deep background, eh? Hmm.

Billy was right about things heating up, but not, it seemed to Jake, doing so in a bad way. *Opening up*, might be a better phrase. The Human Relations Committee started a program of films and discussions in residence hall areas featuring race relations, even though the first film created such an emotional reaction from the black panel that further films were cancelled. But it was an attempt, at least. A Great Contemporary Issues course was in progress which included classes with separate BUS and SDS panels. A Soc prof was under strong heat from blacks because he said in class that some possibility would be "as absurd as his kissing a Ubangi on the lips." He helplessly failed in his attempt to defend the comparison.

Columns had been opened up in the *Daily Stater* for SDS and for one called "Basic Black" by a black student writer named Lafayette Tolliver. *Don't try to "help" blacks*, he advised his white readers, *try to "understand" them; and don't call them Negroes or refer to their communities as "ghettos."* Also, student government was working on ways to make themselves more relevant regarding administration policy, even suggesting student representation on the Board of Trustees.

It all seemed to Jake as if the BUS walkout had garnered some positive results and that the administration was learning lessons and making useful concessions, yes, after the fact, but better late than never. So as far as tidbits to whisper to Billy Kaplan, Jake had none.

But wait a minute. Maybe there was one. Yes, the Bo Wettman issue, congressional spies sneaking around campus intimidating people into reporting local political events. What harm would Jake suffer at revealing such activity? How would public knowledge of Wettman's presence affect the campus? Exposing the slimy weasel might actually be one slight pleasure in a now pleasureless existence.

39

Saturday, March 1, five weeks later …

Late in the afternoon after Goldenrod's performance in the talent show of the weekend's folk festival, Jake felt exuberant, their having rocked the house with "I'll Fly Away," everyone in the auditorium on their feet singing along. He hugged Adele, then Henry, and finally Wash, all embracing each other in turn. Later that night there would be a vote by judges Judy Collins and Doc Watson, who would hand out the prizes. A lone fellow named Gordon Lightfoot and a group named the New Lost City Ramblers featuring Pete Seeger's brother, would perform with Collins and Watson in the evening show. Meanwhile, Goldenrod packed up their gear and headed for their separate abodes to clean up and revel in their success.

When Jake was undressing for a shower, he heard a light knock on his door. Knotting the sash on his bathrobe, he opened up and gasped at the sight. There stood Natasha!

His heart skipped the proverbial beat, three or four perhaps. She gazed up at him with watery blue eyes.

"May … may I come in?"

Door opened wide, he stood back. She moved past him with her long-familiar scent.

"I saw your show, followed you here ... like a stalker. You have a new car."

"Take off your coat and hat, have a seat."

She handed her things to him and he put them over the arm of the sofa.

"Wouldn't happen to have anything to drink, would you?" she asked. "Like some Thunderbird." She smiled meekly.

Jake was taken aback at her reference to their former intimacy.

"Budweiser is all."

"Anything will do fine."

While she settled on his sofa he poured beer into tumblers and, hands shaking a bit, went back and handed her one. He sat on the easy chair, not knowing what to say next. She took a few deep swallows of brew.

"I guess you're wondering why I'm here," she said.

"You guess right."

"The show was great. They didn't want that last number to end."

"Yeah, it felt pretty good."

"You've developed your stage presence. I love the cap. Really cool."

"Uh, where's Ray?"

"His weekend with the Guard."

"Hasn't gone fulltime?"

"He hasn't lost hope, though."

After an awkward silence, she said, "I had to see you, Jake. At first I was only going to watch you on stage and leave, but..."

"You should finish your sentences, Tasha."

She smiled. "Finishing that one will take some courage."

Looking into her tear-filled eyes, he waited.

"Seeing you up there brought everything back." She gave him an odd look and burst into sobs.

He waited a moment, then went to the sofa, sat beside her. She leaned into his arms and wept. He held her, feelings rushing into his head and heart. But he had no idea what to do. He hugged her as he might have hugged a child.

"Oh, my God, Jake," she said into his chest. "What did I do?"

He had no answer, wasn't exactly sure of her question, kept holding her with swirling emotions.

"I'm so sorry, so sorry," she went on.

He still couldn't find words. Finally, she seemed to settle, backed away, looked into his eyes.

"I must look a fright."

"Not at all," Jake said. "I'm blown away that you're here."

"Not mad?"

"Not mad. But confused."

"I'm about to confuse you more, Jake."

"Meaning?"

"Will you take me to bed? Can we, please?"

He felt an immediate surge in his bloodstream. In spite of his shock, his body was answering her desperate question.

He tilted her head upward and crushed his lips against hers. No time for thought, no time for questions. She was there, her hands on him, their mouths searching, tasting of beer, clothing being frantically undone. He lifted her, carried her to the bedroom, pulled off her remaining garments, shed his and took her like a beast. For him it was a combination of vengeance, wild confusion, and pure love, no mercy, a famished lion gorging on red meat. She moaned, cried out, but he barely heard her. He was only taking what he felt was rightfully his, and he went on and on, turning her, letting her on top, ravishing her in every way he knew. Finally, he let himself explode, inside her, on her belly, her breasts, her cheeks, her avid mouth.

He held above her as if he'd conquered not someone, but some*thing*. A force. A law of nature.

He sank beside her, held her quivering body, heard her weeping, felt her breath on his neck, her sweat against his chest, her wet on his thigh. She was his again. That was all that mattered.

They lay in the darkness, their nakedness covered by a sheet and comforter against the chill. Yes, it seemed that she was his again. As if she were there to stay. She stirred, groaned, stretched against him.

"What time is it?" she asked.

The luminous dial of his clock showed past eight pm. He suddenly realized the evening show was starting, the Lightfoot guy, over in the auditorium. The group would be there waiting for Jake because they might receive an award.

"I have to go," Tasha said. "That was exactly what I needed."

"You're leaving?"

"I have to, Jake. I have a thing with my neighbors, pinochle, drinks; they're worrywarts, assigned to watch over me when Ray is gone."

"But..."

"I didn't think I was coming over here tonight, darling Jake. I couldn't stop myself. Thought about calling you so many times."

"Stay. Don't ever go back."

"I can't. Don't ask."

Jake took a breath, sat up, reality having slugged him dizzy.

"You mean..?"

"I understand you must be confused. No one is more confused than I." She draped herself over his back, kissed his neck. "I'm sorry. I shouldn't have come."

"Of course you should. I was hoping that..."

"What else *could* you have thought, Jake? It's my fault. I'm in the most terrible bind I could ever have imagined. But I really have to go. Joe and Betty have become my guardians when Ray is away, they're having friends over, expecting me. They'll start phoning hospitals if I'm not there."

"Call them. We need to talk."

She reached across him and turned on the bed stand light, sat up, found her bra and put it on.

"I need to think this out," she said. "I'm as shocked as you. I wasn't thinking, only feeling. Give me some time, Jake. I'll be in touch, I promise."

Who is this person?

But he saw her intention to leave, now fully clothed, headed for the bathroom. The door closed, water ran, the toilet flushed, silence. He breathed, steamed, sat up. She came out, hair combed, new lipstick.

"Do you think I'm a whore, Jake?"

"No. But..."

"I don't know what I am. I need to think. I'll be in touch, I promise. But I've got to go, really I do, as much as I'd like to stay with you forever. Okay?"

In abject shock, Jake stood naked, said nothing.

"Don't look at me like that, Jake. You'll break my heart. Let me go for now, please?" She stared at him, came across the room, put her arms around his waist, held him as he stood unresponsive. "Say 'okay,' Jake, please."

"It's not okay, Tasha."

"I know it's not, but say it, I beg you. Believe me, darling, I must go."

"Then go."

She sighed, squeezed his buttocks, backed away.

"But if I call, or write, please tell me you'll answer."

"I'll answer."

"I'm sorry, Jake, sorry." And she was gone.

He stood as still as one of those mutilated marble Greek figures in a museum. Finally he shivered, glanced at the clock, 8:40. Judy Collins would be handing out the awards at nine. He supposed he should be there.

40

Tuesday, March 11, ten days later ...

Still consumed by Tasha's dreamlike reemergence into his life and by her nightmarish re-disappearance, Jake took the long, bitter, wind-in-his-face march up Summit Road, over the rise and down to Satterfield. Under his parka he was sweating when he arrived in his office, having picked up a cup of coffee and a letter envelope with Dr. Shenk's return address, the note inside requesting an immediate, eight am, meeting. Jake hung up his coat and with his coffee went directly down the hall to the Rhetoric & Composition suite. Nan, Shenk's secretary, smelling of lilac, smiled up from above the rims of her glasses.

"Go right in, Jake. He's waiting."

Shenk rose, his thick silver hair slicked back, reading glasses low on his nose.

"Close the door and sit."

Jake did as instructed.

"Thanks for coming promptly."

"No problem, sir."

"It's the Ferguson thing. I assume since the lad is one of your freshmen, you've been following the case."

"Yes. It's clear he's been singled out because of his political views."

"Is it?"

"The same supposedly obscene word used in the flier he passed out was in our own student literary journal. No one in the Department was arrested for using it there."

"In our literary journal, you say?"

"You didn't know?"

"God, forbid. This place is becoming a madhouse of contradictions. Did you read this morning's *Stater*?"

"Not yet, came right here as soon as I opened your note." He sipped his coffee.

"All hell is breaking loose. Over the weekend someone tried to burn down West Hall, I'm sure you heard?"

"No. I've been concentrating on my research. West Hall? ROTC?"

"No, the damned art building next to ROTC. One of those decrepit World War Two barracks that should have been torn down years ago. Admin keeps saying all four of those eyesores will be replaced, but never do it. You *are* aware that the art students have been up in arms about the inadequacy of their facilities, are you not?"

"Vaguely. As I said, I've been..."

"Yes, everyone was lauding them for their 'peaceful' protests, now they up and attempt to incinerate their own building! Anyway, that aside, it's the Ferguson thing I called you over here for. What kind of student is he?"

"Militant, erratic in his writings, spouting slogans, but better than most."

"You don't happen to have any of his essays, do you?"

"No. Handed the last one back. Gave it a B minus."

The professor huffed. "I was hoping you'd have one, dammit."

Jake sipped again, waited as Shenk shifted in his squeaky leather chair.

"Jake, Security has approached me, wants whatever we have on the boy, seem to think he's been planted here by SDS on a mission, part of a national conspiracy. Ah, whatever. Too bad you don't have anything tangible as evidence. Would you be averse to passing his next paper on to me?"

"A bit averse, yes, if it's for security purposes. I emphasize that their essays should be related to the stories in the anthology, and he does that. He has a right to his stands on issues, doesn't he?"

"You embarrass me with such a question, Jake. But these are increasingly troubled times. This boy supposedly has a subversive purpose on our campus, a plant. Outsiders come in and out of here, agitating, conferring with our colony of troublemakers, and now apparently infiltrating our academic programs. Holly McGill and a few others are well-ensconced in our department, and PolySci is a snake pit of radicals, not to mention some actual faculty members over in Soc. You undoubtedly saw how they all attached themselves to the coattails of BUS. They're hell bent on tearing down the university. The Ferguson boy may be only a freshman, but he's right in there with them."

Shenk tapped his fingers on his desk like a bongo player.

"So," Jake said, "I'm right about them singling him out for distributing the flier, arresting him for ostensibly for obscenity."

"Admin is intent on ridding the campus of this element before..."

Jake waited.

"Before there's another incident like the BUS walkout."

"Excuse me," Jake said, "but from my vantage point it seems that Admin deals with issues long after the fact. BUS had legitimate complaints. I have yet to see an African American in one of my classes. Blacks had been seriously ignored until they caused a disturbance. Then they were granted amnesty, and now all kinds of programs have been incorporated. What Admin's approach seems to be telling everyone around here is that agitation works wonders."

Shenk yanked a pipe out of a circular rack, pulled a tin of tobacco from a drawer, and began the process of lighting up.

"So, Jake, not that it matters, but out of curiosity, from your vantage point, what approach would *you* propose Admin to take?"

"Sir, looking from the bottom up, I'd say two things. First, they should get ahead of the curve by dealing with legitimate sticking points before those points rise to the level of demands scrawled on placards. It's not hard to see that a sizeable number of our student body opposes the war and that they believe the university supports the National Administration."

"That is patently absurd. We serve members of the whole spectrum of views. It is not the university's role to take official stands on controversial issues."

"Maybe not, but the students think Admin has taken such a stand. So someone should talk to the kids about it. If it's absurd, why not present the university's point of view. Come out and talk, face to face. Make an intellectual argument about the university's neutrality rather than waiting for things to blow up then arresting people, only causing more furor."

Shenk took a puff. "I can see you've given this some thought. Please continue."

"Some thought, yes. Admin should sponsor occasions for a deep discussion of the issues, give legitimacy to student concerns on a serious scholarly level, even without taking an official stand. Hell, they should explain why they can't and shouldn't take official stands. They should be stealing the leadership on these issues away from the radicals. Lifestyle issues also, lines of communication, like the efficacy of student government, student voices in the matters students are concerned with."

"Yes, yes, but that's not what we're all about," Shenk said dismissively, puffing on his pipe. "Go ahead then with your second point."

"Sir, as I see these kids, the overwhelming majority of them are against the war but are moderate about their views."

"Let us be honest here. You and I both know they simply don't want to interrupt their fun-filled lives to serve their country."

"Okay, maybe, but they're not revolutionaries. Sure, some may question our foreign policy, but..."

"They know nothing, less than nothing, about our foreign policy."

"Maybe that's true of many of them. But if they don't, they should. Thing is, sir, there is no voice for the moderates, no place for them to find out what the issues are about. Either it's the SDS types calling for rallies, or Admin emphasizing that violators of the Code of Conduct will be punished. The moderates have no one to talk to, nowhere to go. The hardcore types know these kids are vulnerable to radicalization and are hard at work to garner their support. Incidents that unmask the intractability of faculty and Admin, like in Bobby Ferguson's case, are the very means to bring moderates to their side. They learn that the way to change things is to raise hell. They see that the administration's strategy is to openly go after dissidents in a country that touts freedom of speech and assembly. There is no effort to keep them moderate, to provide rational discussion. Admin needs to tell them that objection to the war is not an unreasonable position given the history involved and that by working within the system, policies can be changed. Give dissenters respect instead of shoving them off to the dangerous fringes. Keep the moderates moderate."

The room, now filled with clouds of cherry blend smoke, had the addition of Jake's flurry of rhetoric. Shenk held the bowl of his pipe, the stem close to his lips.

"All right, Jake. We're not going to solve the world's problems here. The university doesn't exist to manage international affairs or to provide pathways to indoctrinate students' political ideas and/or methodology."

"What *does* it exist for?" Jake asked.

Shenk checked his watch, took a meditative puff.

"Thank you for dropping by, Jake. I didn't mean this little chat to become a philosophical diatribe on higher education's role in our society. Only to check on this lad Ferguson. I'm afraid I must insist, indeed require, that you show me his future class essays. That will be all for now."

Bobby Ferguson, freshman, long curly blond hair bursting out of his head like fireworks, wearing military attire fashionable among activists, serious blue eyes staring at Jake in class as if waiting for something and not getting it. He had been arrested for passing out pamphlets in the Union promoting a leftwing film called *Garbage*. The missive contained the word *motherfuckers*. Though Dean Matson had approved showing the film, he denied having seen the leaflet. Student government passed a unanimous resolution against the lad's arrest by citing the exact same word in the English Department's literary magazine, which had gone unpunished. A group from the Student Senate took copies of the resolution to the campus police department and shouted the bad word repeatedly. No one was arrested. Yet Admin persisted in charges against young Ferguson so that even the Akron chapter of the ACLU opened an office in Kent in order to provide a defense for the youthful activist. Now Admin was apparently claiming the kid had been strategically planted by the national headquarters of SDS as a fulltime student in order to create further unrest at generally apathetic KSU.

For Jake, still committed to keeping his head down according to his dad's wise advice, the sum of all this tempest in a teapot was that he'd been ordered by his boss to violate the kid's privacy, the lad currently out on bail, by sharing his classroom work with campus security. God-damned shit!

Meanwhile, art students had apparently set fire to their own building!

On the way back to his office Jake grabbed the morning *Stater* from a pile on a bench. In the midst of updating himself on the weekend's and Monday's goings-on (the paper published only Tuesday through Friday), he found a *Stater* editorial objecting to the conflagration as a means of protest and even suggesting that an SDS type might have used the art students' theretofore peaceful protest activities as a way of creating trouble. Whoever set the fire, however, the building was now unusable, many supplies and art creations destroyed. The controversy had been ignited by the Art Department's designated funds for a new building having been transferred to the Business Department, apparently without debate with the art faculty and student body.

None of it had a whit to do with the nation's foreign policy, but now the art community was well on its way to being politically radicalized.

Jake read all this and, added to his frustrating conference with Shenk, felt a simmering rage himself.

And sweeping like a riptide beneath this rage surged his feelings for Natasha.

Natasha. His Tasha. She'd come back to him, needing him, she said, then fled to a card game. No explanation, thinking he must necessarily regard her as a whore. How *did* he regard her? Good question. Certainly not as a whore. But as someone he loved with his whole being and who was surely in trouble. So much trouble she was not using her head. And he worried about how she'd guzzled that Budweiser. As he thought about that point, he remembered there had always been wine around, with dinner, with their flirtations, with their sex games. It didn't seem odd at the time, not as if it was a problem, yet it had always been there.

But worse, far worse, was that she'd hardly noticed him as a person, someone with feelings, someone she loved. He seemed much more like a mere function to satisfy her sexual craving. Ten minutes of talk, two hours of vigorous sex, a five minute escape. Not a word more about it, ten more days of brutal silence.

Didn't she know the cruelty of that? Didn't she care? Used him as a mere utility? Could that be possible? It only signified the depth of trouble she was in. And if it had built up to her surprise appearance once, it would surely happen again. Wouldn't it? And when it did, what then? A repeat performance? Hadn't he been equally desperate? Maybe even more so? Had he put the brakes on? No. Had he said, "Hey, girl, slow down, let's talk this out?" No. Instead, he unloaded every milligram of his own frustration upon her, inside her. Was it a harbinger of their relationship becoming an occasional stolen few hours of sexual release?

Not if he could help it. He needed her. He'd staked everything on his love for her. He no longer controlled his own happiness. Couldn't imagine ever being happy again without her. It had been a conscious choice, a gift of his heart to her. And now his heart lay in her hands, and his future wellbeing depended upon how she handled it. So far not well. Her visit was a cry for help. Now his mission had to be how to provide that help. He knew she was miserable, suffering, captured. She needed rescue. But how, dammit, how?

With all this swirling in his brain, Jake heard a knock on his open office door followed by the entrance of, who else?—Wettman. Here to make the arrest, most likely. Without a word he leisurely pulled off his fedora, his scarf and coat, hung them on the rack then took a seat in front of Jake's desk.

"Should I pack my things?" Jake asked.

Wettman smiled. "Relax, my fine feathered friend."

"So what do you want?"

"Got any of those cups I left here for ashtrays?"

Jake pulled out a lower drawer and handed him one.

"Thanks, heaps," Wettman said, lighting a Lucky with his Nixon lighter, inhaling, leaning back.

"Dropped by for a smoke?" Jake asked.

"Ernst, our relationship needn't be combative. But I want to continue our discussion."

"Wasn't I clear? Go ahead, pull out the damn cuffs."

"Easy, fellow. Chill out. Jesus. You get up on the wrong side of the bed today?"

"What do you want?"

"Thought you should have a heads up."

"About?"

"Some heavy shit is about to come down. Thought you oughtta know. Maybe you'll change your view about some important things."

"I don't really care."

"Yeah, I noticed your fox of a girlfriend moved out and got hitched. Could she be why you're in such a surly frame of mind?"

"Get to the point, Wettman?"

"Call me Bo. Okay, here's the scoop, hold on to your hat. You've heard about SDS's big national 'spring offensive,' right? They've got big plans here at Kent. And we've got plans too. I'll tell you this, Ernst, in strictest confidence. You should know that some of the loudest voices around here are, get this, they are working for us."

"I don't need to know any of this. You don't have me over a barrel any more. Go ahead and arrest me."

"Here's the thing. There's going to be trouble. It's going to start with an attack on the Administration Building about getting ROTC off campus, but they're going to push it much farther than usual. There will be broken noses, arrests. It won't be pretty. That's exactly how we want it to be. SDS is desperate for such an incident as part of the national game plan, and they're playing right into our hands."

Jake shifted uneasily, raked both hands through his hair.

"What's it have to do with me?"

"That's for you to decide."

"Meaning?"

"We want you to understand what's happening."

"Why? And what *is* happening?"

"Ah, I'm glad you're curious." He took a deep drag on his Lucky.

"I'm not curious, just confused."

"Okay, listen up. A shit storm is coming this way. Observe it. Take deep whiffs of it. Keep your eyes and ears open. Then decide where you really stand. The key SDS players in all this are with us, not with the enemy. That's all you need to know. We've infiltrated SDS on this campus. That's right, we're cozily ensconced in the so-called Haunted House. And we're going to make arrests, some of our people among them. Stay in the background. Don't become actively involved. Get it?"

"No."

"If it can happen here, there is no place safe from these shitheads. We've had a good start with the Humphrey walkout, then again with the Oakland P.D. A perfect beginning, not part of our plans but eminently useful, so we joined the dance. The blacks are oblivious to us. We're merely riding the tidal wave they started. We want this sleepy little backwoods nowheresville to explode onto the front pages. And unlike the blacks, certain key SDSers here are well-aware of the plan. Got it now?"

"Okay, I suppose this *is* volatile information. I don't get why you're telling me."

"Like I say, a heads up. We understand that you're not with us, but that may be temporary. Pay attention. When the dust settles, we'll talk again. All right?"

"No. Put me in jail. I'm not with you and never will be."

"Right, right. I understand you, better than you do yourself. So let's play it by ear. Hey, it's been nice chatting, but I'm afraid I have a few more meetings on my docket."

Wettman crushed out his cigarette, took his things, and strolled out of the office.

Weird. Why the hell would he reveal all this to someone who's clearly against him? Local SDS infiltrated at high levels by federal informants? What's to keep me from strolling over to Taylor Hall and spilling the beans to the Stater? Is Wettman a fool, or does he have that exact prospect in mind?

41

Sunday, March 23, Spring Break, two weeks later . . .

Jake sat at a window table in the library, looking at the barren pre-spring lawn of front campus. With his many worries he'd been using all his power of concentration to fulfill his duties. He had two term papers to complete, a stack of compositions to grade, heartbreak and concerns about the woman he loved, and the huge confusion from Wettman's visits. Whatever was supposed to happen on campus hadn't yet occurred, so maybe Wettman was simply all wet, merely toying with him for his own demented need to hold power over people.

But Jake had time to thoughtfully consider Wettman's contentions, and they began to make sense in an incredible way. Foment violence at a former teacher's college in the middle of nowhere to scare the general public into accepting a national law and order crackdown. Supreme Court Justice Arthur Goldberg had spoken on campus in February, emphasizing that the need for law and order is basic in any society. He disparaged its seeming lapse in America. There lay the theme. Next comes a disruption at secluded Kent State, not Berkeley, not Columbia or Harvard, but out here in the heartland. Now all of America is scared of these anarchists. Finally comes the crackdown – arrests, prison sentences, manipulation of public opinion. Okay. But how does Wettman see Jake being involved? Why let him in on this secret strategy? It makes no sense. No sense at all.

Whatever – a word receiving active use in Jake's vocabulary. Like, *what the fuck*! His life had swirled out of his control.

In the mostly empty library he forced his mind onto articles about *For Whom the Bell Tolls*, the excruciatingly slow march toward Robert Jordan's inevitable death. With the close of the library at five, he trod the two blocks up the hill toward town for a bite at the Golden Flash Diner, then back home. On his bike, Billy Kaplan arrived at the same moment. They acknowledged each other briefly and went into their separate digs. Jake settled in with his guitar, strumming chords with a vengeance to a Richie Havens piece.

Then he had a lightning idea. He stopped playing, thought, considered, juggled his judgments. Half an hour later, his brainstorm accepted, he went downstairs and knocked on Billy's door.

With the promise of strictly deep background, they talked for two hours. Jake told Billy about Wettman, about his own possible jail sentence, his background, his views, Billy pacing, lighting one cigarette with the butt of the former.

"Okay, okay," Billy said, "Lemmie get this straight. This guy Wettman is actually from the old House Un-American Activities Committee? Are you sure?"

"Sure? No. But he's around Satterfield. My boss ordered me to talk to him."

"Who is that exactly?"

"My supervisor, Byron Shenk."

"And the Wet-guy is saying something's coming down, and that McGill and Engle are in cahoots with the White House?"

"I don't know which exact SDS leaders he was referring to, but yes, that's what he told me."

"And you have no idea why he's telling *you* this?"

"Why me in particular? No clue. He wants me to keep him informed of campus activities, an objective view, so he says. I told him to get lost, that I'll take the jail sentence."

"Jesus fuck! And he told you Nixon wants to incite an incident here?"

"Yes. And that some local SDS leaders are government plants. You haven't heard of Wettman's being on campus?"

"I sure have now. I need a beer. Want one?"

"Sure."

They drank Pabsts together, mostly quiet in the newspaper strewn apartment, the smell of newsprint and cigarette fumes.

"Maybe he's just trying to freak you out," Billy said.

"He's doing a good job."

"It's a helluva story if it's true."

"You promised to keep me out of it."

"Yeah. You're not a major player. Only a source. I don't reveal sources."

"Can you expose Wettman? Make his presence known to everybody?"

"I can try. I'll need a photo."

"How?"

"I'll lend you one of my Instamatics. After you meet with him, maybe you can trail him and get a shot."

"Sure, like tell him I want a souvenir? I don't think so. I'm in enough trouble already. But I have my own camera. I'll start carrying it, see if a chance comes up."

"Super. That would be a real *coup.*"

Billy stood abruptly, a clear signal for Jake to leave.

"You've given me some work to do. Interesting, Jake. Keep me informed. Don't worry, off the record. Thanks. This is some freaky weird shit, for sure."

With Jake at the doorway, Billy added, "Hey, does this asshole know where you live, by any chance?"

"Yes. He knew Natasha lived here, knows she moved out."

"Natasha? Man, were you banging that?"

"Billy, don't take that tone, okay?"

"Sure. Sorry. Maybe that explains all this."

"Me and Natasha?"

Billy smiled. "No, man. If he knows about her, he must know about me."

"Yeah, and Phil across the hall. So what?"

"Connect the dots, partner."

Jake tried to puzzle it out.

"Maybe you're a carrier," Billy said. "Maybe he figures you'll talk to me. Maybe he wants this story out, and you're the messenger, like one of those diseases someone spreads without knowing it."

"The idea did pass my mind that maybe he wanted me to go straight to the *Stater*."

"Maybe he wants to discredit McGill, Engle, and the rest. Make people think they're working for the government. That would shake things up, wouldn't it? Spread paranoia within the ranks?"

Jake's head buzzed.

Billy lowered his voice to a mere whisper. "Look, man. From now on, we shouldn't be seen together, okay? They're watching this place, maybe even have our pads miked, phones bugged." He glanced around his living room. "Be careful. I'll find a way of reaching you from now on. If this is right on, but even if it's simply misinformation they want published, I'm going to have to make myself invisible while I track it down. They probably know you're here right now, hoping I'm dumb enough to go straight to my typewriter."

"If that's what they want you to do, there's nothing to fear, is there?"

"There is if I uproot their plan, discredit Mr. Wet Guy instead of SDS leadership. And my editor isn't going to do a story until we know what's up, until it's absolutely straight. They probably think that out here in the back woods we don't know what we're doing. So let's keep a safe distance, all right? And if you happen to get that shot, slip the film in the tool pack on my bike. I'll be in touch if need be. Holy blazes, brother!"

Jake inspected his apartment to see if anything seemed awry. All appeared normal. He had no knowledge about surveillance techniques so if devices had been installed he probably wouldn't find them. Then again, maybe Billy's fears were totally unwarranted.

To distract himself he picked up his guitar and worked on a run. It didn't work this time. He was awash with all the wrong sensations.

What had Wettman said?—that he knew Jake better than Jake knew himself?

He lay back on his sofa, his mind drifting to even more personal matters, Tasha.

Poor Tasha! Were she to appear again, they would talk. He would hold off his desire to make them one physically and try to understand her, to find out how he can help her besides overwhelming her with sensation. At present he could view sex with her as little more than his exploiting her misery. She needed a more permanent solution.

He went to his desk, found her letter, read it carefully. Tears filled his eyes. Her writing revealed a woman in tremendous crisis, having no choice but to submit to the pressures surrounding her. One line troubled Jake more than any other: *They don't know about us, never should, my darling.* Right out of a melodrama. He'd been cast as Christopher Newman in *The American,* the woman he adored held captive in a castle with a moat. Would this end as tragically?

Okay, was there a strategy he could come up with? He'd gone over his options *ad infinitum*, come up empty every time. The moat was wide, the castle walls thick, the prisoner too weak to meet him halfway.

The crux of the situation was her refusal to tell them the truth. She feared the consequences of revealing her infidelity. The truth was that her marriage to Ray constituted the real infidelity, her betrayal of herself. She wouldn't be able to live without the approval or at least the acceptance of her family. Were she to have come to Jake, she would have been equally as tortured. Poor, beautiful soul, too fragile to exert her true self.

Which torment was worse for her? Jake wondered. Sacrificing herself to the lie, or living the truth and seeing herself as a whore and outcast. More important, how could he help her? Simply by being there when her need for love overwhelmed her faulty reason? Could he accept that? Could he live to perform only that function in her life?

As he descended into the dark regions of his psyche, he realized why lovers sometimes kill. Imagine, he hypothesized as he drifted deeper, Ray goes fulltime into the army, and shot dead in the jungle. She would be honorably free. Ray was the obstacle. Once removed, she could come where she belonged. Or if Ray were in a tragic accident here, on a Guard exercise, or racing that Camaro, or getting stalled on the railroad tracks, or ...

He sat up, gasped from this dark reverie.

He showered, tried his guitar, leaned it aside, read her letter yet again, sat up straight with an idea.

What if ... what if they all knew about him? The letter in his hand was undeniable proof. What if they saw that letter? What if he, himself, revealed the truth to them? He knew where her family lived, could find the house in Akron where he'd visited with the French students. He could drive there, show them her very words. They'd been acting in a vacuum, with no knowledge of her deepest feelings. If they knew, saw it with their own minds, their hearts, would they not weep with the agony they'd caused her?

But suddenly his inspiration imploded. The problem with this scenario was he, himself, a liberal minded, antiwar fugitive from another part of the country, liable to take their daughter away from them. They could never accept him as an alternative to Ray, could they?

No way in hell.

And she'd be left in the exact situation with the added bane of her sin having been revealed.

He crushed the letter in his fist.

42

Tuesday, April 1, a week later ...

On the way out of his apartment with his camera in a side pocket, Jake saw a slip of paper at his door, apparently having been slid under during the night. A note from Tasha? No, unsigned but it took Jake only a moment to figure it was from Billy: *Make sure to catch this morning's* Stater.

The note hastened Jake's march up the hill past the looming water tower and down to Satterfield where a stack of newspapers lay on a lobby bench. He grabbed one, poured a cup of coffee in the lounge and settled in his office. On the front page he saw a headline referring to the former House Un-American Activities Committee. The article contained an informational presentation of Wettman's interviewing various people in reference to campus activists. Admin claimed to have had no advanced warning of his visit and no knowledge of his actions. He would return after Easter to continue interviews for use in possible federal legislation. Campus police were cooperating, and the material he gathered could be used to subpoena Kent students, faculty members, administrators and staff to testify in House hearings.

Jake noted the article's absence of Wettman's assertion to him about SDS leadership being government agents or about an impending campus uprising fomented by Dirty Tricks. If, indeed, Jake had been set up as a carrier, Wettman would be disappointed that his principal message had gone unprinted. But the exposure of the guy's activities would be enough to stir things up. If this was Billy's work, he'd played it cool, maybe realizing that a photo might be pushing things over the line. Or perhaps he didn't have time to wait. Jake wondered if his own tale to his downstairs neighbor had sparked this article though submitted to the student paper rather than the countywide one Billy actually worked for.

Another column caught his eye. Apparently Admin had created a committee to study the Bobby Ferguson case, not to help him with his legal difficulties but to see what mistakes they might have made regarding the First and Fourteenth Amendments. Better late than never, Jake thought, but this seemed to be the M.O. of Admin—to examine problems after they occur. Now they're eating proverbial crow and have the ACLU breathing down their necks.

Jake closed the paper and took a satisfying swallow of coffee.

Next came the problem of using his office for informal discussions with his students. He would have to explain that they needed to move to some other location. He couldn't use his own apartment; Mrs. Whitcomb would surely not renew his lease.

He headed for the main office in Satterfield to check on space availability. Clara, one of the secretaries, several pencils tucked into her hair-bun like a geisha, leafed through some forms, checked some charts. Nothing from eight to six. Same for night classes, even Saturdays. Sundays, only the mimeograph room was open.

"We seem to be bursting at the seams," Clara said. "Ever since they moved the Romance Languages from Bowman to our third floor. What do you need it for, poetry discussions?"

"Something like that."

Jake would talk it over with his students, but vowed not to desert them. And he wanted to assure them that it was not a case of the English Department refusing students the opportunity to discuss their concerns.

At this stage in his academic career he was about to finish his course work. If he completed his thesis on Eliot's *The Sacred Wood*, he would have his master's degree next June. Time had come for him to consider what to do after that, his goal to receive a doctoral fellowship at a more prestigious university. By now he felt certain of a 4.0 grade point average and of solid recommendations from his profs. With Dr. Thrillwell's blessings he'd sent his first paper, significantly revised, to several scholarly journals. He'd received several polite rejections, but two editorial boards had not yet replied. Thrillwell had warned him the process could be agonizingly slow. Publication could go far regarding a fellowship.

Thrillwell had ties to Rutgers; also, Jake's American Transcendentalism prof, Dr. Walpole, knew people at the University of West Virginia. Such ties might take him far as well. Then he remembered his former teacher at Millersville, who'd once bailed him out of jail for disorderly conduct related to the first time he'd been drunk. Groff now taught at LSU. Jake decided to write to him.

After his two seminars he grabbed a tuna salad sandwich and Coke at the Union and headed on to the library where he continued his research on Hemingway. But the more Robert Jordan described his love for Maria, the more Jake thought of Tasha. In the crowded study room, beneath the rustling of pages and student whispers, he sank into the continuing despair of his helplessness. His desperate idea of driving to Akron and revealing Tasha's letter to her parents kept popping up, but he constantly suppressed it with the realization that the mission had to be more concerned about *Tasha's* well-being than his own. His exposing her would only add to her misery. Mostly he longed to talk things over with her face to face, to let her know his feelings and to explore options.

He strolled outside for some fresh air. On the cold, windy entranceway students were smoking and chatting. He moved down the walkway toward Main Street. Maybe he would have to give her up. But how does one give up such a love? One way might be to see his feeling as a mistake, or even to find some fault with the one he loved, a fault previously unnoticed or ignored. What culpability could he find with Tasha? He searched his memory. None. Even her submitting to her family's will showed more virtue than deficiency, her willingness to sacrifice her own happiness for that of others.

Regarding her flawlessness, it had been the same with Christine in high school, and with Ainsley, his ex-fiancé—no defects in evidence. He'd loved them, and to have done so couldn't be twisted into a mistake. The same with Tasha. Thus, what remained but for him to honor her decision, as he had his two former loves? Ah, but the anguish of losing them!

Did they not comprehend the depth of his feeling for them? If so, how could they have missed it? Was the final answer that he was simply not worthy of them? Or was it *karma*, a concept he'd learned in his Transcendentalism course? Not a present lack within himself but within a former self, his own past action coming back to him? Christ, what did it matter? He'd lost Tasha, as he had the others. Nothing left but the pain and loneliness, each time exponentially greater. And something even worse was the bitterness now creeping around at the bottom of his being, the cynicism of all hope destroyed, life as a pile of cow shit.

He thought of his dad, wounded in war, his hard work and constant struggle. But never bitter. There was a big difference, though—his dad had Jake's mom.

And crashing through all this philosophizing suddenly appeared the most horrible fact—the woman he loved was suffering and he could do nothing about it. Let the bastard be called to Vietnam and blown to smithereens! Then Jake confronted a fate much more terrifying than bitterness—the fate of hatred.

He'd never felt it before. It was the worst he'd ever felt.

Wednesday, April 2, next day …
With five minutes left in his nine o'clock writing class, Jake came from behind the small podium and leaned on the front edge of the desk. He announced that he would no longer use his office for their Wednesday discussion sessions and explained the lack of available space in Satterfield.

"How 'bout the Union?" Jake asked.

"Too crowded," Audrey said.

"Too many distractions," echoed Aaron.

He noticed students gathering their things. "Those who aren't involved can leave," he said. Only seven remained. Students from the next class started coming in.

"I know," Steve said. "Let's establish a student club. Then they'll have to give us space."

"Yeah," Audrey said. "I organized the Hiking Club. I know the ropes."

"S.F.M.," Aaron said. "Students for Moderation."

"Sounds like a sex club," Steve said, causing laughter. "Should bring in a lot of members."

"We'll need a faculty advisor, though," Audrey said. "How 'bout it, Mr. Ernst?"

"Whatever the name," Jake answered, "I'm not officially considered faculty, more like a hired hand."

"Like playing ball in the minor leagues," Steve quipped.

Jake smiled. "Exactly, and on the bench. Maybe someone from the Speech Department."

"Screw that," Audrey said. "We want you."

"Schedule permitting, I'd be glad to sit in."

"I have an idea," meek, mousy Naomi spoke up.

They all turned to this unfamiliar voice.

"What idea?" Audrey asked, showing her frustration at all these difficulties.

"Uh, while you're setting this club up, we can use the Pit over at Tri-Towers. The cafeteria is almost empty in the afternoons, only a few kids sitting around studying and talking. We could take a corner there."

That afternoon Jake slogged through a snowstorm over to the three tall dorms, architecturally misfit to the general style of the campus as if someone wanted to show that Kent State belonged in the modern age. The towers all connected to a community hub known as "The Pit," which contained the general eating area. When Jake found it, he spotted Naomi and her compatriots gathered in an alcove, which would do nicely for their talks. They were drinking sodas and eating cupcakes and chips.

After some excited chitchat about girls' curfew being eliminated (except for freshmen), Audrey brought up the strange story that someone from the U.S. Congress was snooping around campus.

"Why Kent State, of all places?"

In these informal talks Jake took on less of a role, the kids learning how to carry on without his steering them in the direction of rational decorum.

"Maybe they're really scared of that guy McGill," someone said. "A girl down the hall from me has his wife for lit class. She's really nice, but he's scary, always with the dark glasses and scruffy clothes, always pissed off."

"His sidekick Engle is worse, what a loudmouth!"

"What's their problem?" Naomi asked, beaming apparently at the success of her suggestion of the meeting place.

"Yeah, Mr. Ernst," Aaron said. "What do they want besides causing trouble?"

"What do you think they want?"

"I'm not sure," Aaron said, "but whatever it is, they're working hard at it. They want people to go on a bus to a march in Chicago this weekend. Supposed to be a rally about it on the Commons tomorrow. I'm tempted to go. I've never been to Chicago."

"I doubt it's a tourist trip," Steve said, raising laughter.

"Do they think we can stop the war, here at Kent?"

"No, man, it's a movement all over the country. We're a small part of it. The kids over in Columbus are really into it."

"Because they don't wanna go and fight?"

On the conversation went, showing clearly to Jake that they knew little about the war itself, its origins, its history, the international issues involved.

"They think the war is part of our government's aim to control the world," Jake said, "to make other countries *de facto* colonies. I don't think the 'scruffy' guys you mentioned are afraid to fight, do you?"

"I read that the guy with the shades is the son of Canton's mayor," Audrey said. "The guy Ronnie, his parents are communists."

"I think they want our country to be communist," someone piped up. "They keep talking about a revolution, like the blacks."

On it went. Clearly these kids were uninformed, confused observers of the campus scene.

At four o'clock, Jake said, "Okay, I have an assignment for you."

Boos and moans.

"This isn't a class, Mr. Ernst," Audrey said.

Jake chuckled at their display of independence. "I meant to say 'an announcement.' I guess the wrong word slipped out by habit. But if you go over to the reading lounge in Rockwell Library, you'll find a display of books and articles about Vietnam. You should inform yourselves. You'll find out some startling facts."

"Like what?" Naomi asked.

"You should decide things yourself. I don't want to bias you one way or another. The facts are out there. But you see how the war is affecting the whole country, especially the young men forced to fight it. So you should know the issues, but not from people who are trying to radicalize you on one side or who want to appeal to your blind patriotism on the other. The most patriotic thing you can do is learn the facts. So if you really care, get on over there and spend an hour or two. The picture will begin to clarify, then you can decide which way to go. And we can talk more about it next week."

43

Tuesday, April 8, six days later …

Jake was taking notes on Professor Lyman's lecture on Hemingway's journalistic revision of modern American prose stylistics when the door burst open and two bearded, longhaired young men in semi-military attire charged in.

"All this is for killing! Stop the war! Come to Admin with us! Join the fight!"

Such class disturbances were occurring throughout the building, shouts and general clamor arising in the hallways. The two activists withdrew as quickly as they'd entered, leaving the grad students and Professor Lyman aghast.

"Come on," one student said loudly. "This course is bullshit." He grabbed his knapsack and rushed out.

Though clearly agitated, the others remained while, flustered, Dr. Lyman shuffled to find where he'd left off in his talk.

"What's happening, Professor?" someone asked.

"Your guess is as good as mine, but it has nothing to do with the subject at hand. Let us turn to the handout and contrast the paragraphs from James' *Ambassadors* with Hemingway's *The Sun Also Rises.*"

Highly distracted from the prof's droning lecture, Jake endured the remainder of the presentation. Curious to find out whether Wettman's prophecy about an upheaval was coming true, he hurried to his office, grabbed his coat and, with several others along the way, strode on Portage toward the Administration Building.

Someone came from the other direction handing out fliers. Jake took one and read as he moved along with the growing crowd. In bold typeface the paper listed four demands: *Abolish ROTC; Abolish the Liquid Crystals Institute; Abolish the Northeast Ohio Crime Laboratory; Abolish the Kent Law Enforcement Training Program.*

As spectators flowed from all directions, several patrol cars, sirens wailing. lights flashing, separated the procession and made their way down the slope to the entrance of Admin where a throng of protestors with signs and a Viet Cong flag shouted slogans. A number of cops with nightsticks in hand jumped out of the cruisers and headed toward the protestors.

"SDS is presenting their demands to White," someone shouted. "They crashed his office."

Police who'd already been there tussled at doorways with dissidents, fisticuffs breaking out here and there amid the shouting. Jake had never witnessed such a melee, even in the several peace marches he attended in D.C. Students wanted to get into the place, and cops were fending off their efforts although not retaliating.

When Jake felt the crowd shoving him toward the building, he edged outward and observed the fracas from the top of the hill. It went on for over an hour until at last a number of handcuffed students, McGill and Engle among them, were forced into patrol cars which pulled up the driveway through the throng now pounding on the roofs and hoods and screaming obscenities.

And not a single black in the whole place, Jake noted.

Finally, with the dropping of temperature and the oncoming of dusk, the gathering slowly dispersed, many seeking warmth in the nearby Union. Jake continued down the hill past the library to Lincoln and then to his apartment.

He turned on his radio and collapsed onto the sofa, the story of today's events being recounted by the campus station. Apparently, a dean had offered SDS leaders entrance into the building to present their demands directly to Vice-president Matson, not to President White. But McGill had declined the offer, insisting that the group stood as one and would enter the building only *en masse*. That was when the mob rushed various entrance points, the leaders having actually broken through and up the stairs where they were stopped by waiting guards who'd apparently been forewarned of the intended invasion.

Forewarned by whom?

Jake tried to imagine all this having been led by FBI plants. If so, the student leaders would probably be let off from prosecution. He would wait to see if that happened. But then, maybe Wettman was simply full of shit. Then again, it had gone off as he'd predicted, hadn't it? The guy had to have known something, from somewhere.

With the radio on, Jake made himself some bacon and eggs. The announcer said that the campus disturbance might have been much worse except that over a hundred fifty campus activists had been at an antiwar rally in Chicago that afternoon. At Kent, seven SDS members were arrested for unlawful trespass, riot, and assault and battery. President White immediately suspended them and their organization from the university. Some were identified in photographs of the crowd. Later, three more SDSers were arrested at a disturbance in the Union.

Maybe the whole thing had been arranged by Admin working with Wettman to get the SDS leaders and the organization itself banned from campus. Jake felt a whirl of confusion.

He particularly noted the announcement that city police in military gear had been inside the building prepared for trouble, another sign of forewarning. In addition, expecting a commotion at an unrelated conference on Asian affairs, a group of fraternity men had assembled to fight off possible protestors though not much had happened there due to the goings-on at Admin. Eventually campus police told the Greek-boys to go back to their frat houses.

As Jake washed his dishes, Matson came on air live. He decried the interruption of classes as well as the invasion of Admin. He stated unequivocally that disruptive tactics like the ones that afternoon would not be tolerated, emphasizing that police procedures would be used whenever necessary. He said that a restraining order would be issued against those arrested, restricting them from reentering the campus.

Though exhausted from standing in the cold for several hours, Jake pulled on his coat and headed back to the University Auditorium to hear Muhammad Ali speak as part of the Campus Lecture Series. The fighter's appearance was yet another in a vast array of attempts to placate campus blacks. The poet/activist Leroi Jones would visit the campus in the near future along with other black poets, novelists and journalists. Back in February, the *Stater* had given extensive coverage to the Black Arts Festival, and a few weeks later did the same for the Uhuru Dance in honor of black African freedom fighters. Then Professor Levitt of Sociology led a tribute and a special panel in honor of Malcolm X. Levitt also spoke in the Current Issues course about his having cancelled his classes during the BUS walkout. He'd paid a price for that action in terms of his career, but emphasized that acts of civil disobedience indeed require the resultant penalties. And even more important for the advancement of campus blacks, Admin intended to establish an official academic Black Studies program.

Jake had attended an Ali presentation several years before at Franklin and Marshall College in Lancaster. There, the heavyweight champ had mostly made hilarious jokes about the absurdity of the black man's role in killing nonwhite people far away who'd never called him "nigger." This time there was little joking around. His point had fallen adamantly in line with Elijah Muhammad's, leader of the Black Muslims, advocating complete separation of the races. Several times Ali stated that whites were devils and that blacks should take no part in their colonialist war. He insisted that, instead, they must take control of their local economies. *Self-sufficiency* appeared to be the current war cry.

Jake spotted Ella, her afro now a badge of her commitment to her race, amid a solid corps of African Americans seated in the front. They cheered wildly at Ali's comments. Walking back home against a harsh wind, Jake felt a vast sadness in his soul.

44

Wednesday, April 16, eight days later ...

His guitar case over his shoulder, Jake entered the Pit at Tri-Towers and found his group, grown to about twenty, in a corner of the cafeteria. As he leaned the case against the wall and pulled off his coat, Audrey introduced him to the new attendees. Jake wondered if she'd been recruiting. A gathering this size was bound to be more unruly than usual. As things proceeded, however, none of the students seemed to be there to push their own agenda. Mainly, they seemed disoriented about the extraordinary days since last week's disruption at the Administration Building.

"Mr. Ernst," Aaron spoke up, "what do you think about White messing with the Student Code of Conduct?"

"Why don't you explain *your* view to the group?" Jake answered.

"Students are supposed to have a hearing to defend themselves against suspensions, aren't they?"

"Apparently so. I read that two of the hearings have been scheduled for today."

"I don't like SDS," a female newcomer said, "but White was wrong to suspend those boys without hearings. He's violating his own code."

"Anyone here want to defend the president?" Jake asked.

Low muttering passed through the group.

"Does anyone give him credit for trying to fix his mistake?"

"Okay," a pale, shaggy haired male newcomer said, "but he should have listened to the demands. He never comes out and talks to us. It's like he's afraid. He only writes letters to the paper."

"Yeah, why doesn't he talk to us, face to face?" came yet another unfamiliar voice. "He sends Matson, like a hatchet man."

"A Mafia enforcer," someone added.

"What do you think the primary duty of a university president is?" Jake asked.

"Get money," someone piped up.

"Enforce rules."

"Build an ice rink."

"Tell lies to students."

"Okay, okay," Jake said. "Let's not forget the purpose of our little group here—rational discussion, objectivity. Wouldn't you say that one of White's main duties is to provide a safe place for higher education to take place?"

"By calling in military police?"

KENT STATE — 1969

"How many of you were over at Admin last week and saw what happened?" Jake asked.

Only a few hands went up.

"I was there, saw a lot of it. The student leaders weren't peaceful. They were in full attack mode, shoving policemen, calling them pigs, shouting obscenities, spitting, throwing punches, trying to force their way into the building. It seemed like they actually *wanted* to go to jail."

"What's all that stuff about 'Liquid Crystals'?" someone shouted. "What are Liquid Crystals anyway?"

"Something for the war," someone answered. "Like napalm."

"I checked it," Audrey said. "*Not* like napalm. There's an article in *Life* about it in the library. It helps against cancer."

"That center is sponsored by the Defense Department," someone added.

As the meeting went on, Jake felt disturbed by the seeming anger of the participants. He didn't want to lose touch with the original four, but the flow of the talk was anti-White, anti-Admin, yet, thankfully, without being pro-SDS. SDS had finally managed to be seen as victims instead of perpetrators, and Jake doubted his usefulness in the current atmosphere. He wanted to defend White's ardent stand against campus disruption, yet these kids were correct that the president had mistakenly violated his own Code by immediately suspending students without their right, written in the Code, to defend themselves.

And ever since White kicked the agitators out, the campus had been in an uproar with more arrests, with the campus TV station's footage being subpoenaed to identify more students, with Admin's powerful, dictatorial statements about putting down disruption, and with *Stater* editorials decrying SDS violence but also accusing White of hypocrisy. Letters from Greeks mocked the militants; letters from SDS sympathizers praised the tactics of confrontation for bringing out debate. The once slumbering issues had now awakened. Jake thought of Wettman's prophecy.

He let this meeting take its course, the process becoming more of a venting session than a discussion.

"We want to know what you think, Mr. Ernst," Audrey finally announced. "You always turn the question back to us, but most of us here don't know what to think."

"We're like the blind leading the blind," someone added.

Jake took a deep breath. "I don't want to influence any of you. I'm not an expert, just an observer..."

"Are you afraid to tell us what you really believe?" Aaron asked.

"Afraid?" Jake chuckled. "Maybe."

"We won't rat you out," Steve said with his usual wit.

"Understand, everyone, this is only my personal opinion. I'm here to maintain rationality, objectivity and moderation, all of which we seem to be drifting away from. So for what it's worth, here is my viewpoint about all of this."

The group settled down to listen, the only sounds the rustling of potato chip bags.

"I don't believe that disruption and violence will get us anywhere. Wait, let me change that. I don't believe it *should* succeed. I believe that Admin, maybe President White, is not prepared for the kind of disruptive tactics SDS used last week. He's an educator, we're all educators, and this kind of thing is not supposed to happen on campuses, so no one is trained in how to handle it. I think SDS sees this weakness, not only here at Kent but across the land, and they want to exploit it on campuses because if they did this kind of thing in the general community it would be quickly squelched by law enforcement. Or, if need be, by the military. So campus authorities are learning. And they're often fumbling as they go. Of course, they must maintain order and safety. Your parents sent you here expecting you to be safe, to be preparing for a successful future, not to be arrested."

"Sounds like you blame SDS," someone shouted.

"I think SDS knows well what they're doing. They are not typical students, like you here. They have a non-academic agenda and they're serious about it, but they're an extremely small minority, let's say three hundred out of twenty-one thousand students. So they need help. The process of getting help is called radicalization. Until now, around here, they've been working on the level of information, occasional rallies..."

"Occasional? Rallies are the main source of campus entertainment."

Laughter broke out.

"And at the ROTC drills, how the radicals march around with buckets on their heads and brooms as guns."

More merriment.

Jake smiled. "Maybe so, but they've been mostly peaceful, more hecklers and spectators than actual participants. But with the so-called National Spring Offensive, they've been directed to up their game to draw attention to the issues. When police brutality occurs or when authorities make missteps, SDS pounces on the opportunity to look like victims and to expose hypocrisy and ineptness. President White made a mistake by violating the Code, but he's admitted it and..."

"But why doesn't he come out and talk to us," Aaron said, "like you're doing right now?"

"Aaron, do you have any idea how low-level I am? I'm a second year TA. It's my way of working toward my master's degree. White has responsibilities I can't even imagine."

"Why doesn't he come out and tell us about them?"

"Maybe there are security issues. Maybe he's shy."

More laughter.

"Don't you believe he should?" said a new voice.

"It's not for me to tell the president what to do," Jake said. "But here's what I would say. And I believe this strongly. SDS is wrong, both in their goals and their methods. They want to close the universities as a way of disrupting our government. They want some kind of revolution. I believe there needs to be changes in our society, less rigidity, more openness, and I believe we should stop the war, but I also think we can make these changes within the system. As someone who teaches you, I advise you with my pretty much irrelevant voice to stay away from SDS. Form your opinions based on facts and knowledge, not on emotion and ignorance. If after careful thought, you want to work to change our society in specific ways, do it through the system. Rallies, speaking out, making your voices heard are all okay, but last week SDS went too far."

"What about King?" someone said. "Didn't he use the same tactics to get attention?"

"Not as far as I know," Jake said. "King always insisted on nonviolence. His idea was for the *authorities* to show violence and for the protestors to pay the price, never fighting back. Look, I'm not here to argue with you. If you'd been at Admin last week you wouldn't have seen any blacks. That should tell you something. You have to make up your own minds, but from knowledge and facts, not from emotions. Let's go around, one at a time, and tell the group *your* feelings about what's going on. I can stay longer this afternoon. Let's listen to what everyone has to say. Audrey, why don't you start?"

At 4:30, about half way through this process, a middle-aged woman dressed in white and wearing a hairnet hesitantly approached the gathering and announced that they would have to disband because the cafeteria was about to open for dinner. She asked politely that everyone put their chairs back properly and drop their trash in the bins.

"Let's not protest *this* policy, okay?" Jake said with a smile. But before leaving, he asked to say one more thing, and the group quieted down to listen.

"Think about this, everyone. It is President White's goal to protect this place for all of us. He is working for the university. SDS clearly states it wants to bring the university down, to close it, to destroy it. They will jump on any cause, not to improve the school but to tear it down. I don't think anyone here wants that. Why would you? You came here for an education, didn't you? How will anyone benefit from SDS's program? Think about it. Admin might make some embarrassing mistakes, but they want what all of us here want, right?" With a smile, he added, "To keep good old KSU alive and well."

To everyone's amusement, Steve ended things by saying, "Okay, Mr. Ernst, next week please bring President White along with you."

With a Goldenrod rehearsal meeting at five when most of the practice rooms were vacant, Jake wended his way up the steep, tiered parking lot toward the Music and Speech Building. He realized he'd given a lecture. He hadn't meant to do that. He justified it because personal candidness had been innocently demanded of him. Students were languishing in the absence of their teachers' honest views. He remembered Professor Lyman's nonresponse to the extraordinary event of two radicals' bursting into his seminar passing out pamphlets and shouting slogans. It seemed to Jake that Lyman should have put down his lecture and opened the class to a discussion about what was happening. If he thought Hemingway's writing style was more important than campus issues, he should have argued the point, laid out his logic. At certain times, leadership must trump scholarship. It had hardly been the moment for business as usual.

Sometimes events require a pause in the routine. What might be Dr. Lyman's thoughts on all these unprecedented happenings?

Half way up the long series of steps Jake's line of reasoning was interrupted by the sounds of a disturbance of some sort coming from the direction of the performance center. When he got to the top of the hill, he was shocked to see a brawl going on, people trying to get in and others trying to keep them out. A Viet Cong flag rippled in the wind. At the periphery of the tussle, he spotted Wash and Adele bundled up and holding their instrument cases.

"What's happening?" he asked when he reached them.

"What's *not* happening?" Wash cryptically replied.

"Not really sure," Adele said. "When we got here, a line of frat guys blocked the entrance. Then a parade of demonstrators marched around the corner of Dunbar, chanting, and when they got here the Greeks stopped them and this fighting started."

Jake saw bloody noses, fists flying, shoving matches.

"A protestor broke one of the glass doors," Wash added, "and some of them crawled through."

"Now they're running around the building trying to find another entrance," Adele said.

"Hang around," Wash added, "enjoy the show."

"Why the hell all the way over here?" Jake asked.

"Something about the suspension hearing being transferred here because not enough room in Admin."

KENT STATE — 1969

"Not enough room for what?"

"I don't know," Adele said. "The kid demanded an open hearing, so I guess for media and spectators. The other hearing was closed, which, apparently, they usually are, but this guy insisted on his being open, I guess a tactic to get more attention."

"And the Greeks apparently decided to spoil the party," Wash said. "The campus cops recruited them last week for the Asian conference too. Vigilantes."

"And that leaves us out here freezing," Jake said. "Any chance of getting some practice in tonight?"

Wash shrugged, opened his arms as if the scene spoke for itself.

"Aren't you going to hang around for all the excitement?" Adele asked.

"I'm in enough of the protest pictures the cops are always taking," he said. "If we're not rehearsing, I'm going home."

"By the way," Wash said, "the owner of the Blind Owl called me about a gig. We're working out the details. They'll pay us."

"Saw us at the folk festival," Adele added.

"Wow," Jake answered sarcastically, "we've hit the big time. Right up there with the Measles."

"The Measles aren't bad," Wash said, "for a rock group. That kid Joe Walsh plays a wicked electric guitar."

On his way around the sprawling building toward Main Street, Jake saw a pair of cops at every entrance, except for one door at the rear, strangely unguarded, standing wide open, militants flowing in.

Someone yelled, "The building is ours! Let's take it!"

In the direction of the president's house, Jake hurried across the brown grass, the shortest way home. Then with the sound of sirens coming closer from the east, he saw three commercial buses, escorted front and back by state patrol cruisers. Lights flashing, alarms wailing, they turned onto Midway Drive.

Three buses. What the hell!

He slung his guitar case from one shoulder to the other and quickened his pace out of there.

At home, breathing hard from his stride, he turned on the radio and slipped a TV dinner into the oven. Adele's details had been correct about the transfer of the hearing from Admin to Music and Speech. An SDS spokesman, however, claimed the change was a trick by Admin to hide the location from the enraged protestors, who, when they heard about the correct location, charged across campus, gathering supporters from the dorms.

Breathless at times, with the noise of the live ruckus in the background, the radio commentator said that Engle and McGill had been freed on bail from the county jail to take part in the happenings because the student sub-

239

ject of the hearing had demanded their presence as two of his seven allowed witnesses. Some three hundred demonstrators had been trapped on the third floor of Music and Speech, doorways blocked and elevators turned off, police having allowed them *into* the building through a back door but their escape cut off. At this point the kids, including Engle and McGill who hardly seemed youthful, were being loaded into buses charged with unlawful trespass and inciting to riot. They'd been placed under arrest and were being hauled off to the Portage County Jail in Ravenna.

Certainly seems like a well-planned snare.

Frat boys had been brought out and posted ahead of the arrival of the protestors. And a back door unguarded. And busses on their way for those detained. If it was a trap, SDS would only get more support from the student body. White must be thinking he can quell the rebellion by arresting the protestors, but in Jake's mind, he would be sadly mistaken. As a renowned educator, why didn't the university president understand the fact that automatic support for the underdog is a truism about human behavior?

45

Friday, April 18, two days later ...

As Jake climbed Summit Road, tension seemed to hang over the campus like a pulsating veil. SDS forces were gaining power, once-apathetic students being radicalized in droves. Admin had made the blunder, in Jake's mind, of drawing battle lines, leaving no room for negotiation. They were at open war with SDS, trying to suppress them with raw, undisguised entrapment and armed force.

He pulled a *Stater* off the pile and headed for his office where he saw a young English professor waiting at his door. He'd seen her around, didn't think she was an activist. She held out a slim, pale hand and smiled.

"We haven't officially met," she said, "but I've seen you at readings and heard good things about you. I'm Leslie Robbins. Friends call me Leslie. Do you have a moment, Mr. Ernst?"

"Sure."

He unlocked his door, turned on the light and ushered her in. After hanging up his coat, he gestured for her to take one of the two seats in front of his desk. He pulled the other farther away and sat on it rather than the one behind, thus equalizing their status.

Leslie smiled. "We've formed a faculty/student committee in regard to last week's situation, want to go on record and also influence future events to the extent we can. We're going to issue a resolution, for the good it might do."

"What's it going to say?"

Jake wasn't winded enough from his hike to miss Leslie's attractiveness, her auburn hair a mass of waves and curls, green eyes bright and clear, skin radiant, like Julie Christie in "Far from the Madding Crowd." Her demeanor pleasant yet businesslike, she wore a dark pantsuit with a green and blue neckerchief.

"The resolution states that the university should handle situations without intervention from off campus and that we should all go about our usual activities. But mainly we want to tell students not to attend these CCC rallies."

"CCC?"

"With SDS abolished, they organized a new group, Concerned Citizens of Kent."

"Then, shouldn't it be CCK?"

"I guess some PR type thought CCC had a better ring. Whatever. In our resolution we say that student hearings should be held according to the rules stated in the Code of Conduct and should be open to the public if the defendant so wishes."

"Sounds like you found some middle ground in all this."

"Will you join us?"

"What do you want me to do?"

"Sign the petition, maybe point out the resolution in your classes. Not like we're forming protest lines or anything."

"I don't know, Leslie. I don't like signing things. Something like this faculty committee of yours might start out sensibly and end up something else."

She smiled. "So you're a cautious one, are you?"

"I have my reasons. But I support your ideas, absolutely. What do you teach, anyway?"

She leaned back, crossed her legs. "They have me doing the Western Civilization survey courses, but my research is in the pre-Victorian novel, Austin in particular. You?"

"I'm about to do my master's thesis on Eliot."

"T.S. or George?"

"The one who wrote a long critical essay in defense of the canon, called *The Sacred Wood*. Big on generalities but thin on details."

"Yes, I know it." She lifted her eyebrows. "The Objective Correlative. Extremely intellectual. Look, are you sure you won't simply sign?"

"Can I have some time to think about it?"

"Mr. Ernst, we intend to present it to the president today, and to have it come out in Monday's edition of the *Stater*."

"Monday's edition? I thought the *Stater* skips Mondays."

"Special edition, about all the fuss around here."

"I'm sure *my* name won't add any force to your resolution."

"Look, we're trying to give voice to the so-called silent majority on campus, feel we can't be silent any longer. Please, won't you sign? We need to take a stand. Look here." She pulled a folder from her briefcase and handed it to him. "You can see that none of these signatures are from anyone associated with any side in all this. But we all believe in protecting the wellbeing of our students. We fear there's going to be more trouble. We're planning to send faculty/student duos for open discussions in the dorms, try to hold back the tide of radicalization."

This statement set Jake back on his chair. It was exactly what he'd been trying to do.

"We're afraid," Miss Robbins went on, "that President White has forced the campus into two sides. This is dangerous. Most of the campus is somewhere in the middle, and we want to give expression to that third constituency. I'm not saying this to flatter you, Mr. Ernst, but..."

"Please do me a favor, Leslie. Call me Jake, and go ahead and flatter me all you want."

She smiled sweetly. "Sure. Jake. You have a reputation for having a good rapport with your students, and we're hoping you'll be willing to take part in one of our diplomacy teams."

"*Diplomacy teams*, I like it." He stretched easily. "Actually, Leslie, I've already been kind of doing that."

"Really?"

He explained how his out of class discussions got started and where they stood today.

"They want me to bring White to the next session," he said.

Leslie looked wide-eyed.

"You should ask him," she said. "It's precisely what he should be doing."

"The president of the university rapping with a bunch of kids in a cafeteria? Fat chance, Leslie."

"You never know until you ask."

"I don't think he likes to *rap*. I think he hides behind procedures."

"Won't hurt to suggest the idea." She leaned toward him. "I'll help. I know one thing about him—he wants to save this university. And to do that he has to communicate with the vast majority of students. I'm afraid that by next Wednesday we'll be closed down."

"I doubt it will come to that," Jake said.

She smiled her sweet smile. "I can't believe you've predicted exactly what we want to do, and gone ahead and done it."

"I doubt White will tag along, but I'd like to invite you, Leslie. Most of the students there are girls, they could relate to you."

She blushed, wiped an errant curl back from her cheek.

"Since I'm free at that time, I accept your invitation. Now will you please put your John Hancock on this paper?"

He pulled a ballpoint from a Golden Flashes mug filled with pens and pencils.

"But, really, Leslie, I don't want to be on a committee. I'm signing this only in support of the ideas written here. No membership cards, I beg you."

"Thank you, kind sir. I assume by the case in the corner, you're a guitarist."

"I wouldn't put it that way. I play rhythm in a bluegrass group."

"Right! Yes, now I know where else I've seen you. Goldenrod! I love that group." As she reached down for her briefcase, she looked up at Jake with an expression that startled him, unmistakably sensuous, almost lascivious, a stark contrast to her sweet professionalism. It was only a glance, but one he was meant to see. Then she closed her satchel and stood, resumed her former attitude, smiled her bright smile.

"I guess I'll see you Wednesday," she said. "Should we meet here and head over to Tri-Towers together?"

With Miss Robbins on her way having achieved her purpose, Jake, that odd, mind-blowing glance lingering in his head, opened the morning's *Stater* and soon discovered the reason behind her sense of urgency about the faculty/student resolution. In a dramatic front-page statement President White exclaimed his fear for the survival of the university, charged that outside professional agitators were behind the disruptions, claimed the trouble was straining university services and finances, and praised law enforcement for their handling of the Music and Speech crisis. His tone would be enough to frighten any reader concerned about the continued existence of the institution.

Another article revealed that fifty-two of the students arrested at last Wednesday's sit-in had been released on one thousand dollar bail and were charged only with trespassing, not rioting. And the day's official editorial rubbed salt in the president's wound by insisting that student suspension hearings follow official protocol and should be open to interested parties upon the student's request. Then Jake reviewed his presentation notes on subordinate clauses for his nine o'clock freshmen.

When he walked into the classroom, he felt the tension immediately. Students' faces were buried in the *Stater* and, still feeling the stress of the president's statement about the survival of the university, he wondered if this wasn't one of those moments when leadership trumped academics. Hardly anyone noticed his arrival.

From her usual seat in the back, Audrey Kraft spoke up.

"Did you read what White wrote, Mr. Ernst?"

The question brought most of the heads up, eyes toward him.

"I did."

"What do you think about it?"

"What do *you* think, Audrey?"

"He says this place might not survive. Is it just a scare tactic?"

"He praises the pigs like they're some kind of heroes," Bobby Ferguson spoke up, still out on bail from his obscenity charge. In standard SDS semi military garb, tangled blond hair, and a tired looking pale face, he glowered at Jake

"White broke his own rules," Aaron added.

"Is that the real issue here?" Jake asked, pulling off his sports coat and rolling up his sleeves.

"What'd a' ya mean?" Aaron answered.

"True, he broke the procedure about immediate suspension," Jake said, "but hasn't he resolved that mistake by deciding to hold the hearings, even open them to the public?"

"Yeah, and trying to hide the location all the way over in Music and Speech," came another voice. "Are you defending him?"

"He has only the pigs to defend him," Bobby said. "He has no argument, only force."

Jake tried to be calm. He detested the term *pigs*, but there were more important issues than rhetorical terminology.

"Okay, let me ask you all this. Do you want the university to close down?"

"Damn straight!" Ferguson said.

"Let me see a show of hands," Jake went on. "How many in this room want be forced to apply to a new school for your college education?"

No hands went up.

"That's not a fair way to ask the question," Bobby objected.

"I decided to come here because I like Kent," Audrey said. "I could've gone to a lotta schools. I don't want Kent to close just because White screwed up on a technicality."

"Look," Jake said. "Let's be clear, like I said last Wednesday over at the Pit. Excuse me Bobby, but you just confirmed SDS's stated goal to destroy Kent State University. President White's goal is to save it. That's the bottom line here, behind all the distracting issues. The sides are clear. SDS is not trying to improve Kent. For them destroying it would be, in their heads, a fantastic victory, right Bobby?"

"You got it, man. This place is part of the whole imperialist system, and everyone in this class is being brainwashed into serving it."

"At least Bobby is saying it as SDS sees it, not focusing on whether or not White made a mistake. They seize on any issue whatever, not because they give a damn about the issue itself but because they need a wedge to get to all of you. They know the huge majority of students here don't want to ruin the school, so they need something you can all relate to, like, for instance, some violent students being denied due process. This is not about due process. It's not even about the war in Vietnam."

"What is it about?" someone asked.

"That is a good question," Jake answered. "Let's ask Bobby what it's all about?"

"Revolution," he said. "Power to the people."

"Exactly," Jake said. "Those of you who have actually read SDS statements know this. So in the *present* craziness, what do they really, really want?"

"To bring down Kent," someone else said.

"Yes, but even more than that," Jake asked.

"Bring down the government."

"Right on, brother," Bobby said.

"That's right," Jake said. "How many of you and your friends want a national revolution that would put SDS in charge of the country?"

No hands went up.

"Bobby Ferguson for president!" someone said, causing laughter.

"Yes, we need changes," Jake said. "But our Founding Fathers made sure change was possible within the system—orderly change, yes, slow, but feasible, much preferable to violent overthrow. Imagine another civil war. Yes, we want to stop the mess in Vietnam, we want fairness and justice for minorities, we want more relaxed lifestyles, changes..."

"Legalize pot," someone yelled.

Jake smiled. "All right, if it's no more harmful than tobacco, why not?"

"It's *less* harmful," came the same male voice.

"And we want some changes around here," Jake went on now sitting on the front edge of the desk. "Legitimate changes. And we've seen that Admin recognizes it. Look what Admin is doing to bring blacks into the mainstream community."

"Only after they had to walk out," Aaron said.

"True, but Admin realized the virtue of the demands, better late than never. And it seems from this morning's paper, they've compromised about the charges for the kids who took over Music and Speech."

"Not for all of them, and there's no amnesty like they did for BUS."

"True, Admin is always a step behind, but they try to make things right. They're not prepared for all this upheaval. They're scholars, used to being holed up in libraries, not to extracting building occupiers. Give them a break."

"They're supposed to be the smartest people in our country..."

"No," Audrey interrupted, "advertisers are much smarter."

"And SDSers," Bobby added.

Laughter broke the serious mood. Jake joined in, felt things softening up.

"Let's get back to the point," he went on. "Do you want the university closed or not? Do you want to fill out applications to other schools, delay your progress, be suspected by admissions officers at other colleges for fomenting revolution? Get drafted? Or do you want to solve these campus issues through rational, logical discussion and keep on moving toward your careers and futures? In his statement, love him or not, the president laid the ultimate issue on the line. He's fighting to save this place; SDS is trying to destroy it. Sorry, Bobby, but isn't which side to be on a no-brainer? President White may be wrong about a lot of things, but he's dead right about the most important issue of keeping our university open."

Jake was surprised to see smiles appearing on the faces of his students, then shocked to actually hear applause. But Bobby Ferguson grabbed his knapsack and walked out.

"Wow! Mr. Ernst," Audrey said, grinning. "We never figured you had such passion. Thought your main protest was against comma splices. You need to get out there and tell everyone else what you just said."

"Better yet," Steve piped up. "White should."

"I'm afraid he did the best he could in this morning's paper," Jake said. "I don't think he's a face-to-face kind of guy. Now let's get back to your education—not commas this morning but the fascinating adverbial clause—which is why you all came to college, right? Not as thrilling as revolution, I know, but imperative in improving your writing style."

46

Saturday, April 19, next day ...

At dinnertime Jake sat alone at the counter of the Golden Flash devouring a hot beef sandwich and mashed potatoes when someone reeking of cigarettes slipped onto the stool next to him. Billy Kaplan.

"Hey, neighbor," Billy said. "What's happening?"

"Good sandwich, like back home."

"Gettin' homesick, eh? Can't blame you, all this shit hittin' the fan."

"I was trying to forget about all of it."

Billy nudged Jake in the ribs. "And now I show up. How'd you like the article I managed about Wettman?"

"That was your piece? I'm shocked you gave up the byline."

"Yeah, my paper wouldn't print what I wrote, so I gave it to a kid from the *Stater*, watered down, but effective. Forced the jerk out into the open, at least. You ever get that snapshot?"

"Haven't had a chance. But I have my camera ready."

Billy ordered a cherry Coke from the cute counter waitress. Jake was beginning to notice the bounty of beauty around campus, couldn't quite get that powerful glance of Leslie's out of his head.

"Yes," he said to Billy. "You handled that article with aplomb."

"At least with a banana." He nudged Jake again. "Get it? Aplomb, a banana?"

"Witty as hell."

"Any more news about old Boris? Did he contact you again?"

"No."

"I've been watching out for any surveillance, man. I don't think there is any. Did you notice anything?"

"No. Don't really know what to look for."

"Hear a strange buzz on your phone?"

"Rarely use my phone."

"Were you at last Thursday's rally on campus?"

"Had class."

"Biggest one so far, maybe fifteen hundred. Lotsa catcalls, heckling, but they were out there in multitudes. Then last night after the rants in the auditorium, a good three-thou marched around campus. Things are heating up. They demanded amnesty for the sit-in at Music and Speech, like BUS did for the walkout. I doubt White's gonna go along with it this time because these kids are white. And there are definitely outsiders here, real pros."

"Hey, Billy, I guess Wettman's ruse about McGill and Engle was exactly that, with their getting arrested and all, no way they'd be working for Nixon."

"Maybe, maybe not. Serving some jail time would only up their credibility. Did you notice how easily they managed to get over to Music and Speech from the county lockup, supposedly as witnesses for that kid's hearing? Word is, those two were the real agitators in there. And released on bail that precise day. That little ratface Engle gave a fiery speech down at Fred Fuller Park yesterday afternoon, passed the hat for bail donations for the others. So they're still out and about, right?"

"Hmm, so you think...?"

"Don't know what to think, but my boss has me on the case. He needs foolproof verification before he prints it. Gonna be a big rally Monday at the Commons. Something's gonna blow."

He slurped the rest of his Coke up through his straw.

"If you hear anything, let me know. I gotta split. Gonna bar hop on the strip see if I can catch any scuttlebutt, maybe even scrounge up a date."

Yeah, a date, Jake thought with Billy gone. *I wonder what they're like.*

After his meal he headed back toward Willow and decided to go on past the crowded head shop to Lincoln. He took a right a few short blocks and went into the DuBois Bookstore across from McGilvrey Hall. Kent had a dearth of good book stores, the several around catering to textbook and souvenir buyers, but Jake wanted an excuse not to go back his apartment. Besides the usual fare, DuBois had a decent music section, and as Jake was flipping through the folk category, his eyes lit up.

Groff! His former professor at Millersville, now in Baton Rouge, who wrote whimsical, ironic ditties about prairie life. He had an album out. On the cover he sat beside a railroad track that stretched to the horizon. In jeans, boots and a Stetson, he held his guitar and gazed down the rails. Jake pulled the record out of the rack and opened his wallet. He couldn't move fast enough to get back to his place and play it. Rugged looking and unabashedly gay, Groff used to play at college parties but Jake never imagined him putting out an album. Jake had seen some of his poems in the *New Yorker*, though.

When he got back to his place, he had another shock—Natasha's Rambler in the driveway. No one was in it. Heart thumping, he unlocked the downstairs door and saw her sitting at the top of the steps holding a bottle of wine.

Taken far aback, Jake climbed upward as she rose.

"Hi, Jake," she said forlornly, clutching the bottle to her chest. "Is it okay I'm here?"

"Of course."

She looked tired, worn, certainly not the old Tasha. He unlocked the door, ushered her in.

"Let me use your corkscrew, okay?" she said, dropping her coat on the arm of the easy chair.

"I'll do it," he answered, taking the bottle into the kitchen as she followed. She opened a cabinet and pulled out a pair of tumblers.

"Are you glad to see me?"

"Yes."

"You don't sound enthusiastic."

He popped the cork, poured the red vino, and they went back and settled, not closely, on the sofa.

"I came here, Jake, because I just craved seeing you."

"And Ray?"

"His weekend in the woods."

"Right. No change?"

"Like his getting active duty? No."

"I meant like you two breaking up."

"No, not that." She chugged all the wine in her glass and poured more into it. "I need to feel your love, Jake, if there's any left. My life is so utterly barren."

"You could change that, Tasha."

"Oh, Jake, do we have to talk? Can't you hold me?"

She emptied her drink again and slid close to him. She wore a long ski sweater, tights, and calf high boots. Her hair was longer, to her shoulders in soft waves. He put his arm around her and she nestled against him. His body instantly responded. She placed her hand on his groin and clenched what had grown inside his jeans.

Jake allowed the sensation to dissolve his thoughts. If this was what she needed, he'd give it to her; it was what he needed too. But the feeling, harsher, less love and more lust, was different than ever before, rougher, though she didn't seem to notice the tinge of anger behind it. When they were finished, their clothes scattered around the sofa, they clung together, sweaty, satiated. She finally eased away, sat up, finished her wine, found her purse, took out a pack of Lark cigarettes and lit one with a butane lighter.

"You started smoking," Jake muttered.

"I succumbed. Ray smokes, chews snuff too. My world isn't exactly one of high culture."

"I think of you as being held prisoner. You once told me if I went to jail you'd bring me a file in a cake. What can I do to help you escape?"

"Nothing, Jake. Yes, I'm in prison, but if I came to you, I'd bring you down with my misery."

"Don't you and Ray...?"

"Make love?" she finished his sentence. "No, we satisfy Ray's physical needs. I perform my wifely duties. For me, I take hot baths and imagine us, you and me, think of you all over me, like a mountain of love."

A wave of pity passed through Jake, the anger gone.

"Isn't there some way we could talk sometimes?" he asked.

She rose, walked into the bathroom, dropped her cigarette in the toilet, flushed.

"Talk?" she said. "I don't see how?"

Back in the living room she began to dress.

"Letters? I could mail them to your school."

"My mail slot is right next to his."

"Of course, with the same last name."

Combing her hair, she sat beside him. "Jake?"

"What, Tasha?"

"May I come and see you sometimes? Like this?"

Jake paused.

"I know it's a lot to ask. I know how attractive you are to girls. I'm sure you must have a ... tennis partner, as you used to say. I can live with that. I have to. I can't expect you to be strictly devoted to me. But, maybe sometimes, like this? Please say, yes. I need you so. I love you, Jake, down to my toenails."

She moved closer to him, gazed into his eyes.

He took a deep breath.

"Yes, I know, Jake, how I betrayed what we had. It's the worst thing I've ever done. But, darling man, I had no choice. It was a terrible decision, but the thing is, Jake, I'd have been miserable either way, and I didn't want to give that misery to you. I let you go because I thought it was the right thing, not for me really, but for you."

Jake took this in. He believed her, but didn't at all agree with her logic.

"I thought...," he began.

She grasped his hand, pressed it against her breasts now covered by clothing.

"I know exactly what you thought, exactly what you wanted. It's so beautiful. There's nothing beautiful about Ray. He's controlling, macho, self-absorbed..."

"Leave him then!"

"Oh, Jake."

"I'll take your misery. We'll work out your parent problems. They don't want you to be miserable. They love you. You only have to convince them that I'll be good to you, that I'll make you happy, that I'll..."

"You dear, dear man." She caressed his cheeks, stared into his eyes. "You don't understand. You think love solves everything, but with my parents it will just begin the problems."

"Tasha, you must be true to yourself, not to them. They'll get over it."

"Be quiet, Jake. I *am* being true to myself, don't you see that?"

She pulled away, got into her boots, zipped them up.

"You didn't answer my question, Jake."

"About seeing you like this?"

"Say *yes*, please."

"You mean once a month when Ray is off playing soldier?"

"Yes, and maybe a few other moments when I can get away. I need you, Jake. I can live with your having tennis partners, it's..."

"Stop saying that, dammit!"

"Sorry, darling, but..."

"I'll see you like this, Tasha. How can I not? But you must think about breaking free, about..."

Her eyes narrowed into a squint with a hint of evil in it.

"Do you know what I think about, Jake? Do you want to know how bad I am? I think about him being activated, about him going away, far away, about..."

He put his hand on her mouth. "I know, Tasha. I've had the identical thought, maybe even worse."

"Oh, my God, Jake! Stop it right there, don't even think that, and don't ever say it. Promise me."

"But look what this situation is doing to us. There's a way. There must be."

"Okay, then, I'll see you in a few weeks. I'll come to you as long as you let me. I know someday you'll find the woman who is right for you, but until..."

"You're the woman who is right for me," Jake said adamantly, at the same time wondering faintly if, now, it was true.

47

Monday, April 21, two days later ...

With his morning brew Jake sat at his office desk pouring through the special Monday edition of the *Stater*. The fact of this interruption of campus routine indicated a crisis. Jake was having trouble focusing on his lessons and studies, and was certain that the current campus uproar was having the same effect on others. The Special Edition articles centered on CCC's (the new SDS, formerly KCEWV) having called for a one o'clock rally on the Commons today. One column described an emergency Saturday night meeting of Student Senate leaders, who, fearing violence, were appealing to their fellow students not to attend the rally. They claimed that over two hundred outside radicals had poured onto campus from a national SDS conference in nearby Akron. They said that CCC had been taken over by revolutionaries led by none other than wee but indefatigable Rachel Gibbs.

The Special Edition also contained the resolution Jake had signed under the persuasive powers of Leslie Robbins, appealing to students and faculty to avoid the rally and go about their daily business. The resolution added that this group was working on opening channels to hear student grievances.

Adding to the appeal for boycott of the rally, a *Stater* editorial entitled "Don't Go!" pressed hard, warning of violence between conservative students (Greeks) and radicals. The editorial repeated the assertion that outside provocateurs would be there and reminded readers that Admin had been following stated procedures, the suspensions now being handled properly, open to TV, and charges against thirty-one of the fifty-six already dropped.

Unfortunately, in Jake's opinion, to avoid further disruptions of normal university functioning Matson had issued a statement endorsing the threat of immediate suspensions. President White proposed that the Code of Conduct be revised to include *immediate* suspensions in the case of violent protest. Another article said that CCC vehemently opposed Admin's attempt to violate due process.

Dr. Levitt of Sociology, the prof who'd cancelled his classes during the BUS walkout, had signed on to the steering committee of CCC and said the rally could be cancelled if violence seemed imminent. He added that he could organize at least fifty faculty marshals to keep things under control. The president of the Student Senate, however, reiterated that CCC, which filed for student organization status, had done so with a description of moderation but had lied, planning to be even more radical than the abolished SDS.

In the midst of all the panicked hoopla, a small article said that CCC insisted the rally would go on as planned.

A tap on his open door caused Jake to look up from the newsprint. Audrey stood there, a worried look on her lovely, usually optimistic face. He waved her in, gestured for her to take a seat.

"Is spring ever going to get here?" she asked, unzipping her heavy jacket.

"You're up bright and early, Audrey."

"I'm scared, Mr. Ernst."

"Where's Aaron? I think this is the first time I've seen you without him."

"He can barely wake up for your nine o'clock. Most people think we're lovers, but we're not. More like brother and sister, protecting ourselves from all the free love around here. So we don't mind others thinking we're a couple."

"Yes, I thought you were. Are you scared there's going to be violence today?"

"I think that all the articles telling us to stay away will only cause everyone to be more curious. I think it's crazy to make such a big deal out of it. And I've been upset ever since our meeting last Wednesday when we talked about White being scared, like the school will be closed down."

"I think you're right about all this special attention to today's rally."

"Don't they understand that people are curious, like at an accident or a fire? Everyone wants to see what's happening."

"Apparently they *don't* understand that, Audrey. Are you going to be among the curious bystanders?"

"My parents called me and told me not to go. They heard it in the news, all the way in Chevy Chase. Aaron said he's definitely going."

Jake caught a fresh, minty scent coming from his visitor.

"So, what are you going to do, Mr. Ernst? I saw your name on the Student/Faculty Resolution. Are you going to the rally?"

"I haven't had time to think about it."

"I have an idea."

Jake chuckled. "Hit me with it."

"If you go, I'd like to hang out with you, and if you don't go, we could have lunch somewhere, like maybe the Venice, for pizza? We could just talk."

What is this?

Apparently noting his confusion, she said, "I feel safe with you."

At a loss for words, Jake shifted uneasily.

KENT STATE — 1969

"Don't get the wrong idea," she said. "I know you must have a girlfriend, or be engaged or something. It's not like that."

Jake cleared his throat, suddenly looking at Audrey in an entirely new way. It struck him that she was much more mature than most of his freshmen, self-confident, bright, articulate, and really pretty. He tried to get a read of the situation and quickly came up with the solution of simply taking her at her word.

"I guess so, Audrey. Don't you want to make sure Aaron stays out of trouble?"

"He made up his mind. He can be impulsive, no one's going to take care of Aaron but Aaron. I don't want to stay in the dorm alone."

"Which do you prefer, witnessing the rally or having a pizza at the Venice?"

"I guess, Mr. Ernst, I'd prefer pizza. Or lasagna, or rigatoni, or whatever."

"All right, Italian it is. Please invite Aaron or Naomi, any of the others. We can make it a pizza for peace."

"Twelve-thirty, then? Meet you there?"

"Okay, are you coming to class?" He checked his watch. "My God, ten minutes."

"When have I ever missed your class, Mr. Ernst?"

Audrey on her way for the moment, Jake leaned back, astonished at this turn of events. The girl had suddenly become more than one of his students. He'd feel much more comfortable if a few others joined them. Thus, he decided to announce the opportunity in class. He would phrase the invitation as if he, himself, had come up with the idea as an alternative to going to the rally. Pizza for peace – the phrase had a nice ring to it.

And he did so, taking time out of the lesson on *who*, *whose* and *whom* to discuss some of the issues in the Special Edition and adding his advice not to go to the rally.

"We should be working toward preserving the university. Think about it. Twelve-thirty, downtown, the Venice."

He noticed a twinge of disappointment on Audrey's face, confirming his suspicion about her motives.

Known for its great food and its live music and dancing on weekends, the Venice Café was a mom and pop place all the way downtown on West Erie Street. Besides painted frescoes of Italian scenes, it had checkered tablecloths with candles in vino bottles, drippings down the sides. Jake had walked back to his apartment and taken his van, arriving a few minutes late. In the dim interior, not crowded on a Monday, he happily noted four of his students at a large round table. Naomi waved at him enthusiastically. Audrey

253

seemed grim. Steve had made it, along with a knockout sorority girl named Beth from his class. Jake settled in, and they ordered two large pizzas with a variety of toppings.

While they waited in awkward conversation, the "mom" of the operation stood on the customer side of the cash register and called for the few patrons' attention. Known as Big Mama, she was a hefty woman with frizzed salt-and-pepper hair, a shade of a mustache, and an intimidating baritone voice. She served as bouncer on weekend nights, stamping wrists of customers and maintaining general order.

"Because unusual times," she announced, "we gonna play the radio news instead of music. We wanna know what'a happens up'a on the Hill, if we gotta lock'a our doors from these'a crazy kids."

The voice of a female announcer came on the student station WKNT.

"I thought we wanted to get away from this," Audrey said grumpily.

"I want to listen," Naomi answered.

"Might as well know what's happening," Steve added.

From the radio background of garbled crowd voices, they heard the tolling of the Victory Bell, like a call to arms. The commentator gave a recap of the last few days' happenings, described the growing crowd. A speaker came on directing everyone to sit down on the grass.

"This is a peaceful rally," she, perhaps Rachel Gibbs, said. "Please find a place and relax."

The pizzas for peace arrived, and on the speaker system the commentator described what sounded like orderly proceedings, several would-be orators decrying the hard line taken by Admin and announcing CCC's three demands: dropping all charges related to Music and Speech; reinstatement of SDS; and the university's abiding by the Code of Conduct as passed in November, 1968. In an almost whispered voice, the announcer said that as she looked around she didn't see any unfamiliar faces, no sign of outside agitators.

"But there is a new person," she went on, "who looks like part of CCC's leadership, tall, lean, dark beard and hair."

Indeed, soon a deep, moderated voice came on the public mike. The newcomer introduced himself as Simon Shapiro, a doctoral candidate in PolySci. He denied any present or former association with SDS.

"Everyone is saying this rally will be violent," he said slowly, his voice rising. "Let's show them we don't need to be violent to be victorious!"

A wild cheer went up.

Steve was the only one in the restaurant who was eating.

Shapiro said that White's refusal to compromise was unacceptable and that the next step was to hold a four day boycott of classes and to have a referendum on Wednesday, two days away, the ballot listing three options for future actions:

"One: do nothing..."

Boos and catcalls went up.

"Two: have a teach-in about local and national issues..."

More shouts of rejection, some sparse clapping.

"Three: have a four day boycott of classes."

Wild cheering.

Shapiro announced that Wednesday's voting would take place at various sites around campus.

By this time the peace pizza was cold, and Big Mama lifted the pans from the table for reheating. The rally disbanded, apparently without any violent incidents. Milling voices served as a backdrop for the commentator's wrap-up.

While the Venice group waited for their food, Jake said, "How will you all vote?"

"I'm not here to miss my classes," Naomi answered without hesitation.

"I'll have to think about it," Audrey said.

Steve dittoed that. "Either way, I won't miss baseball practice, though."

Beth said, "I could go for another spring break. Four days plus the weekend. I'm in Daytona, baby, with some of my sisters."

They all laughed and dug in to the newly delivered pie, now piping hot.

"How will you vote, Mr. E?" Naomi asked.

"I'll boycott the boycott. I'll be waiting in my classroom for whoever shows up. Maybe just you and me, Miss N."

After they all paid their share, including a nice tip for Big Mama, the group piled into Jake's camper for a free ride back to campus, up the hill on Summit Road and left to the entrance of Satterfield, Audrey riding shotgun. She remained after the other three got out of the sliding side door.

"Can we talk?" she asked.

"Sure."

He pulled up Portage to a small faculty lot, left the engine running.

"What's up, Audrey?"

"Don't you know?"

"Afraid not."

"I didn't mean for today to be a group thing."

"You didn't?"

"I wanted some private time with you, to talk."

"Hmm. I see."

With the heater on, Audrey wriggled out of her jacket. Her face was slightly flushed, her long dark hair over the shoulders of her Kent sweatshirt, her hazel eyes gleaming.

"*Do* you see?" she asked. "Really?"

"Sure, Audrey. Conversation."

"Did you make it a group thing to avoid being alone with me?"

"Not at all. It seemed like a good idea to keep people away from the demonstration."

"Is there somewhere we can go to talk? Like, where do you live?"

"We can't go there."

"Why not? Roommates?"

"Audrey. I think I know what's going on here, but..."

"But ... what?"

"Let's say we'd better not spend too much time together, especially in my apartment, okay?"

"You're kind of square, Mr. Ernst. But that makes you ever more attractive. I think you're a really beautiful man. I thought so the first time I saw you play at the Eye."

"Thank you, Audrey. You're a really beautiful girl."

"Do you think so?"

"Yes, absolutely."

"Then why can't we get to know each other? I have so many questions I'd like to ask, not about writing, but about you, the real you, not the professional you."

"Come on, Audrey. I'm your teacher, you're my student. There's a boundary line. An important one."

"I understand that. But, like, what if we had met in a bar, a bookstore, the Union?"

"That's not the case, Audrey."

"I know, but it doesn't make sense that we can't talk together like two human beings. I don't have anything in common with the kids around here, not even Aaron. He's even more of a kid than most. What's the harm in sitting down somewhere, the Hood, the Hot Dog King, anywhere?"

"So, let me get this straight, Audrey. You want to go somewhere and ask me personal questions?"

"You're not being nice, Mr. Ernst."

"I'm being careful. For your sake and mine."

"You don't have to be careful for my sake, and if you're being careful for yours, you're being awfully square. You're blocking someone who needs adult conversation and adult feelings. I know I'm younger than you, but I'm more grown up than I seem. And there are plenty of girls in my dorm who are friends with their profs, more than friends actually."

Unable to deny her attractiveness, Jake fought against the not-too-subtle invitation she was giving him.

"That's all I'm asking," she quickly added. "Some personal connection, do you see? It's not like you're in your fifties or anything. I bet you're not even thirty."

"Good guess, Audrey. Twenty-nine."

"So ten years, big deal."

"Excuse me, Audrey, and please forgive me if I'm wrong. But it sounds to me as if you're suggesting an affair."

"Not to ball, if that's what you're thinking. I'm not that kind of girl. Maybe if I got to know you, I'd decide on plain friendship. It's only that you're a mystery to me, and I imagine what you really are, and maybe I'll find out I'm wrong. That happens sometimes. I'd like to find out."

"Audrey, you're exactly right-on when you say I'm square. I don't think you're at all square. So, excuse the analogy, but square pegs don't fit into round holes, you know? And more important, teachers shouldn't have affairs with their students. The fact that some do doesn't make it right."

Audrey surprised him by lunging over and kissing him on the cheek. "You're so adorable," she said, grabbing her coat, getting out of the van. "A conversation," she said, "that's all I'm asking." She closed the door and sprinted off toward Bowman Hall, pulling on her coat as she ran.

48

Wednesday, April 23, two days later …

After two-thirty, Leslie Robbins popped into Jake's office in a maroon pantsuit, briefcase in hand. She had a rolled up poster under one arm, her coat tucked under the other, and a bright smile on her mildly freckled face.

"Ta-ta," she said cheerily, "ready to head over to the Pit?"

"It's only a ten minute walk," Jake said, smiling. "You're a real eager beaver this afternoon."

"Yes, this is such a good idea. I'll need a few minutes to set up."

"Set up?"

"I drew a flowchart to show the kids the structure of the Faculty Senate, Admin, the Board of Trustees, and the State Board of Regents."

"Whoa there, Leslie. We don't make presentations at these get-togethers. The kids decide the agenda, not us. Have a seat, let's talk."

He explained he'd been mainly staying in the background, only providing some stability, keeping the kids away from partisan speeches, and emphasizing rational discussion.

"This meeting is for them, not us. My being there validates their right not to have to decide for one side or the other. It gives validity to their moderation and even to their confusion."

"So you don't want me to say anything?"

"I'll introduce you, but please don't try to bring this thing under the umbrella of the Resolution, or a committee. Let's keep it an impromptu rap session for those who don't want to be radicalized. Just make yourself available to answer questions if asked, like we're all sitting around a big kitchen table."

"And you're the dad. And that makes me the mom, right?"

"Older siblings might be a better way to look at it."

"I like it. I'll leave my flowchart here, pick it up later when we get back."

"I won't be coming back. I have a practice session with Goldenrod over in Music and Speech."

"Oh, I thought we might have a bite to eat."

Her chart back in her own office, they headed out, the day chilly and overcast.

"Did you vote in today's big referendum?" she asked.

"No."

"I voted for the teach-in. Why didn't you vote?"

"I don't want to give any support to this Concerned Citizens of Kent group. This referendum is a means for them to assert control. Any of the three votes is a vote for them. I don't trust this Shapiro guy, and we both know where Rachel Gibbs stands, with her spray paint."

"At least they're trying to get everyone's voice heard."

"It's a ruse."

"Are you solidly in Admin's camp? Did you see they established committees on Student Senate and Faculty Senate to..."

"...To find facts and make recommendations? Yes, I saw it. Always too late, always showing appeasement rather than leadership, always trying to look like they're doing something. But in the same breath they issue a statement that anyone can recruit on campus, they print some candy-ass, feel-good article about White's secretary, trying to show what a nice, homey fellow he is, and they press on with charges from Music and Speech. To top it all off, they propose changes to the Code that allow the very thing students are protesting against. And rather than coming out of their refuge in the admin building and talking to these kids, they send messages via the *Stater* who seems to agree with all their proposals."

"Wow, Jake," Leslie said, keeping up with his angry strides, "sounds like you're becoming a militant yourself."

Jake slowed his pace, realizing she was right about his rising temper, that he should calm down.

"All this is getting on my nerves. I'm here to build a career not to fight against a revolution."

When he escorted Leslie into the cafeteria he was shocked to see the group had once again doubled. It was now a crowd. Several tables had been pulled together, and Jake knew immediately that it would present a problem for the cafeteria director. As the buzz of conversation settled, Naomi rose and pointed to a vacant chair, gave up the one beside it that had apparently been hers and motioned for Leslie to take it. Jake spotted Audrey and Aaron toward the corner in back and nodded.

The formerly meek and mousy Naomi spoke up. "I have an announcement," she said, showing a power in her tone that Jake would not have predicted. "We have formed an official student group, Students for Moderation, and all we have to do to get funds and an actual meeting place is find a faculty advisor. Mr. Ernst is not a faculty member exactly, so if anyone knows a prof that might sponsor us, that's all we need."

"Great," Jake said. "This started with four students from Comp 101, now it looks like a movement. I had no idea Naomi was working on a club, so congrats, young woman. I'm sure you'll find an advisor."

"I'll volunteer right now," Leslie said, standing. "I'm an assistant professor in English, official faculty."

Sporadic applause arose, most of those in attendance not fully aware of what this was all about.

"But only if Mr. Ernst keeps coming," shouted Aaron.

After nodding that, of course, he would, he said, "For the newcomers, Naomi, why don't you explain what this group is doing?"

And there was Naomi, taking over, clarifying quite lucidly the usefulness and the need for moderate students to share concerns and discuss their reactions to campus events.

"Last week," she said, "Mr. Ernst made it clear that it's becoming a choice between President White and SDS. But we want to have a choice somewhere in between, and our voice is never heard. And some of us don't know what we want. We need the student body to have a way to understand things, to talk about things, to keep our studies going, which is why we're in college, not to overthrow the government."

"And to stay out of the draft," came a male voice.

"How many of you voted in the referendum today?" Leslie asked, still on her feet.

And so the meeting proceeded, calmly, rationally, Leslie taking the reins of designating whose turn it was to speak, Jake delighted to have a back seat. He even saw a possible means of escape altogether, now that the group had grown and was on its way to something other than a kitchen table conversation. And he noticed Audrey's constant stare, her smiles, her seeming tolerance of his professional mask. Her lovely eyes seemed to say, *that leaves just we two, doesn't it, Jake?* Or maybe that's what he wanted her eyes to say.

No, squash that thought, if it exists. Don't allow it to exist.

So he shifted to wondering if, like Admin's scurried attempts to quell the uprising, Naomi's vision for her now official organization hadn't simply come too late.

On the way out of the cafeteria, he noticed a pamphlet labeled Yippie Events lying on a table for various campus fliers. Not having heard of this student organization, he picked it up. On the way to his practice session he flipped it open and saw an announcement for an open Yippie meeting featuring one Bernadine Dohrn, a name he'd seen somewhere as a national leader of SDS. She was to speak at this meeting the following Monday. The fact that SDS and its literature had been legally banned on campus peaked his interest. Could the Yippie group be an SDS cover, like the CCC?

Monday evening, April 28, five days later ...
Curious about Miss Dohrn's appearance at the Yippie meeting in Williams Hall, Jake had hung around into the night doing research in the library. He grabbed a quick bite at the Union and hiked across to the southeast corner of campus to find out what the infamous SDS celeb had to say. The room was crowded with scruffy militants, all seats taken, so Jake stood in the back. It was only the second such indoor meeting he'd attended. His information stream about campus radicalism came from the daily student paper, Mark Rudd's appearance in the auditorium, radio commentary, playing for Goldenrod at rallies and demonstrations, and scuttlebutt from Adele and other casual acquaintances. At this gathering, however, he had the feeling he was in the midst of serious radicalism. It felt chilling. These people weren't messing around. They were excited and smelled victory.

The noise of chatter in the large classroom was almost an uproar, and after some testing of the mike, a number of announcements were made about bail, court proceedings, a notice of Holly McGill's acquittal from her riot charge, all of which garnered clamorous applause and cheers. Then came a strong-armed expulsion of several members of the law enforcement program. When everything settled down, Miss Dohrn finally took the stage, looking quite professional compared to the general ilk of the crowd.

Surprisingly fresh-faced, she was about Jake's age, her long brown hair parted in the middle and hanging over the front of her brown turtleneck. She knew how to speak, and her subject involved congratulations of the successes happening at Kent as well as the subject of carrying guns. She insisted that after the treatment of the Black Panthers, blacks everywhere had the right to wield firearms for self-protection, and she extended this right to SDSers as well. She even stated that she, herself, would be willing to kill in self-defense, and for revenge, though she stammered here and tried to take the revenge idea back by suggesting the comment was figurative, not literal.

Though Jake was stunned by the atmosphere of violence in the room, his principal shock came when he saw Wettman standing against the side wall in semi disguise, unshaven, baseball cap, camping attire, but gray hair and pot belly identifying him without doubt. He whispered now and then to several student types standing next to him.

Not wanting to be seen by the government agent, Jake edged himself toward one of the back exits and, having got adequate sense of what was going on, made his escape into the spring chill of the night.

On his way back past Satterfield, he felt a wave of fear pass though him, not only for himself but for this innocent community and even the world beyond. Miss Dohrn was a dangerous person, of this he was sure, and a national intent was descending upon poor little Kent.

49

Thursday, May 8, two weeks later ...

When Jake walked into the faculty section of the Union carrying a tray with a grilled cheese, fries and a lemonade, he saw Leslie at a window table. She stood and waved at him. He wove his way through crowded tables and joined her. She wore her usual business suit and bright neckerchief, her hair pulled back, making her look like a stock broker.

"Several people have asked for that chair," she said, "but I saved it. Didn't know why, but now I do."

Spring had finally broken, a shower last evening allowing students to use the wet grass of Blanket Hill across the Commons as a water-slide down into a mud patch.

"Rite of spring," Leslie said. "Dirty, but less demeaning than panty raids."

"When I first heard the name of that hill, I thought it was named for an esteemed Professor Blanket."

She laughed. "You didn't guess it's a make out place?"

"At Penn State we used the grounds around the stadium."

"At Ohio State we used a little park by the river. Do you have a girlfriend, Jake? A fiancé? A spouse?"

"None of the above."

She gave him a wry look. "Hmm, I wonder why?"

"*Et vous?*"

"Just out of a three-year relationship. Free as a bird at the moment."

"No scars?"

"Not deep ones. He's an engineer. After we graduated from OSU he moved to Peoria to work for Caterpillar. I ended up here. Oil and water. So you're remaining celibate to work on *The Sacred Wood?*"

"It's complicated. Hey, have you noticed a downturn in the quality of your students' work?"

"Changing the subject, huh? Yes, I have. Attendance is way down, papers not turned in, test scores even more pathetic than usual. I liked what you said at the meeting yesterday about maintaining their focus. But with all the campus turmoil, now we have a hunger strike on Admin's lawn. How can anyone concentrate? Shapiro is pushing hard, man. How 'bout you, Jake. Keeping your mind on your research?"

"Trying to. At least the library is less crowded."

"Maybe we could both use a little break," she said, looking down at her hands, which were smooth and pale, clear lacquer on her nails, a small opal ring on a pinky, a charm bracelet on one wrist, a leather banded watch on the other.

She looked up and hit him with that sensuous look she'd given him in his office. Such angelic hands didn't match that look, the message of which was absolutely clear. He now knew exactly where the phrase *bedroom eyes* came from. She held it longer than a glance, making her message unmistakable, then smiled. Jake felt himself responding, checked it.

"A break, yeah," he said. "If we can make it through this month without the place combusting. This morning on my way into Satterfield, someone had sprayed 'Going Up in Smoke' on the pavement."

She smiled tolerantly. "Maintenance was trying to get it off when I went in. Are you planning to watch White on TV tonight?"

"No, all this is starting to give me a pain in my gut. It's like watching a train wreck about to happen. I'll glance at the aftermath in tomorrow's paper."

"Jake?"

"What, Leslie?"

"Let's have dinner together tomorrow night. I know a place out in the country, the Rusty Nail. On me."

"That sounds nice, Leslie, but my bluegrass group is playing at the Eye."

"The Eye?"

"The Needle's Eye, coffee shop, next to the Hood. Come by if you like, I'll introduce you to the others. And they serve dynamite apple cider, cinnamon stick and all."

"Count me in. Maybe we can go somewhere for drinks afterward."

"Leslie..."

"I won't *hurt* you," she said with those eyes again. "What's the harm in a little libation on a Friday night? Forget all this campus drama for a while. It'll be therapeutic."

Therapy with this girl?

He could use some treatment, had even thought about calling Lil, an impulse immediately squashed.

Leslie leaned toward him across the small table. "Ever hear of tantric yoga?"

"You mean like the *Kama Sutra*?"

"Ever tried it?"

"No."

"It's incredibly ... enlightening."

Jake shifted at the annoying disturbance in his slacks, beginning to forget that she was entering his weakest area. This young woman leaning toward him, speaking in a near whisper, her green eyes saying simply that she wanted to fuck, must have sensed his weedy inner core. She was close enough for him to pick up her subtle scent, and he had a flash of her pale, naked body beneath him.

"I'll show you the positions," she said in a tone that matched her eyes.

He backed away. This was dangerous but irresistible.

If this creature wants to fuck, then I'll fuck her. Why not? Why the hell not?

But he knew this voice was coming from an indecent part of him, one he really didn't want to listen to.

With an unavoidable coldness in his voice which acknowledged her intention thoroughly, he said. "A drink after our show might just be pretty damn nice."

Later in the library Jake sat in the smoking lounge, the day's *Stater* in his hands as a few other students puffed away and chatted. Since Bernadine's appearance, of which, oddly, not a word showed up in the paper, he marginally kept abreast of the campus turmoil. In full swing, Shapiro, the newly arrived leader, was keeping the heat on Admin, White in particular—demonstrations, debates, rhetorical challenges, lawsuits, outcries against more arrests from photos, and now a hunger strike on the lawn outside White's offices. White was smart, often leaving town on a schedule of academic appearances and conferences to discuss higher ed. On campus, he gave speeches on the student TV channel and sometimes in the paper.

CCC members had confronted him with four demands and said they wouldn't eat until he answered them, camped on Admin's lawn. So he finally answered them in today's edition, predictably denying them all four, which, in turn, also predictably, gave the radicals fuel for their radicalization fire. The demands were the oft repeated list to abolish four university sanctioned programs: ROTC, the Law Enforcement Department, the Liquid Crystals Institute, and the Northeastern Ohio Crime Lab. Shapiro insisted that these demands were nonnegotiable.

In White's published reply, the president stated in summary that Admin would continue to fight against any violence and disruption. In addition, he defended all his past decisions and ended by reminding Shapiro that CCC's own campus referendum clearly indicated that disruptive tactics were unwanted by the vast majority of students. He affirmed student arrests and emphasized that decisions about dropping charges lay purely in the hands of the county prosecutor. No university-proclaimed amnesty was forthcoming.

What did his answer portend other than more tension? And the mass of the student body was torn in-between as indicated to Jake not only in the confused voices of the ever growing moderation group in the Pit, but by downward class attendance, shoddy work and inattentiveness to their studies. How could anyone concentrate on learning in such an environment? President White insisted on maintaining order but was accomplishing the very opposite. And the dissidents sensed their advantage and pressed on. Jake pitied White and detested the militants. And he was determined not to permit the stress of the campus to deter him from his purpose for coming here in the first place.

He was pierced by the irony of his having arrived in this backwoods location seeking a refuge. It seemed that no escape from all this uproar existed anywhere in the country. Certainly if it had hit Kent, beautifully secluded and forested Kent, Ohio, City of Trees, no place was immune. So, what the hell, maybe he could find a brief escape in tantric yoga. Or maybe not. Could he venture into Leslie's domain with Tasha in his heart? Though his heart told him one thing, his body told him quite another.

And even at this very moment, here he was, a campus newspaper in his hands, worried about it all. No! No! Back to *The Sacred Wood*. Back to his future. He tossed the paper aside and returned to the study room. Two more courses plus his thesis and he'd be out of here.

Friday, May 9, next evening ...

Goldenrod finished their first set on the small corner stage under a malfunctioning spotlight, Jake having stepped forward for two guitar licks of his own devising and a solo vocal on "Kisses Sweeter than Wine." Wash rounded out the set with a rousing singalong to his perfect imitation of Tennessee Ernie Ford's "Sixteen Tons." As the group settled at their table in the back, Jake felt a tap on his shoulder and turned to see Leslie, wearing a beret over her flowing; shoulder length, fashionably disheveled hair. Her eyes shone wide with astonished delight.

"You guys are totally out of sight!"

"Yeah," Wash answered, "that spotlight wasn't working for shit."

Laughing, Jake introduced Leslie all around and found an empty chair for her. Adele eyed him as if to ask, what happened to Natasha. The place became noisy with chatter, and the group did their second set.

After midnight Leslie and Jake went upstairs and out into a warm spring night. She wore low-cut bellbottoms, revealing her bare midriff, and a gauzy blouse which showed a black bra underneath. Now that they were alone, he felt ready for what lay ahead. He led the way to his van.

"This car is really cool. Do you go camping?"

"Just got it Christmas break. Looking forward to the summer."

"Only three weeks away. I wish I would be here."

"What are your plans for the break?" he asked when they were aboard.

"England, for my dissertation research. Going to immerse myself in Jane's environment. Her home is now a museum, in Hampshire, and there's a library there with a lot of original documents."

"When are you leaving?"

He was headed out 43-South toward the Holiday Inn where he'd once gone with Lil.

"June twelfth, after a few days in the Big Apple."

For some reason Jake felt gratified to hear she was leaving town.

"Did you see White on TV last night?" she asked.

"No, how was it?"

"He's a lousy speaker, hems and haws, repeats himself, needs some lessons in public oratory."

"Maybe that's why he hides in his office rather than coming out and talking to the kids."

"Maybe. But I give him credit for facing his attackers. They got into a big discussion about changing the conduct code to deal with emergencies. The CCC guy, Shapiro, insisted that any changes go through a neutral mediation board. Then they argued about the makeup of that board. And White agreed to write a weekly column in the *Stater* as a way to open channels of communication, but only if invited. Jake, I don't want to think about all that right now."

She slid across the bench seat and caressed his thigh.

"I reserved a room," he said.

"Cool. I told my roommate not to wait up."

Jake had applied a cynical veneer over his decent side, now expecting a tennis match *par excellence*. Leslie didn't seem to notice the transformation. After several screwdrivers and a few dances, they went outside, up the stairs to the second level and into room B222, nothing fancy but clean smelling. They took turns in the bathroom, and when he came out, she was sitting on one of the double beds lighting a small pipe.

"What's that?" Jake asked.

"What do you think it is, baby?"

She'd undergone a transformation herself; perhaps just allowed that expression in her bedroom eyes take over her entire presence.

"Pot?" Jake asked.

She looked at him quizzically. "Don't tell me you're opposed. Don't you dare tell me that."

"Not opposed, but..."

"You mean ... you never smoked?"

"Right. I never."

"Holy Moses! Come on, sit here, I'll show you. Turning on with a virgin will be a blast,."

His lack of experience in the world of dope undermined the confident seducer he'd been playing.

"Come on," she said. "Sit."

He kicked off his shoes. She lit the pipe with a small lighter, inhaled and held her breath. After fifteen seconds or so, she let out a flow of pungent smoke and handed him the pipe.

"You don't smoke cigarettes either?"

"Nope."

"It's the same, but we hold it in. This is really potent shit, called Maui-Wowwie. So don't take too much at first."

He took the pipe to his lips and she held the flame of the lighter to it. He sucked in the smoke, broke out coughing.

"Too much, silly lad. I warned you."

She took another hit herself, and relit the pipe for him, her spittle on the stem. This time he was more careful, felt a mild burn in his throat, held his breath.

"Let's turn on the radio," she said. "Take another toke, I'm going to get us some Cokes. Then we'll get down to the funky business of this little *tete-a-tete.*"

He did as instructed and in somewhat of a haze waited for her return. She rushed into the room with a flow of warm night air. More than soft drinks, she was loaded now with chips, cupcakes, and Snicker bars. On the top forty station, the 5th Dimension's hit "Aquarius" came on.

The world is going to hell. I might as well go along with it.

But this hell was pure heaven. His body never felt more alive, more virile, and Leslie made a sterling tennis partner with a tantric twist, long moments of silent titillation. In the dim light from the bathroom, the match went on and on, several overtime sets. Sex for sex's sake. Raw senses, her body, her tongue, her firm breasts, ripe nipples, moans, her hands and mouth all over him. They gorged upon each other, a banquet of music, color, scent, touch, surging through a warm sea.

It wasn't until afterwards, lying in this enchantress's arms that he thought of Tasha. Yes, he wanted to show her the effects of this magic herb. He had to find a way for them to be together for all time; he just had to.

50

Friday, May 23, two weeks later ...

"You've achieved hero status in the Department," Adele said at their window table in the Union.

Jake munched a French fry loaded with ketchup. "What are you talking about?"

"That group you started over at Tri-Towers. The whole place is talking about it."

"The kids started that group, and Leslie Robbins is the sponsor."

"Activist moderates. Oxymoron in action."

She took a bite of her BLT. Wash showed up with a food-laden tray. He pulled a chair from another table and squeezed his huge frame between Jake and Adele.

"Did she tell you the news?" he asked Jake.

"I didn't start that club," Jake said. "The kids did."

"What club?" Wash asked.

"This big lug and I are tying the knot," Adele interrupted, leaning against Wash. She held out her left hand to show off her diamond.

Jake smiled. "That's great. But I thought you two *were* married."

"Gotta make it official now that she's..."

Jake took a breath. "Wow. That kid will be one musical genius."

"Probably rather play baseball," Wash said.

Jake grinned at his two best friends at KSU. "I'll be damned. At least something around this place finally makes perfect sense."

"Yeah," Wash said, his mouth stuffed with burger, "and, hear the other news? Somebody chained the doors of the Liquid Crystals Institute up on Lincoln Street. The cops hadda get a special device to cut through. Outside, when I got here, there's a rally going on, and some blond chick is standing on an upside-down trash can cussing her butt off and saying SDS did it."

"The militants aren't letting up, are they?" Jake said.

"Some other kid said they're gonna start buying guns, blowing up buildings, anything to shut down the university. It's getting outta hand. They're really pissed off about Admin's confirmation of ROTC. They're raising hell but not scoring any points. I guess chaining the doors of a building for half an hour gave them some satisfaction."

"Summer break is a week away," Adele said. "That should take care of it."

"Yeah," Wash said, "but we're not playing at the rallies any more. At least not me. And the Owl booked us for next fall," he added, "and we're playing at Blossom in July, plus a couple fairs. Other than this SDS shit, life is good. Maybe we should shoot for the really big time, the Hinckley Buzzard Festival next spring."

Wash has the right attitude—let all this SDS disruption slide over us and focus on what really matters, love and music.

Jake wished he could do it. As he headed back up the hill toward Satterfield, he heard the Victory Bell tolling. From the hillside past the ramshackle ROTC building he saw some two hundred students gathered on Blanket Hill. On the Commons below, the cadets marched in their weekly drill. The field had been officially lined off to indicate a "classroom," any infringement a punishable violation. In mockery, a band of jesters made the intrusion. Carrying brooms and mops over their shoulders and wearing buckets on their heads, they high-stepped alongside the aspiring soldiers, jeering as the spectators on the hillside laughed and yelled out catcalls. Most of the gathering had paused on their way to and from class. Many stopped and watched from the walkway in front of Taylor Hall.

Media were there too, including photographers from Taylor, which housed the Journalism Department as well as the *Stater*. The cadets obeyed the shouted orders of their commanders, bearing as best they could the ridicule going on around them.

For several months a special committee set up by White had reviewed the academic efficacy of ROTC, involving numerous departments in which military courses were taught. White had formed the review in the light of several prestigious schools having banned the government-sanctioned program. All of the departments involved affirmed both the academic value of the courses and the teaching credentials of the ROTC instructors. White's final decision to support the program only enraged the militants further and gave them another issue to use on their non-ending radicalization campaign. From the group in the Pit, Jake knew that the campaign, if not radicalizing many students, was at least causing stress and anxiety in the student body at large.

And in Jake as well. He lacked Wash's ability to let the crap wash over him. Maybe if things had worked out with Tasha, he'd have been able to do the same.

He left the rowdy ridicule happening on the Commons and continued to Satterfield where he picked up a stack of final student essays, then headed home. Tonight he would meet up with Leslie for another fun filled evening of mystical pleasure. They'd have dinner, catch "Camelot" at the Kent Theater, then drive out to the Holiday Inn, their own little, stoned, sex filled castle. Back on Willow he saw an unfamiliar car, an Olds sedan, in the driveway of the house where he lived. And when he turned onto the walk leading to the porch, a man, mid-thirties, in casual clothes, light jacket, Indians cap, got out and approached him with a large envelope.

"Jacob Thomas Ernst?"

"Yeah?"

He handed the envelope toward Jake, who took it, puzzled.

The man grinned. "You've just been served."

With Jake standing there stunned, the man hurried to his car, backed out the driveway and peeled out toward Main. Jake looked at the envelope, nothing written on it. He tore the top off and pulled out another one. The return address said United States House of Representatives, Committee for Internal Security, Legal Department, etc., etc.

He sat down on a porch step and pulled out the contents, a letter of subpoena to provide testimony at a committee hearing in D.C., June 23: subject of the hearing—SDS activity at Kent State University.

Jake's head dulled, swirled. He gave up reading the boiler plate about penalties for not appearing, etc., etc. Dazed, he sat on the steps, papers in hand until Billy cruised up the walkway on his Schwinn, smoking a cigarette.

"Gazing at the lovely scenery?" asked the ever sardonic reporter.

Jake handed him the notice.

"Great balls of fire!" Billy said. "Wettman must be behind this."

"Must be."

"Thought the asshole was out of here."

"I saw him at the Bernadine Dohrn thing a couple weeks ago."

"Bernadine Dohrn? And you didn't tell me? Shit, man!"

"You're not going to write about this, are you?"

"Hey, does a bear shit in the woods? It's a story. It's how I earn my enormous salary. No way to keep this off our pages. It's public info."

"I shouldn't have shown you. You caught me off guard."

"You the only one from here testifying?"

"How should I know?"

"Surely not. Are you an insider with SDS?"

"Hell no."

"Are you leveling with me?"

"Yes, dammit."

"So why you?"

"Maybe Wettman spotted me at that meeting. I went out of curiosity, like quite a few others there. A big mistake. I'd been to Rudd's thing too."

"I didn't know the Dohrn chick was here. She's the deep shit. Wants to blow up Macy's, the NYPD, carries dynamite around in her purse. Why have you been keeping your downstairs blood brother in the dark?"

"There were fliers about that meeting all over campus," Jake noted. "I did wonder why it wasn't in the paper, though."

"Cause you didn't give me a heads up, man."

"Cause you fell asleep at the wheel. Should have noticed those fliers."

"Okay, let's go inside. You can fill me in on all the details."

"No way. That's the last scoop you're getting out of me. Anyway, I have a date."

Billy smiled. "Dig it. First things first. We'll talk later. That flutist, used to live upstairs?"

"No."

"She could tootle my oboe any time."

"Shut the fuck up, Billy." Jake rose, headed inside.

"Hey, sorry, pal. Later, okay?"

"I'm not talking to anyone about this." He closed the door solidly behind him and went up the stairs, rolling the papers into a ragged cone.

Leslie lived with a roommate in a downtown apartment. Still baffled about this new wrinkle in his existence, Jake picked her up for their movie date and drove to the Brown Derby Restaurant on East Main, rumored to be one of White's haunts, close to his campus home but far enough not to be bothered by many students. The food was good, but Jake's taste buds weren't exactly at their peak performance on his pineapple ham steak. And later in the crowded theater the film passed by him like a blur, Leslie's hand under his jacket on his thigh.

He was looking forward to the magic weed that would take him to a realm where subpoenas were no more significant than passing clouds. But would that be the case this night? After the movie they stopped at Hahn's and picked up two chocolate éclairs and a dozen assorted cookies.

"What's wrong?" Leslie said on their way out of town. "You seem on another planet tonight."

"No, I'm here, old planet earth."

"You could have fooled me. This being our last date until next fall, I expect full participation."

"I hope you brought some of that Hawaiian Wowwie."

"Maybe we can skip the dancing," she said, "go straight to the room."

"Great idea."

"Why do you always rent a room, anyway? You said you live alone."

"Thin walls."

As usual on a weekend night the motel lot was packed with cars. After checking in to their reserved room, they bought orange sodas and chips from the vending machine and went right up to 222 where the magic herb, top forty hits, and Leslie's silky, supple body took him on a sensual ride to outer space.

51

Thursday night, May 29, six days later ...

In a Bowman Hall classroom Jake filled out a form to take a three day course in meditation. The lecturer, a German man with gleaming eyes and slicked back silver hair, had talked about reducing stress by using a meditation technique brought to America by the Beatles' Indian guru. On the form, the final question asked whether the applicant had smoked marijuana or taken hallucinogenic drugs in the last two weeks. Not about to admit to having committed a crime, Jake left the meeting, tore up the unsigned document and deposited it in the nearest trash barrel. So much for this method of obtaining transcendental consciousness. He'd have to stick to tantric yoga.

Monday morning, June 2, three days later ...

In his office Jake completed his grade sheet and carried it along with his finalized lesson plans and attendance report to the main office where he handed it all to Violet, the head secretary, mid-forties, dark hair cut as short as a man's, and dangling brass Hindu earrings. She looked the papers over and checked off his name on a list of instructors.

"Are you here for the summer, Jake?" she asked, the scent of lilacs wafting from a huge bouquet on her desk.

"I am. Trying to finish my master's by next spring."

"I wanted to tell you, your student evaluations are off the charts." She smiled wryly. "I was wondering how much you pay them for such nice comments."

"I save up from my huge stipend each semester."

"On a more serious note, I have a message here. Dr. Shenk would like to see you right away. I think he's in his office as we speak."

Jake had informed Lord Byron of his June appointment in a House hearing room. When he entered the composition office, Nan waved him to go right into the inner sanctum. Seated behind his pipe paraphernalia, Shenk gestured for him to close the door.

"Extraordinary!" the professor said, motioning Jake to sit. "Testifying in Congress? Do you have access to some special information our nation needs?"

"No, but do you remember telling me that man Wettman wanted to talk? I guess it all came from that."

"I know you formed a group over in Tri-Towers. Could that be it?"

"I didn't form that group, only participated until Leslie Robbins became their sponsor. I attended on my free time, which I'm sure is my right."

"Your right? Quite so, no one is debating that. But are you associated with any of the activists here in the Department? There are quite a few, you know. Dr. Filbert is chairman of the new chapter of ACLU, and others have submitted petitions and resolutions siding with the radicals. I think I saw your name on a few of them. Still others are actual members of SDS, Yippies, Young Socialists and whatnot. Of course, Holly McGill was even arrested, although acquitted at her hearing. But she has other charges pending. Her husband is now in prison, I've heard."

"That was Leslie Robbins' resolution I signed. Exceptionally moderate. I push the idea of students' not sacrificing their studies because of all the noise flying around."

Shenk puffed on his pipe. "I checked wherever I could and didn't find anything against you, talked to some of your students, all of whom said you insist on teaching the subject matter of the syllabus and avoid discussing politics. And you've done a fine job supervising the new TA's. But I have one lingering problem regarding keeping you on in that capacity."

Jake waited in silence.

"It's about that Ferguson boy. I gave you a direct order to show me his writing, an order which you seemed to have ignored."

"Bobby Ferguson walked out of my class, hasn't returned. I have nothing to show you. I had to fail him for the course."

"I suppose your attendance records will confirm that. I won't tolerate insubordination, Jake."

"I should have informed you. Sorry."

"Yes, you should have. It would have avoided my concern."

"My mistake. But my attendance forms will check out."

"Good enough. I really didn't want to let you go. It seems you're one of the sensible voices around this madhouse. So, that little matter concluded, I'm glad to tell you I'm keeping you on. Things will settle down for the summer with the great majority of the students gone. We'll cover for you the days you'll be in Washington. You know, don't you, President White will be testifying too?"

"I wasn't aware of that."

"And Dean Matson, and Campus Security. So you're in good company. It probably means you're not to be accused of anything."

Somehow this assurance didn't ease Jake's mind.

Back in his own office, his official duties completed for the spring quarter, Jake turned his attention to the issue of testifying at a congressional hearing. It seemed an overwhelming prospect. Should he get a lawyer? Check on his rights? How much would that cost? He'd have to make travel arrangements. He'd drive, of course, seven hours or so. Maybe he could stay at Ainsley's place, twenty minutes outside of D.C. She'd be amazed that he'd become a witness about SDS activities. Any of his undergraduate roommates might have been called, perhaps, but hardly he, who'd had to be dragged into protest events. Stephen O'Shea would be no surprise, but he'd found safety in Canada.

Then the thought hit Jake that his appearance at the hearing might prelude his arrest for ripping up his draft card after he'd received his 4F. Would they haul him off in handcuffs right after he answered their questions? And what kind of questions would they ask him? Was he on some kind of trial? Was this Wettman's revenge for Jake's having exposed the man's presence on campus? Other than smoking pot, had Jake done anything actually illegal since he'd come to Kent? He'd gone to some meetings, signed a couple of petitions, spent some of his own time talking to students. These would be the rights of any citizen, nothing subversive about them. Certainly the U.S. Congress wouldn't be interested in his mild objection to the war. Not when people like Bernadine Dohrn and Mark Rudd were traveling around inciting militants to carry guns and blow up buildings. Or any number of Kent State revolutionaries, McGill or Engle, *et al.*

So why him, Jacob Thomas Ernst, a farm boy from Amish country, trying his best to keep his head down?

In the library a flirtatious young librarian with an engagement ring helped him locate information about congressional hearings, rights, procedures and whatnot, all written in nearly indecipherable legalese. But he discovered that in the hearing context his legal rights were far less than in a trial. Counsel was permitted but without coaching. And documents could be subpoenaed as well as witnesses. Other than his shredded draft card, what documents might they have found that incriminated him? He'd written several letters to the editor back in Lancaster and signed two petitions at Kent. Big deal! Nothing worthy of Congress's attention. Christ!

On his subpoena he'd been given nothing but the time and date of the hearing and the number of the meeting room. The subject matter was *SDS at Kent.* In the library he learned that the jurisdiction of the hearing had to be clearly expressed and that all hearing questions had to be within the stated jurisdiction. So Jake doubted that the subject of his draft card or his having smoked pot could come up.

He jotted down information he might actually have about SDS on campus. The specific reference to that group seemed to leave out the now defunct KCEWV or the newly formed CCC. His SDS contact under the stated jurisdiction on his subpoena had been minimal. So what did they want with him?

After a burger and soft drink at K-Shoppe, he went home, dug Ainsley's phone number from a seldom used slot in his wallet, and dialed her number. He heard her unmistakable voice. After she settled from her shock at his calling her, he explained his situation.

"Of course you can stay here," she said. "You'd better not come to town and not."

He didn't want to ask if she'd married the Scottish folksinger or found someone new. Her romantic status hardly seemed relevant when he had no doubt their own relationship had finished. So he checked the calendar and told her when to expect him.

"Still a commune going on there?" he asked.

"Kind of, but a different sort. We're getting the school started, the barn torn down, the cottages being revamped for staff, some bulldozers rumbling around. Jake, I can't wait to see you again, find out what's been going on with you. How did you ever end up at Kent State in Ohio? Never heard of it."

52

Sunday, June 22, three weeks later …

Late afternoon Jake nervously pulled into the driveway of what used to be called Alloway on a small sign, now Alloway School. The once worn great house had been freshly painted. Several cars were parked outside, the big barn gone indeed. In slacks and blouse, Ainsley ran out the front door, across the porch and greeted him with a strong, lengthy hug.

"It's so good to see you, Jake. You're as handsome as ever."

"I don't know about that, but you're as beautiful."

She grabbed his hand and led him into the house. After he used the rest room and waited in the living room, she came out of the kitchen carrying a tray with a tea pot, cups and condiments.

"Come into the office and fill me in on what's happening."

The piles of folders on the desk, on the chairs and tables indicated much work in progress, some of which she explained. He returned fire with the details about the hearing next day, info about his parents and how he'd landed in Kent.

"We should have kept in better touch," she said. "You came alone. I'm surprised. I thought there'd be a significant other."

"A significant other? That's a strange way of putting it."

"Would bed buddy be better?" she said, smiling.

She was really lovely, engaging brown eyes, thick dark brown hair, most of it cut off since he'd seen her last, more professional, less Joan Baez, but a shapely, gorgeous woman. As they talked on a divan by a bay window overlooking a shadowed green expanse of lawn, he couldn't help but feel the old attraction coming back, though he was intent on not showing it.

"I'm seeing a Marine," she said. "He's assigned to ceremonial functions here in D.C., color guards and that kind of silliness. He's, you know, the Greek God type."

"Is it serious?"

"I'm trying to avoid serious. I'm too busy with this project. Little did I know the hoops we'd have to jump through, construction permits especially. And zoning. The natives around here are fighting us, want to keep the area exclusively for their plantations. Then there's the whole accreditation process. Did you know, Jake, that in order to get academic accreditation you must first have a graduating class? Who's going to enroll in an unaccredited school in the first place?"

"Catch 22."

"We have several investors, and my inheritance was huge, Jake. I had no idea how much Daddy had saved for us, and Mother left every cent to me."

"The clairvoyant didn't get anything?"

"Nothing. Except her walking papers from me. Mother was much wiser than I gave her credit for."

They had dinner in a group, seven, the former hippie atmosphere replaced by nicely dressed, well-groomed professionals intent on building a K-12 academy on the A.S. Neil model. Most of the meal of lentil soup, salad, lamb with mint jelly was cooked and served by a middle-aged black woman named Norma, the conversation taken up by Jake's trying to explain his having to testify before a House committee.

"And no attorney?" asked a tall spindly fellow with wire rimmed glasses.

"But I did a lot of research. I'll go in there and tell the truth."

"The truth? So you're taking a radical approach."

After a chuckle all around, the guy said, "SDS, Weathermen, etcetera, etcetera, are fuckwads. I hope you nail the bastards."

After an evening of catching up and laughing over old stories, Jake was drifting off to sleep in the guest room when he heard the door creak open. Soon Ainsley slid out of her bathrobe, pulled back the covers and got in with him.

"How can I resist?" she said. "And after all, we've already done it so many times."

Jake didn't object to this flawed logic. Their intimacy was as luscious as it always had been, only better, like something cherished in one's memory and now revived as a final punctuation mark.

Monday, June 23, next day ...

When the uniformed guard checked off Jake's name on the official witness list, Jake parked in the lot, crossed C Street and climbed the stairs into the Cannon House Office Building. Inside the lobby with its twin marbled staircases, he paused, gazed up at the dome, listened to the echoed voices, and inhaled the history, never having thought he'd possess any reason to be in this hallowed place. He boarded a packed elevator and got off on the third floor where he followed others down a polished corridor and found Room 311. Half an hour early, he waited as the guard cleared him on a list and told him to take a seat in the area behind the witness table where a few others were already waiting, one of them a female student he recognized from rallies. Also, several campus cops.

"Doubt they'll get to you today, Mr. Ernst," the guard said. "These things run as slow as molasses in January. Tomorrow morning would be my guess."

Jake knew that President White would be testifying, but he hadn't planned on staying an extra night. He nodded to the guard and took a seat on a pew-like bench.

In front between two flags stood a long elevated table with microphones and unoccupied high-backed leather chairs. Forty-five minutes later several members and staff entered, followed by others. On the Republican side, Jake saw Wettman come in talking to a balding man with disheveled gray hair. Wettman surveyed the room, sneered when he caught Jake's eye and took a seat along with other staff members against the wall behind the dignitaries.

Thirty more minutes, things finally organized, the Republican chairman from Minnesota pounded his gavel. After a few preliminary remarks, Jake heard President White's name announced as the first witness. White entered from a side door with an entourage that included Dean Matson. A few minutes later they were seated at and behind the witness table ready to proceed. The Chairman said that although not necessary the oath would be given in order to assure any later skeptics that standard protocol had been followed. Several flashbulbs went off.

The Committee concerned itself with the method Kent State administrators had used to quell campus disturbances. Kent was contrasted to recent issues at Georgetown, the difference being that Georgetown had handled matters without external law enforcement while Kent had utilized outside forces. The Committee members were considering whether federal legislation should be passed in order to deal with campus disruptions. White didn't think so. He believed current laws were satisfactory and that further legislation would only inflame the situation. Though several members seemed adamant about creating new laws, they all lavishly praised President White for his wise, strong arm approach to the problem.

It seemed to Jake, incredibly, that the Committee was preparing to present the Kent strategy as a model for institutions nationwide, that is, of employing successive levels of local and state law enforcement depending on the urgency of the situation. White went on to propose that the Committee create a map with statistics to demonstrate the actual occurrences of campus violence throughout the country. His proposal was greeted with unanimous approval.

After lunch, a Kent senior, Mary Alice McVeigh, testified at length about her undercover work for the campus police. As a reporter for the *Daily Stater*, she'd attended meetings and conducted interviews with SDS leaders and their off campus guests, then secretly submitted accounts to law enforcement. She was presently employed fulltime at the campus security office. From her written reports, she presented detailed information of SDS activities and identified members shown in photographs at all the incidents, including pictures of herself among the crowds to verify her presence.

Answering questions from the Committee lawyer, she systematically covered each and every SDS event from the time she was a freshman.

Not having expected to stay an extra day, Jake considered calling Ainsley, but came to think their parting had been sweet and final. He had his camper, after all, and knew of a state park off the freeway toward Baltimore. He still couldn't figure out how he fit in to this hearing, but it was clear that the Committee was primarily concerned with campus enforcement procedures, having already taken for granted the danger SDS presented to national security. He was amazed at how comfortably President White and the tactics he employed were praised by the congressmen, especially in the light of how seriously flawed these methods appeared to be to Jake. Only one Committee member mentioned the idea of techniques of prevention being preferential to those of enforcement.

Despite his continued anxiety about his own appearance there, Jake quietly relished the opportunity he was receiving to see the inner workings of the nation's government, particularly as it applied to campus unrest. The Committee's brutal attitude toward dissent was chilling. He could see the congressmen, especially the two from Ohio, jockeying for positions that would receive approval from their mainstream constituencies, not about to express the idea of freedoms of speech and assembly as they might apply to the clearly reviled Students for a Democratic Society. The Committee's aim toward this group seemed not at all toward accommodating dissent but simply toward stamping the organization and its sympathizers out.

The only speck of light was the lone representative who expressed the idea of prevention through foresightful leadership rather than sheer repression.

Tuesday, June 24, next day ...

The continuation of the hearing involved Dean Matson and several Kent campus law enforcement officials recounting procedures and policies contrived and executed to stem the tide of SDS protest at KSU. Jake took in the testimony, surprised at the planning almost to the level of setups and entrapment, especially the hubbub that bordered on trickery at Music and Speech. Then Wettman testified from his notes, also identifying SDS leaders in photographs as well as presenting incriminating literature he'd gathered.

Finally, well after the lunch break, Jake, the final witness, stood for the oath and sat alone at the polished table, again surprised at his calmness, perhaps from two days of acclimating himself to the scene.

Chairman: Thank you for coming, Mr. Ernst. I understand you have a short statement. Proceed, sir.

Jake began reading: "Ever since I was served with a subpoena to come here, I've been wondering why. My knowledge about SDS is extremely limited. I am not a member nor am I associated with any members. I've seen them around campus and don't agree with their goals or methods, and have said as much when asked. I am opposed to the war in Vietnam and have said as much also. I am hoping that by the time I leave today, I'll understand the purpose of my having been called."

Some mild laughter arose in the room.

Chairman: I hope we'll *all* understand why we're here.

More laughter.

Jake read on: "I can only say what I believe. I believe the current unrest in our society stems from two main sources: the war in Vietnam and our national history of unfairness to blacks. The resistance to the war comes not from cowardice but from the sense of folly in our national foreign policy, a folly that violates the conscience of anyone who has taken the time to study it. And Reverend King revealed to all of us our nation's tradition of racism. I believe that when these two monumental errors have be rectified, organizations like SDS will simply disappear."

Chairman: Thank you, Mr. Ernst. We'll start the questioning with the Representative from Iowa, the Honorable Mr. Johnson.

Mr. Johnson: r. Ernst. I understand that you're on the faculty of Kent State University, is that correct?

Jake: I'm a teaching assistant in the English Department. I teach freshman composition in exchange for a small stipend and tuition toward my master's. I don't have faculty status.

Mr. Johnson: I stand corrected. Let me get directly to the point. On Tuesday, October 29, 1968, you attended a lecture by an SDS leader named Mark Rudd, is that correct?"

Jake: Uh, yes, I did.

Mr. Johnson: At that meeting did Mark Rudd state that the purpose of SDS is to overthrow the United States Government?

Jake: I think he said "bring it down."

Mr. Johnson: Which means overthrow, does it not?

Jake: Yes. But I am not sympathetic to that goal."

Mr. Johnson: Just answer the question, Mr. Ernst. And did Mr. Rudd say "by any means necessary?"

Jake: That meeting was long ago. I don't remember him saying those exact words, but he certainly implied it.

Mr. Johnson: Now Mr. Ernst, on Monday, April 28, 1969, did you attend a meeting in which Miss Bernadine Dohrn spoke?

Jake: Yes.

Mr. Johnson: Did Miss Dohrn also advocate the violent overthrow of the United State Government?

Jake: Yes.

Mr. Johnson: Did she advocate SDS members carrying guns?

Jake: Yes.

Mr. Johnson: Did she say she would be willing to kill for her cause?

Jake: If I remember correctly, she said she'd be willing to kill in self-defense.

Mr. Johnson: Did she also say she'd kill for revenge?

Jake: But she backtracked from that.

Mr. Johnson: Backtracked? In what way?

Jake: As if she'd meant it metaphorically.

Mr. Johnson: But she was advocating violent action against the government, was she not?

Jake: Yes.

Mr. Johnson: And the audience was made up of mostly SDS members, correct?

Jake: "I assume there were many members there. But I was only a spectator, as I'm sure others were too. I'm not a member of SDS and don't know much about the internal workings of their organization.

Mr. Johnson: During your attendance at other sundry presentations on and about campus did you hear local Kent State SDS leaders speak of violent revolution?

Jake: Yes.

Mr. Johnson: Would it be fair to say that according to the leaders you've heard and literature you've read, violent overthrow of the United States Government is key on SDS's agenda?"

Jake: Yes, that would be fair to say. But I've always taken those statements as inflated rhetoric to incite thought, not actual armed revolution.

Mr. Johnson: That's all I have for this witness, Mr. Chairman.

Chairman: Thank you, Mr. Johnson. I give the floor to Mr. Gregg from Vermont.

Mr. Gregg: Thank you, Mr. Chairman, and thank you for appearing today, Mr. Ernst. Are you feeling a little nervous?

Jake: A little, yes.

Mr. Gregg: Never thought you'd be called before such an august body, did you?

Jake: No sir, especially with my limited knowledge of the subject.

Mr. Gregg: You'd feel more at ease discussing Shakespeare, wouldn't you?

Jake: Several of his plays, but I'm hardly an expert.

Mr. Gregg: Have you ever been a member of SDS?

Jake: No sir.

Mr. Gregg: Ever attend one of their planning meetings?

Jake: No.

Mr. Gregg: Ever consult with their leadership?

Jake: No. I was approached to get involved, but declined.

Mr. Gregg: What is the extent of your knowledge of this organization, Mr. Ernst?

Jake: As a spectator I heard Rudd and Dohrn speak, heard the Kent State SDS leadership speak at rallies, read their statements in the student paper, saw fliers, pamphlets, graffiti. Anyone in the Kent State community would have to say much the same. SDS has become quite visible.

Mr. Gregg: Would you call yourself an expert on SDS, Mr. Ernst?

Jake: Definitely not.

Mr. Gregg: That's all I have. Thank you, sir.

Three more congressmen questioned Jake. He finally realized why he'd been called. It was all about SDS and violent overthrow, especially Rudd and Dohrn. The committee didn't seem to be after him personally although the three Republicans seemed nasty, the two Democrats polite, almost apologetic, as if they saw Jake's appearance at the hearing as a sham.

As he walked toward the lobby in the wide corridor, he felt a presence by his side. He turned and saw Wettman.

"Thought you fucked me, didn't you?" Wettman said as though he'd had a victory. "Guess now you see the power I have to screw up your measly life.

And I want you to know I'm holding that ace of spades in the hole. Can send you to Allenwood whenever the hell I want."

Jake walked on, the final little piece of the puzzle about why exactly he'd been brought here, solved. Simple revenge for his having leaked the story to Billy and exposing the guy's presence on campus. By four o'clock, his direct experience with Washington power completed, Jake was back on the road to Kent.

As he drove through the darkening Appalachians, Jake thought of his night with Ainsley, the memory of her once familiar scent still with him, her soft moans, her bright eyes, her quivering orgasm. Most remarkable in his mind was how easily they parted, a brief interlude then back to their current lives, a seamless farewell, no further expectations in either's mind. He guessed he was becoming a seasoned adult. Since Tasha left him six months ago, he'd now slept with two other women, tennis partners, but deeply intimate and with emotion, if not for the person exactly, surely for the game itself. What was happening to the love and devotion he felt for Tasha, which he'd once thought inviolable? Would he have to accept their separation as permanent?

He fought against that idea. He needed desperately to talk to her, not simply to have her rush into her apartment, hit the sack and depart, leaving him raw, his emotions in turmoil. She was deteriorating, the woman he loved, his Tasha, being layered over with realities that he couldn't control. Or so it seemed.

But, Jake, she has *been making decisions. She could have fought, stood up for what we had. Yes, there would have been unhappiness in her defying her family, but would her parents have really disowned her simply because she was in love with someone who loved her totally in return but who didn't fit in with their politics? Someone who would have done anything to make her happy, to protect her, to serve her? What kind of people are they?*

Tennis matches all well and good, fun and games were not what he imagined for his life. So what could he do to swim the moat and smash down the walls of the fortress between him and his true love?

He found himself speeding through a long tunnel beneath an Allegheny ridge, no light yet visible at the end.

53

Thursday, July 3, ten days later …

Eager to read what most of the campus would learn about President White's testimony before the House Internal Security Committee, also Wettman's, and of course his own, Jake hurried into the front entrance of Satterfield and picked up the student paper, which during the summer came out only on Thursdays. He settled at his desk with a cup of coffee and saw the article on the front page beside White's picture. The Committee was probing the national threat of SDS, and Kent was the second university examined, Georgetown the first.

The *Stater* report stated what it saw as White's most salient point: SDS is a danger to democratic procedure, to academic freedom, and to the basic needs of the university. White recommended a national chart of state-to-state campus destruction caused by the organization. He suggested that federal retaliatory legislation might simply inflame the situation, and lamented that a university should need to maintain an extensive peacekeeping apparatus. Finally he revealed that during the summer of 1968, the university had held a secret retreat to confer with police agencies about past actions and future contingencies.

In sum, White's general tone was one of enforcement, of lines of defense, rather than of reaching out to solve student concerns. The account concluded that in the hearing White saw himself in a defense position, more intent upon lauding his successes than in defining the true nature of the problem and in coming to some useful conclusions about how to solve it. He seemed to be drawing a line in the sand against his opponents, SDS in particular. Jake thought the Kent reporter had got it right.

According to the article, Wettman produced ten notebooks containing statistics, photographs and reports of disruptions during the so-called Spring Offensive. He focused on the family backgrounds of the major dissidents, apparently uncovering their communistic roots. He made a point of SDS headquarters being located across the street from the home of a former communist. To Jake, Wettman's testimony was McCarthyism all over again.

Miss McVeigh's appearance was not mentioned. Nor was Jake's. He leaned back in his chair, rolled the paper up and tossed it into his circular file. A shudder of trepidation passed through him. Yes, everything felt relatively peaceful during these summer days, but nothing seemed to be happening to protect the masses of students whose ability to focus on their studies was threatened by what now seemed to be an outright war going on around them. He seriously doubted the future existence of Kent State University and perhaps of many others. Higher education itself was in crisis. The battle lines were drawn. The summer would soon end with the contending forces back on campus assembled in full confrontational mode.

And Jake's quest in it all? – only to get his program completed before it all came crumbling down.

That evening when Jake walked down Willow Street on his way home from intensive work in the library, he saw a shiny new red Mercury Cougar behind his van in the driveway. He wondered if someone had finally moved into Tasha's vacated apartment. Because Edith Whitcomb had demanded full payment of the lease, Tasha's father had required Tasha to keep the rights to the place although most of her things had been removed. As a furnished apartment, however, the basics remained.

Whoever the new occupant is, they must have some bucks. That car is a gem.

Upstairs, some junk mail in his hands, he noticed the door to the other apartment standing open a crack. He heard some rustling inside. Then he caught a whiff of a familiar cooking aroma, excitingly familiar. His key still inside his lock, he went immediately to the adjacent door.

"Tasha?"

"In the kitchen, Jake."

And there she was, stirring something in a pot, short shorts and halter from behind, the sash of an apron around her waist, flip-flops on her feet.

"Thought you might like a good supper," she said, still at work.

Her hair was short, as he'd originally seen it, straight and silky to the nape of her neck. His heart thumped as he stood uncertainly at the door to the kitchen.

"There's a good Beaujolais I picked up for the occasion. I've tried it out. Pour yourself a glass. It's usually for Thanksgiving, so a bit old, but good enough for the Fourth, I think."

Jake had completely forgotten that tomorrow was Independence Day.

"I ... I'm sure it's better than Thunderbird."

She turned, her face lovely, tanned, no sign of tiredness or stress. She wore dark-framed glasses, something new.

"Nice specs," he said. "You look like a professor."

She smiled. "You don't, though. You look like an amazing stud."

He poured some wine from the already half empty bottle. He could use it, took a long swallow.

"I thought someone had moved in here. New car?"

"Daddy's gift for my compliance to his wishes."

There it was, a sore subject for Jake. But it seemed she'd grown accustomed to her situation. Gone was her desperate need to rush into his arms. Jake's wish for exactly that hadn't gone one whit, however.

"It's good to see you," he said, immediately embarrassed at having stated the obvious.

"I took the chance of your not climbing those steps with some gorgeous female. Just a minute, I want to hug you, but I need to finish stirring this sauce. Chicken parmesan tonight."

He didn't know whether to be happy or sad at her apparent quite healthy condition. Then she turned and rushed to him. There was that wonderful clinging embrace as if she needed him as much as breath.

He inhaled her scent, the same, and felt her body pressing, pressing, as before. And he felt his passion for her, precisely as always.

She moved slightly backward so they could kiss. And kiss they did, the taste of wine and marinara, the smooth wetness of her tongue. He could have skipped the meal.

Though she might have undergone some changes, the feeling was still right.

"Oh, my God! How I've missed this, Jake. If only you could know."

"Believe me, Tasha, I know."

"It's the love. The love."

They kissed again, held each other.

A kitchen timer went off.

"Sorry to interrupt this," she said, turning. "But it's time to eat."

"You're not in a hurry like your other visits?"

"That's one of the surprises I have for you. Guess what. We have two whole weeks. That is, if you're free."

She was back at the stove, arranging their plates.

"Have to study, teach, but I'll squeeze you in somehow."

She turned, smiled. "Thank you, kind sir."

He bowed, feeling easier inside, yet still confused.

"Ray's in Oklahoma, training. And I'm not teaching summer school this year. Also, I'm no longer under house arrest. I guess they believe I've succumbed to my fate. And in a way I have, but we can talk about difficult things later, okay?"

"Okay."

"Please be seated, *monsieur*."

"*Oui, madam*."

"Please think of me as still *mademoiselle*," she said. "I'm a *madam* only on paper, not at all in spirit." She finished off the last of the wine. "Don't worry, Jake, there's another bottle in my bag. I came prepared. Oh, and I told my parents I'd be here a lot these days, moving stuff out, cleaning up for the security deposit. Aren't I a clever conniver?"

Jake smiled without feeling it. "I'm glad you're here."

"Speaking of conniving, I have another surprise. I applied to Kent for a teaching assistantship in French. Brilliant idea, don't you think? And I have an *in* with the chairman from helping with those French students last summer. It suddenly struck me as a marvelous move. Took the Graduate Record Exam last week. Imagine, we two working in the same building."

"Wow! You have been conniving. I should warn you about something, though."

"What, that every woman there is in love with you?"

"Besides that. Actually something serious."

"Oh, no, don't tell me you're in love with someone else. I won't believe it, though I wouldn't blame you."

"Just that things have become really crazy on campus. I'm trying to get my program completed before the place really blows up. I'm not sure how long this university will be viable."

She stared at him. "Really, Jake? That serious?"

"These SDS people aren't going to relent. Neither is Admin. They can't. But the thing over in Music and Speech really set off a snowball rolling downhill. More and more kids getting radicalized each day. The only thing that slowed it down is summer break. But come fall, it's going to heat up again. I didn't have a chance to tell you, but I was subpoenaed to testify in front of Congress."

"The student senate, you mean?"

"No, the damn U.S. House Committee on Internal Security, the old Un-American Activities Committee."

"My God, Jake! What for?"

As she listened intently, he told her all about his testimony and about Wettman and President White.

"So like I said," he summed up, "it's getting really nuts. Dangerous nuts. I'm working with a group to help kids stay focused on what they're in school for, but Admin keeps making mistakes, and more and more students are drifting into activism. Something's going to blow, I can feel it."

"Something like what? More demonstrations, more marches?"

"Yes, and more confrontations with law enforcement, arrests. There are rumors about the ROTC building going up in flames. You should hear the rhetoric these people are using—burning, bombing, shooting. And SDS is well-organized, national leaders coming in and out, and Admin is not prepared to deal with armed insurrection, and most of the students are caught in between. Are you sure you want to be part of all this?"

She took a deep breath. "I'm sure I want to be as close to you as possible, Jake. That's what I'm totally sure of. I might even be able to play recorder for Goldenrod. I've been practicing. I have a music book of bluegrass classics. I'll have all kinds of excuses to get out of that dreadful domestic detention center at Twin Lakes. So I guess a little campus turmoil is a small price to pay. You'll be around to protect me from the revolutionaries, won't you? I'll just run down to your office. God, I can't believe you were called to Washington."

"Yeah, my fifteen minutes of fame."

As he reached for more pasta, Jake puzzled at Tasha's new approach to their relationship. Was she planning to set up a double connection, sharing her time between him and Ray? But in the midst of her merry mood, the scrumptious meal and what would be an even better dessert, he cut short his impulse to quiz her. It looked as if this visit would allow time for more serious matters later. So for now, he submitted to her control of their circumstances, the entire weekend of the Fourth ahead.

Friday, July 4, next morning …

When Jake awoke he was vaguely surprised to roll over and find Tasha beside him. He'd trained himself to accept the rhythm of her sudden appearance, their intense lovemaking and her hasty retreat. Now here she was still in his bed, snoring a little, a strand of hair loose across her brow.

He rose, used the bathroom, made some instant coffee and settled at his desk to grade a stack of essays. Finally she stirred, sat up, stretched, lipstick smeared, her full breasts beautifully on display.

"You're wonderful," she said to him, smiling. "Like an avalanche of love coming down on me."

"That's exactly what it is. A veritable Swiss alp of love."

"No. Mount Everest."

"The whole Himalayan range," he added.

She stood, gave him a hug around the neck, kissed his cheek. Even her morning breath was a joy to him.

"Remember how we camped over in Cuyahoga Park?" she asked.

"Indeed," he answered, using his mock professor voice.

"Darling Jake, we still can't be seen in public around here, not even in the woods. I'm sure you understand. Can we use that new camper for the long weekend?"

"Quite assuredly," he said.

She punched his bicep. "Let's do it! I was thinking we could drive over to Presque Isle State Park on the lake near Erie, far away from prying eyes." She shimmied. "How 'bout it, daddy-o?"

She waggled her ass on her way to the bathroom.

54

Thursday, July 17, two weeks later …

Because Jake was taking Dr. Hollingsworth's course on Melville, he'd been recruited along with the other seminar members to help prepare for the professor's brainstorm of staging a one-hundred-fiftieth birthday party for the author of *Moby Dick*. Jake found himself on a small stepladder helping Hollingsworth's effort by hanging related South Pacific art work in the first floor hall of Satterfield. Jake imagined running off to the islands with the woman he loved.

Besides the prints, sketches, and photographs, the celebration would include music, poetry, lectures and guest speakers. It all intruded upon Jake's real summer focus, namely his research on Eliot. About "Prufrock" itself,

Jake had to look into Dante, Michelangelo, Andrew Marvell, *Twelfth Night*, *Hamlet*, the Greek poet Hesiod, and the entire *New Testament*. Eliot believed that a poet should be in intimate touch with the tradition of Western literature, a scholar as well as an artist, and to reflect that tradition in his or her own work. Thus, Eliot's critical treatise, *The Sacred Wood*, and the need for a host of footnotes attached to his poems. Jake now knew his thesis topic had been ill chosen exactly as Professor Thrillwell had warned. But too late to back out. He still hadn't heard from two of the journals he'd sent his paper to nor the schools to which he'd applied for a Ph.D. fellowship.

As he stepped off the ladder and checked to make sure the painting of a Tahitian beach hung straightly, he heard Tasha's voice behind him.

"A little to the left, sir."

He turned to discover her in professional attire. She was beaming.

"When I got back to Twin Lakes this morning," she said, "I found a letter from Professor LaGuardia. They wanted to interview me right away. And guess what, I'm hired. I now share a TA office up on the third floor with someone named Phoebe."

"No kidding?" Jake said in shock.

"Now you'll have to watch out who you flirt with. Or here in these hallowed halls should I say, *with whom you flirt?* I'll be teaching two sections of French 101 and taking a course on the plays of Moliere. Thrilling, isn't it, Jake?"

He looked her up and down. "I'm floored."

"Didn't think I'd qualify?"

"Didn't think you'd actually go through with it. Does Ray know?"

"He'll be back tonight. I'll tell him then."

"How will he take it?"

"He'll have to take it or leave me," she answered haughtily. "Preferably the latter."

"Come on, I'll show you my office."

Jake unlocked the door and ushered her in.

"Oh, you have an office all to yourself."

He closed the door and hugged her.

"Because I supervise the TA's, not the ones in French, though."

She looked around. "You don't decorate much, do you? Only your guitar case in the corner."

"I like bare walls, like Bartleby the Scrivener."

"I guess I'll have to get used to scholastic allusions," she said. "One seldom hears them in the halls of Roosevelt High."

"Sorry, been reading too much Eliot."

During the two weeks in which they'd slept together every night, Jake had refrained from talking about their future. He didn't want to break her vibrant mood, usually wine supported, and she didn't bring it up herself even though the topic seemed to him to be the proverbial elephant in the room.

"I have a serious question to ask you," he said.

"Oh, do you have to?"

"Does Ray have any hint about me-us?"

"Only that we were neighbors and that he put a stop to your helping me with my poor old Rambler. Oh, and that we went to a jazz concert in the city and he thought I looked like a whore."

"And I-us, never came up in your family discussions?"

"You see, darling Jake, keeping you tightly under wraps was the only way I could protect you-us. Otherwise not only your existence but also my morals would have become the subjects, and they'd have despised me and blamed you. Believe me, I know these people."

"Even your mother?"

"She serves Daddy, totally."

"I had the idea of driving over to Akron, visit her seamstress shop, show her your parting letter."

"Oh, my God, Jake! I'm so glad you didn't."

"I thought if she understood your feelings..."

"No, Jake, that would have ruined their opinion of me and caused Ray to confront you."

"I would welcome a little powwow with him."

"There are enough riots around this town without you two making the evening news. Jake, I know what I'm doing. Trust me, please."

He stifled the urge to ask if she slept with him regularly. He'd have to assume as much. During the last several weeks she hadn't once quizzed him about possible tennis partners. The elephant had to remain silently in the corner next to his guitar.

Was it a hint she'd dropped about the possibility of Ray's leaving her? That would solve the problem, wouldn't it? Is that what she's working on? The question left him thinking of his own needs, what he could live without and what he could live with.

For the time being he'd see her almost every day. That was all right with him. It had to be. As far as sharing her, he'd have to block that from his mind.

"Anyway," she said, "where does a person get a bite to eat around here?"

Saturday, August 23, five weeks later ...

Side by side with other workers, Jake found himself in the brutal sun cutting the stems of the mature five-foot-tall tobacco plants. He snapped them off at an angle so they fell in line for the spearers, who followed. It was the kind of manual labor Jake needed, strengthening his grip, his wrists, forearms and biceps. Whimsically he wondered if he might challenge Ray in arm wrestling for Tasha. Today was his birthday, the last week of August and most of September off from school. As his shears snapped the rigid stems, the rhythm of the job and the silence of the laborers induced a meditative state, and Jake recalled Levin's mystical experience as he swept his scythe to and fro with the peasants in *Anna Karina*.

Despite Ray's furious objections about Tasha's enrolling in grad school, she and Jake had become secretly close again, finding spots in their days for interludes at his apartment, for stolen kisses in his office, a private touch of fingertips as they passed in the corridors of Satterfield or ate together in the comfortably uncrowded Union. He fought away the image of what might be happening when she went home at night. But it wasn't easy.

Here in his father's field, the sweat on his back and shoulders drying quickly in the summer heat, he moved easily, in step with the other cutters, the plants toppling nicely to the left, one after another.

He'd had time in the evenings to talk to his parents, and privately with his dad in the shop. His dad had refurbished the MGA and sold it, putting the profit in Jake's old bank account, which also held savings from his four years of teaching; he didn't spend much. Jake told his father about the chaos soon to return to the Kent campus and revealed the amazing tale of his having testified before Congress. Chewing Black Jack gum and sipping Royal Crown Colas, his dad expressed disgust as the conversations went on. Jake spoke much more reservedly with his mom, focusing on the positive highlights of his time in Ohio and protecting her from worry, an art he'd learned from observing his dad.

"I'll have one more seminar," he told her that evening as he gorged on roast pork loin and corn on the cob. "Then I'll have two full terms to write my master's thesis." He avoided, however, trying to explain the intricacies of Eliot's poetics.

"What happens when you graduate?" she asked, handing him a basket of biscuits she'd made.

"I applied to some other schools for my doctorate. Hopefully I'll get a full ride, but I might have to keep on teaching."

"And do you have a girl?" she asked. "Someone special?"

"Much too busy for that complication," he answered, "but don't worry, Mom. You'll have some grandkids sooner or later."

"I'd better," she said with a wink. "And wherever you go on to study, I hope it's somewhere not so far away. If you do provide us with grandchildren, we'd like to see them more than once a year."

"I'll try to work that out." He didn't mention LSU.

"And did you work out that darned draft card problem?"

Jake glanced at his dad with whom he'd discussed the issue.

"Yeah, Mom, I'm pretty sure that no news is good news."

55

Wednesday, October 8, six weeks later ...

The fall term underway, Jake was deciphering Joyce's *Ulysses* in his office, having completed the great author's two earlier books over his three week stay at home, a time of hard work, camaraderie with his dad, and fabulous home cooking and affection from his mom. He learned that retreating to this agrarian way of life would not give him any feeling whatever of having been diminished. With the way things were progressing on campus, he might have to make such a flight. And the idea of removing Tasha from the geographical confines of her family seemed actually a plus.

As he was trying his best to care about one Leopold Bloom's life in Dublin on June 16, 1904, someone knocked on his door. When he said come in, the door opened and his long-ago officemate Ella Curlew burst in. She had transformed her once sorority girl appearance into army fatigues, a Malcolm X tee shirt, huge hoop earrings, and a raging afro. Her eyes showed anger as she plopped down on the chair used for student conferences.

"I want you to know I'm going against the Department's order to hold classes next week. What's wrong with these people? The whole campus wants the moratorium. I'm passing a petition around and I want you to sign it."

She breathed heavily, probably because she'd been walking up and down stairs gathering signatures, quite a few of them, as was apparent when she laid the paper on his desk along with a ballpoint ready to write.

"How have you been, Ella? Everything going okay with your teaching?"

"Yeah. Just sign. I'm busy with this."

"I can see that. Your student evaluations are going up every term. Thought you should know."

"Like I could give a fuck. Sign, okay?"

"Sorry, no."

"Why the fuck not?"

"First, the decree against cancelling classes didn't come from the Department. It came from On High."

"Who cares where it came from? It came from the pigs. You're either with us or against us."

"Then on this tactic, I'm against you. White is one hundred percent correct that by cancelling classes we're denying the right of students who are here paying for those classes. And after all, he said the absences won't be counted as long as the students make up the work—and he even left that up to the instructor. Maybe no one will come, but I'll be in class where I'm being paid to belong."

Fire in her eyes but speechless, she stared across the desk at him.

"And," he added, "I'm sorry to learn BUS has joined up with SDS."

"The pigs around here have forced that. What can we do after Music and Speech? Some sisters were trapped in there."

"Use whatever word you want for your opponents, Ella, they're trying to keep this place open. SDS and now apparently your group are trying to close it down. At least White listened to your side. What about the new Afro-American Studies program, the Human Relations Center, the new black profs being hired, black guest speakers? Don't you see Admin is trying over there? Don't you see that?"

"Yeah, and what about the pig massacres over in Cleveland? I guess you support that also. I'm shocked at you, Jacob's Ladder."

"And are you going to call me a pig now, Ella?"

"If the name fits, right on! Just sign the petition."

"No. I'll be there to teach my classes. You should be too. Let the students decide where they'll be next Wednesday. Respect their right to choose. You're trying to force Admin to join the very enemies that are trying to destroy them. You should fight your wars in a way that doesn't interfere with why we're all here, even you."

She glared at him almost wickedly. "Some things are more important than this fucking place. All right, I'll say it. You're a pig! And if you think that resisting the moratorium is going to keep this school open, you're completely wrong. It only shows you think rules and power will win this war. And, man, are you in fucking outer space, like those white pigs on the moon!"

She snatched her papers from his desk and whirled out of the office.

If Jake was to be compared to the likes of Neil Armstrong, he'd be happy to bear the designation. But his concern about Kent's survival was not lessened by Ella's little visit. It all added up to his completing this course on Joyce, finishing his thesis, somehow grabbing Tasha and getting out of this place. But how to escape, with her now enrolled in the grad program?

Later that day, with his mind back in Bloom's stream of consciousness, another knock sounded on his door. Bracing himself for a visit from BUS's leadership, he swiveled and said come in.

At first, he felt relieved to see Audrey, then immediately concerned on a whole new level. Tanned, bright-eyed, her long dark hair parted in the middle and streaming straight over her shoulders, she entered meekly in jeans and a wild tie-dyed tee shirt that said *I Survived Woodstock*.

"Did you have a nice summer, Audrey? Your shirt tells me you might have."

"Outta sight. Talk about mud fights."

"I saw it on the news, quite a traffic jam. You and Aaron?"

"A bunch of his friends from Rochester, yeah. Did you know that even though Dylan lives right there, he didn't show up?"

"Sounds like Dylan, always defying our expectations. Seeger still doesn't forgive him for going electric."

"So, Mr. Ernst, I dropped by to remind you that I'm no longer your student. I purposely didn't sign up for your 102 class."

Jake feared what was coming.

"So now," she went on, "we can meet somewhere and have a real conversation."

His silence continued.

"So, how 'bout it?"

"Uh ... all right." He opened his schedule book. "Sorry, Audrey, but everything's booked up for a while. We could meet, let's see here, Friday a week."

She grimaced. "Not until then?"

"Sorry. But let's have lunch in the Union that afternoon, okay?"

"You can't have a conversation in that madhouse."

"Okay, how 'bout if the weather is like today, we get something from the Union and talk in that little plaza in front of Admin, where the fountain is."

She shifted a bit. "What time?"

"My seminar lets out at one. So one-thirty?"

"Like a picnic?"

"Sure. Why not?"

"But let's skip the crappy food at the Union. I'll bring something special. But you better not forget."

"I'll be there. If it rains, the Union will have to do. Deal?"

She nodded grimly.

"You can fill me in about that mud bath in upstate New York."

An hour or so after Audrey left, yet another knock came on his door, Leslie, briefcase in hand, a pressed pinstriped suit, skirt mid-thigh.

"Hi, handsome. Time for our meeting with SFM. Sounds kinda like S&M, doesn't it? That's not good. Then again, maybe it will draw more people."

He'd forgotten but grabbed his guitar in its battered case. On their way through the miraculous autumn day, trees in various shades of fall, leaves strewn on hillsides, they passed the construction site of the soon-to-be thirteen story library, also a new student center. Bulldozers rumbled, cranes towered above expanses of mud, and workers in hard hats scurried about.

"Did you happen to notice," Leslie said, "that one of White's 'innovative' programs is precisely the one you invented last year? *Tete-a-tetes* with administrators at the dorms? Not as if he'd ever attend one himself. You were miles ahead of the curve, Jake, even beat *me* to it, remember? You're an unsung hero around here."

"Yeah, right. One of our TA's called me a pig this morning."

"No way. Why?"

As they strolled, he recapped Ella's visit to his office.

"I signed that petition," Leslie said. "Figured I'd go on record. The idea of cancelling classes is going nowhere anyway. Might as well go along with the crowd."

"I guess I'm not political. I'll be in class in case anyone shows up."

"Fortunately I don't even teach on Wednesdays. Hey, Jake." She brushed her hand against his. "Let's hit the Holiday Inn Friday night. I scored some fantastic shit."

The invitation ignited a controversy that had been festering in his skull for weeks. He walked on in silence trying to fit the pieces of his quandary together, the meeting room in, where else, Tri-Towers Pit, not far away.

"Well?" Leslie said with a nudge to his upper arm.

"I'll have to cease and desist with our little rendezvous, Leslie."

"Really? Why?"

"I'm into it with someone else, kind of seriously, though it's complicated."

"That's horrible news, Jake. I thought we had something good going on."

"It was good, but..."

"Is what you're into so serious that you can't have a harmless but ecstatic diversion once in a while?"

"It is, but..."

"But what, lover man?"

"I have a favor to ask."

"You reject me," she teased, "then have the balls to ask me for a favor?"

He grimaced. "Yeah, I guess so."

"All right, what favor?"

"Could you spare a bit of that Hawaiian stuff? I'll pay you, of course."

"What am I, a drug pusher? Anyway, this weed is from Jamaica."

56

Thursday, October 16, eight days later ...

Although the overwhelming majority of students, student organizations, the *Stater* editorial staff, and faculty supported today's moratorium, Jake entered his first floor classroom prepared to teach his class as per the syllabus. Out of thirty students, only five showed up. According to Admin's guidelines, Jake had announced on Tuesday that students would not have to make up homework, a decision Admin had left up to the individual instructors. He wouldn't, however, suspend the lesson, which involved the usual quiz, exercises on parallel structure, and an analysis of Matthew Arnold's "Dover Beach."

The five dedicated freshmen had taken seats in various spots in the room, and Jake gathered them together in front and pulled the desk chair around to join them. He gave them the quiz, went through the chapter in the grammar book and turned to the famous love poem.

"Okay," Jake began, "anyone get the feeling that the speaker of this poem is talking to someone specific, other than us, the readers?"

A thin young man with glasses and a prominent nose spoke up. "He's talking to his girlfriend during World War Two."

"How could it be World War Two?" asked a conservatively dressed young woman with red hair and freckles.

"What'ya mean?" the thin boy answered.

"It says right there in the book Arnold died in 1888."

"Yeah. So?"

"Jeez, that was way before World War Two. It couldn't possibly be World War Two. That didn't start until 1940."

The kid with glasses blushed. "What war was it, then? World War One?"

Jake intervened. He asked the boy, "What makes you think it was any war at all, Kevin?"

"There in the last line it talks about armies. They're clashing. It says so right there."

"So you agree, Kate," Jake said, "that there might be a war going on?"

She huffed. "But not World War One or World War Two. It couldn't be them."

"So which war?" Kevin challenged. Jake half expected him to address Kate as smarty-pants.

"Maybe it's no war at all," Kate returned. "Maybe he's using war as a metaphor, maybe the armies are ideas not actual soldiers. Ideas clashing."

"That's an interesting interpretation," Jake said. "What do you think, Fred?"

Fred was a solemn student who, as if trying to hide, usually stared directly down at his desk from the beginning of class to the end. He was clean shaven with raging acne.

"Excuse me?" he answered. "What did you say?"

"Well, Fred," Jake said, "Kate has proposed that the armies might not be of soldiers but ideas. What do you think?"

"What kinda ideas?"

"Kate?" Jake said, giving her the floor.

"The idea of the old Sea of Faith against the growing idea of atheism. He's saying when there's no God to believe in, we only have each other, so he's saying to his lover they should be true to one another because that's all they have."

"Yeah," another young man spoke up, clean-shaven, blue-eyed, wearing an ROTC cadet uniform, "like the Beatles say, 'Love is all ya need.'"

No one laughed at this intended levity.

"How can *ideas* be ignorant, though?" Kevin came back to Kate's notion.

"Because," Kate said, "an idea is only an idea, not facts, not proven, so any *idea* might be wrong. Religious people are simply going on faith, not proof. Same with atheists. They don't really know if there's no god, like religious people don't really know if there is. No one really knows one way or the other, see what I mean? We're all ignorant, fighting each other with ignorance, making a mess in the whole world."

The class coming to a close, the final voice came from a second girl, chewing gum, her dark blond hair in pigtails, large braless breasts in a tight Harvard tee shirt. "If this poet thinks he can rely on love, boy, is he wrong! Guys'll cheat on you sooner or later, no better than ignorant dogs. He's stringing his girlfriend along, like they all do."

Jake was glad they didn't get back to which war it was, however, because he wasn't sure of that himself, and he didn't care to express his own ignorance on the subject.

On the campus in general the moratorium was in full swing on the crisp autumn day. The *Stater* had issued a special edition strictly about the war, no debate about which one. A huge crowd gathered on the Commons, the Victory Bell tolling. Various speakers gave various views, all opposing America's foreign policy; a folksinger sang a few antiwar songs; someone read poems; then the march began on its designated route, Jake not among the throng of over three thousand. So far, everything had been peaceful.

He and Tasha observed the proceedings from a window table in the faculty section of the Union. Had she not been there, he probably would have tagged along with the massive procession given that the event seemed to be moving on in a nonviolent way. The demonstration was headed downtown on a predetermined route, all parade requests granted by the community, local cops and state troopers at the ready.

"I know you're against the war," Tasha said, "and would like to be out there, but I don't know what to say. I don't want to be seen in town like I've suddenly become a dissident."

"I understand," Jake said.

"Maybe we could take our own march, down to your apartment."

Jake grabbed the last half of his burger, and they hurried out of the Union, down the hill to College Avenue, right on Willow, into his house, up the stairs and into his pad.

"I'll pour us some wine," she said, headed straight for the kitchen.

"Wait."

She stopped in the doorway. "What's wrong?"

"Nothing. I have a little surprise. Come into the bedroom."

"I'd really like to have a drink."

"Come on. I'll show you." He held out his arms and backed up.

Sluggishly, she followed.

"Sit down on the bed."

Seated beside her, he opened the drawer of the side table, took out a film canister and handed it to her.

"You want to take pictures?"

"Go ahead, open it."

She did so, looked inside. "Is this? ... Oh, my God! It is!" She sniffed it. "Ugh! Stinky."

"Let's do it today, instead of wine."

"Where'd you get it?"

"A friend in the Department."

"Have you done it before?"

"Yes. Come on."

He pulled out a small pipe he'd bought at the head shop, snipped off a bud and put it in the bowl.

"I don't want to get into this," Tasha said.

"Come on, try it."

"I don't want to be a druggie, Jake."

"This isn't hard drugs. And no hangover, no addiction."

"So you think I'm an alcoholic?"

"Jesus no. A new adventure. Give it one try. If you don't like it, we won't do it again."

"Do I have to, Jake?"

"No, but I'd like you to. Once."

"You're the only one in the whole world who could get me to do this."

"I'll take that as a yes. Here, I'll start and you do it like I do, okay? Only don't take too much in, it's strong, just a little and inhale it like a cigarette."

He demonstrated. Holding his breath, he said, "See? Like that. Hold it as long as you can, but take in a small amount."

She shook her head in doubt. "Don't know why I'm doing this."

He waved for her to go ahead. She did, handing the pipe back to him and finally letting out her breath.

"Good girl," he said, taking another hit, handing the pipe back to her.

He got up, went into the living room and put on his Brazilian music album. When he returned, she was leaning back against the pillows, grinning.

"I don't think this is working. But it's quite funny."

"What's funny?"

"Remembering the night you got that record."

"That *was* funny. You were amazing. Bridgette Bardot from Ipanema."

"Ridiculous, you mean?"

"No, not ridiculous. You told me afterwards that you wanted me never to forget that night, and I never will, couldn't possibly."

She laughed a little. "I must have really shocked you."

"But in a terrifically good way."

She laughed some more, like chuckling but a little harder than that.

"This isn't working, and it tastes yucky. I much prefer that excellent Chianti in your kitchen cabinet. But give me another puff, maybe I didn't do it right. Did you? Do you feel anything?"

"It takes a few minutes, but I'm beginning to feel a buzz. Relax, there's plenty of time. Everyone is marching around town, and we have the whole afternoon to ourselves while ignorant armies clash in the daylight."

"Huh?"

"We were working on Arnold's 'Dover Beach' today." He looked into her eyes. "*Ah, love, let us be true to one another.*"

"Anyway," she said, "these clothes feel too tight and clingy." She pulled off her sweater. "Do you remember my makeup that night?"

"How can I forget?"

"Don't your clothes feel tight and clingy, Jake?" She giggled. It grew into laughter. "I was ridiculous, I really was. You must have thought I was wacko."

She unsnapped her bra, allowing her breasts to fall free. She lay back, her laughter growing. "I don't know why, but this is all tremendously amusing." She took another drag, inhaling deeply, accentuating her fantastic bust while Jake took off his clothes, which were, by now indeed, too tight and clingy.

57

Friday, October 17, next day ...

On another glorious Indian summer afternoon, as Jake sat on a bench in the garden-like plaza near Admin, he stared at the slate walkways with sculptures depicting books by famous authors. While he waited, he plodded on in *Ulysses*. When he heard Audrey say *hi* some distance away, he looked up and saw her, carrying a picnic basket.

Her dark hair lifted with her pace and with the light breeze. She wore jeans and a plaid hunting shirt, her skin glowing freshly in the sunlight. Jake rose.

"You were serious about the picnic."

"Yeah, it's corny, but fun."

She sat on the bench, opened a flap of the basket and took out a checkered napkin which she spread between them.

"I hope you like ham and cheese."

"I love ham and cheese."

"I also brought carrot sticks and grapes. I know they're boycotting grapes in front of the supermarket, but some things shouldn't be banned."

"I agree, grapes among them."

"And cherries, and watermelon. But the one is out of season, and the other much too heavy to lug across campus."

Jake smiled as she unwrapped a sandwich and handed it to him. "I hope you like the mustard. It's Grey Poupon."

"My favorite."

She'd included crisp lettuce and tomato. He took a bite and gave her a thumbs up.

"Did you go on the march yesterday?" she asked, eating also. "I looked around for you but there were so many there."

"No, I ... was busy."

"Somebody threw a rock through the window of the army recruiting office, but other than that it was really great. The whole focus was on the war, not on all the campus craziness."

"That's the way it should be, trying to stop the fighting, not closing the school. Are you keeping up with your studies?"

"Yeah, I have a 4.0 so far. So does Aaron." She smiled at him, some mustard on her cheek. "It's nice to finally have you all to myself."

This comment gave him pause, but he smiled.

"Sure is a magnificent day," he said.

"So, I've been saving up some questions. Is it okay if I ask?"

With a paper napkin, he reached across and wiped the bit of yellow off her cheek. She smiled, blushed, and for an instant he saw the kid break through her usual adult demeanor. He also realized he'd spontaneously done something intimate.

"Thanks," she said, rubbing the spot with her finger. "Uh, ready for question number one?"

He took a dramatic breath. "Ready as I'll ever be. Shoot."

"Okay. What are you studying exactly? I see you're reading Joyce, but I mean in general, for your degree."

Jake briefly explained his work on *The Sacred Wood*. She listened intently.

KENT STATE — 1969

When he finished, she said, "I often wondered how they choose the things in our book. There's hardly any women writers there, almost no blacks, either. Almost all dead white guys. Who decides?"

"Hmm. That's a great question, Audrey. I guess professors decide, and literary intellectuals, established critics."

"Aren't there great women writers?"

"Yes, some. Not so many ancients, but Victorian women made some inroads into the canon. Austin, Woolf, George Eliot ..."

"Yes, but that last one had a male pseudonym."

"True."

"And they're all British. What about in our country?"

Jake thought a moment, crunched a purple grape. "Emily Dickenson, of course. Certainly some moderns, Willa Cather, Edna St. Vincent Millay, Dorothy Parker."

"What about blacks? I don't think there's a single thing in our text from a black."

"Wow, Audrey, you're onto this. Blacks, let's see. Isn't there a poem by Langston Hughes?"

"'My soul has grown deep like the rivers,'" she quoted.

"So you know your poetry," Jake said.

"I'm going to major in English. I write poetry, and songs too."

"Really, Audrey?"

"Yeah. Okay, question number two. Ready?"

He braced himself. "Ready."

They sat in the sun, grapes and almond cookies consumed, for over two hours. She asked him about his home, his parents, an extended biography, and he spoke honestly and from the heart. He told her about his antiwar activities in Lancaster, but left out ripping up his draft card.

"One last question, Jake."

"Yes, I've got to get down to the library."

"You told me about Ainsley, and that's sad. Do you have a girlfriend now? I thought maybe that woman who sponsors our group."

"I do have a girlfriend, more than a girlfriend actually. But Leslie Robbins is a colleague and a friend."

Audrey wrinkled her brow.

"It's complicated. You know, the adult world."

"Are you happy? I mean sometimes you seem not to be, like you're lonely or something."

"*Happy?* Not a simple word. Things have been in turmoil, no need to go through it all. Let's say Natasha and I are both working on a way we might be together completely, but there are some difficult barriers."

"But you love her?"

"Yes."

"Oh."

"And what about you and Aaron, any closer than before?"

"No. We're platonic. I'm waiting for the really right guy."

"I'm sure you have lots of offers."

"Yeah, that's why I hang with Aaron. He's my shield."

"You say you write songs, Audrey. What kind?"

"I don't know quite how to describe them. I don't like pigeon holes. They're about feelings I have. I try to put feelings into words, then I can deal with them better."

"Is there an artist who inspires you?"

"Joni Mitchell."

"Wow, she's great, the best. Do you play?"

"Piano mainly, guitar a little. Not nearly as good as you, though. You really stand out when Goldenrod plays at the Eye."

"Wash is the real star. Hey, we have a gig next Tuesday at the Blind Owl. Not sure why the Owl wants us, but we'll give it a try. I wonder if you'd show me your songs. You know, Wednesdays after our meeting at the Pit, we rehearse. Maybe you'd like to sit in."

"Really? I'd love to hear you."

"Do you sing, Audrey?"

"Not like Joni. I love her voice, but I'm not as operatic, can't touch her range. I'll come to the Owl. Aaron and I go there sometimes. We like the Measles, especially that guitarist Joe Walsh. He's a trip."

"Thanks for the picnic, Audrey. I've got to go now. I hope you got the scoop on my bio."

"It's not only the facts I wanted. I wanted to back up my feeling about you. You know how sometimes you have a feeling about someone, but then when you get closer you see a discrepancy. But there's no discrepancy with you, Jake. You're a really beautiful man. I'm sorry to hear that you're not completely happy, though, because someone like you should be."

Jake smiled. "That's a sweet thing to say, Audrey. But please don't worry about me. I'm doing fine. You're a beautiful young woman, too."

"Do you really think so?"

"I know so."

Things packed into her basket, she rose, leaned down over him and kissed his cheek. Then she hurried across the plaza and up the hill.

Jake had the weekends to himself, most of the time spent in the library. As he sat at the window table looking out at the dimming, leaf strewn front campus, his mind wandered away from the book on Swinburne he was looking at to his afternoon with Audrey.

Are you happy? she'd asked.

Good question. He was beginning to think that happiness was not a state to be sought. The pursuit of happiness—yes, a pursuit, not a state. Happiness is a mood, he thought, nothing permanent. He drifted to the images Matthew Arnold used in his poem, which seemed an accurate, though grim, description of the world. Happiness seemed to lie only within the little room with his lover, the poem written on his honeymoon in, where else, Kent. England, of course. But the poem expressed doubt even about their love, as if being true to one another was just as futile as the world outside.

Where is Tasha at this very moment? Home with Ray. How can she go there? She must be sleeping with him on a regular basis, mustn't she? Of course, you dope! Of course she sleeps with him. Okay, so apparently it disgusts her, but, Christ, she does it! Yes, it's not with the same feeling as she does it with me ... but she does it.

And I accept it. Why? Because I love her, and there's no other way. I can't kidnap her. When you love someone, when two people love each other, they're a team, right? Like Mom and Dad. They work together to solve problems, each doing their part. She's working on separating from Ray, apparently hoping he'll be the one to make the break. Or that he'll do something that will give her the indisputable right to do so. Indisputable to her father, that is. That's her strategy, isn't it? And I do nothing, demand nothing, grant her total control of her side of this problem. But what if I do make demands, what if I demand she leave him, give her an ultimatum? Look, girl, it's him or me. Choose.

Then I lose her, that's what. Or she chooses me and is miserable beyond repair, disowned, cast out.

Jake never felt more helpless except maybe about the abortion thing with Daphne. That was bad. But this was worse, far worse. Imagining the woman he loved and who loved him in bed with someone else, Christ!

In this mood, Jake saw the plain darkling, all right, like the light now fading into the shadows of the lawn outside.

Then earlier, Audrey, lighting the place up like a sunbeam. Her fresh, hopeful innocence, her life before her, no inkling of the complications that lay ahead.

He had to smile at her picnic, her list of questions, her search for discrepancies. What a gem!

But wait a minute. Get focused. Get back to Algernon Charles Swinburne of the decadent *school.*

58

Monday, October 27, ten days later ...

Fall had turned to winter by the evening of Dr. Benjamin Spock's presentation in the packed auditorium, attended by radicals and moderates alike. Jake listened with satisfaction at the pediatric physician's appeal for working within the system and for avoiding violence, though he did justify defensive violence on the part of blacks, who had been victimized by force for centuries. He clarified the difference between the quest for civil rights and the need to stop the war, although the two cases overlapped. His voice was strongly antiwar yet at the same time antiviolence, and he spoke from an underpinning of compassion and love.

Jake walked outside with the crowd, everyone bundling up in the face of a biting, northwest wind. He felt a tug on the sleeve of his parka.

"That is a great man," Audrey said.

Jake smiled. "Yes, the same tone as Pete Seeger, without the banjo."

"Will you join me at the Flash?" she asked. "I'm in the mood for pancakes."

The restaurant was on his way home. "Where's Aaron?"

"He was at the lecture but has some studying to do. He's in the aerospace program, and his prof is a bear. It's freezing out here. Did you hear about the fence?"

They forged into the wind along East Main.

"What fence?"

"The one that just suddenly showed up along Blanket Hill, blocking the Commons."

"You're kidding."

"I kid you not. We can't get onto the Commons from Taylor any more, can you believe it?"

"What's the explanation from Admin?"

"Guess we'll see in tomorrow's paper," Audrey said. "It's like they're doing everything they can think of to alienate us."

When the two reached the restaurant, its windows steamed, it was busy with students seeking refuge, buzzing with conversation, the juke box playing "Come Together" by the Beatles. They found a small table for two at the back wall.

"You're group was fantastic at the Owl," she said. "Not many people, but you got us all singing, and you're right about that big guy—he's outta sight."

Jake nodded.

"But you're more than backup. You're a cool dude."

He smiled. "Get off it."

"You are."

"Speaking of cool, I looked over your songs. Fantastic, Audrey! I've been playing through them, the chord sequences are original, and the lyrics are spellbinding."

She blushed. "You're saying that to give an amateur some encouragement."

"Nothing amateurish about them. Have you sent them out?"

"You and Aaron are the only ones I've shown them to."

"They have the whole range of emotions. You should send them to someone, make a demo. Do you mind if I let Wash see them?"

"I guess you can, but they're not bluegrass, anything but."

Her pancakes arrived. She spread the butter, soused them with syrup and dug in. Jake sipped his hot chocolate.

"The one you call 'Daisy Mountain' is almost bluegrass. And I want you to come to our practice. There's a piano. We're soon adding a recorder to the group, the girlfriend I mentioned; she's a classical flutist. When, or if, she can get away."

"Natasha? Get away from what?"

"Uh ... she's married, Audrey."

She looked up from her blueberry flapjacks. Again her furrowed brow.

"I told you it was complicated. She's stuck there for the moment. Anyway, you can hang around after the practice and play some of your stuff for me. How 'bout it? I feel we've made a discovery here, and ... it's more than simply music, Audrey."

Her eyes brightened. "It is?"

"Yes. We're singing our way through the chaos, aren't we?"

Friday, November 11, two weeks later ...

In his apartment Jake was studying at his desk when the phone rang. It was Adele.

"Wash wants you over here right away," she said.

"Is he okay?"

"He wants to talk to you. You know how when he wants something it has to be on the spot, immediately, if not yesterday."

Jake bundled up, got into his camper and drove out South Lincoln. The porch light was on. Adele stood in the doorway before Jake turned off his engine. Inside, Wash was sitting on the sofa with what Jake immediately recognized as Audrey's music sheets spread all around. He looked up.

"Why didn't you tell me about this chick?"

"I did. That's why you have her songs. You've had them for two weeks."

"Yeah, but you didn't tell me..."

"Didn't want to prejudice you."

Adele took his coat. "Beer or tea. We're all out of Thunderbird."

Jake smiled at the year old joke. "Tea."

"Herb or black?"

"Black."

"Beer for me," Wash said. He was wearing striped pajamas. "Pull that ottoman over and sit."

"Yes, boss. What's the emergency about?"

"Hell, man, what're we gonna do about this girl?"

"Use some of her songs, if she'll let us."

"Agreed, but..." He motioned toward the kitchen. "We'll have to convince you-know-who to violate her sense of purity."

"I heard that," Adele yelled.

"You gotta admit," Wash returned.

"You mean *sub*-mit, don't you?"

"We got to use this kid before she knows how good she is."

"That's called exploitation," Adele said, coming back in with the tea.

"Here, listen to this," Wash said, lifting his banjo.

He picked and strummed through a piece called "Under the Covers."

"Brian Wilson might have come up with a chord progression like that," Wash said.

Adele sat cross-legged on the carpet. They talked, discussed the future of Goldenrod with her pregnant and about to complete her doctorate and Jake to finish his master's in the spring.

"Why don't we go out with a new sound?" Wash asked. He shuffled some papers. "This stuff deserves to be heard, and I'd like to be the first. Who else knows about this girl, Jake?"

"No one, I think."

"So why you?"

"Because she's in love with him, you dope," Adele said. "Ever since long ago at the Eye."

"She was in my writing class last spring," Jake said. "We respect each other, that's all."

"Men," Adele said dismissively. "Blind as bats."

"Will she let me do some arrangements for our group?" Wash asked.

"Probably be thrilled."

"Can you get her over here right now?"

"Wash, it's Friday night. She's eighteen. Probably down at J.B.'s doing the funky chicken. Anyway I don't have her number."

"She sure doesn't write like she's eighteen. Adele, get that student directory. What's her last name, lover boy?"

"Cut that crap. Kraft, with a *K*. Audrey Kraft."

"Right," Wash said, "like Velveeta."

"Can she sing?" Adele asked.

"Can she ever," Jake said. "She did some stuff after our practice session. Lovely alto voice, natural, Carole King, kinda. Good with the ivories, too."

Jake dialed and heard the phone ringing.

"Prentice, second floor," a girl answered with a background of shouting and rock music.

"Audrey Kraft, please."

"She's outta town. Cleveland. With Aaron." The girl hung up.

"What do you think of this idea of branching out a little, Adele?" Jake asked. "Seriously."

She shook her head sadly. "I guess Wash is right about our breaking up. That is unless we all stay right here in Kent. I'm pretty sure the English Department will give me an offer, especially with the new American Studies program, and I don't know why a mom can't keep on singing unless giving birth affects the vocal cords. What about you, Jake? Will you be hanging around this fantastic town?"

"No. I've applied for doctoral fellowships elsewhere."

"Where's elsewhere?" Wash asked.

"Rutgers, West Virginia, LSU."

"LSU?" Adele said. "All the way down there?"

"An old prof of mine teaches there. Has a record out."

He told them about Groff, including the crazy times they had in Lancaster and New York. The conversation went on late into the night, turning to Jake's having testified before Congress, the happenings on campus. They agreed that Admin had screwed up mightily regarding the Blanket Hill fence, the director of maintenance having confessed that he'd neglected to inform Admin of his plans to protect the hill from becoming a series of muddy paths. Dean Matson publically stated his regrets that students hadn't been consulted. Nevertheless, the fence remained as a symbol of Admin's restrictive stances. Student anger mounted against it.

They also agreed that since the expulsion of SDS from campus, the activists were contained within acceptable boundaries of non-disruption. The huge moratorium march had gone well, and the almost daily demonstrations and rallies, though a nuisance had been kept within the constitutional dimensions of freedom of speech and assembly. Dow recruiters as well as the Oakland Police had kept their distance; the *Stater* had become an open forum for all points of view; and two frats had come out in opposition to the war. President White had cancelled his policy of immediate suspension; faculty reps were meeting with students in the dorms; and everyone was learning about the ins and outs of the Faculty Senate, the Board of Directors, and even the Board of Regents in Columbus.

Yes, hot rhetoric continued as did daily sandblasting of obscene antiestablishment graffiti from sidewalks and walls. Court cases were still pending against the key rioters of Music & Speech, and Ronnie Engle got himself arrested among the Kent presence at the Weatherman disturbances in Chicago. But the hottest issues on campus now seemed to be merely the despised fence and the constant destruction and replacement of the new traffic gate at the Taylor parking lot.

The good friends talked about national news, especially Nixon's speech the week before.

"He's turning up the heat on the protestors after the moratorium," Wash said. "And bracing himself for the Coretta King March this weekend. Christ, the kids at M.I.T. took over their administration building for three days, threatened to blow the place up. Must have taken a lot to get them away from their slide rules."

"And what did Agnew call us?" Adele asked.

"'An effete corps of impudent snobs,'" Jake said.

"Yeah," Wash added, 'nabobs of negativism.' What a goofball!"

"You two going to D.C. for the big march?"

"Yeah, we are," Wash said. "Got our tickets for the bus ride. Never a dull moment. You driving down?"

"No. Gotta read *Finnegan's Wake.*"

As they drank, talked and devoured chips and dip, Jake and his two best pals at the university all agreed that the place was becoming almost livable, especially in that the campus dissidents, though highly active, now seemed to be focused on the D.C. event. After two that morning Jake headed home into a snow flurry with the express assignment of getting Audrey and Wash together at the earliest possible moment.

59

Sunday, November 16, five days later ...

Jake and Tasha lay in each other's arms beneath a heavy comforter after a rare night together allowed by Ray's weekend with the Guard.

"What's it like between you and him?" Jake asked. "I want you to tell me."

She pressed against him. "No you don't. Let's just think about us, being together like this."

"I want this to be permanent."

"I'm working on that."

"Do you have sex with him?"

"Jake, don't."

"I'll take that as a *yes.*"

"It will be better not to think about it," she said.

"Is it like this?"

She backed away. "How can you even ask that, Jake? It's not even in the same galaxy."

"If you don't tell me, I'll imagine the worst."

She sat up, pulling the blankets up to her chin in the chilly room.

"And what might the worst be?"

"That it's like us."

"I should slap you."

"What is it, then?"

"It's nothing. I don't feel it. He does his thing and it's over. You know, a girl only has to lie there. Then I get up and shower, wash him off me." She started to cry. "Don't make me think of it. I'm one hundred percent here with you, Jake. With him, I close my eyes, grit my teeth and try to picture you. Don't torment me with questions."

"We have to do something. I can't bear thinking of you in that situation. Not to mention how I feel."

"Don't bother my mother, okay? That would ruin everything."

He stared across the room at a photograph he'd taken of the farmland back home.

"Doesn't he complain?"

"Not about that. He doesn't notice as long as he gets off. He wants me to stop taking birth control. And he didn't like me coming to grad school, not at all, and he complains about my not being home to make him dinner sometimes. But it has improved with you and me, hasn't it, now that we see each other so much more?"

"But this situation drives me crazy."

"Don't think about it, then."

"That would be a nice trick."

"Let's just count our blessings." She moved down with him again, kissed his cheek.

"When's it going to change," he asked, "his slow plan of yours? When will you be free?"

"He'll have to get sick of me sooner or later. Maybe he'll have an affair. How I wish! He's an attractive guy. Women like him. I used to."

"You know, Tasha, I'll most likely be moving away after I get my degree next spring. Not sure where, but somewhere. I want you to come with me, a real couple, man and wife."

"I know that's what you want, Jake. I want that too."

Jake's turn to sit up. "Then break it off with him. Bear the consequences. Tell your mom what's going on. Sure, your parents might be upset at first, but they love you; they don't want to lose you. They'll adjust when they have to face the fact of it."

"I know my limits, Jake. You shouldn't make me do what I couldn't cope with."

"Maybe you underestimate their concern for your happiness."

"Damn it, Jake! I know them. You don't. Now stop pestering me, please. I love you, I'm with you whenever possible, and that will have to do for now. Do you want other women? Tennis matches?"

She ripped off the blankets and fled to the bathroom.

"That's exactly what I don't want," he shouted.

He stared at the ceiling, began to calm down. At least she hadn't asked him about the tennis he'd already played. She had more self-control than he, more ability to compartmentalize. Their sex was great, the best ever, because love dominated it. That made the difference. And they were active enough so he had no need of anything else.

But he wanted *her*, totally. And he didn't want it to come down to a choice between staying here at Kent and moving on without her. He wanted to advance with her at his side.

Hearing the shower, he rolled over and turned on the radio to the university station that was reporting about the March of Death yesterday in D.C. Peaceful, apparently; only minor incidents. Huge, half a million, a sizeable Kent State contingent among them. In apparent defiance of what was going on outside the White House windows, Nixon had watched the Ohio State/Michigan game in the Oval Office. The House of Representatives had passed a plan for a draft lottery system with no exemptions. It would release half the now eligible men from having to serve, the implication being that the number of antiwar fanatics would be reduced by fifty percent as well. Clever devils in Washington.

The campus had been busy with events preparing for Friday's moratorium, during which Jake had followed White's stated policy of teachers not cancelling classes. Only two students had attended. Then he'd gone to Prentice Gate at front campus where various members of the English Department took turns reading forty thousand names of those killed in Vietnam. He'd read a list of those from Montana. Thursday night there'd been an attempt at a candlelight march, but the weather was cold and damp with the wind blowing out the flames.

Jake had started in the procession but the presence of a Viet Cong flag bothered him too much to continue. He was still an American. So he'd taken a solitary march back to his apartment where he listened on the radio to the events happening in the auditorium. From four o'clock Friday, he'd been in another universe with Tasha. Now he caught up on the radio about the weekend in D.C. in an effort to divert his thoughts of having to share the woman he loved with another man. Life was becoming extremely weird.

Tuesday, November 25, two days later ...

After his seminar meeting on Joyce, Jake found a slip of paper in his mail slot saying that a Professor Levitt from the Sociology Department requested a three o'clock meeting in his Lowry Hall office. Jake assumed this was the famous, or infamous, Jonah Levitt, known for his involvement with radical students and their causes. He had been castigated by Admin for cancelling his classes last year during the BUS walkout, and since then had been part of most negotiations going on among students, faculty and Admin. Recently he'd been on the steering committee of CCC and had been chosen to be on a faculty group to help the ombudsman deal with Admin. Where problems occurred, one was certain to see Professor Levitt's name show up in the newspaper accounts.

What's he want with me?

He remembered his unsatisfactory meetings with Wettman and Shenk regarding student issues. He also recalled the pressure Drew had put on him to get more involved with the antiwar efforts. Also visits to his office by Gibbs, Engle, and the McGills.

He didn't need any more such encounters.

But at quarter to three, he pulled on his parka and hurried across campus to Lowry through a chilling wind and light snowfall. In Levitt's first floor office he found a young, goateed Woody Allen lookalike—dark-framed glasses, short, slim.

"Come in, come in," he said genially when he saw Jake in the doorway. He rose, came around his desk and shook Jake's hand with both of his.

"Sit, sit. I know it's a long walk from Satterfield. The hills keep us all fit here at Kent."

Jake assessed that they were close in age, Levitt probably a few years older. The office was cozy, as if well-used by visitors, a small divan and two upholstered chairs, bookshelves packed to the ceiling, and a picture on the desk of an attractive woman and two infants.

"Some java?" he said. "I can ring our secretary to bring us some."

"Not for me, thanks," Jake said, following the professor's gesture to be seated on one of the chairs.

"Right, and I can do without the caffeine." He sat on the small sofa, smiled widely, took a deep breath. "You undoubtedly want to know why I called this little chat."

"Yes, sir."

"Please call me *Jonah*. I like first names; they level the playing field. I like things even-steven. No value in pulling rank."

"All right."

"So, Jake. I've been talking to a young assistant professor in your department, Leslie Robbins. Not bad." He winked. "Frankly, she's been raving about the commonsense position you've carved out amidst all the turmoil."

Jake nodded. "I think most kids here want to get on with their education. Or their parties. Or both."

"Leslie said you started the moderation movement."

"Actually several of my writing students did. I simply provided a forum, now in Leslie's hands."

"Cool. Way cool. So I've called you over here to solicit your help on a project a number of us faculty members are working on. You see, Jake, things seem relatively calm at the moment. Everyone is hung over from the big march in D.C., and Thanksgiving break is almost upon us, and then end of term. But the atmosphere is definitely going to heat up again when winter quarter begins, and then another spring offensive to follow. Sure to make last spring look like a picnic."

"Yeah, the dissidents aren't about to give up the advantages they've gained."

Levitt grimaced. "Exactly. So this faculty group, led by Graham Fisk over in the Geology Department, wants to keep things on an even keel. Professor Fisk came up with the idea of a marshalling program, you know, concerned faculty and students dedicated to preventing the kettle from boiling over. We'd like you to join us."

"I'll be working on my thesis the next two terms, graduating in June. Pretty busy."

"But this is well worth a sacrifice. Our group merely wants to be on hand during major rallies. We'll wear armbands—Professor Fisk's idea—faculty blue, students white. We'll make our presence known, representing neither Admin nor SDS, or whatever the current title may be. No authority whatever, just a presence, to let both sides know that neutral eyes are watching."

Jake smiled. Levitt noticed.

"What are you thinking, Jake? Please be candid."

"From what I've seen in the paper, you hardly seem neutral."

"Yes, yes. I've made some mistakes in my efforts to help students voice their views. My cancelling classes during the BUS thing really snuck up and bit my behind. Yep, I have a nice scar on my butt about that one. Also, I didn't expect the subversion of CCC by the leftover SDSers. Don't know why I stuck my nose in the middle of that."

"I read your analysis of President White's summer survey," Jake said. "You hit him pretty hard."

"Hey, man, we couldn't let him pull off that stunt. Half those students were only here for the summer, and the fourteen-thousand-dollar P.R. firm had no clue about a scientifically valid survey. Trickery from top to bottom. Here's where we must draw the line with Admin. They see this whole thing as them against the world, creating division every step of the way. We've got to get them to realize this is a family, that we're all in it together, even the revolutionaries who are students here. Admin need to see that such deception, like that bogus survey, only creates more resentment."

Jake's opinion exactly.

"So, yeah, we here in Soc who happen to know something about how to do a valid survey, blasted them for that piece of garbage. But that doesn't mean we're pushing the SDS agenda, anything but. So I'm in there, trying to bridge the gulf. Gotta give me a merit badge for effort, at least. And I'm not alone. There's Fisk from Geology, Hildebrand and others from here in Soc, some from Poly Sci, from Psych, and a lot of strength in English, too—I'm sure you know the names. I certainly do not advocate violence, but I believe in free speech and assembly, of which there will be a lot come springtime."

Jake nodded in agreement. "I respect your efforts, Dr. Levitt, but..."

"*Jonah*, please. I'm still working on my doctorate. So what about it, Jake, will you take one of these blue armbands? After break there'll be a meeting to discuss strategy, tactics, what to expect from law enforcement, etcetera, etcetera. I promise not to take up too much of your time. It'll give you a breather from that thesis you're working on. What's your topic, anyway?"

They talked briefly about Eliot and the issue of who establishes the literary canon. Jake liked this man. In these few minutes Jake's view of him as a radical like Drew had greatly improved.

"Is Leslie involved with the armband thing?" Jake finally asked.

"Only if she pushes hard, which she might, in those pantsuits she wears. But it might get dicey and, chivalrous as we are, we're not recruiting women. But not turning them down either."

Levitt rose, went to his desk, opened a drawer and pulled out a scrap of blue cloth.

"Glad to have you aboard, Jake. Incidentally, I'm having a few people over to the house Saturday night. Nothing formal—turkey leftovers, kosher of course, some libation, useful chatter, bonding. Feel free to bring a guest, although Leslie will be there." He winked again. "Hey, if I were single..."

60

Saturday, November 29, four days later ...

Jake arrived later than most for Professor Levitt's soiree, having to park a block and a half away from his home on Stow Street on a bank above the river. As he rang the bell he heard the buzz of conversation inside. Holding a child at her shoulder, a young woman whom Jake recognized from the photo on Levitt's desk, opened the door, smiled and ushered him into the crowded living room. On the mantle above a crackling fire sat a gleaming menorah, the nine candles as yet unlit.

Mrs. Levitt pulled Jake through the throng to the chairless dining room where the near skeleton of a well-carved turkey sat on a platter with side dishes on warmers.

"Help yourself to whatever's left," she said, smiling. "Jonah's holding court in the den. Please don't smoke inside. You can use the deck off the kitchen. Give me your coat, I'll put it upstairs with the others. And welcome—Happy Thanksgiving, two days late. You can call me Heather, by the way."

The place epitomized the phrase "lived-in," the furniture vintage and toys here and there, a toddler peddling about on a tricycle. Vivaldi's "Four Seasons" played in the background. As Jake poured gravy on some stuffing, he noticed Leslie in the corner, sipping a drink while listening to two tweedy men in animated discussion. Her eyes lit up when she saw Jake. In a green blazer, slacks, and a neck scarf, a red ribbon holding back her tangle of dark auburn curls and waves, she gave him a "save me" look.

Holding his plate, he strolled over. "Are there chairs in the kitchen?" he asked.

"Yes, let me show you." She excused herself from the debate, apparently about the upcoming draft lottery. "Jonah's place is always Grand Central. He said you might show up."

Plates and glasses filled the sink. She led him to a Formica topped table by a window looking out onto the deck. Two highchairs sat at the table along with two regular ones. They sat. Hungry from his long day in the library, Jake immediately dug in to his meal.

"So, Jake, how've you been?"

"Fine. Working on the connection between James Joyce and T.S. Eliot."

"Didn't know there was one. Can't imagine two more disparate spirits."

"In terms of social refinement, maybe, but there was an unbelievably complex relationship, both men modernist to the core. I've been swimming around in it for the last three days, so please let me focus on this turkey."

"Sounds like you could use a little more diversion than that."

He looked up from his plate. Her expression confirmed her meaning.

"You are temptation itself, Leslie. Damn it."

"Why 'damn it,' Jake?"

"Because I can't indulge in any more diversions with you."

"Really? Why not?"

"Because I'm into something that has become more serious. Couldn't live with myself."

"You haven't struck me as much of a moralist."

"No? I guess I haven't shown you that side. It all comes from my one and only conversation with my mother about sex. I think I was about seven."

"How intriguing. Please give me the gist."

"I'll give you her entire advice: there are good girls and bad girls. Stay away from the bad ones."

"I suppose in that dichotomy, I'm one of the latter, is that it?"

"But it so happens that I have a fatal flaw regarding the latter."

"For ones like me, you mean."

"Not exactly. For a long time I thought so, but I came to realize my flaw is the inability to distinguish one from the other."

"This sounds like a T.S. Eliot dialogue," Leslie said. "Let's keep it simple, shall we? Why don't we have sex tonight? My roommate's gone home for the break, I scored some fabulous weed, and I couldn't be more in the mood."

"I can't."

"Come on, Jake. Don't make me go on the prowl."

"Around here, that should take less than two minutes. Did you ever happen to run into Lil Lassiter in the Department?"

She looked puzzled at the non sequitur. "Lascivious Lil? Department vamp? its in the front row at all our guest lectures? I couldn't believe how immediately she caught Gary Snyder's eye. Why bring her up in this discussion?"

"You remind me of her."

"Please. We're both sluts, is that it?"

"You're both modern women."

"The kind of woman your mother warned you against?"

"And the kind I find almost irresistible. And I emphasize the word *almost*."

"Jake, do you realize how absolutely divine you are in bed?"

"Flattery will get you nowhere, Leslie. Really, I can't. But don't think I wouldn't like to at the moment."

"Damn you, then, you asshole." She got up from the table and left the room.

Sulking, Jake finished his meal, the gravy now cold. He added his plate to those in the sink and stepped out onto the deck into the cold night. At one end a couple were whispering to each other, smoking. Jake leaned on the railing, the deck on stilts against the steep forested slope to the Cuyahoga. He heard the distant wail of a freight train, the barking of a neighbor's dog, tree trunks creaking in the breeze.

Tasha. God damn this situation!

Shivering, he went back inside, pulled a bottle of beer from a tub of melting ice, and popped the cap off with a church key tied to a handle of the tub. Back in the living room he saw Leslie leaving with one of the tweedy guys who'd been discussing Nixon's new draft plan. Her departure hit him like a sucker punch to his libido. He knew Tasha was in Akron visiting her family with Ray, probably half sauced in preparation of having to perform her wifely duty in a few hours.

He made his way through the academic buzz to the open doorway of the packed den where Professor Levitt slouched on a worn leather chair, his slippered feet on an ottoman and a beer in his hand. The men leaned against bookshelves and sat on a few folding chairs, all holding drinks of various kinds.

"White is simply the wrong man, in the wrong place, at the wrong time," said a tall fellow in a herringbone jacket with an ascot. Jake recognized him as John Westbrook, the English Department's Shakespeare man. "He has the political acuity of a backyard mole."

"And always responding rather than leading," someone Jake didn't know chimed in. "He should be *seen*, and I don't mean on closed-circuit TV. And he needs to be *heard*, and not in newspaper columns. He needs to be out there on the front lines with a bullhorn, lining up the students behind him, behind the university, winning the war of ideas."

"The man couldn't create a simple sentence," a third jumped in, "if his life were at stake."

"And couldn't inspire a gnat," Westbrook added.

"Moles and gnats aside," Levitt said, "you won't find a finer, more civilized man anywhere."

"But we're not talking about quality, we're talking about competence. No one is saying he's not a decent, fair-minded gentleman. He shares our opinions on race, the war, the draft. Just doesn't think it's the university's job to solve these problems."

"He's right about that," someone spoke up. "But dammit, the barbarians are knocking on his front door and no one is answering."

"Wait a minute," Levitt said. "Let's be fair-minded here. He did a good job with the blacks."

"Only after they walked the hell out. And you think the SDSers didn't notice that? It's exactly what I mean about his reacting rather than leading. We should have had a Black Studies Program five years ago. And his only plan for our sweet little revolutionaries is to line up more cops. Did you see his testimony in front of Congress? He's proud no one was hurt, proud there wasn't any police brutality, gloating about the deftness of the arrests. There shouldn't have been any arrests, damn it!"

"What do you mean?" someone asked. "Just allow them to smash into a building and free them up with slaps on their dainty little wrists?"

"That mob should never have known the location of that hearing," Westbrook said.

"Not sure what you're getting at, John," Levitt said.

"You saw the testimony from our cops. They let the cat out of the bag about the supposedly secret pickup place for the so-called witnesses."

"Which witnesses, John?"

"The Haunted House crew, McGill, Engle. They were still in jail, hauled over from Ravenna supposedly to testify for the defendant in the damned fiasco. At the transfer point from the county sheriffs to the campus cops, those inmates told the new location to one of their friends who took off across the Commons toward Admin like a track star. The cop's exact words, *a track star*. The protestors had been waiting at Admin, and with the new info from the track star, they headed across campus. It's almost as if ..."

"Go on," Jonah said, "as if what, John?"

"For Christ's sake. As if Admin was expecting a riot, had the Highway Patrol all lined up, had hired busses for the arrests, kept a back door wide open, let the kids go up to the third floor then shut down the damned elevators. They planned to trap those kids over in Music and Speech."

"Wait a minute," someone piped up. "How did McGill and Engle know about the change of location?"

"Bingo!" Westbrook said, red in the face. "How indeed?"

"Are you a conspiracy theorist?" someone said. "One of those who believe there was a second shooter on the grassy knoll in Dealey Plaza."

The group chuckled.

"You really think our local Keystone Cops are that brilliant?" another man asked.

"Highly doubtful," yet another pitched in. "One blunder after another. And, man-oh-man, this Blanket Hill fence debacle—holy hell!"

Laughter broke out in a room actually filled with amiability. These men saw eye-to-eye about Kent's situation.

"And no conspiracy about the fence," Levitt said. "White didn't know Maintenance decided to put it up. What do you expect him to do, Stan?"

"What do I expect him to do? As soon as he heard about that damn fence, he should have grabbed a shovel, marched out there and started throwing up dirt, that's what. Soon half the campus would have been out there pitching in. He'd have been a hero with the kids. These militants wouldn't have stood a chance after that."

"They stomp our hallways yelling 'Ho Chi Minh,'" someone added, "and he responds with another paragraph from the Code of Conduct."

"I rest my case," John Westbrook repeated. "Wrong man, wrong place, wrong time. Say what you want, Jonah. Sure he's a good guy, but I just don't know what's going to become of this ship with someone like him at the helm. And incidentally, there *may well* have been a second shooter in Dallas."

"Have Graham Fisk's armbands ready," Jonah said.

"Relax, everyone," Stan added. "According to our top cops, we're the nation's leader in controlling campus uprisings. Everything's under magnificent control."

"Yeah," Westbrook added, "like the God damned Titanic!"

LOVE and WAR at KENT STATE

PART FOUR: 1970
Four Dead

61

Tuesday, January 13, 1970, six weeks later ...

When Jake finished his climb up frozen Summit Road lined with four-foot piles of gray snow, he saw a hand-printed sign on the front door of Satterfield: *All Classes in the Building Cancelled Today.* He immediately thought a sit-in had taken place or, God Forbid, an arson. False fire alarms were often closing the building; maybe this time it wasn't a hoax.

The problem was more banal, however. Over the weekend the pipes had burst because of the big freeze. A maintenance crew was cleaning up the place, so Jake planned to trek over to Rockwell Library. The next two quarters would be devoted exclusively to his thesis, with one class of honors 101 Composition to teach each session. After having been publically accused by a colleague of being insane, the regular honors prof had left campus to file a libel suit, and Jake felt the dubious privilege to have been chosen as the replacement. It would look good on his *curricula vitae*. As yet, however, he hadn't heard about his fellowship applications from the three universities to which he'd applied for the following fall.

Like a snow day, he thought, immediately on his way up to Natasha's office.

But wait. She teaches over in Bowman, dammit, and her seminar is over there too.

Tuesdays were not a good days for them to share time.

In her office, still bundled from the lack of heat, she rose and rushed into his arms. He felt her ardor, loved her deeply at such moments.

"You're off today, aren't you," she said, "you lucky boy. I wish I could play hooky with you. Just have to wait until tomorrow afternoon. What will you do, take in a movie?"

"Maybe sledding on old campus."

On his way to Rockwell Library, however, he dropped into the Union to warm up with a cup of coffee. When he finally found a seat in the crowded place, Audrey plopped down beside him.

"How was your Christmas?"

"Good enough, Audrey, how was yours?"

"Great, except for the constant battle with my dad about the war. He thinks I'm involved in the revolution even though I told him I'm in the moderation group. In Dad's eyes, questioning the old lifestyle is branding myself a radical. Also, he wants me to be a virgin until I'm a grandma."

"You'd make the Guinness Book of Records."

She grinned. "I've been working on Wash's arrangements of my songs. He's brilliant. I can't believe they'd sound right with mandolins and fiddles. He wants me to debut week after next at the Eye."

"You sound excited."

"I've never played for an audience before. He wants me to sing backup for the bluegrass songs too."

"Great. You'll give us sex appeal." This statement slipped out before he realized it.

"Do you really think so?" she said, seeming puzzled at such an innuendo from him.

"Sorry, that just popped out."

"It means you think I'm sexy. I'll take that as a compliment. Actually, I hope I'll add an extra bit of harmony. Did you say your girlfriend was going to start playing recorder?"

"I doubt that will happen. She's pretty busy."

"You're still together?"

"More or less. She's in the French Department."

"Aaron got some terrible news. His birthday came up fifth in the draft lottery."

Jake took a breath. "That's too bad, Audrey. But he'll have his student deferment."

"No, they're eliminating deferments except for medical or hardship needs, like if you have a brain tumor or twelve kids. He can finish out until June, though. He's thinking of moving to Canada."

"I have a contact there," Jake said. "In Vancouver. If he wants to work in the antiwar movement."

"I'll tell him. Wasn't it great that the fence came down?"

"Yeah, mysteriously during break. White should have capitalized on that. Instead it just disappeared, no victory for anyone."

"According to the paper," she added, "it cost fourteen hundred dollars to put it up and only thirty-five to take it down. They're saving it for somewhere else."

"Maybe around the Haunted House," Jake quipped.

"Are you going to hear Segovia Friday night?"

"Absolutely."

"With your girlfriend?"

"Yes."

"Won't she go with her husband?"

"He'll probably be watching professional wrestling on TV."

"Really?"

"Only guessing."

"Why's she with someone like that?"

"It's a long soap opera, Audrey."

"So she'll sneak away for the concert?"

"Yeah, we have seats together."

"I don't know, Jake. I can't see you with a married woman. It doesn't seem to fit you. How'd it happen?"

"She was only engaged when we started. I don't want to go back over it all, Audrey, okay?"

"Sure. Can't picture it, though."

"Don't try to. So you like Wash's arrangements? I told you he's a genius."

In the library Jake took a sheet with the general categories of his research, regretful that he hadn't chosen a poet like Williams or even Stevens rather than Eliot. What he had so far was an understanding of the latter's critical philosophy and a huge stack of three-by-fives back in his apartment with Eliot's connections to a host of other literary figures from Jake's seminars thus far. Over the next two terms his job would be to put it all together with a coherent topic. He wished he could simply entitle his thesis something like *Eliot's Connection with Numerous Other Literary Figures*. How simple would that be? Merely place his previous term papers in chronological order, type up the transitions, and slide through until June. But Professor Thrillwell would never go for that. So Jake was thinking about taking five most major of them and applying Eliot's critical parameters to selected pieces, something akin to a contest to decide which of those particular five would win the "Eliot Prize."

He could use the figures Eliot mentions in *The Sacred Wood*, but that would mean a mountainous amount of research into writers Jake had not already connected to Eliot. So nix that idea. Maybe for his doctoral dissertation. He looked over his general notes to make a list of five that would be manageable in five months. He could cut his effort significantly by choosing individual pieces by those authors instead of their entire bodies of work.

Snow starting to fall again on the white expanse of bare-treed lawn outside the window, Jake began selecting possible writers: *Blake (high risk high* reward because of all Thrillwell's biases), Arnold, Browning, Yeats, and, let's see, throw in an American, Whitman. Okay, choose some typical examples and apply Eliot's critical approach to each, centered on the "objective correlative." He'd already done that on his first paper, one he'd sent out, regarding Blake, so that one chapter was virtually in the can. That left four, two for each quarter.

No, wait. Maybe finish up with Eliot's criteria applied to one of Eliot's own poems as a kind of grand finale. Sounds like a plan.

He started as he always did by drawing up a work schedule: first the reasons for Jake's selections other than his already having done some investigation, then research on the comments of other critics, followed by Jake's own considered assessments, then writing and editing time, then transitions between the parts, final conclusions and the construction of a bibliography. Done. Graduation and a move to parts unknown with Tasha by his side!

All parts of this plan but one were under his total control, Tasha being a matter of an entirely separate hue. Would he eventually be forced to present her with an ultimatum?

Friday, January 16, three days later ...

In the darkness of the auditorium, Jake held Tasha's hand. The maestro's performance was divinity itself. Jake couldn't even fathom a human being's fingers moving like that. He felt himself a fraud for even thinking of lifting a guitar again. Tasha had parked her car in her former space, and they had a short, downhill walk from the theater, bundled against the cold. Inside, she poured red wine that she always kept on hand. As soon as she'd guzzled her first drink and poured another, they were undressed and in each other's arms. Their being together like this always constituted the fabulous release of built-up tension and affection. Now, they snuggled under the warm covers with less than an hour before she would have to leave.

These were times for lolling, but for Jake they were always clouded with the strife of having to part. And now, with his study strategy in place, he felt they needed to create a schedule of what needed to happen between them.

"I can't possibly make a timetable," she said. "We'll just have to take things as they come."

"But, Tasha, I have a cutoff date."

"Forgetting about the little matter of my divorce," she answered, "your places are all so far away."

"Look, your parents are going to be upset, right?"

"*Totally freaked* would be more accurate."

"So maybe some distance away from them isn't a bad idea. We could establish ourselves, then deal with the mileage. For instance, even living fifteen miles apart, how often do you actually see them?"

She moved slightly away from him. "That's not the point. The point is they're close, in case..."

"In case of what?"

"An emergency, for them or for me. It's good knowing they're only half an hour away."

"Morgantown isn't that far, even New Jersey for that matter. There are airplanes, you know. As for the usual holidays, birthday visits, we can buy flight tickets. Or *you* can, if I'm not welcome."

"I can't imagine it, that's all. And when I do envision it, I get back to leaving Ray. I don't think he'll ever give me a divorce. I'm like ... his prize."

"Jesus, Tasha."

"He doesn't care whether I love him, whether I'm miserable, drinking myself half to death, as long as he has me. Like a car he loves but that gives him a lot of trouble, like that sports car used to give you, yet you hung onto it."

"Yeah, until I couldn't take it anymore."

"I don't think he'll ever reach that point with me. That's where the metaphor breaks down."

"Then ..."

"Then what, Jake?"

"*You'll* have to do it."

"That's where I run into real trouble with all this. Deadlines, schedules, distances, divorces, family reactions, battles, angers. It's overwhelming, Jake. God help me."

"You know what I think, Tasha?"

"No, Jake, what do you think?"

"If you were really strong about it and simply said, *this is what I want and I'm going to do it*, everything would eventually fall into place. Your parents love you too much to disown you, and Ray would go to another carnival and win another prize."

"There's only one problem with your theory, Jake."

"And that problem is, Tasha?"

"I'm anything but strong. I'm helpless. Helpless to leave him. Helpless to stop seeing you. Like I'm suspended between two overwhelming forces, hanging in the middle of space."

62

Saturday, February 14, one month later ...

The members of Goldenrod, including the new addition of Audrey Kraft, stood together backstage for the announcement of their entrance at the annual folk festival. A large black female guitarist who'd belted out songs like Odetta received a standing ovation.

"Tough act to follow," said Henry, the fiddler.

"Not with our new superstar," Adele said.

Audrey had now played twice with the group at the Eye, to a tremendous response. Jake stood by, holding his old Martin, disappointed that Tasha had not yet found the wherewithal to overcome Ray's fervent objections to her joining the group. She hadn't even been able to get away for tonight's five-song performance because on Saturday nights she was required to refill pretzel bowls and wipe up spilled beer for her husband's late night poker parties. Jake was growing more and more restless at her inability to defy Ray's edicts. Ray currently wanted her to drop out of grad school and go back to teaching at Roosevelt High.

On stage Goldenrod did two standard numbers, then Wash introduced Audrey as a new member debuting in front of a large audience, emphasizing that the following two pieces were written by her, "Daisy Mountain" and "Wavering Waters." They finished their set with a rousing, singalong version of "By and By." The response was strong but didn't match that of the Odetta lookalike, who was voted first by the contest judges, Goldenrod second.

"Two hundred bucks ain't bad," Wash said.

Afterwards, Aaron followed the group along to the second floor of the Robin Hood where to the rowdy sounds of a Stone's wannabe rock band from downstairs they ordered one of the Hood's famous buckets of beer.

"Nobody was gonna beat out that black chick," Henry said. "All she had to do was show up."

"Now don't get racist about it," Adele answered.

"Reverse racist," Wash said. "Hey, the girl was good."

"She was loud," Henry was willing to concede. "A female Richie Havens."

"You were great," Adele told Audrey, who was all smiles. "I love doing your songs. And appearance-wise you add some real style."

Peeling the label from his beer bottle, Jake wished Tasha were there, enjoying the *esprit de corps*, grinning, happy. She would triple the style. After one beer, he excused himself and headed home. Outside in the freezing night, he felt a tug on his sleeve.

"Let me come with you," Audrey said. "After this magic night, I want to be with someone special."

"That's not a nice thing to imply about Aaron," Jake said in his somber mood.

"He understands."

"Audrey..."

She grabbed onto his gloved hand. "Come on. What's the harm? Just to talk, to share the afterglow. I know you're taken."

"You should find a boyfriend."

"A good friend suits better right now."

"How about pancakes at the Flash?"

"I'm not hungry. Hey, there's a bitchin' band at the Ron-de-Vous. I feel like dancing. Come on." She dragged on his arm toward downtown.

"The Strip?"

"Sure, why not?"

"Never hung out down there, that's all."

"Too seedy for an intellectual like you? Were you planning to go back to your place and brood? Screw that."

He allowed himself to be dragged. "There's no set ratio between intellectualism and seediness," he said. "Ever read about the American expatriates in Paris? Henry Miller and his crowd?"

"Jake, the Vous isn't as raunchy as Orville's. We could go there if you prefer bikers with tattoos."

"I'll let you be my tour guide on North Water Street."

"My pleasure."

The word *seedy* fit. One could have added *squalid, shabby,* and *sordid.* Also *packed.* Bar after bar, not at all like Penn State's College Avenue where it was bar after occasional bar. The Kent strip was raucous and raw, students mixing with the working class. Of course, in Pennsylvania you had to be twenty-one to drink; in Ohio eighteen year olds could buy three-point-two beer, if the owners checked IDs at all.

"I can't believe you've never been down here," Audrey said, still pulling him by the hand. "Hi, Randy," she said to a bouncer massive enough have played offensive guard for the Browns.

"Hey, Aud."

"This is Jake."

"Hi, Jake. Welcome to the Vous. Where's Aaron?"

"At the Hood, trying to find someone to pick up. He got drafted. Number five."

"Bummer. I got off, 301. Hey, go on in. You'll freeze that gorgeous butt off out here."

"How do you know my butt's gorgeous?"

"The evidence speaks for itself."

Crowded and noisy, the place had a five piece band on a corner stage, people dancing to sounds resembling the Grateful Dead. Audrey led him to a small table near the back, rough Parisian murals on the walls, candles in Eiffel Tower holders. Jake ordered a screwdriver, Audrey a 7-Up.

"You know," she added to the waitress, "the usual."

"You're well-known around here," Jake said.

"Yeah, the usual is a shot of vodka." She winked. "Invisible to the naked eye."

The loud music made talking a challenge, so they sipped their drinks until Audrey grabbed his hand and pulled him toward the dance floor in front of the band.

What am I doing here? Pretty damned pathetic, letting this girl drag me around.

"I'm a lousy dancer," he shouted.

"Look around," she answered. "See any good dancers? Just feel the music."

The floor was too packed to move much anyway. When a slow song came on, Audrey immediately pressed against him. He smelled her shampoo, her mild perfume, felt the length of her well-curved body.

"You were great tonight," he said into her ear.

She pressed closer, beyond being with a friend. His moral alarm system clanged in his brain. Yes, he was no longer Audrey's teacher, but he couldn't regard her as a tennis partner either. She was of the highest quality of anyone around, and, unfairly or not, he didn't place tennis partners in that category.

"We need to have a quiet talk," he said into her ear.

She backed away, looked up at him. "Okay. This isn't a good place for that."

"We'll go to my place."

"Now?"

"Yes."

"Cool!"

Out on the streets people were lined up to get into the plethora of bars. Audrey held onto his hand as they passed the flour mill, reached Main Street and headed up the rise, then down to Willow where they turned toward Jake's house.

"So this is where you live," she said as he unlocked his apartment. "I often wondered."

"Yep, this is it."

Inside, he helped her off with her coat. Pretty as they come, she wore the simple black long-sleeved dress she'd worn on stage, her long hair tied back, with a wisp over her forehead, her hazel eyes eager, expectant.

He put on water for tea and gestured for her to sit at the kitchen table, the right place for the conversation he intended to have. He sat across from her.

"We cannot be lovers, Audrey."

She met him eye to eye. "I love you, Jake," she said as firmly as he'd been blunt. "I do."

"And I care for you, and respect you. You're a superb human being, and a beautiful one, beautiful down to your soul. And attractive, sexually. If I were Aaron, I'd be working hard, as I'm sure many guys are. You could be a model, and you're talented, and bright. A total winner. And I'm proud to be loved by someone like you."

"I'm not someone *like* me. I'm actually me."

"But I can't get involved romantically with you because..."

"I'm too young?"

"No, you're not too young, and you're mature beyond your years. It's because I'm already committed to someone."

"But..."

The kettle whistled. Jake got up, made them tea, sat down again, his guest watching his every move.

"Now listen, Audrey. I'm going to tell you all about my situation so that you can understand, okay?"

"Okay, if you think that will help me."

"It has to help you." He went on for half an hour or so describing his predicament. "Now, do you get the picture?"

"I get it, but I don't agree."

"This isn't a debate, it's an account of where things stand."

"May I ask a question?"

"Go ahead," he said. "Let's get everything as clear as we possibly can."

"Are you saying that if it weren't for Tasha, we might have a chance?"

"I don't know."

"Why don't you know, Jake?"

"Because I'm blocking you. I'm not allowing the part of myself that might let me think of you like that. I'm keeping you from entering that restricted area."

"You can do that? Like a *Do Not Enter* sign? Wow!"

"Don't you do that with Aaron?"

"No. I would never be attracted to him that way."

"Why not? He's nice looking, smart, energetic."

"*You* get involved with him then. Look, Jake, I want someone exactly like you want, someone for all time, not just someone to ball. We'd be perfect for each other."

"Tasha is the woman for me," he answered. "I decided that the moment I met her."

"Even though she was engaged?"

"Yes, like your feelings for me. I'm a lost cause for you, Audrey."

"So all this time, from the first time you saw her, in her apron, you've never got it on with anyone else, even though she sleeps with another man?"

To his former account of the state of his life, he was now forced to add the "tennis partner" concept, which, by her eyes as he spoke, seemed to shock her.

"Tennis?" she said, scowling.

"Whatever. Chess. Ping pong. Mud fights."

"Or Musical Chairs." She pondered, sipping cold tea. "I don't think I could do that."

"It was before I was with her, and then after she left me. When she came back to me and said I was the one she wanted to be with, I felt recommitted. But in between those times, I played some tennis, yes."

Her eyes lit up, but before she could go where he thought she was going, he cut her off.

"But I couldn't do that with you, Audrey."

"You couldn't?"

"For one thing, you couldn't do it with me. And for another, you would be much more than that kind of partner for me. I couldn't possibly put you in the same category as Lil and Leslie."

"And your ex-fiancée in D.C.?"

"Nor her. Because I know how you feel about sex, about saving yourself for the right person. You shouldn't violate that. The right person will come along for you. Only a matter of time. When I was younger I fell in love several times, and it didn't work out, and then, you know what?"

"What, Jake?"

"I fell in love again. There's more than one person out there. I didn't believe that was true, but my experience proves it."

"Do you really think Tasha is going to leave this National Guard guy?"

"I don't know. I'll have to wait and see."

"I don't get how you can do that."

"Simple. I love her, understand her situation. It's about my feeling for *her*, not my feeling for myself. Maybe I'll reach my limit eventually. In June I'll have to decide where I go from Kent. That will force the issue."

"Why don't you stay here?"

She got up, gathered their cups, saucers and spoons and rinsed them off.

Looking back over her shoulder, she said, "Maybe if I put an apron on, you'd fall in love with me."

He didn't smile.

"Just kidding," she said, joining him again. "About the apron. What's wrong with good old Kent State?"

"My original plan was to use Kent as a stepping stone, after I established some impressive scholastic credentials, to get my doctorate from a more prestigious university."

"Kent isn't prestigious?"

"Not really. And all this revolution bullshit—I'm getting tired of it."

"But isn't that everywhere? And hasn't it calmed down a lot since last fall?"

"That's the power of blizzards and ice. Wait until spring. Revolution is rumbling underneath us like molten lava. Come on, Audrey, I'll drive you over to your dorm."

They bundled up and got into Jake's van. At Williams Hall, he pulled up front.

"I'm sorry for you, Jake. You're really in a sad bind. But you said something important tonight."

"Really? What?"

"That it's not how you feel about yourself but how you feel about the one you love. It's exactly the same with me. I love you. You're the most beautiful person I've ever known." She leaned over and kissed his cheek. "Happy Valentine's Day. Maybe I'll just wait and see what happens the end of spring, when you decide your next step. But, right now I'm going inside and cry my eyes out for you."

63

Monday, March 16, one month later ...

Jake and Tasha lay in Jake's bed after four o'clock on a cold afternoon during spring break, the campus deserted though the library remained open. Tasha had employed the ruse of studying there to meet Jake at his place and to loll a few hours away without academic and teaching pressures. And loll they had until they were startled by some furious blows on his door. Jake leapt from bed and peered out his window expecting to see a police car, time to haul him away. Instead, a black Camaro was parked behind Tasha's Mercury.

Placing a finger to his lips to indicate silence to Tasha, he waved his other arm for her to get moving. Then they heard Ray's voice.

"Natasha! You in there?"

Jake motioned her to the bathroom, grabbed her garments and handed them to her.

"Natasha!"

Holding her clothes, she shut the bathroom door. Jake pulled on a tee shirt and with one leg in his jeans hopped to the door.

"Who is it?"

"Ray Sweeny. Is my wife in there?"

"Natasha?"

"Hell, yes, Natasha."

"Yes ... yes, she's, uh, not feeling well. Stopped by, uh, to throw up."

"What the hell? Open the door."

Still barefoot, Jake at least had managed to fasten his belt. He opened the door, saw a tall, lean, red-faced man, trench coat, jacket and tie. He glared at Jake.

"She's in the bathroom." Raising his voice so Tasha could hear, he added, "Had an emergency. Stopped in to throw up."

"That's a bullshit story if I ever heard one. Natasha!"

"In a minute," her voice came from the bathroom. "Be right there. Not feeling well."

"She used to live next door," Jake said.

"I fuckin' know that. What's wrong with her?"

"Food poisoning, maybe. Said she ate at Chicken Manor."

"Chicken Manor?"

"That's what she said. Made it to the bathroom in the nick of time."

"She just got here? Is that what you're saying?"

"Yeah, not long ago."

"Wait a minute. I'll be right back."

Jake closed the door, leaned back against it. Tasha came into the living room, panic in her eyes.

"Where'd he go?"

"Don't know. You're sick, ate at..."

"I heard you."

Jake looked out the window. "Christ! He's feeling the hood of your car. He wouldn't happen to carry a shotgun in his trunk like some of the bozos around here, would he?"

"No, Jake." She struggled to get into her coat.

"What are you doing?"

"Leaving, what else? How did he find me?"

"How should I know? Maybe you should stay here with me, in case there's trouble."

"Let me handle this. Chicken Manor, food poisoning? Where'd you get...?"

"He's coming back."

She slipped out the door, slamming it behind her. Jake opened it, stepped onto the landing. Ray burst into the vestibule as Natasha reached the bottom of the stairs.

"What the hell?" he said, bumping into her.

"Let's go home." She tried to go by.

"Your engine is cold. You've been here a while."

"Let's talk about this at home."

"No. Right here. I want to know what's going on. Tell me, now." He shoved her back toward the stairs.

"Careful!" Jake yelled from above.

Ray glanced up, then back toward his wife. "I thought you were at the library."

"We'll talk at home. Let me through."

He looked puzzled. "Hey, wait a minute. Are you two..."

"Don't be silly, Ray. Settle down and follow me home."

"Chicken Manor? You wouldn't be caught dead at that place. What is this shit?"

He blocked the door and shoved her backward again.

"Hey, back off!" Jake yelled.

"He's an old neighbor," Tasha said, "helped me with my car, remember? I stopped by on my way home to say hello. That's all there is to it."

"Like hell! Then what's up with the lies?"

"I don't know why he told you about Chicken Manor. I hate that place."

Jake searched futilely for a plausible explanation.

Phil opened his apartment door downstairs, peered out. "What's all the noise?"

"Nothing, Phil," Natasha said.

"Should I dial emergency?"

"Please don't. We're leaving. Aren't we, Ray."

He scowled up at Jake, gritted his teeth, and let Tasha pull him outside. Still barefoot, Jake ran down the stairs and watched them get into separate cars. They backed out the driveway and headed toward Main Street.

"Everything okay?" Phil asked.

"Let's hope so."

"You two caught in the act? Apparently he doesn't know how often she drops by. And anyway, what's wrong with Chicken Manor? They really give you your money's worth."

Same day ...

Time passed that afternoon and evening as slowly as a freight train pulling through town. But the possible ramifications of this ten minute incident didn't reverberate through his consciousness entirely unpleasantly. He hoped she was at her lakeside home revealing his presence in her life to her husband. The time for that was long overdue. And with the food poisoning and the cold hood of her car, what could she do but confess? He fretted about whether she would actually hit Ray with the truth or have had time on the drive to Twin Lakes to concoct a tale that would prove convincing.

He paced, worked on some guitar licks, tried to read some Yeats but couldn't, paced some more. He expected his phone to ring at any moment, but hours crept by until a fitful sleep took over. He woke with a rosy-fingered dawn.

What was going on in that cozy bungalow? Had she convinced her mate that she and Jake were only friends? Had she somehow managed to reconcile the Chicken Manor story with her only having stopped by to visit an old neighbor? Maybe she'd persuaded him that her old neighbor was whacked out on drugs. After all, she'd been living in a world of lies and deception for months, was good at it, could rely on her reputation of being virtuous.

Jake worried further that if she had managed to cover things up, she'd be bound even more firmly to Ray, maybe even making some dreadful act of appeasement like ... like dropping out of grad school. Maybe this incident would cement her marriage.

Then Jake had another thought. Maybe her inability to escape would be better than ... better than the current situation of her living two lives, of his having to share her. Maybe it would free both of them. He shuddered to think it, but. how long could this go on?

What did he want to happen? That was easy. He wanted her to show up in her car packed with belongings, that's what. Ready to move in with him. Ready to forge a life with one another. There would be problems, problems galore, but they could face them, hand in hand, like a real couple.

Don't real couples face their troubles together, for better or worse?

The rosy fingers had fused with a general gold, the light of day, the brown grass of lawns, the bare branches of maples and oaks.

Or maybe the silence of his phone meant she'd been beaten to a pulp, crushed, subdued. She'd be capable of being so victimized. She wasn't strong. He remembered seeing her as strong, raking leaves, shoveling snow, handling her kitchen, but all that was physical, not psychological.

Perhaps he should drive out there, see if police cars were parked along their street, a lane really, or call the hospital.

Or take a walk over to the Flash for some bacon and eggs. No, not that. He needed to be at home in case the phone rang, or in case, much better, she showed up ready to move in.

But the phone didn't ring, and she didn't show up, and the day drifted onward in its petty pace, the sun shining coldly, clouds moving across the sky, Jake surviving on canned soup and stale bread, instant coffee and cereal with almost spoiled milk.

64

Wednesday, March 18, next day ...

Jake was blessed with the ability to attend to work even in the face of crisis, a skill he undoubtedly picked up from his father on the farm and in the shop. Even with his dad's many worries, animals still needed feeding and motors mending. For Jake, this ability meant presently applying Eliot's critical theories to the verse of William Butler Yeats in the nearly deserted library. Yes, he'd called the hospitals, not only in Kent and Streetboro but in Akron as well. The police departments too, asking about possible incidents. He refrained, however, from calling the Sweeny household and Tasha's parents. He had to assume that she wasn't sunk to the bottom of one or other of the twin lakes. He had to assume that she would contact him when she could. In the meantime, work needed to be done, and he attacked it with a vengeance. At the least, he would get his well-earned degree in June.

Shortly after he'd returned from a quick lunch across the street at the Hood, he delved into Yeats's "A Prayer for My Daughter." As he pondered whether he would ever have a daughter of his own and what prayer he might offer her, Tasha slipped onto the chair next to him. He caught her familiar scent, now so intimate to him. She looked at him, put a hand on his forearm.

"Sorry."

He took a breath to steady himself. Her tone seemed foreboding. He smiled weakly.

"Let's go outside, Jake."

He got into his coat, and they went out into the sun of old campus where they sat on the long line of steps going up the steep hill.

"I managed to patch things up, at least for now, but he's shaky about it. He's going to be cruising by your place, calling me in the French Department, watching me like a hawk. So we're going to have to play it cool for a while."

"Play it cool?"

"Yes, Jake. Back off for the moment."

"So, you didn't tell him about us?"

"I couldn't do that."

"Why not? It was an opportunity to set things straight."

"I'm not ready for that chaos, for the destruction it would cause all around. You understand that, don't you, darling?"

"Will you ever be ready, Tasha?"

"I don't want to be the *cause* of the breakup, don't you see? I want *him* to do it. I want to catch him at something, even if I have to drive him to it."

"That's crazy. He just caught *you* at something."

"Then you're in love with a crazy person. I can't help it. Please try to understand."

"How long do you want me to wait?"

She paused, looked at him. Her face was pale, dry, dark half circles under her eyes.

"I know it's a lot to ask. I wouldn't blame you for leaving me."

"Maybe that's exactly what you *do* want."

"It would kill me, Jake. You're all I live for, all I have. Without you, I don't know." She gazed at the shadowed lawn.

"How'd you patch it up with him? If you don't mind my asking."

"I eventually convinced him that you must have been afraid he'd be thinking we were having an affair and that you made up that wild story about my throwing up. I said you're concerned about me like a brother and were trying to protect me even though there was nothing to protect me from. I had to swear it on a Bible, on my parents' future graves, and worse, promise to spend more time at home."

"Jesus, Tasha."

"Yes, I swore to Jesus too. A lot of oaths from me and a lot of a different kind of swearing from him. But I stuck to my guns. You're simply an over-brotherly ex-neighbor, Jake. And we'll have to be extra careful for a while."

"Tasha..."

"What, Jake?"

"There isn't much time anymore. I'll soon be leaving Kent. In June. Rutgers accepted me, at least for a teaching assistantship. Professor Groff is working with the fellowship committee at LSU."

"You can't stay here?" she said, pleading in her eyes.

"God, Tasha. Stay here as a brotherly ex-neighbor? With our future in Ray's hands? It's tearing me apart, don't you realize that?"

"I do. I do, Jake. God, I love you so much."

"I can't stand your sleeping with Ray, I can't stand..."

"We hardly ever do it. I know that's not enough for you. I understand how you must feel, darling. I know most men would dump me. Have you been sleeping with anyone?"

"Yes. You."

"I mean anyone else, a tennis partner. Beautiful young Audrey, maybe."

"No."

"She has a thing for you. It's obvious."

"She understands I'm unavailable."

"Your seeing someone else is something I accepted, didn't want to know. So I haven't asked. It would drive me insane to know."

"There's no one, Tasha. Only you."

A pair of pitch black squirrels romped through leftover winter leaves.

"What an awful mess I am," she said. "I should tell everyone I love you and we should get married and have some beautiful children, and you should become my world, which you already are, and I should do everything to make you happy, to make up for all the suffering I've put you through."

"Yes, you should. That would be the right thing to do—not easy for you, but right. It's time to do the right thing, Tasha. Ray will move on, and your parents will adjust to the real, the exquisite, you. If not, they're not worthy of having you for a daughter. They should be working for *your* happiness instead of their own."

"Yes, yes, I agree, Jake. That's what I should do. Why can't I then? Why can't I?"

Coming down the steps, a young couple passed them, laughing, arms around each other.

"You must do it, Tasha. Not only for me, but for you. You can't perpetuate this hell you're living in. We love each other, and we need to have a life together, and the Red Sea will simply have to part for us. We must demand it. Then all the right pieces will fall into place. We must take control and stop allowing others to be controlling us. Because..."

"Because what, Jake?"

"Because that is what is right. And you shouldn't have to do it alone. We'll do it together. We'll face Ray together, and your parents, too. Side by side, hand in hand."

"Oh, my God, Jake!"

"We can do it. These people are thinking about themselves, Tasha, not about you. It's you and me, forever, standing together, fighting for each other, fighting for what's right."

She uttered a soft note of sadness, of panic.

"I..."

"What, Tasha?"

"I guess I've been thinking that *we're* not right, Jake. That you're my sin. I've been tormented that being with you is anything *but* what's right. But I can't resist it, can't be pure enough to do what is right."

"No. It's their sin, not yours. It's a sin to try to control someone else's life for your own purposes. I'm not your sin. I don't want to be that. I'm not with you because I can't resist you. I've chosen you. I love you. I care about you. If I thought for one second that you'd be happier with Ray, I'd let you go. If I thought that would be right, I'd do it. *Ray* is your sin, Tasha, not I. Ray is a slow, certain death for you. *I'm* your life."

"Oh, my God. Ray is my sin? Why not just stand me on my head, Jake?"

"It would look a little odd to passersby."

She elbow-punched his arm. They sat, pondering.

"I read somewhere," she said, "that with all the acorns squirrels bury, they don't remember where."

"Yes, isn't nature ironic as hell?"

"I'm cold, Jake."

"Yeah, spring takes forever to get to this place."

"Let's sit in my car and warm up. You can hold me."

They walked around to the nearly empty parking lot and got into her Cougar, pushed immediately into each other's arms, kissed passionately.

"Okay," he said, breaking away. "Let's go talk to Ray."

"We can't right now. He's out hunting with his teaching buddies. They're on break too."

"When will he be home?"

"Late, they always go out drinking afterwards."

"Don't start putting up barriers, Tasha."

"I'm not putting up barriers. But we can't find them in the fields, can we? And he has guns in the house. The other day I had to block the doorway to stop him from coming back to your place with a double-barreled shotgun."

"I'm not scared of him, Tasha. He's weak. I can handle him, gun or no gun."

"Don't be macho, Jake."

"I'll come out there first thing tomorrow. I'll be waiting when you wake up."

"You don't even know where we live."

"Yes, I explored once, after I got your letter two years ago. I saw your Rambler. I should have knocked on your door back then. But your letter was so definite. I went down to the lake and yelled my guts out, instead. Thought maybe you might hear me, I guess. Anyway, I'll come tomorrow."

"No, don't. I have to think about this, Jake. For some reason I've never seen things from your eyes before, the way you put it back there on the steps. That Ray is my sin. I feel like Anna must have, between Vronsky and Karenin."

"Don't say that, Tasha. Anna threw herself under a train. Tomorrow morning it is, then."

The windows of the car were steamed.

"Come on," she said, "let's get into the back. I want to feel you inside me."

A few minutes after ten that night, Jake's phone rang.

"Don't come tomorrow, Jake."

"I'm coming, dammit. It's time, Tasha."

"No. I'm leaving right now for Akron, to see my parents. I called them and told them we needed to talk. I want to try something other than confessing to adultery."

"Try what?"

"To convince them that I don't love him. That it's not working out for me, that I only went along with the marriage to make everybody happy. I'll tell them I want a divorce and that I'll get one even if they don't support me. It will hurt them but not as much as seeing me as a scarlet woman."

"Do you think that'll work?"

"I'll make it work. I'll be firm, Jake, I promise. I'll do it for you. For us."

"What if it doesn't work?"

"Then, I'll tell them about you. I'm going to leave Ray. I pledge it to you."

"When?"

"Soon. A few days. It'll take some time in Akron. I'll call you. I know now that you're not my sin, Jake. You're my life. Say you love me."

"I love you."

"Say you'll be patient and let me handle this for now."

He sighed. "All right."

"And say you won't come to our house tomorrow morning. That you won't confront Ray."

"Okay, I'll wait."

"And say you trust me."

He hesitated, not sure he could say that in all honesty. "I'll wait for your call. This creaky house on Willow Street is waiting for you, along with this creaky heart of mine."

She chuckled. "Oh, Jake, that's a great title for a song."

65

Easter Sunday, March 29, eleven days later ...

The time had passed at the pettiest pace Jake had ever known. His life seemed suspended, in the hands of strangers, avid opponents. Registration for the new term had taken place on Good Friday, classes to begin tomorrow, the Christian community up in arms for the university's having scheduled the opening of the quarter over the Holy Days. The weather had remained frigid, windy, misty, dark.

Intent upon keeping his schedule, Jake had plodded on by revising his teaching materials and spending an hour in the Department's mimeograph room, copying, collating, stapling and stacking for another honors composition class. For his thesis, he'd finished with Yeats and could now start with Whitman, the real challenge—then fit all the pieces together, write a complete draft, proofread, type the whole thing, and hope for Thrillwell's final approval.

In only ten weeks he'd have his degree, hopefully his woman, and his new program in a new place. A new place, yes. But could he really haul Tasha off to Baton Rouge? Maybe distance from all the trauma would be good for her. They could concentrate on each other, a new life together. She'd be sure to get work in the French Department there. But ... the distance issue might simply replace one trauma with another. West Virginia had offered him an assistantship also, which was geographically closer, but if it was prestige he was seeking, that was not the place. And Rutgers ... then Jake had a sudden idea. He'd been neglecting the obvious. Jesus, why hadn't he thought of Ohio State before? Columbus! Only an hour and a half away, Tasha's alma mater. With Ohio's open enrollment policy causing a dire need for TA's in freshman comp, he could surely get a job there, even on short notice. There was still time. And the distance problem for her would be solved.

What had he been thinking, or not thinking?

Yes, there was continuing SDS trouble there, protests about the student newspaper's editorial policy, arrests made. The Akron paper, even the *Stater*, had devoted more space to those troubles than to Kent's, which seemed to be well under control just as White had testified at the hearing. But trouble existed everywhere and was bound to go on until Nixon fulfilled his promise to get the country out of the war. The draft lottery should ease the tension, ridding half those protesters who simply didn't want to go and were now free to party their youths away without the interruption of being shot to ribbons in a far off jungle.

So, hello Columbus! He wrote immediately for the applications and told Thrillwell of his new intent, who preferred his old haunt in Piscataway. But Thrillwell met the idea with nothing but approval. Yes, a doctorate from OSU would carry more clout than any of the other three, and Tasha would have the comfort of remaining in her own realm. Brilliant! He couldn't wait to tell her about this new twist in his plan.

But when would she call? Maybe she was packing at this very moment and he'd soon hear a knock on his door and she'd be standing there with a couple of suitcases, and her car out in the driveway loaded with her stuff.

Surely she'd contact him tonight. She was due to teach French 101 tomorrow. But what was taking her so long to call, to send a card? How was she doing? *What* was she doing? Was it the best plan to have left things entirely in her hands?

Before midnight, as he was working out a lick for one of Audrey's songs, his phone rang. He dropped his guitar and leapt for the receiver.

"Tasha! Where are you?"

"Tasha?" It was a male voice. "So you're waiting for a call from my wife?"

Jake took a step backward as if Ray were actually in the room.

"And you call her 'Tasha'? Isn't that sweet?"

Caught speechless, Jake scrambled to assess this situation.

Ray filled the silence. "You're not gonna get away with this, fuckface."

"Where is she?"

"I know your game. You just proved it. *Tasha*, really? But it won't work. I won't let it. If you want war, okay then it's on."

"Is she all right?"

Ray hung up.

Jake grabbed his coat, raced for the door. The phone rang again. He took his hand off the knob and grabbed the receiver.

"What!"

"Jake!" Tasha's voice.

"Where are you, Tasha? You okay?"

"I think so. I'm in town, the payphone at Hot Dog Inn. I was going to come to your place, but I'd better not."

"I'll be right there," Jake said.

"I should get a room somewhere."

"Hang cool. Order me a dog, light on the mustard."

"This isn't funny, you fool."

Five minutes later Jake pulled his van into the parking lot of the neon diner. He jumped out and ran inside. Tasha sat at a back booth, the place still busy with recently-returned students, "Bridge over Troubled Water" playing on the juke box. She gave him a quick wave and he slid in beside her, pulled her against him.

She spoke rapidly, barely pausing to breathe. "I got out with none of my stuff. We were arguing. It was getting rough, so I went into the bathroom, climbed out the window and took off. Turned north on Forty-three instead of south and circled around through Ravenna. I'm certain he figured I was headed to your place. We'd better get out of here. He's sure to see our cars."

"Okay, we'll take Lincoln and cut over to the Holiday, park in back. Let's go."

Thirty minutes later they were in a comfortable room, the blower on to warm it up.

"God, I need a drink," she said.

"I'll get us some sodas."

"Guess that'll have to do on Easter."

Finally they were settled, able to pull away from each other to clarify the situation. She'd gone home to Akron as planned and taken a few days to ease her parents into the idea of her divorcing Ray. Her father hit the proverbial ceiling, stormed about, got himself under control, after which they began serious discussions which stretched out the entire weekend.

"My case was weak, Jake," she said as they sat face to face, cross-legged on the double bed. "All I could say was that I don't love him, can't love him. Daddy badgered me with all the logical questions: was Ray cruel to me, did he hit me, abuse me, was he inattentive? Blah, blah, blah. I tried to tell him about being on different wave lengths, incompatible personalities, and he answered that we'd been together long enough to know each other perfectly before we got married. I didn't have any rational response except that I'd already cancelled the first ceremony. 'I don't love him,' I kept saying."

"That should have been good enough," Jake said.

"Yes, it should have, but he asked why I married him then, and I tried to explain I did it because everyone else wanted me to, and I didn't want Daddy to stop loving me, and he shucked that off as if the idea were absurd. I told him that I tried, tried hard, but I can't love Ray and no longer want to be a maid and a sex slave, and the expression *sex slave* ignited a whole new fury, and Ma*ma* sat there horrified."

"How'd it all get resolved?"

"It's not resolved. I finally put my own foot down, surprised myself, but Daddy was acting so illogically and dictator-like, it pissed me off so much, so I said, 'I'm leaving Ray, and I'm sorry if you don't like it, but I have to do this for myself.'"

"Good, Tasha. Great! It's about time."

"So now I'm a selfish child who doesn't listen to reason and doesn't try to keep a problematic marriage together, who should at least get counseling, like from our church, and I said, okay, I'd do that, but over here in Kent, and not from a preacher but from a real licensed marriage counselor, and I hugged Ma*ma* and left. That was about eight o'clock tonight."

"Then you presented all this to Ray, and jumped out the bathroom window?"

"Not exactly. He was late getting back from his Guard weekend. I guess there's going to be trouble with a truckers' union in Akron, and they had special training or something, so he got back about eleven, and I was packing, and we started arguing, and I knew he wasn't going to let me go, so I escaped."

"Jesus, Tasha!"

"Yeah, Jesus!"

"But nothing about me?"

"That subject came up from Ray about the other day when he saw my car at your place. But I stuck to my story about your being a brother-like ex-neighbor and your trying to protect me with the Chicken Manor story. Holy Moly Alabama, where'd you come up with that one? Anyway, he gave me the fifth degree about that but I stuck to it. No one could make up a story like that, so it had to be the truth."

"He called me right before you did, and by answering with your name like I was expecting you, he got the message loud and clear."

"A brother-like neighbor could have been expecting a call, couldn't he?"

"Maybe."

"We'll insist on it. I'm not ready to admit to adultery."

"Then we'll insist."

"Because Daddy is not about to see me as his baby girl having an affair. So, the only explanation about all this is that I'm a selfish, ungrateful child who needs counseling. So all right, I'll get counseling. If that will satisfy them, then we're free and clear. They'll have a few weeks for the divorce idea to germinate, and when my freedom is professionally supported, we'll begin dating and our neighborly feelings will become romantic."

"*Germinate.* Good word choice."

"As a single woman, I'll be free to meet a new person, you, and move on with my life without being a whore and an adulteress. I hope you're proud of me."

"You should be proud of yourself, Tasha."

She grinned. "Yes, I guess I am. Now let's take a shower together and wash all this hellish grime away."

"Yes, let's. But I have a little news of my own. I decided to apply to Ohio State, so you won't have to be so far away from home."

"Hell, no," she answered, "let's go all the way to Louisiana."

66

Tuesday, April 7, nine days later ...

Not about to move in with Jake, Tasha found a room in a house with three other grad students in the French Department, two gay men and one straight woman, Janine. The four-bedroom house at the dead end of College Avenue was a mere two blocks away from Jake with a parking lot in back where the Cougar could be safely out of sight. Though Ray had withdrawn everything from their joint checking, Tasha had a private savings account with a comfortable balance. She had also arranged an appointment schedule with a well-respected psychologist in town.

The weather had not yet broken, the days chilly, foggy and windblown, the sun hardly seen, but Jake and Tasha kept each other warm with his nightly visits in the French commune and savoring the vegetarian entrees prepared by her and Janine. An aura of silence pervaded the well-kept home with the three original occupants all having begun the art of Transcendental Meditation, the course Jake had been prevented from taking because of his having indulged in an apparent nirvana-blocking substance. Ravi Shankar, Donovan, the Beatles and sound tracks of ocean waves pervaded the musical menu around the place, with the constant aroma of sandalwood incense. Jake found the atmosphere pleasantly relaxing. Things were definitely looking up, and once Ray had the sense to cooperate with the divorce, the happy skies that were bound by nature eventually to come would be endless.

As Jake walked into the grad office that morning, however, he found a note from Professor Levitt in his mail slot. It reminded Jake to keep his armband handy because rallies, demonstrations and moratoriums would be popping up like overnight mushrooms (Jake's interpretation, not Levitt's imagery). The idea was that in the case of these occurrences, the marshals would make their presence visible on the scene as impartial witnesses and as a discouragement to violence. Levitt emphasized that the marshals were to stay out of confrontations, involvement therein being the auspices of law enforcement.

"We're not risking life and limb in our endeavor," he wrote.

Jake got his morning coffee, went to his office and opened his copy of the *Stater* to learn what he could of the mood on campus, the winter quarter having been almost uneventful. But today's paper showed Jake the reason for Professor Levitt's note. The Young Socialist Alliance was about to come to trial by the Student Senate for distributing leaflets in a dorm without official permission of the dorm council. The new organization had brought suit. Now the YSA president, Mike Alwitz, a relatively new name in campus organizations, was complaining about the university's attempt to silence their message. A hearing was scheduled, and Alwitz demanded it be open. Everyone on campus recalled the mess that the last such open event had caused.

Also, the Student Mobilization Committee planned a referendum in which students would vote yes or no to the question, "Should the United States withdraw all troops from Vietnam immediately." The validity of such a vote would have set the Soc Department's membership on their collective ears. Also, in planning the events for the SMC's national moratorium, the local chapter was demanding expansive office space, with every kind of communications equipment. They also decried President White's statement published in Friday's paper in which he pronounced his hope to provide freedom of speech and assembly. He refused, however, to lead the April 14 march and to make a blanket statement on behalf of Admin in opposition to the war.

In addition, an editorial said that the state of Massachusetts had officially allowed residents to refuse to go to Vietnam, with such bills also in numerous other state legislatures, including Ohio's, and that the *Stater*'s editorial staff supported such bills, which, of course, if passed, would be headed to the Supreme Court.

So, Jake concluded from today's news that although the weather remained wintery, the political atmosphere was definitely heating up, centered around events simmering to their boiling points by next week. On the fifteenth, the date of the national event, buses were scheduled to take Kent protestors to Cleveland's Festival of Freedom where Jerry Rubin of the Chicago Seven would speak and lead a march on the headquarters of AT&T. Jake considered this scheduling positive for calm because any disturbance on the fourteenth would be quelled by the troublemakers' departure on the following day. The trick would be to get through next Tuesday without any broken heads. Last October's march had resulted in only one broken window downtown. Maybe they'd manage to get through this one with no more destruction than that.

Jake dropped the newspaper into the circular file, picked up his briefcase and headed to his nine o'clock class. Though hardly candidates for Harvard, these thirty honors students wrote more proficiently than the usual cut of Kent State freshmen. Most knew what a sentence was and that plural subjects took plural verbs. That was a start anyway. Today's work began with the principles of narrative writing, first-person as opposed to third, present tense as opposed to past, and the use of flashback and of background information. Assignment: think about an account of something humorous that happened to you or that you witnessed, to be written in class on Thursday.

As they turned to Shirley Jackson's short story, "The Lottery," one militant type in an army fatigue jacket, long brown hair and leather headband, spoke out.

"Why do we have to read these stories and poems? What good is English anyway? I can see going to college for math or science, even world events, but why should we read stories written by a bunch of dead people? I mean what good is it to society?"

The name Meyers was printed above the left pocket of the young man's jacket. *Joel* Meyers, on Jake's register.

"Were you in the service, Mr. Meyers?"

"My brother was. He's in the state hospital now, can't count to ten."

"I'm sorry to hear that."

"Okay, but I'm in the aeronautics program, don't see why I need to read stories, or to take art history, or music appreciation, or read poetry."

"Anyone have an answer for Mr. Meyers?" Jake asked. "Why the liberal arts?"

"Makes you well-rounded," someone offered.

"Makes you see our history," another said.

"So what?" Meyers countered. "Look what it all got us, into a stupid war, getting busted for expressing our opinions, racism, economic exploitation, advertising. At least with engineering you can solve problems."

"But science got us the Bomb," a young woman spoke up. "What kind of way is that to solve problems?"

"Look," Jake said. "There are different types of problems. In science and math you work on problems that have definite answers. Maybe you don't know those answers, but you're working for a definite solution. And you have a method to find it. That's all well and good, necessary. But there's another kind of problem, one that is ambiguous, where opinions are involved, where there's a gray area between right and wrong."

"Yeah," yet someone else said, "like the campus vote coming up to get out of the war immediately. That's crazy. We've been there a long time, people depend on us. Sure we should end the war, but there's more than one way to do that and I doubt that packing up and running is the best way."

"That's a good point," Jake said. "There are options to be considered, and we'll never know for sure if the one we choose is the best one. The answer is ambiguous. Stories, poems and such deal with that end of things."

"How does reading a dumb story about how a village gets together and draws numbers to see who's gonna get stoned to death show us how to deal with anything?"

"Anyone have an answer for Mr. Meyers' excellent question?" Jake asked.

"The story shows the stupidity of ancient traditions," someone said.

"So why not just say 'traditions are stupid'?" Meyers asked.

"Mr. Meyers is bringing up valid points," Jake said. "Who has an answer for that one?"

"Because that's only stating an opinion. This story makes you *feel* the problem. I felt the horror of everyone waiting to see if they would be the one to be killed."

"It's like the draft lottery," a new voice. "We were all waiting that day to see who would go and die."

A murmur of agreement and revelation passed through the room.

"Art," Jake said, "*dramatizes* problems, activates the emotions, causes thought and discussion. Science discovers immutable laws, like gravity. Math calculates the interactions of these laws. But human beings throw a monkey wrench into the universe because we are not immutable. We are unpredictable. The liberal arts deal with that little problem – *us*. What do we do with *us*? In the story, some people think this tradition of annually choosing someone to kill is savage, but others defend it in the name of what's been done year after year for centuries. They're doing it because of tradition not because it's right or wrong. The story brings that issue into the spotlight and makes it compelling by causing us to *feel* the issue rather than merely stating it. How can a savage custom be changed? It also provides a format in which we can discuss the issue in a specified way, an actual instance to put our minds to."

"Like how to get out of Vietnam," the voice about the draft lottery added.

"Do you remember a little while ago when I asked Mr. Meyers if his coat meant he'd served in the army? Remember how he answered?"

"That it was his brother's coat and his brother was in the hospital," someone said.

"That now his brother can't count to ten," someone else recalled.

"That one brief image," Jake said, "made us *feel* the tragedy of the war, didn't it? It immediately got into our hearts. There are people who believe that Mr. Meyers' brother made a noble sacrifice, and others who think it's a horrible waste. Science will not solve this problem. But by learning how to debate human ambiguity, in an effort to come to the best conclusions possible involves the Humanities. This is the domain of literature, art, history, psychology, even music. The liberal arts. Take for instance the epitome of solving human problems, a court trial, which is really a process of interpretation. Something happens, a tragedy occurs, and we must determine responsibility. One side says this, the other the exact opposite. What process do we use to find the best answer? We look at the case, all the evidence, and leave it to a jury. The jury debates, argues, discusses and ultimately decides. Are they one hundred percent right? Do they ever really know? Yet, they must decide. So they must employ, hopefully, the tools that the humanities teach us. You will seldom have such a discussion in a math class. We need math, of course, but even dismissing entertainment as a basic human requirement, we need stories and poems equally as much in the process of dealing with the problems of being human."

Jake caught himself doing something he always resisted, lecturing. And the time was up.

"Thank you, Mr. Meyers, for stimulating this discussion. And, again, we're all sorry about your brother."

67

Friday, April 10, three days later …

Wearing his blue armband, Jake met up with Professor Levitt, who'd brought his Collective Behavior class to this event as a field trip. They stood among a crowd of a thousand or so gathered on front campus to hear Jerry Rubin, a convicted felon from the '68 Democratic Convention debacle. Rubin was scheduled to address a rally sponsored by one of the new activist organizations on campus. Spring still hadn't broken, so people were bundled up under cloudy skies listening to a rock band trying to warm things up for this revolutionist celebrity.

An hour late, Rubin, in jeans, coat and wool cap, arrived with his entourage. As the mike was being tested, two young men Jake didn't recognize sidled up on either side of the pair of self-appointed faculty marshals.

"What's with the armbands?" asked a large, full bearded fellow. "Are you guys pigs?"

"We're neutral faculty observers," Levitt answered.

"You got cameras? Cameras ain't allowed here."

"No cameras," Levitt said. "Strictly observing."

"We catch you taking pictures, you're going down, hear?"

The two ruffians wandered off through the crowd.

Rubin received an enthusiastic reception from the group in front of the platform, but Jake soon realized that most of the audience were there for entertainment. Rubin advised his young listeners to buy guns and kill their parents. "They're your first oppressors," he said. He said high schools should be destroyed. The general reception was as cool as the weather, with a lot of heckling. He ended his obscenity filled harangue with the statement that things around Kent State might seem mild at the moment but would heat up. Not many appeared to take him seriously.

As the crowd dispersed, Levitt invited Jake to attend a panel discussion that afternoon at the Eye, right across the street. Some Soc profs, himself included, would discuss their research on utopian communities. Jake declined but said Goldenrod was playing there tomorrow night, perhaps their final appearance because most of the group members, himself included, planned to move on at the end of the quarter.

"Don't know much about the local bands," Levitt said as they walked toward the library. "I go from my house, to my office, to my classroom, and back home. That's my circuit. So you're planning to leave Kent, Jake? Where to?"

"LSU offered me a full fellowship. Got the news yesterday. Probably because I know a professor on the committee there."

"LSU? Wow, you'll experience some culture shock. Do you know the Deep South?"

"Never been south of D.C. Dr. Groff says I'll be a rare Yankee in their midst."

"Yeah, maybe revisiting the Jim Crow era. Have you considered hanging around here? We could use a man like you. We're building, you know, and I mean more than the new library and hockey rink. Recruiting top scholars, developing more graduate programs, involving minorities. It's a place of the future, and you could help build it."

"I'm moving on. Hopefully I won't be skewered by the Johnny Rebs down there."

"I'm sure the academic community won't be *overtly* combative to your invasion from the Union, but beware the undertones. Thanks for coming out today. That fellow Rubin is no threat. How can anyone with half a mind take his rhetoric seriously? You know, Jake, I share many of these people's views but certainly not their methods. I guess there are lunatics on both sides of the spectrum. The idea, as I see it, is to rein them in to rational discussion, not the bilge we were just treated to. Anyway, next outing for our vanguard of marshals will be the moratorium march next Tuesday. We don't intend to go to the main demonstration in Cleveland on Wednesday. Can you make it to the local thing?"

"Maybe you could get the weather to warm up a little."

Levitt chuckled. "I'll make a few calls."

After some work in the library Jake left for his apartment. Tasha taught a late afternoon class, but Jake didn't go over to Satterfield for her. They avoided walking together off campus. Tasha had a faculty parking permit, and even though the campus lot was farther away than where she lived, she drove rather than going on foot and revealing her residence. She rode the bus loop to and from the parking lot. And she felt safer in her car than exposed on foot. Shortly before five Jake turned from Main onto Willow. Half way down the block a black Camaro coming from Summit pulled over beside him. A man Jake didn't recognize rolled down the passenger side window and leaned back, revealing Ray in the driver's seat.

"Where is she?" Ray yelled.

Jake caught his breath. "Who?"

"You know who. Where's my wife?"

"How should I know?" Jake said, resuming his pace.

The car backed up with him. "I need to talk to her. Emergency."

"Can't help you."

"You better play ball," the other guy said, lifting a large pistol above the rim of the window and squinting at Jake.

Noting the move, Jake walked on.

"Tell her to call me," Ray hollered. "It's in her interest, hippie boy."

"Yeah," his pal said. "This poor jerk didn't get laid in a month."

Ray peeled off past College, made a right on Main, probably intending to cruise the campus, Jake surmised. And now weapons were in play. He wondered if he should inform the authorities. Showing that pistol seemed an absurd gesture. But maybe telling the cops would be useful. Maybe Tasha would be able to use it to get a restraining order. He'd talk to her before calling the police. Hopefully those guys wouldn't catch her in her car.

An hour later, careful that he wasn't being followed, he found her at her meditation ashram warming up a curried chili and sipping red wine. He rejoiced that her need for alcohol seemed to be decreasing. After eating together in the kitchen, they went upstairs to her room for privacy. He told her about the incident with the gun.

"God damn him! What did his friend look like?"

"Dark hair, squinty eyes, clean shaven, rough complexion."

"Roger Dougherty, probably. Two drips."

"Should we go to the cops? Get a protection order?"

"Let me think about it."

"You're living like a fugitive, Tasha."

"Only a couple more weeks. He's not about to shoot anyone, Jake. It would ruin his life. He's still trying to get promoted, for God's sake. Maybe it was strictly Roger's idea to flash the gun. They're in the Guard together. Roger is a wacko. He uses squirrels and crows for target practice, probably just showing off today. Anyway, a few more weeks and we're out of here, right?"

"We have till September to get to Baton Rouge. They're on the semester system, so they start earlier than here."

"I'll have to do some research as to why they'd name a town 'Red Stick.' So we have the whole summer. But let's not hang around here. Why don't we take a trip?"

He smiled. "Yeah, why not? Where to?"

"I'd love to see California. We could be summertime hippies."

"Funny, Ray called me hippie boy today. Maybe time for a haircut."

She shook her head in comic despair. "I can't believe I used to love that dope. Beach Boy territory, could we, really?"

"I have the perfect vehicle. We can leave the day after finals. Simply submit our grades, and we're out of here. I can have my degree mailed back home."

"How'd the rally go today?"

"Rubin said we should buy guns and kill our parents," Jake said. "And while we're at it, burn down the high schools and blow up the suburbs."

She shook her head again. "How can they be serious about revolution and talk the way they do? Were the kids sucking it up?"

"Some, but not most. I think the great majority saw the guy as a circus act."

68

Saturday, April 12, next day …

The Eye was packed. As Goldenrod was finally getting a following, they were about to split up, but Wash said nothing to the crowd about this show possibly being their last. He wanted to feature Audrey because, sure to get her own group going, she would be Goldenrod's legacy. After their final number, the audience singing along to "I Saw the Light," Adele was crying. Jake reflected at how much he'd learned by knowing her, coming from strumming as a form of meditation to actually performing and inventing guitar runs. Also, he respected her dignity and dedication.

They joined Tasha at their table. The crowd settled in conversation.

"You guys are fabulous," Tasha said. "Stupendous! *Fantastique!*"

"You were supposed to join us on the recorder," Wash answered. "What happened?"

"I'd be a nervous wreck, and didn't have the time."

In a simple flowered dress, her hair pulled back, Audrey sat on the other side of Tasha from Jake, all of them drinking the Eye's famous apple cider.

"What happens to me with this band splitting up?" she asked.

"I'm still here," Henry said. "Another year at least. If you need a fiddle."

"I don't know what I need."

"We'll work that out," Wash said. "You have a real future. I'll introduce you to some people and maybe all of us can get together one more time and make a demo for you."

"Do you really think our sound is what she's looking for?" Adele asked. "She's much more mainstream, a special vibe, but not like us."

"I love *us*," Audrey said.

"But you're going someplace," Adele went on. "Wash will get you on your way."

Jake looked at both Tasha and Audrey sitting side by side in the dim light as if in relief, the difference in their ages and in their innocence showing, though Tasha had once had Audrey's vibrancy. Then he had a horrible thought: had he stolen that freshness from Tasha? She'd been happy until he moved in next door. He remembered seeing her that first time in her apron on their fire escape as he'd been playing the chords to "Light My Fire." She'd had Audrey's glow back then, long gone now. At the moment, she smiled, listened intently to the group's chatter. But she didn't glow.

Should he have left well enough alone? He'd thought, back then, that he'd be good for her but instead had thrown chaos into her life. Maybe she'd come to know a new kind of happiness, but she'd surely paid a price. And their problems weren't over. Life wasn't what she'd hoped it would be, and he wondered if she could handle the disillusion he caused her. He'd been so certain he was right for her. Now he wasn't so sure. Seeing the two women in such contrast stung him to the quick.

Tasha turned toward him and smiled. He smiled too, put his arm around her shoulder and pulled her close.

But of one thing he was sure—he'd never leave her now.

Tuesday, April 14, three days later …

On his hike to Satterfield, Jake saw only a few signs of spring along the way, a bed of purple crocuses, russet buds on branches under seemingly perpetually darkened skies. He found a note in his mail slot to drop by the Chairman's office before his nine o'clock. That would be Professor Armand Rudolf Madison, expert in Restoration drama and famous for his backbreaking course on Dryden and Pope. In his two and a half years at Kent, Jake had had minimal contact with the determined looking, white haired gentleman resembling Spencer Tracy. Jake had only exchanged pleasantries at Department readings and receptions. Not particularly caring for the subject matter, Jake had ducked Madison's course. Consequently, he was surprised at the note. He went straight to the main office.

A sprig of forsythia in a vase on her desk, Violet smiled and used the intercom to inform her boss that Jake had arrived. In a moment the door to the inner sanctum opened, and the short, stocky chairman extended a solid hand. After shaking Jake's hand firmly, Madison stood aside as if greeting an honored guest.

Nonplussed at the cordiality of the welcome, Jake entered the carpeted confines complete with a conference alcove toward which the Chairman gestured Jake to be seated. He asked Violet to bring coffee.

Jake sat on a cushioned settee, Madison on a chair across a round coffee table on which lay a carefully placed selection of *Restoration Quarterly* as leisurely reading for guests.

"Will the air of spring ever find its way to our little corner of the world?" Madison asked, adjusting his rimless glasses.

"It *is* taking its own sweet time, isn't it?" Jake answered.

"But when it finally arrives, it's spectacular. At least the forsythia are out, and I spotted a pair of robins in our back yard this morning. So the harbingers have arrived. But where are Wordsworth's daffodils?"

Jake nodded, smiled.

"You're probably wondering why I summoned you here. You know, Mr. Ernst, we haven't had much contact, you and I, but I've been quite aware of your presence in the Department."

"Favorably so, I hope."

"Do you recall a fellow who visited us last year. A Mr. Boris Wettman?"

Jake straightened. "Uh, yes. I remember him."

"We don't like such a fellow in our midst, but it was an official visit from the federal government, so we could hardly object. We might have, but what a stink it would have caused."

Violet came in with a tray. No Styrofoam here. Real cups and a silver service with linen napkins.

What is Wettman all about, after the talk of flowers and robins?

Violet poured their coffee, and Jake waited until the Chairman added sugar and cream to his. In unison, they sipped.

"That unwelcomed guest," Madison continued, "appeared at our doorstep with a dossier on you, Mr. Ernst. He approached us as if we had a hidden subversive among us, even as much as suggesting that your arrest on federal charges was imminent. But he thought you might be useful to the committee he represented and wanted us to continue your assistantship under close supervision. By that time you'd been selected by Professor Shenk to coordinate the new teaching assistants, and he preferred that you be permitted to do so until a legitimate reason arose to remove you from that position."

"Excuse me, sir. Does this have anything to do with my graduation in June?"

"Mr. Wettman? By no means. I didn't intend to cause you a moment's distress, which I see I have done. My apologies. Actually, I mean only to develop the narrative leading to the good news I mean soon to present."

"I'm sorry, I don't understand."

"Of course not. How could you? Wettman is a sour note, has been for the university in general. But his visit caused us to keep a close eye on you, Mr. Ernst, and that has worked out quite well to your benefit. Your academic work has been outstanding, your administrative tasks laudably handled indeed, your teaching evaluations of the highest level, and your ... how should I put this ... your behavior regarding campus tensions, exemplary."

Still confused, Jake nodded.

"Most certainly Wettman used you for his own ends, and we did not interfere. This caused you undue stress and inconvenience in terms of your required testimony, but you complied without protest. What has been so extraordinarily admirable has been your attempt to reach the so-called silent majority of students here in order to show them someone cared about them as much as about those who have been acting up. In this, you foresaw a need even before the many committees concerned about the atmosphere on campus."

Jake remained puzzled.

"You appear baffled, Mr. Ernst. It's because I ramble. Let me finally get to the point of this meeting."

"Thank you, sir."

"Quite. All right, then. Due to inquiries from several other universities, we are aware that you are seeking a doctoral fellowship, are we correct?"

"Yes, sir."

"And we, here in the Department have discussed the matter and unanimously agree we would like you to stay on with us. We would like to offer you our William Marlow Sinclair Research Fellowship, our most prestigious and, I might add, our most lucrative award for doctoral study. Virtually faculty status, no required committee work, no teaching requirements, and even a fully paid semester of travel related to your dissertation. All you have to do is study to your heart's content and let your interests take you where they may."

Jake was speechless.

"You are surely aware, Mr. Ernst, that we have no Eliot man in the department, so we foresee some time for you in England, if, indeed, you continue in the direction you've taken in your studies so far. Perhaps it will lead to a tenure track position here."

Madison lifted a large envelope from the coffee table and handed it to Jake.

"You will find all the details in this packet. Several of the recipients of the Sinclair have remained here with us, myself for one. Others have found excellent positions elsewhere. This award is a steppingstone to a great career. And it is indeed an honor to offer it to you, Mr. Ernst. We have not a shred of doubt that you will do it justice. Perhaps a little late in coming, but not the least insincere. We heartily hope you haven't finalized your plans for the fall."

Holding the envelope, Jake caught his breath.

"Again my apologies for not having approached you sooner. The committee made its decision only last evening. What with the campus unrest settling down, we finally have the time to devote to our usual responsibilities."

"I'll have to think about this," Jake said.

"Have you made other commitments?"

"LSU has given me an offer. One of my former professors teaches there. And West Virginia and Rutgers offered me assistantships. And I've put in a late application to Ohio State."

"But nothing of this stature, I assume."

"No. I'll have to process it. When must you know?"

"We were hoping the decision would be an easy one. How about the end of the month?"

"Two weeks. Yes. I'm grateful for your trust in making me this offer."

"It's a trust well-earned and well-proven. Clearly an award for your performance. Please let us know as soon as you decide. There's a brief departmental ceremony, a celebration, if you will. We'd like to get on with the arrangements before end of term, and grant you the award at post-Commencement tea."

Envelope in hand, Jake nodded at Violet's beaming smile and stepped out into the main corridor. It was time to meet his freshmen, a lesson on parallel structure and a discussion of Faulkner's "Barn Burning." After that he'd pull on his armband and attend the campus moratorium events. In the meantime, his mind buzzed not only with the Chairman's offer but with the strange and unpleasant prospect of remaining in Kent.

A cold rain not only kept attendance low at the well-publicized rally on the Commons but also chilled the spirits of those who actually showed up. Under umbrellas, the speakers stood on the brick housing of the Victory Bell and shouted the usual slogans while marchers used their signs, soon smeared, to keep themselves dry. Forgoing the speeches, about two hundred fifty true believers filed around campus trying to increase their numbers. The entire group finally proceeded through Prentice Gate toward downtown.

Jake had the pleasure, even if the discomfort, of sharing a large umbrella with the illustrious Professor Fisk of the Geology Department, the originator of the faculty marshal idea. The most popular prof on campus, Dr. Fisk surprised Jake by his reserve and his quiet voice. Jake decided he would stop by one of the professor's always overbooked classes to see from whence his reputation came.

Jake shivered as the procession ensued, the now soaked motley group in military surplus garb, chanting "Ho-Ho, Ho Chi Minh" and causing clusters of spectators to peer from shop and office windows along East Main.

"The university is like a hotel," Professor Fisk said, a twinkle in his pale blue eyes. "These people we walk with are our paying guests. They prefer, however, the analogy of the democratic city-state, where they have voting rights. In a way they do have such rights—they can vote simply by not checking in, by choosing to board somewhere else, but they don't quite look at it that way, do they?"

"You have an interesting way of viewing it," Jake said.

"They are consumers, purchasing a service. If they don't like the product, they don't have to buy, or they can complain, but they should not try to take over the hotel. This group doesn't view it as such. Nevertheless, since they're here, we need to see to their safety as well as to the safety of the inn."

Jake wasn't sure of the applicability of the metaphor, but it was impossible not to like this soft-spoken, humble man dedicated to creating happy customers. It explained his standing-room-only classes about rocks.

The march through cold, doused Kent ended back on campus with a series of speeches in dry, warm University Auditorium, a string of speakers advocating the immediate withdraw of troops from Vietnam and a definitive antiwar manifesto from the university as a whole. No doubt about it, the march was a bust, and the spirits of the participants were as dampened as the budding chestnut trees. Indeed, it seemed to Jake as if, at least here in Kent, the revolution had faded with the whimper Eliot had predicted of the world's end.

69

Tuesday, April 21, Earth Day, one week later ...

The earth of northeastern Ohio's struggle to bloom resembled a prolonged childbirth, the event inevitable, but when? Nevertheless Jake exuberantly strode down the hallway of Satterfield and into Professor Thrillwell's tidy office. He lay a seventy-six-page document on his mentor's desk.

"For your final approval, sir."

Thrillwell rose and extended a hand. "Congratulations, my boy. And on time, a rare occurrence around here. Please, sit down. And additional congratulations on the Sinclair offer. But word is you're having difficulty with your decision."

Jake sat. "Staying here has never been part of my game plan. And..."

"And what, Jake?"

"I'm not the only one involved."

"Ah, I see. A significant other?"

"I haven't told her yet. I figure I should work out my own feelings first."

"And they are?"

"You know, Dr. Thrillwell..."

"Please, call me Paul. Titles are no longer needed between us. You were about to say?"

"That the last week as I've gone from here to there on campus, I've been seeing the place with new eyes. I hate to say this, but I've never really seen it as anything other than temporary. It was the only school that offered me an assistantship, so I'm afraid I came here as a last resort. And I'm having difficulty viewing it as more than that."

"What is your vision of a place more permanent?"

"Hmm. I'm not sure I envision any place as permanent. I mean, I want permanence, crave it even, but..."

"Then why not Kent? From the way you put it, Kent seems as good a place as any."

"Except for..."

"Except for what, Jake?"

"I hate to sound superficial, but no one has ever heard of this place except maybe in terms of campus disruptions. I mean academically. I intend to raise a family, want to advance..."

"If advancement is on your mind, young man, the Sinclair should settle the matter. That award is as prestigious as any in the country. I hope you've had time to review the career paths of past winners. Several have attained professorships at Ivy League institutions. And we're building, as you can see by the mud and bulldozers. Opportunities abound. You might consider our at-present anonymity as akin to getting in on the ground floor of General Motors back when it was in its metaphorical diapers. And as far as raising a family, I could recommend no place better."

"Except for the winters," Jake said unable to counter the professor's logic with anything more substantial.

Thrillwell smiled. "Yes, that is our one liability."

Except for his composition class, Jake was now free of academic toil. Whether it would be LSU, Ohio State or even obscure Kent, he would not forge a future in Eliot studies as much as he admired the man's erudition. But as Jake's future of literary scholarship unfolded, the prospect of viewing literature as an extension of the canon cherished by T.S. seemed hopeless. *The Sacred Wood* was being overgrown and would soon be seen, if not already, as *The Tangled Bog*. Invaders from women's studies, black studies, competing theories of literary criticism, global influences, the advancing breakdown of form must have Eliot turning in his proverbial grave.

Jake now saw his professional future as the investigation of the leadership tools to be learned from the study of literature, a topic which had grown out of the discussion about the matter with his writing students. The raging issue of the present era had become *relevance*. Why study, especially forcibly, lit at all except as a pleasant curiosity?

He'd been toying with seeing the interpretive process learned by literary analysis as embodying the process of adjudication, of decision making, choosing the best of available alternatives. He wanted to prove beyond all reasonable doubt that studying the humanities was *useful*. So that every literature professor could easily answer the question recently posed to himself, namely, "Why must we learn this stuff?"

He was certain that at present few such professors could answer that question easily. Maybe, with its tradition of education studies, Kent, despite its anonymity, could be the very place to compile such an answer and to demonstrate its efficacy. And both Thrillwell and Madison were certainly correct that Sinclair Fellows went on to lofty careers.

True, there were the winters here, wet, dreary, frigid, storms with little or no notice, and lasting it seemed into June. But such discomfort should not be the basis of his decision. Of course, he'd love to see Groff again, but on their summer trip cross country they could swing by Baton Rouge. Conclusion? The weather in Kent might be endured.

But how would he counteract his basic dislike of the place. Not to mention Tasha's seeming eagerness to break her chains. Once a small crack opened, the whole wall had come tumbling down. And there was the looming, ever more threatening presence of Mr. Ray Sweeny, cruising around town with friends wielding lethal weapons. So with a deadline for decision closing fast, it was time to bring the matter up to his beloved. If she left the decision entirely to him, he'd reject the fellowship and move on, now confident he could succeed in any academic setting. So if she said she could bear Kent no longer, off they'd go. As practical as the Sinclair was, Kent itself held no appeal whatever.

He'd give her one more chance to choose staying here. If she took it, Kent it would be, for her sake. But if not, a welcomed change of scenery was in store.

Jake arrived at Janine's house that evening to find the group having dinner with a guest, a blond, blue-eyed young man, clean shaven and wearing a blazer and tie. He might have been an insurance agent. Janine introduced him as Lance Bellamy from Santa Barbara, here to teach a course in meditation over the weekend. Jake had seen the ad in the *Stater*, the course he'd been denied due to his experiment with marijuana. Lance was touring the Ohio schools with a program designed by an Indian guru named Maharishi Mahesh Yogi.

"We'll be using the house," Janine said, "for the initiations on Saturday and then the next three evenings for the follow-up sessions. So we'll have to be pretty quiet around here."

"I came to the lectures a while back," Jake said to Lance, "but couldn't take the course."

"No time?" Lance asked with a sleepy smile.

"The two week ban on weed."

"Ah. I've been there, done that. Pot is nothing compared to transcending. Maybe this weekend, if you're clean."

Jake looked at Tasha, went around the table and put a hand on her shoulder. "We'll talk about it."

"Lance has been informing me. Let's try it, Jake. We could both use some peace and quiet."

Jake smiled. "All right, Lance, then sign us up."

"A little more than peace and quiet," Lance said, speaking slowly. "Raising consciousness. All the stress these days comes from a lack of consciousness. The way to solve problems, personal or societal, is to use more of the potential of our minds."

"Lance knows the Beatles," Janine said. "And Mia Farrow. Mike Love, too. They all studied together with the Maharishi in India. I already told Natasha we'll be needing your guys' room for the next week."

"Can we leave her car in back?" Jake asked.

"No problem."

The guest from the West Coast turned his attention back to the vegetarian stir-fry Janine had made, and Jake took a plate and scooped some from the big wok on the stove.

After dinner he carried a duffle bag with Tasha's things as they walked back to his place in the cold night. They'd have to be careful about her being seen there, that's all. And Jake wouldn't mind eating meat for dinner again, not to mention having Tasha a little more to himself. After all, they had some things to talk about besides mantras and expanding their consciousness. Settled in his digs, Tasha poured them both some wine, and Jake finally told her about the Sinclair Fellowship.

"So," she said after leafing through the folder, "you're actually thinking about staying in Kent?"

"How would *you* feel about that? It's a good deal, that's all. I can go to LSU also. Which would you prefer? Would you rather get out of Dodge?"

"I was looking forward to it. A fresh start, different setting, just the two of us."

"I was too. Okay, Baton Rouge it is."

"It seems you've really turned some heads here," she said.

"They gave me a hell of an offer. But I intend to do well wherever we go. I won't miss this place. As long as you're with me, I can enjoy a change. So that's that. I'll tell them tomorrow so they can find someone else. Louisiana, here we come."

"Not so fast, Superman. Can't we mull it over a bit? It's a surprise. I need to think about it. After all, I'm doing pretty well myself in the French Department, and making progress with my therapist. We'll still be taking our trip to California, won't we?"

"Can't wait to be on the road with you, kiddo."

"Do they need your decision tomorrow?"

"No, but soon."

"Okay, let's do this meditation number and make our decision when our consciousness has been expanded." She raised her wine tumbler. "To our future together, wherever we might ramble."

He easily joined her in such a toast, far better even than having been offered the Sinclair. He could go anywhere with her, dig ditches if need be.

"Did you hear the rumor going around campus today?" he asked.

"We never hear rumors up on the third floor."

"Tomorrow in front of the Union, an SDS idiot intends to napalm a dog."

"You're kidding."

"That's the scuttlebutt. Jonah Levitt called me to join him over there with my armband."

"God, they've got to prevent that."

"Probably a bluff for attention. I'll attack the guy myself if he tries it."

70

Wednesday, April 22, next day ...

Like for the antiwar moratorium, the weather squelched plans for Environmental Week, buds having forced themselves into lacy green leaflets, daffodils trying to bloom, but everyone still wrapped in winter garb and carrying umbrellas.

When Jake got to Satterfield that morning, waiting at the door, his back toward Jake, stood a shortish, stocky fellow in a denim jacket and a baseball cap. When the young man turned, Jake recognized him immediately, stubbled cheeks and a thick Fu Manchu mustache.

"Mr. Munson!"

The young man smiled, held out his hand.

"Damn, it's cold up here. Nothin' like down in Tampa."

"What a shock! Come on in. I've been following you in the papers as best I can. What are you doing here—coming back to school to finish up?"

"Yeah, when hell freezes over." He handed Jake a small box wrapped in brown paper. "This is for all the grief I gave you reading my English papers."

Jake held the small, weighty, square box. "What is it, Thurman?"

"Go ahead, Mr. Ernst, open it."

Jake pulled the paper off and found a Spalding baseball carton. He smiled. "Thanks, Thurman."

"Keep going."

Inside, Jake yanked away some issue paper. The ball had signatures all over it.

"The whole team," Thurman said. "Just got back from spring training down in Florida to visit my folks in Canton. Thought I'd stop by on my way to New York City, just bought myself a Caddy. Finally made the Big Show last season."

"Yes, I saw your name in the paper."

A brief look at the baseball showed Jake the autographs of Mel Stottlemyre, Roy White, Bobby Murcer, of course Thurman's, and a host of others. Then as he turned it over he got an even bigger surprise.

"Mickey Mantle, Yogi Berra?"

"They dropped by our camp. Might be valuable after we win the Series this year."

"It's already valuable, Thurman. Wow, thank you. I'm surprised you even remember this place."

"Hell, yeah. Old man Houck gave me a week off 'cause of my wrist. Hadda drop by and see Steve Stone, Coach Paskert and the other knuckleheads. Did Stevey-boy ever take your course like I told him to?"

"He did."

"His writing stink as bad as mine?"

"Actually, he was in the honors class."

"That figures. I used to hate the bum, always played against him in high school 'til we ended up being the battery here at Kent. He's like a brother now, Jewish, so of course he studies. The lousy jackoff just got drafted by the Giants."

"He graduates in a couple of weeks," Jake said.

"Yeah, don't know who he hadda pay off for that."

They laughed and chatted for another half hour, Thurman updating Jake on his progress through the minors and last year as a backup and pinch hitter in New York. When he left the office, Jake wrapped the ball in tissue and put it back in the box.

Dammit, I'm beginning to feel like I'm about to leave home. Who would have figured that?

After Mr. Munson departed, Jake opened the day's *Stater*. Last night in the auditorium, guest speaker Stuart Udall had kicked off the weeklong series of teach-ins, lectures, films and tree-plantings. No blue armbands needed there. Jake was happy to see radical causes being trumped by concern for the planet's wellbeing. Perhaps it signaled the demise of the revolution movement on campus. Still, there was the napalm demonstration at noon.

Equally disturbing was an article bylined by the Black United Students. It viciously attacked President White for his earlier published comments about Admin's progress regarding black causes. The BUS column went so far as to suggest the use of guns in a violent confrontation. They demanded a new cultural center, five thousand black students by the fall, more financial support for blacks, and additional black faculty members and administrators. They accused White of regarding BUS's first ever meeting with him as the completion of negotiations; whereas BUS had seen the meeting as only the opening round in a *series* of talks.

At noon Jake stood beside Professor Levitt in front of the Union in a group of three hundred shivering students. On a platform with a German shepherd on a leash, a tall man introduced himself as Bill Arthrell, history major. He began his highly rumored presentation. The audience was on edge, as if Arthrell had a capsule of napalm hidden in the inside pocket of his funereal black suit. He explained how napalm worked, where Dow produced it, what their profit was, etcetera, etcetera. Jake was comforted to see a number of campus police standing near the platform.

Eventually Arthrell said, "I will now demonstrate exactly how napalm works by using it on Shep here."

The crowd gasped and spontaneously shoved forward. Arthrell stopped, shouted, "How many of you turned out to stop me from doing this?"

Many raised their hands and hollered their response.

"And how many intend to use action to stop me?"

The response was even louder.

"So you're willing to fight to save a dog, but do nothing to stop thousands of Vietnamese villagers from being burned to death? Is that what you're saying?"

People muttered, buzzed.

"You may have noticed the cops standing by. There are also agents of county animal services, and even the county's chief prosecutor. Everyone is concerned about Shep here. More concerned, it seems, than for real, living human beings. Shame on you all. Law enforcement, and notice, I don't call them pigs, are good people doing their jobs. They're standing by because using napalm in this country is a felony. Yet we use it every day in Vietnam. If it's a crime here, it's a crime there. And we must fight to stop it, precisely as you were all ready to use action against me."

He reached down and ruffled Shep's chin. The dog wagged its tail and seemed to grin at the powerful rhetorical trick.

Levitt laughed out loud. "Brilliant! Fabulous!"

Jake had to agree.

"Going to hear Ralph Nader tonight?" Levitt asked as they headed back up Portage Drive in the thinning crowd.

"Couldn't get tickets," Jake said, "not even for standing room. Guess they should have booked the gym rather than the auditorium. Hey, Jonah, can I ask you a personal question?"

He smiled a droll Woody Allen smile. "No, I never slept with one of my students."

Jake laughed. "Not that personal. I wanted to know how you like living and teaching here in Kent."

"Why do you want to know that?"

"I have to decide my next step. I've been offered a full ride here for my doctorate."

"Ah, congrats, my fine feathered friend. About Kent, I like it. Good place for a family. Lived in Boston for a while working on my master's. Bad place for a family. Sure, dynamic, exciting, but lots of crime, and pollution and sirens. And would you guess it?—as racist as Birmingham. No place for a kid, at least mine. Of course, you're single, maybe the big city would appeal to you."

"I've been thinking Baton Rouge."

Levitt grabbed Jake's arm and stopped short. "Like hell you have."

"Got a full ride there too."

"Don't do it. I repeat, Jake. Do not do it! I'll block your way on 43-South out of here."

Jake smiled. "Why so adamant, Jonah?"

"Hell, man, it's the South! And worse than that, it's the worst of the South. Your decision should be a no-brainer, my friend. If that's the alternative, stay the hell right where you are and count your blessings."

71

Saturday, April, 25, three days later ...

In his stocking feet Jake sat on the sofa in Janine's living room having brought his fifteen dollars, a half dozen carnations, an apple, and a white hanky – all as instructed for learning the Maharishi's brand of meditation. Tasha was already upstairs in Janine's room meditating while one of Janine's male roommates, a chubby, bearded man, in stocking feet also, led Jake up the stairs and ushered him into the room where Jake and Tasha had resided together and made love numerous times.

For today the dresser had been converted into a makeshift altar with gleaming brass implements on top, a burning candle, a framed picture of an Indian guru in a saffron robe, and vases of roses on both sides. In a three piece suit, blond hair drooping over his forehead, stocking feet, Stan motioned Jake in and explained that TM was part of an ancient tradition and that the picture was of Maharishi's master. The room smelled of incense and flowers.

With Jake standing by his side Stan performed a lengthy chant in Sanskrit. He asked Jake to kneel and whispered a two-syllable mantra with the instruction to think it, never to say it aloud and never to tell anyone what it was. Jake thought the organization was trying to protect its product.

In spite of what Jake viewed as ritualistic silliness, he followed Stan's quiet instructions and ended up sitting on one of the straight back chairs, his eyes closed, repeating the meaningless sound in his head. Stan had told him not to try to hold on to the mantra or to concentrate on it, merely to think it easily, let it be replaced by other thoughts, and then come back to it when he realized he wasn't thinking it. He felt disappointed to stop when Stan told him to open his eyes. Then Janine came in grinning, and silently led him into her room where he was to continue meditating until she came back for him.

Despite the absurdity of flowers, fruit and mysterious rites, and the seeming mumbo-jumbo about the vibrational qualities of silent sounds, Jake found the experience enjoyable, especially the meditation itself. Their instruction completed, he and Tasha walked hand in hand in the persisting chilly weather back to his place on Willow Street.

Thursday, April 30, five days later ...

Jake was grading papers in his office when Ella Curlew knocked on his open door. Her raging afro jiggled as she entered for the appointment Jake had requested as coordinator of the freshman composition teachers. Ella didn't smile. She wore baggy jeans, a blue long-sleeved shirt and a black vest with a Black Panther button on it.

"There's a big mud fight going on over by Korb Hall," she said. "Can you believe these white kids? They're pulling people in who're just passing by. They didn't mess with me, though."

"They're trying to wrestle spring out of its cocoon."

"It's damn cold out to be splashing around, mud all over their clothes. Anyway, why you want to meet with me? Is it about the Ralph Ellison story I had my classes read? So what if it's not on the syllabus? These people need to know a little about black culture."

"Nothing about Ralph Ellison. I intend to nominate you for my job. I'll be leaving after I get my degree in June. Shenk asked me who would make a good replacement."

"This some kinda joke?"

"A joke? Hell, no. You're a great teacher, Ella. From what I saw, you've improved each quarter, got it down to an art. And your student evaluations are tops."

"I'm a BUS activist. They'll never accept me. Didn't you read our statement in the paper?"

"I was hoping you didn't help write it."

"Why's that?"

"Guns? Overt threats of violence? Not to mention all the clichés and slogans. I know you're way beyond that. And Ellison aside, you've played it pretty straight in your classes. You're students say you're 'way cool.'"

She scoffed. "Some of them hate me, out-and-out racists."

"Only a few imbeciles. There seems to be a direct correlation between low grades and complaints. You're a good teacher, Ella, and you've learned to separate your personal agenda from your classroom job. I respect you for that. I noticed you weren't even in the BUS march on Tuesday."

"Did you see any *sisters* in the march?"

"Now that you mention it, I don't think I did."

"That's not because I don't back the demands. President White's scared to answer them, so we had to force the moment. And only brothers were in that march. They're still behind the times as far as giving equal rights to women. They think protecting us is giving us freedom. Probably picking up the Muslim attitude toward the sisters. But that'll change."

"Anyway," Jake said, "despite the weak writing in that statement, BUS made a good factual rebuttal to White's gloating about all he's done for you guys. The argument was well-constructed even if the rhetoric was outlandish. So do you want the job or not?"

"Does it pay more?"

"Two hundred more, plus you only teach one class."

"You think they'll actually give it to me?"

"You're my choice. Can't guarantee they'll hire you. Lord Byron instructed me to submit my candidate. That's you, Ella, for the job you've done."

She softened a moment. "They looking for a token black to promote? Nominate me then choose a white? That's the oldest game in the book."

"Absolutely a matter of merit. You're the best person for the job."

She smiled as if she couldn't stifle her delight.

"Okay, go ahead, nominate your ass off, but I'm telling you there's no chance I'll get it. Like a snowball in hell. Where are you heading off to anyway?"

"Most likely LSU."

"LSU? Dang, brother, that's Whitey country even more than Kent!"

After she left, Jake grinned about her spontaneous use of the word *brother* in his regard.

Jake and Tasha meditated twenty minutes each morning before breakfast and each evening before dinner. They had attended the three successive evening meetings in Janine's living room during which they meditated in a group with the twelve other new practitioners. Stan indoctrinated them into the Maharishi's Vedic principles which Jake listened to with scholarly skepticism. But he couldn't argue with the feeling of relaxation induced by the process itself, and he especially felt it would be good for Tasha. This meditation might be an effective substitute for the wine she relied on.

While he graded papers that evening in his own apartment, she whipped up a supper of canned tomato soup, hamburgers and oven heated crinkle-fries. The grilling meat smelled good to Jake. At the table he mentioned Nixon's scheduled address to the nation tonight and wanted to listen to it. They had no TV, Tasha's still at the cottage in Twin Lakes.

"And Dr. Madison is pushing me to decide about the Sinclair. I promised him a decision Monday. You know, even if I turn it down, I can still stay here, Tasha."

"You mean you don't want to come down south with me?"

He smiled. "The way I figure it, either place I'll have my doctorate in three years, maybe here a little longer if I don't commit to the fellowship on Monday. Same with Rutgers, but I'll have to teach there, so maybe a year longer. And, hell, there's always Columbus. All options are still open. So what I really want is what will be most comfortable for you, babycakes."

He took another bite of burger.

"Well, hot buns," she said, "I have an announcement that might be relevant to all this."

"An announcement? Proceed, *Madame.*"

"This is serious, ketchup-face."

Jake wiped some red stuff from his cheek. "Okay, now proceed."

"Ma*ma* is coming to my Saturday morning counseling appointment with Peggy McCleary. Secretly, without Daddy's knowledge."

"Wow!" Jake laid down his sandwich.

"Yes, wow! I talked to her today and had to tell her I'm thinking about studying somewhere else. I didn't mention you, *us*. Just that I need to get away from you-know-who, that I can't go anywhere without the fear of him stalking me but don't want to get an order against him and ruin his career in the Guard. You know, they promoted him to corporal as compensation for his not getting active duty."

"How will your mom get away from your old man tomorrow?"

"Don't call him that, Jake. I still love him in spite of his thick skull. He works at the bank Saturday mornings, then has a tee time at the Firestone, first golf since last fall. So she'll close her shop and slip away."

"Are you sure she won't tell him? It doesn't sound like their relationship."

"I stressed the point. It might come out eventually, depending what happens at the appointment. But I can't leave town in the dead of night, Jake, so she'll have to know. And I have to tell her about California. That's only four weeks away."

"And about me?"

"No, not yet. I'll tell her I'm going with friends. I want to keep you out of it as long as I can."

She took a full swallow of wine, which she drank like water at every dinnertime.

"What's Peggy have to say," Jake asked, "about keeping *us* out of all this?"

"That *is* a sticking point with her. She doesn't want to lie to my mother. I tend to disagree with her about the healing power of truth. So I'm hoping to structure everything to prevent your handsome face from coming up. My goal is to finalize the divorce before we leave and to convince Ma*ma* to side with me at least. Daddy tells Ray to play the waiting game and keep an eye on me, and Ray is telling him that he can't find me."

"And you're sure your dad won't end up crashing the party Saturday morning?"

"I'm counting on that not happening. Hopefully Saturday will decide some things."

"I don't want to add pressure to this stew, but I promised Chairman Madison I'd give him my decision about the Sinclair after the weekend."

At precisely nine o'clock that night on NBC Radio, Jake sitting at his desk, Tasha ironing her pleated skirt for her Friday classes, President Nixon's voice came on. Soon Jake rose and paced, muttered emotional reactions with rising anger. The President made the same hackneyed case of gaining peace by winning the war, of maintaining America's appearance of military strength. Then to all this he added that he was sending troops into Cambodia.

"Cambodia?" Jake yelled. "No fucking way!"

Nixon claimed that a heretofore neutral Cambodia had requested U.S. intervention against an invasion from North Vietnam.

"Just a damned excuse to expand the war!" Jake shouted.

Nixon added that the intervention was needed to protect his promise to withdraw a hundred-fifty-thousand American soldiers from South Vietnam over the next year.

"Makes no God-damned sense!"

The President said that failing to rid Cambodia of North Vietnamese strongholds would risk losing the war. He also took some pointed swipes at those opposed to the war by saying anarchists were attacking American universities. He'd already referred to antiwar believers as "bums," a little more direct than Agnew's "effete nabobs of negativity."

"You're the anarchist!"

Tasha looked up from her ironing board. "Calm down, Jake. You heard all this before."

"That's just it. I heard it all before. Like a broken record from hell."

Jake's past several days of twice-daily meditations had done nothing to quell his rage. The huge peaceful demonstrations in D.C. had done nothing to change the country's course, nor had the rising tide of antiwar opinion by leading media voices, Walter Cronkite among them, and even politicians.

"And how stupid does Tricky Dick think we are, saying he needs to expand the war to lessen the troop levels? And telling us we'll get out of Cambodia the moment the sanctuaries are removed. As soon as we get out, the North Vietnamese will go back in. This is the Domino Theory in reverse, instead of the communists taking over the countries one by one, it's us."

"I don't understand any of it," Tasha said. "But I think the government must know more than these creeps on campus. They're just putting on shows, like marching around the dorms and threatening to napalm the family pet."

"They're the extreme, Tasha. We are not the good guys in Viet Nam. And Nixon expects to get away with our CIA dividing Vietnam into two parts and stealing one of them away. He's such a liar. And the gall of him saying we must support him to save our soldiers over there—how will expanding the war save lives? It will only add to the death count, on both sides and to those poor peasants in between."

Tasha went to him, tried to hug him.

"I'm too mad," he said, backing away.

"But what will swearing at the radio do about it?"

"And if you think *I'm* mad, wait'll you see campus tomorrow. These *anarchists* and *bums* Nixon refers to will be out in force, not only here but nationwide. This Cambodia thing is simply fuel for the fire. The Guard is already fighting the kids in Columbus, Woody Hayes trying to calm them down, as if these radicals will listen to a football coach. How crazy is that? How out of touch can administrators be? And our own President White writing about how wonderful he's been to campus blacks. And how using law enforcement, arrests and restraining orders have won the battle here. Jesus Christ Almighty!"

"Come on, Jake. Why don't we sit down and think our mantras?"

"Fuck our mantras! I'm going out for a walk. I need some air." He paused, looked at Tasha. "I'm sorry, honey, but I'm upset."

"Oh, really? I hadn't noticed."

"Let me walk it off, half an hour, okay?"

"Only if I can come with you. I'll finish with this skirt when we come back."

72

Friday, May 1, next day ...

Jake woke to rays of sunshine flowing through the Venetian blinds, a first for over a month. Stirring slightly, Tasha lay beside him, her golden hair strewn over the pillow. By the time he came out of the shower, she was sitting in the kitchen in her robe, waiting to start their meditation. She smiled.

"Mantra time," she sang. "Please put your clothes on or I'll be too distracted to transcend."

After their session, as they ate scrambled eggs, she said, "I've never seen you as pissed off as last night."

"Don't remind me."

"You were thrashing around in bed. I thought I was going to have to do something I'd never imagined before—kick you out of bed."

"There's trouble ahead, methinks. The crazies are thirsting for an issue, and I think Tricky Dick just gave them one."

"Looks like a nice day at least, finally."

"Yeah, more mud fights. And perfect for rallies."

"I heard something," Tasha said, "about someone burying the Constitution over at the Victory Bell."

"Yeah, I'll have to be there with Jonah and my armband."

Hand in hand they walked to campus, not concerned about Ray, who according to Tasha's mother had been called a week ago to Akron with the Guard during a truckers' strike. They were bivouacked in Rubber Stadium.

At Satterfield someone had paint-sprayed "Kill the Pigs" on the sidewalk. The couple grabbed *Stater*s and parted ways, her to the third floor and he to the grad lounge for coffee. He noticed several rough posters taped to the walls about a noon rally on the Commons, others announcing a BUS gathering on front campus at three. Jake felt relieved that he'd already handed his thesis in, so monitoring these demonstrations didn't eat into his study time. And it wasn't hard to convince Tasha to stay away from them. In spite of Jake's diatribes, she remained agnostic regarding the war.

As he was reading about student clashes with the Guard at Ohio State – the campus had been closed and martial law declared – he heard a wolf-whistle at his door. He turned and saw Lil leaning sensually against the jamb. She wore a gauzy dress and a floppy hat with daisies in the band, her light brown hair loose over her shoulders.

"What's up, handsome?" she said, imitating Mae West.

Jake smiled tolerantly. "Come in, Lil. What can I do for you?"

"Just checking in before we all split. You graduating in June?"

"Yeah, you?"

"Have to work on my thesis, but I can do it in Chattanooga over the summer."

"Really? Still seeing that Christian poet."

"He wants me to marry him. I'll go down for a trial run. He might be sick enough to shack up with for life. But I highly doubt it. It'll be a good environment for me to finish this damn paper on Lawrence, though."

"As I remember it, when we first went out you were embarking on a grand experiment."

"And grand it's been. Some freak-outs now and then, like getting gang raped that night in the frat house. Thanks for taking care of me."

"So, in a nutshell, Lil, what did you learn?"

"Hmm, in a nutshell, eh? I guess I learned to separate sex from morality, that morality is the white man's way of keeping women in their place. All in all, I've had a blast, and intend to go on doing exactly what I want. Like you slimy males. So I wanted to drop by and bid you a fond farewell. You were my breakout moment. You and that flick, *I, a Woman*. What about you, Jake? I've seen you around the halls with that French student. You've been with her a long time, haven't you?"

"With ups and downs. But things look like they're leveling out."

She smiled. "You're kind of a one gal guy, aren't you?"

"Not kinda."

"And a real professional. Word is they offered you the Sinclair. So you'll be hanging around this looney bin a couple of more years, will you?"

"No."

"Wow, why would you turn down such an opportunity?"

"Change of scenery," he answered flippantly. "Seriously, though, I can't beat the feeling that Kent State is a loser."

"You mean like you want to go to a *real* university?"

"Something like that."

They chatted a while, wished each other luck.

"Have a great life," she said. "I'll always remember you, Jakey-boy." And she swished out into the corridor.

The day was divinely glorious with bright sunshine, warming breezes, trees a rich green, blossoms and flowers in full bloom, robins bounding on the lawns, girls in short-shorts and miniskirts, guys in cutoffs and no shirts. The Commons had become a kind of beach replete with blankets, Frisbees, dogs, a real celebration of spring, intensified because of the interminable wait. The wait was over at last.

It was in this bacchanal atmosphere that Jake and Levitt stood on the Taylor Hall sidewalk overlooking the vast scene below. A blond, longhaired lad was ringing the bell incessantly, and a crowd of a few hundred gathered around as two roughly bearded men, one short, the other tall, climbed up on the casing with a bullhorn. The short one was dressed like Fidel down to the stub of cigar. Both were about to address the group, many of whom were simply passersby who paused out of curiosity.

"The cigar guy," Levitt said, "is Bob Franklin, teaches chem. Out on bail from his arrest at the Cleveland AT&T thing a few weeks ago. The other guy is Simon Shapiro, possibly an SDS plant. This is more of a stunt than anything else. Some grad students in History came up with the acronym WHORE. Cute, eh?" He pulled a folded flier from his jacket pocket, opened it and read: "World Historians Opposed to Racism and Exploitation." This burying the Constitution trip is nothing but a little joke. The kids are having too much fun to pay any attention to revolution at the moment."

The audience paid more attention, however, to a dynamic young ex-soldier dressed in fatigues who announced he was about to burn his discharge papers. He ignited them with a lighter and held them as they burned. Another vet pulled out his and lit them too. Then with a shovel Shapiro dug a hole, laid to rest the supposed copy of the Constitution, and covered it up. A brief scuffle took place caused by a few male students who objected to treating our sacred founding statement with such disrespect.

"Hey," Jonah said, nudging Jake, "a cutie down there is waving at us."

Jake turned his head to the right and spotted Audrey down the hill, Aaron with her, both waving. Jake waved back.

She cupped her hands around her mouth and yelled, "Pretty boring stuff on such a beautiful day."

Jake watched her break into a run to catch a Frisbee.

"Now *there's* a lovely young thing," Jonah said. "The perfect embodiment of a day like this."

At the end of the presentation, the final speaker said they should have another rally, suggested noon Monday, to resurrect the Constitution so that it could be dusted off and actually followed. The participants responded to this idea with enthusiastic cheers.

By now it was 2:10, the BUS rally on front campus to start at three. Jonah headed back to his office over there, and Jake strolled with him, to get a bite to eat at the Union. A young bearded man moved by in the same direction, slowing down to whisper, "Downtown, tonight. Gonna raise some hell."

Jake watched the fellow move along the path ahead, telling everyone he passed as if spreading a delicious secret.

Well, it's spring. Hormones flowing.

He easily recalled the vast lawn in front of Penn State's Old Main on breakout days like this. And the late night masses on College Avenue.

What university life is all about.

BUS members wearing black jumpsuits stood around a podium in the shade of maples on front campus, Jake's favorite place at KSU, often viewed from the library which was about to be replaced by a thirteen story monstrosity on the other side. Jonah had rejoined Jake, standing on the long flight of steps, armbands on. Approximately a thousand had gathered as a tall bearded speaker ferociously read off a list of demands having been made by the black organization at Ohio State. It was a long list, each item punctuated by "Right On's" and the Black Power fist-in-the-air salute.

"We've done almost all of these things here," Jonah said softly. "Way ahead of the game. Got to give President White a pat on the back for that."

While the presentation went on, Jake noticed white males wearing bowler hats being chased on the hillside by young women in spring dresses, all as if oblivious to the BUS event.

"May First," Jonah explained. "Derby Day, a Greek tradition. The girls pursue the boys around, catch them, give them a kiss. Kind of a maypole thing, sociologically speaking."

"Strange traditions around here," Jake said. "Mud fights, weird hats, a rock to paint announcements on."

Though intense, the BUS presentation was orderly, controlled, not a hint of violence, and little said about Kent besides the demands having already been announced in the *Stater* article minus the mention of buying guns. Nor was there levity. The black-suited guards stood straight as sentries, scowls on their faces. With the crowd dispersing, Jonah went over toward Lowry and Jake down toward Main on his way home. On the hillside frat boys continued their frolic with barefoot sorority girls as little caring as the black squirrels about the plight of black students.

73

That evening …

"I have an idea," Jake said as he and Tasha ate dinner in his kitchen.

"Anything to do with visiting my parents, forget it."

"No. A Kent sociological tradition. Why don't we take a blanket up to Blanket Hill and, uh, look at the stars."

She grinned. "I don't think stargazing is what that tradition is all about."

"We can roam free these days with you-know-who tied up with the Guard in Akron, enjoy this fine evening. We'll be leaving here for good. Why not take a walk around on this beautiful night for nostalgia's sake? It would be a shame to make our exit without partaking in one of Trent's major delights."

"You can look at it like that, Jake, because you already left your home. But for me it will be like cutting an umbilical cord. Leaving scares me."

"We have to view *each other* as our home, not a piece of geography."

"What if some of our students see us out there on the hill?"

"We'll point out Orion's belt to them."

When night fell, each carrying a blanket, one to lie on, one to cover with, Tasha wearing a blue wool hat over her blond hair, they hiked up Summit Road, down to Portage, and between classroom buildings and dorms to the famous hill. The night was warm, almost sultry, and many spots were already taken. A crescent moon glowed amid an infinity of stars. Tasha had a bottle of red wine hidden in her tote.

"Can't do this without some fortification," she'd said.

A few security lights glowed from Taylor Hall, the building deserted for the weekend with only the several bluish beams casting shadows amid the trees. Down the slope on the Commons, the Victory Bell sat silent in its brick housing. Students wandered in both directions on the Taylor sidewalk. Jake and Tasha found an open spot near an odd structure known as the Pagoda, a distinctive, Japanese looking, roof-like sculpture at the top of the hill. They spread a blanket, lay down and pulled the other one over them. From their fellow astronomers they heard rustling and whispers, a few spontaneous moans. Tasha opened the bottle of Chianti, took a swig and handed it to Jake, who did likewise.

On their backs, they looked up at the heavens.

"Where is Orion, anyway?" Tasha asked.

Jake pointed. "See those three stars right in a row, almost horizontal to us?"

It took her a while, several pointings, but then she said, "Oh, yes. There they are."

"That's his belt. Lower, there's his sword, and below are his dogs. Orion is a hunter."

"Are you sure that's his *sword*?"

"Maybe *sword* is a euphemism. Phallic symbolism."

"All I know is the Big Dipper," she said, "and how the outer rim points to the North Star."

"Shhh!" came a voice from someone near.

The two snuggled, pressed, opened buttons, drew down zippers, jostled garments, touched skin to skin. It reminded Jake of hayrides during his high school days, doing what they wanted in secret. With him inside her, they lay wriggling, kissing, prolonging the moment until it could be held no longer. Still, they lay side to side, enjoined.

"I love you, Tasha," he whispered in her ear.

"I love you too, Jake. My wonderful Jake."

Couples rose and left. Others arrived, voices low. To Jake, it felt like a sacred rite, somehow. Yes, it was college kids getting laid, but the silence, the shadows, the warmth of spring, even the silly sense of tradition, seemed to sanctify it. And the knowledge that he would be leaving this place soon with the woman he loved. He'd found something here in this remote, often crazy place. He'd found a life. It was what he'd come here for, wasn't it?

He inhaled Tasha's scent, moved inside her again, revitalized, rolled on top of her and sanctified the tradition once again, feeling her warmth, the spring air on his shoulders and neck, her hands gripping his buttocks.

After this round Tasha pulled the cork out of the bottle and they both took drags.

"Let's go back," she said. "I keep feeling we'll get arrested."

"Yeah, can't you see the headlines?"

They shook out their blankets, folded them and headed across campus, down the long steps to the library and home. As they climbed the several stairs of their porch, Billy came rushing out the front door, several cameras on straps around his neck.

"What's up?" Jake asked.

"Can't talk. All hell is breaking out on the Strip. Gotta go."

"What kind of hell?" Jake yelled toward Billy's back.

"Spring riot. And Cambodia. The Kent Four were released from county jail today. I'm sure they're stirring things up."

He jogged off toward Main Street.

"Who are the Kent Four?" Tasha asked.

"The ones arrested for rioting at Music and Speech, from the Haunted House. I guess their sentences are up."

Having seen his share of football celebrations in State College, shop windows broken, toilet paper streamers hung from telephone wires, traffic stopped, Jake's interest in something of the like on North Water Street was not piqued for a moment. With Phil's car gone from the driveway, and Tasha's former apartment still unoccupied, they had the place to themselves. After showers, in their pajamas they played some music together from the Pete Seeger songbook, Pete now dedicating his life to sailing a sloop up and down the Hudson River using his music to fight pollution.

At about midnight they put their instruments away and were preparing to turn in when from his bedroom window Jake noticed an odd glow in the sky. It was in the direction of downtown. He went to the window and looked out. It seemed to be from a fire, nothing clear because it came from beyond the rise between campus and town, a wavering reddish-gold light. Then a distant siren added to the ominous glow.

"Something's happening," he said to Tasha, who was in the bathroom brushing her teeth.

"What did you say?"

"Looks like a fire downtown."

Still brushing, foam at her mouth, she joined him.

"Maybe one of the bars." She went back to the bathroom.

"Must be the riot Billy talked about," Jake said.

"It's about time they burned those dives down. They give our town a bad reputation."

"Didn't you ever hang out down there?"

"Hardly ever. Ray likes to go to the Eleventh Frame, south on Water."

"The bowling place?"

"He and his pals have a team."

Guessing he'd learn what was happening in the news tomorrow, Jake got into bed, a grin remaining from their night as amateur astronomers.

An hour or so later, they were awakened by doors slamming and a ruckus downstairs. Jake went out to the landing and saw Billy, harried, coming out of his place.

"What's going on?" Jake called down.

Billy looked up. "Things out of hand," he said, out of breath. "Just a normal riot until they closed the bars. Everyone watching the NBA finals, ended up sorely pissed, out on the street. Big fire, the Chosen Few doing wheelies on their choppers, old people stopped in their cars, windows broken. Christ Almighty! Ran out of film." He coughed. "Tear gas, too. State cops, driving the kids back on Main toward campus. Gotta go back, get this story."

Jake went in and grabbed his jeans.

"You're not going out there, are you?" Tasha cried.

"Yeah. Jonah will be there sure, and the other marshals. Don't worry, I'll be okay."

"Tear gas?"

"We won't get too close. Don't worry."

He had a sweatshirt on now and was pulling on his sneakers.

"Then I'm coming too. I'm not going to sit in here and worry."

"Come on then. Hurry up. Bring a wet towel to cover your face."

Main and Lincoln, where the university began, was only two blocks away. Wrung-out towels over their shoulders, Jake and Tasha ran out into the warm night. Sirens wailed, some close, some distant. The glow over downtown was gone, but they heard shouting, someone's voice on a bullhorn. The end of Willow had been closed off by squad cars, state troopers, so Jake and Tasha found a way between buildings up to Lincoln, which was blocked by a line of cruisers, lights flashing.

The central scene seemed to be the intersection of Main and Lincoln, but Jake couldn't figure out how to get there except to go back to Willow and up over the hill on Summit, then across campus. On the run he caught Tasha's hand and pulled her with him. Summit was steep and exhausting at their pace, then they had to go down Portage. As they neared the Union, they saw students streaming toward them, yelling, angry, coughing, holding cloths to their faces.

"Fucking pigs!" someone shouted.

Several helped others who were hurt.

Jake had never seen anything like this. Now it was difficult to make their way against the flow. Finally they reached the steps down to front campus, where students milled, lights flashed down on Main.

From a bullhorn they heard, "This assembly is illegal. Go back to your dorms immediately or you will be arrested."

"I guess that's what they call the Riot Act," Jake said. "Is that the National Guard down there?"

"It can't be," Tasha said. "They're in Akron. For tear gas, must be State Troopers, county sheriffs."

"Yeah, all according to White's established hierarchy of campus, town, county, state."

"It's certainly not only the campus and the town, not to stop this mob."

"I'm not sure they're stopped," Jake said.

In spite of the oft repeated bullhorn announcement to disperse, a stand-off appeared to be happening at the intersection. The police seemed hesitant to cross the line onto KSU grounds, and the students reluctant to retreat any farther. It seemed they viewed campus as a sanctuary. Jake and Tasha stood at the landing halfway down the staircase when they heard shots and saw projectiles arching over the streetlights into the crowd. The teargas burst into a fog, panicking the students, who ran up the steep hill, some rushing by Jake and Tasha on the steps, screaming, cursing, gagging. Jake grabbed Tasha's hand and pulled her back up the stairs. They gave their towels to a coughing couple and managed to stay ahead of the gas cloud as they climbed upward, shoved along by the throng.

"Nothing to be done here," Jake shouted to her.

They managed to reach Hilltop Drive unscathed, but Jake couldn't help being moved by the sense that something nearly catastrophic had taken place. The students were furious, some crying, some still shouting obscenities, some comforting their friends. By now it seemed the cops had stopped at Lincoln and Main but had gathered in force behind a barricade of vehicles, lights still flashing.

Except for a few diehard student warriors amid the smoke, picking up canisters and hurling them back toward the police, the front campus had been cleared. But the regenerative glory of the spring night had been replaced by something portentous and frightening, the stars obscured by drifting clouds of gas, and the kids, earlier high on hormones, three-two beer and weed, having become a fuming and terrified mob.

"I wonder if Ma*ma* will be able to make it through for our appointment tomorrow morning," Tasha said, shaking against Jake. He held her close as they hurried back down Summit toward home.

74

Saturday, May 2, next day ...

Jake and Tasha slept fitfully until the phone rang at nine. Bleary-eyed, Jake got up about to answer it on the sixth ring.

"Wait," Tasha said. "It's probably Mama. I'll get it."

"Yes, he's here." With a puzzled look she held the phone toward Jake. "It's Jonah Levitt."

Jake took the phone.

"Hi, Jonah. What's going on?"

"Jake, there's a meeting with the marshals at ten. I'm sure you heard about the commotion last night."

"Yeah, saw part of it, front campus."

"It's serious. Downtown was badly damaged, and we don't think it's over, what with the SDSers getting out of jail and the Cambodia thing. Reports are that outsiders have been brought in, a couple of carloads spotted coming off the Interstate. So we have some planning to do. Graham got us a *control center* in Admin, do you believe that? But that room is too small for a general marshals' meeting, so come to the atrium in Lowry Hall."

Jake said he'd be there. After he hung up, he heard Tasha in the bathroom, the toilet flushing.

"You still have an appointment this morning," he said gently when she came out. "Now I do too. It seems the Columbus riots might be coming here. Jonah thinks last night might have been only Round One."

He turned on the student radio station, all talk about the night's events, store windows shattered, jewelry stolen, fire damage, not only a bonfire in the street but a shed in flames, students arrested, nonstudent agitators, policemen hit by rocks, automobiles smashed, then the tear gas on campus. The mayor and local authorities were meeting, phone calls to alert the governor about a possible state of emergency. On the station, students recounted their harrowing experiences, several revolutionaries saying the town is going to burn, the gloves are off.

To Jake it was a nightmare without a preface, a sleeping volcano suddenly awakened. Such spring outbreaks at Penn State had simply been followed up next day by cleanup crews and everyone sleeping in until three in the afternoon. But this seemed, somehow, to be a declaration of war.

Outside, the sun shone purely on the green of the chestnut trees. Sparrows chattered in the eaves of the house. Two kids sped by on skateboards. No sign of conflict whatever. But according to the radio, downtown presented a picture of tens of thousands of dollars of devastation.

Wrapped in a towel, Tasha found her counselor's number and dialed. Peggy was already in her office on the second block of East Main and said the area was busy with clean up and cop cars but open for appointments. Then Tasha called her mother and confirmed their meeting.

"No, Mama," she said, "they're cleaning everything up. College kids on a spring spree. They're all sleeping it off this morning. See you soon."

A group of faculty and grad students were crowded into the atrium of Lowry Hall. Graham Fisk rehashed an earlier meeting at the fire station among a meek group of administrators and a strong contingent of local leaders and law enforcement officials. President White was in Iowa visiting family.

"Here's the thing," Fisk said. "No one knows exactly what to do except to line up police. They don't know the extent of the threat. But we all know the longstanding rumors about burning down ROTC. We all know that the damn structure has been on their agenda for years now, but last night didn't seem like any of that. Kids in a drunken frenzy. Yes, the agitators were there in the shadows, urging things along, and if the rumors are true, now they've brought in the pros to keep fuel on the fire, and, God help us, that might be literal."

"That old crap of a building will go up like kindling," someone said.

"Yes, and campus police have a game plan. They've been hearing serious threats for weeks now. But there's a conflict about exactly when community cops come onto our turf, not to mention county and state. There's even talk of alerting the Guard. The mayor is calling the Governor's office for a heads up, at least. The troop from the Ravenna armory are hunkered down over in Akron at the moment."

"So when do you issue us bayonets," someone asked.

After the snickers Fisk said, "Our armbands are all the weapons we have. Remember, we are neutral observers. Stay out of any lines of fire, any clashes, keep your distance. But use your voice, your persuasive powers. Remember we're there to prevent violence if we can, but don't risk life or limb. And of course be seen by both sides. They need to know that eyes are watching."

"Cameramen are being threatened," another voice piped up. "Some with their lives."

"Let your eyes and memories be your cameras. Then fill in your logs. We are monitors, not participants. I know it's hard sometimes, but try to hold your tempers. And here's what I think, strictly personally, I love these kids. After my family, they're my life. It's a new breed, grown up being entertained, slow to tolerate boredom, rebellious of their parents' ways. I see it as a cultural clash going on here, a wave of change on the way, the old guard trying to hold it back. Who knows how it will all shake out? And the university is on the front line, and somehow, someway, it's up to us to forge a transition between the old and the new, to create a middle ground instead of polarized opponents bent simply upon destroying one another. Sorry, I know I'm preaching to the choir, and there's not much we can do except witness and persuade. So when you're out there this afternoon and evening, don't get your head knocked in. By either side."

"So what's the next step?" someone asked.

"Pray, meditate, cross your fingers, knock on wood or whatever, find a rabbit's foot, and get out there. I doubt much will happen until nightfall, so maybe after dinner time, meet at the ROTC building. Everyone's guess is that old shack is a prime target, and if it goes up in flames, the SDSers will have a major victory, as much as we'd all like to see all four of those old barracks go. And God bless you all for trying to help save lives. Because it might come to that tonight."

Or it might not, Jake thought. Maybe the great majority of students had enough of tear gas and destruction. Maybe last night was enough for them to realize law enforcement was serious. Burning down buildings, even ram-shackle ones? Here in this little town on this virtually unknown campus? It seemed absurd.

Over in the Union, however, where he stopped in for a sandwich, things were buzzing. The place was packed, high energy, students recounting their adventures, talking issues, and the tone wasn't pleasing to Jake's ears. He overheard talk of a seven o'clock rally on the Commons, of brutality from the "pigs," and of revenge. The feeling from many who'd been elsewhere last night was that they'd missed a helluva show. Something besides a bonfire had been ignited, for sure, excitement and eagerness in the air.

Jake thought of Graham Fisk's words: *I love these kids.* He wondered if he, himself, felt the same and soon realized that, no, he didn't. He felt sorry for them. He felt sorry because they were being led, exploited, by a really evil group, a group willing to propagate total destruction and to use these naïve innocents to do their bidding. But as far as loving them? No, he didn't feel quite that. And as far as the hardcore leaders, for them he felt almost hatred.

Outside, on his way home to find out how Tasha's session had gone, he ran into Audrey and Aaron.

"We saw you and your girl last night on the steps," Audrey said, excit-edly. "Did you get gassed?"

"Not really. You?"

"Yeah we did. That stuff is horrible. My eyes are still burning. I don't know why they had to do it. We were back on campus, headed back to our dorms. They're animals. We were gagging all night."

"I'd stay home tonight if I were you," Jake said.

"Are you kidding?" Aaron said. "Did you hear about Columbus? The pigs are out to get us."

"Then get out of town. I'll lend you my van."

"That serious?" Audrey said.

"Haven't you heard the rumors?" Jake asked.

"About ROTC?" Aaron said. "Who'd miss that shack?"

"I'd like to think you two especially aren't going to be out there."

"But you'll be there, won't you?" Audrey asked. "With your armband?"

"Not that I think it will do much good."

"The time for armbands is over," Aaron said. "Now it's time for action."

"Don't let this situation radicalize you," Jake said. "It's exactly what the professional agitators want. They jump on an opportunity, create a crisis, then get you all on the bandwagon. Last night had nothing to do with the war. It was just spring hormones that got out-of-hand."

"Right on!" Aaron said. "The kids didn't create this crisis. The pigs did. If they come on this campus, they'll get their asses kicked."

"You have my number, Audrey. You know where I live if you need someplace. Don't let Aaron here do anything stupid, okay?"

"I always try to stop him," she joked, "but it's like trying to stop a charging bull at Pamplona."

The weather was splendid. The tennis courts across the Commons were busy, an impromptu softball game in progress on the broad lawn, students sunbathing, dogs chasing squirrels, a guy flying a kite. Someone having newly arrived on campus would have witnessed an idyllic college scene.

Jake took the Commons path to check out ROTC. Several campus police leaned against a university cruiser. The building was a rectangular, wooden structure, painted white, indeed, like a nondescript barracks that had seen more than its day. It and its three mates were definitely out of place here in a community proud of its forward thinking, with the new tower library now looming in the distance over Blanket Hill. Admin would have been smart to have already taken these misplaced structures down, especially since the art students had already tried to incinerate one of them. It would have been an ounce of proverbial prevention, but foresight was not one of Admin's strengths. Response was their forte, or so they thought. But until last night they were contending with a small, manageable foe; last night, Jake now knew, things had changed. Aaron, a heretofore committed moderate, had told him that.

75

Same day ...

With the radio on, Jake strummed his guitar to the simple tune of "Let It Be," linking the lyrics to one of Stan's favorite phrases regarding the mantra: "Take it as it comes." He liked his meditations, vowed to read one of the Maharishi's books. It was two in the afternoon. Where was Tasha? Why hadn't she called? Probably having lunch with her mom at Hahn's, be back soon. Things for her were approaching the breaking point. Maybe Peggy McCleary had pushed her toward telling the truth. It's what should have been done the first time he and Tasha slept together. The period of sharing her was a bad memory.

At two-thirty, Jake found the appointment card Tasha had left on the kitchen table. He dialed the psychologist's office. Expecting a receptionist to answer, Jake was surprised to hear, "Peggy McCleary. How can I help you?"

"Oh, Dr. McCleary. Is Natasha there? This is Jake."

"Hello, Jake. Natasha left with her parents two hours ago."

"Her *parents,* plural?"

"Plural, yes."

"I thought it was her mom, alone."

"No, both."

"Was everything okay?"

"Jake, as well as I think I know you from my talks with Natasha, I can't discuss a client. All I can say is that they left before noon. Gotta run. Have a nice day, Jake."

His head spinning, he hung up.

What now? Her dad in this picture? No phone call? No note?

He raced down the stairs and out into the warm sunshine. At Janine's place he ran around back. Tasha's Cougar was gone. He knocked on Janine's door.

"She came here with her father," Janine said, wearing a sari. "Got her things and he drove her car as she followed him with her mom."

Jake ran back to his place, checked if her things, spare as they were, still hung in the closet. They did. She hadn't been back here, which most likely meant he, himself, hadn't come up in the discussion. She must know he'd be worried, so no call meant she was deep into something and couldn't escape, most certainly back at her parents' home by now. Christ!

Could she possibly be leaving him again? No. Inconceivable. The family were having it out. But in that sentence, what was *it*? More of her attempt to leave him out of their picture? To make them believe she was simply tired of Ray and wanted her own life, later to take up with Jake in a way they might deem respectable? That line of crap would only leave her parents to persuade her to go back to Ray, to try to make a troubled marriage work; with all the time, hopes, and dreams she'd spent on that relationship, not losing the investment. Every marriage has its problems, demands compromise, and Ray such a good, patriotic, dedicated fellow, etcetera, etcetera. Son of a God damned bitch!

Jake grabbed his keys, charged outside, started up the camper and made a left onto Main, saw the cops downtown, the cruisers, the boarded windows and cleanup crews, a group of students helping. He crossed the railroad tracks and sped over the bridge on State Route 59. Of what he intended he wasn't sure, but he knew well where he was headed. He'd lost his patience with this God awful charade. He'd lost patience with this whole fucking town.

In the village of Cuyahoga Falls he felt himself calming down. At a stoplight he realized he was lucky not to have been stopped for reckless driving. A mile or two later, he pulled into a drive-in mobbed by little-league players. He stopped under some oak trees. What was he doing? What did he think he'd accomplish? Would he storm the Van Sollis split-level residence on peaceful Heritage Way? Would he arm wrestle the senior Van Sollis for his daughter's hand?

Come on, now, get a grip. You're acting on zero knowledge.

Well, not zero.

We know her mother broke Tasha's plan by spilling it to her husband who'd upset his tee time to drive to Kent and corral his baby girl. We know all three had returned to their home town. We know Tasha didn't have the wherewithal to make a phone call. Hell, maybe she was calling him at this precise moment while he watched preadolescent kids buying milkshakes.

He got out of the van and paced. Life was moving with its petty pace in this little town, no notion of the turbulence in Kent or of the turbulence in this pacing fellow's heart. Calm down. They'd all been with McCleary, talked about something, McCleary being, according to Tasha, a proponent of speaking the truth. But also a proponent of Tasha's independence for a while, of her freeing herself from reliance upon males. That all worked in his favor, didn't it? But when?

On his mad dash on a rural Ohio roadway, Jake had been thinking only of himself.

What about Tasha? Of course, she must be working hard to solve all this in the best way possible, the best way within her means. Could she really go back to Ray? No way in hell. Out of the question. So calm down, man. Give her some credit. What will you do in Akron but really screw things up? She loves you, you jerk! Wants to be with you. This isn't some romantic comedy where you two will end up riding away in the back of a bus. You both have your jobs to do in this situation. Hers is to deal with her folks, yours is to trust her, believe in her, and ... the hell of it all ... to wait!

She knows you're waiting. She trusts you to wait. She certainly doesn't want you to burst into her suburban home and grapple with her dad. So relax. Think. Go back to Kent and know she's struggling to get free. Put on your armband and see what can be done to keep these much more significant forces from causing a bloodbath.

But on the way back, driving in a more reasonable fashion, he remembered the horror of her former letter, words he'd never expected. That trauma had gone deep, made him trust her now only with a great effort of will, and ... with a depressing surrender to the inevitable, whatever that might be. The truth was that he'd put his happiness, his future, in someone else's hands and now could only hope she'd handle it with care.

76

Same day ...

Back in Kent, police presence was strong, cruisers cruising, patrolmen patrolling the downtown, and an atmosphere not of what's done is done but of what will happen next. Waiting for a phone call, Jake hung out in his apartment, occasional cop cars passing by in both directions. Would she break free? Or would she submit to Daddy's will? Jake could only imagine the pain she must be feeling at her mother's betrayal. She'd walked into a trap.

No phone call came, which told him she was embroiled. She knew he was waiting, needed to hear, so the only reason no call came was that she'd been denied the right, almost by force, or that the news was horrific—that there would never be a call, and all was lost. Probably another letter. Escaping to LSU looked more attractive by the minute.

Toward evening, hunger pangs, he tried to meditate but thoughts kept flooding his mind. He barely started the mantra than worries shoved it out. So he stopped, made a sandwich, downed a glass of milk to fortify himself against what could be a difficult night.

Would they really try to burn down a building? Surely the place would be well-guarded, so if they tried something as crazy as that, there'd be a serious conflict. The marshals had only their voices, weren't about to enter a fray. So there'd be a ring of cops with tear gas at the ready, and some brave and stupid kids would end up choking and telling stories back in the dorms. Surely the bars would be closed, and perhaps a curfew in place. Details on WKSU were sparse, rock music having replaced the oft recounted details of the night before.

And as six approached still no call.

Jake donned jeans, a sweatshirt and sneakers, tugged his armband on, and headed up College to Lincoln then climbed the hill between Engleman and McGilvrey to the Union, already packed with students. From there he strode on Portage to the small lot behind ROTC. What he saw astounded him. There, standing alone, Graham Fisk leaned against the hood of a car. No police in evidence. A lone professor with a blue armband.

Okay, Jake thought. It's still early, an hour before sundown. Certainly some security is about to make an appearance.

Professor Fisk smiled grimly as Jake approached.

"Where are the police?" Jake asked.

Fisk shrugged.

Across the field a scraggily kid with long blond hair began ringing the Victory Bell. A few activist types joined him while others gathered on the Taylor Hall walkway above. The twilight was serene, warm, robins probing for their final meals of the day, two boys throwing a football.

"Seems like Security figures the threat is over," Jake said.

"Communications are a joke," Fisk answered. "Admin threw us a bone giving us a crisis center. They're not around, don't like dealing with faculty, see me as a pain in their backside. Law enforcement seems confused about turf, not wanting to come onto campus unless ordered by Admin, so they're protecting downtown, enforcing the eight o'clock curfew. And here sits ROTC waiting to spontaneously combust."

"Maybe the cops are guarding the president's house," Jake offered.

By now a small crowd had gathered at the bell, someone making a speech. Jake couldn't hear the words, but some power fists were being raised in response. The sun was slowly sinking behind the new library tower. Then, suddenly, the bell group took off up Blanket Hill, between Prentice and Taylor and out of sight.

Fisk sighed. "Okay, then. Maybe that's that. Maybe campus police know what they're doing."

"But those kids might be headed over to Tri-Towers," Jake said. "To amass reinforcements."

"Let's hope you're wrong about that."

Several other marshals, Jonah among them, showed up as the sinking sun shone red in the sky. Fisk directed Jake and two others to go toward the Towers to reconnoiter, while he would remain at his post.

"Wish they'd given us walkie-talkies," he said. "Wonder where the other marshals are."

"Seems pretty quiet here," someone commented.

"Yeah, *too* quiet, kemo sabe," someone answered, causing some chuckles. But it was true.

Jake and his two cohorts jogged across the Commons and climbed the steep hill. He recalled his surreptitious evening with Tasha there. If she'd been trying to call him, she must be aware that he's out on this madness of a job.

As they approached Tri-Towers, he realized that the activist group was trying to increase their numbers by marching through the dorms, calling for others to join them. And students were doing that. The group had grown to a throng as it flowed into the Manchester-Allyn complex. This did not bode well.

"Someone should head back and warn Fisk," Jake said.

One young marshal took off. Someone approached the remaining pair from behind.

"You two better back the fuck away. You're no better than the pigs, and don't think those armbands will protect you."

After coming around Manchester, the march numbered at least a thousand, chanting "Fuck the Pigs!" and "Down with Rot-cee." Someone carried a Viet Cong flag. In flaming red and orange, the sun had nearly set.

"I'm sure the cops are there by now," Jake said. "These kids are not crazy enough to burn down a building."

"I'm not so sure about that," his partner answered.

The horde surged across the practice football field and up the hill behind Taylor. Jake and his mate flanked them on the right and ended up back between Taylor and Prentice, the Commons below them, no cops, only Fisk and a few marshals at their former spot. When they saw the swarm of students rushing toward them, they quickly fled back toward the Union. The ROTC building stood a prize for the taking.

Jake was not about to enter this battle. Incredibly, defying all reason, nothing stood in the way to stop what was about to happen. He and his partner stood on the Taylor walkway with many students converging on the scene from all directions, the Union apparently emptying out as well. Some sparks flew; what looked like a Molotov cocktail was thrown. Jake could barely make out what looked like a garbage can being used ineffectively as a battering ram. Windows were broken, something burning thrown inside. A brief interior blaze soon went out. Screaming and yelling erupted, cheers from spectators on the hillside, obscenities, laughter.

Jake heard sirens, far away but growing closer. He'd never seen anything like this. It was a mob set on destruction. It made him sick. What would be accomplished by this madness? Now the building was actually burning inside, casting a wavering glow from the smashed windows. he sirens came closer, then a fire truck arrived on Portage, eased through the masses, hoses unfurled, students impeding progress, a general ruckus, some water flowing from a hose and then suddenly stopping. The kids were not about to allow a few firemen to douse the flames. A dark column of smoke rose into the dim sky, cheers going up, shouting, merriment, a chant of "Burn it down!"

Jake could hardly see now. Nothing but darkness punctuated by a serious fire, swirling conflagration and smoke. The fire hoses had apparently been cut, the workers held back. No saving the place now. It was a scene of savages dancing in jungle firelight.

This operation had to have been planned, Jake thought. They'd brought equipment to set the fire, though the efforts at first had fallen flat. And they were ready to fight the firemen. And still not a single cop.

The blaze set the sky aglow. It must have been seen for miles. Even up on the hill, Jake heard its roar, felt its heat.

"Nothing we can do now," Jake's partner said. "I'm outta here. Won't be long till the fuzz shows up with tear gas. Come on, let's split this scene."

"Where were they hours ago?" Jake said.

"Who knows? It's fucked up. But this is dangerous."

The guy went back down the hill toward the parking lot, disappeared in the darkness.

Jake took his armband off to look like one of the crowd. He watched as the wooden walls of the building crumbled, sending up a shower of sparks and more cheers of victory. Suddenly a series of gunshots rang out, scattering the crowd in panic until they realized it was stored ammo bursting from the fire. The panic calmed, laughter and cheers replaced the fear.

Jake's partner was right, time to leave. But what Jake witnessed infuriated him. Yes, the building was little more than a shack, but letting it go was wrong, wrong, wrong. Hadn't Professor Fisk mentioned that the campus police had a plan to stop it? What the hell happened to that plan? And if the cops didn't get there soon, and in force, the whole campus would burn.

As he retreated he heard shouts amid the melee: "The president's house. The president's house."

77

Same night ...

Jake hoped that when he got home Tasha would be there. Or that in his absence, she'd have called Phil downstairs and left a message. Instead he found Billy on the front steps, head down, soot and blood on his face, photo vest torn at the shoulder, cigarette in his hand.

"What happened to you?" Jake asked.

He looked up with war-torn eyes. "They took my cameras, ripped out the film."

"Who did?"

"Goons. I never saw them before. They were beating up media people."

"You look like you just got back from Iwo Jima."

"All this was planned out," Billy said in despair. "Coordinated."

"Come upstairs. I have some beer. You could use one."

"Naw, gotta go back there. Came here for my Instamatic, take a breather. This is a helluva story, never seen anything like it."

"Where are the cops? That's what I want to know. Those mobsters were yelling about burning down the president's house."

"That's where the cops are," Billy said. "With such limited personnel, they had to choose the targets, figured the president's house is more important than ROTC."

"Then the whole campus could go."

"Word is the mayor called the governor for the Guard. They're on their way from Akron."

"They better get here soon."

Billy flicked his cigarette butt away and stood up. He went inside and soon came back without his vest, holding a small camera, then headed up the back way toward campus.

Jake went upstairs to his place and sat in the dark. He wanted the phone to ring. The story of Kent State's fire must be on the news by now. Maybe Tasha's family are watching. If so, she'd call even if she had to scratch her way to the phone. Maybe he should drive there, this time not turning around. What was there to lose? Maybe everything. He had to trust her, had to. She'd call and come when she could. Maybe she'd been calling all night.

Ten minutes later as he was musing angrily, the phone rang. He leapt up and grabbed the receiver.

"Tasha!"

"Uh, no, Jake. It's Audrey."

"Audrey? Are you okay?"

"It's chaos in the dorm. Kids are trashing everything. Jake, can I come to your place?"

"Here? Sure, Audrey."

"I'm scared, Jake."

"Where's Aaron?"

"That fool is out there somewhere. They burned down ROTC."

"Yes, I saw the whole thing."

"Can I bring my roommate?"

"Sure."

"Okay, we'll bring blankets, and food. Thanks, Jake."

Leaving his door open to hear the phone, he went downstairs and sat on the stoop, which faced away from campus. Kids passed under the streetlight, trickling down from the hill. Students in other houses were out on their porches, a little after ten o'clock, excited voices in the darkness, music playing.

Jake heard a distant roaring sound. It grew louder, coming from the south, louder still. Then he heard the motors of what must have been many trucks, coming north on Lincoln, a block away. Suddenly, a jeep whizzed by on Willow toward Main. Then another, this one loaded, two helmeted soldiers holding rifles and sitting up on the back. It was like an invasion, no sound but of the motors. Jake stood.

Good! About time.

From the sidewalk he could see up to the intersection of Willow and Main. A barrier was being constructed, probably to prevent the rioters from heading downtown. The main Guard force must have been turning onto campus at the library parking lot, also swinging onto Summit from Lincoln and going in Portage Drive.

Then he saw a small group of kids sprinting down College toward Willow. In the corner streetlight he recognized Audrey, carrying a bundle as were the five or six with her. Out of breath, they arrived at his porch.

"I brought some friends," she said. "Hope it's okay."

Shocked, he took a breath and smiled. Six girls. "Sure, Audrey. We'll start a commune. A couple of you can camp out in my van."

"There's a whole army convoy on Lincoln," she said. "We could hardly get through."

Indeed, he saw others filtering out from campus in the darkness, an exodus, arriving at nearby houses or just running away.

It was a night of no sleep, the sounds of nearby gunfire, the glow of flames, the rumble of vehicles, the shouts of commands, and wisps of tear gas drifting by in the spring darkness. Adding to the chaos came the throbbing of helicopters, beams flashing down and loudspeaker announcements to get inside and stay there. A night of stories, of arguments, of philosophy, of laughter, tears, speculation about futures, worries about boyfriends, peanut butter sandwiches, popcorn, Cokes and beers, the radio going with frantic live commentary. The Guard had set up a line around the shambles of ROTC, which continued to burst into flames, die out and flare up again. The mob had been pushed back up Blanket Hill and ordered to go back to their dorms, then saturated with tear gas which eventually dispersed them.

A secondary fire had been set, a storage shed for archery gear destroyed and a tree ablaze, all described by the radio commentators over a background of cursing and yelling. By two a.m., things had settled down and the broadcasters hosted excited interviews and recapped events. A second fire truck had arrived and put out the flames. The president's house had, in fact, been approached by rioters who'd been successfully thwarted by town police. The small, impotent cadre of campus cops had shown up at the ROTC scene two hours late, in the safety of the Guard. They were jeered for their incompetence. Campus officials were entirely missing but for a few faculty marshals. President White was out of town. Graham Fisk had greeted the Guard commanders as if he represented the university.

It all dumbfounded Jake. There seemed to be no other conclusion than that Admin had sanctioned this disruption, had stood back and let it happen. What else could one think? But why?

Jake recalled his several visits from Wettman, the idea that SDS leaders were working for Nixon, even their jail time simply verifying, falsely, their dedication to the revolutionary cause. And what was Wettman's contention? – that the National Administration wanted things to blow up at Kent to show Middle America, the silent majority, that anarchy could happen anywhere. Nixon knew that the great majority of citizens didn't like the protestors and would support their being roughly handled to maintain order. The Democratic Convention riots in Chicago had proven that. A violent incident in the heart of the nation involving a strong law and order response, exactly President White's approach, would create more national backlash against the dissidents. Not only that, a tough response would show the radicals the physical risk they were taking and make them think twice about their personal

safety. Nixon's strategy: create fear of stark reprisal on the part of the protestors and gain added support for the Republicans and, thus, for the war.

Amid these lines of reasoning, Jake's mind whirled. It was like trying to
grasp the concept of infinity. On the other hand, and much more likely,
maybe the whole thing was simply a matter of sheer ineptitude all around.

In the meantime, he was hunkered down with six scared girls and waiting
for his phone to ring.

78

Sunday, May 3, ongoing …

Jake was asleep on his sofa, three girls in his bed, one on the bedroom
floor, and two in the camper, when his phone awakened him. Shafts of sunshine filtered through the blinds, almost seven a.m. Jake threw off the sheet
and rushed to the phone.

"Tasha?"

"Jake, are you okay?"

"Yes. Are you?"

"Can you come over here and rescue me?"

"I'm on my way."

"Not my house. I broke out. Daddy hid my car keys. I'm at the Arby's,
Market and Sieberling. Take the interstate, Market Street exit, then two
blocks."

"You bet."

He pulled on jeans and sweatshirt, roused the girls from his van, and
headed down Summit, which, one block east at Lincoln, was barricaded by
two army trucks. He took a left onto 43-South and after waiting restlessly at
several interminable traffic lights, pulled onto I-76, then ten more minutes
off onto Market Street in Akron. Finally he saw Tasha in jeans and sweater,
standing like a streetwalker looking to be picked up. She waved. He pulled
over. She climbed aboard and scrambled furiously into his arms.

"Oh, Jake, I love you, love you. I was too worried to go on with my parents a moment longer. You are my life, only you, only you."

She wept against his shoulder. He held her, never wanting to let her go
again.

"It's okay, okay."

"I couldn't call. They wouldn't let me out of their sight. We'd better get
going. Daddy will certainly be out looking for me."

She slouched down in her seat, her face pale, eyes bloodshot.

"I'm not his daughter, I'm his slave. He'll never let go, never listen to reason, even when Peggy told him it was time to let me go, to let me make my
own decisions."

"That's a decade overdue."

"I can't wait to get as far away from here as possible. Maybe the moon. Could you get a fellowship there?"

"Yeah, we can get a cottage with an incredible view."

"Oh, Jake. Were you worried?"

"Was I worried? Nah, it was like a little vacation."

She punched his arm.

"I was trying so hard to get Daddy to accept the divorce. He wouldn't budge. As if Ray was more important to him than his own flesh and blood. Well, he used to say he always wanted a son. So be it. Now he has one. And poor Mama, she's his puppet—not a speck of free will. I couldn't believe she actually brought him along to Peggy's. So I'm disowned now, an orphan, nothing but the clothes on my back, not even underwear. You'll have to adopt me, Jake."

"Hmm, I think they'd call that incest."

"Then marry me."

"That would be my fondest wish come true."

He merged onto the freeway, headed east amid farms and fields aglow in the morning sun, "but first I have to tell you something."

"Don't you dare tell me you found a new girlfriend."

"Six, actually."

By the time Jake pulled into Kent, he'd recounted last night's experience. A checkpoint had been set up at Willow and Summit, a line of cars backed up, some having to turn around, others being let through. When Jake and Tasha got to the barrier, a young, weary looking Guardsman in full combat gear asked for his ID. Jake showed him his Ohio driver's license, with his Willow Street address.

"You a student?"

"Grad student. Teach English."

He asked for Tasha's ID, which she pulled from her purse.

"Any relation to Corporal Sweeny?" the soldier asked.

"Wife," she answered leaning across Jake. "Separated."

The fellow looked confused.

"I'm in the French Department," she said.

"Going to this guy's address?"

"Uh, yes. I have an apartment in the same building. Didn't change my license yet."

The sentry stepped back and waved Jake onto Willow.

The girls were still sleeping, the two dislodged from the van now on the living room floor.

"We'll have to take up residence in the camper," Jake said to Tasha.

"Anything to eat?" She found cereal and milk, which they devoured at the kitchen table.

"Mrs. Whitcomb would freak out at this scene," Tasha said. "She's so protective of her property."

"My lease is up in a month anyway."

Later, the traffic checks eased up and people were being allowed on campus. Jake and Tasha strolled up to the Commons, now a surreal combination of a spring picnic day and smoldering remains of ROTC, ribbons of smoke still lifting from the ruins, only the frame of the entrance still standing. Guard headquarters had been set up next to the rubble, and checkpoints had been established throughout the campus, the atmosphere relaxed, almost festive.

The place had become a tourist attraction, families out and about with their cameras, kids racing around, and students fraternizing with the soldiers, who were not much older. Girls flirted with them as sunshine glinted from M1 barrels.

"Maybe everyone is satisfied now," Jake speculated. "The students have finally had a major victory and Admin has gotten rid of an eyesore and can move ahead with building plans. And the Guard has bravely restored order, in line with White's enforcement policy. Maybe this is the end of it."

"Do you really believe that, Jake?" Tasha clung to his arm as they looked at the scene from the Taylor walkway.

"Why not? It's just as crazy as these soldiers standing around with daisies in their gun barrels. No feeling of tension at the moment. Maybe the whole episode has served as a release valve."

"But I don't see any sign of the military going away."

"Ray must be somewhere around here," Jake said. "Aren't you scared he'll spot you?"

"He can hardly break ranks and take me captive. And I'm done with him and with my dad."

Jake pulled her close.

"Then all the madness has been worth something."

Admin had declared that the university would remain open as usual. Satterfield was unlocked, a few teachers there preparing for Monday's classes. Jake and Tasha used the mimeograph machine for quizzes and class agendas. Jake gathered student essays to take home and grade, figuring the girls would soon be back in their dorm.

"Isn't there supposed to be a rally tomorrow," Tasha asked, "to restore the Constitution that was entombed on Friday, or some such nonsense?"

"I doubt any more rallies will be allowed," Jake said. "As soon as a group starts to congregate, gas canisters will fly again."

On their way out of Satterfield, they saw a covey of helicopters parked in the meadow behind the University School, students gathered around talking to crewmen, being shown inside, taking pictures. A copter took off, flew low and loudly over toward the Commons in the splendid spring sky.

"Now, Tasha," Jake said, feeling oddly relaxed, "what are we going to do about us?"

"I vote for new scenery. This place is a mess, going downhill fast. I don't want to be running into Ray and his gang around town. And who knows what Daddy's going to do. He's probably driving around the streets searching for me now."

"Are you really ready to make a huge move?"

"Yes," she said, leaning against him. "Wherever we go, we'll have to play it by ear, take our reactions as they come."

"You sound like Stan: 'take it as it comes.'"

"Ancient Vedic wisdom."

"So tomorrow I turn down the Sinclair, then we finish out the term, tie up loose ends, gas up the van, go to Lancaster so you can meet my folks, head across country, summertime hippies, and end up in Red Stick. Game plan?"

"Game plan. I checked that map you gave me. We'll get a quaint place, maybe a view of the river, near campus. I'll apply for an assistantship, and we'll have wild sex every night. You'll become a famous scholar. We'll have three beautiful children, two boys and a girl, and become old people sitting in a park with smiles on our faces from having led an idyllic life."

"Right on! Out of sight! Groovy! Count me in!"

"But a few of these last loose ends I'm worried about."

"Which ones, Tasha?"

"Getting Mr. Ray God-damn Sweeny to sign the divorce papers, and keeping Daddy from hauling me back to Akron in shackles."

"Before he can do that," Jake said, "he'll have to crawl over my dead body."

79

Same day, evening …

When Jake and Tasha got back at his apartment, the girls were cooking a big pot of spaghetti. They'd bought supplies at the Dazzle Market and looked as if they were moving in. Audrey told Jake his mother had called, worried about what she'd seen on the television news. Jake called her immediately and told her everything had calmed down and that the danger had passed. Amused at the apartment situation, Tasha helped with the meal and the cleanup. Jake got into the bunk of the van for some shuteye. As he was falling asleep, Tasha opened the camper door and said Jonah Levitt was on the phone. Jake roused himself and groggily went inside.

"The marshals are assembling," Levitt said. "Rumor is students are going to torch the Air Force ROTC tonight. We'd better get out there."

"Damn," Jake answered, "I thought all this had been settled. Isn't the Guard taking care of things?"

"Yes, and they're tired and pissed off. Lord knows what will happen after dark. They'd better be aware that our eyes are watching. So get your butt in gear."

Jake pulled on a sweatshirt and tugged on his frayed armband.

"I'll come with you," Tasha said.

"No. Stay here and be a mother hen for these wayward chicks."

"Everyone was behaving so nicely on campus today."

"According to Jonah, apparently not everyone."

"Be careful then. Remember our game plan."

They kissed long and passionately, then Jake headed out, taking Summit Road, then Portage down to the Commons near the crumbled, foul-smelling ROTC shambles. A group of marshals had assembled behind a line of weary soldiers. A kid was ringing the Victory Bell, students beginning to gather on Blanket Hill. Someone must have been spreading the news of a rally because kids were filtering in slowly from all directions. It seemed to Jake that in terms of numbers the odds did not favor the Guard. Levitt and Fisk were conversing with the commander of the troops, one General Canterbury. Then the two profs led a contingent of faculty marshals across the field to the students at the bell.

Though the peacemakers were greeted with a chant of "Pigs go home," they continued on and conferred briefly with a few kids who seemed to be leaders. The marshals appeared intent on nipping any trouble in the bud, but returned shaking their heads in frustration. They again conferred with the general.

The group of student leaders climbed the hill away from the confrontation, others following. They disappeared down the other side behind Taylor. Soldiers slapped hands and congratulated each other as if a crisis had passed in their favor.

The sun had fully set, only streetlights and search beams from helicopters lighting the area. Several choppers hovered above the students, indicating they were headed toward Tri-Towers. Constant chatter came through on the radios held by Guard commanders, and eventually half the contingent was ordered about face. They moved out toward front campus. Most of the marshals, ten or so including Jake, trailed along.

Watching the searchlights in the sky, Levitt said, "Looks like students are headed for the president's house. Guess they realized getting to the other barracks was useless."

"I thought peace had set in today," Jake said.

"Wishful thinking," Levitt answered, intent on his task. "Our esteemed Governor Rhoades didn't help pacify things in his downtown press conference this morning. He called the students 'brown-shirts,' 'dregs of society' to be defeated by 'any means necessary.'"

"He said that?"

"He's pandering to popular opinion in all this, trying to stir up votes for his election to the Senate. But not making our job any easier."

"He should be trying to ease emotions, not inflame them."

"Hey, man, he's a politician. An *Ohio* politician at that. Sniffing the air for support, backed up by our local officials. Doesn't bode well for these kids."

The throbbing of the copters, the moving beams of light, the footsteps of the troops, orders being barked – all set a surreal scene.

"White's house is well-guarded by city cops," Levitt said as they moved to the top of front campus's hill. "My guess is the kids will either divert back to the Commons or in this direction, maybe try to head downtown."

"One thing is sure," someone else said, "they're intent on a confrontation."

A contingent of students had flanked the Guard on their march, and as the troops moved down the hillside, they were greeted with thrown bottles and stones. With almost no light, the kids hid behind trees, close to the soldiers, so that on their way Guardsmen actually had physical confrontations, using bayonets and billy clubs. Students had gathered at the library. Things were getting nasty—fisticuffs, obscenities from both sides, cries of pain. A fire next to Rockwell flared and was quickly put out.

Jake wondered what role the marshals could play in all this. To deaf ears, Levitt was shouting for the kids to back off. Eventually the troops reached Main Street in front of the library and joined another formation that blocked the street at the intersection with University Drive. That barrier seemed insurmountable. Guardsmen, local police with cruisers flashing, state troopers, and military halftracks and armored vehicles waited in ready reserve one block west at Main and Lincoln. The kids might destroy the campus but they wouldn't touch downtown.

The main force of students now came marching and chanting down the campus side of Main. They stopped when they saw what they were up against.

"Sit down!" someone yelled. "Take the street!"

Fifty or so rushed into the thoroughfare and sat down. Local travelers in a Pontiac sedan were trapped between them and the barricade. Chants of "Pigs off campus" erupted.

Jake saw no chance of the marshals intervening except as pure observers. He stood on a slight rise on the campus side of Rockwell. Levitt and Fisk were on the sidewalk next to the front line of soldiers, and Jake feared that the two men might try to walk between the opposing sides. Rocks, bottles, cans of beer, and obscenities were being hurled toward them as part of the military blockade.

"How could all this happen?" Jake asked himself. "Where did all this hatred come from? This is not about the war, or civil rights. What did the students think they'd gain from it except the destruction of their school? It's all emotion and zero thought, and the more it escalated, the more kids who were there only as spectators were drawn into the upheaval.

Now it was a standoff, having backed off half a block, the troop line now at their principal location of Main and Lincoln, local police on one flank and state police on the other. Now it was all chanting, kids sitting in the street and lining the campus sidewalk. After a while, a student leader moved bravely across no man's land and conferred with the police captain. The kid seemed to be presenting demands. The captain left and conferred with the Guard commanders, came back and issued the student into a cruiser. From the loudspeaker inside the car, the student announced, incredibly, that President White and Mayor Satrom would come and talk with the students.

"They're not going to arrest us! We've won!"

A rousing cheer went up.

Won what?

Chants intensified. Students milled on the sidewalk and around the library, several thousand according to Jake's estimation. Finally the student leader was summoned back across to the cruiser. Soon he made another announcement.

"They lied to us. White and Satrom won't come."

"Liars! Liars!" the chant arose.

From police bullhorns, the announcement was made that the gathering was illegal and had to disperse immediately.

"You are in violation of curfew."

This riot-act announcement came several times, greeted by boos and filthy words. It wasn't long until the troops lowered their bayonets and moved toward the students, who rose in panic and scattered but were blocked by their own masses. Jake saw a student take a bayonet in the back, falling, rising and fleeing."

Mayhem now, choppers throbbing, lights flashing, screams, commands, then the blasts of tear gas canisters fired into the crowd, now yelling and clambering up the hillside. It was the most hellish scene Jake had ever witnessed. The last of the kids hurled rocks, but the mob was defeated utterly, nowhere to flee but back to their dorms.

Jake leaned behind a thick elm close to the library, luckily for him the breeze wafting the gas in the other direction. Yelling curses, the panicked crowd flowed past him. The minimal role of the marshals had ended; time to vacate the vicinity. As soon as it was possible, Jake jogged behind the library to the parking lot, south on Lincoln to College, and back down to Willow. He caught a whiff of errant gas, gagged, coughed, tried to breathe. His eyes watered profusely. He struggled to get air into his lungs. He knelt, stretched out on his stomach on a lawn, gasped for fresh air. Back on his knees, he threw up.

Several jeeps and a truck loaded with troops roared past toward Summit, headed, Jake assumed, back to protect the Air Force shack. A helicopter hovered overhead, the beam directly into Jake's face.

"Get inside, now!" a voice descended from a depraved heaven. "Clear the street!"

Jake staggered toward his front porch, up the steps and into the vestibule where he collapsed on the floor.

80

Monday, May 4, next day ...

Fatigued from stress and lack of sleep, Jake climbed the hill toward campus, Tasha at his side. After showing their ID cards, they passed through a Guard checkpoint at Lincoln and Summit. At the barrier blocking the campus entrance on Portage, one of the Guardsmen did a double take when he saw Tasha.

"Natasha. What are you doing here?"

"Oh, hi, Russ. I teach here now."

"Since when?"

"Since last fall. Here's my campus ID."

He took it, looked it over, handed it back.

"I thought you worked at the high school with Ray."

"No, not anymore."

"Didn't know that. Think these morons will act up again today?"

"I doubt it, Russ. Probably all worn out from last night."

"Yeah, I'm glad I was stationed over here. Ray's team was in the thick of it, though."

"Okay, have a nice day, Russ."

"I sure hope so. Tired of this shit. Wanna go home, sleep in a real bed, eat real food. We been over in Akron two weeks, now this shit."

Tasha and Jake walked on. Sprayed on the walkway in front of Satterfield: "Fuck the pigs."

"I can't believe campus is open for business as usual today," Tasha said.

"I guess Admin and the Guard feel they made their point last night. Cancelling classes would be like surrender for them, not victory."

"Some of the girls' parents told them to stay put at your place. You're going to have a big phone bill, Jake. Those gals seem unfamiliar with the concept of calling collect."

Inside Satterfield, Jake said, "I'll go straight to the Chairman's office and tell him I'm not taking the Sinclair. Let's get together for lunch."

With a parting kiss, they separated at the staircase, Tasha headed up to the third floor, Jake to the Department office, Violet at her desk beside a vase of tulips.

"Dr. Madison isn't in yet," she said pleasantly. "Meeting with a faculty group over at Admin. Strategy powwow, no doubt. Leave a message, Jake?"

"Uh, no. I'll catch him later."

"About the Sinclair Fellowship?"

"But I'd like to talk to him myself."

"I hope congratulations are in store. We need more like you around here. Terrible weekend, wasn't it?"

"Hopefully everything's settled now."

Jake moved on to the lounge for his coffee. At his desk he prepared for his nine o'clock class. He wondered how many would actually show up. When he went into his classroom, he saw a message scrawled on the blackboard: *Rally at noon, the Commons, don't miss it.* He immediately used an eraser.

Several students filtered in, ten in all, each one looking harried and worn.

"Can we talk about what's going on?" one of them asked. "I was home in Ashtabula all weekend."

"Sure," Jake said. "Seems a little more important than how to write an intro and conclusion, doesn't it? What do you guys think about all this?"

"Do you know what time the curfew is?" someone else asked. "It kept changing last night."

"No, I don't know that."

"Who's in charge of the campus? The Guard?"

"Seems that way."

"So, is today's rally illegal, the way they say?"

"Apparently. Look, I'm as confused as you guys."

"When are the soldiers going away?"

"I guess as soon as they figure no one's going to start any more fires."

"That was beautiful Saturday night," a young man named Rick spoke up, a hard core revolutionary who was serious about his academics as well. "We showed the motherfuckers. And I'm going to the rally. The more illegal they make it, the more students will show up. Don't they know that?"

"I'll tell you, Rick. I saw a kid get bayonetted last night, in the middle of the street. And cops getting hit with rocks. It wasn't at all beautiful. I caught some tear gas too, not at all pleasant. You know what I think?"

"No, what?" Rick asked, still smiling.

"You're messing with disaster if you confront these troops. You may see them as invaders but, like it or not, they're here. By defying them, you're liable to get hurt. My advice is to stay as far away from the noon rally as you can. You know, those guys are worn out. They're scared and tired, not much older than you. They don't want this, and they're not responsible. What do you expect if people start burning down buildings?"

"We wouldn't have to burn them down if they start listening to us. The military doesn't belong on campus. Other schools have kicked them out. We should too."

"Okay, but we're not in the negotiating stage at this point, Rick. Look, if you go out there today, and tempers flare, and you get hurt, it will be your own fault. They have weapons and..."

"But their guns are not actually loaded, are they?" a girl named Ginger spoke up.

"Only with blanks," someone else said.

"I heard them say, 'Lock and load,'" Jake answered. "I'm sure they're using real bullets."

"Then they'll just fire in the air," Rick said.

"Not if they're in fear for their lives," Jake answered. "Or totally pissed off at the abuse they're taking. Come on, think. There are thousands of you, only a few hundred of them spread out all over campus. And they are in charge, with the support of Admin and apparently the State of Ohio. Do as they say, please. Don't get hurt. And if you do get hurt, don't blame anyone but yourself. Sure, it may all appear amusing, and getting national attention, but use your heads and stay away from the Commons today if you have any sense at all."

"Where did this stuff come from?" Ginger asked despairingly. "What's it all about?"

"Maybe Rick can explain it," Jake said.

"It comes from years of the administration not listening to the students. *We're* what this campus is all about. All they want to do is control us, push us where they want us to go, like it's all for them. They don't understand *us*, that things are changing, and we don't want their shit way of life."

"But," Ginger said meekly, "what's so bad about life, like the way our parents live? It seems okay to me."

393

"Same shit, boring life?" Rick countered. "Working day in and day out for a country that wages war against peasants and discriminates against blacks and arrests us for smoking a little dope? And uses our parents' money for atomic bombs? That bullshit has got to stop."

"I guess so," Ginger held on, "but this is just college."

"College, yeah," Rick said. "The whole military industrial complex is based on what they do to us here. They're training us to perpetuate capitalistic exploitation. Sure, it looks like democracy because we can vote when we're twenty-one, but actually we're getting brainwashed. So we have to stand up and fight it."

"Okay," Jake intervened. "Many people agree with Rick about the need to change society. The issue is *how* we change it. If we want to win, we must fight battles in a manner to become victorious. Like King. King knew he couldn't defeat the whole system of white oppression by confronting it with its own tactics. No, they had to use peaceful means and expose the oppression to the whole nation, gain allies, get the good whites on their side. He knew black violence would only alienate possible supporters. The approach of the Panthers, of Malcolm X, was doomed to failure. So who do you think you're kidding, Rick, by confronting the Guard on this little campus in the middle of nowhere?"

"We're getting attention," Rick came right back. "Raising awareness. Teaching in the national classroom of CBS and ABC. Every movement needs martyrs. Ask Che, ask Chairman Mao. Fidel started with twelve peasants in the jungle. Jesus started with twelve impoverished disciples. Fighting inside the system only perpetuates the system. It's exactly what the pigs want us to do. It keeps them safe at their pig troughs."

"Fight the battles you can win," Jake said. "Avoid the ones you can't. And I repeat, stay away from today's rally. And if you decide to go, even just for entertainment, or curiosity, understand that you are taking responsibility for what happens to you. I guess, if you want to be a martyr for whatever cause is out there, it's your choice. Make sure you understand that. Right or wrong, people won't blame the Guard, they'll blame you."

"So, you're not going, Mr. Ernst?" a new voice was heard, Cindy, combing her long red hair.

"Cindy, I'm a marshal. We go to keep an eye on things, to be neutral reporters. So I guess I'll be there, but not because I want to be. It's a responsibility I've committed myself to, so I suppose I'll go. But I sincerely hope only a few students, like Rick here, will show up. I hope the rest will be smart enough to stay away. I don't want to see anyone hurt on either side. And Rick, if you really decide you belong out there, remember that those guns will be locked and loaded, and not with blanks and not to be shot at the clouds. And also be aware that those Guardsmen are as angry as you and probably itching to demonstrate the power they have. And chances are, you won't go down a martyr like Jesus or Che, but like a damn fool who will simply be blamed for his own stupidity."

"So you think I deserve to die if I go out there. Is that what you think, Mr. Ernst?"

"No. But I think you must be aware of the risk and take responsibility for it. And if you don't want that risk, stay the hell away. Listen, Rick, whatever statement you have to make has already been made. ROTC is a charred ruin, for everyone to see. You know Admin, President White, always responds with concessions after such provocations. Things have opened up for blacks on campus, maybe not completely, but much for the better. More voices are being heard. He'll respond to this too. He's slow, but he's fair-minded, wants to listen, but of course can't abide violence and disruption. Now's the time to back off, or God forbid, maybe..."

"Maybe what, Mr. Ernst?"

"Or maybe this university will be forced to close down, a tragedy for all of us. I came here to get my master's, and all of you have come for your degrees. What will happen to all that? And for what?"

"I hope this dump does close down," Rick said. "Permanently. That sounds great to me. What a splash it will make for the university no one has ever heard of, until fucking now."

81

Same day ...

After class Jake revisited the main office only to see Violet shake her head.

"He's still in meeting, Jake. Stop back after lunch."

He climbed the stairs to the French Department, tapped on Tasha's office door, went in. She turned from a pile of papers on her desk and smiled. She gave her hair a quick brush, and they went downstairs and out into the marvelous spring day.

"It's actually getting hot," she said.

"Yeah, winter to summer in four days."

As they strolled toward the Union, students changing classes after their ten o'clocks, the campus seemed completely normal until they heard the steady clanging of the Victory Bell. They passed the black, burnt-out ROTC building, soldiers guarding it, standing casually about. According to Russ, the sentry at the barricade, Ray would be there among them. But beyond the firing line, a small group of hardcore students stood around the housing of the bell, conversing and glaring at the troops. Many students sat on the hillside, studying and sunbathing, and even a few families wandered here and there taking snapshots. The crowd grew larger from students passing between classes.

In the packed Union, Jake and Tasha saw Wash and Adele at a table in the faculty section, grabbed two unoccupied chairs and pulled them over. Adele appeared significantly pregnant in her maternity dress; Wash had some mayo caught in his chest-long beard.

After they exchanged pleasantries, the new arrivals went to order the soup and sandwich combo and eventually returned. The chatter in the place was all about the weekend, many of the kids having been home and now learning details.

"Figure the trouble is over, Jake?" Wash asked.

"Not if that crowd out there gets much bigger. Both sides are really pissed off. Last night, the hatred was real. Lots of confusion, kids got sliced, billy-clubbed, not to mention gassed. Guardsmen were hit with rocks and bottles. It was warfare, no fun about it. There are grudges now, and the radicals are hell-bent on making a splash in the national news."

"You were out there because of the armband group?" Adele asked.

"Yeah, and got gassed. That stuff is lethal. As an expectant mom, you should probably go home."

"It's all too amazing," she said.

"We should both go home too," Tasha said to Jake. "You've done enough."

"I can't leave now."

"Why not?" Wash asked. "You're leaving Kent, right?"

"Right. But you should see these faculty marshals. They're really dedicated, and brave."

"Sure, fighting for their jobs, gotta keep this place steamin' along."

"More than that," Jake said. "It's for the kids. Fisk, Levitt, others, trying to keep common sense alive, trying to defend..."

"Defend what?" Adele asked.

"Those guys are what the university is all about, defending the right to speak freely, to argue issues. And the duty of the university is to maintain order and safety."

"Sounds like the marshals are caught right in the middle," Wash said. "A dangerous place to be. Trying to keep this place functioning. Trying, hell, to keep the peace. Only faculty, right? Any administrators wearing those armbands?"

Jake paused. "Not that I know of. So what?"

"Says a lot, doesn't it?"

"We can't let law enforcement have a free hand. These kids are just that, kids. Don't know what they're doing, think they're Che Guevara. Stupid, yes, but not deserving tear gas and bayonets, or worse. Not deserving helicopters keeping them awake all night and tear gas drifting through their dorms."

"So," Tasha said, "I guess you're going out there again today."

"Yes. If I have to be with someone in all this, I choose Fisk and Levitt. They're the ones with the right perspective. I can get you an armband, Wash."

"Hell no. I'd make too massive a target."

Outside, Jake told Tasha he'd meet her back at the house.

"Go back there and tell the girls how to make their parents pay for the calls. More important, try to keep them off campus."

"No, Jake, I'm staying right here with you."

"I won't have that, Tasha. Please, go back to my place, or at least to your office. This could get bad, and you won't accomplish anything here."

"What will you accomplish, Jake?"

"I'm not sure. I'll be here, watching. Mainstream students respect us, Tasha. Maybe I can keep some of them from taking part, persuade them to go back to their dorms or their cars, get out of here."

They looked down the path toward the ROTC shambles. The crowd was growing, students standing behind the line of soldiers, others gathered around the ever-clanging bell, many seated on the hillside viewing the amphi-theater-like Commons, still others on the walkways between buildings and more on the Taylor Hall portico. Many were merely using the area to go to and from their classes and pausing to take in the astounding scene.

The ones at the bell began chanting, "Guard off Campus. Guard off Campus."

"Please don't stay here, Tasha."

"I'm afraid for you, Jake."

"I'll know when I can't be of use."

"Really?"

"Go home. You can be of use to those girls. They'll be listening to the radio. Try to keep them there. I know Audrey is worried about Aaron, but try to keep her from coming up here, okay?"

Sadly, Tasha looked into his eyes. "All right, Jake. But if you get killed, I'll never forgive you."

He smiled. "I won't get killed. Don't worry."

"I love you, you goof."

He paused, looked into her eyes. "I love you too. You're my life."

He kissed her and watched as she blended in with the crowd flowing past the Union toward front campus. She was precious to him, beyond life itself. He quietly rejoiced that she had listened to reason.

Armband on, he moved toward the rear of the military line where he saw Graham Fisk conferring with two officers at a jeep. Professor Levitt greeted Jake.

"Come on, man. Let's go up to Taylor. That's the best view and maybe we can keep traffic flowing, minimize the spectators. You know, the hardheads are a small group. Most of these kids are too curious to keep away, like people gathering around a car wreck."

"Doesn't all this look like serious trouble to you, Jonah?"

"Potentially. The problem is the Guard's reaction to this big crowd, especially as they've been publicizing martial law and the consequent illegality of gatherings. And Admin has pronounced this rally as prohibited. I mean, look at those weekend warriors down there all lined up. How many do you figure, Jake?"

"A hundred or so, I guess. The others are scattered around at checkpoints."

"Yeah, maybe a hundred down there, and how many kids here on the hill?"

"A thousand, maybe."

"Yeah, and growing. The huge majority are nonviolent, but those troops down there don't know that. They're shaking in their boots. They're thinking that a mad rush from these students could overwhelm them in spite of rifles, bayonets and tear gas. Sure, there'd be a lot of bloodshed, but the outcome is clear."

"No way that's happening," Jake said.

"But the troops don't know that. Graham was talking to the general, who said if things look worse they'll have to take offensive action to defend themselves." Jonah checked his watch. It's eleven-thirty. Soon classes will be changing again, and this crowd will compound. Word must be out by now that something's going on. Look, I'll head over to the other side of Taylor and try to keep kids moving along. You stay here, do the same thing. Don't take any chances, okay? Don't be a hero. We're not here for that."

"I'm no hero," Jake said. "You and Graham and the others are."

Jonah smiled a helpless smile. "Give me a break." He wended his way up the walkway toward the trees at the east side of Taylor.

Half way up the hill, Jake took a stance.

"Keep moving," he said to passersby. "Nothing here for you. Don't gawk. Move along."

It didn't take him long to realize his words were useless. From the troop line, above the voices of the gathered students and the ringing bell, he heard a campus police officer shouting something through a bull horn but too far away to be clear. He heard the words *disperse, illegal, arrests,* but only faintly, no one paying any attention. The chant, "Guard off Campus," grew louder in cadence with the bell.

Though clearly futile, Jake kept up his own chant about moving along, now getting answers like, "*You* move along, pig," and "Fuck you, traitor."

Then he felt a tug on his shirt sleeve. He turned.

"Audrey!"

She looked up at him with worried eyes.

"Jake, have you seen Aaron?"

"No. You shouldn't be here. Go back to the house."

"I have to find him. I haven't heard from him in two days."

"This is no place for either of you. Get out of here."

"Then it's no place for you. I'm going to find him. He's probably down there at the bell." She moved downward through the crowd.

Soldiers in a jeep drove out from behind the firing line and came close to the students, a campus cop using a bullhorn to read the Riot Act: "This gathering is illegal. Disperse immediately or you will be arrested."

The jeep was greeted with stones and rocks, probably gathered from the construction site of the unfinished library. The cop with the bullhorn ducked. The jeep continued, circulated the fringe of the student crowd three times telling them to leave. Their efforts had no effect whatever.

"Pigs Leave Campus!" the multitude chanted. Steadily, harshly, the bell clanged.

Across the open field, orders were barked. The soldiers hustled to form a tighter line. They pulled on gas masks. More orders were shouted. The Guardsman began marching across the Commons, in step, rifles lowered, bayonets glinting in the spring sunshine.

In reaction to the Guard's forward movement, the voices of the students lowered for a moment, then came obscenities, raised middle fingers, fists, from males and females alike. Fifty yards away the soldiers gradually came closer. Behind them the two smokestacks of the power plant, spewing coal soot into the pale blue sky, stood like goalposts on a surreal football field of war.

Fear tightened Jake's gut. He could do nothing now but watch. The troops marched, a hundred of them, if that, moving in a single line toward a teeming mass of maybe two thousand if you included the entire scene down at the Union and on the porches of the dorms. At the bell, the hardcores, both genders, held their ground, screaming, gesturing. The line of olive green trudged closer.

Then shots rang out. Trailing smoke, canisters arched toward the students at the bell. The students turned toward the hill, fleeing. Several young men charged at the canisters, picked them up, ran headlong toward the troops and hurled them back. Cheers rang out. Close to the soldiers, a skinny, longhaired kid waved a black flag back and forth.

The troops trod closer. More canisters sailed through the air. A breeze moving west to east drifted the gas toward Prentice Hall next to Taylor where Jonah Levitt had stationed himself. The walkway became a mob of bolting students, shoving against one another, log jammed and hemming Jake in on all sides. The bell stopped ringing. The hardest of the hardcores retreated. Jake spotted Audrey climbing the steep incline, Aaron by her side.

A small cadre of troops, ten or so, veered off from the main line, moving toward the east of Taylor. One of them knelt and fired a canister in that direction, then another round and another into the gap between Taylor and Prentice. It looked as if that line was headed through the trees toward the space where Jonah, holding an arm over his face, furiously gestured kids to move toward the dorm.

Then Jake, shoved along the walkway back toward the Union, saw something even more frightening. Tasha! Against the flow, she fought her way toward him. His heart sank, and his mission, hopeless as it had become, immediately changed. He struggled to pass students in the bottlenecked current toward the Union. He needed to get her out of there. Fortunately the gas was drifting the other way. But canisters kept coming, the report of the launchers heard even above the roar of the fleeing crowd.

By the time he and Tasha met up, the main line of troops had started its ascent up the west side of Blanket Hill toward Taylor. Rocks, bottles and vile epithets flew toward them, and Jake, looking with annoyance at Tasha, pulled her up the hill toward some trees near the Pagoda. Most of the students were racing down the other side of the hill toward the parking lot and the practice field beyond. But Jake, holding Tasha's hand and surveying the area, yanked her through the flow then along the south wall of the building and up the steps to the porch that went all around. The porch, too, was crowded, people rushing out through the doors, coughing, covering their noses and mouths. The gas must have penetrated the structure.

He pressed Tasha close to him at the railing. Students from the Journalism Department and the office of the *Stater* were photographing the phantasmagorical scene as the line of soldiers passed by them close enough for Jake to hear their muffled panting behind their masks.

"Oh, my God!" Tasha whispered. "There's Ray."

"How can you tell?"

"His corporal stripes, the way he walks. And that's his company, the Hundred-and-Seventh. It's him."

The soldiers' peripheral vision must have been extremely limited. In a few seconds the Guardsmen had passed them headed down the hill in steady pursuit of the panicked, bolting students.

"Are you crazy?" Jake said to Tasha. "Why did you come here?"

"I had to be with you. The radio was saying how bad things looked."

"Jesus, Tasha. You made things worse for me by showing up."

In a tight line, the soldiers moved faster down the hill, chasing the kids, who were scattering, impossible for this small company to capture, making the military maneuver seem bizarre.

Jake pulled a handkerchief from his back pocket, handed it to Tasha.

"Here, cover your face. You don't want any of this gas, believe me."

He raised his forearm to cover his mouth and nose.

"Did you see Audrey?" she asked.

"Yeah, she found Aaron. They're in the group running away down there."

The battle formation kept moving all the way down across the practice field where it suddenly stopped. They seemed confused, turning this way and that. Then Jake remembered there was a chain-link fence at that point, barbed wire along the top. The troops were hemmed in. They whirled. From the other side of the fence, a small group of students hurled rocks. The only way out for the troops was the exact way they'd entered, now caught on three sides, students closing in, throwing debris, hurling graphic insults. One scrawny young man, long hair held back by a headband, was especially aggressive, running close to the Guardsmen, taunting them, flipping them the bird with both hands, dancing a jig. The other boy persisted with his black flag.

Jake heard an order being barked. A line of soldiers sank to their knees, pointed their rifles.

"Oh, God, no!" Tasha yelled. "Ray!"

"Jesus," Jake said almost to himself. "This is it."

"Don't worry," someone on the porch shouted. "Their guns aren't loaded."

"Or only with blanks," someone else added.

But the soldiers didn't shoot. Stones bounced off helmets, but they held fire. Ducking, four or five officers conferred furiously. They appeared to be out of tear gas.

Someone is going to be massacred, but on which side?

Was it true they only had blanks? Maybe. Jake desperately hoped so.

An officer yelled an order, and the kneeling riflemen rose. The entire company moved out in the direction from which they'd come, students fleeing to let them pass. They marched in a wedge, the officers inside, retracing their steps up the steep hill.

When they got close to Taylor, to the crest near the Pagoda, Jake could hear their exhausted breathing. Two choppers hovered above them. Though they hadn't fired any more gas, they still wore their masks. They looked like monstrous alien insects. The students were reassembling back down the hill in the parking lot, shouting, cheering, jeering, taunting. Several had trailed the retreating troops, maybe twenty yards behind. Photographers on the porch fired their cameras. People on the portico shouted, cursed.

In the chaos Tasha clung to Jake's arm.

At least the Guard had the sense to retreat. They have a free path all the way across the Commons to where they started. But then what? Everything back to square one?

This thought was cut short by a move from the soldiers now at the top of the hill. In unison, a number of them did a sudden about-face, some kneeling, all pointing their guns in the direction of the students in the parking lot, none close. Without any order that Jake could make out, these troops fired. Several guns were aimed toward the sky, but others right toward the crowd. The sudden noise, the smoke, were ghastly. Jake blinked in amazement. One soldier turned and fired directly at a photographer along the base of the wall, missed. Jake heard the rip of metal in a piece of iron sculpture decorating the slope. After an eternity of seconds the firing stopped. Now shrieks came from the students, all of them racing away or dropping to prone positions, diving behind trees and vehicles.

Tasha was nearly quaking with seizures as she gripped Jake's arm.

Jake held her from falling.

Even worse screaming arose, a different kind, of shock, despair. With the firing now stopped and the troops retreating out of sight down Blanket Hill, Jake saw what the shrieking was about. Several bodies lay flat, the closest one, fifty yards or so, the longhaired kid who'd been taunting the firing line at the practice field. Students gathered around, kneeling. And the small squad of soldiers on the east side of Taylor charged down toward two of the fallen victims.

"He's dead!" a girl, her arms stretched to the sky in horror, yelled toward the troops. "You killed him, you motherfuckers!"

"Oh, my God!" Tasha gasped.

"So much for the blanks," someone on the porch said.

Other students farther down the lot lay motionless also. Still others gripped bleeding wounds.

"Ambulance!" someone yelled. "Call an ambulance!"

Most of the students had fled, but stragglers remained, standing above the fallen. The kid with the black flag dipped the fabric in the boy's blood, soaked it in a bizarre ritual, then raised the fabric and whipped it back and forth spraying the gore into the air and onto bystanders.

"See what you did?" he cried. "See what you did?"

Students harassed the small contingent of troops who were guarding the two bleeding bodies but kept back, now knowing the lethal force against them. The troops who'd fired had retreated with the larger group up past the Pagoda out of sight.

"Was Ray one of the ones who fired?" Jake asked Tasha.

"I couldn't see well, but I don't think so. I think he was standing behind them. I can't believe what I just saw, Jake."

Students on the porch were aghast at what had happened, some speechless, others cursing the Guard.

"They didn't have to fire," someone said.

"No one was following them," came another voice. "Not even close."

"Murderers."

"Blatant homicide."

Jake pulled Tasha with him around the porch. He wanted to find Jonah. At the east end of the walkway, he spotted the professor leaning against the trunk of a tree, his face wan, astonished, unbelieving.

Jake tugged Tasha along.

"Jonah!"

The dismayed professor stared blankly down toward the bloodletting. Sirens sounded in the far distance, and now the mass of students in a rising fury, with tear streaked, anguished faces, began to climb the hill toward where the troops had retreated. A siren sounded close from the direction of the Commons, soon came around the west end of Taylor and down toward the first fallen. It skidded to a stop, and the first one out was Professor Fisk, who rushed to the longhaired kid stretched out, face down, his blood streaming into the gutter.

82

Moments later …

Jonah, his eyes in shock behind his horn-rimmed glasses, took a deep breath as if gathering his wits.

"Holy hell!" he gasped. "That may have been only Round One."

Students now poured out of Prentice Hall as others charged up the hill from the parking lot around both sides of Taylor to gather again on Blanket Hill, all fury and vengeance.

Christ Jesus! Jake thought. Where is Audrey!

"Do you think they shot to kill?" he asked Jonah. "I saw some firing in the air."

Jonah pointed toward the parking lot. "Can't you see the blood?"

The longhaired kid, mostly blocked by a small crowd, still lay flat on his face, a pool of blood beside his head. Others lay farther down the lot. Siren wailing, lights flashing, another ambulance arrived from the direction of the Commons, immediately trailed by yet another.

403

Audrey! Was she among the ones hit? Or Aaron? Hell, it could be anyone. It was random, a turkey shoot.

"A lot of those kids down there were probably just going to class," Jonah said. "Or faculty headed to teach."

It was all fathoms out of Jake's frame of reference, but he didn't have any time to speculate about who'd been shot or about why the Guard had fired with live ammo, any of it, because a new, much more frightening crisis had arisen in the other direction, down toward the military line that had been renewed at its starting point next to the charred shell of ROTC. Turning in that direction, Jake saw the officers in a flurried conference. The mass of furious students had retaken Blanket Hill and the bell at its base.

"We might as well *all* die!" someone shouted.

Some were weeping, howling, others reddened with anger.

"We should charge them, take their guns."

"No!" Jonah yelled. "No more of this. Go back. Go inside, back to your dorms."

"Fuck you!" someone answered. "Let's kill those pigs."

"Let them butcher us all!"

"Make them pay the price!"

The enraged crowd grew ever larger, gathering strength.

"Tasha," Jake said. "Get out of here. Go see if you can help the ones hurt. See if you can find Audrey down there."

"Only with you, Jake."

Jake shook his head hopelessly. "Go back to your dorms," he shouted with Jonah. That was equally hopeless. The students pressed farther down toward the now tolling bell. A violent confrontation with the Guard seemed certain.

"Ray's down there," Tasha said.

"Are you sure he wasn't one of those who fired?"

"There was so much smoke and noise. God, I hope not. They'll be in all kinds of trouble."

"They deserve it. No reason for them to shoot, especially live rounds. No one was even close to them, and they had a clear way back."

"Jake," Jonah said. "Graham and the others have set up a line down there in front of the students. I'm going down where I belong. You stay here and try to talk some sense into these kids. They're out of control. Understandable, but..."

He wedged his way down the hill through the mass of seething students in the small woods.

"I should go down there too," Jake said.

"Then I'm coming with you."

"No way I'm taking you down there."

"No way I'm letting you go alone."

"Jesus, Tasha."

"No, Jake, if you're committing suicide, I am too."

"You're as crazy as these kids."

"Maybe Ray will see me and call off his team."

"Are you out of your mind, Tasha? Maybe he'll see me and fire."

"This is no time for that, Jake. Let it go. Ray is a closed book."

Jake yelled at the kids to go to their dorms. Useless as it was, it was all he could do under the circumstances.

Below on the Commons, he saw Graham Fisk and two others trotting across toward the Guard. It was a spectacular act of courage. All three held up their armbands as a signal of peace. At the troop line, they conversed with the Guard leadership.

Students chanted, "Kill the Pigs!" They meant it. The sound of choppers pulsated above them. Word filtered through the crowd: "Four killed, lots wounded." Cries of horror rose, screams of sadness. The chant grew louder. The crowd pressed forward, now on level ground, the bell clanging.

Fisk and his three partners marched back across no man's land. Fisk carried a bullhorn, walked with determination, a short man in shirt and khakis, flat top haircut, humble, unassuming, dauntless.

At the line in front of the students, he pleaded, begged. "Back off for now. Call it a day. Go back to your dorms. Go home. They won't fire, won't arrest you as long as you disperse."

"They're liars!" someone screamed.

There was real fear in Fisk's voice. He handed the bullhorn to a prof whose name Jake didn't know and who spoke more coherently, calm but ardent.

"There is live ammunition in their guns. They will shoot to kill. Please stop this. Only you have the power. Go home. Go home."

At first, students yelled back epithets, but the tall, bland-looking professor continued. Three disheveled profs against a screaming mob.

"You will get killed. Please, stop this. Go home."

Then, as if miraculously, the message of this small cadre of determined faculty members seemed to sink in. The other several marshals, Jonah not yet having arrived there, joined the plea. Their desperate sincerity, their act of love, of concern, of anguished heartfelt caring, began to take effect. Students wept, others continued cursing but less intensely, and the forward surge let up, and kids began leaving toward Prentice, or across in front of Taylor, or back up the hillside. Slowly, dirge like, the chants became mutters of sorrow, muted fury, and the flood gradually dissolved, leaving only a few determined potential martyrs facing the faculty marshals. Fisk spoke into the bull horn: "Go home. It's over. Go home."

Students brushed both ways against Jake and Tasha. Across the field, the firing line held motionless, rifles aimed. Jake felt a wave of hatred grip his mind against them.

Four killed. Was it true? He thought of Audrey. *No, it can't be.*

But it could be any one of them. It had been haphazard, shots unconscionably fired into an anonymous mass. It was Kent State they'd fired at, a new, misunderstood generation. Any student or worker or visitor could be one of the four. In a way it was *Audrey, and Aaron, any one of his past students, any Kent personnel at all, himself included, Tasha, any and every one pursuing a higher education, the whole young, up-and-coming future of the nation.*

As retreating students jostled Jake both ways on the crowded path, he felt as if a world had ended, that the moving mass embodied an exodus from innocence.

"Come on," he said to Tasha, tears wetting his eyes. "Let's go home."

As they moved across the walk in front of Taylor, he saw Fisk and his cohorts still arguing with the persistent radicals at the bell, keeping them from charging hopelessly and absurdly to their deaths. Jonah finally joined the fragile line maintaining the still uncertain peace. Those few faculty marshals were the bravest, most honorable men Jake had ever seen. He felt more tears welling, and not from the clouds of gas still wafting in the May breeze, but tears from deep down in his bowels, tears of brutal loss.

He tugged Tasha off the walkway and up the hill back toward the Pagoda where below them in the parking lot several ambulances, gatherings of EMT workers and students in small groups labored around the stricken.

"I want to see if Audrey or Aaron are down there," Jake said.

"Don't even think that," Tasha answered.

The first victim, the longhaired boy, had already been taken away, a pool of blood and its stream toward the gutter of the driveway, mourners lingering. Then farther down, Jake saw a dark-haired girl on the ground, EMT's attending. His heart jumped. He ran, pulling Tasha with him.

"That could be her."

She was on a gurney, her long dark hair streaming, and he saw it wasn't Audrey, but a beautiful young woman, eyes closed as if asleep.

"She didn't make it," someone said.

Wounded people were being helped, some bandaged and on their feet, others on the ground, one in a body bag on an ambulance cart.

"Boy or girl?" Jake asked urgently.

"Boy," someone answered. "Very straight arrow."

"It's not Aaron," Jake muttered as if it mattered who it was. They were all human lives taken or wounded, all of equal value.

One young man lay on the ground, bloodied, shot in the back, conscious but apparently unable to move. It was a scene of pain and death, several emergency vehicles arriving as others departed, appalled witnesses standing all around, weeping, in shock.

Jake found relief at least in Audrey and Aaron's not being among the fallen.

But they could have been. That's the real tragedy of this madness. It could have been any teacher's student, anyone's friend, any parent's child, any innocent American youth. It's our country that lies here, torn.

83

Moments later ...

In silence Jake and Tasha meandered their way westward toward Satterfield Hall. They passed the building, neither of them at all inclined to go inside to hear the inevitable stories, endless accounts and even more opinions and rumors of this hellish day's events. Soon blame would be cast, sides taken, columns printed, media commentators spouting opposing viewpoints. Today in this hitherto obscure place had emerged clearly the thus far culmination of the antiwar movement though Jake wondered what it had to do with the war. It was more like a street brawl, no issues, only a primitive mutual hatred, two angry tribes.

Except ... except for those glowing few who fought against the insanity, who tried to stop it, and in the end had ... yes, had saved lives. Without Professor Fisk and his comrades it all might have been much, much worse.

Those brave, conscientious academicians, while others hid, while others found sanctuary in their ivory tower existences, and while administrators thought their work had ended by calling in enforcers, those crazy, splendid profs had been out there for those kids. How many in that blessed crew? Five, finally, standing there pleading into a bullhorn, holding back the tide.

Of far lesser importance in light of the immediate crisis, they'd shown Jake something deeply personal, something profound about true manhood, true courage, something he'd seen in extremely few, possibly only his dad. Those handful of glorious, determined, moral men had stirred something in Jake, something about responsibility, sanity, dedication. It all made him ... he began to feel it now as he climbed with the woman he loved toward the summit of Summit Road ... it all made him, yes, begin to ... cherish this place. It was a most extraordinary emotion—a place he'd detested, wanted to abandon, could hardly wait to leave behind like a moth its smothering cocoon, now seemed miraculously ... hallowed.

He squeezed Tasha's hand. No words spoken, she squeezed his in return.

As they approached the checkpoint at Lincoln Street, Jake saw the same two soldiers they'd passed that morning.

"Glad to see you're still alive," the guard named Russ said to Tasha.

"It's not funny," she answered. "There were people killed."

"Should have been more than four of those assholes," Russ answered.

Jake felt a sudden urge to pummel the guy, forced the impulse back. In this matter, he had no compassion for the Guardsmen. They'd clearly been criminals to fire.

"Four?" Tasha said. "There were four?"

"So far. Guess now the fuckwads know we mean business."

Jake held his tongue.

"Did you run into Ray over there?" Russ asked.

"No," Tasha said.

"Hope he got one or two. The whole town hates those traitors. They deserved everything they got and more."

Jake and Tasha were now a few paces past the barrier.

Yes, a primitive tribe. Not even murder had altered that reality today.

"I'll tell Ray I ran into you," Russ said. "Sorry you two are breaking up."

"You don't need to tell him anything," Tasha answered over her shoulder.

"I will anyway," Russ said, sarcasm in his voice. "I'm sure he'd like to know you made it out in one piece."

The door open, Jake's apartment stood empty of coeds and their belongings as if a mass exit had occurred. The radio was still on. As Jake and Tasha hugged, they heard the news that President White had closed the campus for the rest of the day. He'd been having a leisurely lunch at the Brown Derby Restaurant, his usual noonday haunt, when he'd been informed of the shootings.

Jake heard two car doors slam. He went to the window.

"Your car," he said, puzzled. "Two men."

"Oh, my God! It's Daddy." She peered out. Two men in business suits strode up the walkway and onto the porch.

She ran out. Jake followed as her father and another man started up the stairs.

"Ray said we'd find you here," her dad commented. "Called us last night. This place is all over the news. You're coming home with me."

"No need to come up here, Daddy. I'll come out. Give me a moment to get my things."

"Hurry up; it's time."

She backed inside, closed the door.

"You're not going, are you?" Jake asked.

"I'd better, Jake."

"The last time, you were captured for weeks. Don't you think it's time you stay with me?"

"I just can't."

"Why not?"

"Because ... I don't know why. I just can't. I'll get my stuff from the bath-room."

"Not this time, Tasha. It's time now for you and me—for us."

"Oh, Jake."

"I'll talk to him."

As she objected, he was out the door, down the stairs and outside. The two men were leaning against the trunk of the Mercury, smoking.

"She's not coming," Jake announced from the front stoop.

"Who the hell are you?" Van Sollis asked, straightening.

"I'm the guy she's going to marry."

The man stared at him. "Like hell you are. Didn't I meet you once? Weren't you in our home? A left-winger, if I remember."

"Tasha and I have been together since even before that."

"Together? You and my daughter?"

"Together, that's right."

Van Sollis's brow wrinkled as he pondered this information.

"Sure, together as neighbors, correct? Is that what you mean *together*?"

"Much more than that. And she's staying here."

Tasha burst out the door. Stopped short. "Oh!"

"This character is pulling my leg, baby. Making some pretty outrageous accusations about you."

Frozen, she stared at Jake.

He father chuckled. "Okay, baby, or should I say 'Tasha'? Hop in. They're talking about closing down traffic out and in of this entire town. So let's get a move-on."

Jake stood, a fortress wall between Tasha and her dad.

"Uh ... Daddy. I guess I can't."

"What do you mean, you can't? Let's hop to it."

"Daddy, this is Jake. Jake Ernst. I, uh, I guess I'm with him now."

Van Sollis shifted his weight. "What the hell are you talking about?"

"Jake and I, well, we're going to get married, Daddy."

Van Sollis coughed as if something was caught in his throat.

"We don't have time for this, baby. You're coming home where you'll be safe and sound."

"No, Daddy, safe or not, I'm here with Jake. I love him, and ... and he loves me. We're together now."

"There's that word again, *together*. Since when are you together with this ...? What are you talking about?"

He took an angry step toward her. Jake blocked his way.

"You'd damn well better move aside, young man."

"No. You'd better listen to your daughter, at long last."

Van Sollis turned toward his associate, still at the car.

"Back me up here, Harry."

"Sure." Harry pulled off his suit jacket, flung it onto the hood of the Cougar.

"Stop it, Daddy!"

"Then this sorry soul had better step aside, or he'll sorely regret it."

The two middle-aged men now stood side by side.

Fists clenched, Jake stood at the ready.

"Jake. Come inside. Let me talk to my father like civilized beings."

"Not a chance."

Van Sollis shoved Jake, but Jake was ready and barely budged.

"Are you kidding me?" the older man said.

"Does it look like I'm kidding?"

Van Sollis took a short step backward. "Do you understand what's at stake here, honey?" he asked Tasha, who was still on the steps.

"Nothing need be at stake, Daddy. You'd better not hurt Jake. You'll get arrested. Your reputation as a model citizen will be destroyed."

He shook his head in disbelief. "Arrested? I have a feeling the local cops have other business to attend to at the moment."

"I'm sorry, Daddy. I don't want to hurt you, and especially Mama, but I want to stay here with Jake. And I'll fight you too, if you force me to."

Van Sollis looked dumbfounded, his mouth agape, speechless.

"You better go home, Daddy. We'll talk again when things have calmed down. Things are a little confrontational around here right now. Go home, okay?"

"Since when do you tell me what to do?"

"I guess since now, since it seems Jake won't budge."

"Maybe the girl is right," Harry suggested behind Van Sollis.

"How the hell can she be right? I'm her father!"

"I mean about your reputation. I mean, she is of age, isn't she? Coming with us is a matter of her choice, isn't it? That brings up all kinds of problematic charges, assault, battery, kidnapping, invasion of..."

"Shut the fuck up, Harry. I'm in charge here."

"It would appear not," Harry countered. "She's right. You can work things out later." He took hold of Van Sollis's arm. "And if you're intent on sullying your good standing, all friendship considered, I'd rather not do the same for mine."

Van Sollis ripped loose, shifted, reddened. "All right. All right. But Natasha, you think long and hard about this. You'll never find a better man than Ray Sweeny. Out there today, defending America, everything a man should be."

"Except the man I love," Tasha said quietly. "The man I love is standing right in front of you."

"The hell, I say. We'll see about that. That's God damned impossible."

He turned, strode with his friend Harry, and both got into the Mercury. Spewing gravel, he backed out of the driveway and sped on Willow toward Summit where he turned westward, squealing rubber on his way.

Jake turned toward Tasha who stood on the steps looking at him blankly as if in suspension.

"Well," Jake finally said. "I guess that's enough bullshit for one day."

Pale, shaken, she offered a meek smile. "Yes, Jake, I guess it is."

84

Monday, May 11, one week later ...

Jake sat across a table from Jonah at Mancino's Restaurant off the square in downtown Kent. A middle-aged waitress cleared away their breakfast plates and refilled their coffee cups. The feeling in the town had resembled a giant hangover. Though evidence of national and regional media investigators remained, the town was slowly recovering a semblance, at least, of normality. But the students were gone, the campus closed even to staff and faculty as if it were an expansive crime scene. When it would reopen was anyone's guess.

"Yeah, Jake," Jonah said, "I can dig your wanting to get out of here, but we need you, man. With all these crazy rumors flying around, we need people who were there. I mean the talk of student snipers, that Guardsmen were killed, kids with pistols, Soviet led communists, students charging up that hill two feet from the troops. Somebody's got to set the record straight."

Jake sighed. "I know, but Tasha and I had an important trip planned. A lot of people saw what happened."

"Hey, a lot of those people with agendas. Everyone spinning, even the journalist profs. The whole point of the marshals was to keep an objective eye. Of course, none of us expected what happened. Four kids dead, one paralyzed, eight wounded. Christ! The university shut down. Hey, you're going to stay on after the summer, right?"

Jake smiled meekly at the Woody Allen lookalike, sincere brown eyes big behind his thick lenses, hair line receding, necktie always undone, sports jacket specked with dandruff. A good man. A marvelously good man. A role model, what a college professor should be.

"Look, Jake. We're meeting over at Akron at the Unitarian Church, a hundred of us or more. Formulating a statement, arranging places to meet with our students to finish up our courses, and, hell, for a communion of sensible souls. Why aren't you there with us? Come along with me today. We'll make room in the car."

"I'm going through some things with my girl," Jake said.

"Sure, the one you were with last Monday. A knockout. Bring her along; she's in the French Department, right?"

"She wants to stay as far away from Akron as she can. She's warring with her parents. She grew up there."

"Understandable. But you can come, can't you? Only once. If it's not something you can join, no problem. You can leave your marshal report with us and take off for the territories, as Huck Finn said."

Jake smiled. "All right. Sorry you even have to recruit me. It's embarrassing."

"Why's that, Jake?"

"I don't deserve to be hanging around with the likes of you and Graham. Fisk, and the others. You're all heroes."

"None of us are heroes, just concerned for our students, that's all."

"You're heroes to me," Jake said. "Shining like beams of hope out of all this horror. I saw what you guys did out there. You saved lives. That's heroic. I never expected to see kids murdered in front of me. Never. It was the worst thing..."

"I know, Jake. For me too. Who would have thought? At Berkeley maybe, but here? No way. That's why we need each other right now. Shouldn't try to handle it on our own. And we must focus on keeping the story from being spun out of control. You used the word *murder*. Maybe, but those Guardsmen were under unbelievable pressure, and I'm telling you, those kids were on the verge of a wholesale charge."

"They weren't charging when the troops fired. It was the shootings that blew things totally out of control. What did those goons think they were going to accomplish by marching down to that fenced-in practice field? What kind of tactic was that?"

"For one thing, Jake. They were following orders. This whole mess is one complication piled on another. It's exactly what we're all discussing over in Akron. Now listen up. You need to join us, my friend. For your own sake as well as for our project, if you can call it that. We need your voice. So if not today, think about it and at least come along tomorrow. You can always drop out. Say yes."

"All right," Jake answered. "After this little chat, it would be an honor. Tomorrow it is. Sorry you had to even ask twice."

When Jake got back to his place, he saw an unfamiliar car in the driveway, a three year old Chevelle.

Maybe someone wanting to rent the apartment, he thought.

Before he opened the upstairs door, he heard two female voices from inside.

"You shouldn't have taken such a risk, Mama," Tasha was saying. "Leaving Daddy to drive over here. He'll make your life a living hell."

Jake tapped on the door before going inside. Tasha rose.

"Jake, this is my mother."

He extended his hand and walked over to where she sat on the sofa. She shook it weakly.

"Yes," she said. "I believe we met before, with the girls from France."

"That's right." He wondered if her husband was lurking somewhere.

"She came here alone," Tasha said.

"Would you like me to leave so you two can talk?" he asked.

"No, Jake. We've talked a lot on the phone. he came here specifically to meet you, to get to know you a little. So join us. I'll make some tea."

Hesitantly, Jake sat on the easy chair. Mrs. Van Sollis smiled timidly. She wore a high collared buttoned blouse and a maroon skirt with polished pumps, everything in meticulous order. She looked like an older version of her beautiful daughter.

"I wanted to meet you for myself," she said calmly. "All of this has come as a shock."

"For me," Jake said gently, "I'm glad the truth has finally come out."

"Natasha has told me you met over Tolstoy."

"Yes, she said you used to read *War and Peace* to her in French. I knew then that you must be an exceptional person."

"He wrote it in French, you know."

"Did Natasha tell you I met his daughter?"

"Yes, she showed me the book she signed."

Tasha came back with a tray and placed it on the coffee table. They all took a few minutes to arrange their refreshments.

"Mama would like to know about your family, Jake."

Jake spoke about his parents, his dad being wounded in Africa, his uncle killed, about the farm and the shop. Mrs. Van Sollis listened with tearful blue eyes. He took the photo from his wallet and handed it to her.

"And you love my daughter?" she asked after Jake's faltering, five minute ramble.

"From the first moment I saw her. Right out there on our fire escape. She was wearing an apron and holding a dishtowel."

Mrs. Van Sollis smiled. "So you believe in *coup de foudre*." She spoke slowly as if measuring her words.

Puzzled at the French phrasing, Jake turned to Tasha.

"Love at first sight," she said.

He smiled. "Yes, Mrs. Van Sollis, I guess I do. It never happened to me before, though."

"It was how I felt about William. He was the American liaison with the Resistance in our village. I first saw him in a cave, by lantern light."

"That's why he should understand about Jake and me," Tasha said.

"William is not romantic. He's more the commandant, you see. He's been commandeering his little family and his subordinates as long as I've known him. I was happy for him to do it, his commands were always quite satisfactory. That is, until you entered the narrative, Jake. Natasha must have been terrified of him to have kept your existence a secret for so long."

"Before Jake *entered the narrative*," Tasha echoed, "Daddy's commands were quite satisfactory for me also."

Her mother smiled. "You see, Jake. You've quite toppled our applecart. We are now whirling through space. About your presence in the novel, of course, but now Natasha tells me you plan to take her off to Louisiana. I wish you could comprehend the tragic loss that would be for us. Almost like..."

"Like what, Mama?"

"Like those children killed last week. What their parents must feel! The endless grief."

Jake didn't know what to say

"And now our own little girl leaving us."

"I, uh, understand your sentiment, Mrs. Van Sollis, but pardon me for not being able to place our moving away in the same category. There are phones, letters, flights home for vacations. The loss of those four kids is permanent."

She looked at him, humbled herself even more than before. "Yes, yes, but of course. I over sentimentalize, but having my Natasha so far away feels like such a loss to her Mama. And her daddy. I cannot imagine, ooh-la-la!"

"Will Jake and I have to go into hiding, Mama? Last time Daddy came over here, there was almost a brawl in the front yard."

"Lord knows, when he hears that your very good and decent paramour is going to steal you away across the continent."

"You do over sentimentalize, Mama. Even my psychologist says a long-distance break may be useful, at least for a while."

"Ah, another subject that infects your father's goat, as the American expression goes. You with a therapist, as if he has caused you psychological problems? He claims that it is Jake here who has done that to you. You were perfectly well until..."

"Until he entered the novel? Yes, Mama, I know how hard it is to see things differently from Daddy. I used to be exactly like you, just as subservient, instinctively trusting his every command. But those days are over. Just because I must go my own way doesn't mean I don't love him, and certainly you. And look how far he took you from your family, across a whole ocean. But I have my own mind, and it's time for me to exert it. I'm not like one of those students shot over there. I'm still here, Mama." She smacked her own arm. "You see? Flesh and blood. Now let's think rationally about this. Let's make *our* book, at least, have a happy ending, shall we? Unlike those lost students, we can still choose our fates."

Tuesday, May 12, next day ...

Jonah's station wagon packed with riders, Jake edged into the middle seat. During the commute to Akron he listened to the discussion as it wove from one topic to another, the general theme emerging: what to do next. How long would the university be locked down? Would there be a commencement? What should be done about student grades, given that a full four weeks of the term would be lost?

Even deeper than such practical matters was the issue of who bore responsibility for the deaths and injuries, what kind of criminal actions should be brought, what sort of lawsuits, and how to keep the Kent State chronicle from going completely haywire.

They talked about the rash of national protests in honor of the now martyred Kent Four. Some blamed Nixon for Cambodia and his calling student protesters "bums." Others blamed Governor Rhoades who, using the burning of ROTC as a platform for election rhetoric in his run for the Senate, echoed Nixon by calling Kent protestors "brown-shirts." Still others blamed Mayor Satrom for his clumsy use of law enforcement. Much of the faculty charged President White for administrative negligence, and many accused the Guard officers with incompetence and the troops themselves as trigger happy.

But by far the townspeople and the larger society blamed the students for having long fomented violence and disruption, for their blatant arson, their bad manners, worse dress, their music, long hair, obscene language, dope smoking, communes and radical political ideas. How to officially filter all the confusion and cross-purposes presented a mindboggling problem.

In the church chapel the conversation continued with many more voices, the pews filled and participants, Jake among them, standing against the walls. At this meeting, an English professor known for her quality teaching and common sense, read a draft of a statement intended for publication which expressed the sentiments of this faculty group.

Leaning against the wall of the sanctuary, Jake listened, feeling the appropriateness of this gathering going on in a place of worship. There was a sacredness about it. A sincere urgency, no one spinning, no one with an agenda except how to save the school and preserve the truth.

Leslie Robbins sidled in next to Jake.

"Good people," she said.

"They sure are."

"They're trying their best to structure something out of chaos."

"Yeah."

"So what're your plans? Hanging around Kent, hoping for the best?"

"No. Traveling across country with my girl, then to LSU on a fellowship. How 'bout you, Leslie?"

She held out her left hand.

"Nice ring. Congratulations. Someone in the Department?"

"No. I'm leaving Kent as soon as we figure out what to do about grades. Peoria, Illinois, my old beau, the engineer. He couldn't build bulldozers without me, I guess. But you and I had some good times, didn't we, Jake."

"We sure did."

"I have a nice little stash. Don't want to travel with it. Would you like to have it as a parting gift?"

"No, thanks. We meditate now, transcendental style. It's nice. Calms you down."

"Okay, then. Think of me sometimes, how we helped salvage those moderate kids. A member of our group, Sandy, was one of those killed. She was quiet as a mouse, smiled all the time, no one sweeter. Not even part of the protest, just going to her one o'clock class. Breaks my heart, Jake, really does. How else to think of campus now except as a cemetery."

She squeezed his hand and slipped away.

Jake hadn't known Sandy was in the moderate group, it had grown so large. The others killed had been identified also: Jeff, the longhaired boy who'd been obnoxiously harassing the troops but certainly didn't deserve to be shot down; another girl, Allison, a sophomore, the one Jake had thought at first was Audrey; and Bill, the one described as a "straight arrow," an ROTC cadet also on his way to class. A young man named Doug had been permanently paralyzed. The eight others hit would recover from their physical wounds. But more than physical damage had been done that day. Much more.

In unison and unanimously, the shooters, all identified through military investigative protocol, had claimed they'd thought their lives were in danger and had fired in self-defense. They expressed no remorse. No names had been released. All had engaged defense attorneys.

On the way home in the crowded vehicle, farms and fields, copses of woods drifting by, Jake detached his mind from these matters. He felt a communion of spirit he'd never felt before, an *esprit de corps*, a unified purpose. What that purpose might be, he didn't analyze. He only felt it for the moment, let it penetrate his being. Amid the several conversations going on at once, the lush spring air rushing through the open windows, he simply closed his eyes.

85

Thirty minutes later ...

"How'd it go?" Tasha asked when he got back to the apartment.

"Let's go for a walk."

"I was just about to start dinner."

"Let's eat out. Lejeune's maybe. They have those good chicken pot pies."

"So you worked up an appetite, did you?"

"I want to walk for a while. It's nice out."

The students having vacated the town, the streets were quiet. Some of the residents were mowing their lawns, weeding their gardens. Kids rode bikes, played catch in the streets. All Norman Rockwell ordinary.

Hand in hand, Jake and Tasha strolled aimlessly, up one tree lined street, down another, not saying much, comfortable in each other's company.

Jake let out a long, melancholy sigh.

"What's wrong?" Tasha asked.

"I don't know."

"But it's something, isn't it? With a sound like that?"

"Maybe it's something, yes."

"So what kind of something? You're breaking up with me?"

He stopped. "Hell no. Never. What would make you think that?"

"Infected by my mother's appeal yesterday. Saving everyone's feelings. I've spent the last two years sighing like that."

"No, that's not it, not at all."

"So, something's on your mind. What is it?"

"I was thinking about those kids who were shot."

"Oh. Yes, I think of them a lot."

They strolled again.

"Each one of them was precious," he said. "Beautiful. Yeah, the one called Jeff was a little out of hand, but he wasn't an SDSer, got agitated, that's all, like everyone else."

"That's right," Tasha said, "the SDSers were nowhere to be seen, were they? I didn't see them, anyway. Or the blacks either, for that matter."

"Two of the ones shot, Sandy and Bill, were just going to class, for God's sake."

"Is that what you all discussed in Akron today, Jake?"

"Not specifically, but the root of it all, of course."

"I forgot to tell you. Audrey dropped by today, to pay her phone bill. She was sorry to miss you, said she'd see you next fall. I told her we were leaving and..."

"I don't want to leave," Jake heard himself blurt.

It was Tasha's turn to stop suddenly. "Pardon? What did you say?"

Jake laughed in surprise. "I don't believe I said that. Or felt it."

"You don't want to leave. Did I hear you right?"

"Jesus, I did say that, didn't I?"

"Jake, do you mean it?"

"Uh, I don't know." He shook his head in amazement. "Maybe I do."

"Jake, what's got into you?"

"I don't know, Tasha. Something happened to me today. Being with those people, all planning to stay and fight. I don't mean like before, antiwar and all that. But to save the school. To keep it alive, to keep all this horror from being in vain."

"Do you really mean it, Jake? I thought Kent was the last place you wanted to be, even before all this happened."

"Yeah, but..."

A coal black squirrel raced into the street and almost got hit by two boys racing on their bikes. It tumbled a few times and arrived safely on the other curb and up a maple tree.

"So what's going on inside that head and heart of yours?" Tasha asked as they picked up their pace once more.

"I guess I had the sudden impulse to ... help out," he said, trying to piece his feelings into words. "There's a job to be done here. Those kids deserve something, the people in that church today, Jonah and Graham, all of them. Those guys risked their lives out there. If it wouldn't have been for them..."

"So now you're thinking of staying here in Kent, like for your Ph.D.?"

"Not without you, Tasha. Never that."

"So, you're asking me to stay here with you, here in this town that only a week ago you were hell-bent on leaving?"

"Uh, can we think about it, at least? I mean, when this feeling settles down? I know you wanted to get away as much as I did. And, we can. Sure we can. Why not? Except..."

"Jake. Wait a minute. This isn't like you. You plan everything out, make schedules down to the minute, analyze everything until every question is answered. I've never seen you like this."

"It's just that something good needs to grow out of those deaths, Tasha. Those kids, starting out in life, not hurting anyone, and their parents, and families. They can't be shot down to be forgotten, can they? They can't, God forbid, be blamed. It's like ... I don't know. Something should be preserved in their names. And Jonah and Graham, the others, they're coalescing, Tasha, into a force for good, for justice. I don't think I can walk away now, at least without feeling something less than ... a man. I mean, I will, Tasha, if you think that's best, if you feel you can't stay here. Man-oh-man, I can understand, with your dad and, hell, Ray driving around with his henchmen, and..."

"Be quiet, Jake."

"Yeah. Yeah, Tasha, sorry.   don't know what's happening here. I know it's a crazy idea."

"Will you shut up a minute, you jerk?"

"Sure, sure. I'll shut up. I'm sorry. I apologize. Don't mean to infect your goat, to upset your applecart."

"Enough!" she yelled, turning several neighbors' heads toward them.

Jake was silent.

"There, that's better. Can you listen a moment and keep your big trap shut?"

He nodded.

"Okay. Now, what if I told you that staying here would suit me just fine? Just perfectly fine."

Jake remained silent.

"Okay, you can respond," Tasha said.

"It would? It would be perfectly fine?"

"Yes, Jake, perfectly."

"No Beach Boy land? No Red Stick?"

"There will be time for us to tour the whole wide world. The west coast and the Mardi Gras can wait. I agree, there's work to be done here."

"Okay, but wait. Let me think about this. It seems rash."

"And God forbid you would do anything rash, Jake, like almost beating up my dad, like making love on Blanket Hill, and that nutty story about Chicken Manor. Oh, no, you wouldn't want to do anything rash."

"Staying in Kent?" he mused. "Holy moly, Alabama!"

"Now you sound like Daddy."

"Oh ... Yeah, I guess you taught me that dumb expression. What's it mean, anyway?"

"Can we at least take a weekend to visit your parents?" she asked.

"My parents? Sure, we can do that. You'll love them, and they'll love you."

"And can we go camping sometimes?"

"Yeah, that too. Sure. Of course."

"And have some babies?"

He looked at her and smiled. "I guess we could fit that in."

"Good. And as for practical matters, now that we're staying here."

"Practical matters? Such as?"

"Jake, is the Sinclair still available? You weren't foolish enough to turn it down as of yet, were you?"

"No. I was going to, that Monday as a matter of fact, but the Chairman was out, then the riot and school closed down..."

"So it's just hanging there like a ripe peach on a bough?"

"A peach on a bough? Yes, I suppose it is. If the school ever opens again."

"Okay, so let's go back and call the Chairman at his home, okay?"

"Yeah, yeah. Good idea."

They did an about-face and moved more quickly.

"Oh, and where are we going to live?" she asked. "Mrs. Whitcomb has already leased your place. You should have seen her face when all those girls were there. She almost blew a gasket."

"I can believe that. But she must be relishing what happened on campus, like everyone else in town. Believes the kids deserved it."

"Maybe we could rent a cottage on one of these lovely, quiet streets."

"A cottage, sure. Maybe we could, Tasha. You didn't resign your assistantship, did you?"

"No, Jake."

"Okay then, dammit," he said, his mind whirling into certainty. "We'll stay here, right here, a cottage in Kent, Ohio."

"Yes, my wonderful darling. And it will make Mama so very, very happy."

END

RESOURCES USEFUL IN CREATING THIS BOOK

Kent State: What Happened and Why – James A. Michener
Kent State & May 4th: A Social Sciences Perspective – Thomas R. Hensley & Jerry M. Lewis, eds.
Kent Daily Stater – Digitalized Archives
Kent State Library's Special Editions Department
Hippies – Peter Jedick
Life's What Happens – Kathy Clark
Kent State May 4th Memorial – On Campus
House Internal Security Committee Hearings – Transcripts

OTHER WORKS BY JON MICHAEL MILLER

GOOD GIRLS, BAD GIRLS – 2014
(For Jake Ernst's coming of age, 1959-1967)

FIVE PATHS CROSSING – *2016*
MURDER & MAYHEM IN TROPIC GARDENS – 2015
ARUBA BLUE – 2016
THE VIRGIN, VIV – 2013
CLOSE ENCOUNTERS OF THE JAMAICAN KIND – 2012
NEGRIL BEACH (stories) – 2012
ROZ – 2011
PHOTO SESSIONS – 2011
DRIFTWOOD HOUSES (stories) – 2008
MAHARISHI, TM, MALLORY & ME (memoir) – 2006
THROWN TOGETHER – 2005

All books available in print and eBook formats at Amazon & other book-selling venues,
or
Visit the author's website:
www.JonMichaelMiller.com.

Made in the USA
Middletown, DE
18 June 2018